The Hunchback

The Hunchback

by
Paul Féval

Translated from the French by
Stuart Gelzer

A Black Coat Press Book

For Lisbeth,
S.G.

Visit our website at www.blackcoatpress.com

ISBN 978-1-64932-066-7. First Printing. June 2021. Published by Black Coat Press, an imprint of Hollywood Comics.com, LLC, P.O. Box 17270, Encino, CA 91416. All rights reserved. Except for review purposes, no part of this book may be reproduced or transmitted in any form or by any means, electronic or mechanical, including photocopying, recording or by any information storage and retrieval system, without permission in writing from the publisher. The stories and characters depicted in this book are entirely fictional. Printed in the United States of America.

TABLE OF CONTENTS

PIERRE BLANCHAR

dans

LE BOSSU

d'après
l'œuvre célèbre de
PAUL FÉVAL

avec Paul BERNARD

Réalisation de JEAN DELANNOY   Adaptation et Dialogue de Bernard ZIMMER   Production JASON-REGINA

Introduction
Cape and Sword

First, the title: An Anglophone reader might easily assume that Paul Féval was trying to ride the coattails of the enormous success and prestige of that big Victor Hugo novel featuring a hunchback. But what English speakers know as Hugo's *The Hunchback of Notre-Dame* (1831) was a quarter century old by the time Féval's *Le Bossu* ("The Hunchback") appeared in 1857, so it wouldn't have offered much of a sales boost; more importantly, in French Hugo's novel is named, not after the disfigured bell ringer, but after the cathedral at the center of the story—*Notre-Dame de Paris*.

With *The Hunchback* Féval was actually chasing another and much closer rival: Alexandre Dumas, the enormous success of whose swashbuckling tales of gallant swordsmen set in a more or less historical France—*The Three Musketeers* (1844) and its sequels; *La Reine Margot* (1845) and its sequels; and many others—had inspired a whole generation of popular novelists. As is often the case with a new genre, the name came later; most of the major "cape and sword" landmarks were already in place by the time Amédée Achard published a novel actually called *La Cape et l'Épée* (1875).

But the category didn't need a name to be well defined and thoroughly recognizable to its avid readers. Some of the "cape and sword" peaks encircling (before as well as behind) the mountain that was Dumas's own opus include Alfred de Vigny's *Cinq-Mars* (1826), Prosper Mérimée's *La Chronique du Temps de Charles IX* (1829), Eugène Sue's *Latréaumont* (1837), and Théophile Gautier's *Le Capitaine Fracasse* (1863), and without a doubt Féval's *Le Bossu* ranks among the highest and most visible of those peaks.

Later notable "cape and sword" contributions, from writers of the next generations as well as from outside the French tradition, include Robert Louis Stevenson's *The Black Arrow* (1888), Edmond Rostand's *Cyrano de Bergerac* (1897), Baroness Orczy's *The Scarlet Pimpernel* (1905), Johnston McCulley's Zorro novels beginning with *The Curse of Capistrano* (1919), and Rafael Sabatini's *Scaramouche* (1921). Féval's own son, Paul Féval *fils*, added dozens of titles to the genre between the 1890s and the 1930s—contributing quantity perhaps more noticeably than quality, as will be discussed in the first Appendix to this volume. By the 1930s, certainly by the Second World War, the venerable and long-popular "cape and sword" cycle had reached its natural fadeout—or to be more accurate, moved to Hollywood with Douglas Fairbanks and Errol Flynn—and any examples written since then should be considered self-conscious "neo-swashbucklers," by analogy with "neo-noir."

But let's back up: the earliest "cape and sword" stories—even before Dumas, those of Vigny, Mérimée, Sue—themselves arose out of, and constitute just one subset of, the genre of historical adventure novels pioneered in English by the true founder of the type, Walter Scott, whose long series of Waverly novels marks the genesis of the very idea (obvious now, not so much then) of a fiction set in a time not the writer's own. Scott's *Ivanhoe* (1820) is a good bet for the very first swashbuckler. Scott's formula—a real historical period, preferably in a colorful chaotic violent time (not hard to find, whether in English history or in French), serving mostly as background to the adventures of a set of fictional characters (or sometimes real people, but about whom so little is known that the writer can take full license), period-costumed characters gallant and chivalrous on the one hand or dastardly and treacherous on the other—laid the sturdy historical fiction foundation that all of the "cape and sword" novelists built on. In a few cases, and *The Hunchback* is one of them, an author will deviate from Walter Scott's recipe to pull a genuine major historical figure forward from the scenic background into the thick of the action; Dumas's Cardinal de Richelieu remains a distant cloudy presence in the d'Artagnan novels, but Féval makes the real-life Regent Philippe d'Orléans not only a cornerstone of his *Hunchback* plot, but a fully rounded, fallible man of flesh and blood.

Beside "cape and sword," there's another category, another writing discipline—with its own rules and constraints and expectations and audience—in which the work of Paul Féval so clearly belongs that *The Hunchback* can only be understood in light of it. The mid nineteenth century, both in England and in France, was the golden age of the serialized novel, the *"roman feuilleton."* Here, besides some of the French writers already mentioned, like Dumas and Sue, belong the great Victorian English novelists, Charles Dickens and Wilkie Collins notable among them. Books by all these writers—enormously long novels, some of them—appeared, and were devoured by their readers, in little pieces sprinkled like a trail of breadcrumbs over many months, whether in daily newspapers or in weekly or bi-weekly literary periodicals like Dickens's own *All the Year Round.* The "cape and sword" stories were just one kind of serialized novel; the *roman feuilleton* phenomenon to which they belonged was itself much larger. Pseudo-Gothic horror tales about vampires and werewolves, and contemporary crime world (proto-detective) stories that have a not-quite gaslight, not-quite Conan Doyle atmosphere well before Sherlock Holmes, were enormously popular, and Féval wrote lots of each. (In fact, the publisher of this present volume takes its name from Féval's criminal underworld series of novels, *Les Habits Noirs.*[1])

In France most of the *roman feuilleton* novels appeared in daily newspapers, at the rate of about a chapter a day. The cliffhanger or sudden reveal chapter endings of *The Hunchback* show Féval's care in structuring his story to en-

---

[1] Available from Black Coat Press as *The Black Coats.*

tice the reader to buy tomorrow's paper too, and the next day's and the next. Some notable examples of the *roman feuilleton* form—choosing for now the criminal underworld rather than swashbuckler genre—are Eugène Sue's *Les Mystères de Paris* (1841-42) and Ponson du Terrail's Rocambole novels; Ponson's first Rocambole book, *Les Drames de Paris* (1857), came out at exactly the same time as Féval's *Le Bossu*, going head-to-head with it, day by day in a rival newspaper.

It took a lot of nerve to write a serialized novel. (Stephen King—not an author at a loss for words—tried it with *The Green Mile*, and never again.) Féval and his peers may have worked from a rough plot outline or sketch of the whole story, but they surely weren't writing very far ahead of their readers, and probably just ahead of deadline, day after day and week after week. *The Hunchback* certainly shows signs here and there of Féval starting down one track and then abandoning it—without the modern novelist's luxury of going back in a later draft to suppress the road not taken: a few minor characters are developed but never paid off, some locations are described in great detail as if their layout will matter later but it doesn't, a gypsy possesses useful occult powers early on that would come in handy in a crisis later but by then Féval seems to have forgotten about them, that kind of thing. But those are quibbles: the larger point is, it's extraordinary that any long complex novel written under those publication constraints actually holds together and makes sense at all.

Besides nerve, and of course a fertile imagination, what a successful *roman feuilleton* novelist needed most was speed. The story goes that one evening Ponson du Terrail—maybe the speediest of them all—had friends over for dinner and lost a lot of money at cards; to get himself out of the hole, when the guests went home at midnight he sat down and banged out an entire novel, *Les Oranges de la Marquise*, in time to turn it in to his publisher in the morning. (Nobody ever claimed it was a good novel.) Féval may not have been as fast as Ponson, but he was fast. He certainly spent a lot less time writing *Le Bossu* than I spent translating it—and he cranked out two more complete novels that same year, *Les Errants de la Nuit* and *Les Dernières Fées*, not to mention the two whose serialization ran over from the year before or on to the year after, *Les Compagnons du Silence* [2] and *La Fabrique de Mariages*, respectively. For some writers that would be a whole career.

One of the fascinations of *The Hunchback* is that—in spite of his obligation to write fast, to produce those five chapters a week, week after week—from the start Féval ties one hand behind his back by giving himself a significant structural constraint: he imposes unities of time and place more usual in theater than in novels. Indeed, for long stretches *The Hunchback* conforms to dramatic constraints of unity that would satisfy Racine or even Sophocles. To reveal nothing and spoil nothing:

---

[2] Available from Black Coat Press as *The Companions of the Silence*.

* Part One takes place in and around a single castle on a single day, between noon and midnight.

* Part Two, in and around a single villa on a single day, between morning and evening.

* Part Three, in a single house, at dusk that same day (though admittedly it also frames a long flashback covering many years and locations).

* Part Four, in the palace gardens, still that same day, from evening to dawn.

* Part Five takes place on the following day (from dawn to dawn) but is the first to divide its location: back at the same villa to start with, then in a pleasure house nearby.

* In Part Six, on the following day—still only the third day in a row since the start of Part Two—Féval finally allows himself the kind of crosscutting between near-simultaneous actions in different settings that movies and novels ordinarily rely on all the time.

The result is not an idle "look what I can do" stunt; on the contrary, Féval's exercise in unity of time and place gives his story a clear, vivid arc. I would argue that when you finish *The Hunchback* it remains clearer in your mind than does the more conventionally designed plot of *The Three Musketeers*; the simplicity of its structure makes *The Hunchback* a more easily visualized and more memorable story.

Féval certainly had plenty of experience to draw on when organizing a plot and deciding what would work and what wouldn't; over a span of forty years, he wrote more than two hundred and fifty novels—many of them very long novels: *The Hunchback*, which falls more or less midway in his career, is as long as *Moby Dick* or *Crime and Punishment*. Maybe fifty of those books would qualify as "cape and sword" stories. To keep the conveyer belt moving, Féval freely, even cheerfully, drew on a standard repertoire of plot devices and ingredients common to *roman feuilleton* novels, whether "cape and sword" or not—well-worn elements that were not only within easy reach of a busy writer but were actually in demand by readers, with an appetite unslaked from one story to the next. *The Hunchback* includes lots of them: vengeance sworn, mysterious poisons and philters, children lost (usually stolen) and found again—Féval actually pokes fun at this cliché even while he's using it—miscarriages of justice, prison breaks, a private diary to cover missing years, messages written in blood... and so on.

Since he wasn't wasting his energy on originality of device or prose expression, Féval could devote it instead to trailblazing whole sub-genres: he wrote pioneering vampire stories such as *La Vampire* and *La Ville-Vampire* [3]; his *Habits Noirs* series qualifies him one as one of the fathers of modern crime

---

[3] Available from Black Coat Press as *The Vampire Countess* and *Vampire City*.

and detective fiction; and *Le Loup Blanc* (1843)[4] presents arguably the first example of a hero who fights for justice using a disguise and a double identity—the source for every masked crusader from Zorro/Don Diego de La Vega through Batman/Bruce Wayne and beyond.

The Hunchback itself works that hidden-hero vein, with a disguise much more complex than any mere phonebooth costume change. One of the fascinations of the book is watching Féval wrestle with the narrative challenges (relatively new at the time) that follow from his premise. Though at the scene of the original crime he has the materials at hand—dark night, concealing cloak, unknown voice, etc.—to leave the identity of his villain in doubt, right from the start Féval discards mystery: *The Hunchback* is not a "whodunit," it's a "how will he avenge it." Féval generates suspense by keeping his hero's (rather than his villain's) plans and actions largely out of sight. As a result, as Lagardère necessarily moves into the background of the narrative for the sake of mystery and suspense, the vacuum in the foreground is filled by the villain: by the time we reach the climax of the story Gonzague seems to have more inner life than Lagardère, and the chapters devoted to Gonzague's maneuvers to enslave the souls of his flock of weak-willed followers offer more believable psychological dynamics (he's like a cult leader) than anything that happens to the good people in the story.

Besides the evergreen hidden-identity premise, what in *The Hunchback* still endures after a century and a half? For one thing, surprisingly, the comedy. In general the passage of time is tough on humor, which is so deeply embedded in its culture and era—most of Shakespeare's jokes have long since turned to dust and drifted down the page to the footnotes—but the buddy comedy Féval finds in his pair of reprobates, Cocardasse and Passepoil, still leaps off the page with the power of classic comic duos: Laurel and Hardy, Abbot and Costello, etc.—but with the difference that Cocardasse and Passepoil are not well-meaning bumblers but unsavory, unprincipled rogues with nothing to redeem their badness except hearts of gold.

A very different vein of humor runs through the long historical background set pieces—on Regency morals, architectural fashions, John Law's banking system, and so on; they may seem dry at first glance, but Féval deploys a wicked satirical wit to light up the social commentary with sharp asides. He also uses those set pieces to control the narrative pace and build suspense: almost invariably, after a major section-ending heart-stopping cliffhanger, he opens the next section by taking a long step back from the story to reestablish some aspect of the historical background—allowing himself pages in a row with no mention of the story's characters, and leaving the plot-hungry reader effectively suspended, heart still pounding. He can be downright mischievous about it: at one point a

---

[4] Available from Black Coat Press as *The White Wolf.*

major character is on his final walk to the scaffold—and Féval cuts away to discuss the history of a nearby church.

What notably does not endure, I would say, is the half-paternal, half-erotic romance plot problem—is he her father or her lover or both?—which may have been just another conventional *roman feuilleton* formula and raised not a single eyebrow in 1857, but which I imagine may leave a modern reader a little queasy.

Le Bossu appeared first in the daily newspaper *Le Siècle*, running beneath the news along the bottom quarter of each page including the front page, parceled out at the rate of about a chapter a day, usually five days a week, between May and August 1857. It was published in book form in 1858. A translation into English appeared five years later: *"I Am Here!" The Duke's Motto; or, The Little Parisian* was published in New York in 1863, and the same text was reissued in 1887 with a new title, *"I Am Here!" Lagardère; or, The Hunchback of Paris.* Having used up so many words just for the title, the (anonymous) translator apparently didn't have enough left for the text: the 1863/1887 English version is not so much a translation as a brutal abridgment of the original—even wrapped in the flowery, long-winded language of Victorian times, the whole thing clocks in at about a third of the word count of this present rendering. (Enormous vital chapters—long chunks of the original plot—are deleted between one sentence and the next.) The version of *The Hunchback* in front of you now is therefore the first and only faithful and complete English translation of Paul Féval's swashbuckler monument, *Le Bossu.*

Stuart Gelzer
Santa Fe, 2020

THE HUNCHBACK

BOOK I: THE LITTLE PARISIAN

PART ONE: THE MASTERS OF ARMS

1. The Louron Valley

A city stood here once: Lorre, with its pagan temples, amphitheaters, and palaces. Now it's a deserted valley, where the Gascon peasant's lazy plow shies away from blunting its iron blade against the buried marble columns. The mountains rise close by: right in front of you the snowy horizon of the high Pyrenees cuts across your view and reveals the blue sky of Spain through the deep pass used by smugglers from Benasque. A few miles away, at the Bagnères de Luchon hot springs, consumptive Parisians cough, dance, joke, and imagine they're curing the incurable. A little further away in the other direction, arthritic Parisians expect to leave their sciatica at the bottom of the sulfur pools at Barèges les Bains. It's not iron or magnesium or sulfur that'll cure Paris—it's faith!

This is the Louron Valley, lying between the Aure and Barousse valleys, though less familiar to the bustling tourists who come each year to discover this untamed country. This is the Louron Valley, with its flowering oases, its rushing streams, its extraordinary boulders, and its river, the brown Clarabide, a dark crystal flowing between steep banks past its mysterious forests and its arrogant old castle, as swaggering and improbable as a chivalric poem.

As you come down the mountain, to the left of the pass, on the slopes of little Véjan Peak, you can see the whole landscape at a glance. The Louron Valley lies at the tip of Gascony and spreads out like a fan between the Ens Forest and those beautiful Fréchet Woods that stretch across the Barousse Valley between the paradisiacal villages of Mauléon, Nestes, and Campan. The soil is poor, but the view is rich.

Almost everywhere the ground cracks open violently. The ruts tear apart lawns, wash away the roots of giant beech trees, expose the base of the rocks; the vertical banks are split from top to bottom by the invasive roots of the pines. At the foot of the cliff some caveman once dug his home, and at the top a trail guide's or shepherd's hut now perches like the high, solitary aerie of an eagle.

The Ens Forest follows the foot of a hill that ends abruptly in the middle of the valley to let the Clarabide flow by. The eastern end of that hill is marked by a steep bluff no path has ever climbed. The hill lies crossways to the mountain ranges around it and would close off the valley, like a wall stretched between the mountains, if the river didn't stop it short. The locals call this remarkable place the Hachaz, the ax blow. Of course, there's a legend involved, but I'll spare you. Here stood the palaces of the city of Lorre, which probably gave its name to the Lourron Valley. And here can still be seen the ruins of the Castle of Caylus-Tarrides.

The ruins look imposing from a distance. They cover a large area, and more than a hundred paces from the Hachaz the broken tops of the old towers still poke through the trees. Up close it's like a fortified village. Trees have sprung up everywhere in the rubble, and here and there a pine has had to force its way through a stone vault. But most of those ruins are humble buildings of wood and clay rather than granite.

Caylus-Tarrides was the name of the local branch of a noble family important mostly due to its wealth. According to tradition, one of them, Baron Gaston de Tarrides, built a wall around the little village of Tarrides to protect his Huguenot vassals after the abjuration of Henri IV. If you visit the ruins of Caylus you'll be shown the baron's tree. It's an oak, rooted on the bank of the moat to the west of the castle. One night lightning struck it. It was already a big tree, and when it fell it came to rest lying across the moat. It's been there ever since, alive only through its bark, which is all that survived at the split. But oddly one shoot has sprung from the trunk, thirty or forty feet out from the banks of the moat. That shoot has grown and become a mighty oak, an oak suspended in the air, a miraculous oak, on which twenty-five hundred tourists have already carved their names.

Those Caylus-Tarrides died out early in the eighteenth century, and the last of them was François de Tarrides, Marquis of Caylus, one of the characters in this story. In 1699 the Marquis of Caylus was a man of sixty. Early in the reign of Louis XIV he had attended at court, but without much success, and he'd retired disappointed. He lived now on his estate with his only daughter, the beautiful Aurore de Caylus. His local nickname was Caylus the Jailer. Here's why. Around his fortieth year, the marquis, a widower whose first wife had given him no children, fell in love with the daughter of the Count of Soto-Mayor, Governor of Pamplona. Inez de Soto-Mayor was then seventeen, a Madrid girl, with eyes of fire and a heart burning hotter than her eyes. The marquis was rumored to have given little happiness to his first wife, who'd remained shut up in the old castle of Caylus, where she died at twenty-five. Inez told her father she'd never marry that man. But in the Spain of tragedy and comedy, overruling a girl's will was an elaborate business: city officials, duennas, corrupt valets, and—at least according to storytellers—the Holy Inquisition itself existed for just that purpose. One fair evening poor Inez, hidden behind her blinds, was serenaded for the last time by the magistrate's youngest son, a fine guitar player. The next day she left for France with the marquis. He took her without a dowry, and on top of that he paid the Count of Soto-Mayor who knows how many thousand pistoles. The count, nobler than the king and greedier than he was noble, couldn't resist his offer.

A fever broke out among the young gentlemen of the Louron Valley when the marquis brought his beautiful veiled bride back from Madrid to Caylus Castle. There were no tourists around then, no wandering Lotharios setting fire to provincial hearts wherever discount train fares take them. But the permanent war with Spain kept bands of partisans busy at the border, and the marquis had to be ready. He prepared himself and took on the challenge. The lover who wanted to attempt the conquest of the beautiful Inez would first have to procure some siege cannons. The challenge wasn't just a heart, it was a heart hidden behind the ramparts of a fortress. Tender love letters couldn't reach her, soft lovers' looks wasted their heat and languor, even the guitar was powerless. The beautiful Inez was unapproachable. Not one gallant, or bear hunter, or country squire, or army captain could boast of having glimpsed so much as the spark in her eye. And that's how matters stood. After three or four years, poor Inez finally left that terrible castle—to go to the cemetery. She died of loneliness and boredom. She left a daughter.

The resentful foiled gallants gave the marquis his nickname, the Jailer. From Tarbes to Pamplona, from Argelès to Saint Gaudens, not a man, woman, or child called the marquis anything but the Jailer. After the death of his second wife, he tried again to remarry: he had Bluebeard's good nature, immune to discouragement. But the Governor of Pamplona had no more daughters, and the marquis's reputation was so well established that even the boldest marriageable girls drew back from his approach. He remained a widower, waiting impatiently for his daughter to reach the age when she'd have to be locked away. The gentlefolk of the area didn't like him, and in spite of his wealth he was often alone. Boredom drove him out of his castle. He got in the habit of visiting Paris every year, where younger courtiers borrowed money from him and made fun him.

While the marquis was away, his daughter was supervised by two or three duennas and an aged castle attendant. Aurore was as beautiful as her mother; Spanish blood ran in her veins. The year she turned sixteen, on many a dark night people in the village of Tarrides could hear the castle dogs barking. Around that time one of the most distinguished noblemen at the French court, Philippe de Lorraine, Duke of Nevers, came to stay at his castle in Buch, near Jurançon. He was barely twenty, but having burned through life too fast he was

15

dying of some wasting illness. The mountain air did him good: by early spring he was leading the hunt as far afield as the Louron Valley.

The first time the Caylus Castle dogs barked at night, the young Duke of Nevers, overcome by fatigue in the Ens Forest, had asked a woodcutter for shelter. Nevers spent a year at his castle in Buch. The Tarrides shepherds said he was a generous lord. Those shepherds talked about two nighttime incidents from his stay there. One midnight they saw lights moving behind the windows of the old Caylus Castle chapel. The dogs hadn't barked; but a dark shape, one people in the village had spotted so often they'd begun to recognize it, had crept into the moat after nightfall. All those old castles are full of ghosts. Another time, toward eleven at night, Dame Marthe, the younger of the Caylus duennas, left the castle by the main door and ran to the woodcutter's hut where the young Duke of Nevers had once been a guest. A little later a sedan chair crossed the Ens Forest, and then a woman's cries could be heard coming from the woodcutter's hut. The next day the woodcutter had vanished, and his hut was free for the taking. Dame Marthe also left Caylus Castle the same day.

Four years passed. Nothing more had been heard of either the woodcutter or Dame Marthe. Philippe de Nevers had left his castle at Buch. But another Philippe, no less notable, no less a lord, honored the Louron Valley with his presence. He was Philippe Polixenes of Mantua, Prince of Gonzague, to whom the Marquis of Caylus intended to give his daughter Aurore in marriage. Gonzague had a slightly feminine face, but overall, he was a man of rare looks, none nobler. His black hair fell soft and shiny around his forehead—whiter than a woman's—and formed naturally the thick, somewhat heavy hairstyle Louis XIV's courtiers could only achieve by adding two or three heads of hair to the one they were born with. Gonzague had the clear proud black-eyed gaze of Italian men. He was tall and well built, and his movements and gestures had a theatrical majesty. We need say nothing of his family: the house of Gonzague stands as high in history as Bouillon, Este, or Montmorency.

Gonzague's connections were as lofty as his rank. He had two friends, as close as brothers, one a Lorraine, the other a Bourbon. The Duke of Chartres (Louis XIV's nephew, later to be Duke of Orléans and Regent of France), the Duke of Nevers, and the Prince of Gonzague were inseparable. The court called them the three Philippes. Their closeness recalled the great classical models of friendship. Philippe de Gonzague was the eldest at thirty, the future Regent only twenty-four, and Nevers a year younger.

You can imagine how the idea of such a son-in-law flattered the vanity of the old Marquis of Caylus. Rumor credited the Prince of Gonzague with immense wealth in Italy. What's more, he was first cousin and sole heir to Nevers, whom everyone thought destined for an early grave. And the properties of Philippe de Nevers, himself the sole heir to that title, were some of the finest in France. Of course, no one could accuse Gonzague of wishing for his friend's death; but there was nothing he could do to prevent it, and the fact is it would make him a millionaire ten times over. The intended father-in-law and son-in-law had more or less settled the matter. As for Aurore, she hadn't been consulted—the Jailer's system.

It was a fine autumn day in 1699. Louis XIV had grown old and grown tired of war. The Peace of Ryswick had just been signed, but skirmishes between partisans continued along the Spanish border, and the Louron Valley played host to lots of those inconvenient visitors. Half a dozen guests sat around a well-furnished table in the dining hall at Caylus Castle; the marquis may have had his faults, but at least he was a good host. Besides the marquis, and Gonzague, and Mademoiselle de Caylus, who sat at the head of the table, the company were all people of middling rank who served them.

One of them, Father Bernard, was chaplain of Caylus and priest of the little village of Tarrides, and in the chapel sacristy he kept the register of births, deaths, and marriages. Another, Dame Isidore, from the Gabour estate, had replaced Dame Marthe as Aurore's lady in waiting. A third, Monsieur de Peyrolles, a gentleman attendant on the Prince of Gonzague, we should present more fully, since he'll play a role in our story. He was a man of middle age, tall and a bit stooped, with a thin pale face and scanty hair. Nowadays we'd have trouble picturing someone like him without glasses; but they weren't in fashion then. His features seemed unassuming, but his myopic eyes had a certain boldness. Gonzague claimed Peyrolles was handy with the sword that hung awkwardly at his side. In short, Gonzague made much of him: he needed him. The other guests, officers at Caylus, were mere sidekicks.

Aurore de Caylus did the honors with cold and silent dignity. In general, even the most beautiful women show their emotions plainly: a woman can be charming around those she loves, and almost unpleasant elsewhere. But Aurore was one of those women who can be captivating even against their will, and who attract admiration without meaning to. She wore Spanish dress; three layers of lace fell amid the jet-black waves of her hair. Though she wasn't yet twenty, the pure proud lines of her mouth already expressed sadness. But what light might shine from a smile on those young lips! And what rays might gleam from those eyes, now hidden by the arching silk of her long lashes. It was long since anyone had seen a smile on Aurore's lips. Her father said, "All that'll change when she's a princess."

At the end of the second course, Aurore rose and asked for permission to withdraw. Dame Isidore looked long and regretfully at the pastries, jams, and preserves being brought out. Duty required her to follow her young mistress.

As soon as Aurore was gone, her father became more cheerful. "Prince, you owe me a rematch at chess. Are you ready?"

"Always at your command, dear marquis," replied Gonzague.

Caylus ordered a table and a chessboard to be brought out. The game now about to begin was at least their hundred and fiftieth in the two weeks the prince had been a guest at the castle. In someone of Gonzague's rank and looks, at the age of thirty a passion for chess would make you wonder. It had to be one of two things: either he was desperately in love with Aurore, or he desperately wanted to get his hands on the dowry. Every day, after lunch and after dinner, out came the chessboard. The Jailer was a fourth-rate player. Every day Gonzague let himself be beaten a dozen times, after which the triumphant Jailer, without leaving the field of battle, fell asleep in his easy chair and snored like a righteous man. And that's how Gonzague courted Aurore de Caylus.

"Prince," said the marquis while setting up his pieces, "today I'm going to show you a gambit I found in a learned treatise by Cessolis. I don't play chess like other people, and I make sure to draw from the best sources. Most people don't know chess was invented by Attalus, king of Pergamon, to entertain the Greeks during the long siege of Troy. It's only ignoramuses or liars who give the credit to Palamedes. All right, now please pay attention to your game."

"Marquis," said Gonzague, "I can't tell you how much I enjoy playing chess with you."

They began, with the other guests still around them. When Gonzague had lost the first game, he signaled to his factotum Peyrolles, who tossed aside his napkin and left. One by one the chaplain and the other officers did the same. The Jailer and Gonzague were left alone.

"The Romans called the game *latrunculi*, or little thieves," continued the old man. "The Greeks called it *latrikion*. In his excellent book Sarrazin observes..."

"Marquis," interrupted Gonzague, "I beg your pardon for my absent-mindedness. May I have your permission to take back this move?"

By mistake he'd moved a pawn and won the game. The Jailer hesitated, pulling on his ear, but generosity won out. "Take it back, prince, but don't do it again. Chess isn't for children."

Gonzague sighed deeply.

"I know, I know," said Caylus mockingly, "we're in love."

"To distraction, marquis!"

"I know all that, prince. Focus on your game! I'm taking your bishop."

"Yesterday," said Gonzague, like a man trying to shake off painful thoughts, "you didn't finish the story about the gentleman who tried to sneak into your house..."

"Ah, you sly trickster!" cried the Jailer. "You're trying to distract me! But I'm like Caesar, who could dictate five letters at the same time. Did you know he played chess? Anyway, the gentleman got half a dozen sword cuts down there in the moat. That kind of thing happened more than once. The conduct of the ladies of Caylus has never given slander anything to chew on."

"And what you did as a husband, marquis," asked Gonzague casually, "would you do it as a father?"

"Of course. I don't know any other way to guard the daughters of Eve. *Shah mata*, prince, as the Persians say! You're beaten again." The old man stretched out in his chair and arranged himself for his siesta. "From those two words, *shah mata*, which mean the king is dead, we've derived checkmate, according to Ménage and according to Frère. As for women, believe me, good blades around good walls, that's the recipe for virtue!" He closed his eyes and fell asleep.

Gonzague quickly left the dining room. It was about two in the afternoon. Peyrolles was pacing in the corridor, waiting for his master.

"Our men?" said Gonzague as soon as he saw him.

"Six have arrived," replied Peyrolles.

"Where are they?"

"At the Adam's Apple tavern, on the other side of the moat."

"Who are the two missing?"

"Master Cocardasse Junior, from Tarbes, and Brother Passepoil, his second-in-command."

"Two good blades!" said the prince. "And the other business?"

"Dame Marthe is with Mademoiselle de Caylus right now."

"With the child?"

"With the child."

"How did she get in?"

"By the low window in the baths that opens onto the moat, under the bridge."

Gonzague thought for a moment. "Have you questioned Father Bernard?"

"He won't talk."

"How much did you offer him?"

"Five hundred pistoles."

"That Dame Marthe must know where the register is. Don't let her leave the castle."

"Done," said Peyrolles.

Gonzague paced with long strides. "I want to talk to her myself," he murmured. "But are you sure my cousin Nevers got Aurore's message?"

"Our German carried it."

"And Nevers is due to arrive?"

"This evening."

They'd reached the door to Gonzague's rooms. At Caylus Castle, three corridors met at right angles: one going to the main living quarters, two going to the wings. The prince's rooms were in the west wing and ended at the stairs leading down to the baths. There was a noise in the central corridor. It was Dame Marthe, coming out of Mademoiselle de Caylus's rooms. Gonzague and Peyrolles ducked quickly into Gonzague's rooms, leaving the door open.

The next moment Dame Marthe came fast and stealthy down the corridor. It was broad daylight, but it was siesta hour, and the Spanish custom had crossed the Pyrenees: everyone at Caylus Castle was asleep, and Dame Marthe had every reason to hope she'd meet no one. As she passed Gonzague's door, Peyrolles threw himself on her and pressed his handkerchief hard against her mouth, stifling her first cry. Then he took her by the waist and carried her, half-fainted, into his master's room.

II. Cocardasse and Passepoil

One straddled a work horse with long tangled mane and hairy knock knees; the other sat sidesaddle on a donkey, like a lady of the manor on her palfrey. In spite of his humble mount, who let his head hang sadly between his legs, the first man carried himself proudly. He wore a laced doublet of buffalo hide with a heart-shaped breastplate, moth-eaten tartan stockings, and a pair of those fine funnel-shaped boots so fashionable at the time of Louis XIV. He topped it all off with a swashbuckling hat and an enormous rapier. Behold Master Cocardasse Junior, a native of Toulouse, formerly a fencing master in Paris, now eking out a living in Tarbes.

The other man, shy and humble, was dressed like a shabby clerk: he wore a long black doublet cut straight like a cassock over black leggings shiny with use, a wool cap carefully pulled over his ears, and stout fur-lined boots in spite of the heat. In contrast to Master Cocardasse—who prided himself on his rich curly hair, as tousled and as black as an African's—nothing but a few locks of faded blond stuck to his companion's temples. Likewise, while two frightening hooks served Cocardasse as a mustache, his second-in-command made do with three off-white whiskers sticking out below his long nose. For this peaceful traveler was indeed a provost of arms, and we can assure you that when he had to he could swing with vigor the great ugly sword that slapped the sides of his donkey. He was named Amable Passepoil. He came from Villedieu in Lower Normandy, a town that rivals Condé sur Noireau in its output of mercenaries. His friends called him Brother Passepoil, either because of his clerical dress or because he'd been a barber's assistant and a pharmacist's flunky before strapping on a sword. In spite of the sentimental gleam in his beady blinking blue eyes when a skirt of red fustian crossed the road, he was ugly in all ways possible. Cocardasse, on the other hand, could pass anywhere for a handsome rogue.

The pair of them stumbled along under the sun of the South of France. Every stone on the road made Cocardasse's cob shy away, and every few paces Passepoil's charger threw a fit.

"You know, brother," said Cocardasse in a thick Gascon accent, "we've been looking at that same damned castle on that same damned mountain for two hours now. It seems to be moving as fast as we are."

"Patience, patience!" answered Passepoil in a nasal Norman singsong. "We'll get there soon enough for what we have to do there."

"God's hat!" sighed the Gascon. "Passepoil, if we were better behaved, with our skills we could be choosier about our jobs."

"You're right, Cocardasse," replied the Norman, "but our passions have ruined us."

"Gambling, wine..."

"And women!" And Passepoil raised his eyes to heaven.

They were following the banks of the Clarabide, through the middle of the Louron Valley. The Hachaz rose before them like an immense pedestal for the massive walls of Caylus Castle. There were no ramparts on this side, so you could see the whole ancient structure, from the foundations to the rooftops, and for an admirer of fine views this would have been an obligatory stop. Indeed, Caylus Castle formed a worthy crown to that great cliff, the result of some forgotten geological convulsion.

Local people said the castle was much older than the Caylus family itself. The firm hand of the Roman army must have passed there, and beneath the moss and bushes covering its approaches could be seen the traces of pagan construction. But only hints of that remained, and everything that rose above the ground belonged to the Lombard style of the tenth and eleventh centuries. The two main towers that flanked the central building to southeast and northeast were square and squat rather than tall. The windows, always placed above an arrow slit, were small and plain, and their arches rested on simple pilasters devoid of moldings. The builder's only indulgence had been a sort of mosaic: the stones, symmetrically cut and placed, were separated by protruding bricks.

That was the foreground, whose austere form matched the bleakness of the Hachaz. But behind the straight lines of the central structure, which could have been built by Charlemagne, a jumble of gables and turrets followed the rising slope of the hill and formed an amphitheater. The keep, a high octagonal tower topped by a Byzantine balcony with cloverleaf arches, crowned the hodgepodge of roofs like a giant standing amid dwarves.

Two ditches, to right and left of the two Lombard towers, formed the moat, whose ends had once been closed by walls to hold in the moat water. The edge of the village of Tarrides could be seen through the beech trees beyond the moat to the north. Within the circle of the moat stood the chapel, built at the beginning of the thirteenth century in the ogival style, showing its twin transepts with glittering windows. Caylus Castle was the gem of the valleys of the Pyrenees.

But Cocardasse and Passepoil had no taste for the fine arts. They went on their way, and only glanced up at the somber castle to judge how far they still had to go. They were headed to Caylus Castle, and though as the crow flies it was barely half a league away, since they had to go around the Hachaz they faced another hour of travel. Cocardasse must have been a cheerful companion when his purse was full, and even Passepoil's cunning face showed signs of customary good humor, but today they were sad and had their reasons for it: empty stomachs, empty pockets, and the prospect of probably dangerous work, the kind of work you can afford to turn down if you have food on the table. Unluckily for Cocardasse and Passepoil, their passions had eaten up everything.

And now Cocardasse said, "God's hat! I'll never touch another card or another glass!"

"I renounce love forever!" added Passepoil.

22

And both of them built fine virtuous dreams on their future savings.

"I'll buy all the right gear!" cried Cocardasse enthusiastically. "And I'll become a soldier in our little Parisian's company."

"Me too," added Passepoil, "a soldier or the head surgeon's valet."

"Wouldn't I make a fine cavalryman for the king?"

"The regiment I join would at least be sure of being properly bled."

And together they said, "We'd see the little Parisian again! We'd be sure to fend off some attack against him now and then."

"He'd call me good old Cocardasse again!"

"He'd make fun of Brother Passepoil the way he used to."

"Thunder and lightning!" Cocardasse punched his cob, who could do no more. "We've fallen pretty low for swordsmen, brother, but for every sin there's a mercy. I feel like with the little Parisian I'd reform."

Passepoil shook his head sadly and gave his clothes a despairing look. "Who knows if he'd even choose to recognize us?"

"Oh, come on," said Cocardasse, "that boy's got a true heart!"

"Such skill," sighed Passepoil, "and such speed!"

"Such poise with a weapon! And so direct!"

"Remember his crosscut in retreat?"

"Remember his three straight lunges, called in advance in that attack on Delespine?"

"What a heart!"

"A true heart! Always lucky at gambling, God's hat. And a fellow who knew how to drink!"

"And who drove women wild!"

With every answer they grew more animated. By mutual agreement they stopped to shake hands with deep, sincere feeling.

"God's death," said Cocardasse, "we'll be his valets if the little Parisian wants, won't we?"

"And we'll make him into a great lord!" added Passepoil. "That way Peyrolles's money won't bring us bad luck."

So it was Monsieur de Peyrolles, right-hand man to Prince Philippe de Gonzague, who was making Cocardasse and Passepoil travel like this. They knew Peyrolles well, and his master Gonzague even better. Before teaching the country squires of Tarbes the noble art of Italian fencing, they'd kept a fencing school in Paris, on the Rue Croix des Petits Champs, near the Louvre. And without the difficulties their passions inflicted on their business they might have made their fortune, because the whole court came to them. They were just a pair of decent rascals, who had—no doubt in a moment of weakness—committed some indiscretion. They were so good with their swords! Let's be merciful, and not try too hard to find out why one day, slipping the key under the door, they'd left Paris as if a fire were at their heels. Certainly in Paris in those days fencing masters associated with the highest noblemen. They often knew more about what was going on than the courtiers themselves. They were the gossip columns come to life. And you can imagine that Passepoil, who'd been a barber, must have known some things! As a result, they both counted on making a living from their skills.

As they set off from Tarbes Passepoil had said, "This job is worth millions. The Duke of Nevers is the greatest blade in the world after the little Parisian. If it involves Nevers, the pay has to be good." And Cocardasse had agreed enthusiastically.

It was two in the afternoon when they reached the village of Tarrides, and the first peasant they met pointed the way to the Adam's Apple tavern. The small downstairs taproom was already almost full when they came in. A girl in the traditional bright skirt and laced corset of Foix was busy bringing out pitchers, tin goblets, light for pipes in a clog—everything to restore six hearty men after a long slog in the sun of the Pyrenees valleys.

On the wall hung six stout rapiers and their related gear. Every forehead might as well have been branded with the words "hired killer." They had tanned faces, bold looks, insolent mustaches. An honest citizen coming in here by mistake would have fainted away just at the sight of their swashbuckling profiles. Three sat at the first table, near the door: three Spaniards, by their looks. At the next table sat an Italian scarred on brow and chin, and across from him a frightful devil whose accent betrayed his German origin. At the third table sat a lout with long tangled hair who growled in Breton dialect. The three Spaniards were named Saldaña, Pinto, and Pépé, known as El Matador; all of them were swordsmen, one from Murcia, one from Seville, the third from Pamplona. The Italian was an assassin from Spoleto named Giuseppe Faenza. The German was named Staupitz, the Breton Joel de Jugan. Monsieur de Peyrolles had recruited all of these blades; he knew his job.

When Cocardasse and Passepoil, after stabling their sad mounts, entered the Adam's Apple taproom, they both took a step backward at the sight of this respectable company. The low room was lit only by a single window, and in the half-light and the cloud of pipe smoke they saw at first just the projecting tips of mustaches on narrow faces, and the rapiers hanging on the wall. But six hoarse voices called out together, "Master Cocardasse! Brother Passepoil!" accompanied by assorted oaths from the Papal States, from the banks of the Rhine, from Brittany, from Murcia and Navarre and Andalusia.

Cocardasse shaded his eyes with his hand. "Crooked ace! *Todos camaradas?*"

"All old friends," translated Passepoil, his voice shaking. He was a coward by birth, whom necessity had made brave. He got goose bumps for a trifle, but he fought like a demon.

Handshakes all around, the kind of firm handshakes that crush fingers, a flow of hugs that pressed together silk doublets, old cloth, threadbare velvet—everything except clean linen. Nowadays fencing masters, or as they prefer to be called, "professors of fencing," are serious hardworking men, good husbands, good fathers, following an honest trade. But in the seventeen century a virtuoso of the cut and thrust was either a kind of polished charlatan and a favorite of court and town, or else a poor rascal who had to do unspeakable things just to drink his fill of bad wine in cheap dives. There was no middle ground. Our friends at the Adam's Apple had no doubt seen their good days, but the sun of prosperity had set on all of them. They'd all been drenched in the same storm.

Before Cocardasse and Passepoil arrived, the three groups had had nothing in common: the Breton knew no one, the German mixed only with the Italian, and the three Spaniards kept proudly to themselves. But Paris was already a center for the noble arts, and men like Cocardasse and Passepoil, who'd held forth on the Rue Croix des Petits Champs, behind the Palais-Royal, were likely to know all the braggarts of Europe. They connected all the groups, who had so much in common. The ice was broken, tables pulled together, pitchers mingled, introductions made, résumés recited.

It was enough to make your hair stand on end: those six rapiers hanging on the wall had carved up more Christian flesh than all the axes of all the executioners of France and Navarre combined. The Breton, if he'd been a Huron, would have carried three dozen scalps on his belt; the Italian's dreams were haunted by twenty and some ghosts; the German had massacred two fifth-rate princes, three fourth-rate princes, five third-rate princes, and one second-rate prince, and he was still looking for a first-rate prince. And that was nothing compared to the three Spaniards, who could easily have drowned in the blood of their countless victims. Pépé El Matador spoke of nothing but skewering three men at a time. We can think of no higher praise for our Gascon and our Norman: they were the toast of this band of cutthroats.

When the first round had been drunk and the noise of the boasting had dwindled a little, Cocardasse said, "Now, my beauties, let's talk business."

They called in the barmaid, trembling amid these cannibals, and ordered more wine. She was a big cross-eyed brunette. Passepoil had already aimed the artillery of his amorous gaze at her. He tried to follow her out, on the pretext of getting better wine, but Cocardasse grabbed him by the collar. "You promised to overcome your passions," he said solemnly. Passepoil sat back down with a sigh. When the wine came, the wench was dismissed with orders not to return.

"My beauties," resumed Cocardasse, "Brother Passepoil and I didn't expect to meet such beloved company so far from the populated spots where you generally exercise your talents."

"Alas, Cocardasse, *caro mio*," said Faenza, "do you know any towns where there's work now?"

And all of them shook their heads like men who feel their virtue isn't sufficiently recognized.

Then Saldaña said, "Don't you know why we're here?"

Cocardasse was opening his mouth to answer when Passepoil stepped on his boot. Though nominally the leader, the Gascon was in the habit of following the advice of his second-in-command, who was a wise and prudent Norman.

"I know we were summoned," he answered.

"That was me," interjected Staupitz.

"And that for any ordinary assignment," went on Cocardasse, "Passepoil and I would be more than enough for the job."

"Hell! Usually, when I'm around," said El Matador, "they don't need to hire anyone else."

They all agreed, each according to his degree of eloquence or vanity.

Then Cocardasse said, "So are we going up against an army?"

"Our business," answered Staupitz, who worked for Monsieur de Peyrolles, right-hand man of Prince Philippe de Gonzague, "is with a single man."

A loud laugh greeted this announcement. Cocardasse and Passepoil laughed louder than the rest, but the Norman's foot was still on the Gascon's boot. That meant, "Let me handle this."

Passepoil asked innocently, "And what's the name of this giant who's going to take on eight men?"

"Of whom each one—God's blood!" added Cocardasse, "is worth half a dozen good mercenaries!"

"It's Philippe de Nevers," answered Staupitz.

"But they say he's dying!" cried Saldaña.

"Wheezing!" added Pinto.

"Run down, broken down, tubercular!" cried the others.

Cocardasse and Passepoil now said no more. The latter shook his head slowly and pushed away his glass. Cocardasse did the same.

The others couldn't help noticing their sudden seriousness. "What's going on? What's the matter with you?" they were asked on all sides.

Cocardasse and Passepoil looked at each other in silence.

"What the hell is this about?" cried Saldaña, astonished.

"It almost looks like you want to back out of the job," said Faenza.

"My beauties," replied Cocardasse, "if you thought that, you wouldn't be far wrong."

Objections drowned him out.

"We knew Philippe de Nevers in Paris," added Passepoil gently. "He came to our fencing academy. That's a dying man who'll cut you a new butt crack."

"Us?" they shouted, and all of them shrugged with disdain.

Cocardasse looked around the circle. "I see you haven't heard of the Nevers attack."

They all opened their eyes and ears.

"Old Master Delapalme's attack," added Passepoil, "which laid low seven fighters between the town of Roule and the Saint Honoré gate."

"Those secret attacks are all piffle!" cried El Matador.

"With good footwork, a good eye, a good garde," added Joel de Jugan, "I care no more for secret attacks than for Noah's flood!"

"Crooked ace!" said Cocardasse haughtily, "I'm confident I've got good footwork, a good eye, and a good garde, my beauties..."

"Me too," said Passepoil.

"...As good footwork, as good an eye, as good a garde as any of you..."

"To prove which," said Passepoil with his usual gentleness, "we're ready to try our skills against any of you, if you like."

"And yet," continued Cocardasse, "the Nevers attack doesn't seem like piffle to me. I was beaten by it in my own academy."

"Me too."

"I was hit between the eyes, three times in a row."

"And I, three times in a row, between the eyes!"

"Three times, without once finding his blade to parry it!"

The six cutthroats were now listening carefully. Nobody laughed anymore.

"So," said Saldaña, crossing himself, "it's not a secret attack, it's a spell."

Jugan put his hand in his pocket, where he must have kept a rosary.

"It's a good thing they summoned us all, my beauties," said Cocardasse solemnly. "You talk about an army—I wish we were an army! Believe me, there's only one man in the world who can face Philippe de Nevers, sword in hand."

"And that man?" asked six voices together.

"Is the little Parisian," replied Cocardasse.

"Oh, him!" cried Passepoil, suddenly enthusiastic. "He's a devil!"

"The little Parisian?" said the whole circle. "Does your little Parisian have a name?"

"A name you all know, gentlemen. His name is the Chevalier de Lagardère."

It did indeed seem like the cutthroats all knew that name, because a silence followed. Finally, Saldaña said, "I've never met him."

"All the better for you," replied Cocardasse. "He doesn't like men of your type."

"Is he the one they call handsome Lagardère?" asked Pinto.

"Is he the one," added Faenza, "who killed those three Flemish men under the walls of Senlis?"

"Is he the one," began Jugan, "who..."

But Cocardasse forcefully interrupted him. "There aren't two Lagardères!"

III. The Three Philippes

The only window in the downstairs taproom at the Adam's Apple opened onto a beech wood sloping down to the castle moat. A cart track through the wood led to a plank bridge thrown across the very deep, very wide moat that surrounded the castle on three sides and hung open at both ends in midair above the Hachaz. The moat had drained out when the walls that held in the water were knocked down, and its dry bottom now yielded two fine hay harvests a year for the castle stables. The second crop had just been mown. From where they sat our eight hired killers could see the haymakers baling hay under the bridge. Though dry, the moat was intact, and its walls rose sheer to the bordering slope. There was only one break in the wall, made to give access to the hay carts, at the end of the cart track that ran past the tavern window.

From ground level to the bottom of the moat the castle ramparts were pierced by many arrow slits, but there was only one opening big enough for a person to get through: a low window located under the fixed bridge that had long ago replaced the drawbridge. That window, barred and heavily shuttered, had once brought air and light to the castle steam room, a large basement room that still retained some of its grandeur. It's common knowledge that in the Middle Ages, especially in the South of France, the practice of bathing had been taken to the point of luxury.

The tower clock had just rung three. Since the terrible killer known as handsome Lagardère wasn't there—and since he wasn't the man they were waiting for anyway—once their first panic subsided the swordsmen resumed their boasting.

"Well, I'll tell you, friend," said Saldaña to Cocardasse, "I'd give ten pistoles to see your Chevalier de Lagardère!"

"Sword in hand?" Cocardasse took a long drink and smacked his lips. "That day, brother, make sure you're in a state of grace and trust to God!"

Saldaña put his hat on sideways. It's a miracle no blows had yet been exchanged, but the dance might have been about to begin when Staupitz, who was at the window, called out, "Peace, boys! Here comes Monsieur de Peyrolles, the Prince of Gonzague's factotum."

He was indeed coming up the slope on horseback.

"We've talked too much and said nothing," said Passepoil quickly. "Nevers and his secret attack are worth gold, my friends, that's all you need to know. Do you want to make your fortune in one stroke?" No need to report the others' response. He went on, "If that's what you want, leave things to Cocardasse and me. Whatever we say to Peyrolles, back us up."

"Understood!" they cried in chorus.

Passepoil sat down. "At least that way tonight those who haven't had their hide punctured by Nevers's sword will be able to pay for a Mass for the deceased."

Passepoil was the first to doff his wool cap in respect as Peyrolles entered. The others greeted him in turn. He had a big bag of money under one arm, which he dropped loudly on the table. "Here you go, men. This is for your refreshments." He looked around and counted them. "Well, you're finally all here. I'll tell you briefly what the job is."

"We're listening, Monsieur de Peyrolles," replied Cocardasse, putting his elbows on the table.

"Oh yeah," said the others, "we're listening."

Peyrolles struck an orator's pose. "This evening around eight o'clock a man will come along the track you can see here, right under the window. He'll be riding. After going down over the rim of the moat, he'll tie up his horse to the bridge posts. Look there, under the bridge; you see a low window with oak shutters?"

"Of course, Monsieur de Peyrolles," replied Cocardasse. "Crooked ace! We're not blind."

"The man will approach the window..."

"And that's when we'll accost him?"

"Politely." Peyrolles gave a sinister smile. "And your pay will be earned."

"God's hat!" cried Cocardasse. "Good old Monsieur de Peyrolles, what a wit!"

"You understand?"

"Of course. But you're not leaving us yet, I hope?"

"I'm in a hurry, friends," said Peyrolles, already making a move to go.

"What!" cried Cocardasse. "Without telling us the name of the man we're supposed to... accost?"

"His name is none of your business."

Cocardasse winked, and all the swordsmen muttered discontentedly. Passepoil declared he was shocked. Cocardasse went on, "And without even telling us the name of the honorable lord we're working for?"

Peyrolles looked at him nervously. "What's it matter?" he said, trying to sound lofty.

"It matters a lot, Monsieur de Peyrolles."

"Even though you're getting paid well?"

"Maybe we'll decide we're not getting paid well enough."

"Which means what, friend?"

"God's hat!" Cocardasse rose, and all the others did the same. Then his tone changed. "My beauty, let's speak frankly. All of us here are masters of arms, and therefore gentlemen. Me especially, being a Gascon with a touch of Provençal. Our rapiers"—and he slapped his own, which he'd kept by him— "our rapiers want to know what they're doing."

"Here," said Passepoil, politely offering Peyrolles a stool. The other swordsmen warmly approved.

Peyrolles hesitated a moment. "Gentlemen, since you want to know so badly... You could easily have guessed: whose castle is this?"

"The Marquis of Caylus's, God's blood! A nobleman whose wives don't grow old. It's Caylus the Jailer's castle. So?"

"Well, aren't you sharp!" said Peyrolles. "You're working for the Marquis of Caylus."

"You believe that, men?" asked Cocardasse rudely.

"No," answered Passepoil.

"No," echoed the others obediently.

The blood rose to Peyrolles's hollow cheeks. "What? You scoundrels!"

"That's right," said Cocardasse. "Be careful—my distinguished friends are murmuring. Instead let's talk this over calmly like reasonable people. If I understand you, here's the situation: the Marquis of Caylus has found out that a fine handsome gentleman has been getting into the castle by night now and then, using that low window. Is that right?"

"Yes."

"He knows his daughter, Mademoiselle Aurore de Caylus, loves that gentleman."

"Quite right."

"That's according to you, Monsieur de Peyrolles! That's how you account for our being here at the Adam's Apple tavern. Other people may consider that a good explanation; I have my own reasons for thinking it's not. You haven't been telling us the truth, Monsieur de Peyrolles."

"Damn your insolence!" cried Peyrolles.

But he was shouted down by the other swordsmen. "Speak, Cocardasse, speak on!"

Cocardasse needed no encouragement. "First, my friends and I know that this night visitor, the man you're aiming our swords at, is no less than a prince."

"A prince!" Peyrolles shrugged.

"Prince Philippe de Lorraine, Duke of Nevers," went on Cocardasse.

"You know more than I do."

"I doubt it, God's hat! That's not all. There's another thing, and that other thing my distinguished friends might not know. Aurore de Caylus isn't Monsieur de Nevers's mistress."

"Oh?"

"She's his wife!"

Peyrolles turned pale. "How do you know that?" he stammered.

"I know it, that's all. How I know it doesn't matter. I'll soon show you I know even more. There was a secret wedding in the castle chapel almost four years ago, and if I'm well informed you and your noble master"—he stopped to take off his hat mockingly—"were present as witnesses."

Peyrolles didn't deny it. "And what's your point with all this gossip?"

"To learn the name of the honorable patron we're working for tonight."

"Nevers married the girl against her father's will. Monsieur de Caylus wants revenge. What could be simpler?"

"Nothing simpler—if the Jailer knew about it. But you were discreet. Monsieur de Caylus knows nothing. God's hat! The sly old man would certainly take care not to kill off the richest son-in-law in France! Everything would've been settled long ago if Monsieur de Nevers had said to the old man, 'King Louis wants me to marry his niece Mademoiselle de Savoy, but I can't because I'm secretly married to your daughter.' But Caylus the Jailer's reputation worried the poor prince: he feared for his wife, whom he adores."

"So where's all this going?"

"Where it's going is, we're not working for Monsieur de Caylus."

"That's clear!" said Passepoil.

"As day," growled the chorus.

"So who do you think you're working for?" asked Peyrolles.

"Who indeed? Do you know the story of the three Philippes? No? Then I'll make it short. They're three noble lords. The first is Philippe of Mantua, Prince of Gonzague—your master, Monsieur de Peyrolles—a nobleman who's bankrupt and on the run, and who'd sell his soul to the devil at a discount. The second is Philippe de Nevers, the man we're waiting for. The third is Philippe de France, Duke of Chartres. All three of them young and handsome and distinguished. And if you tried to imagine the strongest, most heroic, most impossible friendship, you'd still have just a feeble notion of the tender mutual bond between those three Philippes. That's what they say in Paris. Let's leave aside the king's nephew and focus on Gonzague and Nevers, Damon and Pythias."

"So," cried Peyrolles, "now you're going to accuse Damon of wanting to murder Pythias!"

"Well," said Cocardasse, "the original Damon, in the days of the tyrant Dionysus of Syracuse, was comfortably off. And the original Pythias didn't have an income of six hundred thousand écus!"

"Which our Pythias does have," added Passepoil, "and to which our Damon is the heir presumptive!"

"So, Monsieur de Peyrolles, you see how much that changes the picture. I should add, the original Pythias didn't have a lover like Aurore de Caylus, and the original Damon wasn't in love with her, or rather with her dowry."

"And there it is!" concluded Passepoil.

Cocardasse filled his goblet. "Gentlemen, to Damon—I mean, to Gonzague—who as of tomorrow will have six hundred thousand écus in income, plus Mademoiselle de Caylus, plus her dowry, if Pythias—I mean, Nevers—departs this life tonight!"

"To the health of Prince Damon of Gonzague," cried all the swordsmen, led by Passepoil.

"Well, what do you say to all that, Monsieur de Peyrolles?" added Cocardasse triumphantly.

"Daydreams!" growled Peyrolles. "Lies!"

"That's a harsh word. My distinguished friends will decide between us. I take them as witnesses."

"You spoke true, Cocardasse, you spoke true!"

"Prince Philippe de Gonzague," said Peyrolles, striving for dignity, "is so far above such insults, there's no need to defend him."

"All right, Monsieur de Peyrolles, sit down," said Cocardasse.

But Peyrolles resisted, and Cocardasse had to push him down onto a stool by force. "Passepoil, are we going to move on to a greater villainy?"

"Cocardasse!" replied Passepoil.

"Since Monsieur de Peyrolles won't give up, it's your turn to preach."

Passepoil blushed to his ears and lowered his eyes. "But I'm no good at public speaking!" he stammered.

"Get on with it!" ordered Cocardasse. "Crooked ace! These gentlemen will forgive your youth and lack of experience."

"I count on their indulgence," murmured the shy Passepoil. And then, in a voice like that of a girl facing questions at catechism, he began. "Monsieur de Peyrolles has good reason to hold up his master as a perfect gentleman. Here's a detail that struck me; I don't see any harm in it, but meaner spirits might disagree. While the three Philippes were having fun together in Paris—so much fun that King Louis threatened to rusticate his nephew to his country estates—I'm talking about two or three years ago... I was working for an Italian doctor, a student of the great Exilius, named Pierre Garba."

"Pietro Garba Gaete!" cried Faenza. "I knew him. He was a wicked villain."

Passepoil smiled gently. "He was a tidy man, of peaceful habits, pious and scholarly. He made his living preparing a wholesome cordial he called the elixir of long life."

The hired killers all burst out laughing.

"Crooked ace!" said Cocardasse. "You're telling it like a god! Go on!"

Peyrolles mopped the sweat from his brow.

"Prince Philippe de Gonzague," resumed Passepoil, "often came to visit Pierre Garba."

"Not so loud," said Peyrolles.

"Louder!" cried the swordsmen. They were highly entertained, and the more so because they could see the story leading to an increase in their pay. "Speak, Passepoil, speak, speak!" they said, pulling their chairs closer.

And Cocardasse, rubbing the back of Passepoil's neck, said paternally, "The little rascal is a hit, by God!"

"I'm sorry to have to repeat something that seems to displease Monsieur de Peyrolles," went on Passepoil, "but the fact is, the Prince of Gonzague often came to Garba's, no doubt for lessons. Around that time the young Duke of Nevers fell ill with a wasting sickness."

"Slander! Vile slander!"

"Have I accused anyone, sir?" said Passepoil innocently.

Peyrolles bit his lip till it bled.

"Monsieur de Peyrolles isn't talking so big now, is he?" said Cocardasse.

Peyrolles rose suddenly. "I supposed you'll allow me to leave!" he said angrily.

"Of course." Cocardasse laughed heartily. "And we'll even escort you back to the castle. The old Jailer must have finished his siesta, and we'll go talk it over with him."

Peyrolles dropped back onto his stool. His face looked greenish.

Cocardasse, pitiless, offered him a glass. "Have a drink to recover, because you don't look so good. Take a deep drink. No? Well then, relax and let Passepoil finish: he's talking better than a lawyer at the High Court."

Passepoil bowed his thanks and went on. "Soon everyone was saying, 'That poor young Duke of Nevers is dying.' The court and the city grew anxious. The noble house of Lorraine is so distinguished! The king himself asked after him. Philippe the Duke of Chartres was inconsolable."

"Not as inconsolable as Philippe the Prince of Gonzague!" interrupted Peyrolles.

"God forbid I should contradict you," said Passepoil, whose steady politeness ought to serve as a model to anyone in an argument. "I believe indeed that the Prince of Gonzague was saddened. The proof is, every night he came to Master Garba's, disguised as a servant in livery, and every night he complained, 'It's taking too long, doctor, it's taking too long!'"

Every man in the downstairs taproom at the Adam's Apple was a killer, and yet they all shuddered. Their blood ran cold. Cocardasse struck the table with his big fist. Peyrolles bowed his head and said nothing.

"One evening," went on Passepoil, lowering his voice, "Philippe de Gonzague showed up earlier than usual. Garba took his pulse; he had a fever. 'You've won a lot of money gambling,' said Garba, who knew him well. Gonzague laughed. 'I've lost two thousand pistoles.' But then he added, 'At the fencing academy today, Nevers tried to lunge; he's now too weak to hold the rapier.' 'So,' murmured Doctor Garba, 'it's the end. Maybe tomorrow...'" Passepoil paused, then went on quickly and happily, "But every day is different from the day before. The next day, in fact, Philippe the Duke of Chartres put Nevers into his carriage and rode hard for Touraine. His Highness took Nevers to his own estate. Since Master Garba wasn't around, Nevers got better. From there, in search of sun, warmth, life, he moved on to the Mediterranean and reached the Kingdom of Naples. Gonzague came to my master one night and asked him to take a trip down there. I was packing his bags when, unfortunately, his alembic cracked. Poor Doctor Garba breathed the fumes of his own elixir of long life and dropped dead."

"Ah! The honest Italian!" cried all the men.

"Yes," said Passepoil simply, "I miss him. But here's the end of the story. Nevers was away from France for eighteen months. When he returned to court everyone said he looked ten years younger. He was strong, alert, tireless! In short, as you know, second only to handsome Lagardère, Nevers is now the greatest blade in the world." Passepoil fell silent and waited modestly.

"In fact," said Cocardasse, "so great that the Prince of Gonzague felt he needed to hire eight swordsmen to face him. Crooked ace!"

There was a silence, finally broken by Peyrolles. "Where's all this chatter going? You want more money?"

"Lots more," said Cocardasse. "In good conscience, what we charge for a father avenging the honor of his daughter wouldn't be enough to cover a Damon who wants to hurry up his inheritance from Pythias."

"How much do you want?"

"Triple."

"Done." Peyrolles didn't hesitate.

"Secondly, after the job we all get hired on by the house of Gonzague."

"Done."

"Thirdly..."

"You're asking too much," began Peyrolles.

"What a shame!" cried Cocardasse to Passepoil. "He thinks we're asking too much!"

"Let's be fair," said the conciliatory Passepoil. "The king's nephew might want to avenge his friend, and in that case..."

"In that case," answered Peyrolles, "we cross the border, Gonzague buys back his Italian properties, and we're all safe there."

Cocardasse looked at Passepoil, then around at the other men. "It's a deal."

Peyrolles held out his hand, but Cocardasse didn't take it. Instead, he slapped his sword and added, "This is the lawyer who'll guarantee the contract, Monsieur de Peyrolles. Crooked ace! You wouldn't try to cheat us!"

Peyrolles, now free, headed for the door. He stopped on the threshold. "If you don't get him, the deal's off."

"That goes without saying. Sleep well, Monsieur de Peyrolles!"

A loud laugh followed Peyrolles out the door, and then as one the happy voices shouted, "More wine! More wine!"

IV. The Little Parisian

It still wasn't yet four o'clock; our cutthroats had some time. Except for Passepoil, who had gazed too long at the cross-eyed barmaid and was now sighing heavily, everyone in the downstairs taproom at the Adam's Apple was merrily drinking, shouting, and singing. At the bottom of the castle moat, now the heat of the day was past, the haymakers were back at work baling the mown hay. Suddenly the sound of horses came from the edge of the Ens Forest, followed a moment later by cries from the moat: the haymakers shouted as they fled from a band of partisans who struck at them with the flat of their swords. The partisans were after fodder for their horses, and nowhere could they have found a finer harvest.

Our eight bravos watched out the tavern window.

"Those fellows are bold!" said Cocardasse.

"Riding right up under the marquis's walls!" added Passepoil.

"How many are they? Three, six, eight..."

"Just as many as us!"

Meanwhile the raiders calmly took their fodder, laughing and loosening their hot collars. They knew the old castle cannons had long ago fallen silent. Most of them were handsome young men, with two or three gray mustaches among them. They wore buffalo doublets, warlike hats, and long rapiers—the remnants of the recognizable uniforms of assorted regular armies. But, unlike our cutthroats, they also had pistols hanging from their saddles. Two were Italian cavalrymen, one was a Flemish gunner, one was a Catalan guerrilla from over the mountains, and one old crossbowman must have been a veteran of the French civil wars of fifty years earlier. Like worn-away medals, the remainder had lost all distinguishing marks. All of them together could be mistaken for a fine band of highway robbers. And in fact these rogues, who called themselves royal volunteers, weren't much better than bandits.

When they'd finished the job and loaded up their horses, they rode back up the cart track. Their leader, one of the two Italian cavalrymen, who wore a corporal's stripes, pointed to the Adam's Apple tavern. "This way, men. This place will do nicely."

"Hurrah!" they shouted.

"Gentlemen," murmured Cocardasse inside, "I suggest you get your swords."

In a moment all the sword belts were buckled on, and the masters of arms had left the window and sat back down at the tables. You could smell a fight coming a mile away. Passepoil smiled peacefully under his three-whiskered mustache.

"So as we were saying," began Cocardasse for the sake of appearances, "the best way to defend against a left-handed swordsman, which is always dangerous..."

"Hey!" said the leader of the marauders, showing his bearded face at the door. "The tavern's full, men!"

"Then we'll have to empty it," answered his followers. That was only logical. The leader, whose name was Carrigue, had no objections. They all dismounted and boldly tied up their horses—laden with the stolen hay from the castle moat—at the rings set into the tavern wall.

Our masters of arms hadn't moved. Carrigue came in first. "You! Scram, and fast! There's no room here for anyone but the king's volunteers!"

No one answered. But Cocardasse turned to his friends and murmured, "Mind your manners, boys. Let's not get carried away, but let's make the king's volunteers dance in tempo."

Carrigue's men already filled the doorway behind him. "Well?" he said. "What did I just tell you?"

The masters of arms rose and bowed politely.

The Flemish gunner said, "Ask them to go out the window." And he picked up Cocardasse's full glass and brought it to his lips.

Carrigue said, "Hey, yokels, can't you see we need your pitchers and your tables and your stools?"

"Crooked ace!" said Cocardasse. "We'll give you everything, boys." He smashed a pitcher over the gunner's head while Passepoil threw a heavy stool at Carrigue's chest. Sixteen rapiers sprang forth at the same moment. All of the men were brave veteran swordsmen, and brawlers by nature. They went at it hard.

Cocardasse's tenor rose over the tumult. "Give it to 'em! Give it to 'em!"

To which Carrigue and his men replied by charging, heads down. "Forward! Lagardère! Lagardère!"

That was a thunderbolt. Cocardasse and Passepoil, who were at the front, backed up, and put the big table between the two armies. "Crooked ace!" cried Cocardasse. "Lay down your arms, everybody!"

Three or four of the volunteers were already wounded. Their attack had gained them nothing, and they could see only too well what they were up against.

"What did you just say?" asked Passepoil, his voice trembling with emotion. "What did you just say?"

The other masters of arms muttered, "We were about to gobble them up like starlings."

"Quiet!" said Cocardasse firmly. Then he turned to the scattered volunteers. "Tell me the truth. Why did you shout 'Lagardère'?"

"Because Lagardère is our leader," said Carrigue.

"The Chevalier Henri de Lagardère?"

"Yes."

"Our little Parisian! Our darling!" cooed Passepoil, a tear already in his eye.

"One second," said Cocardasse. "Let's avoid any misunderstanding: we left Lagardère in Paris, in the king's light cavalry."

"Well," said Carrigue, "he got bored of that. He kept only his uniform, and now he leads a company of royal volunteers here in this valley."

"In that case, boys," said Cocardasse, "it's over. Sheath your swords! God's life, any friends of the little Parisian's are friends of ours. Let's all drink to the finest blade in the world!"

"Good idea," said Carrigue, who had a feeling his gang was getting off easy. The royal volunteers quickly sheathed their swords.

"Don't we at least get an apology?" said Pépé El Matador, that proud Castilian.

"You'll get the satisfaction of fighting me, if you insist," said Cocardasse. "But as for these gentlemen, they're under my protection. Have a seat, everyone! More wine! I'm not feeling the joy." He held out his glass to Carrigue. "Allow me to introduce my second-in-command, Passepoil, who—no offense—was just about to teach you a lesson you can't even imagine. He is, like me, a devoted friend of Lagardère."

"And proud of it!' interjected Passepoil.

"As for these other gentlemen," went on Cocardasse, "you'll have to forgive their bad mood. They had you, boys, and I took the morsel out of their mouths—still no offense. Let's drink!"

They drank. Cocardasse's last comment had given satisfaction to the masters of arms, and the royal volunteers seemed to think better of objecting. They'd seen the curry comb from too close up. While the barmaid, whom Passepoil had almost forgotten, went to get more wine from the cellar, they carried the stools and tables out onto the lawn, because the downstairs taproom of the Adam's Apple wasn't big enough to hold all of this valiant company. Soon everyone was comfortably settled around the tables on the slope.

"Let's get back to Lagardère," said Cocardasse. "I'm the one who gave him his first fencing lesson. He wasn't yet sixteen, but what a promising future!"

"He's barely eighteen now," said Carrigue, "and God knows he's kept his promise."

Instinctively the masters of arms grew interested in the supposed hero they'd been hearing about all day. They listened, and none of them now wanted to meet him anywhere except at table.

"Yes, he certainly has kept his promise," went on Cocardasse, growing animated. "He's still handsome, still as brave as a lion."

"Always lucky with women," added Passepoil, reddening to his ears.

"Always scatterbrained," went on Cocardasse, "always stubborn."

"Fatal to showoffs, and gentle with the weak."

"A window-breaker, a husband-killer!"

They kept on alternating verses, like two shepherds in Virgil.

"A fine gambler!"

"Throwing money out the window!"

"Every vice!"

"Every virtue!"

"No brains!"

"But a heart, a heart of gold!" It was Passepoil who had the last word. Cocardasse embraced him warmly.

"A toast to the little Parisian! A toast to Lagardère!" they shouted together.

Carrigue and his men raised their glasses enthusiastically. They all stood up to drink. The other masters of arms couldn't say no.

"But damn it all," said Jugan, the Breton, putting down his glass. "Tell us at least who this Lagardère is!"

"Our ears are ringing with his name," added Saldaña. "Who is he? Where does he come from? What does he do?"

"He's as much a gentleman as the king," said Cocardasse. "He comes from the Rue Croix des Petits Champs and calls it home. Satisfied? If you want to hear more, pour me some wine." Passepoil refilled his glass, and after a moment's reflection Cocardasse went on. "It's not a great story, or at least it doesn't tell well. You have to see him at work. As for his birth, I said he's nobler than the king, and I'll stand by that. But in fact, no one knows his father or his mother. When I met him, he was twelve. It was in the Fountain Court at the Palais-Royal. He was getting beaten up by half a dozen street kids bigger than him. Why? Because those delinquents were trying to rob the little old lady who sold meat pies under the arch at the Villa Montesquieu. I asked him his name: 'Little Lagardère.'—'Where are your parents?'—'I have none.'—'Who takes care of you?'—'No one.'—'Where do you live?'—'In the ruined attic of the old Villa Lagardère, at the corner of the Rue Saint Honoré.'—'Do you have a job?' He had two: he dove at the Pont Neuf, and he disarticulated himself at the Fountain Court. Crooked ace! Those are some fine jobs!"

He paused. "The rest of you don't know what it means to dive at the Pont Neuf. Paris is a city of gawkers. At the Pont Neuf the gawkers throw coins into the river, and children risk their lives diving for them. That entertains the gawkers. My God! Nothing would make me happier than to take a blackjack to some of those bourgeois scum! Well worth the price! As for disarticulating: you see contortionists everywhere. That little rascal Lagardère could do anything he wanted with his body—make himself bigger, make himself smaller, make his legs into arms, his arms into legs—I can still see him mimicking the old beadle of Saint Germain l'Auxerrois, who was hunchbacked in front and behind...

"Anyway, I liked the little fellow, with his blond hair and his rosy cheeks. I pulled him out of his enemies' hands and said, 'Want to come with me, you little rascal?' And he said, 'No, I have to watch over old Mother Bernard.' Mother

Bernard was a poor beggar woman who lived in a cranny in that ruined attic. Every night little Lagardère brought her the proceeds from his diving and his contortions. So I described to him all the pleasures of a fencing hall. His bright eyes shone. He sighed and said, 'When old Mother Bernard gets well, I'll come find you.' And he ran off. I thought no more about it.

"Three years later, a big timid cherub showed up at our fencing academy. 'I'm little Lagardère,' he said. 'Old Mother Bernard is dead.' A few gentlemen who were there started to laugh. The big cherub blushed and lowered his eyes, got angry, and threw those gentlemen to the floor. A real Parisian! Slim, agile, as graceful as a woman, but as hard as iron. Six months later he quarreled with one of our provosts, who'd made a snide reference to his talents as a diver and a contortionist. Damn! He manhandled that provost as if he weighed nothing. At the end of a year, he could fence with me the way I could fence with one of these king's volunteers here—no offense, of course.

"So then he became a soldier, and killed his captain in a duel, and deserted. Then he joined a mercenary army headed for Germany, and stole the commander's mistress, and deserted. Then Monsieur de Villars recruited him for a sneak attack on Fribourg. He came back out all by himself, with prisoners—four enemy soldiers roped together like sheep. Villars made him the regimental bugler. He killed his colonel in a duel and was cashiered. Sweetheart! What a boy!

"But Monsieur de Villars liked him—who wouldn't? Villars let him take the king the news of the victory at Baden. The Duke of Anjou saw him and wanted him as a page. So then he became a page, and the women of the Dauphin's household fell in love with him and fought over him from morning to night. He got fired. Finally, fortune smiled on him: he joined the royal light cavalry. And now I don't know whether he left the court on account of a man or a woman. If it was a woman, good for her; if it was a man, may he rest in peace!" Cocardasse stopped and downed a glass. He'd earned it. Passepoil shook his hand in congratulation.

The sun was setting behind the forest. Carrigue and his men began to talk of heading out, and they were all going to drink one last round to toast their lucky meeting, when Saldaña noticed a child creeping along the moat and trying to pass unseen: a shy, frightened boy of thirteen or fourteen, dressed like a page, but without insignia, and wearing a messenger's belt. Saldaña pointed him out to the others.

"By God," said Carrigue, "that's quarry we've already hunted. He wore out our horses last time. The Governor of Benasque sends out spies like him. Let's catch this one."

"Agreed," said Cocardasse, "but I don't think this joker belongs to the Governor of Benasque. There are lots of eels under the rocks around here, mister royal volunteer, and this quarry is ours—no offense." Every time Cocardasse used that expression he gained a point with his friends the masters of arms.

There were two ways to reach the bottom of the moat: by the cart track and by steep stairs at one end of the bridge. The men split into two groups and went down both ways at once. When the poor boy saw he was cornered he didn't try to run, and tears came to his eyes. His hand slipped furtively into his doublet. "Kind lords!" he cried. "Don't kill me! I have nothing! I have nothing!" He took the men for simple robbers—and that's certainly what they looked like.

"Don't lie," said Carrigue. "Did you come through the mountains this morning?"

"Me?" said the boy. "The mountains?"

"The hell with that," said Saldaña. "He came straight from Argelès. Isn't that right, kid?"

"From Argelès?" echoed the boy, and he glanced toward the low window under the bridge.

"Crooked ace!" said Cocardasse. "We're not going to skin you alive, young fellow. Who's that love letter for?"

"Love letter?" echoed the boy again.

Passepoil cried, "You must have been born in Normandy, little duckling!"

Again the boy echoed, "In Normandy, me?"

Carrigue said, "Let's search him."

"No! No!" cried the boy, falling to his knees. "Don't search me, kind lords!" But that was trying to put out the fire by blowing on it.

"He's not from around here," said Passepoil. "He doesn't know how to lie."

"What's your name?" said Cocardasse.

"Berrichon," said the boy without hesitating.

"Who do you work for?"

The boy said nothing. Around him the mercenaries and the volunteers began to lose patience. Saldaña grabbed him by the collar while all the men repeated, "Come on, answer! Who do you work for?"

"You little piece of trash!" said Cocardasse. "You think we have time to play around? Search him, boys, and let's get this over with."

There followed a surprising sight: the page, up to now so timid, suddenly broke free from Saldaña's hands and drew from his doublet a little dagger that looked like a toy. With one leap he passed between Faenza and Staupitz and sprinted toward the eastern side of the moat. But Passepoil had often won first place in the footraces at the Villedieu fair. Young Hippomenes, who ran fast enough to win the heart of Atalanta, couldn't have beaten him. In a few strides he'd caught up with Berrichon. The boy fought fiercely. He scratched Saldaña with his little dagger, he bit Carrigue, he kicked Staupitz in the shins. But it was an unfair fight.

Berrichon, thrown to the ground, could already feel the swordsmen's big hands reaching into his doublet when suddenly a thunderbolt struck his attackers—a thunderbolt! Carrigue went rolling away, his feet flying. Saldaña spun in a circle and slammed into the rampart wall. Staupitz bellowed and collapsed like a stunned ox. Cocardasse himself went end over end and kissed the dirt.

Well! One single man had caused all that, in the blink of an eye and you might say in one stroke. A wide circle formed around the newcomer and the boy. Not one sword was drawn from its scabbard. All the men lowered their eyes.

"The villain!" grumbled Cocardasse as he got up, rubbing his sides. He was furious, but under his mustache he was smiling in spite of himself.

"The little Parisian!" said Passepoil, trembling with either affection or fear.

Without helping Carrigue, who still sprawled dizzily on the ground, his men touched their hats with respect and said, "Captain Lagardère!"

V. The Nevers Attack

It was indeed Lagardère, handsome Lagardère, the breaker of heads, the executioner of hearts. He faced the sixteen rapiers of sixteen masters of arms, sixteen cutthroats—not one of whom dared draw his blade against an eighteen-year-old boy who smiled and folded his arms. And this was Lagardère! Cocardasse and Passepoil hadn't exaggerated. All of their boasting about their idol fell short of the truth.

It's youth that attracts and seduces, youth that even the winners in the game of life look back on with regret, youth that can't be regained even by wealth wrested from—or genius rising over—the cowed common man, youth in its proud godlike bloom, with its curly golden locks and a smile on its lips and the spark of victory in its eyes! People say everybody's young once. Then why sing the praises of a glory shared by all? Have you seen any truly young men? If so, how many? I myself know children who are twenty and old men who are eighteen; I'm still looking for young men. By that I mean men who—giving the lie to the truest of old saws—have wit alongside strength; men who, like the blessed orange trees of sunny lands, bear fruit next to flowers; men who have everything in abundance—honor, courage, vitality, folly—and who, hot and bright as a sunbeam, pour out with both hands the inexhaustible treasure of their lives. Sadly, they often last only a day, because the touch of the crowd acts like water dousing a flame. And often all that splendid treasure is spent in vain, and the brow marked by God as a hero's wears only the crown of debauchery. Often. That's the law: like a moneylender on the street, humanity keeps in its great ledger a column of profits and a column of losses.

Henri de Lagardère was a little taller than average. He was no Hercules, but his limbs had the agile, graceful strength typical of Parisians, as far from the heavy musclebound North as the bony leanness of street boys immortalized in popular comedy. He had slightly curly blond hair above a high forehead marked by intelligence and nobility. His eyebrows were black, as was the thin mustache curling over his lip. Nothing gives a more nonchalant look than that contrast, especially when a pair of laughing brown eyes light up the rather flat pallor of that kind of face.

The shape of his long but symmetrical face, the high arc of his eyebrows, the strong line of his nose and mouth, all added a touch of nobility to the humor of his usual expression. The fun-loving smile didn't erase the swordsman's proud stare. But what can't be captured in writing was the attraction, the grace, the youthful freedom of all his features together, and the mobility of his changeable expression, which in a romantic hour could languish like a woman's soft face and at the hour of battle sweat terror like Medusa's head. Only those he'd killed, or loved, had really seen him.

He wore the elegant uniform of the king's light cavalry, a little disheveled and faded, but improved by a fine velvet cloak thrown carelessly over one shoulder. A sash of red silk with gold fringe marked his rank among the partisans. The recent vigorous exercise seemed barely to have reddened his cheeks. "Shame on you!" he said scornfully. "Roughing up a child!"

"Captain..." began Carrigue as he got back to his feet.

"Shut up. Who are these braggarts?"

Cocardasse and Passepoil stood before him, hat in hand.

Well," said Lagardère more cheerfully, "my two guardians! What the devil are you doing here, so far from the Rue Croix des Petits Champs?" He held out his hand, but like a prince extending his fingers to be kissed. Cocardasse and Passepoil touched his hand worshipfully. It must be said that that hand had often opened to give them gold coins: his guardians had no reason to complain of their protégé.

"And the others?" Lagardère looked at Staupitz. "I've seen that one somewhere before. Where, you?"

"In Cologne," said the German awkwardly.

"That's right: you made one hit land."

"Out of a dozen!" mumbled Staupitz.

"Aha!" Lagardère now looked at Saldaña and Pinto. "My two heroes from Madrid. Good soldiers!"

"Oh, Your Excellency," said the two Spaniards together, "that was a challenge. We weren't used to fighting outnumbered ten to one!"

"What? What?" cried Cocardasse. "You mean two to one in your favor!"

"They claimed they didn't know you," added Passepoil.

Cocardasse pointed at Pépé El Matador. "And this one was looking forward to facing off against you."

Pépé did his best to return Lagardère's look. Lagardère said only, "Him?" And Pépé, muttering, bowed his head. "As for these two heroes," said Lagardère, pointing to Pinto and Saldaña, "in Spain I went by Henri." With one finger he pantomimed the path of a fencing maneuver. "Gentlemen, I see we've all met before, more or less, because here's an honest fellow whose head I split open with the weapon of his own country."

Jugan rubbed his temple. "I still have the scar," he murmured. "You handle a staff like a god, that's for sure."

"Friends, none of you had any luck against me," continued Lagardère. "But at least just now you were all picking on someone your own size. Come here, kid."

Berrichon obeyed. Cocardasse and Passepoil began talking at the same time, trying to explain why they'd wanted to search the boy.

Lagardère silenced them. To the boy he said, "What're you doing here?"

"You saved me, and I won't lie to you," answered Berrichon. "I came to deliver a letter."

43

"To whom?"

Berrichon hesitated, and his glance slid again toward the low window. But he answered, "To you."

"Give it to me."

The boy pulled a folded note from his doublet and held it out. Then he stretched up to Lagardère's ear. "I have another letter to deliver."

"To whom?"

"To a lady."

Lagardère threw him his purse. "Go ahead, kid. No one will bother you."

The boy ran off, and soon disappeared around the bend of the moat. When he was gone Lagardère opened his note. "Back off!" he said, as the volunteers and mercenaries crowded around him. "I like to keep my correspondence private."

They all backed away promptly.

"Hurrah!" he cried after reading the first few lines. "That's what I call good news. This is exactly what I came here for. By God, that Nevers is a staunch nobleman."

"Nevers!" echoed the astonished swordsmen.

"What's this about?" asked Cocardasse and Passepoil.

Lagardère led the way out of the moat and back up the path through the woods to the tavern. "I'm well satisfied. I'll tell you the whole story, but give me a drink first. Sit here, Master Cocardasse, and here, Brother Passepoil, and the rest of you wherever you like."

Cocardasse and Passepoil, proud to be favored, sat on both sides of their hero.

Lagardère took a drink. "You should know that I've been exiled. I'm leaving France."

"You, exiled!" cried Cocardasse.

"We'll live to see him hanged," sighed Passepoil.

"Exiled why?"

Luckily that last question covered Passepoil's fond but irreverent remark: Lagardère didn't tolerate liberties. "You know that big rascal Bélissen?" he asked. "The Baron of Bélissen?"

"Bélissen the sword fighter?"

The late Bélissen," corrected Lagardère.

"He's dead?" asked several voices.

"I killed him. The king had ennobled me, you know, so I could join his light cavalry. I'd promised to behave, and for six months I was as good as gold. They'd almost forgotten me. But one night, Bélissen decided to bully a poor little cadet from the sticks who didn't even shave yet."

"Always the same story," said Passepoil. "A regular knight errant!"

"Shush!" said Cocardasse.

"I went up to Bélissen... but when His Majesty knighted me, I'd promised him not to insult people, so I just pulled the baron's ears, the way they do to naughty schoolboys. He didn't like it."

"I can imagine!" they all cried.

"He said so out loud, so out behind the Arsenal I gave him what he'd been asking for a while: a clean stroke—to the heart!"

"Ah, youngster," cried Passepoil, forgetting times had changed, "you sure know how to deliver that lunge!"

Lagardère began laughing. Then he slammed his pewter goblet on the table: Passepoil thought he was done for. "Here's justice for you!" cried Lagardère. "They should've paid me the hunting bounty, since I'd killed a wolf. Instead, no—they exiled me! The honorable witnesses all thought I'd gone too far."

Cocardasse swore—God's hat!—that the arts weren't sufficiently protected.

"Anyway," went on Lagardère, "I submit to the court's decision. I'm leaving. The world's a big place, and I've vowed to find somewhere to live well. But before I cross the border, I have a whim to satisfy—two whims: a duel and a romantic escapade. That's how I want to say farewell to beautiful France!"

Curious, the men drew closer. "Tell us about it," said Cocardasse.

Instead of answering, Lagardère asked, "Have you men by chance ever heard tell of the secret attack of Monsieur de Nevers?"

"By God!" they exclaimed around the table.

"It came up just a little while ago," said Passepoil.

"And what were you saying about it?"

"Opinions were divided. Some said: piffle! Others claimed old Master Delapalme had sold the duke an attack—or a series of attacks—by means of which the duke was guaranteed to hit a man, no matter who, right between the eyes."

Lagardère grew thoughtful. "What do you think of secret attacks in general, you who are all experts and masters of arms?"

The unanimous feeling was, secret attacks were a con, and in the end any lunge could be defended against with a standard parry.

"That's what I thought," said Lagardère, "before I had the honor of facing off against Monsieur de Nevers."

"And now?" The question came from all sides, because the answer concerned everyone: in a few hours the famous Nevers attack might leave two or three of them stretched out dead on the ground.

"Now I feel differently. You know, that damned attack was a longtime obsession of mine. I swear, it kept me awake! You have to agree, this Nevers got himself talked about too much. Everywhere, all the time, since he came back from Italy, I heard nothing but Nevers! Nevers! Nevers! Nevers is the handsomest! Nevers is the bravest!"

"Second to someone else we know," interjected Passepoil. This time he had Cocardasse's full approval.

"Nevers over here, Nevers over there," continued Lagardère. "Nevers's horses, Nevers's weapons, Nevers's estates! His witticisms, his luck at cards, the list of his mistresses—and on top of it all, his secret attack! Hell and damn! It was giving me a headache! One night my landlady served me lamb chops à la Nevers. I threw the plate out the window and left without eating. At the door I ran into my shoemaker, who was bringing me boots in the latest style, boots à la Nevers. I beat up my shoemaker; it cost me ten louis, which I threw in his face. The rascal said, 'Monsieur de Nevers beat me up once, and he gave me a hundred pistoles!'"

"He overpaid," said Cocardasse seriously. And Passepoil resented his dear little Parisian's frustrations so much that he broke into a sweat.

"You understand," went on Lagardère, "I felt like I was going crazy. I had to make it stop. I got on my horse and went to wait for Monsieur de Nevers to come out of the Louvre. When he passed by, I addressed him by name. 'What is it?' he said. 'Duke,' I answered, 'I have great confidence in your courtesy. I've come to ask you to teach me your secret attack, by moonlight.' He stared at me. He probably took me for an escapee from an asylum. But he said, 'Who are you?' I answered, 'The Chevalier Henri de Lagardère, by grace of the king serving in the royal light cavalry, former bugler, former ensign, former captain, always cashiered for lack of brains.' He got down off his horse. 'Oh, you're handsome Lagardère? I keep hearing about you, and I'm getting tired of it.' We were walking together toward the Church of Saint Germain l'Auxerrois. I said, 'If you don't consider me too much of a gentleman to cross swords with me...' He was charming! So charming! I have to give him that. Instead of answering me, he planted his rapier between my eyebrows, so hard and so neatly I'd still be lying there if I hadn't jumped back twenty feet just in time. 'That's my attack,' he said. Well, I thanked him cordially; it was the least I could do. 'One more time, please,' I said, 'If it's not asking too much.' 'At your service.' Damn—this time he broke the skin on my forehead. I was hit! I, Lagardère!"

The masters of arms exchanged nervous looks. The Nevers attack was growing to worrisome proportions.

"You saw nothing but the flash?" asked Cocardasse timidly.

"I saw the feint, by God," cried Lagardère, "but I never got to parry. That man is as fast as lightning."

"How did the story end?"

"Can the night watch ever leave law-abiding people alone? The night watch showed up. The duke and I parted the best of friends, promising a rematch."

"But, hell!" said Cocardasse. "He'll still get you with his attack!"

"Come on!" said Lagardère.

"You have the secret?"

46

"Of course! I worked on it in the privacy of my room."

"And?"

"It's child's play."

The swordsmen breathed again. Cocardasse rose. "Chevalier, if you remember the humble lessons I gave you with so much pleasure, you won't deny my request."

"How could I?" Lagardère reached for his wallet.

"That's not what Master Cocardasse is asking for," said Passepoil with dignity.

"Speak up then. What would you like?"

"I'd like you to teach me the Nevers attack," said Cocardasse.

Lagardère rose. "That's only fair. It's professional interest."

They stood en garde. The other swordsmen formed a circle around them. The hired killers especially were all eyes.

"God's death!" said Lagardère as he pressed against Cocardasse's blade, "you've grown soft! Let's go, engage in tierce, parry my right thrust! Parry! Right thrust, back to the start... Parry my prime and riposte! Slide along the blade, and up between the eyes!" He matched his actions to his words.

"Thunder and lightning!" said Cocardasse as he jumped aside. "I saw a million stars! And what's the parry?" he said as he put himself en garde again.

"Yes, yes, the parry!" cried the cutthroats.

"Nothing to it!" said Lagardère. "Are you ready? Tierce! In time for the remise. Prime two times! Dodge! Lock swords, and the trick is done."

"Did the rest of you get that?" said Cocardasse, wiping his brow. "God's hat! That little Parisian, what a kid!" The other swordsmen nodded. Cocardasse sat back down. "That could come in handy."

"It's going to come in handy right away," said Lagardère as he poured himself a drink. They all looked up at him. He emptied his glass slowly, sip by sip. Then he unfolded the letter the young page had given him. "Didn't I tell you Monsieur de Nevers had promised me a rematch?"

"Yes, but..."

"I had to settle this business before I go into exile. I wrote to Monsieur de Nevers, at his castle in Béarn. This is his answer."

A murmur of astonishment ran around the group of cutthroats.

"He's still so charming!" Lagardère went on. "When I've fought to my heart's content with this perfect gentleman, I think I'll love him like a brother. He agrees to all the terms I proposed: the time of the meeting, the place..."

"And what time is it for?" asked Cocardasse anxiously.

"Nightfall."

"Tonight?"

"Tonight."

"And the place?"

"The moat of Caylus Castle."

Silence: Passepoil had put his finger to his lips. The cutthroats tried to keep countenance.

"What made you choose that place?" asked Cocardasse.

Lagardère laughed. "That's a whole different story! I've been told, now that I'm leading this band of volunteers—just to pass the time before I leave the country—I've been told the old Marquis of Caylus is the greatest jailer in the world. He must be good at it, to be called Caylus the Jailer! Well, last month at the fair in Tarbes I caught sight of his daughter Aurore. I swear, she's pretty as can be! So after my little conversation with Monsieur de Nevers I plan to go console the charming recluse."

Carrigue pointed to the castle. "Do you have the key to the jail, captain?"

"I've taken plenty of other fortresses by storm! I'll get in by the door, or the window, or the chimney, or who knows how, but I'll get in."

A while back, the sun had gone down behind the Forest of Ens. Night was coming. A few lights could be seen in the lower windows of the castle. A dark shape slid rapidly along in the shadows of the moat. It was Berrichon, the little page, who had no doubt finished his job. From a distance, as he ran up the path leading into the forest, he called out his thanks to Lagardère, his savior.

"So, why aren't you laughing anymore, boys?" said Lagardère. "You don't think it's a bold adventure?"

"In fact," said Passepoil, "a little too bold."

Cocardasse said seriously, "I'd like to know whether you mentioned Mademoiselle de Caylus in your letter to Nevers."

"By God, I explained the whole plan. I had to give him a reason for such an out-of-the-way rendezvous."

The swordsmen exchanged a look.

"Come on now, what's the matter with you?" said Lagardère.

"We're thinking," said Passepoil. "We're happy to be here to be able to help you out."

"That's the truth!" said Cocardasse. "We'll do you a big favor."

Lagardère burst out laughing at the absurdity of the idea.

"Chevalier," said Cocardasse with meaning, "You won't be laughing once I tell you a piece of news."

"Let's hear your news."

"Nevers won't be coming to your rendezvous alone."

"Come on! Why not?"

"Because, after what you wrote to him, your encounter is no longer a fencing match for pleasure. One of you must die tonight. Nevers is Mademoiselle de Caylus's husband."

Cocardasse was mistaken if he thought Lagardère was done laughing. The fool now laughed hard enough to hold his sides. "Bravo! A secret marriage! It's like a Spanish novel! By God, this beats all, and I couldn't have hoped for better in my final adventure!"

Deeply moved, Passepoil said, "And to think, men like him get sent into exile!"

VI. The Low Window

It promised to be a pitch-black night. The dark outline of Caylus Castle could barely be distinguished against the sky. Lagardère rose and tightened the buckle of his sword belt.

"Come on, chevalier," said Cocardasse. "No false pride, God's life! Accept our help in this unequal encounter."

Lagardère shrugged.

Blushing deeply, Passepoil tapped him on the shoulder. "If I can be of any assistance in your romantic escapade..." According to one Greek philosopher, moral experience teaches us that blushing is a sign of virtue. Passepoil was much given to blushing, but he was perfectly devoid of virtue.

"God's blood, boys!" cried Lagardère. "I'm in the habit of taking care of my own business, and you know it. Night's falling. One last round, and then clear off—that's all the service I ask of you."

The partisans went to their horses. The hired killers stayed put.

Cocardasse took Lagardère aside. "I'd die like a dog for you, chevalier," he said with embarrassment, "but..."

"But what?"

"Each man to his task, you know. We can't leave this spot."

"Oh? And why's that?"

"Because we're also waiting for someone."

"Really! And who is this someone?"

"Don't get angry. That someone is Philippe de Nevers."

Lagardère started. "Ah! And why are you waiting for Monsieur de Nevers?"

"We were hired by a certain gentleman..."

He didn't finish. Lagardère's fingers gripped his wrist like a vise. "An ambush! And you dare tell me that!"

Passepoil began, "I would just like to point out..."

"Silence, jokers! I forbid it, you hear me? I forbid you to touch one hair of Nevers's head, or you'll have to deal with me! Nevers is mine. If he has to die, it'll be by my hand, in single combat. Not by yours—not while I live!" Lagardère had drawn himself up straight. He was one of those people whose voice in anger doesn't shake but grows deeper.

The cutthroats stood around him, hesitating.

"And that's why you had me teach you the Nevers attack! And I'm the one who... Carrigue!"

Carrigue came when called, along with his men, leading their horses loaded with hay.

"It's a disgrace!" continued Lagardère. "A disgrace that men of their kind made us share their wine!"

"Hard words," said Passepoil with tears in his eyes. And under his breath Cocardasse muttered all the oaths ever invented in fertile Gascony and Provence.

"Saddle up, on the double!" went on Lagardère. "I don't need any help to punish these jokers!"

Carrigue and his men, who'd already gotten a taste of the cutthroats' rapiers, were quite content to move on a little and enjoy the cool of the evening.

"As for you," said Lagardère, "you'll beat it, and fast. Or by God I'll give you a second fencing lesson—to the blood!" He drew.

Cocardasse and Passepoil made their companions back up: the masters of arms, secure in their numbers, had entertained visions of making a stand.

"Why should we complain if he insists on doing our job for us?" said Passepoil. For solid logic, it would be hard to find many Normans better grounded than Passepoil.

"Let's go!" was the general consensus. It's true that Lagardère's sword was whistling as he sliced the air.

"God's hat!" said Cocardasse as he led the retreat. "Common sense will tell you we're not afraid, chevalier, we're just making way for you."

"To make you happy," said Passepoil. "Goodbye!"

"Go to hell!" replied Lagardère, turning his back.

The partisans took off at a gallop, and the cutthroats disappeared through the tavern yard. They'd forgotten to pay, but Passepoil stole a sweet kiss from the barmaid when she asked for her money.

It was Lagardère who settled the whole bill. "Barmaid! Close the shutters and bar the windows. Whatever you hear down in the moat tonight, make sure everyone in this house sleeps soundly. It's none of your business."

The barmaid closed the shutters and barred the windows.

The night was moonless and starless. One smoky candle stub burned faintly in a saint's niche at the end of the plank bridge, but its glow didn't reach more than a few paces, and the shadow of the bridge kept any light from reaching the moat. Lagardère was alone. The sound of hoof beats had faded into the distance. The whole Louron Valley had fallen into deep darkness, broken here and there by the red glow marking a laborer's shack or a shepherd's hut. The mournful sound of goat bells on the wind joined the muted murmur of the Arau, a brook that empties into the Clarabide at the foot of the Hachaz.

"Eight against one, the wretches!" he said as he followed the cart track down into the moat. "Murder! What villains! It's enough to turn you against swordsmanship."

He came to the haystacks torn apart by Carrigue and his men. "By God," he said, shaking out his cloak, "here's what concerns me: that page will warn Nevers he saw a band of cutthroats down here, and Nevers won't come, and the rendezvous won't happen—the best rendezvous in the world. Hell and damn! If it turns out that way, tomorrow there'll be eight villains laid out."

He was now under the bridge. His eyes were adjusting to the dark. Where he stood now, by the low window, the haymakers had left a large open space, which he surveyed with satisfaction, thinking it would make a fine dueling arena. But he was also pondering how to get into the castle, an idea that obsessed him. Heroes who don't use their exceptional powers for good are a great menace. Walls, locks, guards—handsome Lagardère sneered at all that. An adventure lacking any of those obstacles wouldn't have interested him.

"Let's get to know the terrain," he said, giving in to his gleefully mischievous side. "God's death! The duke will show up angry, and I just have to be ready. We'll have to cross swords with care: I doubt we'll even be able to see the tips of our blades!"

He'd reached the base of the high ramparts. The great mass of the castle rose sheer above him, and the bridge formed a black arc across the sky. To climb the ramparts with the help of a knife would take all night. Feeling his way along, he came to the low window. "All right, good! Now, what'll I say to that proud beauty? I can see from here her shining black eyes and her eagle's brows furrowed with indignation." He rubbed his hands. "Delicious! Delicious! I'll tell her... I need something really well turned. I'll tell her... God's blood! This is no time to be stingy with eloquence!... But what's that?" He stopped to listen. "That Nevers is a charming fellow!"

He could hear footsteps up on the edge of the moat, the footsteps of gentlemen, because they were accompanied by the silvery tinkle of spurs. "Well, well," he thought. "Could Master Cocardasse have been right? Did the duke bring company?"

The footsteps stopped. The light from the candle stump at the end of the bridge revealed two men in long cloaks, standing still. They were obviously peering into the darkness of the moat.

"I see no one," said one of them in a low voice.

"I do," said the other, "there, near the window." And he called carefully, "Cocardasse?"

Lagardère stood still.

"Faenza! It's me, Monsieur de Peyrolles!"

"I feel like I've heard this rascal's name before," thought Lagardère.

Peyrolles called again. "Passepoil? Staupitz?"

"What if he's not one of ours?" murmured his companion.

"Impossible," said Peyrolles, "I told them to leave a lookout here. It's Saldaña, I recognize him—Saldaña?"

"Here!" answered Lagardère, taking a guess and using a Spanish accent.

"See?" cried Peyrolles. "I knew it! Let's take the stairs down—here's the top step."

"Hell if I haven't just been given a role in this little play!" thought Lagardère.

The two men began to climb down. Under his cloak Peyrolles's companion looked well built and wealthy. Lagardère thought he detected a light Italian flavor in the man's accent.

"Please keep your voice down," said the man as they came carefully down the steep, narrow stairs.

"No need, my lord," answered Peyrolles.

"So," thought Lagardère, "he's a lord!"

"No need," repeated Peyrolles. "These fellows know perfectly well who's paying them."

"Well, I don't," thought Lagardère, "and I'd like to find out."

"I did my best," went on Peyrolles, "but they just wouldn't believe it was the Marquis of Caylus."

"That's already useful to know," thought Lagardère. "Clearly I'm dealing with two utter scoundrels."

"Did you go to the chapel?" asked the man who seemed to be in charge.

"I got there too late," said Peyrolles apologetically.

The other stamped his foot angrily. "Blunderer!"

"I did what I could, my lord. I found the register where Father Bernard recorded the marriage of Mademoiselle de Caylus with Monsieur de Nevers, as well as the birth of their daughter..."

"And?"

"Those pages had been torn out."

Lagardère was all ears.

"We were warned," said the master, disappointed. "But who did it? Aurore? Yes, it must've been Aurore. She expects to see Nevers tonight, and she wants to give him, along with the child, the record that establishes her birth. Dame Marthe couldn't tell me that, because she didn't know it, but I can guess it."

"What's it matter?" said Peyrolles. "We're in good shape. Once Nevers is dead..."

"Once Nevers is dead," interrupted his master, "the inheritance goes straight to the child."

There was a silence. Lagardère held his breath.

"The child..." began Peyrolles very quietly.

"The child will disappear," said the one he'd addressed as my lord. "I would've preferred to avoid that step, but it won't hold me back. What kind of man is this Saldaña?"

"A ruthless villain."

"Can he be trusted?"

"Yes, as long as he's well paid."

The master thought for a moment. "I would've liked to have no one in-volved beyond ourselves, but neither you nor I could pass for Nevers."

"You're too tall," agreed Peyrolles, "and I'm too thin."

"It's as dark as an oven," said his master, "and this Saldaña is about the size of the duke. Call him."

"Saldaña?" called Peyrolles.

"Here!" said Lagardère again.

"Come here!"

Lagardère came forward. He'd raised the collar of his cloak, and the brim of his hat hid his face.

"You want to earn an extra fifty pistoles, on top of your share?" asked the master.

"Fifty pistoles! What do I have to do?" As he spoke Lagardère did his best to make out the features of the unknown man, but he was as well hidden as Lagardère himself.

"Can you guess?" the master asked Peyrolles.

"Yes."

"Do you agree?"

"I agree. But our man has a password."

"Dame Marthe gave it to me. It's the motto of Nevers."

"*Adsum*?" said Peyrolles.

"He says it in French: Here I am!"

Lagardère couldn't help echoing, "Here I am!"

The unknown man leaned closer to him. "You'll say that very quietly un-der the window. The shutters will open, and then the bars, which are hinged. A woman will appear. She'll speak to you, but you won't say a word, and you'll put your finger to your lips. Got it?"

"To make her think we're being watched? Yeah, I get it."

"Smart boy," murmured the master. "The woman will pass you a bundle, you'll take it in silence, and you'll bring it to me."

"And you'll give me fifty pistoles?"

"Right."

"I'm your man."

"Shhh!" hissed Peyrolles. All three of them listened. There was a sound far off in the countryside.

"Let's split up," said the master. "Where are your partners?"

Without hesitating, Lagardère pointed beyond the bridge to where the moat curved toward the Hachaz. "There, hiding in the haystacks."

"Good. You remember the password?"

"Here I am!"

"Good luck, and see you soon."

"See you soon!"

Peyrolles and his companion climbed back up the staircase. As Lagardère watched them go, he wiped the sweat off his brow. "God will remember, on my dying day, the effort I had to make not to plunge my sword into those wretches' bellies! But I have to follow this thing through. I have to know!" He held his head in his hands, because his mind was boiling with ideas. We can be sure he was no longer thinking about either his duel or his romantic escapade. "What should I do? Run away with the child? Because that bundle must be the child! But who to give her to? I know no one in these parts except Carrigue and his bandits—bad nannies for a young lady! And yet I have to take her! I have to! If I don't get her out of here, those villains will kill the child just like they plan to kill the father. God's death! This isn't why I came here!"

In great agitation he paced back and forth between the haystacks, constantly glancing over at the low window to see if the shutters were turning on their rusty hinges. He saw nothing, but soon he could hear a slight noise from inside. The bars behind the shutters were being opened.

"*Adsum*?" said a woman's voice, soft and trembling.

Lagardère leaped across the hay bales between him and the wall, and under the window he said, "Here I am!"

"Thank God!" said the woman's voice. And the shutters opened.

The night was dark, but Lagardère's eyes had long since adjusted. He could see perfectly well that the woman leaning out the window was Aurore de Caylus, still beautiful, but pale and broken by worry. If you'd reminded Lagardère at that moment that his intention had been to make his way into that woman's room by surprise, he would have denied it, and in good faith. If only for a few minutes, his usual spirit of feverish mischief lay dormant: he was as wise and bold as a lion. Maybe at that moment another man was born in him.

Aurore looked straight ahead. "I see nothing. Philippe, where are you?"

Lagardère held out his hand, and she pressed it to her heart. Lagardère staggered; he felt on the brink of tears.

"Philippe, Philippe," she went on, "are you sure you weren't followed? We've been betrayed, sold out!"

"Have courage, Madame," blurted Lagardère.

"Was that you who spoke?" she cried. "I must be going crazy! I don't recognize your voice!" In one arm she held the bundle Peyrolles and his companion had mentioned; with her other hand she pressed her forehead as if to tame her wild thoughts. "I have so much to tell you! Where should I start?"

"We don't have time," murmured Lagardère, trying to avert the shame of overhearing intimacies. "Hurry, Madame."

"Why that icy tone? Why don't you call me Aurore? Are you angry with me?"

"Hurry, Aurore, hurry!"

"I obey, dear Philippe, I'll always obey! Here's our little darling, take her. She's no longer safe with me. My letter must have explained everything. Some plot is being spun around us."

She held out the sleeping child, who was wrapped in a silk jacket. Lagardère received her without a word.

"Let me kiss her once more!" cried the poor mother, her chest heaving with sobs. "Give her back, Philippe! Oh, I thought my heart was strong enough! Who knows when I'll see my daughter again?" Tears choked her voice.

Lagardère saw she was handing something white out to him. "What's this?"

"You know—but you're as confused as I am, poor Philippe. It's the pages torn out of the chapel registry: our child's future!"

Afraid to speak, he took the papers in silence. They were folded inside an envelope with the seal of the Caylus parish chapel. At the moment he took the envelope, the long mournful sound of a shepherd's horn rang down the valley.

"That must be a signal," she cried. "Run, Philippe, run!"

"Farewell," said Lagardère, playing his role to the end so as not to break the young mother's heart. "Don't worry, Aurore, your child is safe."

Aurore pulled his hand to her lips and kissed it passionately. "I love you!" she said through her tears. Then she closed the shutters and vanished.

VII. Two Against Twenty

It was indeed a signal. Three men with shepherd's horns had been stationed along the road from Argelès, which the Duke of Nevers had to follow to get to Caylus Castle—where he was summoned both by the pleading letter from his young wife and by the insolent note from the Chevalier de Lagardère. The first man was supposed to send his signal when Nevers crossed the Clarabide, the second when he entered the forest, and the third when he reached the edge of the village of Tarrides. All along the way there were good spots to commit a murder. But Philippe de Gonzague was not in the habit of launching open attacks: he wanted to conceal his crime. The murder would be made look like revenge, and—whether he liked it or not—would be credited to old Caylus the Jailer.

Behold now our handsome Lagardère, our incorrigible quarreler, our first-class fool, behold the finest swordsman in all of France and Navarre, with a two-year-old child in his arms. You can imagine how awkward he felt: he carried the child clumsily, the way a shop clerk plays sports; he rocked her in his arms, unused to this new job. He had only one concern in the world now—not to wake the little girl!

"Rockabye baby," he said, his eyes moist, but at the same time he had to laugh.

You could have given his old companions in the king's light cavalry odds of a thousand to one: not one would have guessed what this notorious swashbuckler on his way to exile was doing at this moment. He was fully given over to his new role of nursemaid: he set his feet down carefully to keep from shaking the sleeper, and he wished he had a cotton-filled cushion in each arm.

A second horn call, closer than the first, sent its plaintive note into the night silence. "What the devil is that?" said Lagardère. But he kept his eyes on little Aurore. He didn't dare kiss her. She was a beautiful little creature, white and pink. Her closed eyelids already had the long silky lashes she inherited from her mother. An angel, a sweet angel of God, asleep! He listened to her soft, pure breathing, and admired her deep calm, her sleep that was one long smile. "Such calm, such sleep, while her mother weeps and her father—ah, this changes everything. A child's been entrusted to scatterbrained Lagardère. All right, to protect the child, he'll have to gather his wits... How she sleeps! What thoughts could possibly cross a brow crowned with such angelic curls? There's a soul in there. She'll grow into a woman who can enchant—and, alas, suffer!... How good it must feel to win, bit by bit, by care and tenderness, all the love of these dear little creatures, to watch for their first smile, to wait for their first kiss, and how easy it must be to devote yourself entirely to their happiness!"

And so forth: a thousand foolish thoughts that would never have crossed the minds of most sensible men, and a thousand innocent tender thoughts that would make those men smile but bring tears to the eyes of mothers. And lastly this word, this final word, spoken from the bottom of his heart like an act of contrition: "Ah! I've never held a child in my arms!"

At that moment the third signal sounded from behind the huts in the village of Tarrides. Lagardère started and awoke: he'd been dreaming he was a father. Quick footsteps rang out from behind the Adam's Apple tavern, steps that couldn't be mistaken for those of the cutthroats who'd been there earlier. At the first sound of those steps Lagardère thought, "It's him."

Nevers must have left his horse at the edge of the forest. Less than a minute later Lagardère—who now understood those repeated horn calls had been about Nevers—saw him pass in front of the candle that lit the Virgin's shrine at the end of the bridge. The fine face of Philippe de Nevers, pensive though very young, was brightly lit for a second; then only a proud tall silhouette; then the man disappeared. He came down the stairs built into the wall of the moat. When he reached the floor of the moat, he drew his sword and muttered, "A couple of torch bearers would come in handy here." Nevers felt his way forward, stumbling on the scattered hay bales. "Is that damned chevalier trying to make me play blind man's bluff?" he said with growing impatience. Then he stopped. "Ho there! Anybody here?"

"I'm here," said Lagardère, "and thank God there's no one else!"

Nevers didn't hear the second part, but moved quickly toward the sound of the voice. "Let's get down to business, chevalier! Just draw your sword, so I can tell where you are. I can't spare you much time."

Lagardère was still rocking the little girl, who slept deeper than ever. "Before we start, duke, you have to hear me out."

"Much chance you have of persuading me to do that, after the message I got from you this morning. Now that I can see you, chevalier—en garde!"

It hadn't even occurred to Lagardère to draw: his sword, which usually jumped out of its scabbard all by itself, seemed to be as fast asleep as the little angel in his arms. "When I sent you that message this morning, I didn't know what I know tonight."

"Oh?" said Nevers mockingly. "You don't like sword fighting in the dark, I can see that much." He stepped forward, sword raised.

Lagardère retreated and drew his sword. "Just listen to me!"

"So you can insult Mademoiselle de Caylus again?" Nevers's voice shook with anger.

"No, on my honor! No! I'm trying to tell you—damn it!" Lagardère parried Nevers's first lunge. "Be careful!"

Nevers thought Lagardère was making fun of him. Furious, he threw himself at his opponent with all his might, lunging over and over with all the speed that made him so dreaded a fencer. At first Lagardère parried without backing up and without riposting. Then he tried to give way while still parrying, and each time he blocked Nevers's blade to right or left he cried, "Listen to me! Listen to me! Listen to me!"

"No! No! No!" replied Nevers, each time with a deadly lunge.

Lagardère had now given way until his back was against the rampart wall. He felt his ears growing hot. To resist for so long the urge to deliver one solid counterattack—that's heroism! "Listen to me!" he cried one last time.

"No!"

"You can see I can't back up any further!" said Lagardère in a tone of distress that had its funny side.

"All the better!"

"All the devils in Hell!" cried Lagardère, out of parries and out of patience. "Do I have to split your head open to keep you from killing your own child?"

It was like a thunderclap. The sword fell from Nevers's hand. "My child! My daughter, in your arms!"

Lagardère had wrapped his cloak around his precious burden. In the dark, Nevers had assumed he was using his cloak rolled around his left arm as a shield, as was commonly done. His blood froze in his veins as he thought of the furious lunges he'd delivered. His rapier could have...

"Chevalier," said Nevers, "you're a fool, like me and many others, but you're an honorable fool, a brave fool. If they told me you were in the pay of the Marquis of Caylus, I wouldn't believe them."

"Much obliged." Lagardère was panting like the winner of a horse race. "What a hail of sword blows! You're a lunging machine, duke!"

"Give me my daughter!" said Nevers, and he tried to unwrap the cloak.

But Lagardère knocked his hand away. "Gently! You'll wake her."

"Will you at least tell me..."

"Listen to the man! First, he wouldn't let me speak, now he's trying to force me to speak! Kiss her, dad, come on, gently, gently."

Nevers did as he was told.

"Have you ever seen a match like that at a fencing academy?" said Lagardère with innocent pride. "Holding off a full-scale attack, an attack by Nevers, by Nevers angry, without once riposting, with a sleeping child on one arm, a child who didn't wake up?"

"For God's sake!" pleaded Nevers.

"At least tell me it was well done! I'm drenched in sweat! You'd like to know what's going on, wouldn't you? Enough kisses, dad! Let go now. The kid and I are already old friends. I'd bet a hundred pistoles—if I had 'em!—she'll smile at me when she wakes up."

Lagardère wrapped his cloak around the child again, with more care than many a wet nurse. Then he set her down in the hay, by the rampart under the bridge. "Duke," he said in a more serious and manly tone, "I'll guard your daughter with my life, come what may. In doing so I'll make amends as far as I can for the wrong I did in speaking lightly of her mother, who is a beautiful, noble, saintly woman."

"You're going to kill me," groaned Nevers in agony. "You saw Aurore?"

"I saw her."

"Where?"

"Here at the window."

"And she gave you the child!"

"She thought she was entrusting her daughter to her husband."

"I'm so confused!"

"Ah, duke, strange things are going on here! Thank God you're in a mood to fight, because in a little while you'll have fighting to your heart's content."

"An ambush?"

Lagardère dropped suddenly and put his ear to the ground. "I thought they were coming," he murmured as he got up again.

"Who?"

"Cutthroats hired to murder you." Lagardère quickly reported the conversation he'd overheard, and his own exchange with Monsieur de Peyrolles and an unknown man, and his encounter with Aurore, and what followed. Nevers listened, dumbfounded.

"As a result," concluded Lagardère, "I won my fifty pistoles without doing anything."

Half to himself Nevers said, "That Peyrolles is the right-hand man of Philippe de Gonzague, my best friend, my brother, who's visiting at the castle now to help me!"

"I've never had the honor of meeting the Prince of Gonzague," said Lagardère, "so I don't know if it was him."

"Him!" cried Nevers. "Impossible! That Peyrolles has the look of a villain; he must've been bought off by old Caylus."

Lagardère calmly polished his sword with the hem of his doublet. "It wasn't Monsieur de Caylus. It was a young man. But let's not get lost in speculation, duke. Whoever the wretch is, he's a clever one. His plans were well made—right down to knowing your password. It's thanks to the password I was able to fool Aurore de Caylus. Oh, she certainly loves you! And I wanted to kiss the ground at her feet to make up for my fatuous stupidities!... Let's see, is there anything else to tell you? Only that there's a sealed envelope inside the child's pelisse: her birth record and your marriage record... Ah, my beauty!" he said, admiring his polished sword, which seemed to draw in all the starlight and throw it back in a bouquet of wild sparks, "our toilette is complete. We've done enough mischief; from now on we're going to swing for a good cause, missy. So get ready!"

Nevers took his hand with deep feeling. "Lagardère, I misjudged you. You're a noble soul."

Lagardère laughed. "I have only one goal now: to get married as soon as possible, so I can have my own little blonde angel to kiss. But shhh!" He dropped to his knees. "This time I'm not mistaken."

Nevers leaned down to listen. "I hear nothing."

"That's because you're a duke." Lagardère stood up again. "Someone's creeping along over there by the Hachaz, and also here, to the west."

"If I could only let Gonzague know the position I'm in," reflected Nevers out loud, "we'd have another good blade on our side."

Lagardère shook his head. "I'd rather have Carrigue and my men with their guns. Did you come alone?"

"With a boy, Berrichon, my page."

"I know him. He's nimble and smart. If we could get him to come..."

Never put his fingers between his lips and gave a loud whistle. A similar whistle answered from behind the Adam's Apple.

"The question," murmured Lagardère, "is whether he can get to us."

"He could get through the eye of a needle," said Nevers.

Indeed, a moment later the boy appeared at the top of the moat.

"Good boy!" cried Lagardère, moving toward him. "Jump!" Berrichon obeyed, and Lagardère caught him in his arms.

"Hurry," said the boy, "they're getting closer up there. In a minute there won't be any way out."

Lagardère was surprised. "I thought they were down here."

"They're everywhere!"

"But there are only eight of them?"

"At least twenty. When they saw there were two of you, they recruited the smugglers from Mialhat."

"Bah," said Lagardère, "eight or twenty, what's the difference? Get on your horse, boy. My men are over at the hamlet of Gau. It'll take half an hour to get there and come back. Go!" He grabbed the boy's legs and lifted him. Berrichon reached up and was able to grab onto the edge of the moat. A few seconds later a whistle announced he'd reached the forest.

"Hell," said Lagardère, "we can hold them off for half an hour, if they give us time to prepare our fortifications."

"Look!" Nevers pointed to something shining faintly on the other side of the bridge.

"That's the sword of Brother Passepoil, a meticulous rascal who never lets his blade get rusty. Cocardasse must be with him. They won't attack me. Give me a hand, please, duke, while there's still time."

On the floor of the moat, besides stacked or scattered hay bales, lay all kinds of debris—planks, logs, dead branches—plus a half-filled cart the hay-makers had abandoned when Carrigue and his men fell on them. Taking the cart as their rallying point and the spot where the child was sleeping as their center, Lagardère and Nevers quickly improvised a system of barricades, so as to break their attackers' first assault at least. Lagardère directed the work. It was a shabby and minimal citadel, but it had the benefit of being built in a minute. Lagardère pulled debris together here and there; Nevers stacked hay bales into an embankment; they left openings for sorties. The great Vauban would have envied their impromptu little fort. Half an hour! They had to hold out for half an hour!

While they worked Nevers asked, "Are you really going to fight for me, chevalier?"

"And fight hard, duke! Partly for you, mostly for the little girl."

The fortifications were ready. They weren't much, but in the dark they might serve to slow down the attack. The two defenders counted on that, but they counted still more on their good blades.

"Chevalier," said Nevers, "I won't forget this. From here on between us it's life and death."

Lagardère held out his hand. Nevers took it and pulled him into a hug. "Brother, if I live, we'll share everything in common. If I die..."

"You won't die," interrupted Lagardère.

"If I die..." repeated Nevers.

"Then, to earn my place in heaven," cried Lagardère, moved, "I'll be her father!"

They held their embrace for moment, and never did braver hearts beat one against another.

Then Lagardère disengaged. "Swords out—here they come!"

Muffled sounds filled the night. Lagardère and Nevers held their naked swords in their right hands, while their left hands were still joined. Suddenly the darkness seemed to move, and a great shout enveloped them. The murderers fell on them from all sides at once.

VIII. The Battle

Berrichon hadn't lied: there were at least twenty, including not only the smugglers from Mialhat but half a dozen highway robbers picked up in the valley. That's why the attack had been delayed.

Monsieur de Peyrolles had found the hired killers waiting in ambush and was surprised to see Saldaña. "Why aren't you at your post?"

"At what post?"

"Didn't I talk to you a little while ago in the moat?"

"To me?"

"Didn't I promise you fifty pistoles?"

They explained themselves. When he realized he'd blundered, when he learned the name of the man to whom he'd betrayed himself, Peyrolles was filled with fear. The cutthroats tried to explain that Lagardère himself was there to duel Nevers, that between them it was a fight to the death, but Peyrolles wasn't reassured. He understood instinctively the impression that the sudden discovery of treachery would have on a young and virtuous spirit. By now Lagardère must be in league with Nevers. By now Aurore de Caylus must have been warned—because Peyrolles couldn't guess what Lagardère had done, and couldn't conceive the rashness of a man who would accept the care of a child before a fight. Peyrolles himself took on the job of alerting his master and watching Aurore de Caylus. Meanwhile he sent Staupitz, Pinto, Pépé El Matador, and Saldaña out to recruit reinforcements. In those days, especially near the border, you could always find rapiers for hire. The four masters of arms returned well accompanied.

But how can we express the profound embarrassment, the pangs of conscience, in a word the distress of Cocardasse Junior and his alter ego Brother Passepoil? They were a pair of rascals, we freely admit. They killed for hire. Their rapiers were no better than a cutthroat's stiletto or a bandit's knife. But the poor fellows didn't do it out of malice: it was just their livelihood. Blame a debased age and low morals more than you blame them. It was a shining century, lit by so much glory, but the brilliance was only on the surface, under which lay chaos. And even the surface glitter and brocade showed stains. The war had corrupted everything, from high to low. It had been a mercenary war from the start. For most of the generals, just as for the lowest of the foot soldiers, the sword was just a tool, and valor was just a job.

Cocardasse and Passepoil loved their little Parisian, who stood head and shoulders above them; and affection grows fierce and strong in corrupt hearts. Besides that affection, whose origins we know, Cocardasse and Passepoil were utterly incapable of doing good. They had some seeds of good in them, and that business with the little orphan from the ruins of the Villa Lagardère wasn't the only good deed they'd done in their lives by accident and inadvertence. But their love for Lagardère was their best quality, and though it had an element of egotism, since they saw themselves reflected in their talented student, it must be said their friendship wasn't based on self-interest. Cocardasse and Passepoil would gladly have risked their lives for Lagardère. And yet here tonight fate had placed them against him. No way to retract: Peyrolles had paid for their blades. To skip out or to abstain would be to fail badly in a point of honor rigorously upheld by their professional peers.

They'd spent a whole hour without exchanging a word. Cocardasse had gone the whole evening without using his favorite exclamation, God's hat! They both sighed deeply, in unison. From time to time, they looked at each other pitifully. That was all. When everyone was suiting up for battle, the pair shook hands sadly.

Passepoil said, "What can we do? We'll do our best."

And Cocardasse sighed, "It can't be, brother, it can't be. Do what I'm doing." From his pocket he took the round metal button he used at the fencing academy and stuck it on the tip of his rapier. Passepoil did the same. Then, their hearts lighter, they could breathe again.

The cutthroats and their new reinforcements were divided into three groups: the first went around the moat to approach from the west; the second waited beyond the bridge; the third, made up mostly of highwaymen and smugglers led by Saldaña, would make a frontal attack down the little staircase.

For a few seconds now, Lagardère and Nevers had see them clearly enough to count the men creeping down the staircase.

"Look out!" said Lagardère. "Let's stand back-to-back and stay up against the rampart. The child will be safe behind the bridge post. Be careful, duke. I warn you, they might try to teach you your own attack—if you happen to have forgotten it." And he grumbled bitterly, "To think I'm the one who stupidly did that! But hold tight. As for me, my skin's too tough for those scoundrels' swords."

Without the precautions they'd taken so quickly, the first shock of the cutthroats' assault would have been devastating. They all attacked at once, heads down, shouting, "Get Nevers! Get Nevers!" Above the general cry Cocardasse and Passepoil could be heard sharing words of comfort that at least the attackers hadn't singled out their former student.

The cutthroats didn't know about the obstacles thrown in their way. Those fortifications, which may have struck the reader as a feeble resource, proved wonderfully effective at first. All those men with heavy gear and long rapiers ran up against the beams and tripped over the hay bales. The few who reached our two heroes came away carrying their mark. After a lot of noise and confusion, one bandit lay on the ground. As soon as most of the murderers began to fall back, Nevers and Lagardère went on the attack.

"Here I am! Here I am!" they cried together and threw themselves forward. Lagardère's first lunge ran a bandit through from front to back. Pulling out his sword and swinging behind him, he cut off a smuggler's arm. Then, unable to slow his momentum and getting too close to a third man to swing, he smashed his skull with a blow of his pommel. That third man was the German, Staupitz, who fell heavily backwards.

Nevers too was carving away. Besides a partisan he'd thrown under the wheels of the hay cart, he had seriously wounded both Pépé El Matador and Jugan. But as he was about to finish off the latter, he saw two shadows gliding along the wall, going toward the bridge. "Help me, chevalier!" he cried as he dropped quickly back.

"Here I am! Here I am!" Lagardère waited only long enough to drop a fine cleaver blow on Pinto, who went the rest of his life with only one ear. "God's life!" he said as he rejoined Nevers, "I almost forgot my darling little blonde angel!"

The two shadows had fled. A deep silence filled the moat. A quarter of an hour had passed.

"Catch your breath fast, duke," said Lagardère. "Those jokers won't let you rest for long. Are you wounded?"

"A scratch."

"Where?"

"On my forehead."

Lagardère clenched his fists and said no more: it was the result of his fencing lesson.

Two or three minutes went by, and then the assault began again, but this time it was serious and coordinated. The attackers came in two lines and took care to move the obstacles aside before advancing further.

"It's time to fight for keeps!" murmured Lagardère. "Worry only about yourself, duke. I'll cover the child."

A silent somber circle began to close around them. Ten blades stretched out.

"Here I am!" cried Lagardère, leaping forward once again. El Matador gave a cry and fell across the bodies of two dead bandits. The cutthroats backed up, but only by a few feet. The last men to arrive still shouted, "Get Nevers! Get Nevers!"

And Nevers, who was warming to the game, answered, "Here I am, boys! You want a piece of me? And another! And another!" And each time he drew his blade out wet and red. Ah, they were a proud pair of fighters!

"Your turn, Señor Saldaña!" cried Lagardère. "That's the lunge I taught you at Segorbe! Your turn, Faenza! Come closer—it would take a cathedral halberd to reach you!" He stabbed, he scythed. Already, of the highway bandits who'd been sent in the first wave, not one remained.

Someone waited behind the shutters of the low window. It wasn't Aurore de Caylus. Two men listened, ice in their veins and sweat cooling on their foreheads: Peyrolles and his master.

"Wretches!" said the latter. "They outnumber them ten to one and it's not enough! Do I have to go out there myself?"

"Take care, my lord!"

"We can't risk either one of them surviving!"

Outside, the cry of "Here I am! Here I am!" rose again. In fact, the circle was widening as the attackers dropped back. In just a few minutes the half hour would be up, and help would come. Lagardère was untouched, and Nevers had only that one scratch on his forehead. Both of them could have fought on like this for an hour.

But in the enthusiasm of victory, they began to drift away from their position to attack the cutthroats. Didn't the ring of dead and wounded around them clearly prove their superiority? They exulted—but caution dies as exhilaration is born. This was the moment of greatest danger. They couldn't tell that all those dead and wounded were just reserves, backups sent in first to tire them out.

The masters of arms were still on their feet, except for Staupitz, who had only passed out. They all kept back, biding their time. They said, "If we can separate them, and if they're made of flesh and blood, we'll get them."

For a while now their actions had been aimed at drawing one of the heroes forward while keeping the other backed against the wall. Jugan—twice wounded—Faenza, and Cocardasse and Passepoil were assigned to Lagardère; the three Spaniards took on Nevers; and the remaining auxiliaries were divided evenly between them. At a given moment the first group was supposed to drop back while the other group held firm.

At the first attack, Cocardasse and Passepoil dropped to the rear. Jugan and Faenza each received a well-aimed blow. At the same time Lagardère, turning, slashed El Matador's face as he pressed too close to Nevers.

"Run for your lives!" rang out the general cry.

"Forward!" cried Lagardère.

"Forward!" echoed Nevers.

"Here I am! Here I am!" they both cried.

Everyone fell away in front of Lagardère, and in the blink of an eye he found himself at the other side of the moat. But in front of Nevers stood a wall of steel, and his momentum carried him only a few feet. He wasn't one to call for help. He held on, and God knows the three Spaniards had a job of it. Both Pinto and Saldaña were already wounded.

At that moment the iron bars over the low window a few feet from Nevers ground on their hinges. The shutters opened. Surrounded as he was by noise and movement, he heard nothing. One at a time, two men climbed out into the moat. Nevers didn't see them. Both men had their swords drawn. The bigger man wore a mask.

"Victory!" cried Lagardère, who'd cleared the ground around him.

Nevers replied with a cry of agony. One of the two men who'd come out the window, the bigger, masked man, had just run him through from behind. Nevers fell. The stroke had been aimed Italian-style, as they say, which means expertly, surgically. The cowardly deathblows that followed it made no difference. As he fell Nevers turned and fixed his dying eyes on the masked man with a look of bitter anguish. The moon, in its last quarter, was just rising behind the castle towers; it couldn't yet be seen, but its pale glow indistinctly lit the shadows.

"You! It's you!" murmured the dying man. "Gonzague! You, my friend, for whom I would've given my life a hundred times!"

"I'm only taking it once," said the masked man coldly.

Nevers's pallid head fell back.

"He's dead," said the masked man. "Now for the other one." But there was no need to go after him, because he was coming. When Lagardère heard Nevers's death rattle, he didn't shout, he roared. The masters of arms had closed ranks against him—but try to stop a springing lion! Two cutthroats rolled on the ground; Lagardère got through.

As he reached Nevers, the duke raised his head and said dully, "Brother! Don't forget! And avenge me!"

"By God, I swear it!" cried Lagardère. "Every man here will die by my hand!"

The child under the bridge cried out, as if she'd been woken by her father's death rattle, but the faint sound went unnoticed.

"Get him! Get him!" cried the masked man.

"You're the only man here I don't know," said Lagardère as he rose, now alone against all. "Since I've sworn an oath, I'll have to know how to find you when your hour has come."

Between the masked man and Lagardère stood five masters of arms and Peyrolles. But they weren't the first to attack. Lagardère grabbed a hay bale as a shield and broke through the line of cutthroats like a cannonball. His momentum carried him to the center of the circle. Only Saldaña and Peyrolles now stood between him and the masked man, who raised his blade. Lagardère's sword, slicing between Peyrolles and his master, gashed the latter's hand.

"You've been marked!" cried Lagardère as he retreated. He alone had heard the waking child's first cry. In three strides he was under the bridge. The moon had now risen above the towers. Everyone saw him pick up a bundle.

"Attack! Attack!" gasped the masked man, choking with rage. "It's Nevers's daughter! Spare nothing to get Nevers's daughter!"

Lagardère already had the child in his arms. The cutthroats looked like beaten dogs, without the heart to keep going. Cocardasse—purposely stoking their discouragement—muttered, "The rascal's going to finish us all off!"

To reach the little staircase Lagardère had only to wave his sword, which now glittered in the moonlight, and say, "Make way, scum!" All of them instinctively moved aside. He climbed the stairs. In the distance could be heard the hoof beats of cavalrymen. On the top step Lagardère, showing his handsome face in the moonlight, held up the child, who smiled when she saw him.

"Yes!" he cried. "This is Nevers's daughter! Reach past my rapier and get her, murderer! You who ordered the killing, you who carried it out, from behind like a coward! Whoever you are, your hand will carry my mark. I'll recognize you. And when it's time, if you won't come to Lagardère, Lagardère will come to you!"

PART TWO: THE VILLA NEVERS

I. The House of Gold

Two years had passed since Louis XIV died, having outlived two generations of his heirs, the Dauphin and the Duke of Burgundy. The throne had gone
to his great-grandson, the child Louis XV. The great king had passed entirely
away, powerless to do what lies in anyone's power at death: weaker than the
least of his subjects, he couldn't enforce his own dying will. It's true his ambitions were extreme—to dispose of twenty or thirty million of his subjects by a
flourish of his signature. But Louis XIV alive would have dared even more;
while the will and testament of Louis XIV dead was, it seems, nothing but
worthless paper, soon torn up. No one got upset, except maybe his legitimatized
sons.

During his uncle's reign, Philippe d'Orléans had played the court jester,
like Brutus, but with a different aim. No sooner did the cry come from the door
of the deathbed chamber—the king is dead, long live the king!—than Philippe
dropped his mask. The Regency Council established by Louis XIV fell into lim-
bo. There was only one Regent, the Duke of Orléans. The princes objected loudly, the Duke of Maine got angry, his wife the duchess spread scandal. But the
country cared nothing for all those bickering illegitimates and remained at
peace.

Except for the Cellamare conspiracy [5]—which Philippe d'Orléans expertly
snuffed out—the Regency was a quiet time. It was a peculiar age. I don't believe
it's been treated unfairly; now and then, a few writers protest at the scorn in
which that era is generally held, but most condemn it with deafening unanimity.
History and memory agree: at no other time has humankind, formed from a mud
clod, better recalled its origins—debauchery ruled, and gold was God. When
you read about the folly and corruption and desperate speculation over the bits
of paper issued by John Law, you might think you're witnessing the financial
drunkenness of our own time. But for them the Mississippi alone was the bait:
nowadays we've got lots of other fish hooks. The arts of civilization then were
not so far advanced as now; they were the arts of a child, but a child of genius.

It was now September 1717. Eighteen years had passed since the events
described in the first part of this narrative. The creator of the Bank of Louisiana,
son of the Scottish goldsmith John Law senior of Lauriston, stood at the peak of
his success and power. John Law's invention of government notes, his Bank of

---

[5] See *The She-Wolf*.

69

France, and finally his Company of the West, soon transformed into the Company of the Indies, had made him the de facto finance minister of France, though Monsieur d'Argenson held the actual title. The Regent—whose lively intelligence had been spoiled first by his education and then by over-indulgence of all kinds—was conned in good faith by the splendid mirages of the poet economist. John Law claimed he could do without gold and could change everything into gold. In fact, the time came when every speculator, each a little Midas, could have paper worth millions in his safe, and no bread to eat. But our story won't reach as far as the fall of John Law, the bold Scot, nor is he one of our characters. We'll witness only the dazzling beginnings of his System.

In September 1717, the new shares in the Company of the Indies, known as the daughters—as opposed to the mothers, which were the shares originally issued—were trading at five times their face value. The granddaughters, issued a few days later, would be just as sought after. Our forefathers were paying five thousand livres, in bright jingling écus, for a strip of gray paper bearing a promise to pay a thousand livres on demand. Within three years those splendid bits of paper were going for fifteen cents a hundred. They were used to make hair curlers, and many a lady with a poodle hairdo could have five or six hundred thousand livres tucked under her nightcap.

Philippe d'Orléans treated John Law with the greatest indulgence. Memoirs from the time confirm that his indulgence wasn't granted for free. With every new issue of shares, Law set aside a portion for the court. Noble lords fought over the spoils with repellent greed. Father Guillaume Dubois—who wasn't made Archbishop of Cambrai till 1720, nor cardinal and member of the Académie Française till 1722—had just been named Ambassador to England. He loved those shares, whether mothers or daughters or granddaughters, with a sincere, unshakeable love.

The morals of the time have been described often enough, and we have nothing to add. The court and the city went to extremes to make up for the rigid scruples of Louis XIV's last years. Paris was one big cabaret, a gambling den. If a great nation can suffer dishonor, the Regency would be an indelible stain on the honor of France. But under what magnificent glory the coming century would hide that minor blemish!

It was a cold gray autumn morning. Groups of carpenters, joiners, and masons walked up the Rue Saint Denis carrying their tools on their shoulders. They were coming from the neighborhood of Saint Jacques, where most artisans lived, and all or almost all of them turned the corner onto the little Rue Saint Magloire. Toward the middle of that street, almost facing the church of the same name, which was still surrounded by its parish cemetery, stood a fine gate flanked by crenelated walls rising to gables covered in carvings. The workmen passed through the carriage entrance into a large paved courtyard surrounded on three sides by noble costly buildings.

This was the former Villa Lorraine, occupied at the time of the Catholic League by the Duke of Mercoeur. Since the reign of Louis XIII, it had been called the Villa Nevers. It was now called the Villa Gonzague, and was home to Philippe of Mantua, Prince of Gonzague. After the Regent and John Law, he was without doubt the richest and most important man in France. He enjoyed the wealth of Nevers under two different titles: as the cousin and heir presumptive of the last duke, and as the husband of Nevers's widow, Aurore de Caylus. That marriage had also brought him the enormous fortune of Caylus the Jailer, who'd gone to the next world to rejoin his two wives.

If Aurore's marriage comes as a surprise, we should remind the reader that Caylus Castle was remote and isolated, and two young women had already died there in captivity. Some things can only be explained by physical or emotional violence. The old Jailer didn't beat around the bush, and we've already witnessed the subtlety of the Prince of Gonzague. For the past eighteen years, Nevers's widow had carried the name of Gonzague, but not for a single day had she put aside her mourning clothes, not even to go to the altar. When Gonzague came to her bedroom on the wedding night, with one hand she showed him the door; the other hand held a dagger against her own breast. "I live for the sake of Nevers's daughter," she said, "but human sacrifice has its limits. Take another step and I'll go wait for my daughter by her father's side."

For the income from the Caylus property, Gonzague needed his wife. He bowed low and withdrew. Since that night, the Princess of Gonzague had never uttered a word in her husband's presence. He was courteous, considerate, affectionate; she remained cold and silent. Every day at dinnertime Gonzague sent his head butler to let the princess know. He wouldn't take his seat without having carried out that small formality: he was a great lord. Every day the senior lady in waiting to the princess replied that her mistress felt poorly and begged the prince to excuse her from joining him. That happened three hundred and sixty-five times a year for eighteen years.

Gonzague spoke often of his wife, and in the most affectionate terms. He had expressions at the ready that began, "The princess was telling me," or "As I was saying to the princess," and he used those phrases easily. The world wasn't fooled, but it pretended to be; and for some strong-willed characters that's good enough. Gonzague was very strong-willed, undoubtedly clever, both self-disciplined and bold. He had the somewhat theatrical formality of manners typical of Italians; he lied with an effrontery that was almost heroic; and, though he was the most shameless libertine at court, in public every word he spoke was marked with the seal of rigorous good manners. The Regent called him his closest friend.

Everyone knew of Gonzague's ongoing efforts to find the daughter of poor Nevers, the third Philippe, the Regent's other childhood friend. She couldn't be found; but since her death couldn't be proved, Gonzague remained for several reasons the natural and legal guardian of a girl who was most likely no longer alive. It was in that capacity that he received the income of Nevers. Only the officially recognized death of Mademoiselle de Nevers would have made Gonzague her father's heir—because Nevers's widow, though she gave in to her father's pressure over the marriage, had been inflexible about her daughter's rights. She'd remarried using the publicly claimed title of widow of Philippe de Nevers and had also acknowledged the birth of her daughter in the marriage contract. No doubt Gonzague had his reasons for agreeing to all that. For eighteen years he'd searched for the girl, as had the princess. Their efforts, equally tireless though animated by quite different motives, had remained fruitless.

Late that summer Gonzague had finally begun to speak of resolving his status, and of calling a family council to settle the question of pending interests. But he had so much to do, and he was so rich! For example, all the workers we saw earlier entering the old Villa Nevers were his: all the carpenters, the joiners, the masons, the landscapers, the locksmiths. Their job was to turn the villa upside down. But it was a splendid mansion, one that Nevers after Mercoeur, and Gonzague himself after Nevers, had taken pleasure in improving.

Each of the three main blocks was decorated with ornamented pyramidal arcades running the length of the ground floor and with an overhanging gallery on the second floor, a gallery whose carvings of interlaced buckwheat stalks put to shame the Villa Cluny's delicate garlands and far surpassed the Villa Trémoille's bas-relief friezes. The three main doors, with low arches set into the middle of the pyramidal vault, opened onto colonnades that Gonzague had restored in the Florentine style, fine columns of red marble topped by floral capitals and standing on large square pedestals, each with four lions crouching at the corners. Above the gallery, the central block facing the main gate displayed two stories of square windows; the two side wings, though of the same height, consisted of only one upstairs floor with double-height windows, ending above the roof line in squared mansard-style gables. At the inner angle where the central block met the east wing stood a fantastical turret held up by three sirens whose tails entwined around the projecting corbel base. It was a minor masterpiece of Gothic craftsmanship, a jewel of cut stone.

The expertly restored interior offered a panoply of marvels: Gonzague was both arrogant and artistic. The façade opening onto the garden was barely fifty years old and presented an array of Italian columns supporting the arcade of an overhanging cloister. The garden—immense, shady, and crowded with statues—extended east, south, and west to the Rue Quincampoix, the Rue Aubry le Boucher, and the Rue Saint Denis. Paris had no more princely villa. Gonzague—a prince, an artist, and arrogant—must therefore have had a serious reason to make drastic alterations. Here was his reason.

At the end of dinner one night the Regent had granted the Prince of Carignan the right to open a vast stock exchange in his villa. The commercial establishments on the Rue Quincampoix tottered for a moment on their worm-eaten foundations. According to rumor, Monsieur de Carignan had the right to forbid any stock trade not authorized at his villa. Gonzague was envious. To console him, at the end of another dinner the Regent granted the Villa Gonzague a monopoly on all trading of shares for commodities. It was a staggering gift, worth mountains of gold. But first Gonzague needed to find room for everyone, since everyone would have to pay, and pay plenty. The morning after he received the monopoly, the army of workmen arrived. They started with the garden. The statues took up space and produced no revenue: the statues were knocked down. The trees produced no revenue and took up space: the trees were felled.

From a tall, heavily curtained second-floor window a woman in mourning sadly watched the destruction. She was beautiful, but so pale that the workmen compared her to a ghost. Among themselves they decided she must be the late Duke of Nevers's widow, now the wife of Prince Philippe de Gonzague. She watched for a long time. Facing her window stood a spectacular elm tree in which, winter or summer, birds sang every morning to greet the dawn. When the old elm fell to the ax, the woman in mourning closed the dark curtains and was seen no more.

They all fell, all those grand shaded avenues of trees leading to baskets of wild rosebushes growing in enormous antique pedestal vases. The baskets were trampled, the rosebushes were uprooted, the vases were thrown into storage: they all took up space, space worth money—lots of money, thank God! How much would gambling fever make each of Gonzague's trading sheds worth? From now on speculation could take place only there, and everyone wanted to speculate. A shed like that would rent for at least as much as a mansion. When people were surprised by the demolition or criticized the waste, Gonzague said, "In five years I'll be worth two or three billion. I'll buy the Tuileries from His Majesty Louis XV, who by then will be king and bankrupt."

On the morning in which we're entering the Villa Gonzague for the first time, the work of devastation was almost done. Three stories of wooden cubicles rose around the central courtyard. The hallways had been turned into offices, and the masons were finishing the sheds in the garden. The courtyard was crowded with renters and buyers, because today was the big day: opening day for the trading counters of what was already being called the House of Gold. Inside the villa people came and went freely. All of the ground floor and all of the second floor except for the private apartment of the princess had been set up to accommodate traders and their goods. Everywhere the acrid smell of fresh-cut pine attacked the throat; everywhere the din of hammers attacked the ears. The servants didn't know whom to obey. The trading clerks were going crazy.

On the main stairs, in the middle of a clot of merchants, stood a gentleman draped in velvet, silk, and lace, with rings on all his fingers and a splendid gold chain around his neck. It was Monsieur de Peyrolles, confidant and private counselor and factotum of the master of the house. He hadn't aged much: he was still thin and yellow and stooped, with big frightened eyes that seemed to call for glasses. He had his own toadies, and deserved them, because Gonzague paid him well.

Toward nine o'clock, when the crowd had thinned a little as a result of the bothersome pangs of hunger that affect even speculators, two men who didn't look quite like financiers came through the front gate a few paces apart. Though entry was unrestricted, these two fellows didn't look very sure of their rights. The first covered his unease poorly with an insolent manner; the second, by contrast, made himself as humble as he could. They both wore swords, the kind of long swords that reek of cutthroat three leagues away. It has to be said, that look was a little out of fashion. The Regency had done away with mercenaries. People hardly killed each other anymore, even in high society, except by larceny—clearly a mark of progress, and proof of the benevolence of the new morals.

Our two fellows waded into the crowd, the first using his elbows freely, the second slipping like a cat between clusters of men too busy to notice him. The insolent one, who scraped his worn and tattered elbows against so many brand-new doublets, wore a memorable moustache, a broken hat that came down over his eyes, a buffalo-hide vest, and stockings whose original color was a mystery. His sheathed sword exposed the torn lining of a comic-opera cloak. Our man came from Madrid.

The other man, the shy and humble cutthroat, had three blond whiskers under his hooked nose. His brimless hat fit him like a snuffer fits a candle. An old doublet mended with leather thongs, patched stockings, and gaping boots completed his outfit, which would have gone better with an inkwell than with a rapier. But still he wore a rapier, one as modest as himself and which humbly knocked against his ankles.

After crossing the courtyard our two fellows reached the door to the main vestibule at about the same time. Each examined the other out of the corner of his eye, and both had the same thought: "Now there's a sad loser who didn't come here to buy the House of Gold!"

II. Two Ghosts

They were both right. In a modern stage melodrama, a couple of villainous mustachioed swindlers—say, Robert Macaire and Bertrand—in disguise as starving, threadbare, sword-dangling cutthroats of the time of Louis XIV, would have dressed exactly like them. This Macaire, however, felt pity for his colleague, of whom all he could see was his profile buried in the turned-up collar of his doublet—turned up to hide the absence of a shirt. "How could anyone be as pathetic as that?" he thought. And this Bertrand, seeing his colleague's face lost in a disheveled mass of wooly hair, thought in the goodness of his heart, "This poor devil is living on Christian charity! It pains me to see a swordsman in such a pitiful state. At least I'm keeping up appearances." He glanced with satisfaction at the ruins of his own getup. Macaire, making a similar assessment in return, thought, "At least I'm not an object of charity!" And he drew himself up like one of the Magi with a new coat on.

A smug, insolent valet appeared at the door of the vestibule. Both men thought at the same time, "That other poor fellow won't get in!"

Macaire got there first. "I'm here to buy, sonny!" he said, standing as straight as a capital i and with his hand on the pommel of his sword.

"Buy what?"

"Whatever I want, rascal. Take a good look at me! I'm a friend of your master's and a man of substance, God's life!" He took the valet by the ear, spun him around, and strode by him. "Anyone can see that!"

The valet did a pirouette and found himself face to face with Bertrand, who doffed his candle snuffer politely. "My friend," said Bertrand confidingly, "I'm a friend of the prince, and I'm here on business—financial business."

The valet, still reeling, let him go by.

Macaire had reached the first room and glanced scornfully left and right. "Not bad. In a pinch you could put up here."

Behind him Bertrand thought, "The Prince of Gonzague seems pretty well set up here—for an Italian!"

They were at opposite ends of the room. Macaire noticed Bertrand. "What do you know! Incredible. They let that fellow in. Ah, God's hat! What a getup!" He began to laugh heartily.

"I swear," thought Bertrand, "he's making fun of me! Is that possible?" He turned away so he could hold his sides. "He's magnificent!"

Seeing him laugh, however, Macaire changed his mind. "After all, it's Liberty Hall here. That buffoon might've murdered some merchant on a street corner. He might be loaded. I should engage him in conversation, God's blood."

"Who knows," thought Bertrand at the same time, "they let all kinds in here. Clothes don't make the man. That gargoyle might've pulled off a job last night. What if he's got good money in those nasty pockets? I ought to find out."

Macaire came forward. "Sir..." he said, with a formal bow.

"Sir..." said Bertrand at the same time, bowing to the floor.

As one, they both bounced upright like springs. Macaire's accent had struck Bertrand; Bertrand's nasal singsong had given Macaire a start.

"Crooked ace!" cried the latter. "I believe it's that rascal Brother Passepoil!"

"Cocardasse! Cocardasse Junior!" replied the other, whose eyes, accustomed to tears, were already moist. "Is it really you?"

"In the flesh, God's hat! Give me a hug, baldy!" Cocardasse opened his arms, and Passepoil threw himself against his chest. Between the two of them, they amounted to quite a pile of rags. They remained hugging for a while, with deep sincere feeling.

"Enough!" said Cocardasse finally. "Talk some, so I can listen to your voice, rascal."

"Eighteen years apart!" murmured Passepoil as he wiped his eyes on his sleeve.

"Thunder and lightning!" cried Cocardasse. "You don't have a handkerchief, son?"

"Somebody stole it in the crowd," said Passepoil gently.

Cocardasse checked his own pockets; of course, he found nothing. "Hell! The world's full of thieves. Ah, baldy, eighteen years! We were both young!"

"The age for foolish love! Alas! My heart hasn't aged."

"I still drink as much as I used to."

They looked at the whites of each other's eyes.

"You know, Master Cocardasse," said Passepoil sadly, "the years haven't made you prettier."

"Frankly, Brother Passepoil," replied Cocardasse, "I'm sorry to tell you, but you're even uglier than you used to be, son!"

Passepoil smiled with false modesty and murmured, "That's not what the ladies think! But even while aging you've kept your good features: a shapely leg, your chest well out, shoulders back. A little while ago, when I first saw you, I said to myself, there's an impressive gentleman!"

"Me too, me too, baldy! As soon as I saw you, I thought, there's a fine-looking soldier!"

"What can I say," Passepoil smirked. "The influence of the fair sex never quite fades away."

"So... Whatever became of you, after that business?"

"The business in the moat at Caylus?" Passepoil instinctively lowered his voice. "Don't remind me—I can still see the fire in the little Parisian's eyes."

"It may've been night, God's hat, but you could see the sparks in his eyes."

"The way he handled them!"

"Eight dead in the moat!"

"Not to mention the wounded!"

"God's blood, what a hail of blows! Beautiful to see. And when I think that if we'd chosen sides honestly, like men, if we'd thrown Peyrolles's money back in his face and stood with Lagardère, Nevers wouldn't have died. And our fortunes would surely have been made!"

"Yes," sighed Passepoil, "that's what we should have done."

"Putting the buttons on the tips of our rapiers wasn't enough. We should've fought for Lagardère, our beloved student."

"Our master!" Passepoil unconsciously took off his hat. Cocardasse shook his hand, and they both stood pensively for a moment.

"What's done is done," said Cocardasse finally. "I don't know what's happened to you since then, baldy, but it hasn't been good for me. When Carrigue's men attacked us with their guns, I fled into the castle. You'd disappeared. Instead of keeping his promise, the next day Peyrolles fired us all on the pretext that our being in the area would confirm the suspicions that were already spreading. Fair enough. We got paid something. We left. I crossed the border, asking everywhere along the way for news of you. Nothing! I settled first at Pamplona, then at Burgos, then at Salamanca. I moved to Madrid."

"Fruitful country."

"The rapier is losing ground to the stiletto. It's like Italy, which otherwise would be paradise. From Madrid I went to Toledo, from Toledo to Ciudad Real. Then I got tired of Castile, where I'd gotten in trouble with the magistrates, and I moved to the Kingdom of Valencia. God's hat! I drank some good wine, from Majorca to Segorbe. I had to leave there because I did a job for an old lawyer who wanted to get rid of a cousin of his. Catalonia's worth a visit. There are gentlemen all along the road between Tortosa and Tarragona and Barcelona, but their wallets are empty and their rapiers are long. Finally, I crossed the mountains again. I didn't have a cent left. I heard the call of my motherland. That's my story, sweetheart." He turned out his pockets. "And you?"

"Carrigue's horsemen chased me all the way to Bagnères de Luchon, or just about. I also considered crossing over to Spain, but I met a Benedictine monk who hired me as his servant, based on my honest looks. He was going to Kehl, on the Rhine, to deliver an inheritance on behalf of his abbey. I took his trunk and his suitcase, and maybe his money too."

"Rascal!" said Cocardasse affectionately.

"I reached Germany. What a country of gangsters! You mentioned the stiletto? At least that's steel. In Germany they fight with beer steins. A tavern keeper's wife in Mainz relieved me of the Benedictine's ducats. She was nice, and she liked me. Ah, Cocardasse! Why is it my bad luck to be so irresistible to women! If not for women, I could've bought a house in the country to spend my old age in, with a little garden and a field of red daisies and a stream with a mill..."

"And at the mill, a miller's daughter!" interrupted Cocardasse. "You're dry kindling!"

Passepoil struck his chest. "Desires!" he cried, raising his eyes to heaven. "Desires are the torment of life, and they keep a young man from building up any savings!" Having so wisely expressed his moral philosophy, he went on. "Like you, I moved from town to town, in that wide, flat, stupid, boring country. Skinny sallow students, idiotic poets howling at the moon, fat burgermeisters without the least little nephew they want to see buried, churches where they don't sing Mass, and women... but I can't badmouth the sex whose charms have adorned and ruined my career! Anyway, raw meat, and beer instead of wine!"

"Crooked ace!" said Cocardasse firmly. "I'll never go to that dregs of a country."

"I saw Cologne, Frankfurt, Vienna, Berlin, Munich, and a lot of other big cities, where you meet gangs of young men summoning the devil in song. I did the same as you: I got homesick, I crossed Flanders, and here I am!"

"France! There's nowhere like France, my boy!"

"A noble country!"

"The homeland of wine!"

"The mother of love!"

After this duet, in which they competed for lyrical style, Passepoil said, "My dear master, was it just your lack of cash, plus your love of country, that brought you back?"

"And you? Was it just homesickness?"

Passepoil shook his head, and Cocardasse lowered his fierce eyes. "There was something else," he said. "One evening, crossing a street, I found myself face to face with—can you guess?"

"I can guess. The same thing made me leave Brussels in a hurry."

"On reflection, I began to feel the climate of Catalonia was no longer so healthy for me. After all, there's no shame in giving way to Lagardère!"

"I don't know about shame—but there's definitely prudence." Passepoil lowered his voice. "You know what happened to all of our companions in that business in the moat at Caylus?"

"Yes, yes, I know the story. The little rascal said it: you'll all die by my hand!"

"The work advances. There were nine of us in that attack, counting Captain Lorrain, the leader of the band of highwaymen. I leave aside his men."

"Nine good blades!" said Cocardasse thoughtfully. "They all got out of that moat—gashed, slashed, bleeding—but alive."

"Of those nine, Staupitz and Captain Lorrain were the first to go. Staupitz was a family man, though he came across like a brute. Captain Lorrain was a soldier, and the King of Spain had given him command of a regiment. Staupitz died under the walls of his own estate, near Nuremberg. He was killed by a sword thrust, right between the eyes!" Passepoil pointed to the spot on his own forehead.

Cocardasse instinctively did the same. "Captain Lorrain died at Naples, from a sword thrust right between the eyes. God's blood! For those who know and remember, it's like the mark of the avenger."

"The others had made their way in life," went on Passepoil, "because Monsieur de Gonzague had forgotten only us in his generosity. Pinto married a woman in Turin, El Matador opened a fencing school in Scotland, Joel de Jugan bought an estate in rural Brittany."

"Yes, yes," said Cocardasse, "they were relaxed and at ease. But Pinto was killed in Turin, and El Matador was killed in Glasgow."

"Jugan was killed at Morlaix, all by the same stroke."

"The Nevers attack, God's death!"

"The dreaded Nevers attack!"

They were silent for a moment. Cocardasse lifted his lowered hat brim to wipe the sweat off his brow. "There's still Faenza."

"And Saldaña."

"Gonzague treated those two well. Faenza's a chevalier."

"And Saldaña's a baron. Their turn will come."

"Sooner or later," murmured Cocardasse. "As will ours!"

"Ours too!" echoed Passepoil, shivering.

Cocardasse straightened up. "Well, brother!" he cried, like a man who's come to a decision. "You know, when he's laid me out on the street or on the grass, with that hole between my eyebrows—because I know there's no way to stop him—I'll tell him, just like in the old days, 'Shake my hand, you little rascal, and so I can die happy, forgive old Cocardasse!' God's hat! That's all there is to it."

Passepoil grimaced. "I'll make sure he forgives me too, but not so late."

"Good luck with that, baldy! Meanwhile, he's exiled from France. In Paris at least we can be sure not to meet him."

"Quite sure!" echoed Passepoil, but without much conviction.

"Anyway, our best chance in the whole world to avoid him is this place. That's why I came here."

"Me too."

"And also to pay my respects to Monsieur de Gonzague and refresh his memory of me."

"That fellow certainly owes us something."

"Saldaña and Faenza will protect us."

"Until we're big shots like they are."

"God's blood! We'll make a fine couple of gallants!" Cocardasse made a pirouette.

"I clean up nice," said Passepoil seriously.

"When I called on Faenza I was told, 'The chevalier is not receiving.' The chevalier!" Cocardasse shrugged. "Not receiving! I remember the days when I could make him spin like a top."

"When I rang at Saldaña's door," said Passepoil, "a tall footman looked me up and down suspiciously and said, 'The baron is not receiving.'"

"Well!" cried Cocardasse, "when you and I have strapping footmen, God's death, I want mine to be as insolent as a hangman's valet!"

"Ah!" sighed Passepoil, "if only I had a housekeeper!"

"Crooked ace, my boy, that'll come. If I understand you, you haven't yet seen Monsieur de Peyrolles."

"No. I want to go straight to the prince himself."

"They say he's worth millions now!"

"Billions! They call this the House of Gold. I'm not proud, I'll be a financier if I have to."

"For shame! My second-in-command, a money-grubber!" That was Cocardasse's immediate reaction, from the heart. But then he changed his tone. "A sad fall! But, if it's true you can make your fortune that way, sweetheart..."

"If it's true!" cried Passepoil with enthusiasm. "You can't even imagine!"

"I've heard lots of things, but I don't believe in miracles."

"You should! There are miracles all around us! Have you heard about the hunchback of the Rue Quincampoix?"

"The one who lends his hump to stock speculators?"

"He doesn't lend it, he rents it, and they say in two years he's made fifteen hundred thousand livres."

Cocardasse burst out laughing. "Impossible!"

"So much possible that he's going to marry a countess."

"Fifteen hundred thousand livres! Just off his hump! God's guts!"

"Ah, friend," exclaimed Passepoil, "we lost a lot of years abroad, but we got back just in time. You only have to bend down to pick up money. It's a miraculous harvest. Tomorrow a gold louis won't be worth more than loose change. On my way here I saw some brats shooting craps with six-écu coins."

Cocardasse licked his lips. "Well then, in this land of milk and honey, how much would a sword stroke be worth—delivered with the proper expert lunge, straight to the heart and according to all the rules of the art?" He turned en garde, stamped noisily with his right foot, and lunged deep.

Passepoil blinked. "Not so loud. Somebody's coming." He leaned closer and lowered his voice. "My opinion is, it must still be worth plenty. And before the hour's out I hope to hear exactly that from the lips of Monsieur de Gonzague himself."

III. The Auction

The great hall where Cocardasse and Passepoil were talking so pleasantly stood at the center of the main block. The windows, hung with heavy Flemish curtains, opened onto a narrow strip of lawn bounded by a trellis, which from now on was to be called grandiosely "the private garden of the princess." Unlike the other rooms on the ground floor and the second floor, which already swarmed with workmen of all kinds, here nothing had changed yet. It was the formal great hall of a prince's villa, with opulent but intimidating furnishings—a hall that must have been used for more than just banquets and entertainment, because facing the great black marble fireplace stood a raised dais, draped with a Turkish carpet, that gave the whole space the feel of a courtroom. Here, indeed, members of the noble families of Lorraine, Chevreuse, Joyeuse, Aumale, Elbeuf, Nevers, Merour, Mayenne, and Guise had met more than once in the days when the great barons controlled the destiny of the kingdom. Only in today's chaos and confusion at the Villa Gonzague could our two bravos have been allowed to enter such a place. And here they were much less disturbed than they would have been in any other room. For one more day the great hall preserved its inviolability: a formal family council was to take place here today, and tomorrow the cubicle-building carpenters would take possession.

"One more thing about Lagardère," said Cocardasse when the sound of footsteps that had interrupted them had faded away. "When you ran into him in Brussels, was he alone?"

"No," replied Passepoil, "and when he crossed your path in Barcelona?"

"He wasn't alone."

"Who was with him?"

"A girl."

"Pretty?"

"Very pretty."

"That's odd," said Passepoil. "He was also with a very pretty girl when I saw him in Flanders. Do you remember her figure, her face, her clothes?"

"The dress, the figure, the face of a charming Spanish gypsy girl," said Cocardasse. "And yours?"

"The quiet demeanor and angelic face and fine dress of a noblewoman."

"That's odd. And about how old?"

"The age that child would be now."

"Just like the one I saw. We haven't heard the last of this, baldy. And among those waiting their turn, besides us and besides the Chevalier de Faenza and Baron Saldaña, don't forget Monsieur de Peyrolles, and don't forget Prince Philippe de Gonzague."

The door opened, and Passepoil could only reply, "Time will tell!" before a servant in fine livery entered, followed by two workmen with measuring sticks. The servant was too busy to notice our bravos as they slipped unseen into a window alcove.

"Mark off tomorrow's job and make it fast!" said the servant. "Four feet by four, everywhere."

The two men got to work. While one measured, the other marked off lines in chalk and between them wrote a number, starting with 927 and going up sequentially.

"What the devil are they doing?" asked Cocardasse, leaning out of their hiding place.

"You don't know?" said Passepoil. "Each line marks where a cubicle partition will go, and number 927 shows there are already almost a thousand cubicles in Monsieur de Gonzague's villa."

"And what are these cubicles for?"

"For making money."

Cocardasse stared. Passepoil tried to explain the stupendous present Philippe d'Orléans had just given his bosom friend.

"What!" cried Cocardasse. "Each of those boxes will be worth as much as a farm on the Loire or the Seine! Ah, brother, let's fasten ourselves tight to the great Monsieur de Gonzague!"

The men measured and marked. The servant said, "Numbers 935, 936, 937... You're making them too big! Remember, every cubicle is worth gold!"

"Bless me!" said Cocardasse. "So those little pieces of paper are really worth something?"

"Worth so much," said Passepoil, "gold and silver are about to be overthrown."

"Vile metals!" said Cocardasse gravely. "They deserve it. But crooked ace! Maybe it's just from habit, but I'm still a little fond of pistoles."

"Number 941," said the servant.

"That leaves two and a half feet," said the man measuring. "It doesn't work out evenly."

"Wow," said Cocardasse, "that one'll be for a skinny fellow!"

"Send in the carpenters as soon as the meeting's over," said the servant.

"What meeting?" asked Cocardasse.

"Let's try to find out. Knowing what's going on in a place gives you an advantage."

Cocardasse greeted that bit of wisdom by stroking Passepoil's chin, like a proud father smiling at the budding intelligence of his favorite son.

The servant and the two workmen left. Suddenly loud voices erupted from the direction of the vestibule: "My turn!"—"My turn!"—"I have my registration!"—"No cutting in line!"

"Hello," said Cocardasse, "something new!"

"Quiet! For God's sake, quiet!" ordered a voice of authority from the door.

"It's Monsieur de Peyrolles," said Passepoil. "Keep hidden!" They pushed deeper into the alcove and drew the curtain.

At that moment Peyrolles entered the room, followed or rather pressed forward by a dense mob of petitioners—petitioners of a rare and precious kind, because they were begging to hand over a lot of money for a little puff of smoke. Peyrolles was richly dressed; diamonds sparkled in the flood of lace covering his bony hands.

"Come now, gentlemen," he said, fanning himself with a handkerchief decorated with d'Alençon lace. "Stand back. Have a little respect."

"Ah, the rascal!" sighed Cocardasse. "He's magnificent!"

"He's in his glory!" said Passepoil.

It was true: Peyrolles was indeed in his glory. He was flanked by two assistants carrying enormous account books. He used his walking stick to push back the mob of moneygrubbers. "Try at least to show some dignity!" he said, brushing a few crumbs of Spanish tobacco off his neckerchief. "Can't you contain your greed?" And he made a gesture so fine that our two masters of arms felt the urge to applaud like spectators in a loge.

But it made no impression on the merchants, who shouted, "My turn!"— "Me first!"—"Me!"—"Me!"

Peyrolles stopped. "Gentlemen!" Silence fell. "I've asked you to be quiet. I am the personal representative here of the Prince of Gonzague. I'm his agent. I see some of you still have your hats on." All hats came off. "It's about time! Gentlemen, here's what I have to say to you."

"Quiet! Quiet! Hear him!" said the crowd.

"The trading counters in this hall will be built and delivered tomorrow."

"Hurrah!"

"This is the only space we have left. These are the last spots. Every other room has already been assigned, except for the private apartments of his lordship and those of the princess." He bowed.

The chorus resumed. "My turn!"—"I'm registered!"—"God's blood, I'm not going to lose my spot!"—"No pushing!"—"Are you going to rough up a woman?!" (There were indeed women present, the forbears of the ugly women nowadays who frighten passersby, around two in the afternoon, on the fringes of the stock exchange.) "Clumsy oaf!"—"Boor!"—"Lummox!" Those insults were answered by the curses and squeals of business women. The time had come for hair pulling. Cocardasse and Passepoil were just poking their heads out to watch the fight, when at the far end of the hall, behind the dais, the double doors opened.

"Gonzague!" murmured Cocardasse.

"The billionaire!" added Passepoil.

Instinctively they both doffed their hats.

And it was indeed Gonzague who appeared on the dais, followed by two young noblemen. Though he was nearing fifty, he was still handsome, still tall, still lithe. His face was unlined, and his impressive hair, thick with oil, fell in shining raven ringlets to the shoulders of his simple black velvet tailcoat. His sumptuousness was nothing like Peyrolles's. His ruff cost fifty thousand livres, and there were diamonds worth a million on his pendant, of which only a small corner emerged from under his white satin waistcoat.

The two young noblemen who followed Gonzague—one the rake Chaverny, Gonzague's cousin on the Nevers side, the other the youngest son of the Duke of Navailles—both carried snuff and wore beauty spots. Navailles was about twenty-five; the Marquis of Chaverny was going on twenty. They were charming young fellows, a little effeminate, a little enervated, but, in spite of the early hour, already cheered by just a dash of champagne, and they wore their silk and velvet with admirable insolence. They stopped to look at the mob and burst out laughing.

"Gentlemen, gentlemen," said Peyrolles as he took off his hat, "a little respect, at least, for the prince!" The crowd, on the point of coming to blows, calmed down as if by magic. All the competitors for those cubicles bowed as one, and all the ladies curtseyed.

Gonzague waved his hand vaguely and passed on, saying, "Hurry up, Peyrolles. I need this hall."

"Oh, what lovely faces!" said Chaverny, eyeing the crowd up close.

"Oh, what lovely faces!" echoed Navailles, laughing till he cried.

Peyrolles approached Gonzague. "They've been heated white hot. They'll pay whatever we ask."

"Let them bid!" cried Chaverny. "It'll be entertaining!"

"Shush," said Gonzague. "We're not at supper now, clown." But he liked the idea. "All right, an auction! What should the opening bid be?"

"Five hundred livres a month for a four-foot cubicle," said Navailles, thinking he was aiming high.

"A thousand livres a week!" said Chaverny.

"Let's make it fifteen hundred," said Gonzague. "Carry on, Peyrolles."

"Gentlemen," said Peyrolles to the crowd, "since these are the last spots, and the best, they'll go to the highest bidder. Number 927, for fifteen hundred livres!"

There was a murmur, but no one spoke up.

"God's blood, cousin," said Chaverny, "I'll give you a leg up." He stepped forward. "Two thousand livres!"

The applicants looked at each other unhappily.

"Two thousand five hundred!" said Navailles, whose pride was at stake.

Consternation among the real applicants. A big wool merchant called out in a strangled voice, "Three thousand!"

"Sold!" said Peyrolles hastily. Gonzague glared at him. Peyrolles was a man of limited imagination, and he was afraid of pushing the boundaries of human folly.

"It's going well!" said Cocardasse. Passepoil watched and listened with his hands folded.

"Number 928," said Peyrolles.

"Four thousand livres," said Gonzague nonchalantly.

"But it's no better than the first cubicle!" said a woman who dealt in notions on the Rue Quincampoix, and who'd just married off her niece to a count—which had cost her a dowry of twenty thousand hard-earned louis.

"I'll take it!" shouted an apothecary.

"I'll bid four thousand five hundred!" yelled an ironmonger.

"Five thousand!"

"Six thousand!"

"Sold!" said Peyrolles. "Number 929..." After a look from Gonzague he went on, "going for ten thousand livres!"

"Four feet by four feet!" said Passepoil, astonished.

"Two thirds of a burial plot," added Cocardasse somberly.

But the bidding had begun, and vertigo threatened. Number 929 was fought over like an inheritance, and no one was surprised when Gonzague set the price of the next cubicle at fifteen thousand livres. Let it be noted that payment was in cash—good hard coin or government notes. One of Peyrolles's assistants handled the money, while the other wrote the buyers' names in his account book.

Chaverny and Navailles had stopped laughing; they were impressed. "Incredible folly!" said Chaverny.

"You have to see it to believe it," said Navailles.

"France is a beautiful country, gentlemen," said Gonzague. Then he called out, "Let's get this over with! All the rest are going for twenty thousand livres!"

"That's like giving them away!" said Chaverny.

"Mine!"—"Mine!"—"Mine!" shouted the crowd. Men fought, women fell smothered or trampled—but even in their distress they shouted, "Mine!"— "Mine!"—"Mine!" More bidding, more cries of joy and rage. Gold poured across the steps of the dais, which served as the sales counter. Bulging pockets were being emptied at a speed both hilarious and astonishing. Those who had their receipts waved them over their heads and went off, giddy and crazed, to find their spots and stand in them. The losers tore their hair.

"Mine!"—"Mine!"—"Mine!" Peyrolles and his assistants could barely hear anyone. Frenzy loomed. When it came to the last cubicles, blood ran on the parquet floor. Finally, number 942, the leftover space only two and a half feet wide, went for twenty-eight thousand livres. Peyrolles slammed shut his account book. "Gentlemen, the auction is closed."

There was a moment of total silence. The happy possessors of all the cubicles looked at each other, stunned.

Gonzague called to Peyrolles, "Time to clear this place out."

But at that moment another crowd appeared at the entrance from the vestibule, a crowd of courtiers, gentlemen, and financiers come to pay their respects to the Prince of Gonzague. Seeing the hall was full, they stopped.

"Come in, come in, gentlemen," said Gonzague. "We're kicking these people out."

"Come on in," added Chaverny. "If you want, these good people can sell you what they just bought, at a hundred percent markup."

"They'd be making a mistake!" said Navailles. "Morning, Oriol!"

The man he addressed bowed low to Gonzague. "So this is the gold mine!" Oriol was a promising young merchant. Also in the crowd were the financiers Albret and Taranne; the Baron of Batz, an honest German who'd come to Paris to be corrupted; Montaubert, Nocé, Gironne, the Viscount of La Fare—all of them distant relatives of Nevers or here as their proxies, all of them summoned by Gonzague for the formal occasion we'll soon witness, the meeting mentioned by Peyrolles.

"How did the sale go?" asked Oriol.

"Poorly," said Gonzague coldly.

"You hear that?" said Cocardasse in the alcove.

Sweating heavily, Passepoil replied, "He's right. Those chickens would've given him all the rest of their feathers!"

"You, prince?" cried Oriol. "Make a mistake in business! Impossible!"

"Judge for yourself! I gave up my last cubicles for twenty-three thousand livres each."

"A year?"

"A week!"

The newcomers looked at the spots marked for cubicles, and then at the buyers. "Twenty-three thousand livres!" they repeated, stunned.

"I should've started at that price," said Gonzague. "I had almost a thousand spots. And it just felt like a twenty-three thousand kind of morning."

"So it's a form of insanity?"

"A frenzy! And there'll be more. I've rented out the courtyard, then the garden, then the vestibule, the stairs, the stables, the toilets, the storerooms. I'm down to the sleeping quarters, and then—God's death!—maybe I'll go stay at an inn."

"I'll rent you my bedroom during the day, cousin," said Chaverny.

"As the space remaining shrinks," went on Gonzague, "the fever rises. I've got nothing left."

"Look harder, cousin! Let's give these gentlemen the pleasure of a little auction."

At the word auction, those who'd failed to rent anything quickly drew closer.

"Well..." said Gonzague. "Ah! I have it!"

"What?" they all cried.

"My dog kennel."

The courtiers burst out laughing, but the merchants and financiers didn't: they were thinking it over.

"You think I'm joking, gentlemen," cried Gonzague. "I bet if I wanted to I could get ten thousand écus for it, cash down."

"That's thirty thousand livres!" they cried. "For a dog kennel!" And they laughed twice as hard.

But a strange figure suddenly appeared between Navailles and Chaverny, someone who laughed louder than all the rest, a hunchback with oddly tangled hair. In a thin, cracking voice the hunchback said, "I'll take the dog kennel for thirty thousand livres!"

IV. Largesse

The hunchback must have had his wits about him, in spite of the extravagance he was committing: his eye was bright and his nose was sharp, he had a well-shaped forehead under that grossly disheveled wig, and the light smile playing on his lips hinted at diabolical malice. A true hunchback! As for the hump itself, it was substantial, solidly seated in the middle of his back, and high enough to rub the nape of his neck. In front, his chin touched his chest. His legs were strangely twisted, but without the proverbial thinness that usually accompanies a hump. This odd creature wore a suit of all black, of the utmost correctness, with collars and cuffs of pure white pleated muslin. All eyes were on him, and it didn't seem to bother him at all.

"Bravo, Aesop!" cried Chaverny. "You strike me as a bold and clever speculator."

"Bold enough." The hunchback looked at him unblinkingly. "Clever, we'll see about." His thin voice grated like a child's rattle.

"Bravo, Aesop, bravo!" they all repeated—and from then on he was known by the name Chaverny had given him.

Cocardasse and Passepoil had lost the power to be surprised by anything. Their arms had long since dropped to their sides. But Cocardasse asked quietly, "Have we ever known a hunchback, brother?"

"Not that I can remember."

"God's life! I feel like I've seen those eyes somewhere."

Gonzague was also watching the little man with great attention. "Hey, friend, you know it's cash down, right?"

"I know." Aesop drew a wallet from his pocket and counted sixty government banknotes of five hundred livres into Peyrolles's hand. The hunchback's sudden arrival had been so fantastical, people half expected his paper money to turn into dry leaves; but it was a gullible crowd. "My receipt," he said. Peyrolles gave him his receipt. Aesop folded it and tucked it into his wallet in place of the banknotes. Then he tapped the account book. "Pleasure doing business with you! Till next time, gentlemen!"

He bowed politely to Gonzague and the company. Everyone stood aside to let him pass. They were still laughing, but a nameless cold ran through their veins. Gonzague had grown thoughtful. Peyrolles and his assistants began to disperse the cubicle buyers, who couldn't wait till tomorrow. Gonzague's friends were still staring at the door through which the little man in black had left.

"Gentlemen," said Gonzague, "while they're getting the hall ready, please follow me to my apartment."

"Let's go," said Cocardasse behind the curtain. "It's now or never!"

88

"I'm scared," said Passepoil.

"Really? I'll go first."

Cocardasse took Passepoil by the hand and headed straight toward Gonzague, keeping his hat brim lowered.

"Ha!" cried Chaverny when he saw them. "You're putting on quite a show for us, cousin! It must be dress-up day. The hunchback wasn't bad, but this is the finest pair of cutthroats I've ever seen!"

Cocardasse glared at him. Navailles, Oriol, and the others gathered around our two friends and examined them curiously.

"Careful!" murmured Passepoil in Cocardasse's ear.

"God's hat!' replied Cocardasse. "They're staring at us like they've never seen two gentlemen before!"

"The tall one is gorgeous!" said Navailles.

"I like the short one better," said Oriol.

"There are no more cubicles to rent, so what are they doing here?"

Luckily the two had now reached Gonzague, who started when he saw them. "Ah!" he said, "what do these fellows want?"

Cocardasse bowed with the same noble grace he brought to all his actions. Passepoil bowed more modestly, but like a man who's seen the world. Cocardasse surveyed the mocking sequined crowd and said in a firm clear voice, "This gentleman and I are old acquaintances of his lordship, and we've come to pay our respects."

"Ah!" said Gonzague again.

"If his lordship is busy with more important matters," went on Cocardasse, bowing again, "we can come back at whatever hour he names."

"That's right," stammered Passepoil. "We'd be honored to come back."

They bowed a third time, then stood erect, their hands on the pommels of their swords.

Gonzague called Peyrolles, who'd just finished ejecting the last of the cubicle bidders. "You recognize these fine fellows? Take them to the kitchen, give them food and drink and new clothes, and have them wait for my orders."

"Ah, my lord!" cried Cocardasse.

"Generous prince!" cried Passepoil.

"Go!" ordered Gonzague.

They backed away, bowing at every opportunity and sweeping the floor with the tattered feathers of their hats. When they reached the mocking crowd, Cocardasse stuck his hat back on at an angle and lifted the fringed skirt of his cloak to reveal the end of his rapier. Passepoil did his best to copy him. Then— haughty, splendid, noses in the air, fists on their hips, raking the mockers with terrible stares—the two of them crossed the great hall and followed Peyrolles to the kitchen, where their powerful fork handling astonished all of the prince's servants.

While they ate, Cocardasse said, "Brother, our fortune is made!"

Passepoil, always more cautious, said "God willing!" with his mouth full.

When they were gone Chaverny said to Gonzague, "Seriously? Since when do you make use of tools like that?" Gonzague looked around as if in a daze, and didn't answer.

The noblemen, meanwhile, speaking loudly enough for Gonzague to hear, openly paid him court with hymns of flattery. They were slightly bankrupt aristocrats and slightly corrupt financiers. None of them had as yet done anything strictly punishable by law, but none of them was as pure and stainless as a wedding dress. All of them, from first to last, needed Gonzague for one thing or another. Among them Gonzague was lord and king, like a patrician in ancient Rome surrounded by the throng of his pathetic clients. Gonzague held them by their ambition, by their greed, by their needs and their vices. The only one of them who'd kept any independence was the young Marquis of Chaverny, too scatterbrained to play the markets, too indifferent to sell out. As for what Gonzague aimed to use them for, that'll be revealed in the unfolding of this story—because at first glance, sitting as he did at the apex of wealth, power, and favor, Gonzague seemed to need no one.

"They talk about the mines of Peru!" Oriol was saying while Gonzague stood apart. "The prince's villa alone is worth more than Peru and all its mines!" Oriol was as round as a ball, red-faced, chubby-cheeked, short of breath. The actresses at the Opéra were willing to tease him in a friendly way, as long as he had money and was in a giving mood.

"My God," said Taranne, a thin dull financier, "this is Eldorado!"

"The House of Gold!" added Montaubert. "Or should I say the House of Diamond!"

"Ja," agreed the Baron of Batz, "tiamont inzdet!"

"Many a fine lord could live for a year on what the Prince of Gonzague makes in a week!" said Gironne.

"That's because the Prince of Gonzague is the king of lords!" said Oriol.

"Cousin Gonzague!" cried Chaverny in a tone so pitiful it was funny, "Please, beg for mercy, or these annoying hosannas will last till tomorrow!"

Gonzague seemed to wake from his thoughts. "Gentlemen," he said, without responding to Chaverny, because he didn't like to be teased. "Be so kind as to follow me to my apartment. We have to vacate this room."

When they'd reached his private study he said, "Gentlemen, you know why I've summoned you."

"I heard talk of a family council," said Navailles.

"Better than that, gentlemen: a solemn assembly, a family tribunal in which His Royal Highness the Regent will be represented by three of the highest dignitaries of the state: Chief Judge de Lamoignon, General de Villeroy, and Minister d'Argenson."

"Damn!" said Chaverny. "Is this about the succession to the throne?"

"Marquis," said Gonzague coldly, "we're discussing serious business, so please spare us."

Chaverny yawned in anticipation. "Do you have any picture books to entertain me while you're being serious?"

Trying to keep him quiet, Gonzague just smiled.

"So what's it about, prince?" said Montaubert.

"It's about you proving your loyalty to me, gentlemen."

They all cried as one, "We're ready!"

Gonzague bowed and smiled. "I summoned you specifically—Navailles, Gironne, Chaverny, Nocé, Montaubert, Choisy, Lavallade, and the rest of you—in your capacity as relatives of Nevers; you, Oriol, as proxy for your cousin Châtillon; you, Taranne and Albret, as authorized representatives of the two Châtellux..."

"If it's not the Bourbon succession," interrupted Chaverny, "are we here to discuss the Nevers succession?"

"We'll be deciding the Nevers inheritance," said Gonzague, "and other matters as well."

"And why the devil would you need the Nevers inheritance, cousin—when you're earning a million an hour?"

For a moment Gonzague didn't reply. Then with deep feeling he said, "Am I alone? Am I not going to make your fortunes too?"

All around him the faces softened with gratitude.

"Prince," said Navailles, "you know you can count on me."

"And me!" cried Gironne.

"And me!"—"And me!"

"And me too, by God!" said Chaverny after all the others. "I'd just like to know..."

Gonzague interrupted him coldly. "You're too inquisitive, cousin. It'll be the death of you. Those of you who are with me, understand this well: you'll have to follow my lead, good or bad, straight or winding."

"But..."

"That's an order! Each of you is free to follow or to stay behind. But whoever stops short along the way has chosen to break the pact. I will no longer acknowledge him. Those who are with me must see with my eyes, hear with my ears, think with my mind. The responsibility belongs not to you, the arms, but to me, the head. You hear me, marquis: I want no friends on other terms!"

"And we ask only one thing," said Navailles, "that our illustrious relative show us the way."

"Mighty cousin," said Chaverny, "may I be permitted, humbly and modestly, to ask you one question? What will I have to do?"

"Keep quiet and give me your vote at the council."

"At the risk of offending our friends—whose devotion to you is so touch-ing—I have to tell you, cousin, I value my vote about as little as an empty champagne flute, but..."

"No buts!" interrupted Gonzague.

And all the rest echoed enthusiastically, "No buts!"

"We'll close ranks around your lordship," added Oriol pompously.

"Your lordship remembers so well those who serve you!" said the financier Taranne. The solicitation wasn't graceful, but it was at least direct. All the rest of them put on a distant air, so as not to appear implicated.

Chaverny gave Gonzague a mocking smile of triumph. Gonzague wagged his finger at him as if at a naughty child. His anger had passed. "I like Taranne's devotion the best," he said with a slight note of contempt. "Taranne, my friend, you can have my farm at Épernay."

"Ah, prince..." began Taranne.

"Don't thank me," interrupted Gonzague. "And, Montaubert, would you open a window? I feel ill."

All of them rushed to the windows. Gonzague was very pale, and sweat dripped from his hair. He dipped his handkerchief in a glass of water that Gironne offered him and wiped his brow. Chaverny came to him quickly.

"It's nothing," said Gonzague. "Fatigue. I was up all night, and I had to at-tend the king's morning levee."

"Why the devil do you have to run yourself to death like that, cousin?" cried Chaverny. "What can the king do for you? I might almost say, what can God do for you?"

With respect to God, Gonzague wasn't at fault: if he got up too early in the morning, it wasn't to say his prayers. He clasped Chaverny's hand. He would have paid plenty for someone to ask Chaverny's question. "Ingrate," he mur-mured, "you think it's for myself I do it?"

Gonzague's followers were on the verge of kneeling before him. Chaverny was silenced.

"Ah, gentlemen!" continued Gonzague. "Our young king is a delightful child. He knows all your names, and he always asks me for news of my close friends."

"Really!" sang the choir.

"The Regent was by the royal bedside with his mother Madame Palatine, and when he opened the bed curtains young Louis raised his beautiful eyelids, heavy with sleep, and it seemed to us that dawn had broken."

"Rosy-fingered dawn!" cried the incorrigible Chaverny. Everyone else felt a little like stoning him.

"Our young king," continued Gonzague, "held out his hand to His Royal Highness the Regent, and then, seeing me, he said, 'Ah, good morning, prince! I saw you the other evening at the Cours la Reine Park, surrounded by your people. You really should give me that Monsieur de Gironne: he's such a splendid chevalier!"

Gironne pressed his hand to his heart. The others pursed their lips.

"'Monsieur de Nocé pleases me too,'" went on Gonzague, of course reporting the king's actual words. "'And that Monsieur de Saldaña! God's death, he must be a mighty warrior.'"

"Don't bother," whispered Chaverny in his ear. "Saldaña isn't here." Indeed, no one had seen either the Baron of Saldaña or the Chevalier de Faenza since the previous evening.

Gonzague ignored the interruption. "His Majesty also mentioned you, Montaubert, and you too, Choisy, and several others."

Chaverny interrupted again. "And did His Majesty deign to notice that gallant and noble figure, Monsieur de Peyrolles?"

"His Majesty forgot no one," said Gonzague coldly, "except you."

"Serves me right!" said Chaverny. "That'll teach me!"

"At court they already know about your mining concern, Albret," went on Gonzague. "'And your Oriol,' the king said to me, laughing, 'did you know people say he'll soon be richer than I am?'"

"What wit!" they all cried. "What a great ruler he'll be!"

Gonzague smiled slightly. "But those are just words. We have better than that, thank God. I can tell you, Albret, your concession will be granted."

"Who wouldn't belong to you, prince?" cried Albret.

"Oriol," added Gonzague, "you've been granted your title of nobility. You can go see d'Hozier about your coat of arms."

The fat little financier puffed up like a balloon and almost burst.

"Oriol," cried Chaverny, "now you're cousin to the king—and you're already cousin to everyone on the Rue Saint Denis. Your coat of arms is obvious: gold, with three azure stockings, two over one; and above, a flaming nightcap, with the motto 'A Useful Yes Man,' in Latin of course." Everyone laughed a little, except Oriol and Gonzague. Oriol had been born in a hosiery shop off the Rue Saint Denis. If Chaverny had saved his wisecrack for dinner, it would have been a hit.

"You've been granted your pension, Navailles," continued Gonzague, that living horn of plenty. "And Montaubert, you've got your title."

Montaubert and Navailles were sorry they'd laughed.

"Nocé," went on Gonzague, "tomorrow you'll ride in the royal carriage with the king. As for you, Gironne, I'll tell you later privately what I've gotten for you."

Nocé was happy, and Gironne even happier. Riding the flow of his generosity, which was costing him nothing, Gonzague named each man in turn, forgetting no one, not even the Baron of Batz. Finally Gonzague said, "Come here, marquis,"

"Me?" said Chaverny.

"Come here, you spoiled brat!"

"I know my fate, cousin!" Chaverny laughed. "All of our friends who behaved have gotten straight As. The best I can look forward to is bread and water." He struck his chest. "Ah! I feel like I've deserved it!"

"Monsieur de Fleury, the king's tutor, was at the morning levee," said Gonzague.

"Naturally," said Chaverny. "That's his pupil."

"Monsieur de Fleury is strict."

"That's his job."

"Monsieur de Fleury had heard about your affair with Mademoiselle de Clairmont at the Feuillantines Convent."

"Uh-oh!" said Navailles.

"Uh-oh!" echoed Oriol and the rest.

"And you saved me from banishment, cousin?" said Chaverny. "Many thanks!"

"It wasn't going to be banishment, marquis."

"What was it going to be, cousin?"

"It was going to be the Bastille."

"And you saved me from the Bastille? Many thanks, doubled!"

"I've done better than that, marquis."

"Even better? Should I prostrate myself, cousin?"

"Your estate at Chaneilles was confiscated by the late king."

"Yes, at the time of the Edict of Nantes."

"That estate at Chaneilles brought you considerable rent, didn't it?"

"Twenty thousand livres, cousin, and for half that much I'd sell my soul to the devil."

"Your estate at Chaneilles is restored to you."

"Really!" Chaverny held out his hand to Gonzague. "In that case, I'm selling my soul to the devil!"

Gonzague frowned. The whole group waited only for his sign to start an uproar. Chaverny looked around with scorn. "Cousin," he said slowly and quietly. "I wish you nothing but the best. But if hard times come, these people around you will scatter. I'm not insulting anyone—that's the way of the world. But even if I'm the only one left, cousin, I'll stand by you!"

V. In Which is Explained the Absence of Faenza and Saldaña

The handouts were finished. Nocé planned what he would wear the next day to ride in the king's carriage. Oriol, made a gentleman five minutes ago, was already looking to claim some ancestors from the time of Saint Louis. Everyone was happy. The Prince of Gonzague had certainly made good use of his attendance at the king's morning levee.

But even so the little Marquis of Chaverny said, "In spite of your wonderful gift to me, cousin, I'm not satisfied."

"What do you want now?"

"I don't know if it's because of the Feuillantines Convent and Mademoiselle de Clairmont, but Bois-Rosé stubbornly refused me an invitation to the ball at the Palais-Royal tonight. He says all the tickets have been handed out."

"I should think so!" cried Oriol. "They were going for ten louis apiece on the Rue Quincampoix this morning. Bois-Rosé must have made five or six hundred thousand livres off that."

"Of which half goes to his master, Father Dubois!"

"I saw one ticket go for fifty louis," said Albret.

"I couldn't even get one for sixty!" said Taranne.

"People are fighting over them."

"By now they're priceless."

"That's because it's going to be a magnificent ball, gentlemen," said Gonzague. "Everyone there will be granted riches or nobility. I don't think the Regent meant to hand the tickets over to scalpers. But that's the plague of our times—and I don't see why Bois-Rosé or the priest shouldn't make a little something on the side."

"Even if tonight the Regent's rooms are full of stockbrokers and wheeler-dealers!" said Chaverny.

"That's tomorrow's nobility," said Gonzague. "They're the up and comers."

Chaverny tapped Oriol on the shoulder. "You, the nobility of today, I bet you'll look down on tomorrow's men!"

We need to say a word about this ball. It was the Scotsman John Law's idea, and it was Law who was covering the enormous costs. It was to be the symbolic triumph of his System, as people called it, the loud official proclamation of the victory of credit over specie. To give the announcement more dignity, Law had persuaded Philippe d'Orléans to lend him the halls and gardens of the Palais-Royal. Even better, the invitations were issued in the Regent's own name, and for that reason alone the triumph of the God of Plenty had become a national holiday. It was said Law had donated insane sums to be spent on the Regent's palace so that nothing should diminish the glory of the occasion. Everything lavish expenditure could produce in the way of marvels would dazzle the guests' eyes. People were talking especially about the fireworks and the ballet. The fireworks show, directed by the Chevalier de Gioja, would depict the enormous palace Law planned to build on the banks of the Mississippi. Everyone knew that soon the only Wonder of the World would be that marble palace, decorated with all the useless gold the victory of credit would pull out of circulation. A palace as big as a city, into which would be poured all of the world's metallic wealth—gold and silver being good for nothing else.

The ballet, an allegorical piece in the fashion of the times, would depict Credit, personified as the guardian angel of France, taking its place at the head of all the nations. No more famine, no more suffering, no more war! Credit—that second messiah sent by a merciful God—would spread across the whole globe the recovered delights of the terrestrial paradise. After that night's ball, deified Credit would need no temple, and its pontiffs existed already.

The Regent had set the number of guests at three thousand. Father Dubois quietly tripled that. Bois-Rosé, the master of ceremonies, secretly doubled it again. In an age ruled by speculation fever, speculation spreads everywhere, and nothing is immune to its infection. On the fringes of commercial districts you can see children who have barely started to walk already trading for their toys and taking bids on a half-eaten spice cake or a tattered kite or half a dozen marbles; in the same way, when speculation fever has infected a society, grown children jack up the price of anything sought after or in fashion: menus from trendy restaurants, tickets to hit shows, pews in crowded churches. It happens spontaneously, without any coordination.

When Gonzague said, "There's no harm in Bois-Rosé making five or six hundred thousand livres off those invitations," he was just voicing the general consensus. Now he pulled out his own wallet. "I think I heard Peyrolles say he was offered two or three thousand louis for the stack of invitations His Highness sent me. But too bad! I kept them for my friends."

There was a loud hurrah. Several of those gentlemen already had invitations in their pockets—but you can't have too many invitations when they're worth a hundred pistoles apiece! Nobody could be more generous than Gonzague was that morning. He opened his wallet and tossed onto the table a stack of pink letters decorated with gorgeous vignettes, all of them depicting Credit, almighty Credit, holding a horn of plenty and surrounded by garlands and cupids. The gentlemen divided them out. Each took some for himself and some for his friends—except Chaverny, who was still enough of a nobleman not to stoop to reselling what he was given. The newly ennobled Oriol seemed to have a great many friends, because he filled his pockets.

Gonzague watched them all; his eye met Chaverny's, and they both laughed. If any of those gentlemen thought they were taking advantage of the prince, they were mistaken. He had his reasons, and he had more brains in his pinky than a dozen Oriols multiplied by half a hundred Gironnes or

Montauberts. "Gentlemen," said Gonzague, "be so kind as to leave two invitations, for Faenza and Saldaña. In fact, I'm surprised not to see them here." It was unheard of for Faenza and Saldaña to skip a summons.

While his followers went on dividing the spoils so sought after by the scalpers on the Rue Quincampoix, Gonzague said, "I'm happy to have been able to do this trifling favor for you. Remember: everywhere I go, you'll go. You're a holy battalion around me. Your job is to follow me. My job is to keep your heads above the rabble." Nothing was left on the table but the two invitations for Faenza and Saldaña. The gentlemen gave Gonzague their undivided respectful attention. "I have only one more thing to say," he concluded. "Events will soon take place that will be mysterious to you. Don't try to understand. I ask—I demand—only this: don't look for reasons for what I do, just wait for my orders and follow them. It doesn't matter if the road is long and difficult, since I tell you on my honor that at the end of it your fortunes will be made."

"We'll follow you!" cried Navailles.

"All of us, such as we are!" added Gironne.

And Oriol, round as a ball, summed up gallantly, "Even if it's into Hell!"

"Damn, cousin," said Chaverny quietly, "what firm friends we've got! I'm willing to bet..."

He was interrupted by a cry of surprise and admiration. He himself stopped open-mouthed at the sight of a beautiful girl who'd just appeared in confusion at the door to Gonzague's bedroom. She must not have expected to find such a large gathering: when she first came in, her sparkling smile shone with happy mischief, but at the sight of Gonzague's guests she stopped to lower a veil of embroidered lace and stood as still as a statue.

Chaverny devoured her with his eyes. The others had trouble restraining their inquisitive looks. Gonzague, startled at first, now recovered and went to the newcomer. He brought her hand to his lips with more respect than gallantry. The girl said nothing.

"It's the beautiful recluse!" murmured Chaverny.

"The Spaniard!" added Navailles.

"The one for whom the prince keeps that private little house over behind Saint Magloire!"

Being connoisseurs, they all admired her lithe yet noble figure, her adorable calves and fairy's feet, her thick gorgeous crown of silky jet-black hair. She was dressed in an elegant lady's street clothes of rich simplicity, and she wore them well.

"Gentlemen," said Gonzague, "you were going to meet this dear child today—dear to me in more ways than one. But I didn't count on it happening so soon. I won't introduce you to her now: we don't have time. Wait for me here, please, gentlemen. You'll be needed in a little while." He took the girl's hand, led her into his room, and closed the door behind them.

Immediately all the men's faces changed, except for that of Chaverny, who looked as impudent as ever. The teacher was gone, and all of these bearded schoolboys were free to play.

"All right!" cried Gironne.

"We can relax!" said Montaubert.

"Gentlemen," said Nocé, "the late king made a similar appearance, in front of the whole court, with Madame de Montespan. Your uncle tells the story in his memoirs, Choisy. The Archbishop of Paris was there, the Lord Chancellor, the princes, three cardinals, and two abbesses, not to mention Father Letellier. The king and the countess were supposed to say a formal goodnight and then retire to their separate apartments in the bosom of virtue. But no: Madame de Montespan wept, and the Great Louis teared up, and then they both bowed their way out of the dignified assembly."

"She's so beautiful!" said Chaverny dreamily.

"It just occurred to me," said Oriol. "What if this family conclave is for a divorce!"

They all protested, but then each of them admitted it was possible. Everyone knew about the total separation between Gonzague and his wife.

"That devil of a man is as subtle as amber," said Taranne. "He's capable of dropping the woman and keeping her dowry!"

"And that's what we're here to give our votes for," said Gironne.

"What do you think, Chaverny?" asked fat little Oriol.

"I think you'd all be despicable if you weren't so stupid."

"By God, cousin," cried Nocé, "you're still young enough to be taught to behave, and I have a mind to..."

"Now, now," said Oriol peaceably.

Chaverny hadn't even looked at Nocé. "She's so beautiful!" he said again.

"Chaverny's in love!" they all cried.

"That's why I'll forgive him," said Nocé.

"But what do we actually know about that girl?" said Gironne.

"Nothing," said Navailles, "except that Gonzague keeps her carefully hidden, and Peyrolles is the flunky assigned to cater to her every whim."

"What does Peyrolles say?"

"Peyrolles says nothing."

"That's why Gonzague keeps him around."

"She can only have been in Paris for a couple of weeks at most," said Nocé, "because last month Nivelle was queen and mistress of our prince's little pleasure house."

"Since which," added Oriol, "we haven't dined once at the little house."

"There's a sort of guardhouse in the garden," said Montaubert. "Faenza and Saldaña take turns keeping watch."

"Mystery, mystery!"

"Be patient: we'll find out today what's going on."

"Hey, Chaverny!" The little marquis jumped as if he had woken with a start.

"Chaverny, you're daydreaming!"—"Chaverny, you're too quiet!"—"Say something, Chaverny, even if it's just to insult us!"

Chaverny rested his chin on his hand. "Gentlemen, you damn yourselves to Hell three or four times a day for the sake of a few banknotes. For the sake of that beautiful girl, I'd damn myself once, that's all."

When he'd settled Cocardasse and Passepoil in the kitchen in front of a lavish feast, Monsieur de Peyrolles left the villa by the garden gate. He went along the Rue Saint Denis and behind the Saint Magloire Church and stopped at the gate of another garden, whose walls were almost hidden under the enormous low-hanging branches of an avenue of old elms. Peyrolles kept the key to that gate in the pocket of his handsome doublet. He entered. The garden was empty. At the far end of a path that ran under a bower so shaded as to be mysterious stood a newly built pavilion in the Greek style, whose colonnaded porch was lined with statues. It was a gem of a little pleasure house, the latest achievement of the architect Oppenordt.

Peyrolles followed the shaded path to the little house. A number of servants in livery waited in the vestibule. "Where's Saldaña?" asked Peyrolles. They hadn't seen Baron Saldaña since the day before. "And Faenza?" Same answer. Peyrolles's thin face grew anxious. "What's this mean?" he wondered to himself. Without inquiring further, he asked whether Mademoiselle was available. Servants went back and forth, and a chambermaid's voice could be heard. Mademoiselle was waiting for Monsieur de Peyrolles in her boudoir.

"I can't sleep!" she cried as soon as she saw him. "I didn't sleep a wink all night! I can't stay in this house! The alley on the other side of the wall is a cutthroat's paradise!"

It was the same beautiful girl we already met in Gonzague's rooms. Without slighting her street dress, she looked even more charming—if that's possible—in her negligee. Her flowing white dressing gown hinted at the perfections of her figure, at once slim and solid. Her beautiful unbound hair fell to her shoulders, and her small bare feet played in satin slippers.

To come so close to such an enchantress without danger, a man would have to be made of marble. Peyrolles had every quality to justify his master's trust in him: he was as indifferent as one of Harun al Rashid's eunuchs. Rather than admire the lady's charms he said, "Doña Cruz, the prince wishes to see you at his villa this morning."

"It's a miracle!" cried the girl. "Me, getting out of my prison! Me, crossing the street! Are you sure you're not talking in your sleep, Monsieur de Peyrolles?" She burst out laughing and spun in a double pirouette.

Peyrolles's expression didn't change. "For your visit to the villa, the prince wishes you to dress."

"Me, getting dressed!" she cried again. "*Virgen Santa*! I don't believe a word you're saying!"

"I'm quite serious, Doña Cruz. You have to be ready in an hour."

Doña Cruz looked in the mirror and snorted. Then, exploding like gunpowder, she shouted, "Angélique! Justine! Madame Langlois!—Frenchwomen are so slow!" She seemed angry that they hadn't come before they were called. "Madame Langlois! Justine! Angélique!"

"It takes time..." began Peyrolles.

"You, scram!" cried Doña Cruz. "You've done your errand. I'll be there."

"I'll escort you."

"*Santa Maria*, the boredom!" she sighed. "You have no idea how much I'd like to see a face that isn't yours, Monsieur de Peyrolles!"

Madame Langlois, Angélique, and Justine entered together. Doña Cruz had already forgotten about her Parisian chambermaids. "I don't want those two men in my house all night," she said, referring to Faenza and Saldaña. "They scare me."

"That's his lordship's order," answered Peyrolles.

"Am I a slave?" cried the petulant girl, reddening with anger. "Did I ask to come here? If I'm a prisoner, at least let me pick my own jailers! Promise me I'll never see those two men again, or I won't go to the villa."

The senior chambermaid, Madame Langlois, whispered a few words in Peyrolles's ear. His normally pale face turned white. His voice shook. "You saw it?"

"I saw it," replied the chambermaid.

"When?"

"A little while ago. They just found them both."

"Where?"

"Outside the little door that opens onto the alley."

"I don't like people whispering in front of me!" said Doña Cruz haughtily.

"I beg your pardon, Madame," said Peyrolles humbly. "All you need to know is, you won't see those two men again."

"Well then, dress me!" she ordered.

Madame Langlois continued her account while she led Peyrolles down the stairs. "The two of them ate supper together downstairs last night. Saldaña, who was on guard duty, walked out with Faenza. Then we heard the clash of swords in the alley."

"Doña Cruz mentioned that," said Peyrolles.

"The noise didn't last long. Then a little while ago a servant going out by way of the alley stumbled over two bodies."

At that moment Doña Cruz called out, "Langlois! Langlois!"

"Go ahead," said the chambermaid as she hurried back up the steps. "They're at the far end of the garden."

In the boudoir the three chambermaids began the easy, gratifying task of a beautiful girl's toilette. Doña Cruz soon gave herself over to the joy of seeing herself look so good: her mirror smiled back at her. *Virgen Santa*! She hadn't been this happy since she got to the great city of Paris, of which she'd seen nothing but long dark streets on a gloomy autumn night. "Finally!" she said to herself. "My handsome prince will keep his promise. I'll see and be seen! Paris, that I heard so much about, will finally be something besides a lonely little house in a cold walled-off garden!" She escaped from her chambermaids' hands to dance around the room in joyful circles like the giddy child she was.

Peyrolles, meanwhile, had gone straight to the far end of the garden. Under a dark bower, on a pile of dry leaves, two cloaks had been spread out to cover what looked like human shapes. Trembling, Peyrolles lifted first one cloak, then the other: Faenza and Saldaña. Both had the same wound, on the forehead right between the eyes. Peyrolles's teeth chattered. He let the cloaks drop.

VI. Doña Cruz

There's a tragic tale every novelist has made use of at least once in his career: the story of the poor child stolen from her mother—a duchess—by Scottish gypsies or Calabrian zingari or Roma from the Rhineland or Hungarian tsiganes or Spanish gitanos. I don't know, and I'm not about to go ask her, whether our beautiful Doña Cruz was a stolen duchess or a genuine gypsy girl. The fact is, she'd spent her whole life among gypsies, moving with them from town to town, from hamlet to village, dancing in the plaza for pennies. She herself will tell us how she left that life—free-spirited but low-income—to come to Paris and live in Monsieur de Gonzague's little pleasure house.

We'll rejoin her now, a half hour after her toilette was done, in Gonzague's bedroom, upset in spite of her boldness, and embarrassed by the grand entrance she'd just made in Gonzague's private parlor at the Villa Nevers.

"Why was Peyrolles not with you?" asked Gonzague.

"While I was doing my toilette, your Peyrolles lost his mind and the power of speech. He left me for a moment to go walking in the garden. When he came back he looked like he'd been struck by lightning." She went on in a more flirtatious voice, "But you didn't ask me here just to talk about your Peyrolles, did you, my lord?"

Gonzague laughed. "It wasn't to talk about Peyrolles."

"Tell me, then!" she cried. "You can see I'm impatient! Tell me!"

He observed her carefully, thinking, "I've searched a long time. Could I have found anyone better? She looks like him! It's not an illusion."

"Well?" said Doña Cruz. "Tell me!"

"Dear child, sit down."

"Am I going back to my prison?"

"Not for a long time."

"Ah!" she said sadly. "But I will go back! Today for the first time I saw a little corner of the city by daylight. It's beautiful. My solitude will feel even sadder now."

"This isn't Madrid. I have to take precautions."

"Why? Why all these precautions? What have I done that I have to be hidden?"

"Nothing, I assure you, Doña Cruz. But..."

"Now listen, my lord," she interrupted angrily. "I have to speak—my heart's too full. You don't have to remind me, I can see we're not in Madrid anymore, where I was poor, it's true, and an orphan, and abandoned, it's true, but where I was free, as free as air!" Frowning, she paused. "My lord, you know you promised me lots of things?"

"I'll give you even more than I promised."

"That's another promise, and I'm beginning not to believe in your promises." She stopped frowning, and a veil of daydreaming softened the sharp glitter of her gaze. "Everyone knew me—the common people and the nobles. They loved me, and when I arrived they cried, 'Come see the gypsy girl who's going to dance the Jerez *bamboleo!*' And if I got there late there was always a crowd, lots of people waiting to see me on the Plaza Santa, behind the Alcazar. In my dreams now I see those orange trees at the palace perfuming the evening air, and those houses with lattice-work turrets, with their blinds raised halfway at dusk. Ah, I played my mandolin for more than one Spanish grandee! A beautiful country!" She caught herself, with tears in her eyes. "A land of scents and serenades! Here, the cold shade of your trees makes me shiver." She hid her face in her hands.

Gonzague, his mind elsewhere, let her talk.

"Do you remember?" she said suddenly. "One evening I'd danced later than usual. Turning a corner on the dark street that climbs to the Church of the Assumption, suddenly I saw you near me. I felt both fear and hope. When you spoke, your soft serious voice alarmed me, but I didn't think to run away. You stood in front of me to block my way, and you said, 'What's your name, child?' And I said 'Santa Cruz. I was called Flor when I was with my people, the gypsies of Grenada. But my baptismal name was Maria de la Santa Cruz.' And you said, 'You're a Christian?' Maybe you've forgotten all this, my lord?"

"No," said Gonzague distractedly, "I've forgotten nothing."

Her voice trembled. "I'll remember that moment all my life. How could I already love you? I don't know. You're old enough to be my father, but where could I find a lover nobler, more handsome, more brilliant than you?" She spoke without blushing: she lacked our modern-day reserve. But it was a father's kiss that Gonzague planted on her forehead.

Doña Cruz sighed deeply. "You said, 'You're too pretty to dance in public with a tambourine, wearing a belt of fake sequins. Come with me.' So I followed you. I'd already surrendered my will. When we got to your house I knew it was the Villa Alberoni. They told me you were the Ambassador of the Regent of France to the court in Madrid. What did I care? We left the next day. You didn't let me ride in your carriage. I've never told you these things, my lord, because we barely see each other. I'm lonely, I'm sad, I'm abandoned. I made the long journey from Madrid to Paris, that endless road, in a coach with thick curtains, always closed. I made that journey weeping, full of regrets. I already felt like an exile. How many times, *Virgen Santa*, how many times in those silent hours did I wish for my nights of freedom, my wild dancing, my lost laughter!"

Gonzague, his thoughts elsewhere, had stopped listening.

"Paris!" she cried with a bitterness that made him start. "You remember what a picture you painted me of Paris? Paris, a young girl's paradise! Paris—enchanted dream, inexhaustible wealth, staggering luxury! Happiness without

103

end, a lifelong party! You remember how you intoxicated me?" She took Gonzague's hand and pressed it between hers. "My lord, my lord! In your garden I've seen beautiful flowers from Spain—faded, sad, dying. Do you want to kill me, my lord?" She straightened up and pushed back her thick hair. "Listen," she cried, "I'm not your slave! I like crowds; solitude frightens me! I like noise; silence leaves me cold. I need light, movement, and above all, pleasure! The pleasure that sustains life! I'm attracted to playfulness, laughter, singing! Tintilla de Rota wine puts diamonds in my eyes, and I know I'm most beautiful when I laugh."

"Silly little thing!" murmured Gonzague with a fatherly pat.

She drew back. "You weren't like this in Madrid." Then she added angrily, "You're right, I am silly, but I'm getting wise. I'm leaving."

"Doña Cruz," he said. She was crying. He wiped away her tears with his embroidered handkerchief.

Behind her still-wet tears she smiled proudly. "Others will love me," she threatened. "This paradise is a prison! You tricked me, prince. I have a magnificent boudoir in a pleasure house that might have been broken off a fairytale palace. Marble, fine paintings, velvet curtains embroidered with gold, more gold in the wainscoting, sculptures and statues, crystal chandeliers—but all of it surrounded by damp gloomy shadows, black lawns on which dead leaves fall one by one from the icy cold, silent chambermaids, self-effacing servants, savage bodyguards, and for a majordomo that white-faced Peyrolles!"

"Do you have any complaint against Peyrolles?"

"No. He's a slave to my least whim. He addresses me gently, even respectfully, and when he greets me the feather in his hat sweeps the ground."

"Well then!"

"You're joking, my lord! Don't you know he bolts my door? He's like the guardian of a seraglio!"

"You're exaggerating."

"Prince, a caged bird doesn't even look at the gilding on the bars. I'm unhappy here, a prisoner here, and my patience is at an end. I demand my liberty!"

Gonzague smiled.

"Why are you hiding me like this? Answer me!" She tossed her head.

He was still smiling.

"You don't love me!" She reddened, not from shame but from disappointment. "Since you don't love me, you can't be jealous of me!"

He took her hand and carried it to his lips.

She blushed even more. "I thought..." she murmured, lowering her eyes. "You told me once you weren't married. But when I ask about that, the people around me say nothing. I thought, when you sent me teachers, when I saw I was being taught everything an accomplished Frenchwoman needs to know—why shouldn't I say it?—I thought I was loved." She stopped and glanced sidelong at Gonzague, whose eyes expressed pleasure and admiration. "And I worked hard," she went on, "to make myself better and more worthy. I worked bravely and intently. Nothing was too much for me. No obstacle was enough to overcome my will. You're smiling!" she cried, with a furious gesture. "*Virgen Santa*, don't smile like that, prince, or you'll drive me mad!" She stood before him, and in a tone that brooked no evasion she said, "If you don't love me, what do you want from me?"

"I want to make you happy, Doña Cruz," said Gonzague gently. "Happy and powerful."

"Then first make me free!" cried the beautiful captive in total rebellion. As Gonzague tried to calm her she went on, "Make me free! Free! Free! That's enough, that's all I want." Then she gave rein to her wildest fantasies. "I want Paris! I want the Paris you promised me! The bright noisy Paris I know must be out there beyond the walls of my prison. I want to be seen everywhere. What good is all my finery inside these walls? Look at me! Did you think I was just going to melt in tears?" She burst out laughing. "Look at me, prince: I feel better already. I won't cry anymore, I'll do nothing but laugh, as long as I can go to the Opéra, which I know only by reputation for its parties and dances."

"This evening, Doña Cruz," said Gonzague coldly, "you'll put on your finest things." She looked at him, both distrustful and curious. "And I'll escort you to the Regent's ball."

She was stunned. Her charming expressive face changed color two or three times. "Is that really true?" she said finally, because she still doubted him.

"It's true."

"You'd do that! Oh, I forgive you everything, prince! You're good, you're my friend!"

She threw her arms around his neck. Then, letting go, she began to dance around madly. "The Regent's ball! We're going to the Regent's ball! The walls here may be thick, the garden cold and empty, the windows shut, but still I've heard about the Regent's ball, and I know there'll be wonderful things to see! And I'll be there! Oh, thank you, thank you, prince! If you knew how handsome you are when you're good! It's at the Palais-Royal, isn't it?"

She ran to Gonzague from the far end of the room and knelt on a cushion at his feet. Suddenly serious, she folded her hands on his knee and stared at him. "What shall I wear?"

He shook his head solemnly. "At a ball given at the court of France, Doña Cruz, one thing enhances and adorns a beautiful face more than the finest dress."

"Is it a smile?" she guessed, like a child trying to solve a simple riddle.

"No."

"Is it charm?"

"No. You have the smile and the charm, Doña Cruz. The thing I'm talking about..."

"I don't have. What is it?" He didn't answer, and she added impatiently, "Will you give it to me?"

"I'll give it to you."

"But what can it be I lack?" she said coquettishly, with a proud glance in the mirror.

The mirror could certainly not have offered her Gonzague's reply. "A name!"

And Doña Cruz tumbled from the heights of her joy. A name! She had no name! The Palais-Royal wasn't the Plaza Santa behind the Alcazar. Here she couldn't dance to a tambourine, wearing a belt of fake sequins around her hips. Poor Doña Cruz! Gonzague had made her a promise, but Gonzague's promises... Anyway, what exactly does a name give you?

The prince seemed to anticipate that objection. "Without a name, dear child, all of my tender affection is powerless. But your name has only been lost; and I found it. Your name is distinguished even among the most distinguished names in France."

"What are you saying?" she cried, dazzled.

"You have a family," he continued solemnly. "A powerful family, related to our kings. Your father was a duke."

"My father! He was a duke, you say? So he's dead?"

Gonzague bowed.

"And my mother?" The poor child's voice trembled.

"Your mother is a princess."

"She's alive!" Her heart leapt. "You said she's a princess, so she lives! My mother! Please tell me about my mother!"

He put a finger to his lips. "Not now," he murmured.

But Doña Cruz wasn't one to put up with mystification. She grabbed Gonzague's hands. "You're going to tell me about my mother—right now! My God, I'll love her so much. She's good, isn't she? And beautiful? It's strange: I've always dreamt about this. Something inside me told me I was the daughter of a princess."

Gonzague had trouble keeping a straight face. "They're all the same," he thought.

"Yes, when I went to sleep at night I could always see my mother, bending over my bed, with beautiful black hair and proud eyebrows and a string of pearls and diamond earrings, and such gentle eyes! What's my mother's name?"

"I can't tell you yet."

"Why not?"

"There's great danger..."

"I understand! I understand!" she interrupted, in the grip of some fanciful memory. "That's how it worked in plays I saw at the theater in Madrid: you can never tell young ladies their mother's name right away."

"Never," he agreed.

"Great danger—but I can keep a secret! I'd keep the secret to the grave!" She planted herself, as fine and proud as Chimène in *El Cid*.

"I don't doubt it. But you won't have long to wait, dear child. In a few hours your mother's identity will be revealed to you. Right now all you need to know is, your name is not Maria de Santa Cruz."

"My real name was Flor?"

"Not that either."

"Then what was my name?"

"At birth you were given your mother's name. She was Spanish. Your name is Aurore."

Doña Cruz started. "Aurore!" Then she clapped her hands. "What a strange coincidence!"

Gonzague watched her carefully. "How so?"

"Because it's not a common name," she said pensively, "and it reminds me..."

"It reminds you..." he prompted a little anxiously.

"Poor little Aurore!" she murmured with tears in her eyes. "She was so good! And so pretty! How I loved her!"

Gonzague's effort to hide his feverish curiosity was obvious, but luckily for him Doña Cruz was lost in her memories. He affected cold indifference. "You knew a girl named Aurore?"

"Yes."

"How old was she?"

"My age. We were children together, and we loved each other dearly, though she was well off and I was poor."

"How long ago was this?"

"Years." She studied him carefully. "Does this interest you, prince?"

Gonzague was the kind of man who's never caught off guard. He took her hand and said lovingly, "I'm interested in anything that's precious to you, my dear. Tell me more about little Aurore, your friend from long ago."

VII. The Prince of Gonzague

Gonzague's bedroom, as luxurious as the rest of the villa, opened on one side into an intermediate space that served as his dressing room, beyond which lay the small parlor where we left our financiers and gentlemen. On the other side the bedroom opened onto a library unrivaled in Paris for the size and quality of its collection. Gonzague was very well read, a capable Latinist, familiar with the literary greats of Athens and Rome, a deft theologian on occasion, and fully versed in philosophy. If he'd also been an honest man, nothing could have stood in his way. But he lacked a moral compass. If you have no principles, the smarter you are, the more you'll go astray. Gonzague was like the prince in the fairy tale, born in a golden cradle surrounded by good fairies. They grant the lucky little prince every gift needed for glory and happiness. But one fairy was forgotten. She shows up angry and says, you can keep everything my sisters have given you, but—and that one "but" was enough to make the little prince the most wretched of wretched beings.

Gonzague was handsome, he was born supremely rich and at the pinnacle of the ruling class, he had courage and had proven it, he had learning and intelligence, few men spoke more ably or with more authority than he, his ability as a diplomat was known and proclaimed, everyone at court acknowledged his charm, but... But he recognized neither faith nor law, and his past actions dictated his present course. He no longer had the power to stop on the slope down which he'd started in his youth. He was inexorably driven to commit new crimes to hide and cover up his old crimes. He could have been a great force for good; instead he was a powerful engine for evil. Nothing held him back; after twenty-five years he was still tireless.

As for remorse, Gonzague believed in it no more than he believed in God. There's no need to explain to the reader that for him Doña Cruz was just a skillfully chosen tool, which seemed ready to do its job to perfection. Gonzague hadn't picked this girl at random; he'd hesitated long before making his choice. Doña Cruz brought together all the qualities he'd dreamt of, including a certain resemblance, vague to be sure, but enough so that unbiased people could say the precious words: "She has the family looks"—words that would immediately give deception the weight of truth.

But one detail had suddenly emerged on which he hadn't planned. As a result, in spite of the strange news Doña Cruz had just received, Gonzague was more stirred up than she was. He needed all his diplomatic skill to hide his agitation, and in spite of that skill, she noticed his agitation and was surprised. The last thing Gonzague had said, skillful as it was, left her in doubt. She grew suspicious. A woman can feel wary without fully understanding—but what could have disturbed so self-controlled a man? The name she'd spoken: Aurore.

What's in a name? For one thing, as Doña Cruz had observed, it was an uncommon name. For another, there are such things as omens. The name had struck Gonzague hard—and it was his very awareness of that impact that now troubled the superstitious prince. He said to himself, "It's a warning!" A warning from whom? Gonzague believed in the stars, or at least in his star. The stars can speak; his star had spoken. If that name, fallen into the conversation by chance, was some kind of revelation, then the consequences of that revelation were so serious that Gonzague's astonishment and agitation should no longer surprise us. He'd been looking for eighteen years!

He got up, ostensibly because of a loud noise in the garden, but really to regain his composure. His bedroom stood at the inner corner of the ell formed where the central block met the right wing of the villa, and it looked out onto the garden. His windows faced those of the Princess of Gonzague, all of whose were shut and heavily curtained.

Doña Cruz got up and, merely out of a child's curiosity, wanted to follow him to the window.

"Stay there," he said. "You can't be seen yet." He paid no attention to the dense crowd milling around below his windows and throughout the ruined garden; serious and thoughtful, he looked only across at his wife's windows. "Will she come?" he said to himself.

Pouting, Doña Cruz had sat back down.

"Anyway," thought Gonzague, "at least the battle would be decisive." Then he pulled himself together. "At all cost I must find out..."

He was about to return to Doña Cruz when he noticed in the crowd below him that strange little man whose whimsical eccentricity had made such a stir in the great hall that morning: the hunchback who'd bid for and won the dog kennel. The hunchback now held a devotional book of hours, and he too seemed to be looking up at Madame de Gonzague's windows. In other circumstances Gonzague—a man who overlooked no detail—would have paid closer attention, but he was focused on that name. If he'd stayed at the window another minute he would have seen a woman, a chambermaid of the princess, come down the steps from the left wing and approach the hunchback, who spoke to her briefly and handed her the book of hours. Then the chambermaid went back inside, and the hunchback vanished in the crowd.

"That noise is just my new tenants quarreling," said Gonzague as he sat back down with Doña Cruz. "Where were we, dear child?"

"We were at what my name will be from now on."

"The name that's your name: Aurore. But then something came up. What was it?"

"You forgot already?" said Doña Cruz with a mischievous smile.

Gonzague pretended to think. "Ah! That's right. Some girl you knew who was also called Aurore."

"A pretty little girl, an orphan like me."

"Really! And this was in Madrid?"

"In Madrid."

"A Spanish girl?"

"No, she was French."

"French?" said Gonzague, with excellent indifference. He stifled a yawn. You would have sworn he was keeping up the conversation only to be polite. But all his skill was wasted: Doña Cruz's playful smile should have warned him.

"And who took care of her?" he asked absentmindedly.

"An old woman."

"Sure, but who paid the duenna?"

"A gentleman."

"Also French?"

"Yes."

"Young or old?"

"Young and very handsome."

She was watching his face. He pretended to hold back another yawn.

"But why talk about things that bore you, prince?" laughed Doña Cruz. "You don't know the man. I wouldn't have thought you cared."

Gonzague could see he'd have to do better. "I don't care, child. You don't yet know me well. Of course personally I care about neither the girl nor the man, though I know lots of people in Madrid. But when I ask you questions, I have my reasons. What was the gentleman's name?"

This time Doña Cruz's beautiful eyes were full of mistrust. "I've forgotten," she said coldly.

He insisted with a smile. "I think if you tried..."

"Like I said, I've forgotten."

"Come on, try to remember. I'll help you."

"What difference does his name make to you?"

"Let's work on it together, I said. Afterwards you'll see what I want his name for. Could it be...?"

"Prince, it won't come to me no matter how hard I try." She said it so firmly there was no use insisting.

"Never mind. It's a nuisance, that's all, and I'll tell you why it's a nuisance. A French gentleman living in Spain is most likely an exile. Sadly, there are lots of them. You have no friend your age here, dear child, and friendship can't be willed. I was thinking, I have influence, I could have the gentleman pardoned, and he could come home, bringing the girl with him, so my dear little Doña Cruz wouldn't be so lonely."

He spoke with such an air of plain truth that the poor girl was touched to the bottom of her heart. "Oh, how kind you are!"

"No hard feelings," he said with a smile. "There's still time."

"What you're suggesting is something I was dying to ask you for, but I didn't dare to. Still, you don't need to know the gentleman's name, and you don't need to send a letter to Spain. I've seen my friend."

"Recently?"

"Very recently."

"Where?"

"In Paris."

"Here!" Gonzague went on smiling, but he turned pale.

Doña Cruz was no longer suspicious. "It was the day we arrived," she went on without being asked. "From the time we came through the Saint Honoré gate I was arguing with Monsieur de Peyrolles, asking him to open the carriage curtains, which he was stubbornly keeping closed. He kept me from seeing the Palais-Royal, for which I'll never forgive him. Turning a corner by a little courtyard not far from there, the carriage brushed past the houses. I heard someone singing in a downstairs room. Monsieur de Peyrolles was holding the curtain, but he took his hand away once I broke my fan over it. I'd recognized the voice. I opened the curtain. My friend Aurore, the same as always but even more beautiful, was at the window of the downstairs room."

Gonzague drew a notebook from his pocket.

"I called out," she went on. "The carriage had picked up speed. I wanted to get out. I made a fuss. Ah, if I'd been strong enough to strangle your Monsieur de Peyrolles!"

"You were saying, a street somewhere near the Palais-Royal."

"Very near."

"Would you recognize it?"

"Oh, I know what it's called. I made sure to ask Monsieur de Peyrolles."

"And what's it called?"

"The Rue du Chantre. What are you writing down, prince?"

Gonzague was indeed scribbling in his notebook. "What I'll need so you can see your friend again."

Blushing with pleasure, Doña Cruz rose, joy in her eyes. "You're so kind, so truly kind!"

He shut his notebook and put it away. "You can decide about that soon, dear child. In the meantime we'll have to part for a while. You're going to take part in a solemn ceremony. Don't try to hide your discomfort or distress. It's natural, and no one will think ill of you." He rose and took her hand. "In half an hour from now at most, you'll see your mother."

Doña Cruz pressed her hand to her heart. "What will I say to her?"

"You have no reason to hide the miseries of your childhood—none, understand? You can tell the truth, the whole truth." Gonzague lifted the curtain leading to the boudoir. "Stay in here."

"All right," she murmured. "And I'll pray to God for my mother."

"Pray, Doña Cruz, pray. This is a solemn moment in your life." He kissed her hand.

She entered the boudoir, and the curtain dropped behind her. "It's my dream!" she thought. "My mother is a princess!"

Now alone, Gonzague sat at his desk, his head in his hands. He was the one who needed to collect himself: a world of ideas spun in his head. "Rue du Chantre," he murmured. "Is she alone? Did he follow her here? That'd be bold. But is it really her?" For a moment he stared at nothing. Then he cried, "That's the first thing I have to find out!"

He rang. No one answered. He called Peyrolles by name. Silence. He got up and went quickly into the library, where his factotum usually waited for orders. The library was empty, but on the table lay a folded note addressed to Gonzague. He opened it. In Peyrolles's handwriting it read, *I was here. I had lots to tell you. Strange things have happened at the little house.* Then there was a postscript: *Cardinal de Bissy is with the princess. I'm keeping watch.*

Gonzague crumpled the note. "They'll all tell her, 'Go to the meeting, for your sake, for your child's sake, if she's still alive.' But she'll be stubborn, and she won't come. She's a dead woman! And who killed her?" His face grew pale, and he lowered his eyes. But even so he went on. "She used to be a proud creature, beautiful beyond compare, as sweet as an angel, as brave as a knight! She's the only woman I could ever love—if I could love a woman!" He straightened up, and his cynical smile returned. "Every man for himself! Is it my fault if to rise above a certain level you have to climb steps made from heads and hearts?"

On his way back to his bedroom his eye fell on the curtains covering the boudoir where he'd left Doña Cruz. "She's praying," he thought. "I'm almost ready to believe in that nonsense about the call of the blood. She was moved, but not much, not like a real daughter who's just been told she's about to see her mother again! Bah! A little gypsy! She's only thinking about jewels and parties. You can't tame a wolf."

He put his ear to the door of the boudoir. "Is she ever praying! It's a funny thing. In some corner of their foolish heads, from their first baby tooth to their last dying sigh, all foundling children hang on to the idea that their mother is a princess! They go around with a gunny sack on their back, looking for their father the king. This one's a charmer, a real gem. She'll serve my purpose without ever knowing it. If some good peasant woman, her real mother, showed up now and held out her arms to her, my God, she'd be furious! We'll see some tears when she tells the story of her childhood. Everything turns into theater."

On his desk Gonzague kept a crystal flask of Spanish wine and a glass. He poured a glass and drank it. "Well, Philippe," he said as he sat down to his scattered papers, "this is the big roll of the dice! Now or never, we're going to throw a veil over the past! It's a big gamble, with high stakes! The millions in John Law's Bank can act like those sequins in the Arabian Nights and turn into dead leaves; but the great Nevers estates are solid and real!"

As he organized his long-prepared papers, his brow gradually darkened, as if a dreadful notion had come to him. He paused to think. "Make no mistake, the Regent's vengeance would be implacable. He's fickle, he's forgetful, but he remembers Philippe de Nevers, whom he loved more than a brother. I've seen tears in his eyes when he looks at my wife—Nevers's widow—dressed in mourning. But appearances are on my side. It's been eighteen years, and not one voice has been raised against me." He brushed a hand across his forehead as if to drive away the haunting thought. "All the same, I'll take precautions. I'll find a scapegoat, and once the scapegoat's been punished I'll rest easier."

Most of the notes on the papers spread in front of him were figures, but on one page was written, *Find out whether Madame de Gonzague believes her daughter is alive or dead.* And under that: *Find out if she has the birth certificate.* "For that, it would be better if she shows up," he thought. "I'd give a hundred thousand livres just to know if she has the birth certificate, or even whether it still exists. Because if it exists, I'll have it! And who knows," he went on, his spirits rising, "who knows? Mothers are a little like the foundlings I was talking about earlier, who see their parents everywhere: they see their children everywhere. I don't believe in the infallibility of mothers. Who knows? Maybe she'll open her arms to my gypsy girl. Ah, that'd be victory! Celebrations, hymns of praise and thanksgiving, banquets! Even a *Te Deum!* And all hail Nevers's heiress!" He stopped to laugh. "And then, a little later, a beautiful young princess dies. So many girls die young! Everybody in mourning, funeral oration by an archbishop. And for me, an enormous inheritance that—God's blood!—I'll have earned!"

The Saint Magloire clock tower rang two in the afternoon. It was time for the opening of the family council.

No doubt the noble Villa Lorraine hadn't been built to serve as a stock job-bers' den, but it turned out to be well placed and well laid out for it. The three sides of the garden that bordered the Rues Quincampoix, Saint Denis, and Aubry le Boucher offered three valuable entrances. The first of those especially was worth the weight in gold of all the stone blocks of its new gateway. And as a stock exchange the garden was certainly more practical than the Rue Quincampoix itself, which was always muddy, and was lined with awful dives where merchants regularly got themselves murdered. Gonzague's garden was clearly destined to supersede the Rue Quincampoix; everyone thought so, and for once everyone was right.

For twenty-four hours people had talked about that previous hunchbacked Aesop—the first so-called Aesop, who'd retired rich and married a countess. An old soldier, a veteran of the Royal Guard named Gruel, nicknamed the Whale, had tried to take his place. But the Whale was six foot six, which was awkward: even when he crouched down, his back was too high to make a convenient desk. Still, the Whale had announced openly he would swallow any Jonah who dared to compete with him, and that threat made the hunchbacks of Paris hesitate. The Whale was big enough and strong enough to swallow them all, one by one. He wasn't a bad sort, but he drank seven or eight bottles of wine a day, and wine was expensive in 1717: the Whale had to make a living.

When the hunchback who'd won Médor's dog kennel at auction showed up to take possession of his estate, he prompted lots of laughter in the Villa Nevers garden. Everyone on the Rue Quincampoix came to watch. He was al-ready nicknamed the new Aesop, and his rounded back served perfectly and was an instant success. But the Whale growled, and Médor the dog did too. The Whale saw in Aesop a successful rival. Since Médor had the same complaint, they pooled their grudges. The Whale became Médor's protector, and the dog bared his long fangs each time he saw the new occupant of his rightful home. A tragic ending loomed: everyone expected the hunchback to wind up as food for the Whale. As a result, following Biblical precedent, he was given another nick-name: Jonah. That left him with a longer tag than most straight-backed people, but not too long: "the new Aesop, known as Jonah" accurately and elegantly expressed the idea of a hunchback swallowed by a whale. It was like a whole funeral oration delivered in advance.

Aesop himself didn't seem worried by the terrible fate awaiting him. He'd moved into his kennel and furnished it nicely with a little bench and a trunk. Diogenes in his barrel, which was really an amphora, probably wasn't as com-fortably lodged; and, according to historians, Diogenes was five foot six. From Aesop's belt of rope hung a good burlap bag. He bought himself a board, a writing case, and some quill pens, and he was ready for business. Just like the former Aesop, his much missed predecessor, when he saw a deal about to close, he discreetly drew near. He dipped his quill in ink and waited. When the deal was done, he set his board on his hump; the parties laid the contracts on the board and signed them as conveniently as in any notary's office. Then Aesop took his writing case in one hand and his board in the other. The board became his begging bowl and collected his donation, which ultimately went into the burlap bag. There was no set fee. The new Aesop, like the previous, accepted anything besides copper coins. But anyway, who carried copper coins on the Rue Quincampoix? In that bountiful time, copper was good only as a source of verdigris for poisoning your rich uncle.

Aesop started work at ten in the morning. About one in the afternoon he hailed one of the many peddlers of cold meats who wandered around this fairground of paper. He bought a baguette with a golden crust, a good-looking plump chicken, and a bottle of Chambertin. What can you say—business was good! (His predecessor wouldn't have done that.) He sat on his little kennel bench, spread out his meal on his trunk, and ate splendidly while the speculators stood waiting on him. A living desk has the disadvantage that it takes lunch breaks. But people lined up enthusiastically at the door of his kennel, and nobody thought to use the Whale's broad back. The giant, forced to drink on credit, drank twice as much, and roared. His sidekick Médor ground his fangs with rage.

"Hey, Jonah!" people shouted. "Are you almost done eating?"

Jonah was generous, and referred business to the Whale, but everybody wanted Jonah. It was a pleasure to sign contracts on his hump. Besides, Jonah wasn't tongue-tied. You know how clever those hunchbacks are! People were already quoting his witticisms. But the Whale was lying in wait for him.

When Jonah was done eating, he called out in his harsh little voice, "Soldier friend, you want some of my chicken?"

The Whale was hungry, but envy held him back. "Little bastard!" he cried, while Médor howled. "Do I look like I eat scraps?"

"Then send me your dog, soldier," replied Jonah calmly, "and stop insulting me."

"Oh, you want my dog!" roared the Whale. "You'll get him!" He whistled and called, "Sic 'em, Médor, sic 'em!" The Whale had been in the garden for about a week, and some friendships are formed at first sight; Médor and the Whale were a team. Médor gave a hoarse bark and attacked.

"Look out, hunchback!" cried the speculators.

Jonah stood still and waited for the dog. Right when Médor was about to plunge into his old kennel as if into a reconquered land, Jonah seized the chicken by both drumsticks and brought it down hard on the dog's muzzle. A miracle! Instead of getting angry, Médor began licking his chops. His tongue stretched here and there in search of bits of chicken stuck to his fur.

A general burst of laughter met this savvy battle tactic. A hundred voices cried, "Bravo, hunchback, bravo!"

The Whale shouted, "Sic 'em, Médor, you rascal, sic 'em!"

But that turncoat Médor had changed sides for good. Aesop had bought his loyalty for the price of a flying chunk of chicken. The Whale's fury burst its bounds, and he launched himself at the kennel in turn.

"Oh, Jonah! Poor Jonah!" cried the chorus of speculators.

Jonah emerged from his kennel and stood laughing at the Whale—who lifted him off the ground by the scruff of his neck. Jonah was still laughing. Just as the Whale was about to throw him back down, Jonah stiffened, set the tip of his toe on the giant's knee, and leaped like a cat. No one could say exactly what happened—it went too fast. But the fact was that now Jonah sat astride the Whale's thick neck, and he was still laughing. The crowd let out a long murmur of satisfaction.

"Soldier," said Aesop calmly, "beg for mercy or I'll strangle you."

The Whale reddened, sweated, foamed at the mouth, and made desperate efforts to free his neck. Aesop, hearing no call for mercy, tightened his knees. The Whale stuck out his tongue, turned scarlet, then blue. Clearly the hunchback had strong muscles. After a few seconds the Whale vomited up one last oath and cried for mercy in a throttled voice. The crowd danced. Jonah immediately let go, hopped gracefully down, tossed a gold piece onto his victim's lap, and ran to get his board, his pens, and his writing case, calling out cheerfully, "Let's go, gentlemen, back to work!"

Aurore de Caylus, widow of the Duke of Nevers, wife of the Prince of Gonzague, was seated on a handsome straight-backed chair of ebony, like all the furniture in her private chapel. She maintained mourning in both her clothing and her surroundings. Her dress, plain to the point of austerity, matched the plain austerity of her chapel. The ceiling of the chapel was a four-sided vault whose central boss held a medallion painted by Eustache Lesueur in the ascetic style of his later period. Wall paneling of black oak, without gilt ornament, served to frame fine tapestries depicting religious subjects. Between the two windows stood an altar draped in mourning, as if the last service held there had been the Mass for the dead. Facing the altar hung a full-length portrait of Duke Philippe de Nevers at the age of twenty, signed by Mignard. The duke was in his uniform as a colonel in the Swiss Guards. Around the frame hung black crepe. In spite of the pious images everywhere, the room felt a little like that of a pagan widow: even a baptized Artemisia would have kept up a less showy tribute to the memory of King Mausolus. Christianity seeks in grief more resignation and less insistence. But how rare it is for widows to err on the side of too much mourning! Besides, let's not forget the special circumstances of the princess, who had married the Prince of Gonzague against her will. Her mourning served as a flag of separation and resistance. Aurore de Caylus had been Gonzague's wife for eighteen years, yet she didn't know him: she'd never wished either to see him or to hear him.

Gonzague had done everything possible to gain an interview with her. He'd certainly loved her once; maybe he still did, in his way. He had a high opinion of himself, and with good reason. So sure was he of his own eloquence, he believed that if the princess agreed even once to hear him out he would emerge victorious. But the princess, rigid in her despair, wanted no consolation. She lived alone, and took pleasure in her solitude. She had neither friend nor confidante. Even her spiritual director heard only her confession of sins. She was a proud woman, inured to suffering. The memory of her husband Nevers had turned into a religion. Only one emotion lived on in her walled-off heart: maternal love. She loved—passionately—only the memory of her daughter. The thought of her daughter kept her alive and gave her the faintest hope for the future.

Everyone knows the profound effect physical objects have on us. The Princess of Gonzague, always alone with servants who had orders not to speak to her, always surrounded by bleak and gloomy art, had shriveled in intelligence and emotion. To the priest who was her confessor, she sometimes said, "I'm a dead woman." It was true: she moved through life like a ghost. Her existence passed like a troubled sleep. When she rose in the morning, silent women carried out her funereal toilette. Then her reader opened a devotional book. At nine o'clock the chaplain came to say the Mass for the dead. The rest of the day she sat, unmoving, cold, alone. She hadn't left the villa once since her marriage. The world thought she was a madwoman. The royal court came close to worshiping Gonzague for his marital devotion. In fact, not one complaint had ever fallen from Gonzague's lips.

Once, when her confessor noticed her tear-reddened eyes, the princess told him, "I dreamt I saw my daughter again. She was no longer worthy of the name of Mademoiselle de Nevers."

"And in your dream, what did you do?" asked the priest.

Crushed, paler than a corpse, the princess replied, "I did in my dream what I'd do in real life: I drove her away!"

From that time on, she grew even sadder and gloomier than before. The thought never let go of her. Yet still she went on searching throughout France and abroad. Gonzague's purse was always open for his wife's desires—but he made sure everyone was privy to the secret of his generosity.

At the start of this season, the princess's confessor had brought her a serving woman her own age, a widow like her, who caught her interest. Her name was Madeleine Giraud. She was gentle and devoted. The princess had chosen her as her chief attendant. It was now Madeleine Giraud who spoke with Monsieur de Peyrolles—whose job it was to come twice a day to ask for news of the princess, to ask on Gonzague's behalf for permission to present his respects, and to announce that dinner was served for the princess. We already know the unchanging daily response he got from Madeleine: the princess thanked Monsieur de Gonzague, she was receiving no one today, she was too ill to come to the table.

Madeleine had had plenty to do that morning. Unlike on an ordinary day, lots of visitors had shown up, asking to see the princess. They were all serious, distinguished people: Monsieur de Lamoignon, Chancellor d'Aguesseau, Cardinal de Bissy, her cousins the dukes of Foix and of Montmorency-Luxembourg, the Prince of Monaco and his son the Duke of Valentinois, and many others. They'd all come to see her on the occasion of the solemn family council in which they were to take part today. Without prearrangement, they all wanted to understand the princess's position, to find out whether she had some secret grievance against her husband the prince. The princess refused to see them.

Only one got in, old Cardinal de Bissy, who came on behalf of the Regent, to pass on a message: Philippe d'Orléans assured his noble cousin that he still remembered Nevers, and that all that could be done for his widow would be done. "Speak, Madame," concluded the cardinal. "The Regent is at your command. What is it you want?"

"Nothing."

The cardinal tried to probe, to prompt her to share secrets or complaints. She remained stubbornly silent. The cardinal left thinking she was half mad, and Gonzague must be a man of great virtue.

The cardinal had taken his leave just before we entered the princess's private chapel. She sat, as usual, unmoving and gloomy. She stared blankly at nothing, like a marble statue, paying no attention as Madeleine Giraud crossed the room to the prayer desk beside her and set down the book of hours she'd hidden under her cape. Then Madeleine stood facing her mistress, arms folded, waiting for questions or instructions.

The princess looked up. "Where did you just come from, Madeleine?"

"From my room."

The princess lowered her eyes. A few minutes earlier, when she got up to greet the cardinal, she'd spotted Madeleine in the villa garden, in the crowd of speculators. That was enough to raise suspicion in her mind.

Madeleine, however, had something to say but hesitated. She was a good soul, filled with genuine respect and pity for the princess's great grief. "Will the princess allow me to speak?" she murmured.

Aurore de Caylus smiled and thought, "Another one paid to lie to me!" She'd been duped so often. Aloud she said, "Speak."

"Princess, I have a child, who is my whole life. I'd give everything I have in the world, except my child, for you to be a mother as happy as I am."

The princess said nothing.

"I'm poor," went on Madeleine, "and before the princess's generosity my little Charlie often went without. Ah, if I could repay the princess for everything she's done for me!"

"Do you need something, Madeleine?"

"No! Oh, no! It's about you, Madame, only about you! That family council..."

"I forbid you to speak of it, Madeleine."

"Madame, my dear mistress, even if you have to dismiss me..."

"I will dismiss you, Madeleine."

"...At least I'll have done my duty by saying: don't you want to find your child?"

Pale and trembling, the princess gripped the arms of her chair and rose halfway. As she did so, her handkerchief fell. Madeleine quickly bent down to pick it up, and in her apron pocket something jingled. The princess eyed her coldly. "You have money," she murmured. Then, with a gesture fitting neither her noble birth nor her proud character, the gesture of a suspicious woman who wants answers no matter what, she plunged her hand into Madeleine's pocket. Madeleine wept and clasped her hands as the princess withdrew a fistful of gold coins: about a dozen Spanish doubloons. "Monsieur de Gonzague has just returned from Spain!" murmured the princess.

Madeleine fell to her knees, weeping. "Madame, Madame, my little Charlie can go to school, thanks to this gold. The man who gave it me also just came from Spain! In God's name, Madame, don't dismiss me until you've heard me!"

"Out!" ordered the princess. Madeleine continued pleading. With an imperious gesture the princess pointed to the door and said again, "Out!"

When her servant had left, the princess fell back into her seat and hid her face in her thin white hands. "I could've loved that woman!" she murmured with a shudder of dread. Her face reflected the deep anguish of her loneliness. "No one! No one! God, give me the strength to trust no one!" She stayed that way for a moment, her face in her hands. Then a sob shook her chest. "My daughter! My daughter!" she cried in a heart-rending voice. "Holy Virgin, I pray she's dead! At least I'd meet her again by your side."

Emotional outbursts were uncommon in that muted soul; when they came, they left the poor woman broken for a time. It took a few minutes for her sobbing to ease. When she could speak again she cried, "Death! Savior, grant me death!" She looked at the crucifix on her altar. "Lord God! Have I not suffered enough? How much longer must this martyrdom go on?" She spread her arms, and with all the feeling in her tortured heart she cried, "Death! Lord Jesus Christ, in the name of your wounds and of your Passion on the Cross! Virgin Mother, in the name of your tears—death! Death!"

Her arms dropped, her eyes closed, she fell back in her chair. For a moment it looked like merciful heaven had granted her prayer. But soon she shuddered faintly all over, and her clenched hands moved. She opened her eyes and gazed at Nevers's portrait. She resumed that fixed, blank, dry-eyed, slightly frightening stare.

In the book of hours Madeleine Giraud had set on the prayer desk there was a page to which, from long use and a worn-out binding, the book opened by itself. That page held the French translation of the psalm *Miserere mei, Domine.* The princess read it several times a day. After a while she reached out to pick up the book of hours. It fell open to that psalm. For a moment her tired eyes looked without seeing. Then suddenly she started and cried out. She rubbed her eyes and looked around to be sure she wasn't dreaming. "The book hasn't left its place," she murmured.

If she'd seen the book in Madeleine's hands she wouldn't have thought it was a miracle—for she was sure it was a miracle. She stretched to her full height, and the light in her eyes rekindled: she was as beautiful as in the days of her youth, beautiful and proud and strong. She knelt at her prayer desk with the book open before her. For the tenth time she reread the words in the margin next to the verse of the psalm that ran, *Have mercy upon me, O God*—words written by an unknown hand: *God will have mercy, if you will have faith. Take courage and protect your daughter. Go to the family council, even if you're sick or dying. And remember the old signal arranged between you and Nevers.*

"His motto!" she stammered. "Here I am!" Tears filled her eyes. "My child! My daughter!" She raised her voice. "The courage to protect her! I have courage, and I will protect her!"

IX. The Speech for the Defense

The great hall of the Villa Lorraine, which had been disgraced that morning by the squalid auction, and which starting tomorrow would be polluted by the herd of wheeler-dealers, seemed at this moment to be casting its last and brightest glow. Never, surely, even in the time of the great dukes of Guise, had a nobler company been gathered under its roof. Gonzague had his reasons for wanting nothing to lack from the solemn grandeur of the event. The letters of convocation had been sent in the name of the king. It seemed indeed like a state occasion, one of those famous appellate court sessions held by royal decree, in which the fate of a great nation was settled within the family.

Besides Chief Judge de Lamoignon, General de Villeroy, and Minister d'Argenson, who were present on behalf of the Regent, the seats of honor also held Cardinal de Bissy flanked by the Prince of Conti and the Ambassador of Spain, the old Duke of Beaumont-Montmorency next to his cousin Montmorency-Luxembourg, Prince Grimaldi of Monaco, the two La Rochechouarts of whom one was Duke of Mortemart and the other Prince of Tonnay-Charente, Cossé, Brissac, Grammont, Harcourt, Croy, Clermont-Tonnerre, and so on. We mention only the princes and dukes; as for marquises and counts, they were there by the dozen. The ordinary gentlemen and the authorized proxies—of whom there were plenty—sat below the dais. This august gathering divided neatly in two: those who'd been bought by Gonzague and those who were independent. The first category included a duke and a prince, several marquises, lots of counts, and just about all of the aristocratic small fry. Gonzague was counting on his eloquence and the merits of his case to win the rest over.

In the casual chatter before the session began, it was clear no one knew exactly why the council had been called. Some thought they'd be mediating between the prince and the princess over the Nevers property. Gonzague had his staunch partisans; Madame de Gonzague had the support of a few honest old lords and a few young knights errant.

A new theory went around after the cardinal arrived. His account of the princess's state of mind led to talk of an intervention. The cardinal, who didn't mince words, had said, "The woman is three-quarters mad!" After that the general feeling was that she wouldn't show up. Still, it seemed fitting to wait for her, and Gonzague himself insisted on waiting, with a loftiness that came easily to him.

At half past two, Chief Judge de Lamoignon took his seat. Cardinal de Bissy, Minister d'Argenson, General de Villeroy, and Monsieur de Clermont-Tonnerre served as his advisors. The chief clerk of the Appellate Court of Paris took up his pen as secretary, and four royal notaries assisted him; all five were sworn in. Jacques Thallement, the chief clerk, was asked to read out the act of convocation.

The act stated that Philippe of France, Duke of Orléans and Regent, had intended to preside in person over this family gathering, as much for the sake of his friendship for the Prince of Gonzague as for the sake of the brotherly love that had bound him to the late Duke of Nevers; but the cares of government, whose reins he could not drop, even for a day, to pursue any one particular matter, kept him at the Palais-Royal. In his place His Royal Highness had appointed as royal commissioners and judges Messrs de Lamoignon, de Villeroy, and d'Argenson. The cardinal would serve as royal trustee to the princess. The council was hereby constituted as a sovereign court of last resort, fully empowered to decide, without appeal, all matters relating to the succession and inheritance of the late Duke of Nevers, and specifically empowered to settle all questions of law, even to the point of assigning, to whomever it found in the right, the full and irrevocable possession of the Nevers property.

The Regent's letter couldn't have been worded more to Gonzague's advantage if he'd written it himself. The assembly listened in reverent silence. Then the cardinal asked Chief Judge de Lamoignon, "Does the Princess of Gonzague have an authorized representative present?" The judge repeated the question aloud.

Gonzague himself was about to reply, to request that a representative be appointed for her by the court, without his own involvement, when the big double doors opened and the court ushers entered unannounced. All rose: only Gonzague or his wife could make an entrance that way. Indeed, the Princess of Gonzague appeared in the doorway, dressed in mourning as usual, but so proud and so beautiful that a long admiring murmur ran from row to row at the sight. No one expected to see her; and certainly no one expected to see her like this.

"What were you saying, cousin?" said the Duke of Mortemart in Cardinal de Bissy's ear.

"On my faith!" replied the cardinal. "May I be stoned dead! I've blasphemed—there's some miracle behind this."

From the threshold the princess said calmly and clearly, "Gentlemen, there's no need to appoint a representative. I'm here."

Gonzague leapt up from his seat. Advancing quickly to his wife, he offered her his hand with respectful gallantry. The princess didn't refuse it, but at his touch she started, and her pale cheeks reddened.

At the foot of the dais sat Gonzague's followers—Navailles, Gironne, Montaubert, Nocé, Oriol, and the rest—and they were the first to move aside to make way for the couple.

"What a happy little family!" said Nocé as the two climbed the steps of the dais.

"Shh!" said Oriol. "I can't tell if the boss is pleased or angry at her showing up." The boss was of course Gonzague. And maybe he himself didn't know how he felt.

A seat for the princess had been prepared in advance, at the far right of the dais, next to the cardinal. To the right of her seat hung the curtains that covered a private door to the surrounding gallery. The door was shut and the curtains were closed.

The stir caused by the princess's arrival took some time to die down. After one quick glance around, she lowered her eyes and resumed the stillness of a statue. No doubt Gonzague had to adjust his battle plans, because he seemed deep in thought.

Judge de Lamoignon read the act of convocation a second time, then said, "As the Prince of Gonzague needs to explain to us what he wants, in deed and in law, we await his pleasure."

Gonzague rose and bowed, first to his wife, then to the king's judges, then to the rest of the company. Gonzague was a fine orator: head held high, bold expressive features, bright complexion, sparkling eyes. At the start his voice was subdued, almost shy. "No one here can imagine I would've summoned such a gathering for any ordinary purpose. And yet, before broaching a serious matter, I feel the need to express a fear I have—a fear that's almost childish. When I consider that I have to speak before so many great and distinguished persons, in my weakness I'm afraid, even if just on account of my way of speaking, the accent that a son of Italy can never quite overcome. I would in fact draw back from my task—except that I remember that the powerful are forgiving, and that your great eminence itself is my surest protection."

This highflown rhetorical preface prompted smiles in the rows of the elite. Gonzague did nothing unpremeditated.

"Allow me first," he went on, "to thank all those who have honored our family on this occasion with their benevolent concern. The Regent, first of all—the Regent about whom we can speak frankly because he's not among us—that noble, excellent prince, always taking the lead in any good and worthy cause."

The assembly responded with vehement signs of agreement, and Gonzague's followers waved their hats. "What a lawyer our cousin would've made!" said Chaverny to his neighbor Choisy.

"Secondly," went on Gonzague, "the princess, who in spite of her ill health and her preference for a retired life, has been willing to undergo the ordeal of coming down from the heights where she lives to the level of our mundane human concerns. Thirdly, these high dignitaries of the greatest kingdom in the world: the two lords of the high court that both renders justice and sets the course of the State, the glorious officer—one of those heroic soldiers whose victories will give material to future Plutarchs—a prince of the Church, and all these peers of the realm, so worthy to sit on the steps of the throne. And finally, all of you gentlemen, no matter what your rank. I'm overcome with gratitude, and my thanks, though badly expressed, do at least arise from the bottom of my heart."

All of this had been spoken with a perfect cadence, in the ample resonant tone that belongs by right to Northern Italy. This was the exordium. Lowering his eyes, Gonzague paused to collect his thoughts. Then he went on in a more muted voice. "Philippe de Lorraine, Duke of Nevers, was the cousin of my blood, the brother of my heart. We shared all the days of our youth. I can say that our two hearts were one, so closely did we share both our sorrows and our joys. He was a generous prince, and God knows what glories awaited him had he lived! He who holds in His hand the destiny of the mighty of the earth chose to stop that young eagle at the very moment he first took flight. Nevers died before he reached his twenty-fifth year. Though in my life I've been tested often and tested hard, I can't recall any blow more cruel. I can speak here for all of us. The eighteen years elapsed since that fatal night have not sweetened the bitterness of our sorrow. His memory remains here!"—he placed his hand over his heart and made his voice tremble—"His living memory, eternal, like the mourning of my wife, who has never deigned to take my name after the name of Nevers!"

All eyes turned to the princess. Her face was red, and distorted by great feeling. "Don't speak of that!" she said between clenched teeth. "I've spent those eighteen years withdrawn, in tears!"

Those who were there as serious judges—the magistrates, the princes and peers of France—listened carefully. Gonzague's followers, the men we saw gathered in his apartment, let out a long murmur. That ugly phenomenon commonly called a "claque" in the theater hadn't yet been invented; Nocé, Gironne, Montaubert, Taranne, and the rest were just conscientiously doing their job.

Cardinal de Bissy rose. "Honorable Judge, I'm forced to call for silence. The words of the princess have as much right to be heard here as those of Monsieur de Gonzague." As he sat down again, he whispered into his neighbor Mortemart's ear, with all the glee of an old busybody who senses she's on the track of some grotesque scandal, "Duke, I have the feeling we're about to find some things out!"

"Silence!" ordered Judge de Lamoignon with a glare, and Gonzague's overbold followers lowered their heads.

Gonzague picked up on the cardinal's words. "Not only as much right, Your Eminence, if I may be allowed to contradict you, but even more right, since the princess is the wife and widow of Nevers. I'm shocked anyone here could forget, even for a moment, the deep respect owed to the Princess of Gonzague."

Chaverny chuckled to himself. "If Hell had saints, I'd argue before the Pope to have my cousin canonized!"

Silence was restored. Gonzague had won his bold skirmish across difficult ground. Not only had his wife made no specific allegation against him, but he'd been able to cloak himself in the appearance of gallant generosity. He'd scored a point. He lifted his head and continued in a firmer tone, "Philippe de Nevers died a victim of revenge or treachery. I must touch very lightly on the mysteries of that tragic night. Monsieur de Caylus, the princess's father, is long dead, and respect for his memory seals my lips."

The princess stirred in her seat, close to being taken ill, and Gonzague guessed a second challenge would go unanswered. He therefore broke off to say, with perfect courteous goodwill, "If the princess has something to add here, I would hasten to yield her the floor."

She tried to speak, but her throat, choked tight, let out not a sound.

Gonzague waited a few seconds, then went on. "The death of the Marquis of Caylus—who could no doubt have supplied valuable testimony—the remote scene of the crime, the escape of the murderers, and other reasons most of you know, made it impossible for a criminal investigation to clear up this blood-stained case. Questions were asked, suspicions floated, but in the end justice couldn't be done. And yet, gentlemen, Philippe de Nevers had another friend, one more powerful than I. Need I name that friend? You all know him: Philippe d'Orléans, Regent of France. Who would dare claim the murdered Nevers lacked an avenger?"

There was a silence. Gonzague's followers in the back row exchanged animated gestures and repeated in an undertone, "It's clear as day!"

The princess pressed her handkerchief to her lips to catch the blood, a mark of the violence of her indignation.

"Gentlemen," continued Gonzague, "I come now to the events that prompted this gathering. On the point of marrying me, the princess made public her prior marriage—secret but legal—to the late Duke of Nevers. At that same time she legally attested to the existence of a daughter by that marriage. There was no written proof. The parish register, with pages torn out in two places, offered no record. I'm forced to observe again that the Marquis of Caylus was the only man who could've cleared up this question. But while he lived Monsieur de Caylus said nothing, and now no one can question him in the grave. The sacraments must've been witnessed by Father Bernard, chaplain of Caylus, who noted the first marriage and the birth of Mademoiselle de Caylus in the margin of the act of marriage that gave my name to Nevers's widow. I call on the princess to lend my words the authority of her agreement."

Everything he'd just said was perfectly true. She said nothing. But Cardinal de Bissy, after leaning toward her, rose and said, "The princess disputes nothing."

Gonzague bowed and went on. "The child disappeared on the night of the murder. Gentlemen, you know what inexhaustible reserves of patience and affection a mother's heart holds. For eighteen years, the princess's sole concern, the work of every day, of every hour, has been to find her daughter. I have to say, up to now the princess's search has been fruitless. Not one trace, not one clue—the princess is no closer today than on day one."

Gonzague glanced at his wife. She had her eyes raised to heaven. He looked in vain through her tears for the despair his words should have provoked. The blow had not struck home. Why not? He grew afraid. Summoning all his cool, he continued. "Now, gentlemen, in spite of my reluctance to do so, I must speak of myself. After my marriage the Appellate Court of Paris, under the late king, acting in full session at the instigation of the unfortunate Nevers's uncle the late Duke of Elbeuf, indefinitely suspended my rights to the Nevers inheritance. That was done to protect the interests of young Aurore de Nevers, if she was still alive. And I didn't object, far from it. But that decision has nonetheless caused me deep and irreparable harm."

Everyone paid closer attention, and the men in the back rows cried, "Listen! Listen!" A glance from Gonzague had alerted Montaubert, Gironne, and the rest that the critical moment had come.

"I was still young," he went on, "well placed at court, and wealthy—even very wealthy. My rank was indisputable. My wife was a jewel of beauty, intelligence, and virtue. How could I escape becoming the target of sneaking, cowardly envy? I had one weakness, my Achilles heel: the Appellate Court's decision had left me in an awkward position, because to some low evil-minded people, to those vile souls for whom money is the only motive, it looked like I had reason to want the death of Nevers's daughter."

This was greeted with appropriate cries of protest.

"Yes, gentlemen," said Gonzague before Judge de Lamoignon could restore order, "that's the way of the world! We can't change the world. I had interest, a material interest, and therefore I must have a motive. Slander had a purchase on me, and slander didn't hesitate to take advantage of it. Only one obstacle separated me from a great inheritance. Death to the obstacle! The evidence of my long blameless life went for nothing. I was suspected of the wickedest, vilest intentions. They assumed—I'm forced to tell you—coldness, mistrust, almost hatred between the princess and me; they claimed as evidence the signs of mourning that shrouded the retreat of a saintly woman; they pitted the living husband against the dead one; and—to use a banal word, better applied to the happy lives of humble folk than to those of us called the mighty—they upset my household!" He emphasized that word. "My household, you hear? My domesticity, my peace, my family, my heart! Oh, if you only knew what tortures the wicked can inflict on the good! If you knew the tears of blood you weep as you appeal to mute Providence! If you only knew! On my honor and my salvation, I swear to you, I'd have given up my title and my fortune to be happy the way ordinary people are, people with a household: a devoted wife, the friend of your heart, children who love you and whom you adore, in short a family—that crumb of heaven's bliss a benevolent God has dropped on us!"

You would have thought he'd poured his whole heart into his delivery; he spoke his last few words with such feeling that all the assembled company were moved, their hearts stirred. It went beyond their own interests: they felt respectful compassion for this once-proud man, this lord of the earth, this prince who, with tears in his eyes and his voice, had just laid bare the awful wound of his life. Most of the judges were family men; in spite of the prevailing morals of that time, the ties of fatherhood and marriage tugged hard on them. The others, the rakes and speculators, felt some vague emotion, like blind men guessing at colors, or fallen women going to the theater to weep over tales of virtue besieged.

Only two people present remained unmoved in the midst of the collective softening: the Princess of Gonzague and the Marquis of Chaverny. The princess kept her eyes lowered; she seemed to be daydreaming, and her cold demeanor did nothing to sway the judges in her favor. As for Chaverny, he rocked in his seat and muttered through clenched teeth, "My distinguished cousin is a supreme rascal!" But all the others understood, just from Madame de Gonzague's present attitude, what the poor prince must have suffered.

"It's too much!" said the Duke of Mortemart to Cardinal de Bissy. "Let's be fair, it's too much!" The cardinal brushed Spanish tobacco off his lapel.

Everyone on the judges' bench did his best to remain stern and solemn. But that didn't restrain the back rows. Gironne wiped his eyes, though they were dry; Oriol—more softhearted or just more skilled—wept hot tears; the Baron of Batz sobbed.

"What a heart!" cried Taranne.

"What a great heart!" added Peyrolles, who'd just come in.

"Ah!" cried Oriol with feeling. "What a misunderstood heart!"

"What did I tell you?" murmured the cardinal, who'd recovered a little. "We'll hear some whoppers! But shh—Gonzague isn't done."

Indeed, pale and splendid with emotion, Gonzague went on. "I have no hard feelings, gentlemen. God forbid I should resent this poor afflicted mother. The very strength of their love makes mothers gullible. And if I've suffered, hasn't she also faced cruel torture? A long martyrdom wears down even the stoutest spirit. The intellect fades. They told her I was her daughter's enemy, I had a material motive—think of it, gentlemen: a material motive! I, Gonzague, the Prince of Gonzague, the richest man in France after John Law!"

"Even before Law," interjected Oriol, and no one there could contradict him.

"They said to her," went on Gonzague, "that man has agents everywhere, his people crisscross France, Spain, Italy—that man is more obsessed with finding your daughter than you are." He turned to the princess. "Isn't that what they told you, Madame?"

Without moving or looking up, she said, "That's what they told me."

"You see!" cried Gonzague to the judges. Then he turned again to his wife. "You poor mother, they also told you, if you can't find your daughter, if your efforts have been futile, it's because the hand of that man, acting in the shadows, frustrates and foils your search—his perfidious hand! Isn't it true, Madame, isn't that what they told you?"

"That's what I heard," she said again.

"You see, my judges and my peers, you see!" he cried. "And didn't they also tell you, Madame, that the hand in the shadows, the perfidious hand, was the hand of your husband? And didn't they tell you the child might be dead, there were men despicable enough to murder a child, and maybe—I won't finish the thought, Madame, but that's what they told you."

The princess, as pale as a corpse, replied for the third time, "That's what they said."

"And you believed it, Madame?" he asked indignantly.

She answered coldly, "I believed it."

At her words, exclamations broke out all over the hall.

"You're condemning yourself, Madame," murmured the cardinal into her ear. "No matter where the prince goes with this, you're sure to lose."

She'd resumed her silence and stillness. Chief Judge de Lamoignon opened his mouth to remonstrate with her, but Gonzague stopped him with a respectful gesture. "Let it go, judge, I beg you. Gentlemen, let it go. I've been given a painful duty on this earth; I carry it out as best I can; God will remember my efforts. To tell you the whole truth, the main reason for this gathering was to force the princess to listen to me for once in her life. In eighteen years of marriage, she's never done me that favor. I wanted to reach her—I who've been in exile since our wedding day. I wanted to show a woman who doesn't know me who I am. I've succeeded, and I owe all of you my thanks. But don't stand between her and me—because I have the talisman that will finally open her eyes!"

Then, speaking only to the princess and addressing her directly, as a deep hush fell over the hall, Gonzague said, "They told you the truth, Madame! I did have more agents than you in France, in Spain, in Italy; because, while you were listening to vile accusations against me, I was working for you. My reply to all those slanders was to search harder and more stubbornly than you. I too was looking, looking without cease or pause, using my influence and power, my wealth, my heart. And today—now that you're finally listening to me—today I'm finally rewarded for all those difficult years. I come to you, who scorn and hate me, I who respect and love you, I come to you and I say: Happy mother, open your arms so I can give you your child!"

Turning to Peyrolles, who awaited his orders, Gonzague called loudly, "Bring in Mademoiselle Aurore de Nevers!"

X. Here I Am!

You've read Gonzague's words. What can't be conveyed in writing is the fire of his delivery, the impact of his presence, the profound conviction of his looks. Gonzague was a great actor. He was so deeply immersed in the role he'd prepared that he was overcome by emotion, by a genuine rush of feeling that came from the heart. That's the zenith of the actor's art. In different circumstances, and with different ambitions, this man could have stirred the world.

His listeners included heartless men well-versed in all the tricks of rhetoric, magistrates jaded by oratory, financiers the harder to fool because they were in on the lie to begin with. Gonzague did the impossible and performed a real miracle: everyone believed him, everyone would have sworn he was telling the truth. Oriol, Gironne, Albret, Taranne, and the rest were no longer just doing their job—they were convinced. They all thought, later he'll lie, but right now he's telling the truth! And then they all thought, could there be in one man so much greatness alongside so much corruption? His peers, the great lords there to judge him, were sorry they'd ever doubted him. What gave him his stature was his chivalrous love for his wife and his magnanimous forgiveness for years of abuse. Even the most debased age can set a man on the pedestal of domestic virtue. Every heart in that room beat loudly.

Chief Judge de Lamoignon wiped away a tear, and Villeroy the old soldier cried out, "God's blood, prince, you're a gallant man!"

But the most dramatic reversals were the conversion of Chaverny the skeptic, and the devastating effect on the princess herself. Chaverny resisted as hard as he could, but Gonzague's final words had made his jaw drop. "If he really did that," he said to Choisy, "I'll be damned if I don't forgive him everything else!"

As for the Princess of Gonzague, she'd risen, shaking and pale, looking like a ghost. Cardinal de Bissy had to support her in his arms. She stared at the door by which Peyrolles had left. Dread and hope played in turn across her face. Was she about to see her daughter? Is that what the note meant, the one she'd found on the *Miserere* page in her book of hours? She'd been told to come; she'd come. Would she have to protect her daughter? No matter what the unknown danger, her heart beat above all with joy. Her daughter! Her heart would leap toward her at first sight! The tears of eighteen years would be paid for with a single smile! She waited, and everyone waited with her.

Peyrolles had left by way of the gallery leading to the prince's apartment. He soon returned, leading Doña Cruz by the hand, with her eyes shut tight. Gonzague advanced to meet her.

"She's so beautiful!" came the general cry. Gonzague's accomplices went back to work and repeated in an undertone what they'd been taught: "What a family resemblance!"

But it turned out that the honest men present went even further than the bought lackeys. The two judges, the general, the cardinal, and all the dukes, looking from the princess to Doña Cruz and back again, cried out spontaneously, "She looks like her mother!" For those who were here to render judgment, it was already a given that the princess was Doña Cruz's mother.

And yet the princess's expression had changed again: once more she looked troubled and anxious. She gazed at this beautiful girl with dread. No—this wasn't how she'd dreamt of her daughter! Her daughter could be no prettier, but her daughter had to be different. And that sudden chill she felt—at the very moment when her heart should have leapt toward her newfound child—appalled her. Was she a bad mother? And a second fear followed the first. What kind of past had she had, this charming girl with hard bold eyes and strangely supple lissome figure, whose whole presence showed such grace—too much grace, the kind of grace a strict family upbringing doesn't normally teach the heiresses of dukes?

Chaverny, now fully recovered from his reaction and sorry he'd believed in Gonzague even for a minute, put the princess's thoughts into words better than she herself could have. "She's adorable!" he said to Choisy.

"So you're still in love with her?"

"I was before," said Chaverny, "but the Nevers name doesn't suit her—it weighs her down."

A lively, free-spirited boy off the streets of Paris would look wrong in a cavalryman's dashing helmet. Some disguises don't work. Gonzague had missed it, but Chaverny caught it. Why? First, because Chaverny was French and Gonzague was Italian. Of all the men in the world, a Frenchman comes closest to a woman's capacity for sensitivity and nuance. Secondly, the Prince of Gonzague was almost fifty, while Chaverny was very young. As men age they lose their feminine side. Gonzague hadn't seen it because he couldn't see it. His Milanese subtlety was that of diplomacy, not the senses. To catch those details you'd either have to have the exquisite sensitivity of a wife and mother like the Princess of Gonzague, or else peer as close as the slightly myopic Marquis of Chaverny.

Meanwhile Doña Cruz, blushing, eyes lowered, a smile on her lips, had reached the foot of the dais. Only Chaverny and the princess understood what it was costing her to keep her eyes shut—she wanted so badly to see.

"Mademoiselle de Nevers," said Gonzague, "go embrace your mother!"

Doña Cruz gave a start of genuine unaffected spontaneous joy. It was a mark of Gonzague's great skill that he hadn't chosen an actress to play the role: Doña Cruz was sincere. She opened her eyes, and her tender gaze turned immediately to the woman she thought was her mother. She took a step forward and reached out. But then her arms dropped, and her eyes did too. A single cold gesture from the princess froze her in place.

All the mistrust that had haunted the princess's solitary life returned. Prompted by her own earlier reaction to Doña Cruz's appearance, she said under her breath, "What have they done with Nevers's daughter?" Then she raised her voice. "As God is my witness, I have a mother's heart. But if Nevers's daughter came back to me marked by a single stain, if she'd forgotten her proud blood for as little as a single minute, I would veil my face and say, nothing of Nevers now remains alive."

"God's guts!" thought Chaverny. "I'd bet this girl forgot for quite a few minutes!" But he was the only one who thought so. Madame de Gonzague's severity seemed inappropriate, even unnatural.

While the princess spoke, a small noise came from her right, as if the door behind the nearby curtains was turning on its hinges. She took no notice of it.

Clasping his hands, as if any doubt at this moment was blasphemy, Gonzague said, "Oh, Madame, Madame! Can these really be the words of your heart? Mademoiselle de Nevers, your daughter, Madame, is purer than the angels." A tear stood in poor Doña Cruz's eye.

The cardinal leaned toward the princess. "Unless you can explain your doubts and give us concrete reasons..."

"Reasons! My heart is cold, my eyes are dry, my arms hang at my sides—aren't those reasons enough?"

"Madame, if you have no others, I can't in good conscience oppose the clear consensus of the council."

The princess looked around darkly.

"You see," whispered the cardinal to the Duke of Mortemart, "I wasn't mistaken: there's an element of madness here."

"Gentlemen!" cried the princess. "Have you already passed judgment on me?"

"Stay calm, Madame," said Chief Judge de Lamoignon, "and rest assured that everyone here respects and loves you, everyone—and most of all the great prince who gave you his name." The princess lowered her head. A little more sternly, the judge went on, "Follow your conscience, Madame, and fear nothing. This court is not here to punish anyone. Error is not a crime but a misfortune. Your friends and relatives will sympathize if you've made a mistake."

"A mistake!" echoed the princess without lifting her head. "Oh, yes, I've made lots of mistakes. But if no one here will defend me, I'll defend myself. My daughter must have proof of her birth."

"What proof?" asked Judge de Lamoignon.

She straightened up. "The proof named by Monsieur de Gonzague himself: the page torn from the chapel registry at Caylus—torn out by my own hand, gentlemen!"

"That's what I wanted to find out," thought Gonzague. Aloud he said, "Your daughter will have that proof, Madame."

"You mean she doesn't have it now?" she cried.

A murmur ran around the gathering.

"Take me away!" stammered Doña Cruz, in tears. "Take me away!"

The distress in the poor girl's voice stirred something deep in the princess's heart. "My God, inspire me!" she said, raising her hands to heaven. "What a catastrophe and a crime it would be to reject my own child! My God, from the depths of my misery I beg you, answer me!"

Suddenly her face cleared and her whole body trembled. She'd asked God a question. A mysterious voice, a voice only she heard and that seemed to reply directly to her question, a voice from behind the curtain, spoke the three-word motto of Nevers: "Here I am!" The princess leaned on the cardinal's arm to keep from falling over backward. Had that voice come from heaven?

Gonzague misunderstood her sudden emotion, and decided to strike the final blow. "Madame," he cried, "you've appealed to the Creator of all things. God has answered you: I can see it, I can feel it. Your better angel resists evil counsel. Madame, after your years of suffering, so nobly endured, do not reject happiness now. Forget the hand that put this precious long-sought gift in yours; I'm not asking to be rewarded—I'm only asking that you look at your child. Here she is, trembling, shattered by her mother's welcome. Look within yourself, Madame, and listen to your conscience." The princess looked at Doña Cruz. Gonzague went on with increasing force, "Now that you've seen her, in the name of the living God I ask you, is this not your daughter?"

The princess didn't reply right away. Unconsciously she made a half turn toward the curtains. The voice only she could hear spoke just one word: "No."

"No!" she repeated loudly. She looked around the assembly. She wasn't afraid. Whoever the mysterious advisor behind the curtain was, she trusted him, because he opposed Gonzague. And besides, he fulfilled the promise of the words written in her book of hours, and came to her with the motto of Nevers: "Here I am!"

Meanwhile, exclamations filled the hall. The outrage of Oriol and company knew no bounds.

"This is too much!" said Gonzague, restraining with a gesture the excessive zeal of his loyalists. "There's a limit to human patience! One last time I say to the princess, you need good reasons, serious strong reasons, to reject the obvious truth."

"Exactly what I said," sighed Cardinal de Bissy. "But when a woman gets an idea in her head..."

Gonzague went on, "Do you have such reasons, Madame?"

"Yes," said the mysterious voice.

"Yes," said the princess in turn.

Gonzague was livid, and his lips trembled convulsively. He sensed that, in the midst of this gathering he himself had summoned, some invisible hostile influence must be at work. He could feel it, but he couldn't find it. For the past few minutes everything about Nevers's widow had changed: marble had become flesh, the statue lived. What was the source of this miracle? The change had come at the very moment the distraught princess had called on God for help, but Gonzague didn't believe in God. He mopped the sweat that ran down his face. "Is it because you have news of your daughter, Madame?" he said, doing his best to hide his apprehension.

The princess kept silent.

"There are impostors out there," he went on. "Lots of predators are after Nevers's fortune. Have you been shown some other girl?"

Still silence.

"Did they say, 'This is the real one, we saved her, we protected her'? They all say that! The subtlest negotiator could get taken in."

Chief Judge de Lamoignon and his fellow judges now looked at Gonzague with surprise. Chaverny murmured, "Sheath your claws, tiger!"

The mysterious voice certainly exerted a clever power by its silence. As long as the voice said nothing, the princess said nothing, and in his fury Gonzague lost all caution. His burning bloodshot eyes contrasted with his pale face. "She's around, somewhere," he went on through clenched teeth, "ready to appear—that's what they told you, isn't it, Madame? She's alive, alive! Right? Answer me!"

Staggering, the princess put one hand on the arm of her chair to steady herself. She would have given two years of her life to lift the curtain that concealed the oracle, now so silent.

"Answer me! Answer me!" cried Gonzague.

And the judges themselves echoed, "Madame, answer him."

Holding her breath, the princess listened. Why was the oracle waiting? Half turning, she murmured, "Have pity!" The curtain moved slightly.

"What answer can she give?" said Gonzague's accomplices.

"Alive?" the princess asked the oracle, her voice cracking.

"Alive," came the answer.

She straightened up, radiant, giddy with joy. "Yes, alive! She's alive!" she said loudly. "Alive in spite of you, and by God's protection!"

Like a cresting wave, the crowd rose in an uproar. Gonzague's accomplices all spoke at once, demanding justice. The bench of royal judges turned to each other. "I told you so!" said Cardinal de Bissy to the Duke of Mortemart. "I told you so! But we haven't heard everything yet, and I'm beginning to think the princess isn't crazy!"

Amid the general tumult, the voice from behind the curtain said, "Tonight, at the Regent's ball, someone will address you with the motto of Nevers."

"And then I'll see my daughter?" stammered the princess, on the point of being taken ill.

From behind the curtain came the faint sound of a door closing, then nothing more. Just in time: Chaverny, as curious as a woman and seized with a vague suspicion, had slipped behind Cardinal de Bissy. He flung open the curtain, and saw... nothing—but the princess stifled a cry, and that was enough to make Chaverny throw open the door and leap into the gallery. Night had begun to fall, and the passage was dark. Chaverny saw nothing—except, at the far end of the gallery, the lurching silhouette of the little hunchback with crooked legs, going calmly away down the stairs. Chaverny pondered: maybe his cousin had tried to play some trick on the devil, and the devil had gotten revenge.

Meanwhile, in the great hall, at a sign from Chief Judge de Lamoignon, the company had retaken their seats. Gonzague made a terrible effort and managed at least to look calm. He bowed to the judges. "Gentlemen, I would blush to add a single word. Decide, if you please, between the princess and me."

Several voices said, "Let's deliberate."

Judge de Lamoignon rose and put on his hat. "Prince, having heard the cardinal speak on behalf of the princess, the opinion of the royal commissioners is that no grounds for a verdict exist. Since Madame de Gonzague knows where her daughter is, let her present the girl. Monsieur de Gonzague likewise will make the case for the girl he says is Nevers's heiress. The written proof the prince mentioned and the princess invoked, the page torn out of the chapel registry at Caylus, will be produced, and that will make it easy to decide. In the name of the king, we adjourn this court for three days."

"I accept," said Gonzague quickly, "and I'll have proof."

"I'll have my daughter, and I'll have proof," said the princess. "I accept."

The judges officially brought the session to an end.

"As for you, child, poor child," said Gonzague to Doña Cruz as he handed her again to Peyrolles, "I did what I could. Now God alone can open your mother's heart to you!"

Doña Cruz lowered her veil and moved away. But before she left the room she changed her mind and ran back to the princess. "Madame!" she cried, taking her hand and kissing it. "Whether or not you're my mother, I respect you and love you!"

The princess smiled and brushed the girl's brow with her lips. "You're not complicit, child. I can see that. I have nothing against you. I love you too."

Peyrolles now led Doña Cruz away. The whole noble crowd that had filled the great hall was gone. Night was falling quickly. As the princess was about to leave, accompanied by her women, Gonzague returned from seeing out the judges. At his imperious gesture, her attendants moved aside. He approached his wife. With the grand courteous manners he never dropped, he bent to kiss her hand. "So now it's open war between us, Madame?" he said lightly.

"I'm not on the attack, monsieur. I'm only defending myself."

"Just between us," said Gonzague, who had trouble hiding the rage in his heart under his cold politesse, "let's not debate it, please. I'll spare you that pointless bother. But I see you have mysterious protectors, Madame?"

"I have heaven's mercy, sir, which is the succor of mothers."

Gonzague smiled.

"Giraud," said the princess to her servant Madeleine. "Have my chaise made ready."

"Is there an evening service at the Saint Magloire Church?" asked Gonzague in surprise.

"I don't know, sir," replied the princess calmly. "I'm not going to Saint Magloire. Félicité, fetch my jewel case."

"Your diamonds, Madame!" said Gonzague mockingly. "Will the court, which has missed you for so long, have the honor of receiving you again?"

"I'm going to the Regent's ball tonight."

For a moment he was struck dumb. "You!" he stammered. "You!"

The princess drew herself up—so beautiful and so haughty that instinctively Gonzague lowered his eyes. "Yes, I!" As she led her attendants away she added, "My mourning ends today, prince. Do what you will against me: I'm no longer afraid of you."

XI. In Which the Hunchback Gets Himself Invited to the Ball

The Prince of Gonzague stood watching his wife as she followed the gallery back to her apartment. "She's been resurrected!" he thought. "Yet in this high-stakes game I played my hand well. Why did I lose? Clearly she had hidden cards. Gonzague, you missed something." He began to pace the hall with long strides. "In any case, there's not a minute to lose. Why is she going to the ball at the Palais-Royal? To speak to the Regent? She must know where her daughter is." He opened his notebook. "But I know too, thanks to a lucky break."

He rang, and to the servant who came running he said, "Send me Monsieur de Peyrolles immediately!" The servant left. Gonzague resumed his solitary pacing, and returned to his first thought. "She has a new ally. In this picture there's someone hidden behind the canvas."

"Prince!" cried Peyrolles as he entered. "Finally I can speak to you. Bad news: as they were leaving, I heard the cardinal say to the judges, 'There's some mysterious wrongdoing behind this.'"

"Never mind the cardinal."

"And Doña Cruz is rebelling. She says she was forced to take part in a shameful spectacle. She wants to leave Paris."

"Never mind Doña Cruz. Listen to me."

"Not till you know what's going on: Lagardère is in Paris."

"Bah! I expected as much. Since when?"

"Since yesterday at least."

To himself Gonzague reflected, "The princess must have seen him." Then aloud he said, "How do you know?"

Peyrolles lowered his voice. "Saldaña and Faenza are dead."

Gonzague was obviously not expecting that. The muscles of his face trembled, and he looked stunned, but it was over in a moment. He'd already recovered before Peyrolles looked at him.

"Two in one stroke!" Peyrolles shivered. "The man's a devil!"

"Where did they find their bodies?"

"In the alley outside the garden at your little pleasure house."

"Together?"

"Saldaña against the door, Faenza a few paces away. Saldaña was killed by a single thrust..."

"There, right?" Gonzague pointed between his eyes.

Peyrolles made the same gesture. "There! Faenza was stabbed the same way, in the same spot."

"No other wounds?"

"None. The Nevers attack is still fatal."

Gonzague smoothed the lace of his collar in a mirror. "All right. The Chevalier de Lagardère has left his visiting card twice at my door. I'm pleased he's in Paris. We'll catch him."

"The rope that'll catch that fellow..."

"Hasn't yet been braided, right? I think it has. God's death, Peyrolles, it's about time! Of everyone there in the moonlight in the moat at Caylus, only four of us are left."

"Yes." Peyrolles shivered. "It's about time."

"Two mouthfuls," said Gonzague as he rebuckled his belt. "The two of us in one bite, and in the other bite those two pathetic rascals..."

"Cocardasse and Passepoil! They're afraid of Lagardère."

"Then they're just like you. It doesn't matter, we have no choice. Go get them!"

Peyrolles headed toward the kitchen.

Gonzague thought to himself, "Like I said, it's time to act, and fast! Tonight will bring strange doings!"

When Peyrolles reached the kitchen he said, "Hop to! His lordship wants you."

From noon to dusk Cocardasse and Passepoil had been eating nonstop. What a pair of heroic bellies! Cocardasse was as red as the dregs of the wine forgotten in his glass; Passepoil was ashen. The bottle can have that contrary effect, depending on the constitution of the drinker. But wine acts in just one way on the sense of hearing: after drinking, neither Cocardasse nor Passepoil could put up with more than the other. Besides, the time for humility was over. They'd been dressed from top to toe in new clothes. They wore splendid dress boots, and hats that had only been reblocked three times. Their hose and their doublets were worthy of their accessories.

"Say, brother!" said Cocardasse. "I think this pile of trash is talking to us."

"If I thought this villain..." said gentle Passepoil as he picked up a pitcher in both hands.

"Easy there, baldy," said Cocardasse. "You can have him, but, hell, don't break the crockery."

He grabbed Peyrolles by one ear and spun him toward Passepoil, who grabbed the other ear and spun him back at Cocardasse. Peyrolles made that trip back and forth two or three times. Then Cocardasse said to him, with the great solemnity of a plate-breaker, "Little lamb, you forgot for a moment you were addressing gentlemen! Be sure to remember it in future."

"That's right!" added Passepoil.

They both got up, while Peyrolles did his best to put his clothing back in order. "They're drunk, the pair of them!" he grumbled.

"Hey, hey!" said Cocardasse. "Did the little sweetheart say something?"

"I have a feeling like maybe he did," said Passepoil.

One on the left, one on the right, they reached out to grab Peyrolles's ears again, but he wisely took flight and returned to Gonzague, with whom he did not share his recent adventures. Gonzague instructed him to say nothing to the two about the unfortunate end of Saldaña and Faenza, but he didn't need to: Peyrolles had no appetite for further conversation with Cocardasse and Passepoil.

A moment later they showed up, heralded by an awful rattling. Their hats were askew, their stockings were disheveled, they had wine down their shirts—in short, they were perfectly dressed cutthroats. They swaggered in, their cloaks pulled back to show their swords: Cocardasse as always magnificent, Passepoil as always clumsy and ugly to a tee. Cocardasse turned to Passepoil with his best Provençal manners. "Make your bow, brother, and thank his lordship."

"Enough!" Gonzague glared at them.

They froze. With these heroes, the man who paid them could do no wrong.

"Can you stand up?" asked Gonzague.

"I drank just one glass, to toast your lordship," Cocardasse answered boldly. "God's hat! Sobriety is my middle name."

"It's true, my lord," added Passepoil timidly. "And I went even further and drank only reddened water."

Cocardasse looked at him sternly. "Brother, you drank exactly as much as I did, no more and no less. Crooked ace! I'll ask you not to bend the truth in my presence, because lies make me sick!"

"Your rapiers still work?" asked Gonzague.

"Better than ever," said Cocardasse.

"And at your lordship's service," added Passepoil with a bow.

"Good." Gonzague turned his back, toward which the two friends went on bowing.

"This fellow knows how to talk to swordsmen!" murmured Cocardasse.

Gonzague motioned for Peyrolles to approach. The two of them walked to the far end of the great hall, by the double doors. Gonzague tore out of his notebook the page on which he'd written the information he got from Doña Cruz. Just as the prince was giving the paper to Peyrolles, the hunchback's odd face appeared behind the hinges of one of the wide-open doors. No one could see him, and he knew it. His eyes sparkled with intelligence, and his whole figure had changed. Seeing Gonzague and his factotum talking a few feet away, the hunchback quickly put his ear to the hinged opening. He heard Peyrolles decipher aloud the words his master had scrawled in pencil. "Rue du Chantre... a girl named Aurore."

The expression on the hunchback's face would have shocked you. His eyes glowed darkly. "He knows!" he thought. "How does he know?"

"Understood?" said Gonzague.

"Understood," said Peyrolles. "Talk about luck!"

"People like me have their guardian star."

138

"Where will we put the girl?"

"In Doña Cruz's pleasure house."

The hunchback slapped his forehead. "The gypsy girl!" he murmured. "But how did she herself find out?"

"We just kidnap her?" said Peyrolles.

"No fuss," said Gonzague. "We're not in a position to deal with complications. Cleverness, finesse—your strong suit, Peyrolles. If it were an occasion for fighting it out I wouldn't be asking you. Our man must live there, I'd bet on it."

"Lagardère!" murmured Peyrolles with visible dread.

"You won't confront that braggart. The first thing is to make sure he's away. I bet he's out right now."

"He used to like to drink."

"If he's out, here's the plan: take this card." Gonzague gave Peyrolles an invitation to the Regent's ball, one of the two set aside for Saldaña and Faenza. "You'll get a ball gown, an attractive, fashionable one like the one I ordered for Doña Cruz. You'll have a chaise waiting in the Rue du Chantre. You'll introduce yourself to the girl in the name of Lagardère himself."

"That's like gambling my life on heads or tails," said Peyrolles.

"Oh, come on! Just the sight of the dress and the jewels will drive her mad! All you have to say is, 'Lagardère sends you these and awaits you.'"

"Bad idea!" said a harsh voice between them. "The girl won't budge."

Peyrolles jumped back, and Gonzague put his hand on his sword.

"Crooked ace!" said Cocardasse in the distance. "Look, Passepoil—look at that little man!"

"Ah!" said Passepoil. "If nature had shamed me like that, and I had to give up any hope of pleasing the ladies, I'd try to take my own life."

Like all cowards who've had a scare, Peyrolles began to laugh. "Aesop, known as Jonah!"

"This creature again?" said Gonzague angrily. "You think renting my kennel gives you the free run of my house? What are you doing in here?"

"And you?" said the hunchback impudently. "What are you going to do out there?"

Here was an adversary fit for Peyrolles. "Little Aesop!" he said, squaring away. "We're going to teach you, right now, the cost of sticking your nose in other people's business!"

Gonzague was already looking toward his two hired bravos. Too bad for Aesop, known as Jonah, if he chose to eavesdrop behind doors! But just then the prince was thrown off by the little man's peculiar and daring next move: without a word, the hunchback grabbed the invitation card out of Peyrolles's hands.

"What are you doing, clown?" cried Gonzague.

The hunchback calmly drew his pen and inkwell from his pocket.

"He's crazy!' said Peyrolles.

"Not completely!" The hunchback went down on one knee and settled himself comfortably to write. When he rose again, he held out the card to Gonzague and said triumphantly, "Read it!"

Gonzague read:

"Dear child, this finery comes from me. I wanted to surprise you. Make yourself gorgeous. Two porters will come on my behalf with a chaise to take you to the ball, where I'll be waiting for you.

—*Henri de Lagardère."*

Cocardasse and Passepoil, who were standing too far away to overhear, followed the scene by eye and understood nothing. "God's blood!" said Cocardasse. "His lordship looks like a man who's seeing things!"

"But look at the little hunchback's face," said Passepoil. "Just like last time, I feel like I've seen those eyes somewhere before."

Cocardasse shrugged. "I only worry about men who are more than five foot four."

"I'm only five foot nothing," said Passepoil reproachfully.

Cocardasse held out his hand and said kindly, "Once and for all, baldy, remember you're the exception. God's hat! Friendship is like a crystal prism through which you look to me as white and rosy and plump as Cupid, the only son of Venus risen from the waves."

Passepoil gratefully shook the extended hand.

It was true: Gonzague looked like a man struck dumb. He stared with a kind of dread at Aesop, known as Jonah. "What's the meaning of this?"

"It means," said the hunchback cheerfully, "this note will make the girl trust you."

"So you've guessed our plan?"

"I understood you wanted the girl."

"And do you know what you're risking when you uncover certain secrets?"

"I'm risking getting well rewarded." The hunchback rubbed his hands.

Gonzague and Peyrolles exchanged a look. Gonzague lowered his voice. "But what about the handwriting?"

"I have my little skills. I guarantee it's a perfect imitation. When I've seen a man's writing once..."

"Hell! You can go pretty far with that! And the man?"

"Oh, the man!" The hunchback laughed. "He's too tall and I'm too short. I can't pass for him."

"You know him?"

"Pretty well."

"How do you know him?"

"Business."

"Can you tell us anything?"

"Just one thing: yesterday he struck twice; tomorrow he'll strike twice more."

Peyrolles shivered from head to foot.

"The cellars of my villa make excellent dungeons!" said Gonzague.

The hunchback took no notice of his threatening tone. "A waste of space. Turn them into wine cellars, and you can rent them to wine merchants."

"I think you're a spy."

"Think again. The man we're talking about doesn't have a penny, and you're worth millions. You want me to catch him for you?"

Gonzague stared.

"Give me that card." The hunchback pointed to the second invitation, still in Gonzague's hand.

"To do what with?"

"To make good use of it. I'll give it to the man, and he'll keep the promise I'm making now in his name: he'll go to the Regent's ball."

"God's life, man!" cried Gonzague. "You must be a diabolical fiend."

"Oh," said the hunchback modestly, "there are greater fiends than me."

"Why are you so eager to serve me?"

"That's how I am. I'm devoted to people I like."

"And it's my good luck that you like me?"

"Very much."

"And it's to prove your devotion from up close that you paid ten thousands écus?"

"For the kennel? No, sorry to disappoint you. That was pure speculation, just business." He cackled. "The hunchback is dead, long live the hunchback. The previous Aesop made a million and a half sitting under an old umbrella—at least I have my own office."

Gonzague motioned to Cocardasse and Passepoil, who approached, rattling like old iron.

"Who's this?" asked the little man.

"Men who'll assist you—if I hire you."

The hunchback bowed with great ceremony. "Your servant, your servant. So don't hire me." To the two swordsmen he said, "Gentlemen, don't bother to collect your bric-à-brac. We won't be going anywhere together."

"But..." began Gonzague menacingly.

"There's no but. Hell, you know the man as well as I do. He's brusque, very brusque, you could even say brutal. If he spotted these two sackfuls of gallows meat behind me..."

"Hey!" said Cocardasse indignantly.

"How rude!" said Passepoil.

"I act alone or not at all," said the hunchback firmly.

Gonzague and Peyrolles exchanged a look. Then Gonzague said mockingly, "Your hump is that precious?"

The hunchback bowed. "As precious as a jug of wine is to these bravos. It's my livelihood."

"What guarantee do I have?" asked Gonzague, eyeing him. "Listen. If you serve me faithfully, you'll be rewarded. If not..." He didn't finish, but handed him the second invitation.

The little man backed away toward the door, bowing every few steps. "I'm honored to have your lordship's confidence. Your lordship will have news of me tonight."

On a surreptitious signal from Gonzague, Cocardasse and Passepoil began to follow the hunchback out, but the little man said, "Easy there! What about our agreement?" He pushed them aside with an arm whose strength surprised them, bowed once more, and exited. They tried to follow him, but he slammed the door in their faces. When they opened it, the corridor was empty.

"Quick!" said Gonzague to Peyrolles. "Have the house in the Rue du Chantre surrounded in half an hour, and do the rest as planned."

Out on the Rue Quincampoix, empty now, the hunchback scampered along. "Money was short," he murmured. "Hell if I knew how I was going to get invitations and a ball gown!"

PART THREE: AURORE'S JOURNAL

I. The House with Two Doors

In those days the old, narrow Rue du Chantre still cut like a blight through the neighborhood around the Palais-Royal. Three back streets ran from the Rue Saint Honoré uphill to the Louvre: the Rue Pierre Lescot, the Rue de la Bibliothèque, and the Rue du Chantre—all three dark, dank, and sinister, all three an insult to the splendor of Paris, which found to its surprise that it couldn't wipe the shameful leprous stain off the middle of its face. From time to time you'd hear people talk about some crime that took place there, in the dark of night that even the midsummer noonday sun couldn't dispel. Maybe it was a mud-stained hooker attacked by drunken louts. Maybe it was some hapless solid citizen from out of town whose corpse was found bricked up in an old wall. It was horrifying and disgusting. The vile stink of those slums rose even to the windows of the great palace, home to cardinals and princes and kings.

But is the dignity of the Palais-Royal really of such long standing? And didn't our fathers tell us about what went on in those avenues of trees and galleries of stone? Nowadays the Palais-Royal is an honest stonework square. The avenues of trees are gone. And nothing could be tamer than strolling through those stone galleries. Nobody gathers there except government office drones. But upstairs, in the swarm of cheap restaurants, old-timers from the sticks enjoy talking about the strange doings in the Palais-Royal during the Empire and the Restoration. The old men get excited, and their shy nieces wolf down the *prix fixe* two-franc spread while pretending not to listen.

Where slimy gutters ran down the Rues du Chantre and Pierre Lescot and Bibliothèque now stands an enormous hotel, welcoming all Europe to its thousand-seat restaurant. Its four sides face the courtyard of the Palais-Royal, a straighter Rue Saint Honoré, a wider Rue du Coq, and a longer Rue du Rivoli. From the hotel windows you can see the new Louvre, the legitimate and lookalike scion of the old Louvre. Light and air flow freely. The mud's gone, who knows where; the slums are gone; the hideous leprosy, suddenly cured, didn't even leave a scar. (But where have the criminals and their molls gone?)

In the eighteenth century, those three back streets we've been disparaging were already ugly, but they weren't much narrower or much dirtier than their big neighbor, the Rue Saint Honoré. And along their badly cobbled course stood a few fine doors, a few mansions among the hovels. In general the residents were much like those in nearby streets: small businesspeople, shopkeepers, used goods dealers, piecework tailors. Paris had lots of worse places.

At the corner of the Rue du Chantre and the Rue Saint Honoré stood a tidy, unassuming, nearly new house. The small arched front door stood on a landing up three steps and opened onto the Rue du Chantre. For a little while now the house had been occupied by a young family that drew the interest of the more curious neighbors. There was a young man—young, at least if you went by the youthful beauty of his face and the fire in his eye and the thick blond hair above his smooth, open brow. His name was Master Louis, and he engraved sword guards. With him lived a girl, as pretty and sweet as an angel, whose name nobody knew. They'd been overheard talking together. They addressed each other formally, and were not a couple. Their servants were an old woman who never spoke and a boy of sixteen or seventeen who did his best to be discreet. The girl never went out—absolutely never—to the point where you might have thought she was a prisoner, except that her lovely young voice was heard at all hours singing hymns or ballads. By contrast Master Louis was often out, and came back late at night. When that happened, he didn't use the front door on the landing. The house had two entrances: the second was by way of the staircase of the house next door, and that's the one Master Louis used when he came home.

Since they'd been living there, only one person had visited them, a little hunchback with a gentle, thoughtful face, who came and went without a word, always using the staircase, never the front landing. No doubt he was a close friend of Master Louis. The neighbors had never seen him in the downstairs room where the girl spent her time with the old woman and the boy. Nobody could remember having seen that hunchback in the neighborhood before Master Louis and his household moved in; and he aroused the neighbors' curiosity almost as much as did the handsome, laconic craftsman himself. In the evening, when the work of the day was done and the neighborhood shopkeepers sat on their stoops and chatted, the talk was sure to turn to the hunchback and the new neighbors. Who were they? Where did they come from? At what hour of day or night did the mysterious Master Louis do his engraving—and how did his hands stay so white?

The house was laid out like this: On the ground floor a large low-ceilinged main room, with the small kitchen to its right, looked onto the inner courtyard, and the girl's room looked out onto the Rue Saint Honoré. The kitchen had two under-stair sleeping closets, one for old Françoise Berrichon and the other for Jean-Marie Berrichon, her grandson. The whole of the ground floor had only one outside door, the one opening onto the front landing. But at the back of the main room, by the kitchen, a spiral staircase led up to the second floor.

The second floor consisted of two rooms: that of Master Louis, which opened onto the spiral staircase, and beyond it another room, which had no known exit and seemed to lead nowhere. That second room was always kept locked. Neither old Françoise nor young Jean-Marie nor even the girl herself had ever been allowed inside it. About that, Master Louis, otherwise the mildest of men, was inflexibly strict.

Still, the girl would have liked to know what was behind that locked door. Françoise Berrichon might have been a sensible, wise old woman, but she was dying to know. As for little Jean-Marie, he would have given two fingers just to put his eye to the keyhole—but a cover on the inside of the lock blocked all view. Only one person was privy to Master Louis's secret: the hunchback. He'd been seen entering that room and leaving it. But—as if everything related to this mystery had to be odd and inexplicable—each time after the hunchback went into the room, it was Master Louis who emerged later; and likewise after Master Louis went in, it was the hunchback who came out. No one had ever seen those two inseparable friends together.

Among the curious neighbors was a poet, who lived in the garret (of course) on the top floor of the house. Having racked his brains, he explained to the gossips on the Rue du Chantre that in ancient Rome the priestesses of Vesta or Ops or Rhea or Cybele—the good goddess, daughter of Sky and Earth, wife of Saturn and mother of the gods—were required to keep a sacred fire perpetually lit. According to the poet, the temple virgins took turns: while one tended the fire, the other went about her business. The hunchback and Master Louis must have a similar arrangement. There must be something in that room that couldn't be left alone for even a moment, and Master Louis and the hunchback took turns tending it. They were like vestals, except for their sex and religion. The poet's theory had some impact: he'd always been considered a little touched, and now he was known to be a complete idiot. But no one else had a better explanation.

Toward dusk on the same day Gonzague held the formal family council at his villa, the girl who lived at Master Louis's house was alone in her room. It was a charming little room, decorated simply, but in which every object was clean and eloquent and purposeful. Bright white percale curtains surrounded the cherry wood bed. By the bed hung a small pitcher under a wreath of box. A few religious books on the shelves built into the paneling, some needlework, a guitar on one of the chairs, a little caged bird at the window—those were all the furnishings of this humble, graceful cottage. But we've forgotten to mention a round table, and on it a few scattered sheets of paper. The girl was busy writing. You know the careless way girls strain their eyes, keeping the needle or the pen going long past dusk. You could barely see, and yet the girl was still writing.

The curtains were open, and the last rays of sunlight coming through the window lit her face just enough for us to describe her. She was a laughing girl, one of those sweet girls whose beaming gaiety is enough to bring joy to a whole family. All of her features seemed made to please: her childlike forehead, her nose with its lovely rosy nostrils, her mouth whose smile revealed its pearly treasure. But her big, dark blue eyes, with lashes like a long silk fringe, were dreamy. Except for the pensive look in those fine eyes, you would barely have thought her old enough to fall in love. She was tall, and a little too thin. When no one was there to see her, she fell into a lovely innocent listlessness.

Her expression was gentle, but under the bold arch of her black eyebrows her eyes shone with a calm, fearless pride. Her hair was black as well, with warm highlights of red gold, and so long and thick that sometimes her head seemed to bend under its weight. It fell in waves on her neck and shoulders, a frame and a crown for her sweet beauty. Some women need to be loved fiercely for a single day; others can be cherished for years with quiet tenderness; this girl needed to be loved passionately and forever. She was an angel, but above all a woman.

Her name—which the neighbors didn't know, and which old Françoise and young Jean-Marie Berrichon had been forbidden to utter aloud since they'd reached Paris—was Aurore: a silly pretentious name for a young lady in high society, a ridiculous name for a girl with work-roughened red hands or for some old aunt with a quavering voice, but a gorgeous name for any girl who can weave it, like one more flower, into her coronet of poetic endearment. Names are like jewelry: they crush some and exalt others.

She was home all alone. When twilight hid the nib of her pen, she stopped writing and began to daydream. The thousand noises that reached her from the street didn't rouse her. One fine white hand in her hair, her head tilted back, she gazed toward heaven, as if in silent prayer. She smiled at God. Then amid her smile came one tear, a single pearl that trembled on her eyelid before rolling slowly down her satin cheek. "How late he is!" she murmured.

She gathered together the scattered sheets of paper on the table and tucked them into a small box, which she pushed away behind the headboard of her bed. "Until tomorrow!" she said, as if she were parting from a friend she saw every day. She closed the window and picked up her guitar and strummed a few chords at random. She waited. Today she had reread all the pages stored in the box. She had plenty of time to read, alas. Those pages contained her story—what she knew of her story. The story of her feelings, of her heart. Why had she written it? The opening lines of the manuscript answered that question. Aurore had written:

I begin writing on an evening when I'm alone, having waited all day. This isn't for him. It's the first thing I've done that's not meant for him. I wouldn't want him to see these pages, in which I'll talk constantly about him, about nothing but him. Why? I don't know why. I'd have trouble explaining. Happy are those girls who have companions, other girls with whom they can share their heart's overflow, the sorrow and the joy. I have no companion. I'm alone, all alone. I have only him. When I see him I fall silent. What would I say to him? He asks me nothing.

And yet it's not for myself I pick up my pen. I wouldn't write if I had no hope of this being read, if not in my life then after my death. I think I'm going to die young. I don't wish for it—but God keep me from fearing it! If I died, he'd mourn for me, and I'd mourn for him even in heaven. But maybe from up there I could see into his heart. That thought makes me look forward to dying.

He has told me my father is dead. My mother must be alive. Mother, I write this for you. My heart is all his, but it's all yours too. (I'd like to ask those who understand the mystery of that double affection: do we therefore have two hearts?) I write this for you. I feel like I could hide nothing from you, and that I'd want to reveal to you the most secret corners of my heart. Am I mistaken? Isn't a mother a friend who should know everything, a doctor who can heal everything?

I once saw, through the open window of a house, a little girl kneeling before a gentle, solemn, beautiful woman. The child was crying, but they were good tears. The mother, moved and smiling, bent to kiss her hair. Ah, what divine happiness, Mother! I think I feel your kiss on my brow. You too must be gentle and beautiful. You too must know how to give consolation with a smile. That scene is always in my dreams. I envy that little girl's tears. Mother, if I had both you and him beside me, what in the world could I envy? I've never knelt except before a priest. A priest's words are helpful, but God speaks through the mouths of mothers.

Are you waiting for me? Are you looking for me? Do you miss me? Am I in your prayers morning and night? Do you see me in your dreams, as I see you? I feel like when I think of you, you must be thinking of me. Sometimes my heart speaks to you; do you hear me? If ever I'm granted the great blessing of seeing you, dear Mother, I'll ask you if there were moments when your heart leaped for no reason. I'll say, "That's when you heard my heart cry out, Mother!"

I was born in France, I've never been told where. I don't know my age exactly, but I must be around twenty. Is it a dream, is it reality? The memory, if it is one, is so distant, so vague! Sometimes I seem to remember a woman with the face of an angel, bending to smile over my cradle. Was that you, Mother? Then, in darkness, a great noise of battle. Maybe it's just a child's fever dream. Someone carried me in his arms. A voice like thunder made me tremble. We ran in darkness. I was cold. There's a fog around all of it. He must know, but when I ask him about my childhood he smiles sadly and falls silent.

The first time I can picture myself clearly, I was in the Spanish Pyrenees, dressed like a little boy. I was leading goats out to pasture for a mountain peasant with whom we must have been staying. Henri was ill, and I kept hearing people say he would die. In those days I called him my father. When I came back in the evening he had me kneel by his bed and he joined my hands together and said to me in French, "Aurore, pray God that I live."

One night the priest came to administer extreme unction. Henri confessed, and wept. Thinking I couldn't hear, he said, "My poor little girl will be left alone."

"Think on God, my son!" the priest exhorted.

"Yes, Father, oh yes, I'm thinking on God. God is good; I'm not worried about myself. But my poor little girl will be left alone in the world. Would it be a great sin, Father, to take her with me?"

"To kill her!" cried the horrified priest. "My son, you're delirious."

He shook his head and didn't answer. I crept closer. "Henri," I said, looking hard at him—and if you only knew, Mother, how gaunt and haggard he was—"Henri, I'm not afraid of dying, and I don't mind going to the cemetery with you."

He took me in his arms, which were burning with fever. And I remember he said, over and over, "To leave her alone! To leave her alone!"

He fell asleep, still holding me in his arms. They tried to tear me away, but you'd have had to kill me first. I thought, "If he goes, I'll go with him."

A few hours later he woke up. I was bathed in his sweat. "I'm saved," he said. And, seeing me pressed against him, he added, "Beautiful little angel, it's you who healed me!"

I'd never looked carefully at him. One day I noticed how handsome he was, the way I've seen him ever since. We'd left the peasant's farm to go further into Spain. Henri had regained his strength and was working in the fields as a farmhand. I've since understood that was to feed me. It was on a rich estate near Benasque. The farmer raised crops and sold wine to smugglers. Henri had told me never to leave the little yard behind the house, and never to go into the common room. But one night some gentlemen came to dinner at the farmhouse, gentlemen from France. I was playing in the yard with the farmer's children. The children wanted to see the gentlemen, and I foolishly followed them. Two men sat at the table, surrounded by servants and guards: seven men in all. The leader made a sign to his companion, and they both looked at me. The first man called me over and petted me, while the other went to whisper to the farmer. When he came back I heard him say, "It's her!"

"Saddle up!" said the leader, and he tossed the farmer a purse full of gold. Then to me he said, "Come as far as the fields, kid. Come look for your father."

I asked for nothing better than to see my father a few minutes earlier than usual. I climbed bravely into the saddle behind one of the men. I didn't know the way to the fields where my father worked. For half an hour I bounced along on the back of the trotting horse, laughing and singing, as happy as a queen. Then I asked, "Will we see him soon?"

"Soon, soon," the man answered. And on we went. Night was falling. I grew afraid. I wanted to get down. The leader ordered, "Full gallop!" And the man who was holding me put his hand over my mouth to stifle my cries.

But suddenly, speeding across the fields, we saw a horseman cutting through the air like a whirlwind. He was riding a farm horse, without saddle or bridle. His hair floated in the wind like the shreds of his ragged clothes. The road curved around a wood bisected by a river; he had forded the river and cut through the woods. Nearer and nearer he came. I didn't recognize my calm, gentle father; I didn't recognize my smiling Henri. This man was as frightening and beautiful as a storm cloud. Nearer he came, and with one last leap his horse crossed the hedge along the road and fell exhausted. In his hand Henri held a plow blade.

"Get him!" cried the leader.

But Henri had anticipated him. The plow blade, gripped in both hands, struck twice. Two armed servants fell and lay in their own blood, and each time he struck Henri cried, "Here I am! Here I am! Lagardère! Lagardère!"

The man who held me wanted to run, but Henri had his eye on him. He leaped over the bodies of the two servants and struck him once with the plow blade. I didn't faint, Mother. Maybe later I wouldn't have been so brave. But during that whole terrible fight I kept my eyes wide open, waving my hands as much as I could and shouting, "Courage, Henri! Courage! Courage!" I don't know if the battle lasted more than a minute. Then he mounted one of the dead men's horses and galloped away with me in his arms. We didn't go back to the estate. He said the farmer had betrayed him. And he said, "No place is better for hiding than a town."

So we needed to hide—I'd never understood that. My curiosity was aroused, along with the feeling that I owed him everything. I questioned him. He hugged me in his arms and said, "Later, later." Then, a little sadly, he said, "Are you already tired of calling me your father?"

Don't be jealous, dear Mother. He was my whole family, both father and mother. It's not your fault you weren't there. But when I remember my childhood it brings tears to my eyes. He was good, he was loving, and your kisses, Mother, couldn't have been gentler than his. And yet he was so fierce! So brave! Ah, if you could just see him, how you'd love him!

II. Childhood Memories

I'd never been in a town. When we saw the faraway steeples of Pamplona, I asked what they were. "Those are churches," said Henri. "You'll see lots of people there, Aurore, fine lords and beautiful ladies, but you won't have a flower garden." I wasn't sorry about the flowers or the garden then; I was carried away by the thought of seeing so many fine lords and beautiful ladies. We entered the city gates. Two rows of tall, dark houses hid the sky. With the little money he had, Henri rented a small room. I was a prisoner there. In the mountains and at the farm I had fresh air and sunshine, flowering trees, wide lawns, and the company of children my age. Here, four walls: outside, the long line of gray houses in the bleak silence of Spanish towns; inside, solitude—because Henri went out early in the morning and came home late in the evening. He came back with black hands and a sweaty brow. He was sad, and only my hugs could restore his smile. We were poor, and we ate dry bread. But he still found a way sometimes to bring me chocolate, that Spanish delicacy, and other treats. Those days his sad face grew happy and smiling.

"Aurore," he said one evening, "here in Pamplona I go by Don Luis. And if anyone asks your name, tell them it's Mariquita." I knew him only as Henri. He'd never told me he was the Chevalier de Lagardère. I found that out by chance. I also had to figure out for myself what he'd done for me when I was a baby. I think he wanted me not to know how much I owed him. That's how Henri is, Mother: nobility, self-denial, generosity, bravery, all pushed to the point of madness. You'd only have to meet him to love him almost as much as I do. But at the time I'd have preferred less tact and more cooperation in answering my questions: why had a man so frank and self-assured changed his name? One answer haunted me, and over and over I thought, he's doing it for me, I'm the cause of his troubles.

Here's how I found out what trade he followed in Pamplona, and at the same time his real name long ago in France. One evening, around when he usually came home, two gentlemen knocked at our door. I was putting the wooden plates on our table; we had no tablecloth. I thought it was Henri, and I ran to open the door. At the sight of two strangers I drew back in fear. No one had ever come to visit us since we'd been in Pamplona. They were thin, long-legged Basque swordsmen, jaundice yellow, with long mustaches curled into points. Their long thin rapiers lifted the skirts of their cloaks. One was old and talkative, the other young and taciturn.

"*Hola*, pretty one," said the first. "Isn't this the home of Señor Don Henri?"

"No, señor."

The two Basques looked at each other. The younger one shrugged his shoulders and muttered, "Don Luis!"

"Don Luis, *válgame Dios!*" cried the older one. "Don Luis, Don Luis is what I meant to say." And as I hesitated he went on, "Come on in, Don Sancho, my nephew, come on in! We'll wait in here for Señor Don Luis. Don't you worry about us, *conejita*, we'll be comfortable here. Have a seat, nephew. Shabby quarters for a gentleman, but that's none of our business. Want a cigarillo, nephew? No? As you wish."

The nephew, Don Sancho, didn't say a word. He had a long thin face like a yardstick, and now and then he scratched his ear like an embarrassed schoolboy. His uncle, whose name was Don Miguel, lit a *pajita* and smoked and talked with unflappable garrulousness. I was mortified, afraid Henri would scold me. When I heard his step on the stairs I ran to meet him, but Don Miguel had longer legs than I did, and from the top of the stairs he cried, "Welcome, Señor Don Luis! My nephew Don Sancho and I have been expecting you for half an hour. *Gracias a Dios!* I'm pleased to meet you, and my nephew likewise. I'm Don Miguel de la Crencha, from Santiago, near Roncesvalles, where gallant Roland was slain. My nephew Don Sancho is of the same name and the same country; his father, my brother, is Don Ramon de la Crencha, Lord Mayor of Toledo. We heartily kiss your hand, Señor Don Luis—heartily, *Santa Trinidad!*" Don Sancho had stood up, but he said nothing.

Henri stopped at the top of the stairs. He frowned and looked worried. "What do you want?"

"Come on in!" cried Don Miguel, politely drawing back to make way.

"What do you want?" asked Henri again.

"First, allow me to present my nephew, Don Sancho."

"What the devil do you want?" cried Henri, stamping his foot. I trembled when I saw him like this.

At the sight of his face, Don Miguel took a step back, but he soon recovered—he had the cheerful hidalgo spirit. "Since you're not in the mood to chat, here's what we came for. Our cousin Carlos, from Burgos, was with the Spanish embassy to France back in ninety-five, and he recognized you at the arquebus maker Master Cuenza's. You're the Chevalier Henri de Lagardère."

Henri grew pale and lowered his eyes. I thought he would deny it.

"The greatest blade in the world!" continued Don Miguel. "The unbeatable man! Don't deny it, sir, I'm sure of what I'm saying."

"I won't deny it, señores," said Henri gravely. "But it may cost you dearly to have found out my secret." And he closed the door leading to the stairs. That beanpole Don Sancho began to tremble in every limb.

"*Por Dios!*" cried Don Miguel smoothly. "It'll cost us whatever you say, señor chevalier! We've come here with our pockets full. Come on, nephew, empty your purse!"

Without a word Don Sancho, whose long teeth were chattering, put two or three good fistfuls of doubloons on the table, and his uncle did the same. Henri watched them with astonishment.

"He, he!" laughed Don Miguel as he stirred the pile of gold. "You don't earn this much filing sword guards for Master Cuenza, do you? Don't get angry, señor chevalier! We're not here to betray your secret. We don't want to know why the great Lagardère is stooping to do work that ruins his white hands and damages his lungs, do we, nephew?" The nephew bowed awkwardly. "We're here," continued the talkative uncle, "to hire you for some family business."

"I'm listening."

Don Miguel sat back down and relit his cigarillo. "Family business, simple family business. Right, nephew? I have to tell you, señor chevalier, in our family we're all swordsmen, like the Cid, to say no more. I myself fought two Basque hidalgos from Tolosa, big strong rascals—but I'll tell you that story another time. This isn't about me, it's about my nephew, Don Sancho. My nephew was quite decently courting a young lady from Salvatierra. He's reasonably good looking and rich and not an idiot, but the girl was taking her time deciding. Finally she fell in love—with another man, if you can believe it, señor chevalier. Right, nephew?"

The laconic Don Sancho let out a grunt of agreement.

"As you know," went on Don Miguel, "two roosters and one hen means war! It's not a big town, and the two young fellows crossed each other's path every day. Things heated up. His patience exhausted, my nephew raised his hand—but he wasn't quick enough, señor chevalier: it was he who got slapped. Can you imagine, a de la Crencha getting slapped! Blood and death, right, nephew? Only steel can avenge such an insult!" Don Miguel winked at Henri in a way that was both good-humored and dreadful; only a Spaniard could play Sancho Panza and the Boogeyman at the same time.

"You haven't yet mentioned what you want from me," said Henri. Two or three times his eyes had strayed to the gold spread out on the table: we were so poor!

"Well, well," said Don Miguel, "that's easy enough to figure out, right, nephew? The de la Crenchas don't get slapped. It's the first time in history. The de la Crenchas are lions, señor chevalier! And my nephew Don Sancho above all. But..."

He left a long pause. Henri's face brightened, while his eyes drifted once again to the pile of doubloons. "I think I understand, and I'm ready to serve you."

"*Santiago!*" cried Don Miguel. "Excellent! A worthy chevalier!"

His nephew dropped his impassivity and rubbed his hands together happily.

"I knew we'd get along!" went on Don Miguel. "The rascal is Don Ramiro Nuflez Tonadilla, from the village of San José. He's small and bearded, with sharp shoulders."

"I don't need to know all that."

"Yes, you do! Hell, we don't want to make a mistake! Last year I went to the dentist in Hondarribia, right, nephew? I paid him a doubloon to pull an aching tooth in the back of my mouth. The joker pulled a good tooth instead of the bad one, and kept my doubloon!"

Henri's face clouded over, and he frowned.

Don Miguel didn't notice. "We're paying you, and we want the job done carefully and done right. That's fair, isn't it? Don Ramiro has red hair and always wears a gray hat with black feathers. Every night around seven he passes by the Three Moors tavern, between San José and Roncesvalles."

"Enough, señores. We've misunderstood each other."

"What? What?"

"I thought you wanted me to teach Don Sancho how to handle a sword."

"*Santa Trinidad*!" cried Don Miguel. "In the de la Crencha family we're all first-class fighters! At the fencing academy the boy fences like Saint Michael the Archangel, but out in the field accidents can happen. We thought you'd take on the job of waiting for Don Ramiro Nuflez at the Three Moors tavern and avenging my nephew's honor."

This time Henri didn't reply. His cold smile expressed such contempt that the uncle and the nephew exchanged a look of embarrassment. Henri pointed to the doubloons on the table. Without a word, the uncle and the nephew put them back in their pockets. Then Henri pointed to the door. The uncle and the nephew went out, hat in hand and shoulders hunched. They went down the stairs four steps at a time. That night we ate our bread dry; Henri had brought nothing home to put on our wooden plates.

I was too young to understand that scene completely, but it made a vivid impression. I thought a long time about the way Henri had looked at the gold those Basque hidalgos brought. As for the name Lagardère, I was too young and had lived too much apart to know its strange renown. And yet the name struck a resounding chord in me, like a battle fanfare. I remembered my kidnappers' terror when Henri threw that name in their faces, when he stood alone against them all.

Later I found out what the Chevalier de Lagardère had been, and it saddened me. His sword had toyed with men's lives, his whims had toyed with women's hearts. I was deeply saddened. But did that stop me from loving him? I know nothing about the world, dear Mother. Maybe other girls aren't like me. When I knew he'd sinned, I loved him even more. I felt he needed my prayers to God. I felt I was an important part of his life. He'd changed so much since becoming my adoptive father! Don't blame me for pride, Mother: I felt like I was his gentleness, his wisdom, his goodness. When I say I loved him more, maybe that's not it: I loved him differently. His fatherly kisses made me blush, and I began to weep quietly when I was alone. But I'm anticipating, and speaking of recent events...

It was in Pamplona that Henri undertook my education. He had little time to teach me, and no money for books, because his days were long and badly paid. He was then still just an apprentice in the craft that has since made him famous throughout Spain as El Cincelador, the engraver. He was slow and clumsy. His master treated him badly. And he—a veteran of King Louis XIV's light cavalry, a haughty young man who used to kill for a word, for a look—he patiently bore the reproaches and insults of a Spanish artisan, because he had a daughter! When he came home with a few pennies earned by the sweat of his brow, he was as happy as a king, because I smiled at him. Other people might laugh condescendingly, Mother, but I'm sure that you instead will shed a tear.

Henri owned a single book, an old *Treatise on Fencing* by Master François Delapalme of Paris, licensed master of arms, with degrees from Parma and Florence, member of the Mannheim Handegenbund and the Naples Accademia della Scrima, fencing tutor to His Highness the Dauphin, etcetera, etcetera, followed by a description of all the different lunges, attacks, and points of etiquette in use in the art of standing combat, by Giovanni-Maria Ventura of the aforementioned Naples Accademia della Scrima, edited and updated by J.-F. Delambre-Saulxure, provost of cadets, and published in Paris in 1667.

Are you surprised I can remember it? Those were the first words I learned to read, and I remember them as well as my catechism. Henri used that old fencing manual to teach me to read. I've never held a sword, but I'm an expert in theory: I know tierce and quarte, the natural parries; prime and seconde, the partly instinctive parries; the two universal compound counter-parries; the semi-circular parry; the coupé, both simple and reverse; the straight cut, the feints, the disengages. I didn't get far until Henri had saved up twenty-five pesetas to buy me a Salamanca primer. Believe me, Mother, it's not the book that matters, it's the teacher. I soon learned to make my way through that ridiculous mishmash, put together by a trio of ignorant cutthroats. What did the crude principles of the art of killing matter to me?

Patiently, gently, Henri taught me the letters. I sat on his knees. He held the book, and I used a pie server to point to each letter and name it. It wasn't work, it was a joy. When I read well, he hugged me. Then we both knelt, and he recited the evening prayers. I tell you, he was a mother to me, a tender affectionate mother to his darling little girl! Didn't he dress me, didn't he brush my hair? His doublet went to pieces, but I always had nice dresses. Once I caught him, needle in hand, trying to mend my torn skirt. Oh, don't laugh, Mother, don't laugh! It was Lagardère doing it, the Chevalier Henri de Lagardère, the man before whom the greatest swordsmen fell or bowed down!

On Sundays, when he'd curled my hair and fastened on my hairnet, when he'd made the copper buttons of my little blouse shine like gold and tied around my neck the velvet ribbon of my steel cross—my first present from him—he took me, proud and happy, to the Dominican church in the lower town. We heard Mass; he'd become devout because of me and for me. After Mass we went out the city gates and left the gloomy town behind. How good the fresh air was for our poor imprisoned lungs! How bright and sweet the sunshine was! We went through empty fields. He wanted to join in my games—he was more of a child than I was. Toward midday, when I grew tired, he led me into dense, shady woods. He sat at the foot of a tree, and I fell asleep in his arms. He watched over me, waving away mosquitos and wasps. Sometimes I just pretended to sleep, and watched through half-closed eyelids. His eyes were always on me; he smiled as he rocked me. I have only to close my eyes now to see him again that way: my friend, my father, my noble Henri! Do you love him now, Mother?

Before or after my nap, just as I pleased—because I was queen—we ate lunch on the grass: a little black bread dipped in milk. Think of the most delicious feast, Mother; you can describe it to me, since I've never known one. Still I'm sure our feasts were better: our bread and milk were manna dipped in ambrosia! Joyful hearts, loving embraces, mad laughter over nothing, childish endearments, songs, who knows what. Then more games; he wanted me to grow big and strong. On the way home our idle conversation was interrupted by flowers to pick or bright butterflies to catch or a white goat bleating to be petted.

Without my knowing it, in those talks Henri was forming my mind and my heart. He read secretly and learned what a woman needs to teach her daughter. I learned to know God, and the story of God's people, and the marvels of heaven and earth. Sometimes, when we were alone together, I tried to question him to learn about my family. I often spoke to him of you, Mother. He grew sad and didn't answer. All he said was, "Aurore, I promise you'll know your mother." I hope that promise, made so long ago, will be fulfilled. I'm sure it will, because Henri has never lied to me. And if I believe the stirrings of my own heart, the time is near. Oh, Mother, how I'll love you!

But I should finish this account of my education. I went on having lessons long after we'd left Pamplona and Navarre. I had no teacher besides Henri. It wasn't his fault. When his great artistic talent became known, when every Spanish grandee wanted the hilt of his rapier to be carved—no matter the cost—by Don Luis, El Cincelador, he said to me, "My darling girl, you're going to be educated. There are famous schools in Madrid where young ladies learn everything a grown woman needs to know."

"I want you to be my teacher—always, always!"

He smiled. "My poor Aurore, I've taught you everything I know."

"Well, in that case, Henri, I want to know no more than you do!"

III. The Gypsy Girl

I often cry, Mother, even now that I'm grown up. But I'm like a child: my smile comes out even before the tears are dry. Reading this incoherent babble—my vague impressions of battle, the story of those two hidalgos (Don Miguel the uncle and Don Sancho the nephew), my first learning to read from a fencing manual, the account of my pathetic childhood pleasures—you might have thought, she's mad! It's true, joy makes me crazy; but I'm not afraid of sorrow. Joy leaves me giddy. I'm not familiar with worldly pleasures, and I don't care: what matters to me is the heart's joy. I'm happy, I'm like a child, everything amuses me—alas, as if I'd never suffered.

We had to leave Pamplona, where we were just beginning to prosper. Henri had even saved up a little money, and it's a good thing he did. I think I must have been about ten years old. One evening he came home anxious and full of care. I added to his worries by telling him that all day a man wrapped in a dark cloak had stood watch in the street under my window. Henri didn't sit down at the table. He laid out his weapons and dressed as if for a long journey. When night fell he dressed me in a woolen blouse and laced up my boots. He went out, taking his sword. I was terrified; I hadn't seen him so upset in a long time. When he came back he made up a bundle of his things and mine.

"We're going away, Aurore."

"For a long time?"

"Forever."

"What!" I cried, looking around at our little home. "We're leaving all this?"

"Yes, all of it." He smiled sadly. "I went down to the corner to find a pauper who'll inherit this from us. He's as happy as a king. So goes the world!"

"But where are we going?"

"God knows," he said with forced cheer. "Let's go, Aurore. It's time."

We left. And now I have to write something awful, Mother. My pen stopped for a moment, but I want to hide nothing from you. As we were going down the front steps, I saw a dark object in the middle of the empty street. Henri tried to lead me away toward the city gates, but he was hampered by our luggage, and I got away and ran over to the thing I'd noticed. Henri called out to stop me. I'd never disobeyed him, but it was too late: I could already see a human form under a cloak, and I recognized the cloak worn by the mysterious sentinel who'd paced beneath my window all day. I lifted the cloak: it was the same man. He was dead, and soaked in his own blood. I fell back, as if I myself had received the fatal blow. There'd been a fight, so near me, because when he went out Henri had taken his sword. Once again, Henri had risked his life for me—I have no doubt it was for me.

I woke in the middle of the night. I was alone, or at least I thought I was alone. I was in a room even humbler than the one we'd left: it was the typical upstairs room of a Spanish farmhouse built by poor hidalgos. Barely audible voices came from the common room downstairs. I was lying in a bed with worm-eaten bedposts, on a straw mattress covered with a ragged piece of cloth. Moonlight shone through unglazed windows. The branches of two big cork oaks waved in the night breeze. I called quietly for Henri; no answer. But a shadow crossed the floor, and in a moment he was at my bedside. He motioned me to be silent, and whispered in my ear, "They've found us. They're downstairs."

"Who?"

"The friends of the man under the cloak." The dead man! I trembled from head to toe and thought I might faint again. Henri squeezed my arm. "They were at the door a little while ago. They tried to open it, but I put my arm through the rings like a door bar. They couldn't tell what the obstacle was. They've gone downstairs to find a crowbar to take the door off its hinges. They'll be back."

"But what did you do to them, Henri," I cried, "that they won't stop chasing you?"

"I snatched away the prey those wolves were about to tear apart!"

Me? I understood he meant me, and the thought filled my heart with sadness. I was the cause of everything, I'd ruined his life. This handsome man, once so dashing, so happy, now lived on the run like a criminal. He'd given up his whole life for me. Why? "Father, dear Father, leave me here and escape, I beg you."

He put his hand over my mouth. "Silly thing!" he murmured. "If they kill me I'll have to abandon you, but they don't have me yet. Get up!"

I tried to obey, but I was very weak. Later I found out that Henri, dropping from fatigue after carrying me in his arms, half-dead as I was, from Pamplona all the way to this lonely farmhouse, had asked for shelter here. They were poor people, and they gave him the room we were in. Henri had been about to lie down on the straw bed made up for him, when he heard horses outside. They stopped at the door. He realized he'd have to put off sleep to another night. Instead of lying down, he quietly opened the door and went partway down the stairs. People were talking in the lower room.

The farmer in rags said, "I'm a gentleman, and I won't hand over my guests." Henri heard the sound of a handful of gold thrown onto the table. The farmer was silenced.

A voice Henri recognized said, "Get to work, and do it fast!"

Henri quickly returned to our room and did what he could to secure the door. He ran to the window to see if we could escape that way. The branches of the two big cork trees rubbed against the window frame. Below lay a small kitchen garden, surrounded by a low hedge. Beyond that stood a meadow, and then the Arga River, shining through the trees in the moonlight.

"You're pale, Aurore," he said when I was up, "but you're brave, and you'll help me."

"Oh, yes!" I cried, delighted at the thought of serving him.

He led me to the window. "Can you reach the orchard by way of that staircase?" He pointed to the branches and the trunk of one of the cork trees.

"Yes, Father, if you promise to join me soon."

"I promise, Aurore." Then, as he took me into his arms he added quietly, "Now or never, poor little darling!" I was so shaken up that I didn't really understand, which was lucky. He opened the window just as footsteps could be heard coming upstairs again. "When you reach the ground," he said, "throw a pebble into the room as a signal. Then sneak along the hedge as far as the river."

I climbed into the branches of the cork tree while Henri ran to the door. He used his arm in place of the missing door bar. They tried to open the door, they pushed, they leaned, they swore, but Henri's arm was as good as an iron bar. I was still near the window when I heard the sound of a crowbar being slid under the door. I stayed to watch.

"Go! Go!" said Henri impatiently.

I obeyed. From the ground I tossed a small pebble through the window. Then I heard a muffled crash from upstairs: it was the door being broken open. My legs became useless, and I stood nailed to the spot. Two shots rang out in the room, and then Henri appeared, standing on the windowsill. In one leap, without using the tree, he joined me. "Ah, poor thing!" he said when he saw me. "I thought you were already gone! They're going to fire." He took me in his arms. Several shots were fired from the window. I felt him flinch hard.

"Are you hit?" I cried.

In the middle of the orchard he stopped in the moonlight. Turning to present his chest to the bandits at the window, who were reloading, he shouted, "Lagardère! Lagardère!"

Then he went through the hedge and reached the river. They were after us. The Arga there runs fast and deep. I was already looking around for a rowboat, but Henri, without slowing down, and still carrying me in his arms, threw himself into the river. I could tell it was easy for him. With one arm he held me over his head, with the other he swam. In moments we reached the opposite bank. Our enemies stood on the other side debating what to do. "They're going to look for the ford," said Henri. "We're not safe yet."

I was soaked and shivering, and he warmed me against his chest. We heard horses galloping along the opposite bank. Our enemies were looking for a ford across the Arga so they could follow us. They were sure we wouldn't be able to stay ahead of them for long. When the sound of the horses faded in the distance, Henri got back into the water and crossed the Arga again. "We're safe now, Aurore," he said as we climbed out onto the bank at the same spot from which we'd started. "Now we need to dry you off and bandage me up."

"I knew you were wounded!"

"It's nothing! Come."

He headed back to the house of the farmer who'd betrayed us. The man and his wife were talking and laughing around a warm glowing brazier in the downstairs room. Knocking the man down and tying him and his wife up together in a single parcel was the work of a moment for Henri. "Shut up," he said, as the couple cried out pitifully from fear that he was going to kill them. "There was a time when I would've burned down your hovel, which is what you deserve. But nothing's going to happen to you. Here's your guardian angel!" He ran his hand through my wet hair.

I wanted to help bandage him. The wound was in his shoulder, and was bleeding heavily from all the strain he'd put on it. While my clothes dried I was wrapped up in his cloak, which he'd left upstairs when he fled. I tore up rags and bandaged his wound.

"It doesn't hurt anymore," he said. "You've healed me!"

The gentleman farmer and his wife kept as still as corpses. Henri went upstairs to our room and came back down with our things. Toward three in the morning we left the house, riding on a big old mule Henri had taken from the stable, for which he threw two pieces of gold on the table. Before we set off he said to the couple, "If they come back, give them greetings from the Chevalier de Lagardère, and tell them God and the Virgin will protect the orphan, and right now Lagardère doesn't have time to deal with them, but their hour will come!"

That big old mule wasn't as bad as she looked. We reached Estella before dawn, and made a deal with a muleteer to get us across the mountains to Burgos. Henri wanted to get further away from the French border; his enemies were French. His plan was not to stop till we reached Madrid.

We poor parentless children can give free rein to our imaginations, which are always at work on the mystery of our unknown relations. Are you rich, Mother? You must be important, for your daughter to be the object of such dogged pursuit. If you're rich, you probably can't picture what it's like to make a long journey across Spain, that beautiful, noble land spreading out its proud misery under the dazzling splendor of the sun. Misery is bad for the heart; young as I am, I know that much. The gallant people who defeated the Moors are on the decline now. Of all their ancient outstanding qualities, they've hung onto little besides their theatrical pride, dressed in rags. The landscape is wonderful. The people are contemptible, lazy, up to their necks in shameful filth. That pretty girl going by, so romantic from a distance, carrying her basket of fruit so gracefully—that's not her real face you see up close, it's a mask of dirt. There are rivers, but Spain doesn't yet seem to have discovered what water is for.

When a hundred highway robbers meet, they call it a village and choose a mayor. The mayor and all his staff are gentlemen of the same kind. The countryside around the village remains a wasteland. No matter how empty the road, there are always enough travelers passing by for the hundred and one gentlemen and their families to have an onion a day to eat. The mayor, more of a gentleman than his constituents, is also more of a thief and more of a glutton. Some of those autocrats have been known to eat as many as two onions in the space of twenty-four hours. But those who make a god of their bellies that way end badly: the blunderbuss awaits. Conspicuous consumption is an abuse of the gifts of heaven.

It's rare to find anything to eat at an inn. They're set up to cut travelers' throats—travelers who go into the next world hungry. The proud, laconic innkeeper gives you a small pile of straw covered with a gray rag: that's your bed. If somehow you get through the night without having your throat cut, you pay and leave without eating. No need to mention the monks and policemen: armed robbers are familiar the world over. And everyone knows muleteers are the natural allies of mountain bandits. A Spaniard who has to travel three leagues in any direction summons a notary first and draws up his will.

Between Pamplona and Burgos we had a hundred adventures, but none connected to our pursuers, and it's only about them I need to tell you, Mother. We were to meet them again once more before reaching Madrid. We'd gone by way of Burgos to avoid traveling through the high Sierras of Old Castile. Henri's funds were rapidly running out, and countless obstacles made our progress slow. (The account of any journey through Spain reads like a stack of adventures whimsically tossed together by some fanciful satirical imagination.) Finally we left behind the gingerbread Saracen bell tower of Valladolid. Our journey was more than halfway done.

We were following the frontier of Léon, going toward Segovia. It was dusk. We were both riding the same mule, and we had no guide. The road was good, and we'd heard about an inn on the Adaja River with good food. But the sun was setting over the sparse woods in the direction of Salamanca, and still we saw no sign of the inn. Night was falling; there were fewer muleteers on the road; it was the hour of undesirable encounters. But that night, thank God, we had none—the only surprise was a good one: Mother, that was the evening we met little Flor, my dear gypsy girl, my first and only friend.

We parted long ago, and yet I'm sure she remembers me. Two or three days after we reached Paris, I was downstairs singing. Suddenly I heard a call from the street, and I thought I recognized Flor's voice. A carriage was passing, a big traveling coach without livery markings. The blinds were down. No doubt I was mistaken. But since then I've often gone to the window, hoping to see her graceful figure, her fairy feet just brushing the cobblestones, her black eyes shining behind her lace veil. I must be crazy! Why would Flor be in Paris?

The road followed the lip of a precipice. At the very edge of the precipice lay a child, asleep. I saw her first and asked Henri to stop the mule. I jumped down and knelt by her. She was a little gypsy girl, my age, and so pretty! I'd never seen anything as adorable as Flor: gracefulness, delicacy, gentle mischief personified. By now Flor must be a beautiful young lady. I don't know why, but right away I wanted to embrace her. My kiss woke her. Smiling, she kissed me back—but the sight of Henri frightened her.

"Don't be afraid," I said. "That's Henri, my dear father, who'll love you, since I love you already. What's your name?"

"Flor. And you?"

"Aurore."

She smiled again, and murmured, "The old poet who writes our songs often talks about Aurore's tears that shine like pearls in the flower's cup. But I bet you've never cried, while I cry all the time." I didn't know what she meant by her old poet. Henri was calling us. She put her hand to her stomach and said, "Oh, I'm so hungry!" She grew pale, and I took her in my arms. Henri dismounted. Flor said she hadn't eaten since breakfast the day before. He gave her a little bread and the last of the sherry in his flask. She ate eagerly. When she'd drunk, she looked at both of us in turn, and murmured, "You don't look alike." And then, "Why don't I have anyone to love?" Her lips brushed Henri's hand. "Thank you, señor chevalier. You're as kind as you are handsome. I beg you, don't leave me here to spend all night by the road!"

Henri hesitated: gypsies are cunning, dangerous rogues. The child abandoned here might be a trap. But I spoke up for her, and he finally agreed to bring her along. How happy we were—unlike the mule, who now had a third load to carry.

Along the way Flor told us her story. She was part of a gypsy band coming from Léon and going, like us, to Madrid. The previous morning, who knows why, the group had been chased down by a squadron of the *Santa Hermandad*, and while her companions fled Flor had hidden in the bushes. When the coast was clear she tried to catch up with them, but, whether walking or running, she couldn't find them. She questioned passersby, but they threw stones at her. Because she wasn't baptized, so-called Christians felt free to steal her silver-plated copper earrings and her necklace of fake pearls. She spent the night in a flour mill. Luckily sleep assuages hunger, because she hadn't eaten. The next day, she walked all day without food. Barking farm dogs followed her, and little children shouted at her. From time to time she saw the print of a gypsy sandal in the dust of the road, and that encouraged her. When they travel from one place to another, gypsies usually agree on a rendezvous point to stop at along the way. Flor knew where her band would meet, but it was far, far away, in a canyon below Cerro del Baladron, looking toward the Escurial Monastery, seven or eight leagues from Madrid.

It was on our way, and I got Henri to agree to take Flor that far. She shared my straw bed at the inn, and she shared the splendid *olla podrida* we were served for dinner. Real Castilian *olla podrida* is hard to find elsewhere in Europe. You need a ham hock, a little cowhide, half a goat horn from a goat that died of disease, cabbage stalks, turnip peelings, a field mouse, and a bushel and a half of garlic. At least those were the ingredients we recognized in the excel-

161

lent *olla podrida* we had in the town of Sanlúcar, between Pesquera and Segovia, at one of the finest inns there could possibly be in all of the King of Spain's
lands.

From the moment lovely little Flor joined us, the road became less dull.
She was almost as playful as I was, and much cleverer. She could dance, she
could sing. She entertained us with stories of the hanging offenses of her gypsy
friends. We asked her what god they worshiped. She said, "a jug." But at Zamo-
ra, in the state of Léon, she met a good Misericord friar who told her of the
greatness of the Christian God, and Flor wanted to be baptized.

She was with us for a week, long enough to get from Sanlúcar in Castile to
Cerro del Baladron. When we came within sight of that bleak, rocky mountain,
where I'd have to part from my dear Flor, I grew sad; I didn't know it was a
foreshadowing. I'd gotten used to Flor: for a week we'd ridden the same mule,
holding onto one another and chattering away along the road. She loved me, and
I thought of her as my sister.

It was hot; the sky had been overcast all day, and the air was heavy, like
before a storm. Big raindrops began to fall as we reached the foot of the mountain. Henri gave us his cloak to wrap us both up, and we went on climbing, urging our lazy mule on through a torrential downpour. Flor had promised us the
warmest hospitality on behalf of her friends, and a rain shower wasn't enough to
stop Henri, and Flor and I would happily have faced the most awful storm from
under the shelter we shared. The clouds rolled by, one after another, with occasional gaps through which we saw blue sky. At the western horizon, in a confusion of purple, the last light of day dyed everything red. The steep rocky road
spiraled up. The gusting wind was strong enough to make our mule stumble.

"It's funny how this light makes you see things!" I cried. "There, on that
rocky ridge, I thought I saw two men carved in stone."

Henri quickly looked that way. "I see nothing."

"They're gone," said Flor quietly.

"Were there really two men?" asked Henri.

The nameless fear I felt rising in me was only magnified by Flor's answer.
"Not two, but at least ten."

"Armed?"

"Armed."

"Not your friends?"

"Definitely not."

"How long have they been watching us?"

"They've been prowling around us since yesterday morning."

Henri looked at Flor with mistrust, and I myself couldn't resist suspecting
her. Why hadn't she warned us? She anticipated our reaction. "At first I thought
they were travelers like you. They were following the old road west. Many of
our hidalgos do that. It's mostly the common people who use the new roads.
Their actions have only seemed suspicious to me since we came into the moun-

tains. I didn't warn you because from here on they'll be ahead of us, and on a road where we won't meet them anymore."

She explained that the old road, now abandoned because it was too diffi-cult, ran on the north side of Baladron, whereas ours bent more and more to the south as it approached the canyons. The two roads met at only one place, called El Paso de los Rapadores, well beyond the gypsy camp. And indeed as we went further into the mountains we no longer saw those fantastical silhouettes stand-ing out against the scarlet sky. The rocks were deserted as far as the eye could see, and nothing moved except the beech trees shaking in the wind.

IV. In Which Flor Casts a Spell

Night was falling. We no longer worried about those mysterious prowlers: deep ravines and impassable gorges now separated them from us. All our attention was focused on our mule, whose legs could barely make it up the road. It was nearly dark when Flor cried out with joy, and we knew our struggles were over. A magnificent spectacle met our eyes. For several minutes we rode between two high ridges that hid the horizon and the sky, like two enormous ramparts. The rain had stopped. A northwest wind swept the clouds away and left a clear sky, as always clearer after rain. The moon bathed the ground in white light.

Coming through the pass, we found ourselves in a sort of circular valley surrounded by sharp peaks on which grew a few patches of mountain pines: this was La Taza del Diablillo, the Goblin's Teacup, in the middle of Cerro del Baladron, whose highest peaks lie around it, looking toward the Escurial. At that moment La Taza del Diablillo seemed like a bottomless pit. The moonlight shining on the peaks around the Teacup left the valley in shadow and gave it a frightening depth. Facing us we saw another narrow pass, like the one from which we were now emerging, so that each was the continuation of the other; the Teacup between them must be the result of some great geological convulsion.

Around a fire sat men and women, their thin, strong features reddened by its glow, which also lit the nearby rocks, while pale moonlight shone on the damp slopes. We were spotted as soon as we came out of the pass. Those primitive people have sharper senses than we do. The drinking and smoking and talking continued around the fire, but two scouts ran off left and right. Flor pointed them out a moment later as they crept across the valley toward us. She gave a special cry, and the scouts stopped. At a second cry they turned around and went calmly back to their places by the fire. We were still far away. For a moment I thought I saw dark shadows move behind the sparkling sequined circle of gypsies—but by now I'd seen enough tricks of the light in the mountains, so I kept quiet, and as we drew closer I saw nothing more. I wish to God I'd spoken up!

We'd reached about the middle of the valley when a big swarthy fellow rose from the fireside holding a gun of extraordinary length. He hailed us in an Eastern tongue, and Flor replied in the same language.

"Welcome!" said the man with the gun. "Since our sister has brought you, we'll offer you bread and salt."

The gypsies of Spain, and in general all the gypsy bands living outside the law in the various kingdoms of Europe, enjoy a well-deserved reputation for hospitality. The bloodiest bandit honors his guest—even in Italy, where bandits are worse than lions and hyenas. By common understanding, once we'd been offered bread and salt we had nothing more to fear. They made us welcome. Flor kissed the chief's knees, and he solemnly blessed her with his powerful hands. Then he ordered brandy to be poured into a wooden cup, and presented it with great ceremony to Henri, who drank. The circle closed once more around the fire. A gypsy girl got up and sang and danced inside the circle, playing with the flames and making her scarf flutter over the fire.

Ten minutes later Henri cried out in a hoarse, altered voice, "Villains! What did you put in this wine?" He tried to rise, but his legs wobbled, and he fell heavily to the ground. I thought my heart had stopped beating. On the ground Henri struggled against the numbness that hobbled all his limbs. His heavy eyelids began to close. Around the fire the gypsies laughed silently. Large dark shapes loomed behind them: five or six men wrapped in cloaks, their faces hidden by their hat brims. They weren't gypsies. When Henri stopped struggling I thought he was dead, and I prayed to God for my own death.

One of the cloaked men tossed a heavy purse into the middle of the circle. "Finish the job and you'll get double!" I didn't recognize his voice.

"We need time and distance," said the gypsy chief. "Twelve hours and twelve miles. Death cannot be given in the same place or on the same day as hospitality."

The man shrugged. "Nothing but mumbo-jumbo! Get to work, or leave it to us!" He moved toward Henri, still sprawled on the ground.

The gypsy chief barred his way. "Until twelve hours have passed, until we've gone twelve miles," he said firmly, "we'll protect our guest, even against the king!"

Strange beliefs! A strange code of honor! All of the gypsies surrounded Henri. Flor murmured in my ear, "I'll save you both, or I'll die trying!"

That night I slept in the gypsy chief's tent, on a canvas sack stuffed with dried moss. The chief slept nearby, with his gun on one side and his scimitar on the other. By the lamplight I could see that his eyes remained half open, as if watching even while he slept. A snoring gypsy nestled at his feet like a dog. I didn't know where they'd put Henri, and God knows I didn't dare close my own eyes. I was guarded by an old gypsy woman acting as my jailer. She lay cross-ways, her head on my shoulder; and she took the extra precaution of clasping my right hand between hers as she slept. That wasn't all: outside I could hear two sentinels pacing.

An hour after midnight, by the hourglass, I heard a slight noise from the tent opening. I turned to look, and that simple movement made my duenna open her eyes. Grumbling, she woke halfway. I saw nothing, and the noise stopped. But soon I heard only one sentinel's footsteps. A few minutes later, the other sentinel also stopped pacing. Total silence fell around the tent. The tent flap moved, then rose slowly, and a smiling mischievous face appeared: it was Flor. She nodded to me. She wasn't afraid. Her lithe, slender body followed her head inside. When she stood up, her fine black eyes shone triumphantly. "The hard part's done!" she mouthed.

I hadn't been able to suppress a slight movement of surprise, and my duenna had woken again. For two or three minutes Flor didn't move, holding a finger to her lips. The duenna fell back asleep. I thought it would take magic for me to free my shoulder and my hand. I was right: my dear Flor was magical. She took one careful step, then another—not toward me, but toward the mat where the chief slept between his gun and his scimitar. She stood before him and stared fixedly at him for a moment. His breathing grew quieter. She bent over him and pressed her thumbs and index fingers lightly to his temples. His eyelids closed. Flor looked at me, her eyes like a shower of sparks. "One down!" she mouthed.

The gypsy at the chief's feet was still snoring, with his head on his knees. Flor put her hand on his forehead and gave him the same commanding stare. Little by little his legs stretched out and his head fell back to the ground; he looked dead. "Two down!" mouthed Flor.

Only my dreaded duenna was left. Flor took more care with her. Slowly, slowly, she drew near, watching her like a snake trying to hypnotize a bird. When she was within reach, she stretched out one hand above the gypsy woman's eyes. The old woman shuddered and tried to rise. Flor said, "I won't let you!" The woman sighed heavily. Flor's hand moved from her forehead to her stomach and stopped there. She extended one finger, from which seemed to flow some mysterious fluid. Through the duenna's body, still touching mine, I myself could feel the strange effect of that fluid. My eyes began to close.

"Stay awake!" ordered Flor with a queen's glare. The shadows already dancing around my eyes vanished. But I thought I was dreaming. Flor's hand moved once again to the woman's forehead, and she aimed her finger between her eyes. The old woman's body slumped, and I felt her weight on me. Flor stood erect, serious, commanding. Her hand dropped and rose again. After two or three minutes she came closer and made a sudden spraying gesture over the old woman's head, which lay on me like a lead weight. "Are you asleep, Mabel?" asked Flor quietly.

"Yes, I'm asleep," said the old woman. My first thought was that she was joking.

Before we reached the gypsy camp, Flor had taken a snippet of my hair and of Henri's hair and put them into a small locket she wore around her neck. Now she opened the locket and put Henri's hair into the old woman's inert hand. "Tell me where he is." The woman stirred and grumbled. I was afraid she'd wake up. Flor kicked her roughly, to show me how deep asleep she was. Then she said again, "You hear me, Mabel? Tell me where he is."

"I hear you," said the old gypsy. "I'm looking for him. What is this place? A cave? A cellar? They've taken away his cloak and his doublet. Ah!" She shivered. "I see what it is! It's a tomb!"

The sweat froze in all my pores.

"But is he alive?" asked Flor.

"He's alive," said Mabel. "He's sleeping."

"And where is this tomb?"

"North of here. Where they buried old Hadji two years ago. The man is resting his head against Hadji's bones."

"Tell me how to get to that tomb."

"North of the camp. The first gap in the rocks. Three steps to go down, one stone to lift."

"And how do I wake him?"

"You have your dagger."

Flor casually dropped Mabel's head onto the sack of moss. The old woman lay there like a lump. I was astonished to see that her eyes were wide open. "Come!" said Flor. We left the tent. Around the dying fire a circle of gypsies lay asleep. Flor had taken the lantern, which she covered with her cloak. She pointed to another tent further away. "That's where the Christians are." She meant the ones who wanted to murder poor Henri!

We walked north from the camp. Along the way, Flor had me untie three little Galician horses that were browsing on the lower branches of the trees with their halters secured to stakes. The gypsies never use mules. After a few paces we found the gap between two rocks, and went through it. Three steps carved in the granite led down to the entrance of a cave, which was blocked by a big stone it took both of us to move aside. Behind the stone, lamplight revealed Henri, half-dressed, dead asleep, lying on the damp ground with his head resting on a human skeleton. I ran to him and threw my arms around his neck and called to him. Nothing!

Behind us Flor said, "You love him a lot, Aurore, and you'll love him even more!"

"Wake him up! Wake him up! In God's name, wake him up!"

She put down the lamp and took both of Henri's hands. "My spell has no power here. He drank a Scottish gypsy psaw. He'll sleep until hot steel touches the palms of his hands and the soles of his feet."

"Hot steel!" I echoed uncomprehendingly.

"Quick! Now I'm risking my own life as well as both of yours!" Flor lifted her Basque overskirt, and from the pleats of her skirt, whose hem was lined with bits of sewn-in lead to weigh it down, she drew a small bone-handled dagger. "Take off his shoes!"

I obeyed automatically. Henri was wearing sandals with gaiters. My hands were shaking so much I couldn't untie the straps.

"Quick! Quick!" said Flor, holding the point of her little dagger in the flame of the lamp to redden it. I heard a brief sizzling noise: it was the burning dagger piercing the palm of one of Henri's hands. After another pass through the flame, the blade pierced his other hand. He didn't move. "The soles of his feet!" cried Flor. "Quick! Quick! He has to feel the pain in all four at once." The knife blade passed through the flame again. Flor began to sing in her unknown tongue. When she pierced Henri's feet his lips twitched.

"I owed the kind young lord that much," she said as she watched for him to wake. "And you too, laughing Aurore! Without you I'd have died of hunger. Without me you'd never have come this way: I'm the one who drew you into the trap."

The Scottish witch's psaw is made from the sap of the curly red lettuce the Spanish call *lechuga pequeña,* along with a little distilled tobacco and a simple extract of field poppies. It's a devastating soporific. As for how to bring an end to that sleep, Mother, I'm just telling you what I witnessed. According to Flor, without that gypsy song the piercing with a hot knife would do nothing. In the same way, in the Hungarian tales she told so well, the crystal door to the cave protecting the treasure of Buda can't be opened if the one carrying the magic thimble doesn't also know the enchanted words: *mara moradno.*

When Henri opened his eyes I was kissing his brow. He looked around in confusion. He gave us both a thin, pale smile. When his eyes fell on the skeleton of old Hadji he recovered his usual seriousness. "Ah! So this is the companion they chose for me. In a month we'd have made a matched pair."

"Let's go!" cried Flor. "By sunrise we must be out of the mountains."

Henri was already on his feet. The little horses were waiting for us at the opening to the gap in the rocks. Flor led the way, because she'd been here before. By moonlight we began to climb the heights of Baladron. At dawn we could see the Escurial, and in the evening we reached Madrid. I was happy, because Flor would stay with us. After what she'd done, she could no longer return to her people. Henri said to me, "Dear Aurore, you'll have a sister."

For a month all went well. Flor had asked to be taught the Christian religion, and she was baptized at the Convent of the Incarnation and had her First Communion with me in the children's chapel. She was sincerely pious in her own way. But the nuns of the Incarnation, on whom she depended as a convert, wanted a different kind of piety. My poor Flor, or rather Maria de la Santa Cruz, couldn't give them what she didn't have. One morning she appeared again in her old gypsy clothes.

Henri smiled. "Sweet bird, you've waited a long time to fly away."

I wept, because I loved my dear little Flor, Mother—I loved her with all my heart! When she kissed me goodbye she had tears in her eyes too, but she couldn't help what she was doing. She left promising to return. Alas! That same night I saw her on the Plaza Santa, in the middle of a crowd of common people, dancing with a tambourine and telling the fortunes of passersby.

We lived behind the Calle Real, on a little street whose modest-looking doors opened onto large splendid gardens. (It must be because I'm French, Mother, that here in Paris I don't miss the wonderful climate of Spain.) We didn't lack money. Right away Henri had found his place among the top metalworkers in Madrid. He wasn't yet so renowned that he could easily make a fortune, but the best armorers appreciated his skills. It was a peaceful, happy time. Flor visited in the mornings, and we talked. She was sorry not to live with me anymore, but when I suggested she come back to her old life she ran away laughing.

Once Henri said to me, "Aurore, that child isn't the right friend for you."

I don't know what happened, but Flor's visits grew rarer and rarer, and we acted colder to each other. When Henri speaks, my heart obeys: things and people he no longer likes stop pleasing me too. Isn't that the way to love someone, Mother? Poor dear Flor! If I saw her now, I still wouldn't be able to keep from throwing myself into her arms.

Mother, I should tell you about something that happened just before Henri went away—because I was about to experience the worst suffering of my life: he was going to leave me, and I'd have to be by myself and go a long time without seeing him. Two years, Mother, two years: can you understand that? I'd woken every morning to my father's kiss; I'd never gone a day without seeing him. When I think back on those two years, they feel longer than all the rest of my life.

I knew Henri had put aside money for a journey. He was going to Germany and Italy. France alone was closed to him, and I didn't know why. And the reasons for his journey were also a secret. One morning when he'd gone out, as usual, I went into his room to tidy it. His desk—whose key he always carried—stood open. On the desktop lay a bundle of papers wrapped in an envelope yellowed with age. From the envelope hung two seals with the same signet: a coat of arms and a Latin motto, *adsum*. When I asked my confessor to translate it, he said, "Here I am." You remember, Mother, that when Henri came riding to my rescue in Benasque, as he threw himself on my kidnapers he cried, "Here I am! Here I am!" The envelope had a third seal that seemed to belong to a chapel or a church. I'd seen those papers once before: the day we fled from the farmhouse on the banks of the Arga, outside Pamplona, it was to retrieve that precious bundle that Henri went back to the house. When he found it unharmed he beamed with joy. I remembered all that.

Near the bundle, whose envelope bore no writing, lay some kind of list, written recently. I did wrong, and read it—alas! I wanted so badly to know why Henri was leaving me, Mother. The list consisted of nothing but names and places. I knew none of the names. No doubt they were people Henri planned to visit on his journey. Here was the list:

1. *Captain Lorrain, Naples*
2. *Staupitz, Nuremberg*
3. *Pinto, Turin*
4. *El Matador, Glasgow*
5. *Jugan, Morlaix*
6. *Faenza, Paris*

7. Saldaña, Paris.

Then came two more numbers without any names: 8 and 9.

V. In Which Aurore Has Dealings with a Little Marquis

I'm going to finish the story of that list, Mother. When Henri returned from his travels two years later, I saw the list again. Lots of names had been crossed out, no doubt of the people he'd managed to see. But two new names had been added on the blank lines. Number 1, Captain Lorrain, was crossed out. Number 2, Staupitz, was crossed out. Pinto as well, El Matador as well, Jugan too. Those five were crossed out in red ink. Faenza and Saldaña were still on the list. Number 8 now carried the name Peyrolles, and number 9 read Gonzague, both of them in Paris.

I'd gone two years without seeing Henri, Mother. What was he doing for those two years, and why did he always have to keep his actions a secret from me? Two centuries, two long centuries! I don't know how I survived so many days without him. If I were separated from him now, I'm sure I'd die. I'd been sent to the Convent of the Incarnation. The nuns were good to me, but they couldn't console me. All my happiness had fled with Henri—I could neither sing nor smile. Ah, but when I saw him again it made up for all my suffering. My long martyrdom was over! My dear father, my friend, my protector had come back to me, and I lacked even the words to tell him how happy I was.

After the first kiss he examined me, and I was surprised by the look on his face. "You're all grown up, Aurore, and I didn't expect to find you so beautiful."

So I was beautiful! He found me beautiful! Beauty's a gift from God, Mother, and I thanked God from my heart. I was sixteen or seventeen when Henri told me that. I didn't yet know how happy you can feel just hearing the words, "You're beautiful." He'd never said that to me before.

I left the Convent of the Incarnation that same day, and we went back to our old house. But everything there had changed. Now that I was a young lady, Henri and I would no longer live alone. At the house I found a good old woman, Françoise Berrichon, and her grandson Jean-Marie. When she saw me, old Françoise said, "She takes after him!"

Who was it I took after? No doubt there are things I'm not supposed to know, because no one's told me anything. I guessed right away, and felt even more strongly later, that Françoise Berrichon must be an old family servant. She must have known my father, she must have known you, Mother! How many times I tried to question her! But Françoise, usually so talkative, would fall silent when I brought up certain subjects. As for her grandson Jean-Marie, he's younger than I am and knows nothing.

I hadn't seen my dear Flor even once while I was at the Convent of the Incarnation. I searched for her as soon as I got out. They told me she'd left Madrid. It wasn't true, because a few days later I spotted her singing and dancing on the Plaza Santa. I complained to Henri, and he said, "We were wrong to de-

171

ceive you, Aurore. But we were right to keep you away from that poor girl. Remember, there are certain things that would alienate from you the people you should love."

So whom should I love? You, Mother, first and foremost! Well, would it displease you that I still felt affection for my first friend, and felt grateful to her for saving us from terrible danger? I can't believe that—that wouldn't be the you I love. Henri exaggerates your strictness: you're more good than you are proud. And I'll love you so much—my embraces will leave you no time to be stern!

So I was now a young lady. I had servants. Little Jean-Marie could pass for my pageboy. Old Françoise was a faithful companion. I was less lonely than before, but I was far from being as happy as before. Henri had changed: his manner was different; he was always cold and often sad. It seemed like a wall had risen between us. As I've told you, Mother, it was impossible to get an explanation from him. He kept secrets even from me. I could tell he was suffering, and he got relief from his work. People came from all around asking for his help. We were well off, almost rich. The armorers of Madrid bid for the services of El Cincelador, the engraver. Medina-Sidonia, favorite of King Philip V, had said, "I have three swords. The first is decorated with gold, and I'll give it to a friend. The second is decorated with diamonds, and I'll give it to my mistress. The third is only burnished steel—but since El Cincelador engraved it, I'll give it to no one but the king!"

Three months went by. I'd grown melancholy, and Henri saw it and was unhappy. My room looked out on the enormous gardens behind the Calle Real. The largest and finest of those gardens belonged to the old villa of the Duke of Osuna, who'd been killed in a duel by Señor de Favas, a gentleman serving the queen. Since the death of its master the villa had stood empty. One day I noticed the blinds had been raised. Fine furniture was brought in to fill the empty rooms, and rich curtains were hung at the windows. New flowers were planted in the abandoned garden. The villa had a new tenant. I was as curious as any shut-in; I wanted to know his name. When I learned it, I was struck: the new occupant of the Villa Osuna was named Philippe of Mantua, Prince of Gonzague. Gonzague! I'd seen that name on Henri's list: the second of the names added during the trip, the last of the four that remained—Faenza, Saldaña, Peyrolles, and Gonzague. I assumed Henri was a friend of the great lord, and I might meet him.

The next day Henri had blinds installed on my windows, which till then had been without. "Aurore, please don't show yourself to anyone who might go walking in that garden."

I'll admit, Mother, after that prohibition I was more curious than ever. It wasn't hard to find out more about the Prince of Gonzague: everyone was talking about him. He was one of the richest men in France, and the Regent's particular friend. He'd come to Madrid on a private mission. He carried the rank of ambassador, and brought courtiers with him.

Every morning little Jean-Marie came to tell me the talk of the neighborhood. The prince was handsome, the prince had beautiful mistresses, the prince was throwing millions out the window. His friends were all feckless young men, the kind who went around Madrid by night, climbing balconies, smashing street lamps, breaking down doors, beating up girls' guardians. One of them was barely eighteen, a little demon named the Marquis of Chaverny. People said he had such gentle manners, and looked as sweet and rosy as a girl, with long blond hair above a pale brow, beardless cheeks, and eyes as mischievous as any girl's. He was the worst of them all! That cherub troubled the hearts of all the señoritas of Madrid.

Through the slits in my blinds I could sometimes see, under the shady trees in the beautiful Osuna gardens, an elegant young gentleman, a little effeminate in manner—but he couldn't be that gremlin Chaverny! This little gentleman looked so modest, so well-behaved! He went walking early in the morning, whereas that Chaverny must be a late riser after staying out all night doing mischief. My little gentleman—whether seated on a bench, or stretched out on the lawn, or strolling thoughtfully with his head bowed—almost always had a book in his hand. A studious boy! Whereas that Chaverny would never have been encumbered by a book. It was impossible. My little gentleman was the exact opposite of the Marquis of Chaverny, unless rumor had terribly slandered the marquis... Rumor had done no such thing, and yet my little gentleman was certainly the Marquis of Chaverny. That imp, that demon! If Henri weren't alive I think I might have fallen in love with him. He had a good heart, Mother, a good heart led astray by those who corrupted his youth, but still a noble, passionate, generous heart.

I think the breeze must once have lifted a corner of my blinds, because he saw me, and after that he was always in the garden. I must have kept him safe from lots of mischief! In the garden he was as gentle as a little saint. At the most, sometimes he was bold enough to kiss a flower he'd picked, and toss it toward my window. Once he brought a pea shooter and aimed at my window, and very skillfully shot a little note through the gap in the blinds. I have to say, Mother, it was a charming little note. He wanted to marry me, and said I'd be plucking a soul out of Hell. That would have been a good deed, so it was hard for me to keep from replying. But the thought of Henri stopped me, and I returned no sign of life. The poor little marquis waited a long time with his eyes fixed on my window. I saw him wipe away a tear. My heart was full, but I held firm.

That evening I was out on the balcony of the spiral turret attached to our house, at the corner of the Calle Real, overlooking the main street and a small side alley. I was waiting for Henri, who was late. Suddenly I heard low voices in the alley. I turned and saw two shadows along the wall: Henri and the little marquis. Soon their voices were raised.

"Do you know who you're talking to, friend?" said Chaverny haughtily. "My cousin is the Prince of Gonzague!"

At that name Henri's sword seemed to jump out of its scabbard all by itself. Chaverny drew as well, and stood en garde like a showoff. They seemed so mismatched I couldn't help crying out, "Henri! Henri! He's a child!" Henri immediately lowered his sword.

Chaverny bowed to me and said, "We'll meet again!"

When Henri came inside a moment later I barely recognized him. He looked shaken, and instead of speaking he paced the floor. Finally in a changed voice he said, "Aurore, I'm not your father."

I knew that. I thought he'd go on, and I was all ears. But he fell silent, and went back to pacing. He wiped the sweat from his brow.

"What's wrong, Henri?" I asked gently.

Instead of answering, he asked, "Do you know that gentleman?"

"No, Henri, I don't know him." I must have blushed a little, and yet it was the truth!

After a silence he went on, "Aurore, I asked you to keep your blinds shut." And then with a certain bitterness he added, "It wasn't for me, it was for you."

I was stung. "Have I done something wrong that I always have to hide like this?"

"Ah!" He put his face in his hands. "The time had to come! God have mercy on me!"

I understood only that I'd wounded him. Tears ran down my cheeks. "Henri, my friend, forgive me, forgive me!"

"Forgive you for what, Aurore?" He looked at me with sparkling eyes.

"For the suffering I've caused you, Henri. If you're upset, I must have done wrong."

He looked at me again. "It's time!" he murmured. Then he sat next to me. "Speak openly and fear nothing, Aurore. I want only one thing in this world: your happiness. Would you object to leaving Madrid?"

"With you?"

"With me."

"Anywhere you go, Henri," I said slowly, looking into his eyes, "I would go happily. I like Madrid because you're here."

He kissed my hand. "But," he said awkwardly, "what about that young man?"

I put my hand to my mouth to cover my laughter. "I forgive you, Henri, but don't say another word. And if you want, let's go."

His eyes grew moist. It took an effort for him not to open his arms to embrace me. He was afraid he might get carried away by his feelings, but in fact he has enormous self-control. He kissed my hand again and said with fatherly kindness, "Then if you don't object, Aurore, we'll leave tonight."

"And of course," I cried out with real anger, "this is for my sake and not for yours!"

"For you, and not for me." He got up to leave.

When he was gone I dissolved in tears. "He doesn't love me, he'll never love me! And yet..." Alas, how hard we work to fool ourselves! "He loves me like a daughter. He loves me for my own sake, and not to have me for himself." I was dying young.

We planned to leave at ten that night. I was to go in a post chaise with Françoise. Henri would escort us, along with four bodyguards; he was rich now. While I was packing my bags I saw that the Osuna gardens were lit up. The Prince of Gonzague was throwing a big party that night. I felt sad and discouraged, and it occurred to me that the sparkling pleasures of the world might distract me and ease my pain. You should know, Mother: do girls with broken hearts find relief by escaping into pleasures of that kind?

Now I'm finally coming to recent events—as recent as yesterday. Only a few months have passed since we left Madrid, but the time has felt long: something's come between Henri and me. Oh, how I wish I could pour out my heart to you, Mother!

We left Madrid as planned, while the orchestra was playing its first notes under the big orange trees in Gonzague's garden. Henri rode alongside. Through the carriage window he asked, "Will you miss anything here, Aurore?"

"I'll miss my friend Flor from long ago."

Our route had been planned out in advance. We were headed straight to Saragossa, and from there to the French border, meaning to cross the Pyrenees at Benasque and then go down toward Bayonne, from where we'd travel by sea to Ostend. Henri needed that detour into France: he had to make a stop in the Louron Valley, between Lux and Bagnères de Luchon.

Nothing happened between Madrid and Saragossa, nor between Saragossa and the border. Without our stop at the old castle of Caylus, after we crossed the mountains, I'd have nothing to report, Mother. But, though I can't say why, that visit was one of the most moving experiences of my life. I was in no danger to speak of. Nothing happened to me there. And yet if I live to be a hundred I'll still remember the feelings that place aroused in me.

Henri wanted to talk to an old priest, Father Bernard, who'd been chaplain of Caylus under the last lord of that name. Once we crossed the border we left Françoise and Jean-Marie at a little village on the banks of the Clarabide. We'd left our four bodyguards behind on the other side of the Pyrenees. Henri and I went on alone, on horseback, toward that strange eminence they call the Hachaz, on which the dismal castle stood. It was a February morning, dark and gloomy but without fog. The white summits of the snow-covered range we'd crossed the day before stood out against the dark sky like lacework on the horizon. The pale rays of the sun rising in the east lit up the rime-covered peaks. A west wind brought big slow clouds, hanging like a drab curtain behind the Pyrenees. Ahead of us, high on its giant pedestal against the pallid eastern sky, rose that colossus of black granite, the Castle of Caylus-Tarrides.

It would be hard to find a building that expressed more eloquently the dismal grandeur of the past. In former ages that murderous, pillaging castle stood there like a sentinel, watching travelers go by in the valley. In those days its mute cannons and silent arrow slits still spoke aloud; oaks didn't grow up through its broken towers; the ramparts didn't have that icy coat of damp ivy; the turrets still showed off their threatening crenelation, now hidden by a red or golden crown of tufted spiky snapdragon. Just the sight of it inspired a thousand melancholy awful thoughts. It was both grand and frightening. No one in that place can ever have been happy. And that country abounded in legends as black as ink. People said the last lord alone, known as Caylus the Jailer, murdered his two wives, his daughter, his son-in-law, and more. And his ancestors before him had done their best to equal that.

We reached the Hachaz plateau by a narrow, winding road that ended at what used to be the drawbridge. No drawbridge survived, just the ruins of a wooden footbridge whose rotten beams hung down into the moat. At one end of the bridge stood a small alcove with a shrine to the Virgin. Caylus Castle was now uninhabited, except by a watchman, a grumbling old man, half deaf and totally blind, and hostile at first. He said the current owner, who hadn't visited the castle in sixteen years, was the Prince of Gonzague. (You notice, Mother, how that name had seemed to follow me recently.) The old man told Henri that Father Bernard, the old chaplain of Caylus, had been dead several years. He wouldn't let us see inside the castle.

I thought we would head back down to the valley, but we didn't, and I soon realized that this place evoked in Henri some tragic, touching memory. We had lunch in the village of Tarrides, near the moat. The house closest to the edge of the moat, and to the ruined footbridge I mentioned, was a tavern. We sat on two stools at a shabby beechwood table, and a middle-aged woman came out to wait on us. Henri looked at her carefully. "Ma'am, were you already working here the night of the murder?"

She dropped the jug of wine she was holding, and looked at him suspiciously. "Oh ho! For that matter, weren't you there too?"

My blood ran cold, but I was consumed by curiosity. What had happened here?

"Could be," said Henri, "but that's no business of yours, ma'am. There are a few things I want to know, and I can pay."

She picked up the jug and mumbled, "We double-locked our doors and shutters. It was best not to see what was going on."

"How many bodies did they find in the moat the next day?"

"Seven, counting the young lord."

"And the law came?"

176

"The bailiff from Argelès, and the lieutenant from Tarbes, and others. Yes, yes, the law came, the law always comes, but then it looks away. The judges said the old man was in the right, because that little window was found open." She pointed to a low window in the wall of the moat itself, under the rotting bridge. I understood that the officers suspected the late young lord of having tried to get into the castle that way. But why? The barmaid answered my unspoken question. "And because our young lady was rich."

A sad story told in few words. That low window fascinated me. I couldn't take my eyes off it. No doubt it was used for a lovers' rendezvous. I pushed away my wooden plate, and Henri did the same. He paid for our meal and we left the tavern. The road leading to the moat passed by the front door. We followed it, and the barmaid followed us. "There," she said, pointing to one of the posts that held up the bridge on the castle side, "That's where the young lord set down his child."

"Ah!" I cried. "There was child!"

Henri gave me an extraordinary look I still can't define. Sometimes the simplest thing I say provokes sudden unexplained emotions in him, and that prompts my imagination to run wild. I've spent my life looking in vain for the key to all the enigmas that surround me. Mother, people make fun of poor orphans who see clues to their birth everywhere. To me that instinct seems both deeply moving and a blessing. Yes! It's our job to search without end, and never to give up on the difficult ungrateful task. If the obstacle we've lifted halfway falls back on us and knocks us down, we have to get up again even stronger. The hour despair prevails is the hour of our death. How many times before that hour must hope be cheated! How many chimeras, how many disappointments!

Henri's expression seemed to say, "Aurore, that child was you!" My heart pounded, and I looked up at the castle with new eyes. But then he asked the woman, "What became of the child?"

And she answered, "Dead!"

VI. While Setting the Table

The bottom of the moat was a meadow. From there, beyond the broken arch of the wooden bridge, the sloping lip of the moat revealed the village of Tarrides and the first trees of the Ens Forest. To the right, the pointed, ornate steeple of the Caylus Castle chapel rose above the ramparts. Henri gave the landscape a long and melancholy look. Sometimes he seemed to be orienting himself. He drew in the grass with his sword. His lips moved as if he were talking to himself. Finally he pointed to where I stood and cried, "There—it must be there!"

"Yes," said the barmaid, "that's where we found the young lord's body lying."

I stepped back, shivering from head to foot.

"What happened to the body?" asked Henri.

"I heard they took it to Paris to be buried in the cemetery of Saint Magloire."

"Yes," he mused aloud, "Saint Magloire was a fief of Lorraine."

So, Mother, that poor young lord, killed that awful night, was of the noble house of Lorraine. Henri stood with his head lowered, lost in thought. Now and then he glanced sidelong at me. He tried to climb the little staircase by the end of the bridge, but the rotten steps gave under his weight. He came back to the rampart, and with the pommel of his sword he tested the shutters covering the low window.

The barmaid was following him around like a tour guide. "Solid and reinforced with iron. It's never been opened since the day the magistrates were here."

"And what did you hear that night through your closed shutters, ma'am?"

"Ah! Good Lord, sir, all the demons of Hell seemed to have been unleashed in the moat. We couldn't sleep. The bandits had been drinking at our place during the day. When I went to bed I said, 'May God have mercy on those who won't see the sun rise!' We heard a great racket of steel and shouts and curses, and from time to time two men shouting, 'Here I am!'"

Thoughts crowded in on me, Mother. I knew that motto. Since childhood I'd heard Henri say it, and I'd found it again in Latin on the seals that closed the mysterious envelope he treasured. Henri was mixed up in this story somehow. Only he could explain it to me.

The sun was setting as we headed back down to the valley. My heart was full. I often turned around to look back at the gloomy granite giant standing on its enormous base. That night I saw phantoms: a woman in mourning carrying a small child in her arms and bending over a pale young man with an open wound in his side. Was that you, Mother?

178

The next day, on board the ship taking us across the Bay of Biscay and up the Channel to Flanders, Henri said, "Soon you'll know everything, Aurore. I hope to God it makes you happier!" His voice was sad. Could it be that knowing my family would make me unhappy? Even so, I want to know you, Mother.

We landed at Ostend. In Brussels Henri received a large letter sealed with the crest of France. The next day we set off for Paris. It was already dark when we reached the victory arch on the Flanders road that marks the edge of the great city. I rode in the chaise with Françoise, with Henri on horseback ahead of us. I was lost in my own thoughts, Mother. Something told me you were here. You're in Paris, Mother, I'm sure of it. I recognize the air you breathe.

We rode down a long street flanked by tall gray houses, then into a narrow alleyway that led to a church surrounded by a cemetery. I now know it was the church and cemetery of Saint Magloire. Across from it stood a proud, noble mansion, the Villa Gonzague. Henri dismounted and offered me his hand. We entered the cemetery. Behind the church, in an area enclosed by a simple wooden fence, stood an open rotunda containing several monumental tombs. We passed through the fence. A lantern hanging from the vault feebly lit the rotunda. Henri stopped in front of a marble mausoleum on which was carved the image of a young man. Henri kissed the forehead of the image, and said with tears in his voice, "Brother, here I am. God is my witness that I've done my best to carry out my promise."

I heard a slight noise behind us and turned. Old Françoise Berrichon and her grandson Jean-Marie knelt in the grass beyond the fence. Henri too had knelt. He prayed long and silently. When he rose he said, "Kiss this image, Aurore." I did so, and asked why. He opened his mouth to answer, then hesitated. Finally he said, "Because he was a noble heart, and because I loved him!" I kissed the figure's icy marble brow again. Henri thanked me by pressing my hand to his heart. How he loves, when he loves, Mother! Maybe it's fated that he can never love me.

A few minutes later we reached the house where I'm writing you these lines, Mother. Henri had rented it in advance. Since I first crossed the threshold I've never left. I'm more alone now than ever, because Henri is busier in Paris than he was elsewhere. I barely see him at mealtimes. I'm forbidden to go out. I have to be careful even when I sit at the window. Ah, if he were jealously possessive, Mother, how happily I'd obey him, and veil myself and hide myself and keep myself for him! But I remember what he said in Madrid: "It's not for my sake, it's for yours." It's not for him—you can only feel jealous about someone you love.

I'm alone. Through the closed curtains I watch the busy, noisy crowd. All those people are free. I watch the houses across the street. On every floor there's a family, and young women with beautiful smiling children. They're happy. I can also see the windows of the Palais-Royal, which are often lit up in the evening for the Regent's parties. The ladies of the court go by in their chaises with fine gentlemen riding alongside. I hear dance music. Sometimes I don't sleep all night. But if only he caresses me, if he speaks a single affectionate word, I forget all that, Mother, and I'm happy.

I sound like I'm complaining. Don't think I lack for anything, Mother. Henri overwhelms me with generosity and consideration. If he has acted cold toward me for some time now, is that a crime? Here's a thought I've sometimes had, Mother: since I know Henri's gallant, sensitive nature, I've wondered whether my rank is higher than his, and my wealth greater. That separates us. He's afraid to love me. Oh, if I could be sure of that, I'd renounce my fortune and throw aside my title! What use is birth compared to the joys of the heart? Would I love you less, Mother, if you were poor?

Day before yesterday, the hunchback came to see him. But I haven't yet mentioned that mysterious dwarf, the only person who's allowed into our solitude. This hunchback visits at all hours—that is, he visits Henri, in the room upstairs. We see him come and go. The neighbors think he's some kind of goblin. He and Henri are inseparable, but they never go out together! That's the gossip on the Rue du Chantre. It's the oddest, most mysterious friendship ever: even Françoise, Jean-Marie, and I have never seen those two inseparable friends together. They spend all day closeted together in that room upstairs, then one of them goes out while the other stays behind to guard some unknown treasure. It's been going on since about two weeks after we got here, and in spite of Henri's promises I know nothing more than I did at the beginning.

Anyway, I wanted to tell you, Mother: the other evening the hunchback came to see Henri, and didn't leave. They were shut up together all night. The next morning Henri seemed even sadder than usual. Over breakfast the conversation turned to great lords and ladies. Henri said bitterly, "People who are too high up are liable to vertigo. You can't count on the gratitude of princes." He lowered his eyes. "Anyway, what service can you pay for with that vile currency, gratitude? If a noble lady for whom I'd risked my honor and my life couldn't love me, because she was high and I was low, I'd go so far away I'd never know whether she was insulting me with her gratitude."

I'm sure the hunchback had been talking to him about you, Mother. Well, it's true: he risked his honor and his life for your daughter. He did more, much more: he gave your daughter eighteen years of his proud youth. What could repay such extraordinary generosity? But he's mistaken, Mother, isn't he? Since in fact you'll love him, wouldn't you then despise me if all my heart—except the part reserved for you—weren't his? I don't dare say it to him, because something holds me back. I've grown as shy as when I was a child, but in a different way. But that wouldn't just be ingratitude, it would be treachery! I'm his; he saved me, he raised me—what would I be without him? Nothing but a little dust at the bottom of a pauper's grave. And what mother—even a duchess and a cousin to the king—what mother wouldn't be proud to have the Chevalier Henri de Lagardère—the handsomest, the bravest, the most honest of men—for a son-in-law? Of course I'm just a lowly girl: I'm not acquainted with the mighty of the earth and I can't judge them. But could there be among those great lords and ladies a heart so lost, a soul so damned, as to say to me, "Aurore, forget Henri"?

But I've just had a silly thought, Mother, one that'll drive me mad and leave me in a cold sweat: if my mother—but God keep me from uttering my thoughts—it would feel like blasphemy. No! You're just the way I've dreamt of you and adored you, Mother. You'll kiss me and smile at me. No matter how exalted a name heaven has given you, you have something greater than your name, and that's your heart. That thought I had is an insult to you, and I kneel before you to beg your pardon.

But now the daylight's fading. I'll put down my pen and close my eyes to see your gentle face the way I see it in my dreams. Come to me, beloved Mother, come!

Those were the last words in Aurore's manuscript. Those pages were her dearest companion, and she loved them. As she put them back in their box she said, "See you tomorrow!"

Night had fallen. Lights came on in the houses across the Rue Saint Honoré. The door opened gently, and the naive figure of Jean-Marie Berrichon stood silhouetted against the lamplight from the next room. Berrichon was the son of the little page whom we met in the first part of this story, the one who brought Nevers's letter to Lagardère. That page had died a soldier, and his mother had no one left but her grandson. "Our miss," said Jean-Marie, "Grandma wants to know, should she set the table here or in the big room."

Aurore roused herself with a start. "What time has it gotten to be?"

"Suppertime, our miss."

How late Henri is, she thought. Aloud she said, "Set the table here."

"Good enough, our miss." Berrichon brought the lamp and set it on the mantelpiece.

From the kitchen, at the far end of the main room, Françoise called in her deep masculine voice, "The curtains aren't closed all the way, little one. Close them."

The boy obeyed, shrugging a little and grumbling, "You'd think we were scared of the neighbors." Like Aurore, he knew nothing and wanted to know everything.

"Are you sure he didn't come back by way of the staircase?" asked Aurore.

"Sure? Who can be sure of anything around here? I saw the hunchback come in a while ago. I went to listen."

"You shouldn't have!" said Aurore sternly.

"Just to find out if Master Louis was back! Not snooping."

"And you heard nothing?"

"Less than nothing." He spread the tablecloth on the table.

"Where can he have gone?" she wondered.

"Heck—only the hunchback knows that, our miss, and I have to say it's pretty odd to see a fine upright man like the chevalier, I mean Master Louis, hanging around with a little cripple as twisted up as a corkscrew. The rest of us don't have a clue what's going on, that's for sure. He comes and goes by that back door."

"But isn't that his right, as the master?"

"As for that, he's the master. The master of coming, the master of going, the master of locking himself up with his little monkey, and he doesn't seem to mind. But the neighbors do gossip, our miss."

"You talk too much to the neighbors, Berrichon."

"Me?" cried the boy. "God above, now I'm a blabbermouth! Thanks!" He put his blond head through the doorway. "Hey Grandma, now I'm a blabber-mouth!"

"Nothing new there, little one," said the old woman, "and a lazybones too."

He crossed his arms. "Well, all right then! Go ahead and hang me, since I've got every vice—the sooner the better. I, who've never ever said a word to anyone! I listen to people as I pass by, that's all. Is that a sin? And they're talking about us, I promise you! But as for getting drawn into conversation with those shopkeepers—come on! I know my place." Then he went on more quietly, "But I'll admit, it's hard to hold back when everybody's plying you with questions."

"So they've been asking you questions, Berrichon?"

"Lots, our miss."

"What kind of questions?"

"Awkward questions."

"Well?" said Aurore impatiently. "Like what?"

He began to laugh naively. "They've asked me everything. Who we are, what we're doing here, where we come from, where we're going, how old you are, how old the chevalier is, I mean Master Louis, if we're Catholic, if we plan to stay here, if we didn't like it where we came from, if we fast on Fridays and Saturdays, and if your confessor, our miss, is at Saint Eustache or at Saint Germain l'Auxerrois." He took a breath and kept going. "This and that and so forth and so on, why we chose to come live on the Rue du Chantre instead of somewhere else, why you never go out—and about that, Mother Moyneret the midwife made a bet with Mother Guichard that you only have one good leg—why Master Louis goes out all the time, why the hunchback—Oh! That hunchback intrigues them! Old Mother Balahault says he looks like someone who does business with the Evil One."

"And you get involved in all this gossip, Berrichon!"

"That's where you're wrong, our miss. Nobody keeps himself to himself like I do. But you should hear them, the women most of all. My God, the women! I can't even set foot in the street without getting my ears warmed. The street cleaner from across the way calls out, 'Hey, Berrichon, little cherub! Come over

182

here and try some of my cider!' Not likely! And the big woman at the greasy spoon says, 'Well, well, I bet the little angel would like some soup!' And the butter-maker! And the one who mends old furs! Even the attorney's wife! I just pass by as proud as an apothecary's valet. Guichard and Moyneret and Balahault the street cleaner from across the way and the butter-maker and the fur-mender and all the rest of them are wasting their time. But they never learn.

"Just listen up a little to how they are, our miss. It'll make you laugh. Here's Mother Balahault, the dark skinny one with glasses on the end of her nose." Berrichon switched to falsetto. "'The girl's a cutie and she's got a nice figure!'—she's talking about you—'You say she's twenty, darling?'" He switched back to his normal voice. "'I have no idea.'" Then, in falsetto once again, "'For a cutie, she's a cutie!'—this is Mother Moyneret babbling—'and you wouldn't think she's the niece of a simple metalworker. And is she really his niece, sweetheart?'" Baritone Berrichon, "'No!'" Tenor Berrichon, "'Then she must be his daughter. Right, darling?' 'No!' And I try to move on, our miss. But not a chance! They form a circle around me: Guichard, Durand, Morin, Bertrand. 'But if she's not his daughter, is she his wife?' No. 'His little sister?' No. 'What? What? Neither his wife nor his sister nor his daughter nor his niece! Then she must be an orphan he took in and raised out of charity.' No, no, no!" and by now Berrichon was shouting.

Aurore put her beautiful white hand on his arm. "That wasn't right, Berrichon," she said gently and sadly. "You lied to them. I am an orphan he took in and raised out of charity."

"Really?!"

"Next time they ask you, that's what you should tell them. I'm not ashamed. Why hide my friend's good deeds?"

"But, our miss..."

"And am I not a poor abandoned child?" she mused. "Without him, without his good deeds—"

"The truth is," cried Berrichon, "Master Louis, as we're supposed to call him, would be furious if he heard you now! Charity! Good deeds! For shame, miss!"

"I hope to God they say nothing else when they talk about him and me!" murmured Aurore, her lovely pale brow flushing.

Berrichon drew closer. "So you already know," he stammered.

"What?" She trembled.

"Heck, our miss..."

"Go ahead, Berrichon, I want to hear it." The boy still hesitated, and Aurore drew herself up. "I command you to speak. I'm waiting."

He lowered his eyes and awkwardly twisted the napkin in his hand. "Well—it's gossip, nothing but gossip! The women say, 'We understand! He's too young to be her father. He takes too many precautions to be her husband...'"

"Go on." Her pale face was damp with sweat.

"Heck, our miss—a man who's neither the father nor the brother nor the husband..."

Aurore buried her face in her hands.

VII. Master Louis

Aurore shook with sobs. Her head was lowered, and her beautiful hair fell onto her hands, while tears flowed through her fingers.

Jean-Marie Berrichon thought, "What if the master came in right now!"

When she straightened up, her eyes were still wet, but the color had come back to her cheeks. "A man who's neither the father nor the brother nor the husband of a poor abandoned child," she said slowly, "and whose name is Henri de Lagardère, is a friend and a savior and a benefactor." She clasped her hands and raised them to heaven. "Even their slander proves how far he is above other men. They only accuse him of what they themselves have done. I already love him, and they'll make me worship him like a god."

"That's right, our miss. Worship him if only to drive them crazy!"

"Henri," she murmured, "the only person in the world who protected me and loved me!"

"Oh, as for loving you," said the boy as he went back to his long-neglected chore of setting the table, "no doubt about that, and you heard it from me. We see it every morning. 'Did she have a good night? Did she sleep well? Did you keep her company yesterday? Is she sad? Does she need anything?' And whenever we notice something you want, it makes him so happy. Heck, as far as loving you goes, there's no doubt!"

"Yes," she said half to herself, "he's good, and he loves me like a daughter."

"And another way too," interjected Berrichon slyly.

She shook her head. Her heart longed so much to broach this subject that she considered neither the boy's age nor his rank. Berrichon, still setting the table, became her confidant. "I'm alone," she said, "always alone and sad."

"Bah! As soon as he comes back, our miss, you'll find your smile."

"Night has fallen, and I'm still waiting, and it's been this way every night since we came to Paris."

"Heck, that's just the way it is in the big city. There! The table's set, and not too badly either. Is supper ready, Grandma?"

"It's been ready at least an hour," came the answer from the kitchen in Françoise's deep voice.

Berrichon scratched his ear. "And I bet he's upstairs now, with that hunchbacked demon. It bothers me to see our miss upset like this. If I dared..." He crossed the room and set one foot on the bottom step of the stairs leading to Master Louis's rooms. "It's forbidden," he reflected. "I wouldn't like to see the chevalier as angry as he was that other time. Ye gods!"

He went back to Aurore. "Heck, our miss, why's he hiding anyway? It makes people talk. I know I'd talk if I was one of the neighbors, and even

185

though I'm no blabbermouth I'd be saying like everybody else, 'he's a conspirator,' or 'he's a sorcerer.'"

"Is that what they're saying?"

Instead of answering, the boy began to laugh. "Good Lord! If they knew what I know about what's up there: a bed, a trunk, two chairs, a sword hanging on the wall—that's it. I don't know about the room that's locked; I only saw one thing."

"What?" she asked eagerly.

"Oh, nothing much. One night he forgot to put on the cover that blocks the keyhole from inside, you know."

"I know. But you dared to look through the keyhole?"

"My God, our miss! I didn't mean any harm. I went up to call him for you, and light was shining through the keyhole. I put my eye to it."

"And what did you see?"

"I'm telling you: nothing special! The hunchback wasn't there. It was only Master Louis, sitting at a table. On the table was a box, the box he never leaves behind when he travels. I always wanted to know what's inside. Well! It would hold a lot of doubloons, but it's not doubloons Master Louis keeps in there, it's a bundle of papers, like a big square envelope with three seals in red wax hanging from it, each as big as an écu worth six livres."

Aurore recognized the description and said nothing.

"Well," he went on, "that bundle of papers almost cost me plenty. I guess I made a noise, though I'm light on my feet. He came to open the door. I only had time to throw myself down the stairs, and I landed on my back, and it still hurts when I touch it. I won't try that again—but you, our miss, you can get away with anything, you don't have to be afraid! I'll tell you what, I'd sure like to eat supper early enough to go see everybody arriving for the ball at the Palais-Royal. Couldn't you go upstairs and call him nicely?" She didn't answer. Berrichon may not have been talkative, but he went on, "Didn't you see the carts going by all day, carrying flowers and shrubberies and lanterns and pastries and liqueurs?" He licked his greedy lips. "It'll be beautiful! Ah, what I'd give just to get inside!"

"Go help your grandmother."

"Poor little miss," thought the boy as he withdrew. "She's dying to go dancing!"

Aurore rested her head pensively on her hand, but she was thinking neither of the ball nor of dancing. She said to herself, "Should I go call him? What's the point? I'm sure he's not there. Every day his absences get longer." She shivered. "It frightens me to think about it. The mystery appalls me. He forbids me to go out, to see anything, to have visitors. He keeps his name secret, he keeps his outings secret. I understand all that: it's the old danger come back, the never-ending threat that surrounds us, the murderers' veiled war against us. Who are they? They've shown they're powerful. They're relentless in pursuing him—or rather me. They only want to kill him because he protects me! And he tells me nothing, nothing! As if my heart couldn't guess it all, as if he could close these eyes that love him! He comes in, he accepts my kiss, he sits down, he does his best to smile. He can't see that his heart is bared to me, that with a glance I can read victory or defeat in his eyes. He doesn't trust me, he doesn't want me to know what he's done for me, the battle he's engaged in. My God! Doesn't he understand it's a thousand times harder for me to swallow my tears than it would be to share the work and fight by his side?"

She heard a sound from the main room, clearly a familiar one, because she leaped up, radiant, and opened her mouth to utter a cry of joy. The sound was the door at the top of the inside staircase opening. Berrichon was right: Aurore's beautiful maiden face now showed not a trace of tears or sign of sadness. She was all smiles. Her heart beat, but with happiness. Her drooping body rose graceful and lithe. She was a garden flower that wilts on its stem overnight and rises fresher and more scented with the first rays of sunshine. She jumped up and ran to her mirror—afraid of not being beautiful enough, cursing the tears that can cloud eyes and dim their diamond fire. Twice a day she was a coquette like this. But her mirror reassured her that her fears were in vain, and reflected such a young, tender, charming smile that she thanked God.

Master Louis came down the stairs. Berrichon stood at the bottom with a lamp to light his way. Whatever his actual age, Master Louis was a young man. His bouncing curly blond hair fell around a forehead as smooth as an adolescent's. The Spanish sun had done him no harm: he had the Gallic ivory complexion, and only his masculine features balanced and overcame his feminine coloration. His eyes of fire under the proud line of his eyebrows, his straight blunt nose, his mouth whose lips seemed carved in bronze and were shaded by a thin mustache, his strong chin, all gave his face an admirable look of forceful resolve. He was dressed—leggings, vest, doublet—entirely in black velvet, with matching jet buttons. He was bareheaded and wore no sword.

He was still near the top of the stairs when he began to look around for Aurore. When he found her he repressed a movement. He willed himself to lower his eyes, and though his feet wanted to hurry he slowed down. An observer who could see all and analyze all might deduce this man's secret at a glance. Master Louis spent his life inhibiting himself. He lived in the presence of happiness and wouldn't touch it. And he had a will of steel, stoic enough to quench the naturally tender, passionate, feminine fire of his heart. "Did you hear me coming, Aurore?" he said as he came down the stairs.

Françoise Berrichon poked her red face out the kitchen door and said in her stentorian drill sergeant's voice, "What were you thinking, Master Louis, to make the poor child cry like that!"

"Were you crying, Aurore?" He'd reached the bottom of the stairs.

She threw her arms around his neck. "Henri," she said, presenting her forehead to be kissed, "you know girls are foolish. Françoise is mistaken. I wasn't crying. Look at my eyes, Henri. Do you see any tears?" She smiled with such abundant happiness that Master Louis spent a moment admiring her without meaning to.

Françoise glared at her grandson. "Little one, didn't you tell me our miss had been doing nothing but crying?"

"Heck! Listen, Grandma, I don't know, maybe you heard wrong or maybe I saw wrong—unless our miss just doesn't want it known she was crying." This Berrichon was a chip off the block of Lower Normandy.

Françoise carried out the main course. "Even so, our miss is always alone, and that's no way to live."

Blushing with shame, Aurore murmured, "Did I ask you to complain on my behalf?"

Master Louis offered her his hand and led her into the other room, where the table was set. They sat facing one another. Berrichon stood behind Aurore as usual to wait on her. They spent a few minutes pretending to eat. Then Master Louis said, "Leave us, my boy, we don't need you anymore."

"Should I bring out the other courses?"

"No," said Aurore quickly.

"Then I'll bring dessert."

"Out!" Master Louis pointed to the door.

The boy left cackling. "Grandma," he said as he entered the kitchen, "I believe they're going to have it out." Françoise shrugged her shoulders. "Master Louis looked pretty angry," said Berrichon.

"Just do the dishes! Master Louis is smarter than all the rest of us; as strong as a bull, in spite of being small; and as brave as a lion; but don't worry— our little Miss Aurore could handle four like him!"

"What?" He was amazed. "She doesn't look like it!"

"Exactly." And to end the discussion she added, "You're too young to know. Get to work!"

"Apparently you're not happy, Aurore?" said Master Louis when Berrichon had left the room.

"I see you so rarely!"

"And do you blame me, dear child?"

"God forbid! Sometimes I'm unhappy, it's true. But who can stop silly ideas forming in the mind of a poor shut-in? You know children are afraid of the dark, Henri, but as soon as day comes again they forget their fears. I'm the same way, and it only takes your being here for me to forget my foolish anxieties."

He looked away. "You have a dutiful daughter's affection for me, Aurore, and I thank you for it."

"And do you have a father's affection for me, Henri?"

He got up and came around the table. She joyfully pulled out a chair for him. "That's right, come sit here! We haven't talked like this in ages. You remember how the time used to pass, back then?"

But he was pensive and sad. "Our time's no longer our own."

She took his hands and looked into his face so gently that he felt the warmth in his eyes that precedes and triggers tears.

"Are you unhappy too, Henri?" she murmured.

He shook his head and tried to smile. "You're mistaken, Aurore. I once had a beautiful dream, a dream so beautiful it robbed me of sleep. But that was only one day, and only one dream. I'm awake, I've given up hope, I've taken a vow, I do my duty. The time is coming when my life will change. Dear child, I'm pretty old now for starting over with a new life."

"Pretty old!" she echoed, showing all her teeth as she burst out laughing.

He wasn't laughing. "At my age," he said quietly, "other men already have families."

She quickly grew serious. "And you have none, Henri—you have only me!"

He opened his mouth to answer, but stopped himself. He lowered his eyes again.

"You have only me," she repeated, "and what am I to you? An impediment to your happiness!" He wanted to stop her, but she went on. "You know what they're saying? 'She's neither his daughter nor his sister nor his wife.' They say..."

"Aurore," he interrupted, "for eighteen years you've been my only joy."

"You're generous, and I thank you," she murmured.

For a moment they both fell silent. His embarrassment was visible.

It was she who broke the silence. "Henri, I know nothing of your thoughts or your actions. What right have I to reproach you? But I'm always alone, and always thinking of you, my only friend. There are times when I feel sure I can figure it out. When my heart aches, when tears stand in my eyes, it's because I think, 'If it weren't for me, some beloved woman would cheer his solitude; if it weren't for me, he'd live in a big splendid house; if it weren't for me, he could go anywhere without hiding his face.' Henri, you don't just love me like a good father, you respect me, and because of me you've had to repress your heart's desires."

She spoke from her heart: she had in fact had those thoughts. But diplomacy comes naturally to the daughters of Eve, and her words were meant above all as a maneuver to learn more. Her gambit failed. She got in return only this cold answer: "Dear child, you're mistaken." He was staring into space. "It's getting late," he murmured. Then suddenly, as if he couldn't help himself, he added, "When I'm gone, Aurore, will you remember me?"

Her rosy coloring vanished. If he'd looked up he would have seen her whole heart in the glance she gave him. "Are you leaving me again?" she stammered.

"No," he said uneasily. "I don't know—maybe..."

"I beg you! I beg you!" she murmured. "Have pity on me, Henri! If you leave, take me with you!" He didn't answer, and with tears in her eyes she went on, "You're annoyed because I was demanding and unreasonable. Oh, Henri, you didn't hear about my tears from me! I won't cry anymore. Henri, listen to me, believe me, I won't cry anymore. My God, I know I was wrong. I'm happy I get to see you every day. Henri, won't you answer me? Henri, are you listening?"

He'd turned his face away. She reached for him like a child to make him look at her. His eyes were bathed in tears. She slipped out of her chair and knelt by him. "Henri, Henri, my dear friend, my father. If you were happy you could have your happiness all to yourself, but I want to share your tears!"

He drew her passionately to him. But then his arms dropped. "We're both crazy, Aurore!" He gave a tight bitter smile. "What if someone saw us! What's all this about?"

She didn't give up. "It's about the fact that you're selfish and spiteful tonight, Henri. You've changed a lot, starting the day you told me I wasn't your daughter."

"The day you begged me to spare the Marquis of Chaverny? I remember that, Aurore, and I can tell you the marquis is back in Paris."

She didn't answer, but her gentle, noble face so eloquently expressed her surprise that he bit his lip. He took her hand and kissed it as if he were about to leave, but she held him firmly. "Stay," she said. "If this goes on, one day you'll come home and find me gone. I see I'm a trouble to you, so I'll leave. My God! I have no idea what I'll do, but you'll be rid of a burden that's becoming too heavy."

"You won't have time," he murmured. "You won't have to run away to leave me, Aurore."

"Would you throw me out?" cried the poor girl, straightening up as if she'd been struck in the chest.

He hid his face in his hands. They were still close together: she knelt on a cushion and rested her head on his knees.

"What would I need to be happy?" she murmured. "To be truly happy! Alas, Henri, it wouldn't take much. Has it been so long since I lost my smile? Didn't I used to be cheerful and joyful when I ran to meet you?"

His fingers stroked her thick hair, which shone like burnished gold in the lamplight.

"Do what you used to do," she went on, "that's all I ask. Tell me when you're happy, and especially tell me when you're sad, so I can either rejoice with you or let my heart share your sadness. It'll ease your pain. If you had a daughter, Henri, a beloved daughter, isn't that what you'd do?"

"A daughter!" His brow darkened again.

"I'm nothing to you, I know. Don't remind me."

He passed the back of his hand across his brow. "Aurore," he said as if he hadn't heard her last words, "there's a life you don't know, dear child, a sparkling life, a life of pleasure, of privilege, of luxury, the life of the fortunate of this world."

"And why would I need to know it?"

"I want you to. You need to know it." He couldn't help lowering his voice. "You may have to make a choice. You need to experience it before you can choose." He stood up. His noble face took on an expression of firm and considered resolve. "Aurore," he said slowly, "this is your last day of uncertainty and ignorance. And it might be my last day of youth and hope!"

"Henri, in God's name, explain yourself!"

He raised his eyes to heaven. "I've followed my conscience," he murmured. "He can see me from heaven. I have nothing to hide from him." Then he said, "Farewell, Aurore. You won't sleep tonight. Observe and reflect, and trust your mind more than your heart. I won't tell you more: I want your first impressions to be pure and unprepared. I'm afraid if I warned you I'd be acting out of selfishness. Just remember: however strange they seem, your adventures tonight will be what I intended, acting in your interest. If you don't see me, trust me: near or far, I'm watching over you."

He kissed her hand, and headed back up to his own rooms. Aurore, struck dumb, followed him with her eyes. When he reached the top of the stairs, before entering his room, Master Louis nodded and blew her a paternal kiss.

VIII. Two Girls

Aurore was alone. Her conversation with Henri had ended in such an unexpected way that she remained there, stunned and as if blinded in her wits. Her
thoughts were confused and disorganized. Her head was burning. Her heart, hurt
and unsatisfied, turned inward. She'd done her best to provoke him to explain;
she'd pursued him with all the creative finesse a woman's ingenuity is capable
of. Not only had she gotten no explanation—but now another mysterious horizon, whether threat or promise, opened out before her.

Henri had said, "You won't sleep tonight." And he'd said, "However
strange they seem, your adventures tonight will be what I intended, acting in
your interest." Adventures! Up to now Aurore's wandering life had certainly
been full of adventure. But Henri had always taken care of her and stayed by her
like a watchful bodyguard, an infallible savior, protecting her even from fear.
Tonight's adventures would be different: she'd have to face them alone. But
what adventures? And why the hints and evasions? He'd said she needed to experience a life quite different from the one she'd led before: a sparkling life, a
life of luxury, the life of the powerful and the fortunate. "So you can choose,"
he'd said. No doubt he meant choosing between that unknown life and the one
she had now. Wasn't her choice already made? She only needed to know on
which side of the scale Henri would stand. But then the thought of her mother
crossed Aurore's troubled mind, and her knees buckled. To have to choose! A
sad thought occurred to her for the first time: what if her mother stood on one
side of the scale and Henri on the other? "Impossible!" she cried, and pushed the
thought away. "God wouldn't allow it."

She opened the curtains at her bedroom window and rested her elbows on
the balcony to let the fresh night air cool her burning brow. The street was full
of people. A crowd had gathered around the gates of the Palais-Royal to watch
the guests arrive. A parade of litters and chaises passed between two lines of
gawkers. At first Aurore paid no attention. What did all that activity and noise
matter to her? But then in a passing chaise she saw two women dressed for the
ball, a mother and daughter. Tears came to her eyes, followed by a kind of diz-
ziness. "My mother might be going!" she thought. It was possible, even proba-
ble.

So she began to examine more carefully what she could see of the ball, and
she guessed at other and greater splendors beyond the palace walls. With a
vague and growing yearning she envied those beautifully dressed girls with
pearls around their necks, and flowers and more pearls in their hair—not for
their flowers, or their pearls, or their clothes, but because they were sitting next
to their mothers. She wanted to stop watching, because all that happiness
seemed like an insult to her own sadness. The joyful cries, the bustling people,

the noise, the laughter, the sparks, the strains of the orchestra already playing far away, all of it weighed on her. She hid her burning face in her hands.

In the kitchen Jean-Marie Berrichon was playing the part of the serpent, tempting his mannish old grandmother. There hadn't been much to wash up, thank God—Aurore and Master Louis had used only one plate apiece. In the kitchen, on the other hand, dinner had been lavish; Françoise and her grandson had eaten enough for four.

"For what it's worth," said Berrichon, "I'm going to go to the corner to have a look. Mother Balahault says up there they've got all the magical delights of an enchanted fairy palace. I'd like to have a look for myself."

"Don't be long, little one," grumbled Françoise, who was weak in spite of her deep voice.

Berrichon took off. Mesdames Guichard, Balahault, Morin, and the rest hailed him as soon as he hit the grimy cobblestones of the Rue du Chantre.

From the kitchen door Françoise glanced into Aurore's room. "Well! He's already gone! The poor angel's alone again!" She thought to go keep her young mistress company, but just then Berrichon came back.

"Grandma! Yew trees, banners, lanterns, soldiers on horseback, women covered in so many diamonds that they make the ones who are only dressed in satin brocade look like they're going to church! Come see, Grandma!"

She shrugged. "It's nothing to me."

"Oh, Grandma, right here on this corner Mother Balahault is calling out the names and telling stories about all the lords and ladies going by. It's very educational! Come see, just long enough to step down to the corner."

"And who'll watch the house?" she said, a little unnerved.

"We'll be ten feet away. We'll keep an eye on the door. Come on, Grandma, come on!"

He put his arm around her and dragged her out. The door stayed open behind them. They were only ten feet away. But Mesdames Balahault, Guichard, Durand, Morin, and the rest were proud women, and once they'd conquered Françoise they wouldn't let her go. Was this part of Master Louis's mysterious plan? We doubt it. The crowd of old women dragging Jean-Marie Berrichon toward the Palais-Royal and its dazzling lights had to pass under Aurore's window, but she was lost in thought and didn't see them.

"Not a single friend!" she mused, "not a single companion to give me advice!"

She heard a slight noise behind her in her bedroom. She whirled around and cried out in fear—and her cry was answered by a joyful burst of laughter. Before her stood a woman dressed in a pink satin domino cloak, hooded and masked for the ball.

"Mademoiselle Aurore?" said the woman with a formal curtsey.

"Am I dreaming?' cried Aurore. "That voice!"

The mask dropped, revealing—framed in brand-new finery—the mischievous face of Doña Cruz.

"Flor!" cried Aurore. "Is it possible? Is it really you?"

With the grace of a sylph Doña Cruz came to her with open arms, and they exchanged the quick light kiss of girls. Have you ever seen two doves billing in fun?

"And here I was complaining about having no companion! Flor, my dear Flor, I'm so happy to see you!" Then Aurore had a sudden misgiving. "But who let you in? I'm forbidden to see anyone."

"Forbidden?" Doña Cruz bridled.

"Asked, if that sounds better." Aurore blushed.

"I'd call this a well-guarded prison! The door wide open, and nobody to say boo!"

Aurore hurried into the main room. It was indeed empty, and the double doors stood wide open. She called for Françoise and Berrichon: no answer. We know where they were just then, but Aurore didn't. After Henri's peculiar last words, warning her the night would be full of strange adventures, she could only conclude he'd meant this to happen. She closed the door without locking it, and returned to Doña Cruz, who was busy curtseying in front of the mirror.

"Let me look at you," said Doña Cruz. "My God, you're all grown up and gorgeous!"

"You too!"

They admired each other happily.

"But what about that costume?" said Aurore.

"Just my ball gown, dear," said Doña Cruz a little smugly. "Are you a good judge? What do you think?"

"Lovely!" Aurore pulled open the cloak to see the skirt and the blouse. "Lovely! It's sumptuous. I bet I can guess: you're appearing on stage here, Flor?"

"Come on! Me appearing on stage? I'm going to the ball, that's all."

"What ball?"

"There's only one ball tonight."

"The Regent's ball?"

"God, yes, the Regent's ball, darling. I'm expected at the Palais-Royal, to be presented to His Royal Highness by the Princess Palatine, his mother—that's all, dear."

Aurore stared.

"Are you surprised?" Doña Cruz pushed back the train of her cloak with her foot. "Why would that surprise you? Though actually I'm pretty surprised myself. There's so much to tell, darling, so much to tell. It's raining stories, and I'll have to tell you all about it."

"But how did you find my house?"

"I knew where it was. And I had permission to see you. Because I have a master too..."

"I have no master," Aurore interrupted proudly.

"A slave, if you prefer, a slave who gives the orders. I was going to come tomorrow morning, but I thought, 'I'll just go pay a call on my dear Aurore!'"

"Do you still love me?"

"Madly! But let me tell you my first story. And another one after that one. Like I said, it's raining stories. I haven't set foot outside since I got to Paris, and I was supposed to find my way here from the Saint Magloire Church."

"The Saint Magloire Church! You live near there?"

"Yes, I have my cage just as you have yours, little bird. But mine's prettier: my Lagardère does things right."

"Shh!" Aurore put her finger to her lips.

"All right, all right, I see we're still living in the land of mystery. Anyway, I was a little at a loss for getting here when I heard scratching at my door. Before I could open it someone had come in—an ugly twisted little man, all dressed in black. He bows down to the ground, and I do the same with a straight face, like everything's normal. He says, 'If mademoiselle will follow me, I'll lead her where she wishes to go...'"

"A hunchback?" Aurore was lost in thought.

"Yes, a hunchback. Did you send him?"

"Not I."

"Do you know him?"

"I've never spoken to him."

"Well, I swear I hadn't said a word to anyone about coming to see you tonight instead of tomorrow morning. I'm sorry you know that dwarf—I'd rather have gone on thinking of him as a supernatural being. Anyway, he must at least be something of a magician to have gotten past my Arguses. I don't want to brag, dear, but I'm better guarded than you are. You know I'm not easily scared; the little man in black's offer tickled my sense of adventure, and I said yes right away. He bows even more respectfully than the first time, and opens a little door I'd never noticed—in my own room, can you imagine? He leads me down some hallways I knew nothing about. We get out without being seen. There's a carriage waiting in the street. He hands me in. In the carriage he behaves perfectly. We both get out at your door, the carriage takes off at a gallop, I climb the front steps—and when I turn around to thank him, he's gone!"

Aurore listened, still lost in thought. "It's him," she murmured, "it must be him!"

"What's that?"

"Nothing... But under what possible pretext can you, Flor, my little gypsy girl, be presented to the Regent?"

Doña Cruz pursed her lips and settled into a soft chair. "Darling, you see before you no more of a gypsy girl than would fit in the palm of my hand.

There's never been a gypsy girl, it's a mirage, an illusion, a lie, a daydream. We are quite simply the noble daughter of a princess."

"You?" Aurore was stunned.

"Who else? Unless it's you! Look, dear, it's the gypsy way. They sneak into palaces by coming down the chimney when the fire's out, they grab a few valuables, and they never fail to take along the cradle where the little heiress is asleep. I'm an heiress stolen by gypsies. The wealthiest heiress in Europe, I'm told."

It wasn't clear whether she was joking or serious; maybe she herself didn't know. The flow of her story brightened her brown cheeks. Her bold eyes, blacker than jet, sparkled with intelligence.

Aurore listened, mouth agape, her face a picture of gullible innocence, her eyes shining with pleasure at her friend's good fortune. "Wonderful! And what's your real name, Flor?"

Doña Cruz smoothed out the pleats of her dress and said impressively, "Mademoiselle de Nevers."

"Nevers! One of the greatest names in France!"

"Alas, yes, my dear. It seems we are in some way a cousin of His Majesty."

"But how...?"

"Ah, yes, how?" Doña Cruz dropped her grand airs and resumed the giddy playfulness that suited her better. "That's what I don't know. They haven't yet been kind enough to show me my family tree. When I ask, they shush me. Apparently I have enemies. People always envy the great. I don't know, I don't care, I'm perfectly happy to let things be."

After some thought Aurore said suddenly, "Flor, what if I know more about your own story than you do?"

"It wouldn't surprise me, darling, I swear. But if you know my story, keep it to yourself. My guardian's going to tell me the whole thing tonight, every detail. My guardian and friend, the Prince of Gonzague."

Aurore gave a start. "Gonzague!"

"What's wrong?"

"Did you say Gonzague?"

"I said Gonzague, the Prince of Gonzague, the man who's defending my rights, the husband of the Duchess of Nevers, my mother."

"Ah! So this Gonzague is the duchess's husband?" Aurore remembered her visit to the ruins of Caylus. People unknown to her then had names now. The child mentioned by the barmaid from Tarrides, the child who'd slept through the terrible battle, was Flor. But what about the murderer?

"What are you thinking about?" asked Doña Cruz.

"I'm thinking about the name Gonzague."

"Why?"

"Before I tell you, I want to know whether you love him."

"Moderately. I could've loved him, but he wasn't interested."

Aurore said nothing.

"Well, speak!" Doña Cruz stamped her foot impatiently.

"If you loved him..."

"Speak, I tell you!"

"Since he's your guardian, and married to your mother..."

"*Caramba!*" The alleged Mademoiselle de Nevers didn't hesitate to swear. "Do I have to tell you everything? I saw my mother! I respect her, and what's more I love her for all she's suffered. But when I saw her my heart didn't beat harder, my arms didn't open to embrace her. You know, Aurore," she went on in a passionate flow, "I feel like a girl should die of joy when she meets her mother."

"I feel the same way."

"Well, I stayed calm—too calm. If it's about Gonzague, speak and don't be afraid. Even if it's about Madame de Nevers, speak and don't be afraid."

"It's only about Gonzague. That name, Gonzague, is mixed up in my memory with all my fears as a child and all my anxieties as a girl. The first time Henri risked his life to save me, I heard the name Gonzague. I heard it again the time we were attacked at a farm near Pamplona. The night you cast a sleeping spell on my guards in the gypsy chief's tent, I heard the name Gonzague a third time. In Madrid, Gonzague again. At Caylus Castle, once again Gonzague!"

Doña Cruz became thoughtful in turn. "Did Don Luis, your handsome Cincelador, ever tell you you were the daughter of a noble lady?"

"Never. And yet I think I am."

"I swear," cried Doña Cruz, "I don't like to overthink things, darling. I have lots of ideas, but they're all mixed up in my head and they don't want to come out. As for becoming a grand mademoiselle, I feel like it would suit you better than me. But I also feel like there's no point in cracking your skull trying to solve enigmas. I'm a Christian, but I've hung onto the best part of the faith of my people, the people who raised me: take things as they come, and find consolation in saying, that's fate! For example, one thing I can't agree with is that Monsieur de Gonzague is a highwayman and a murderer: he's too well bred for that. I can tell you there are lots of Gonzagues in Italy—real ones and fake ones; yours must be a fake Gonzague. Plus, if the real Prince of Gonzague is your persecutor, Master Louis wouldn't have brought you to Paris, exactly where everyone knows the Prince of Gonzague lives."

"But what about all the precautions that surround me? Forbidden to go out, forbidden to let myself be seen at the window?"

"Bah! He's jealous."

"Oh, Flor," murmured Aurore reproachfully.

Doña Flor performed a pirouette, and her lips formed the most impish of her smiles. "I won't become a princess for another two hours, so I can still speak openly. Your dark handsome stranger, your Master Louis, your Lagardère, your knight errant, your king, your god, is jealous. And by our lady, as they say at court, isn't he worth it?"

"Flor, Flor!"

"Jealous, jealous, jealous, darling! And it wasn't Monsieur de Gonzague who drove you out of Madrid. Since I have a little bit of witchcraft, I happen to know, mademoiselle, your lovers were already measuring how high it was to your windows!"

Aurore turned beet red. Even with her witchcraft, Doña Cruz had no idea how close to home her shot had landed. She looked at Aurore, who couldn't lift her eyes. "Well!" she went on, kissing Aurore on the forehead. "Here she is, blushing with pride and delight! She's pleased someone's jealous over her. Is he still as gorgeous as the stars? And proud? And gentler than a child? Go on, tell me. Here's my ear to whisper your confession into. You love him!"

"Why whisper?" Aurore drew herself up.

"All right, out loud if you want."

"Out loud, then: I love him!"

"Well done! Good for you! Let me kiss you for telling the truth." Doña Cruz examined her friend with her piercing black eyes. "Are you happy?"

"Of course."

"Very happy?"

"Since he's here."

"Perfect!" cried Doña Cruz. Then she looked around a little disdainfully. "*Pobre dicha, dicha dulce!*"—a Spanish proverb that's been rendered in French by one balladeer as, "A hovel and my sweetheart!" When Doña Cruz had looked all around she said, "You'd need some love here. The house is ugly, the street's gloomy, the furniture's awful. I know, darling, you're going to give me the obligatory answer, 'A palace without him...'"

"I'll give you a different answer," interrupted Aurore. "If I wanted a palace, I'd only have to say the word."

"Oh, come on!"

"It's true."

"Has he grown so rich?"

"I've never asked for anything he didn't give me immediately."

"It's a fact," murmured Doña Cruz, no longer laughing, "he's not like other men. There's something strange and superior about him. I've never lowered my eyes to anyone but him. You never know: in spite of what people say, there are such things as magicians. I think your Lagardère is one." She was perfectly serious.

"What nonsense!"

"I've seen a few," said Doña Cruz gravely. "I want to find out for sure. Here, wish for something while thinking about him." Aurore began to laugh. Doña Cruz sat down next to her. "Just to make me happy, darling," she coaxed. "Come on, it's not that hard!"

Aurore was surprised. "Are you being serious?"

Doña Cruz put her mouth to Aurore's ear and murmured, "I used to be madly in love with someone. One day he placed his hand on my forehead and said, 'Flor, the one you love can never love you.' I was cured. So you see, he's a magician."

"And the one you loved," said Aurore, turning pale, "who was it?"

Doña Cruz rested her head on Aurore's shoulder, but didn't answer.

"It was him!" cried Aurore with inexpressible terror. "I'm sure it was him!"

IX. The Three Wishes

Doña Cruz's eyes were moist. Aurore's limbs trembled feverishly. Both of these beautiful girls found the contrast in their natures reversed at that moment: Doña Cruz, normally bubbly and bold, became gently melancholic, while a bolt of jealous passion shot from Aurore's eyes. "My rival is you!" she murmured.

Overcoming Aurore's resistance, Doña Cruz drew her close and kissed her. "He loves you," she said quietly. "He'll never love anyone but you!"

"And what about you?"

"I'm cured. I can look at your mutual affection happily, with a smile, without hatred. You see, your Lagardère really is a magician!"

"Are you lying to me?"

Doña Cruz put her hand over her heart. Her eyes were wide and her brow clear. "If all it took was my death to make it come true, you'd be happy!"

Aurore threw her arms around her neck.

"But I insist on my test!" cried Doña Cruz. "Don't refuse me, dear Aurore. Wish for something, please!"

"I have nothing to wish for."

"What! Not a single desire?"

"Not one."

Doña Cruz pulled her to her feet and led her to the window. The Palais-Royal glittered. Under its colonnaded porch flowed a river of splendidly dressed women. "You don't even want to go to the Regent's ball?" she asked abruptly.

"Who, me?" stammered Aurore, whose heart began to beat hard.

"Don't lie!"

"Why would I lie?"

"All right, not denying it is admitting it. You wish to go to the Regent's ball." Doña Cruz clapped her hands and counted, "One!"

"But I have nothing," objected Aurore, laughingly joining in her friend's game, "—no dresses, no jewels, no finery..."

"Two!" cried Doña Cruz, clapping her hands a second time. "You wish for dresses and jewels and finery. And make sure you're thinking about him, otherwise it won't work!" The longer the business went on, the more serious she became. Her big beautiful black eyes lost their look of certainty. She believed in black magic; she was afraid, but curious, and her curiosity overcame her fears. She lowered her voice unconsciously. "Make your third wish."

"But I don't really want to go the ball! Let's stop this game."

"What! Even if you were sure to meet him there?"

"Henri?"

"Yes, your gallant affectionate Henri, who'd find you even more beautiful dressed in all your glory."

"In that case," said Aurore, lowering her eyes, "I think I'd go."

Doña Cruz clapped her hands together loudly. "Three!"

"Here's all the trinkets and the gewgaws they brought for our miss, more than twenty boxes' worth—dresses, lace, flowers. Come on, everybody, come on in! This is the house of the Chevalier de Lagardère!"

"Shame on you!" cried Aurore in fear.

"Don't worry, I know what I'm doing," said Jean-Marie Berrichon smugly. "No more hiding! Enough with the mystery! We're dropping the mask, damn it!"

But how can we describe Doña Cruz's surprise? She'd invoked the devil, and the obedient devil had answered her call, and he certainly hadn't dawdled. She was a bit of a skeptic: all skeptics are superstitious. Remember that Doña Cruz had spent her childhood in the camps of wandering gypsies, living in a world of marvels. Her mouth hung open and her eyes were wide.

Through the door of the main room came half a dozen young women, followed by as many men carrying boxes and bundles. Doña Cruz wondered whether those boxes and bundles held real finery or dried leaves.

Aurore smiled at her friend's stunned expression. "Well?"

"He's a magician," stammered Doña Cruz. "I knew it!"

"Come in, gentlemen, come in ladies!" cried Berrichon. "Come in, everybody! It's open house now! I'm going to go get Mother Balahault, who's been dying to see what our place is like. I never tasted anything as good as her angelica liqueur. Come in, ladies, come in, gentlemen!"

The ladies and gentlemen didn't hesitate. Florists, seamstresses, and dressmakers set down their boxes on the big table in the middle of the main room. Behind the provisioners of both sexes came a page without livery. Going straight to Aurore, he bowed deeply before handing her a letter handsomely tied up in silk. He bowed again and left.

"Hey you, at least wait for an answer!" cried Berrichon, running after him. But the page was already at the end of the block, speaking with a gentleman wrapped in a traveling cloak whom Berrichon didn't recognize.

"Is it done?" the gentleman asked the page. Getting a yes, he added, "Where did you leave our men?"

"Near here, on the Rue Pierre Lescot."

"The chaise is ready?"

"There are two chaises."

"Why two?" asked the gentleman in surprise. The lapel of his cloak, which hid his face, shifted a little, and we would have recognized the pale pointed chin of our old friend Monsieur de Peyrolles.

"I don't know, but there are two chaises," said the page.

"Probably a misunderstanding," thought Peyrolles. He wanted to go take a look through the door of Lagardère's house, but further reflection stopped him. "All they'd have to do is see me," he murmured, "and that would botch the whole thing..." To the page he said, "Go back to the villa as fast as you can, you hear me?"

"As fast as I can."

"At the villa you'll find those two bravos who've been taking up space in the kitchen all day."

"Master Cocardasse and his friend Passepoil?"

"Exactly. Tell them the job is all set up for them, and all they have to do is show up... Just now, did anyone mention the name of the gentleman whose house this is?"

"Yes—Monsieur de Lagardère."

"Do not utter his name to them. If they ask, tell them there are only women in the house."

"And where do I bring them?"

"To this corner, and from here you'll point out the door."

The page took off running. Peyrolles pulled his cloak back up over his face and vanished into the crowd.

In the house, Aurore had just torn open the letter the page had brought. "It's his writing!" she cried.

"And that's an invitation card just like mine," added Doña Cruz, not yet through being surprised. "Our fairy godmother has forgotten nothing." She turned over the card: it was decorated with pretty little vignettes of chubby cupids and garlands of grapes and roses, and seemed not at all diabolical.

Meanwhile Aurore read her letter, which ran like this:

Dear child, this finery comes from me. I wanted to surprise you. Make yourself gorgeous. Two porters will come on my behalf with a chaise to take you to the ball, where I'll be waiting for you.

— Henri de Lagardère.

Aurore passed the letter to Doña Cruz, who rubbed her dazzled eyes before reading. When she was done she said, "And do you believe it?"

"I do. I have my reasons for believing it." Aurore smiled confidently: hadn't Henri told her to be surprised by nothing tonight? On her part, Doña Cruz took Aurore's self-assurance in these strange circumstances to be another trick of the devil.

By now the open cases, boxes, and packages had spread their dazzling contents across the big table. Doña Cruz could see that, instead of dried leaves, they held all the apparel needed for a visit to court, as well as a pink satin domino cloak just like hers. The dress was a white weave embroidered with silver; the pattern was scattered roses, each with a small pearl at its center. The train, the collar, the sleeves, were all embroidered with hummingbird feathers—the very height of fashion. The Marquise d'Aubignac, daughter of the financier Soulas, had made her fortune and her fame at court in a dress like that, given to her by John Law. But the dress itself was nothing: the lacework and the needlework were truly magnificent, and the jewelry cost more than an army brigade.

"He's a magician," said Doña Cruz over and over as she took stock of it all. "Clearly a magician! Even El Cincelador doesn't earn enough engraving sword guards to pay for presents like this." And once again she suspected that at some point all this finery would turn into sawdust or wood shavings.

Berrichon admired it all and wasn't shy about saying so. Old Françoise, who'd just come in, shook her grey head in a way that summed up her thoughts.

But there was another witness to this scene, whose presence no one suspected, and who certainly seemed just as interested. He was hiding behind the door to the rooms upstairs, which he held carefully ajar. From up there, over everyone's heads, he could see all the finery spread out on the table. It wasn't the dignified, melancholy Master Louis, but a little man dressed all in black: the man who'd brought Doña Cruz here, who'd forged Lagardère's handwriting, who'd rented Médor's dog kennel—the hunchback, Aesop, known as Jonah, victorious over the Whale. He'd been there since Doña Cruz arrived; no doubt he was waiting for Lagardère. He rubbed his hands together. "God's head!" he chuckled to himself. "The Prince of Gonzague does things right, and that rascal Peyrolles is certainly a man of good taste."

Aurore was a daughter of Eve. The sight of all those fine clothes made her heart race. And that everything came from her friend Henri made it a double joy. It didn't even occur to her, as it had to Doña Cruz, to calculate the cost of all this regal apparel. She surrendered herself entirely to pleasure. She was happy, and the feeling that fills any girl at the moment of her debut in the world was sweet to her. And wouldn't she have Henri there to protect her? Still, one thing worried her: she had no chambermaid, and old Françoise was better suited to cooking than to dressing.

Two chambermaids stepped forward as if they'd guessed her thoughts. "We are at mademoiselle's orders." At their signal, all the delivery people bowed and left.

Doña Cruz pinched Aurore's arm. "Are you really going to put yourself in the hands of these creatures?"

"Why not?"

"And you're really going to put on the dress?"

"Of course I am."

"You're brave! Very brave!" murmured Doña Cruz. "But at least your demon is a perfect model of chivalry. You're right, make yourself gorgeous, it can't hurt."

Aurore, Doña Cruz, and the two chambermaids who were part of the gift all went into the bedroom. Françoise Berrichon and her grandson Jean-Marie stayed behind in the main room.

"Who in the world is that hussy?" asked the old woman.

"What hussy, Grandma?"

"The one in the pink domino."

"The brunette? She's got some sparkling eyes, Grandma."

"Did you see her come in?"

"No, she was here before me."

Françoise pulled her knitting out of her pocket and began to think. "I tell you," she went on solemnly in her deep voice, "I don't understand anything that's going on."

"You want me to explain it, Grandma?"

"No, but if you want to do me a favor..."

"Oh, Grandma, you're kidding: if I want to do you a favor..."

"Then keep quiet when I'm talking. I still say there's some kind of skullduggery going on."

"Not at all, Grandma!"

"We were wrong to go out. It's a wicked world. Who knows but what that Balahault woman lured us out."

"Oh, come on, Grandma! She's a good woman and she makes great angelica."

"Well, I like to see my way clear, boy, and this whole story doesn't sit well with me."

"But it's as clear as day, Grandma. Our miss spent all day watching the wagons full of flowers and shrubberies going to the Palais-Royal. And heck if seeing all that didn't make the poor girl sigh. So she spun Master Louis this way and that to get her an invitation. They're for sale, Grandma. Mother Balahault got one from the valet of the royal wardrobe, a connection of hers through his servant girl—the valet of the wardrobe's servant girl—who gets her tobacco from the younger Madame Balahault, on the Rue des Bons Enfants. The servant girl had an invitation because she found it on her master's desk. So there was thirty louis to share between the two Balahault women and the servant girl. That's not stealing, is it, Grandma?"

Old Françoise may have been the most honest cook in Europe, but she was still a cook. "God, no, boy! That's not stealing—just a stupid piece of paper!"

"So then Master Louis got himself all spun around, and he went out to buy an invitation. On the way he bargained for some ladies' knickknacks and he sent everything here, still warm."

She paused in her knitting. "But it's worth a ton of money!"

He shrugged. "You're so gullible, Grandma! Some old satin with fake embroidery and little bits of glass!"

There was a gentle knock at the street door.

"Who is it now?" said Françoise grumpily. "Bar the door."

"Why bar the door? We're not playing hide and seek anymore, Grandma."

There was a louder knock.

"On the other hand, what if it's robbers?" said Berrichon, who wasn't a brave soul.

"Robbers? When the street's full of people and lit up like noon? Go open up."

"On second thought, Grandma, I'd rather bar the door."

But it was too late, and whoever was knocking had grown tired of it. The door opened carefully, revealing a man with an enormous mustache. The owner of the mustache glanced quickly around the room. "Crooked ace! This must be the turtledove's nest, God's blood!" Then he turned, and to someone outside he said, "Do yourself the favor of coming in, brother. There's nobody here but a worthy duenna and her no-account duckling. We'll hold converse."

As he spoke he came in, nose held high, fist on hip, making the folds of his cloak sway majestically. He had a package under his arm. The one he'd called "brother" now appeared: another fighter, but less frightening to look at. He was much smaller and very thin, and his shabby mustache struggled in vain to suggest the impressive curl so becoming on a hero's face. He also had a package under his arm. Like his leader, he glanced around the room, but slowly and more carefully.

Oh, how bitterly young Berrichon repented not having barred the door in time! Surveying the newcomers, he admitted to himself that he'd never seen two more villainous-looking rascals. (That only showed his unfamiliarity with high society, because Cocardasse Junior and Brother Passepoil certainly qualified as magnificent rascals.) The boy slipped prudently behind his more courageous grandmother, while she asked in her deep voice, "What do you want here, you two?"

Cocardasse touched his hat with the noble courtesy of one who has worn out a lot of shoes in the sand of a fencing academy. Then he winked at Passepoil, and Passepoil winked back. No doubt that meant something, and Berrichon trembled all over.

"Well, good woman," said Cocardasse finally, "you've got a voice that goes right to my heart. How about you, Passepoil?"

As we already know, Passepoil was one of those tender souls who's always deeply moved by the presence of a woman. Age made no difference. He didn't even mind if the female person had more mustache than he did. Passepoil smiled approvingly and glanced off into the corners. Admire, please, the complexity of his character: his passion for the gentler sex didn't slacken his vigilance—he'd already made a mental map of the quarters. The turtledove, as Cocardasse referred to her, must be in that further room, from under whose closed door a ray of bright light escaped. On the opposite side of the main room stood the door to the kitchen, open and with a key in the lock. Passepoil touched Cocardasse's elbow and said quietly, "The key's on the outside."

Cocardasse nodded. "Venerable lady, we're here on important business. Is this the home of..."

"No," said Berrichon from behind his grandmother. "It's not."

Passepoil smiled. Cocardasse curled his mustache. "God's hat! Here's a young fellow full of promise!"

"With a forthright manner," added Passepoil.

"And with wits enough for four—thunder and lightning! But how can he know the person in question isn't here, since I never named him?"

"It's just the two of us living here," said Françoise curtly.

"Passepoil?" said Cocardasse.

"Cocardasse?" said Passepoil.

"Ha! Would you have believed this worthy lady could lie like a Norman rascal?"

"Word of honor," answered Passepoil gravely. "No, I would not have believed it."

"Move along now," cried Françoise, whose ears were beginning to burn. "Less chatter! This is no time to be loitering in people's houses! Out of here!"

"Brother," said Cocardasse, "there's some truth to that. The hour is unwarranted."

"Quite right," said Passepoil.

"And yet, we cannot leave without getting an answer, can we?"

"Clearly not."

"I therefore propose, baldy, that we have a decent, peaceful look around the house."

"I concur." Passepoil took a step closer. "Get your handkerchief ready. I've got mine. You take the boy, I'll take the woman."

At critical moments Passepoil sometimes surpassed Cocardasse himself. Their plans were made. Passepoil headed for the kitchen door. Françoise bravely threw herself in his way, while Berrichon tried to run outside to call for help. Cocardasse snagged him by one ear. "If you call out I'll strangle you, sweetheart!" Berrichon, terrified, made not a sound.

Meanwhile, at the cost of three scratches and two fistfuls of hair, Passepoil securely bound and gagged Françoise. He picked her up and carried her into the kitchen, where Cocardasse also brought Berrichon.

Some people claim Passepoil took advantage of old Françoise's helpless state to give her a kiss on the brow. If he did so, he was in error: she'd been ugly even as a girl. But we decline to take any responsibility for Passepoil's actions. He had weak morals—too bad for him! The boy and his grandmother weren't done suffering: they were bound together and tied up inside the dish cupboard, with the kitchen door securely locked. Cocardasse Junior and Brother Passepoil remained the undisputed masters of the field.

X. Two Dominoes

Outside, all the shops on the Rue du Chantre were closed. Any neighbor-hood gossips who weren't yet asleep had joined the noisy crowd at the gates of the Palais-Royal. Mesdames Guichard and Durand and Balahault and Morin all agreed they'd seen better dressed women, and more of them, arrive tonight than at parties given by His Royal Highness himself. The whole court was here. Mother Balahault, a person of substance, appointed herself the final arbiter of the dresses discussed by Mesdames Morin, Guichard, and Duran. But they ad-vanced smoothly from analyzing silk and lace to dissecting personalities. In Mother Balahault's opinion, very few of those fine ladies would have deserved the virgin bridal attire of Scripture.

But it wasn't to gawk at ladies that our gossips pressed close to the gates of the Palais-Royal, ignoring the shouts of porters and coachmen, defending their spots against latecomers, standing in the mud with admirable forbearance; nor was it to see princes and great lords. They were bored by ladies, and if you've seen one great lord or prince you've seen them all. They'd seen Madame de Soubise go by with Madame de La Ferté; the two beautiful Lafayette girls; the young Duchess of Rosny—that black-eyed blonde who broke up the marriage of one of Louis XIV's sons; the Mesdemoiselles Bourbon-Bisset; five or six Rohan women of different vintages; some Brolies, some Chastelluxes, some Bauffremonts, some Choiseuls, some Colignys, and so on. They'd seen Mon-sieur du Maine's brother, the Count of Toulouse, go by with his wife the prin-cess. They'd stopped counting judges, they barely noticed ministers, they looked right past ambassadors. But still the crowd stayed, and even grew by the minute. What was it waiting for? They wouldn't have persevered like this for the Regent himself. It must be for someone else: the young king! No. Aim higher: that god, the Scotsman, John Law, Providence himself to a crowd dreaming of becoming a crowd of millionaires.

Mr. Law of Lauriston, savior and benefactor! Mr. Law, whom the same crowd would try to lynch on this very spot a few months later! Mr. Law, whose horses stood idle, replaced by humans in harness! The crowd awaited the great Mr. Law. The crowd was determined to wait till tomorrow morning if necessary. To think that poets commonly call crowds fickle and changeable—the excellent crowd, more patient than a flock of sheep, unwavering, stubborn, untiring, jam-ming damp sidewalks for fifteen hours straight to see this or that go by, often not much, sometimes nothing at all! If all the heavy oxen of the last five hundred years only knew how to write...

Though it wasn't far removed from all that noise and light, the dark and deserted Rue du Chantre seemed to be asleep. Two or three pitiful street lamps were reflected in the muddy gutter. At first glance not a sign life was visible.

But a few paces from Master Louis's house, across the street, in a deep recess created by the recent demolition of a couple of shacks, six men in dark clothes stood silent and unmoving. Two porter's chairs sat on the ground behind them. These men weren't waiting for Mr. Law. They hadn't taken their eyes off the closed door of Master Louis's house since Cocardasse Junior and Brother Passepoil had gone in.

Those two, still in the main room after their victorious campaign against young Berrichon and old Françoise, stood looking at each other with mutual admiration.

"God's blood, son!" said Cocardasse. "You haven't forgotten your trade."

"Nor you neither. It's all done properly—though it did cost us our handkerchiefs." If we've sometimes seemed critical of Passepoil, it wasn't out of prejudice against him. To prove which, we won't hesitate to draw attention now to one of his virtues: he was frugal.

Cocardasse, who leaned more toward extravagance, dropped the subject of their handkerchiefs. "Well, the hard part's done."

"As long as Lagardère isn't mixed up in it, a job goes smoothly."

"And Lagardère is miles away, crooked ace!"

"It's sixty leagues from here to the border."

They rubbed their hands.

"No time to waste, sweetheart," said Cocardasse. "Let's survey the ground. We've got two doors." He pointed to Aurore's room and to the top of the spiral staircase.

Passepoil stroked his chin and started toward Aurore's door. "I'll have a look through the keyhole."

Cocardasse's terrible glare stopped him. "God's hat! I can't allow that! The little chickadee is getting dressed—have some decency and respect!"

Passepoil humbly lowered his eyes. "Ah, brother, how blessed you are to have such good morals!"

"Thunder and lightning! That's how I am, and believe me, my boy, if you stick around with me some of it might rub off in the end. A true philosopher is the master of his passions."

"I'm the slave of mine," Passepoil sighed. "But they're so strong!"

Cocardasse pinched his cheek affectionately. "A victory without effort," he said solemnly, "is a victory without satisfaction. Go upstairs and see what's there."

Passepoil climbed the spiral stairs like a cat. He tried the door of Master Louis's room. "Locked!"

"And through the keyhole? In this case decency permits it."

"Black as a pit."

"Come back down, sweetheart. Let's review Monsieur de Gonzague's instructions."

"He promised us fifty pistoles each."

"On certain conditions. Firstly..." Instead of going on, Cocardasse took the package out from under his arm. Passepoil did the same.

At that moment, the door that Passepoil had found locked at the top of the stairs opened quietly. The pale, crafty figure of the hunchback appeared in the shadows. He listened.

The two masters of arms eyed their packages uncertainly. Cocardasse struck his discontentedly. "Is this really necessary?"

"It's just a formality."

"Well, then, get us out of it."

"Easy. Monsieur de Gonzague said, 'You'll be outfitted with servants' clothes.' We're obediently outfitted with them—under our arms."

The hunchback began to laugh to himself.

"Under our arms!" cried Cocardasse enthusiastically. "You've got a devilish wit, baldy!"

"Without my passions' tyrannical reign over me," said Passepoil seriously, "I think I could've gone far."

They both set their packages containing suits of livery on the table.

Cocardasse went on. "Secondly, Monsieur de Gonzague said, 'You'll make sure the chaise and the porters are waiting in the Rue du Chantre.'"

"Done," said Passepoil.

"Well, sure." Cocardasse scratched his ear. "But there are two chaises. What do you say to that, sweetheart?"

"Too much of a good thing doesn't hurt. I've never ridden in a chaise."

"Ha! Me neither."

"We'll take turns being carried back to the villa."

"Settled. Thirdly: 'You'll get into the house.' Here we are."

"'In the house you'll find a girl...' Ah, brother," cried Passepoil, "look at me, I'm trembling all over."

"And you've gone pale. What's wrong?"

"Even just hearing the name of the sex that's the cause of all my miseries..."

Cocardasse struck him hard on the shoulder. "Crooked ace! Between friends you've got to make allowances, and we all have our little failings—but if you wear out my ears one more time with your passions, God's blood, I'll cut yours off!"

Passepoil refrained from pointing out the grammatical error, and understood the threat was to his ears rather than his passions. Though they were long and red, he was attached to them. "You didn't want me to make sure the girl was there."

"The damsel is there," said Cocardasse. "Just listen." A burst of happy laughter came from the next room. Passepoil put his hand on his heart.

Cocardasse went on with the instructions. "'You'll take the girl, or rather, you'll ask her politely to get into the chaise, which you'll have carried to the little pleasure house.'"

"'And you won't use force, unless there's no other way.'"

"That's right! And I say fifty pistoles is good pay for a job like that!"

Passepoil sighed tenderly. "That Gonzague's a lucky dog!"

Cocardasse reached for his sword.

Passepoil stopped his hand. "Brother, just kill me now. It's the only way to quench the fire that consumes me. Here's my breast; deliver the fatal blow."

Cocardasse looked at him with deep compassion. "Sweetheart, you're hopeless! Worthless trash who won't spend even one of your fifty pistoles drinking or gambling!"

The noise in the next room grew louder. Then Cocardasse and Passepoil jumped as a harsh, rasping voice spoke quietly from behind them: "It's time!"

They whirled around. The hunchback from the Villa Gonzague stood by the table, calmly opening their packages.

"Holy...!" said Cocardasse. "Where did this fellow come from?"

Passepoil had prudently stepped back.

The hunchback held out one suit of livery to Passepoil and the other to Cocardasse. "Make it quick!" he ordered without raising his voice.

They hesitated. Cocardasse especially couldn't reconcile himself to the idea of putting on servant's clothes. "God's hat! What business is it of yours?"

"Shush!" whispered the hunchback. "Hurry up."

Through the door they could hear Doña Cruz saying, "It's perfect! All that's missing now is the chaise."

"Hurry up!" the hunchback ordered again, and at the same time he put out the lamp.

The door to Aurore's room opened, throwing a little light across the main room. Cocardasse and Passepoil withdrew behind the spiral staircase to dress quickly. The hunchback opened one of the windows looking onto the Rue du Chantre. A faint whistle echoed in the darkness, followed by the sound of a chaise being picked up.

The two chambermaids felt their way across the main room. The hunchback opened the door to let them out. Then he whispered, "Are you ready?"

"We're ready," answered Cocardasse and Passepoil.

"Go to work!"

Doña Cruz came out of Aurore's room, saying, "Do I have to go find you a chaise? Why didn't your chivalrous devil think of it?"

The hunchback closed the bedroom door behind her, leaving the main room in complete darkness. Doña Cruz was afraid of no man—it was demons she feared in the dark. She'd just made mocking reference to the devil, and now she thought she could already sense his horns in the darkness. She turned back to reopen Aurore's door, but two strong hairy hands grabbed hers. They belonged to Cocardasse. Doña Cruz tried to cry out, but terror closed her throat and choked off her voice.

Aurore, turning coquettishly in circles in front of her mirror to admire her finery, heard nothing over the hubbub of the crowd in the street. Someone had just announced that Mr. Law's carriage, coming from the Villa Angoulême, had reached the Trahoir crossroads. "He's coming! He's coming!" cried voices on all sides, and the crowd stirred wildly.

"Mademoiselle," said Cocardasse, bowing low—a gesture wasted in the darkness—"Allow me to offer you my hand, God's life!"

Doña Cruz had fled to the other end of the room. There she met two other hands, not as hairy but more callused, belonging to Passepoil. This time she managed to cry out.

"Here he is! Here he is!" shouted the crowd, and poor Doña Cruz's cry was lost, just like Cocardasse's bow. She escaped from Passepoil's grip, but Cocardasse cornered her. The two men worked together to block off every escape except the street door. When she reached the double doors, they opened, and streetlight fell on her face—and Cocardasse couldn't help starting with surprise. A man standing outside on the steps threw a cape over her head. She was grabbed, half-crazy with fear, and pushed into the chaise, whose door was immediately closed.

"To the little house behind Saint Magloire!" ordered Cocardasse.

The chaise hurried away. Passepoil appeared, wriggling like a fish on a riverbank. He'd touched silk! "She's adorable! Adorable! Adorable! Oh, that Gonzague!"

Cocardasse looked pensive. Then, as if trying to chase away an unwelcome thought, he cried, "God's hat! I hope that was a job well done!"

"Such a smooth soft hand!"

"The fifty pistoles are ours." Cocardasse looked around like someone not quite sure of what he was asserting.

"And her waist! I envy Gonzague neither his titles nor his gold, but..."

"Come on! Let's go!"

"She'll trouble my sleep!"

Cocardasse grabbed Passepoil by the collar and dragged him away. Then he changed his mind. "Out of kindness we have to free the old woman and the boy."

"Didn't the old woman strike you as well preserved?" asked Passepoil, and got stunned by a punch in the back.

Cocardasse unlocked the kitchen door. Before he could open it, the hunchback—whom they'd almost forgotten—said from over by the stairs, "You did well, men, but the job isn't finished. Listen up."

"That damned little cripple's got a nerve!" grumbled Cocardasse.

"Now that we can't see him," said Passepoil, "his voice gives me a funny feeling, like I've heard it somewhere before."

With the dry repeated sound of striking a light, the hunchback relit the lamp.

"What else do we need to do, if you please, Master Aesop?" asked Cocardasse. "That's what they call you, isn't it?"

"Aesop, Jonah, and other names. Pay attention to my orders!"

"Bow to his lordship, Passepoil! His orders, he says! Damn!"

Cocardasse touched his hat, and Passepoil did the same, adding mockingly, "We await Your Excellency's orders!"

"Good thing!" said the hunchback curtly.

Our two swordsmen exchanged a look. Dropped his mocking tone, Passepoil murmured, "I know I've heard that voice before."

From behind the staircase the hunchback fetched two of those lanterns on handles that were carried in front of chaises at night. He lit them. "Take these."

"Come on!" said Cocardasse grumpily. "You think we can catch up with that chaise?"

"It's long gone by now, unless it waited," added Passepoil.

"Take these!" said the hunchback stubbornly.

Our two bravos each took a lantern.

The hunchback pointed to the room out of which Doña Cruz had come a few minutes earlier. "There's a girl in there."

"Another one!" cried Cocardasse and Passepoil together. And the latter thought aloud, "The second chaise!"

"That girl is finishing dressing," continued the hunchback. "She'll come out that door, like the other one."

Cocardasse nodded at the lit lanterns. "She'll see us."

"She'll see you."

"So what do we do?"

"I'll tell you. You'll greet her openly but respectfully. You'll say, 'We're here to take you to the ball at the palace.'"

"There was nothing about this in our instructions," observed Passepoil.

And Cocardasse added, "Will she believe us?"

"She'll believe you, if you tell her who sent you."

"Monsieur de Gonzague?"

"Absolutely not! And also if you add that your master will wait for her, at the stroke of midnight—remember that!—in the palace gardens, at Diana's Circle."

"God's blood! So now we have two masters?" cried Cocardasse.

"No, only one—but his name isn't Gonzague." The hunchback went to the spiral staircase and set his foot on the first step.

"Then what's our master's name?" Cocardasse tried in vain to keep up his insolent smirk. "Aesop, maybe?"

"Or Jonah?" stammered Passepoil.

The hunchback stared them down, and their eyes fell. He said slowly, "Your master is named Henri de Lagardère."

"Lagardère!" Their voices were muted and shaking.

The hunchback climbed the stairs. At the top he paused a moment to glance down at the cowed and beaten men below. Then he said only, "Behave yourselves!" And he vanished.

"Ouch!" said Passepoil when the door upstairs had closed.

"Crooked ace!" muttered Cocardasse. "We've seen the devil."

"Let's behave ourselves, brother."

"God's hat! Let's be as good as gold, and behave ourselves," agreed Cocardasse. Then he added, "You know, I thought I recognized..."

"The little Parisian?"

"No, the girl, the one we put into the chaise. I thought she looked like the sweet gypsy girl I saw in Spain, on Lagardère's arm."

The door to Aurore's room opened, and Passepoil cried out.

"What's wrong?" asked Cocardasse, trembling—because now everything spooked him.

"The girl I saw on Lagardère's arm, in Flanders!" stammered Passepoil.

Aurore stood in the doorway. "Flor!" she called. "Where are you?"

Holding their lanterns and bowing low, Cocardasse and Passepoil came forward, more and more determined to behave themselves. In any case with their sheathed swords they made splendid lackeys. Few small-town mercenaries could have matched them for poise and style. Aurore looked so perfectly beautiful in her ball gown that they were lost in admiration.

"Where's Flor? Did the silly thing leave without me?"

"Without you," echoed Cocardasse.

And Passepoil reechoed, "Without you."

Aurore gave her fan to Passepoil and her bouquet to Cocardasse. "I'm ready. Let's go!"

"Let's go!" said the two echoes.

As she was getting into the second chaise, she asked, "Did he say where I'll meet him?"

"At Diana's Circle," murmured Cocardasse in a tenor voice.

"At midnight," added Passepoil.

Both of them stood with their heads bowed and their arms hanging. They set off. Over the roof of the chaise they were escorting, lanterns in hand, Cocardasse Junior and Brother Passepoil exchanged one last look, signifying, "Let's behave ourselves!"

The next moment you would have seen a little man dressed all in black come out the alley door that led to Master Louis's rooms and go trotting away along the Rue du Chantre. He crossed the Rue Saint Honoré just as the great Mr. Law's carriage was passing, and the crowd made plenty of fun of his hump, but their mockery didn't seem to bother him. He went around the Palais-Royal and into the Fountain Court. In the Rue de Valois there was a small door that led to the part of the palace called the Privacy of Monsieur, the king's brother. It was here that Philippe d'Orléans, Regent of France, had his private business office. The hunchback gave a special knock. The door opened immediately, and from the far end of a dark corridor a loud voice rang out. "Oh, it's you, Rumpelstiltskin! Come quick, you're expected!"

Admired at court, all-powerful, wealthy, with no one to oppose him but a lowly exile, the Prince of Gonzague might think his triumph was assured. But the Tarpeian Rock stands near the Capitol, and there's many a slip twixt the cup and the lip. No matter how precarious his own position, Henri de Lagardère's vengeance advanced relentlessly, as inexorable as Fate. He was finally about to confront Nevers's murderer. By a trick as clever as it was bold, he would soon use Gonzague to condemn Gonzague—and to name the murderer he would call on the testimony of... the victim himself.

BOOK II: LAGARDÈRE!

PART FOUR: THE PALAIS-ROYAL

I. In the Tent

Stones have their destinies too. Walls have long lives and see generations pass; they've heard some stories! It would be interesting to write the biography of one of those blocks cut from limestone or sandstone or granite or tuff. What dramas would surround it, what tragedies and comedies! What momentous events and what trivia! How much laughter, how many tears!

It was tragedy that built the Palais-Royal. Armand du Plessis, Cardinal de Richelieu, a great statesman, a terrible poet, bought the old Villa Rambouillet from Lord Dufresne and the grand Villa Mercoeur from the Marquis of Estrées. On the site of those two noble dwellings Richelieu asked the architect Lemercier to build him a house befitting his great importance. He acquired four other properties to lay out the gardens. Finally he bought the Villa Sillery to open up the street view toward his façade, displaying the Richelieu crest topped by a cardinal's hat; and he had a broad new street put through to enable his carriage to travel without hindrance out to his country estate at Grange Batelière. The street is still called Richelieu; the country estate—on which now stands the finest neighborhood in Paris—gave its name to the area behind the Opéra; only the palace has preserved no memory of him in its name. While it was still new it swapped the cardinal's title for an even higher rank: Richelieu was barely in his grave before his palace was renamed the Palais-Royal.

How that terrible priest loved the theater! You could almost say he built his palace to house theaters. He included three, though he really needed only one, to stage his own beloved tragedy, *Mirame*—that maiden idolized by her own creator. The hand that chopped off Marshal de Montmorency's head was probably too heavy to excel at light verse. *Mirame* was performed for three thousand boys and girls dragged in off the streets, who were certainly wise enough to clap. The next day a hundred odes, as many dithyrambs, and twice as many madrigals rained blandly down on the city, singing the praises of the poet, and then the craven chorus fell silent. People whispered about a young man who also wrote tragedies, but who didn't happen to be a cardinal, and whose name was Corneille.

One theater with two hundred seats, another with five hundred, another with three thousand: Richelieu would settle for nothing less. While he carried out Tarquin's colorful policy and systematically lopped off all heads insolent enough to rise above average, he still kept busy with scenery and costumes, like the excellent director he was. They say he invented the tossing-sea set piece, which now allows so many stage hands to provide for their families; and gauze clouds; and moving ramps and risers. He thought up the spring that rolled the rock of Sisyphus, son of Aeolus, in Desmarest's play. They say all those little skills, like dancing, mattered more to him than political glory. But rules are rules: Nero was no immortal, in spite of his acclaim as a flautist; and Richelieu too died.

Anne of Austria and her son Louis XIV moved into the Palais-Royal. Outside those new walls France raised an uproar. Mazarin, who didn't write tragic verse, heard the shouts of the crowd gathered under his windows, and he laughed covertly but trembled too. Mazarin had been given an apartment in the east wing, connected to what's now the Nautical Gallery, near the Fountain Court—the same rooms later used by Philippe d'Orléans, Regent of France. That's also where, in the spring of 1640, during the Fronde rebellion, the mob broke into the palace to see for themselves that the young king hadn't been taken away from them. A painting of that scene, hanging in the gallery of the Palais-Royal, shows Anne of Austria holding up the infant Louis XIV in his swaddling clothes for the crowd to behold.

Louis Philippe, King of the French and grandnephew of the Regent, said something memorable on the subject—something that suits the Palais-Royal, that agnostic landmark, charming but cold, free of prejudice, a sharp wit made of stone blocks, a building that one day could wear Camille Desmoulins's green cockade of Revolution behind its ear, and the next day embrace the Cossacks of the Restoration. Looking at that painting by Mauzaisse, Casimir Delavigne expressed surprise that it showed the queen standing amid the mob alone, without bodyguards. The Duke of Orléans, later Louis Philippe, smiled and answered, "They're there, you just can't see them." The same could be said of the Regent, the wittiest prince who ever wasted the nation's time and money on orgies.

In 1672 Louis XIV granted possession of the Palais-Royal as an appanage to Monsieur, his brother and the flower of the House of Orléans. Henrietta Anne of England, Duchess of Orléans, held court brilliantly there. In 1692 the Duke of Chartres, Monsieur's son and the future Regent, was married there to Mademoiselle de Blois, youngest of the illegitimate daughters of the king and Madame de Montespan.

Under the Regency, tragedy was out of vogue. The sad ghost of Mirame must have averted her eyes at the sight of the little suppers the Duke of Orléans hosted, in the words of Saint-Simon, "in very peculiar company." But the theaters saw use, because actresses were in fashion. The beautiful Duchess of Berry, the Regent's daughter, always either drunk or hung over, her nose dusted with Spanish tobacco, joined that peculiar company, which—again according to Saint-Simon—included no one besides "ladies of mediocre virtue and gentlemen of none, but all of them notable for wit and debauchery." But Saint-Simon, though he was close to the Regent, didn't like him. If history can't entirely hide the prince's unfortunate failings, at least it provides evidence of the great qualities even his excesses couldn't smother. His vices were the fault of his wicked tutor, Cardinal Dubois. His few virtues are all the more to his credit given the great effort devoted to snuffing them out. His orgies were exceptional in not involving bloodshed. He was human, and good; he might have been great, if not for the role models and the teachings that poisoned his youth.

The garden of the Palais-Royal was then much larger than it is today. It reached from the houses on the Rue de Richelieu on one side to the houses on the Rue des Bons Enfants on the other. At the far end, toward the Rotunda, it reached all the way to the Rue Neuve des Petits Champs. It was only much later, during the reign of Louis XVI, that Louis Philippe Joseph, Duke of Orléans, built what are called the Stone Galleries, to isolate and beautify the garden. At the time of our story, enormous bowers trimmed in the shape of Italian porticoes surrounded the flowerbeds. The fine avenue of Indian chestnuts planted by Richelieu was then in its prime. The Cracow Tree, the last representative of that avenue, was still alive at the beginning of the nineteenth century. Two other avenues, of elms trimmed into spheres, ran perpendicular to it. Where they met stood a semicircular pool with a fountain. Going back toward the palace, Mercury's Circle stood on one side and Diana's Circle on the other, surrounded by high shrubberies. Behind the semicircular pool, staggered rows of lindens separated two great lawns.

The east wing of the palace—larger than the west wing, which later held the Théâtre Français on the site of the famous gallery by Mansard—ended in a pedimented gable with five windows overlooking the garden and Diana's Circle. The Regent had his private business office there, and the Grand Théâtre, which had seen lots of changes since Richelieu's time, was used for performances by the Opéra. Besides its formal halls, the east wing also held the apartment of the Princess Palatine, Elisabeth Charlotte of Bavaria, Monsieur's second wife and now dowager Duchess of Orléans; that of the Regent's wife, the present Duchess of Orléans; and that of the Duke of Chartres. The young princesses, except for the Duchess of Berry and the Abbess of Chelles, lived in the west wing, which stretched to the Rue de Richelieu.

On the other side, the Opéra stood partly on the lot now occupied by the Fountain Court and the Rue de Valois, and backed onto the Bons Enfants Convent. A passageway known by the gallant name of the Laughter Court separated the Regent's rooms from the private entrance of the nuns; by special permission they enjoyed access to the palace garden. Otherwise the garden wasn't open to the public, the way it is now, but it was easy enough to get in. Almost all the houses on the surrounding streets had balconies, terraces, small doors, and even stairs that gave access to the flowerbeds. The residents felt so much entitled to the use of the garden that later they sued Prince Louis Philippe Joseph d'Orléans when he tried to build an enclosing wall around the Palais-Royal. Writers from the time agree that the palace garden was a delightful spot, and if they're to be believed we should lament its loss. Nothing could be less pleasant than those walkways now, crowded with nannies strolling between two rows of sickly elms. No doubt the addition of the Stone Galleries, by blocking the airflow, harmed the plants. Our Palais-Royal is a fine courtyard; it's no longer a garden.

That night it was magical, a paradise, a fairy palace. The Regent, normally not much for display, had done things magnificently for once. It's true people said it was the great Mr. Law who was paying for the ball. But what did it matter? Lots of people in this world think results are their own justification. If Mr. Law was paying for the violins that played in his honor, it's only because he understood public relations. He deserved to live in our own cleverer times, when a writer can make himself famous by buying up the first fourteen print runs of his book, so the fifteenth can finally sell, or almost; when a dentist spends ten thousand écus on advertising to drum up twenty thousand écus of business; or when a theater director seats three or four hundred humble friends at every night's performance, to prove to the two hundred and fifty genuine spectators that fervor isn't dead in France.

Mr. Law can be considered the true father of modern banking, and not just for his invention of exchange rate speculation. This ball was for him, and it was meant to celebrate his System and himself. If you want to dazzle people by throwing powder in their eyes, you have to throw it from a great height. Mr. Law had felt the need of a pedestal from which to throw his powder. A new stock issue was being readied for the next day. Since money cost him nothing, he could throw a splendid ball. Never mind the palace rooms, decorated for the occasion with astonishing luxury; in spite of the lateness of the season, the ball was mostly taking place out in the garden, which had been draped and roofed over.

The theme was a settlement of Louisiana colonists on the banks of the Mississippi, that river of gold. Every greenhouse in Paris had been requisitioned to supply the beds of exotic shrubs; tropical flowers and the fruits of the terrestrial paradise grew everywhere. The countless lanterns hanging from trees and columns were Indian lanterns, supposedly. The tents of the savage Indians, scattered here and there, seemed a little too nice—but Mr. Law's friends went around explaining, "You have no idea how advanced the natives are there!" Once you accepted the not quite believable tents, everything certainly was delightfully rococo. There were artful vistas, forests on canvas, fearsome cardboard rocks, cataracts that foamed with the help of a little soap.

Above the central pool stood an allegorical statue representing the Mississippi—a river deity made to look a little like Mr. Law—holding an urn from which water flowed. Behind the deity, in the pool, stood a structure meant to represent one of those dams built by beavers in North America. Monsieur de Buffon hadn't yet produced his scientific description of those curious, ingenious, methodical animals. (We include the detail about the beaver dam because it says it all, and would be worth a lengthy digression all by itself.) Around the statue of the river deity an Indian ballet with a cast of five hundred was going to be staged, led by starlets from the Opéra—Mesdemoiselles Nivelle, Desbois, Duplant, and Hemoux—along with Messrs Leguay, Salvator, and Pompignan. The Regent's companions in pleasure—the Marquis of Cossé, the Duke of Brissac, the poet La Fare, Madame de Tencin, Madame de Royan, and the Duchess of Berry—made fun of the whole thing, but not as much fun as the Regent himself. Only one man could outdo the Regent in making fun, and that was Mr. Law.

The Duke of Brissac and Madame de Toulouse had officially opened the ball. The rooms were already mobbed, the garden was crowded, and tables were set up for playing lansquenet in all those supposedly savage tents. In spite of the guards—disguised as comic-opera Indians—posted outside all the houses bordering the garden, more than one gatecrasher had managed to slip inside: some of the domino cloaks passing by looked Catholic enough to belong to nuns from the convent. From all sides came the noise and bustle of a crowd given permission to have a good time. But the toast of the ball had yet to appear: no one had seen the Regent, or the young princesses, or Mr. Law. The people waited.

When the sachems of the great river felt like smoking the calumet of peace, they could withdraw to tables set up inside a wigwam of red-orange velvet with gold piping, not far from Diana's Circle, under the Regent's office windows. Inside that crowded tent, around a marble table covered with a mat, a rowdy game of lansquenet was going on. Gold was being thrown around by fistfuls; people shouted and laughed. Nearby a group of elderly gentlemen talked quietly while playing réversi.

Around the lansquenet table we would have recognized the handsome little Marquis of Chaverny, as well as Choisy, Navailles, Gironne, Nocé, Taranne, Albret, and others. Monsieur de Peyrolles was there too, and was winning—a notorious habit of his. People usually kept a close watch on his fingers; under the Regency cheating at cards was no sin. Conversation was limited to numbers that crisscrossed and bounced off one another—"A hundred louis!"—"Fifty!"— "Two hundred!"—and the occasional oath by the losers, and the uncontrollable laughter of the winners. Naturally all the men around the table were unmasked. Out in the garden avenues, on the other hand, lots of masks and dominoes strolled by in conversation. Servants in whimsical livery, most of them masked to preserve their masters' incognito, waited on the far side of the Regent's steps.

"Are you winning, Chaverny?" asked a little blue domino who'd poked her hooded head through the tent opening. Chaverny emptied the last of his purse onto the table.

"Save us, Cydalise," cried Gironne, "nymph of the virgin forest!"

A second domino looked in behind the first. "Excuse me?"

"She's not a person, Desbois, darling," said Gironne. "She's the trees."

"Well, all right, then!" said Mademoiselle Desbois-Duplant, coming in. Cydalise handed her purse to Gironne.

One of the old gentlemen at the réversi table made a scornful gesture. "In our day, Monsieur de Barbanchois," he said to his neighbor, "these things were done differently."

"Everything's spoiled, Monsieur de La Hunaudaye," said his neighbor, "everything's corrupted."

"Diminished, Monsieur de Barbanchois."

"Bastardized, Monsieur de La Hunaudaye."

"Disfigured."

"Debased."

"Dirtied!"

And then together they sighed deeply and said, "Where are we all headed, baron? Where are we all headed?"

The Baron of Barbanchois touched one of the agate buttons adorning the Baron of La Hunaudaye's old-fashioned doublet. "Who are these people, baron?"

"That's what I want to know, baron!"

"Are you in, Taranne?" cried Montaubert. "Fifty!"

"Taranne?" muttered Barbanchois. "That's not a man, that's a street!"

"Are you in, Albret?"

"That was Henri IV's mother's name!" said La Hunaudaye. "Where do they dig up these names?"

"Where did the baroness's spaniel Fido get his name?" said Barbanchois, opening his snuffbox. Cydalise, who was passing by, rudely stuck two fingers into it. He was left openmouthed.

"Good stuff!" said the actress.

"Madame," said Barbanchois solemnly. "I don't like to share. Please accept the whole box."

Cydalise didn't hesitate. She took the snuffbox and stroked the outraged gentleman's old chin. Then she spun around and went away.

"Where are we all headed?" repeated Barbanchois, choking. "What would the late king say to all this?"

"You lose, Chaverny! You lose again!" rose the cry at the lansquenet table.

"I don't care. I've got my estate at Chaneilles. I'm still in."

"His father was an honorable soldier," said Barbanchois. "Who's he with?"

"With the Prince of Gonzague," said La Hunaudaye.

220

"God save us from the Italians!"

"Are the Germans any better, baron? Like that Count Horn broken on the wheel at the Place de Grève for murder!"

"A relative of His Highness! Where are we all headed?"

"I tell you, baron, soon they'll be cutting people's throats on the street in broad daylight!"

"They've already started, baron! Don't you read the news? Somebody was murdered yesterday near the Temple, a woman named Lauvet, a stock speculator."

"And this morning a clerk of the war department funds, Monsieur Sandrier, was pulled out of the Seine at the Notre Dame bridge."

"Because he talked too loudly about that damned Scotsman," said Barbanchois very quietly.

"Shh!" whispered La Hunaudaye. "That makes eleven in a week!"

"Oriol! Oriol! To the rescue!" cried all the rakes.

That fat little financier had appeared at the tent opening. He was wearing a mask, and the ridiculous extravagance of his costume had made him a comical hit at the ball. "I'm shocked. Everybody recognized me!"

"There aren't two Oriols!" cried Navailles.

"The ladies think one's more than enough!" said Nocé.

They all laughed. "You're just jealous!"

"Gentlemen, have you seen Nivelle?" asked Oriol.

"To think," said Gironne, "poor Oriol has spent the last eight months begging in vain for a chance to be the next financier our dear Nivelle makes fun of and gobbles whole!"

"You're just jealous!" they all said again.

"Have you been to see d'Hozier the genealogist, Oriol?"—"Have you got your parchment scrolls, Oriol?"—"Do you know the name of the ancestor you're going to send off to the Crusades, Oriol?"—And they all laughed.

Barbanchois folded his hands.

"They're gentlemen, baron," said La Hunaudaye, "and yet they're making fun of things that are sacrosanct!"

"Where are we all headed, Lord, where are we all headed?"

"Peyrolles," said Oriol, coming to the table, "I'm in for fifty louis, because it's you—but push your sleeves up."

"Excuse me?" said Peyrolles. "I only joke with my equals, little man."

Chaverny glanced over at the servants waiting beyond the Regent's steps. "By God," he murmured, "those rascals look bored. Go fetch them, Taranne, so our Monsieur de Peyrolles can have someone to joke with."

This time Peyrolles didn't hear—he picked his occasions to get angry—and got satisfaction by winning Oriol's fifty gold louis.

"And all this paper!" said Barbanchois. "Nothing but paper!"

"We're getting our pensions in paper now, baron!" said La Hunaudaye.

"And our rents. What do those scraps of paper even mean?"

"Money's disappearing."

"Gold too. I'll tell you, baron, we're headed straight for catastrophe."

La Hunaudaye discreetly shook Barbanchois's hand. "My friend, that's exactly where we're headed. That's what the baroness says."

Oriol's voice rose over the noise and laughter and mutual insults. "Have you heard the news? The big news?"

"No—let's have your big news!"

"I'll bet you a thousand to one you can't guess it."

"Mr. Law turned Catholic?"—"Madame de Berry started drinking water?"—"Monsieur du Maine asked the Regent for an invitation to the ball?"—and a hundred other impossibilities.

"You're cold! You're cold, my darlings! You'll never get it. The Princess of Gonzague, the inconsolable widow of Monsieur de Nevers, Artemisia sworn to eternal mourning..."

All the old gentlemen pricked up their ears at her name.

"Well," Oriol went on, "Artemisia has finished drinking the ashes of Mausolus. The Princess of Gonzague is at the ball."

"Impossible!" they all cried.

"I saw her with my own eyes, sitting with the Princess Palatine. But I saw something even more extraordinary."

"What?" they all cried.

Oriol puffed himself up; he held the floor. "I saw—and I wasn't hallucinating, and I wasn't dreaming—I saw the Prince of Gonzague turned away at the door."

Silence fell. This mattered to everyone: the fortunes of every man around the lansquenet table depended on Gonzague.

"What's so surprising about that?" asked Peyrolles. "Matters of state..."

"His Royal Highness isn't busy with matters of state at this time of night."

"But if an ambassador..."

"His Royal Highness wasn't with an ambassador."

"Then maybe some new infatuation..."

"His Royal Highness wasn't with a lady."

All of those sharp, categorical rebuttals came from Oriol. The group's curiosity grew.

"Then who was with His Royal Highness?"

"Good question," said Oriol. "Monsieur de Gonzague himself was put out by the answer."

"And what did the servants say?" asked Navailles.

"It's a mystery, gentlemen, a mystery! The Regent's been feeling down ever since he got a certain letter from Spain. And today he gave orders to admit, by way of the little door on the Fountain Court, someone none of his regular servants saw, except for Blondeau, who thought that in the outer office he glimpsed a little man dressed all in black, a hunchback."

"A hunchback!" they all cried. "It's raining hunchbacks!"

"His Royal Highness is seeing him privately. And La Fare and Brissac and even the Duchess of Phalaris all found the door closed to them."

There was another silence. The tent opening offered a view of the windows of the Regent's private rooms, and Oriol glanced that way. "Well, well!" he cried, pointing. "They're still together!"

All eyes turned toward the lit windows. Against the white curtains, the sharp silhouette of Philippe d'Orléans paced by. Another shadow, less distinct because further from the window, seemed to pace alongside him. In a moment the two shadows had gone past the window. When they came back the other direction they'd switched places. Now the Regent's silhouette was blurrier, while that of his companion fell clearly on the curtains: something misshapen, a big hump on a small body, and long arms that gestured intently.

II. A Private Interview

The silhouettes of Philippe d'Orléans and the hunchback disappeared from the curtains: the Regent had taken a seat, and the hunchback stood respectfully but firmly before him.

The Regent's private business office had four windows, two of which looked onto the Fountain Court, and three entrances: one the public door from the outer office, the other two hidden—the essential ingredient of any comedy. One of those hidden doors opened onto the Laughter Court, the other onto the Fountain Court. After a performance at the Opéra the actresses came over, their way lit by lanterns on handles even though they only had to cross the Laughter Court, and hammered violently on the Regent's door. Meanwhile Cossé, Brissac, Gonzague, La Fare, and Gouffier's illegitimate son the Marquis of Bonnivet—whom the Duchess of Berry had taken into her service "to have a tool for cutting off ears"—came and knocked on the Fountain Court door in broad daylight. The attendants at those two doors had plum appointments: the door on the Laughter Court was watched by a staunch old woman who'd been a singer at the Opéra, and the door on the Fountain Court by Master Le Bréant, former groom to Monsieur. This same Le Bréant also kept watch over the garden from a little lodge behind Diana's Circle.

It was Le Bréant's voice we heard from down a dark corridor when the hunchback came in by way of the Fountain Court. The hunchback was indeed expected and awaited. The Regent was alone, and anxious. He was still in his dressing gown, though the ball had long since begun. His fine hair was up in curlers, and he wore special gloves to preserve the whiteness of his hands. In her memoirs his mother writes that he inherited his excessive taste for care of his person from Monsieur. Indeed, to the end of his life Monsieur was just the same, and more fastidious than a woman.

The Regent was past forty-five, and looked older because of the great fatigue that clouded his features. Still, he was handsome: his face expressed nobility and charm, and his eyes, of a feminine softness, suggested goodness bordering on weakness. He stooped slightly when he wasn't in public. His lips and especially his cheeks had the drooping softness characteristic of the House of Orléans. His mother, the Princess Palatine, had passed on to him a little of her German good cheer and ready wit—but she'd kept most of it for herself. If we can believe what this fine woman herself says in her memoirs, which are a masterpiece of observation and originality, she didn't try to give him beauty she didn't have.

Orgies leave little trace on some members of the elite: there are men of iron. But Philippe d'Orléans wasn't one them. His face and posture spoke eloquently of the way debauchery fatigued him. You could already predict that this profligate life was down to its last resources, and that death awaited him at the bottom of a glass of champagne.

A single manservant met the hunchback at the office door and let him in.

The Regent looked him up and down. "Are you the one who wrote to me from Spain?"

"No, my lord," replied the hunchback respectfully.

"And from Brussels?"

"Not from Brussels either."

"And from Paris?"

"No."

The Regent looked him over again. "I had trouble picturing you as that Lagardère," he murmured.

The hunchback smiled and bowed.

"Sir," continued the Regent gently and seriously, "I wasn't referring to what you probably think. I've never seen this Lagardère."

"My lord," answered the hunchback, still smiling, "he was known as handsome Lagardère when he was in your royal uncle's light cavalry. I could never have been either handsome or a cavalryman."

The Regent wanted to move on. "What's your name?"

"At home I'm Master Louis, my lord. Outside, people like me have no name other than the nickname we're given."

"Where do you live?"

"Far away."

"Are you refusing to tell me where you live?"

"Yes, my lord."

The Regent glared at him, then said quietly, "I have a police force, sir, and it's said to be competent. I can easily find out..."

"Since I see Your Royal Highness insists, I'll stifle my objections. I live at the Prince of Gonzague's villa."

"At the Villa Gonzague!" echoed the Regent in surprise.

The hunchback bowed. "The rent's high," he said coolly.

The Regent looked thoughtful. "I first heard of this Lagardère a long time ago—a very long time ago. He was once a bold cutthroat."

"Since then he's done his best to atone for his foolishness."

"What are you to him?"

"Nothing."

"Why didn't he come himself?"

"Because I was available."

"If I wanted to see him, where would I find him?"

"I can't answer that, my lord."

"But..."

"You have a police force, it's said to be competent, give it a try."

"Is that a dare, sir?"

"It's a threat. An hour from now, Henri de Lagardère can be out of reach of all your searching, and the initiative he undertook for the sake of his conscience he'll never repeat."

"So he took that initiative reluctantly?"

"Reluctantly, the very word."

"Why?"

"Because all of his life's happiness is at risk in this move, a move he didn't have to make."

"So he was obliged to make this move because of...?"

"An oath."

"Sworn to whom?"

"To a dying man."

"And that man was named?"

"You know it well, my lord. That man was named Philippe de Lorraine, Duke of Nevers."

The Regent's head dropped to his chest. "It's been twenty years," he murmured in a changed voice. "I've forgotten nothing—nothing! Poor Philippe, I loved him, he loved me. Since the time they took him from me, I don't know if I've shaken the hand of a true friend."

The hunchback watched him closely, with signs of strong emotion on his face. For a moment he opened his mouth to speak, but then with a violent effort he held back. His face regained its impassivity.

The Regent straightened up and said slowly, "The Duke of Nevers and I were close kin. My sister married his cousin, the Duke of Lorraine. As a prince and as a relative, I owe my protection to his widow, who is in any case the wife of one of my closest friends. If his daughter's alive, I promise she'll be a wealthy heiress, and she'll marry a prince if she wants to. As for the killing of my poor Philippe, people say I have only one virtue, which is to forget a wrong, and it's true: the thought of revenge is born and dies within me in the same minute. But I too swore an oath when they told me Philippe was dead. Now that I rule France, punishing Nevers's murderer would no longer be vengeance, it would be justice."

The hunchback bowed silently.

"There are a few things I still need to know," the Regent went on. "Why did this Lagardère wait so long before approaching me?"

"Because he said to himself, 'When I give up the guardianship of my ward, I want Mademoiselle de Nevers to be fully grown, so she can recognize both her friends and her enemies.'"

"Does he have proof of his claims?"

"All but one."

"Which is?"

"The proof that will unmask the murderer."

"He knows the identity of the murderer?"

"He thinks he knows, and there exists a definite mark to confirm his suspicions."

"A mark can't prove anything."

"Your Royal Highness will soon judge. As for the birth and identity of the girl, all is in order."

The Regent pondered. After a silence he asked, "What oath did this Lagardère swear?"

"He promised to be the child's father."

"So he was there at the time of the killing?"

"He was there. The dying Nevers gave him the guardianship of his daughter."

"Did this Lagardère draw his sword to defend Nevers?"

"He did what he could. When Nevers was dead he escaped with the child, though he was alone against twenty men."

"I know he's the greatest swordsman in the world," murmured the Regent. "But your answers aren't clear, sir. If this Lagardère witnessed the killing, how can it be that he merely suspects who the murderer was?"

"It was a dark night. The killer was masked. He struck from behind."

"So it was the leader himself who struck?"

"It was the leader. And as Nevers fell he cried, 'Avenge me, friend!'"

"And that leader," pursued the Regent with evident hesitation, "was not the Marquis of Caylus-Tarrides?"

"The Marquis of Caylus-Tarrides is long dead," answered the hunchback. "The murderer lives. Your Royal Highness has only to say the word, and Lagardère will point him out tonight."

The Regent jumped on that. "So then this Lagardère is in Paris?" The hunchback bit his lip. The Regent stood up. "If he's in Paris, he's mine!" He rang a bell, and to the servant who came in he said, "Send me Monsieur de Machault immediately!" Machault was the Chief of Police.

The hunchback had regained his calm. "My lord," he said, glancing at his pocket watch, "at this very moment Monsieur de Lagardère is waiting for me outside Paris, on a road I won't name even under torture. It's now almost eleven. If Monsieur de Lagardère doesn't hear from me by eleven thirty, he'll ride at a gallop for the border. He has a relay of horses, and your Chief of Police won't catch up with him."

"I'll keep you hostage!"

"Me?" The hunchback smiled. "If you really insist on taking me prisoner, I'm in your power." He folded his arms.

The Chief of Police arrived. Monsieur de Machault was nearsighted and, not seeing the hunchback, he spoke without waiting to be addressed. "Here's news! Your Royal Highness will see whether we can show mercy in a mess like this one. I've got proof of their collusion with Alberoni. Cellamare is in it up to

227

his neck, along with Monsieur de Villeroy and Monsieur de Villars and all the old court that's with the Duke and Duchess of Maine."

"Silence!" cried the Regent. At the same moment Machault spotted the hunchback and stopped cold. The Regent said nothing for a good minute, and while he waited he examined the hunchback a few times covertly. The hunchback hadn't batted an eye.

"Machault," said the Regent finally, "I summoned you precisely to talk about Cellamare and the others. Please wait for me in the outer office."

As he crossed the room Machault eyed the hunchback curiously through his lorgnette. When he had reached the door the Regent added, "And please send in a sealed and countersigned safe-conduct, left blank."

Machault examined the hunchback one more time with his lorgnette before leaving.

The Regent couldn't keep a straight face that long. "Whose idea was it to put a four-eyes in charge of spying?" he muttered. Then he went on, "Sir, this Chevalier de Lagardère is negotiating with me like an equal. He sends me ambassadors, and in his last letter he even dictates the wording of the safe-conduct he wants. I assume his real motive is profit: no doubt he'll demand a reward."

"Your Royal Highness is mistaken," said the hunchback. "Monsieur de Lagardère will ask for nothing. Not even the Regent of France himself has it in his power to repay the Chevalier de Lagardère."

"Hell," said the Regent, "we'll certainly have to meet this mysterious, romantic character. He might be a hit at court, and even bring knight errantry back into fashion. How long do we have to wait for him?"

"Two hours."

"Perfect! He can be the unscheduled interlude between the Indian ballet and the savages' supper."

The servant came back with a safe-conduct countersigned by Secretary of State Le Blanc and Monsieur de Machault. While the Regent himself was filling in the blanks and signing it, he said, "Monsieur de Lagardère did nothing unforgivable. The late king was strict about dueling, and he was right. Mores have changed, thank God, and these days rapiers tend to stay sheathed. Monsieur de Lagardère's pardon will be registered tomorrow, and here's his safe-conduct."

The hunchback reached out, but the Regent held onto the paper. "You'll warn Monsieur de Lagardère that any violence on his part will nullify this document."

"The time for violence is over," said the hunchback solemnly.

"What do you mean by that, sir?"

"I mean that two days ago the Chevalier de Lagardère could not have accepted that condition."

"Because...?" The Regent was haughty and suspicious.

"Because it would have required a violation of his oath."

"So he swore to do more than be a father to the child?"

"He swore to avenge Nevers..." The hunchback stopped.

"Go on, sir."

"Before he escaped with the little girl," said the hunchback slowly, "the Chevalier de Lagardère said to the murderers, 'You will all die by my hand!' There were nine of them. Lagardère recognized seven, and all of those are dead."

The Regent grew pale. "By his hand?"

The hunchback nodded coldly.

"And the other two?"

The hunchback hesitated. Finally, looking the Regent in the eye, he said, "My lord, there are some heads that rulers don't like to see drop at the chopping block. The sound those heads make as they fall can shake a throne. Monsieur de Lagardère will leave the choice to Your Royal Highness. He asked me to say, 'The eighth murderer is just a servant, and Monsieur de Lagardère doesn't count him. The ninth is the man in charge, and he must die. If Your Royal Highness doesn't want the executioner to get involved, give that man a sword and leave the rest up to Monsieur de Lagardère.'"

The Regent held out the safe-conduct again. "The cause is just," he murmured. "I do this in memory of my poor Philippe. If Monsieur de Lagardère needs help..."

"My lord, Monsieur de Lagardère asks only one thing of Your Royal Highness."

"And that is?"

"Discretion. One reckless word can ruin everything."

"I'll be silent."

The hunchback bowed low, put the folded document in his pocket, and went to the door.

"So, in two hours?" said the Regent.

"In two hours." And the hunchback left.

"Did you get what you came for, little man?" asked Le Bréant, the old doorkeeper, when he saw him come back out.

The hunchback slipped a double louis into his hand. "Yes, but now I want to see the ball."

"God's head!" cried Le Bréant. "Check out the fine dancer!"

"And I also want you to give me the keys to your little lodge in the garden."

"What for, little man?"

The hunchback slipped him another double louis.

"The little man's got some funny ideas!" said Le Bréant. "Here's the key to my lodge."

"Lastly, I want you to put the package I left with you this morning into the lodge."

"Is there another double louis in it for me?"

"Two."

"Bravo! An excellent little man! I'll bet it's for a lovers' tryst."

"Could be." The hunchback smiled.

"If I were a woman, I'd love you in spite of your hump, because of all your double louis. But you need an invitation to get in there: those Royal Guards aren't kidding."

"I've got one. Just deliver the package."

"Right away, little man. Go back down the corridor and turn right. The vestibule is lit. Go down the steps. Have fun, and good luck!"

III. A Round of Lansquenet

We won't devote much attention to the conspiracies of the time. Though rich in dramatic incident, the plots led by Monsieur du Maine and his wife the princess, and the intrigues of the old Villeroy faction with the Spanish embassy, don't intersect with our story. Let's just say in passing that the Regent was surrounded by enemies. The judiciary hated him and held him in such contempt that at every formal event there was a dispute over precedence. The clergy opposed him because of the constitutional issue. In the standing army the old generals scorned his easygoing policies. Even within the Regency Council itself, some members systematically thwarted him. It seems clear that only Mr. Law's financial circus kept public opinion on his side. Duclos, the most impartial historian of the period, claims in his *Secret Memoirs* that the Regency of the Duke of Orléans would have been unsustainable without Law's Bank.

No one—except the bastard princes who'd been legitimized—could summon much personal hatred for the Regent, a man of neutral temperament, without an ounce of meanness in his heart, but whose goodness was little more than carelessness. You can only hate someone you might have loved intensely. Philippe d'Orléans had plenty of companions in pleasure, and not a single friend. Law's Bank enabled the Regent to buy off the princes; that's a harsh description, but the judgment of history will countenance no softer one. Once the princes were bought, the dukes followed, and the legitimized princes stood alone, with no comfort but the occasional visit to the Old Woman, as Madame de Maintenon was known after her fall from power. Monsieur de Toulouse, an honest man, surrendered openly. Monsieur du Maine and his wife looked for support abroad.

People say that when Lagrange's satirical poems, *The Philippics*, came out, the Regent was so insistent that the Duke of Saint-Simon, then his intimate friend, read them aloud to him, the duke finally agreed. They say the Regent heard without batting an eye—and even laughed at—verses in which the poet dragged his private and domestic life through the mud, depicting him sitting down to an orgy with his own daughter. But they also say he wept and fainted at verses accusing him of having poisoned, one by one, Louis XIV's entire line of succession. He was right: accusations like that, even if they're lies, leave a deep impression on ordinary people. Beaumarchais, who knew what he was talking about, said, "Something always sticks."

People loved the young King Louis XV. His education had been entrusted to hands hostile to the Regent. And even the public that didn't care either way felt some muted concern about the Regent's integrity: they were afraid Louis XIV's great-grandson would drop dead from one moment to the next, just like his father and his grandfather had. That provided fertile ground for conspiracies.

Of course Monsieur du Maine, Monsieur de Villeroy, the Prince of Cellamare, Monsieur de Villars, Alberoni, and the Breton-Spanish faction weren't plotting in their own interests—come on! They were only working to remove the young king from the unhealthy surroundings that had shortened the lives of his relatives.

At first the Regent met their attacks with indifference: soft ground makes the best fortifications, and a simple mattress blocks a bullet better than an iron shield. For a long time he slept soundly behind his insouciance. When he had to show himself, he showed himself—and since the attackers flocking around him had neither valor nor virtue, he need do no more than show himself. At the time in which our story is set, the Regent was still asleep behind his mattress, and the gossip of the baying mob didn't wake him. But God knows the mob was at full cry, around his palace, under his windows, and even within his home. The mob had lots to say. Except for the insults that went too far—those accusations of poison, which the very existence of the young King Louis XV refuted—the Regent shrugged off slander. His life was a barefaced scandal. Under his rule France was like one of those great disabled ships that have to be towed by another ship: the towing ship was England. And in spite of the success of Law's Bank, anyone who took the trouble to predict the looming bankruptcy of France found an audience.

Present in the Regent's garden that night were both his enthusiastic partisans and the cabal of malcontents: political malcontents, financial malcontents, moral malcontents, other malcontents. That last group—made up of all those who'd been young and splendid under Louis XIV—included the Baron of La Hunaudaye and the Baron of Barbanchois. They weren't especially elderly codgers, but they comforted each other by insisting that in their time the ladies were prettier, the men wittier, the sky bluer, the wind milder, the wine better, servants more devoted, chimneys less smoky. That kind of remarkably naive dissidence was known even in the time of Horace, whose epithet for an old man was *laudator temporis acti*—"flatterer of the past."

But let's be clear: politics didn't figure much in the conversation of the gilded, smiling, elegant, velvet-masked crowd that grew steadily and flowed through the palace courtyards to come have a look at the decorations in the garden—a crowd that was densest around Diana's Circle, beneath His Royal Highness's windows, wondering why the Regent had yet to appear. Everyone was in a festive mood, and if the Duchess of Maine's name appeared on someone's pretty lips it was only to pity her for missing the ball. The VIPs had begun to arrive. The Duke of Bourbon was there, escorting the Princess of Conti. Chancellor d'Aguesseau came in with the Princess Palatine. Father Dubois was paying court to Lord Stair, the English ambassador.

Then a rumor spread suddenly through all the rooms, the courtyards, the arbors—a rumor that panicked the ladies and made everyone forget the Regent's delay and even Mr. Law's absence: the tsar was at the Palais-Royal! Tsar Peter of Russia, led by his "tour guide," General de Tessé, and followed by thirty bodyguards whose order was never to leave him. Not an easy job: Tsar Peter made sudden moves and indulged impulsive whims. Tessé and those body-guards sometimes had to execute awkward maneuvers to catch up with him when he escaped from their respectful care. The tsar was staying at the Villa Lesdiguières, near the Arsenal. The Regent was treating him magnificently, but Parisian curiosity, roused to fever pitch by the visit of this savage potentate, hadn't yet been satisfied, because the tsar didn't like people paying attention to him. When gawkers began to gather around his residence, he sent Tessé out with orders to attack. The poor general would sooner have led ten battle campaigns. The honor he'd been given of guarding the Muscovite prince aged him by ten years.

Peter the Great had come to Paris to complete his education as a royal founder and builder. The Regent didn't want to host this terrible guest, but he made the best of what he couldn't help, and tried to dazzle the tsar with the splendor of his hospitality. It wasn't easy: the tsar resisted being dazzled. When he saw the magnificent bedroom that had been prepared for him at the Villa Lesdiguières, he had an army cot set down in the middle of the room and slept there. He went everywhere, going into shops and talking casually with shop-keepers, but he did it all incognito.

Because Parisian curiosity couldn't make sense of him, and because of the odd stories going around, Parisian curiosity had reached delirium. The lucky few who'd seen the tsar described him this way: tall, well-built, a little thin, olive complexion, light brown hair, very animated, big lively eyes with a penetrating and sometimes even fierce look. Just when you weren't expecting it, a nervous tic convulsed his face, attributed to poison given to him by his equerry Zubov when he was a child. When he first met someone, his expression was gracious and charming. We all know how hard graciousness is for wild animals. The most popular animal in Paris is the bear in the Jardin des Plantes, because he's a cheerful monster. For Parisians of that time a Muscovite tsar was certainly an odder, more fantastical, more unbelievable animal than a green bear or a blue ape.

He ate like an ogre—so says Verton, the king's maitre d', who was respon-sible for feeding him. He didn't like small portions, and he ate four lavish meals a day. At every meal he drank two bottles of wine, plus a bottle of liqueur with dessert, not to mention beer and lemonade between courses, which added up to twelve bottles of alcohol a day. From that alone, the Duke of Antin declared him to be the greatest man of his century. The day the duke hosted him at his castle at Petit Bourg, Peter the Great enjoyed the wine so much he couldn't get up from the table, and they had to carry him away, wondering just how much wine it took to do that to the sturdy Russian. His erotic appetites were even more ec-centric than his dining appetites; Paris discussed them at length—but we won't.

A great stir followed the news that the tsar was at the ball. He wasn't on the schedule. Everyone wanted to see him. Since no one really knew where he was, rumors pulled people in all directions, and the surging crowd ran into itself at every intersection. The Palais-Royal wasn't the Bondy Forest—they had to find him eventually!

All that tumult was of little concern to our lansquenet players in the Indian tent. Not one of them had dropped out. Gold and banknotes spilled onto the floor. Peyrolles had amassed a tremendous bankroll. He was dealing now. Chaverny had turned pale; he was still laughing, but a little hollowly.

"Ten thousand écus," said Peyrolles.

"I'm in," said Chaverny.

"With what?" asked Navailles.

"On my word."

"You can't play on your word at the Regent's," said Monsieur de Tresmes, who passed, adding with deep disgust, "What a clip joint!"

"One from which you're not getting your cut, duke!" said Chaverny, waving to him.

A burst of laughter followed, and Monsieur de Tresmes shrugged and walked away. The Duke of Tresmes was Governor of Paris, and skimmed a tenth of the profits from gambling dens. He was said to own a gambling joint himself, on the Rue Bailleul. That wasn't unusual: the Princess of Carignan's villa was one of the most dangerous clip joints in Paris.

"Ten thousand écus," said Peyrolles again.

"I'm in," said someone, dropping a bundle of notes of credit onto the table. It was a new voice, and everyone turned to see the speaker: a well-built long-legged fellow in a round unpowdered wig and a canvas collar—a marked contrast to the elegant dress of his neighbors. He wore a thick vest of brown wool, gray serge stockings, and good heavy boots of dull greasy leather. His wide belt held a sailor's cutlass. Was he the ghost of the privateer Jean Bart? If so, he was missing his pipe.

Peyrolles turned over a card and won ten thousand écus.

"I double!" said the stranger.

"Double," said Peyrolles, though it was a reversal of the normal roles.

Another handful of bills dropped on the table. Some of those corsairs carry millions in their pockets. Peyrolles won again.

"I double!" said the stranger again, angrily.

"Double it is!" Peyrolles dealt the cards.

"My God," said Oriol, "that's forty thousand gone in a flash."

"I double!" said the man in the brown wool vest even so.

"You must be rich, sir," said Peyrolles, making it a question.

But the man with the cutlass didn't even look up; his hundred and twenty thousand livres lay on the table.

"You win again, Peyrolles!" cried all the spectators.

234

"I double!"

"Bravo!" said Chaverny. "There's a real gambler!"

The man in the wool vest sharply elbowed aside the players who separated him from Peyrolles, so that he could stand directly facing him. Peyrolles won his two hundred and forty thousand livres, and then his half million.

"Enough!" said the man, adding curtly, "Give me room, gentlemen!" Then with one hand he drew his cutlass, while with the other he seized Peyrolles by the ear.

"What are you doing? What are you doing?" came the cry from all sides.

"Can't you see?" the man in the wool vest said calmly. "This man's a crook!"

Peyrolles tried to draw his sword. He was paler than a corpse.

"Look at them going at it, baron!" said old Barbanchois. "That's what we've come to."

"What can you do, baron," said La Hunaudaye. "That's the fashion now." They both looked glumly resigned.

But the man with the cutlass was no duffer, and knew how to use his weapon. One quick whirl, executed by the book, moved backed all the gamblers. One quick well-aimed lunge broke in half the sword Peyrolles had only just managed to draw.

"If you move," said the man with the cutlass, "I won't answer for your life. If you don't move, I'll only cut off your ears."

With choked cries, Peyrolles offered to give back the money. How long does it take for a crowd to gather? A solid mass of people was already pressing around them. The man with the cutlass gripped it halfway along the blade like a straight razor, and was calmly about to begin the promised surgical operation—when an uproar broke out at the entrance to the Indian tent.

Prince Kurakin, a general and the ambassador of Russia to the French court, burst impetuously into the tent, his face bathed in sweat, his hair and clothes in disarray. Behind him came General de Tessé, followed by the thirty bodyguards whose orders were to stay with the tsar. "Sire! Sire!" cried Tessé and Kurakin together. "In the name of God, stop!"

The crowd all looked at each other. Who were they addressing as sire? The man with the cutlass turned around, and Tessé threw himself between the man and his victim, but he didn't touch him, and he took off his hat and bowed. Then everyone realized the big fellow in the wool vest was Tsar Peter of Russia.

The tsar frowned slightly. "What do you want?" he asked Tessé. "I'm rendering justice." Kurakin whispered a few words in his ear, and he immediately let go of Peyrolles and smiled, blushing a little. "You're right. I'm not at home—I forgot." He waved to the astonished crowd with a stately grace that suited him well, then left the tent, surrounded by his bodyguards. They were used to his escapades, and spent their lives running after him.

Peyrolles straightened his clothes and calmly put into his pocket the enormous sum the tsar hadn't bothered to take back. "An insult by a great prince doesn't count, right?" He looked around the table with an expression both cunning and insolent. "I assume no one here has the slightest doubt about my honesty."

Everyone moved away from him, and Chaverny said, "No doubt at all, Monsieur de Peyrolles—we've got all the proof we need."

"Good thing!" said Peyrolles evenly. "Because I'm not one to tolerate an insult."

The crowd that wasn't interested in the game had gone away to follow the tsar's suite. But they were disappointed: Peter left the Palais-Royal, jumped into the first carriage that came along, and went off to have his three bottles of wine before bed.

Navailles took the cards out of Peyrolles's hands, gently pushed him out of the circle, and started a new game as banker.

Oriol took Chaverny aside. "I'd like to ask your advice," he said mysteriously.

"Shoot," said Chaverny.

"Now that I'm a gentleman, I don't want to act like a rube. Here's what happened: a little while ago I bet a hundred louis against Taranne, but I don't think he heard me."

"Did you win?"

"No, I lost."

"Did you pay him?"

"No, since he didn't ask for it."

Chaverny assumed a scholarly look. "If you'd won, would you have claimed your hundred louis?"

"Of course, because I'm sure I made the bet."

"Does having lost make you less sure?"

"No, but if Taranne hadn't heard me, he wouldn't have paid me." Oriol fiddled with his wallet.

Chaverny put his hand on the wallet. "It seemed straightforward at first," he said solemnly, "but it's actually more complicated."

"Fifty louis are bid!" cried Navailles.

"I'm in!" said Chaverny.

"What?! What?!" protested Oriol as he watched Chaverny open his wallet. He wanted to get it back, but Chaverny firmly pushed him away, saying, "The sum under litigation must be deposited with a third party. I'll take it, and split the difference: I declare I owe fifty louis to you and fifty louis to Taranne, and that's as good as the judgment of Solomon!" He gave the baffled Oriol back his empty wallet.

"I'm in! I'm in!" cried Chaverny, returning to the gaming table.

"You're in with my money!" grumbled Oriol. "I'd be safer with highway robbers."

"Gentlemen, gentlemen!" said Nocé as he entered the tent. "Put down your cards. You're playing on the lip of a volcano. Monsieur de Machault has just uncovered three dozen plots, of which the smallest would shame Catiline. The Regent is afraid, and has shut himself up with a little man in black to read his future."

"Bah!" they all said. "Is the little man in black a magician?"

"From head to toe," said Nocé. "He told the Regent Mr. Law would be drowned in the Mississippi, and the Duchess of Berry would get married again, to that scum Riom."

"Stop! Stop!" cried the more sensible voices. The others burst out laughing.

"Everybody's talking about it," went on Nocé. "The little man in black said Father Dubois would get his cardinal's hat."

"Seriously?" said Peyrolles.

"And Monsieur de Peyrolles would stop cheating," added Nocé.

An explosion of laughter followed. Then Nocé, after a glance out toward the steps, cried, "Look, look! There he is! Not the Regent, the little man in black!"

Everyone left the table and went to the opening of the tent. And indeed they could all see him, with his hump and his twisted legs, as he came slowly down the steps of the Regent's rooms. At the foot of the steps a sentry stopped him. The little man in black showed him his invitation, smiled, bowed, and went on.

IV. Remembering the Three Philippes

The little man in black carried pince-nez, through which he examined the party decorations like an authority. He bowed very politely to the ladies, and cackled into his beard just like the hunchback he was. He wore a black velvet mask. As he drew closer to the tent, the rakes watched him more carefully—but certainly no one watched him more carefully than Monsieur de Peyrolles.

"What the hell kind of creature is that?" cried Chaverny. "But—it looks like..."

"Yes!" said Navailles.

"What?" said Oriol, who was nearsighted.

"The man from earlier," said Chaverny.

"The man with the ten thousand écus!"

"The man with the kennel!"

"Aesop, known as Jonah!"

"Impossible!" said Oriol. "A creature like that, in the Regent's private office!"

Peyrolles thought to himself, "What could he have had to say to His Royal Highness? I never liked that rascal."

The little man in black was still approaching, though he seemed not to notice the group gathered at the opening of the Indian tent. He smiled, he bowed, he peered through his pince-nez—the most cheerful and polite little man in black that ever was. He was close enough now for them to hear him muttering through clenched teeth, "Delightful! Delightful! Everything is delightful. No one can do these things like His Royal Highness. Ah, I'm so pleased to have seen it all! So pleased! So pleased!"

Voices rose inside the tent: another group had taken over the table abandoned by our rakes. The new people were almost all of mature age and high rank. One of them said, "I don't know what's happened, but I just saw Bonnivet double the sentries by direct order of the Regent."

Another said, "Two companies of the Royal Guard are waiting in the Laughter Court."

"And no one can see the Regent."

"Machault's going nuts."

"Monsieur de Gonzague himself couldn't get a word out of him."

Our rakes began to eavesdrop, but the new people lowered their voices.

"Something's going to happen," said Chaverny. "I can feel it."

"Ask the magician!" laughed Nocé.

The little man in black bowed amiably. "Positively something, but what?" He polished his pince-nez with care. "Positively, positively something—something highly unexpected. He, he, he!" And now his shrill harsh voice gained a tone of mystery. "I've come out of a hot place, very hot, and I feel cold. I'd be much obliged if you gentlemen would allow me to come inside."

He shivered slightly. The rakes made way, all eyes on the hunchback. Bowing and bowing, he slipped into the tent. When he saw the group of great lords now seated around the table, he shook his head with a satisfied air. "Yes, yes, something's going on. The Regent's worried, the Royal Guard's been doubled, but no one knows what's going on. The Duke of Tresmes doesn't know, and he's Governor of Paris. Monsieur de Machault doesn't know, and he's Chief of Police. Do you know, Monsieur de Rohan-Chabot? Do you know, Monsieur de La Ferté-Senneterre?" He turned back to our rakes, who recoiled instinctively. "And you, gentlemen, do you know?"

No one answered. Rohan-Chabot and La Ferté-Senneterre took off their masks—the polite way of forcing a stranger to show his face. Laughing and bowing, the hunchback said, "Gentlemen, it won't do any good. You've never seen me."

"Baron," Barbanchois asked his worthy neighbor, "do you know this outlandish individual?"

"No, baron," replied La Hunaudaye. "He's quite the oddball."

"I'd give you a thousand to one," said the hunchback, "if you can guess what's going on. But I'd be wasting my time. It's not the kind of thing that comes up in your public meetings and your private thoughts, it's not the subject of your anxiety, my noble lords." He looked at Rohan-Chabot and La Ferté-Senneterre and the other old lords around the table. Then, looking at Chaverny, Oriol, and their companions, he went on, "It's not about what drives your more or less lawful ambitions, you whose fortunes have still to be made. It's not about intrigues in Spain, or unrest in France, or bad tempers in the high courts, or the little solar eclipses Mr. Law calls his System. No, no! And yet the Regent's worried, and yet the Royal Guard's been doubled!"

"So what's it about then, handsome masked man?" asked Rohan-Chabot with an impatient gesture.

The hunchback paused for thought, his chin on his chest. Then he looked up quickly and gave a little bark of laughter. "Do you believe in ghosts?"

The supernatural usually needs the right setting. On a winter evening, in the great hall of a castle, with rain weeping down the windows, around a fireplace of carved black oak, far away in the wastes of Morvan or the forests of Bretagne, people can be frightened by the thinnest legend, the thinnest tale. The dark wood paneling soaks up the lamplight, and vague red reflections dance on the gilded frames of the family portraits. A manor house has its gloomy, mysterious traditions. Everyone knows down what corridor the old count drags his chains, and what room he enters, when the clock strikes twelve, to sit by the cold hearth and shiver away the fever of his sins.

But here at the Palais-Royal—under the Indian tent, in the middle of this celebration of money, surrounded by dubious laughter and irreverent chatter, a

239

few feet from a table set up for cheating at cards—this wasn't the place for those nameless terrors that can sometimes affect bluff swordsmen and even those ready wits who are cutthroats only in their thoughts. And yet ice ran through all their veins when the hunchback said the word "ghosts." He laughed as he said it, that little man in black; but his jocularity made them shiver. In spite of the flood of lamplight, in spite of the joyful noise from the garden, in spite of the soft strains of the faraway orchestra, they felt cold.

"He, he!" laughed the hunchback. "Who believes in ghosts? Nobody, at noon out on the street. Everybody, at midnight in a dark corner, when the night-light just blew out. Like one of those flowers that blooms only under the stars, conscience is a deadly nightshade. Relax, gentlemen—I'm not a ghost."

"Will you be so kind as to explain yourself, handsome masked man—yes or no?" said Rohan-Chabot, rising. A circle had formed around the little man in black. Peyrolles hid in the second row, but he was all ears.

"Duke," answered the hunchback, "we're neither of us handsomer than the other, so let's drop the compliments. This is business from the other world: a dead man who lifts the stone off his tomb after twenty years, duke." He laughed and muttered, "Does anyone here at court remember people who've been dead twenty years?"

"What's he talking about?" cried Chaverny.

"I'm not addressing you, marquis. It was the year you were born, so you're too young. I'm talking to the graybeards." Then suddenly the hunchback's tone changed. "He was a gallant lord, a noble prince—young, brave, generous, happy, well-loved, with the face of an angel and the body of a hero. He had all the blessings God grants in this world..."

"...Where only the good die young," interrupted Chaverny.

The hunchback touched him on the shoulder and said gently, "Remember, marquis, proverbs sometimes lie, and some parties have no morning after."

Chaverny turned pale.

The hunchback moved him aside and approached the table. "I'm talking to the graybeards. To you, Monsieur de La Hunaudaye, who'd now be lying six feet under Flemish ground if the man I'm speaking of hadn't split the skull of the Catalan who had you at his mercy."

The old baron was left open-mouthed, so deeply moved that words failed him.

"And to you, Monsieur de Marillac, whose daughter took the veil out of love for him. And to you, Monsieur de Rohan-Chabot, who fortified the home of your mistress, Mademoiselle Féron, because of him. And to you, Monsieur de La Vauguyon, whose shoulder must still remember the sword thrust..."

"Nevers!" cried twenty voices at once. "Philippe de Nevers!"

The hunchback took off his hat and said slowly, "Philippe de Lorraine, Duke of Nevers, murdered under the walls of the Castle of Caylus-Tarrides in November 1699!"

"Murdered treacherously from behind, they say," murmured La Vauguyon.

"In an ambush," added La Ferté-Senneterre.

"If I'm not mistaken," said Rohan-Chabot, "they blamed the Marquis of Caylus-Tarrides, the Princess of Gonzague's father."

Among the younger men, Navailles said, "My father mentioned it more than once."

And Chaverny added, "My father was a friend of the late Duke of Nevers."

Peyrolles listened and made himself small.

In a deep, resonant voice the hunchback went on, "Murdered treacherously from behind in an ambush, that's all true, but the killer wasn't Caylus-Tarrides."

"Who then?" came the question from all sides.

It was the whim of the little man in black not to answer. He went on, in a light, mocking tone that held a bitter undertone, "It caused a stir, gentlemen. Damn, it even caused a big stir. People talked of nothing else for a whole week. The next week they talked about it less. By the end of a month, anybody still talking about Nevers sounded like Rip van Winkle."

Rohan-Chabot broke in, "His Royal Highness did everything possible!"

"Yes, yes, I know. His Royal Highness was one of the Three Philippes. His Royal Highness wanted to avenge his best friend. But how? Caylus Castle is at the end of the world. That November night kept its secrets. It goes without saying that the Prince of Gonzague... Isn't one of you here a distinguished agent of Monsieur de Gonzague by the name of Peyrolles?"

Oriol and Nocé moved aside to reveal the somewhat disconcerted factotum.

"I was just going to add," went on the hunchback, "that of course the Prince of Gonzague, another of the Three Philippes, moved heaven and earth to avenge his friend. But all for nothing. Not a clue, not a lead! Like it or not, they had to trust to time, which is to say to God, to expose the culprit."

Peyrolles had only one wish: to run and warn Gonzague. Still he stayed, to find out how far the hunchback would dare push his betrayal. As he watched the memories of that November night rise to the surface, Peyrolles felt like a man being strangled. The hunchback was right—the royal court had no memory, and people dead for twenty years were twenty times forgotten. But this case was an exception, because the dead man was part of a trinity, whose other two members were alive and all-powerful—Philippe d'Orléans and Philippe de Gonzague. As a result, judging by the interest awakening on all the faces present you would have said it was about a murder committed yesterday. If the hunchback's aim had been to rekindle the emotions around that mysterious long-ago drama, he'd succeeded completely.

"He, he!" he chuckled, with a quick, piercing glance around the circle. "To leave justice to heaven is the last resort. I know there are wise people who've resigned themselves to waiting for that. And, frankly, gentlemen, you could do worse: heaven has sharper eyes than the police, and heaven has time and patience. Sometimes heaven waits, and days turn into months and years. But when the hour has come..."

He stopped. His quiet voice resonated. The impression he left was so strong, so vivid, that each one of them felt it, as if the unspoken threat veiled in his harsh speech were aimed at all of them at once. Only one man there was guilty—an underling, a tool. But all of them trembled. Gonzague's army of followers, all of them too young to be under suspicion, still stirred under the weight of some mysterious painful burden. Did they already sense that each passing day forged ever tighter the mysterious chain that bound them to their master? Could they see the sword of Damocles already hanging by a thread over Gonzague's head? Who knows. Intuitions aren't subject to reason. They were afraid.

"When that hour comes," went on the hunchback, "and it always comes, sooner or later... a man, a messenger from the tomb, a ghost, rises from the earth, because God wills it. That man—sometimes unwittingly—carries out his fatal mission. If he's strong, he strikes. If he's weak, if his arm is like mine and can't sustain the weight of the broadsword, then he slithers along and keeps going—until he can put his humble mouth to the ear of the powerful. And then when the time comes the astonished avenger hears, whether in a shout or a whisper, the name of the murderer dropping from the clouds."

There was a long and solemn silence.

"What name?" asked Rohan-Chabot.

"Do we know him?" asked Chaverny and Navailles.

The hunchback seemed to have been stirred by his own words. In a shaking, halting voice he said, "Do you know him? What's it matter? Who are you? What can you do? To hear the murderer's name would terrify you like a thunderclap. But up in heaven, on the bottom step of the throne, sits a man. A little while ago a voice dropped from the clouds, saying, 'Your Highness, the murderer is here!' and the avenger started in surprise. 'Your Highness, the murderer is here in this glittering crowd!' and the avenger opened his eyes and looked out at the crowd passing under his windows. 'Your Highness, yesterday the murderer sat at your table, tomorrow the murderer will sit at your table!' and the avenger ran through his guest list in his mind. 'Your Highness, every day, morning and night, the murderer gives you his bloodstained hand!' and the avenger rose and said, 'By the living God! Justice will be done!'"

An odd thing happened: all of them present, even the mightiest and most noble, looked at each other suspiciously.

"And that, gentlemen," added the hunchback nimbly and cuttingly, "is why the Regent of France is worried this evening, and why the Royal Guard's been doubled." He bowed and turned to go.

"The name!" cried Chaverny.

"The damned name!" added Oriol.

"Can't you see," said Peyrolles, "this insolent buffoon has been making fun of you?"

The hunchback stopped at the mouth of the tent. He looked at his audience through his pince-nez. Then he came back, laughing the dry little laugh that sounded like a child's rattle. "There, there! Now you're afraid to go near each other. Each of you thinks his neighbor is the murderer. What a touching sign of your mutual esteem! Gentlemen, times have changed, and fashions with them. Nowadays we don't kill each other with the brutal weapons of the last reign—the pistol or the rapier. Our weapons are in our wallets: to kill a man all you have to do is empty his pockets. He, he, he! Thank God, murderers are scarce at the Regent's court! Don't back away from each other—the murderer isn't here! He, he, he!" He turned his back on the old lords and addressed only Gonzague's followers. "Look at all the long faces! Are you feeling remorse? You want me to cheer you up a little? Look, there goes Monsieur de Peyrolles, running off. He's missing a lot. You know where he's going?"

Peyrolles was already disappearing from view behind the flowerbeds, heading toward the palace.

Chaverny touched the hunchback's arm. "Does the Regent know the name?"

"Oh, marquis, we've moved on. We're having fun! My ghost is in a good mood. He can tell tragedy isn't popular here, so he's going to try comedy. And since that devil of a ghost knows everything, the present as well as the past, he's come to the ball tonight. He, he, he! And he's just waiting for the Regent's finger to point to him." The hunchback pointed into space. "The finger points, you hear? After bloodstained hands come dextrous pointing fingers. The light entertainment always follows the dark drama. You have to wind down with jokes about poison and daggers. The finger points at the able gentlemen who've stacked the deck and marked the cards at the great lansquenet game in which Mr. Law has the honor to be the dealer!" He doffed his hat piously as he spoke Law's name. "The finger points at the players with loaded dice, at the knights of speculation, at the conjurers on the Rue Quincampoix. The finger points! The Regent is a good prince, and free from prejudice. But he doesn't know everything, and if he did, he'd be mighty ashamed!"

There was a stir among the rakes.

"That's the truth," said Rohan-Chabot.

"Bravo!" cried La Hunaudaye and Barbanchois.

"Isn't that right, gentlemen?" said the hunchback. "You have to laugh when you're telling the truth. These young fellows want to throw me out, but they're holding back out of respect for your age. I'll refer you to Messrs Chaverny, Oriol, Taranne, and the rest: fine youths, somewhat faded aristocrats mixed with unwashed commoners, like the multicolored threads in knitting—salt and pepper! By God, don't get angry, noble masters! We're at a masked ball, and I'm nothing but a poor hunchback. Tomorrow you'll toss me an écu to buy the use of my back as a writing desk. Are you shrugging your shoulders? Good! I really deserve nothing but your scorn."

Chaverny took Navailles's arm. "What can we do to this clown?" he muttered. "Let's get out of here."

The old lords laughed heartily. The rakes drifted away one after another.

The hunchback turned again to Rohan-Chabot and his elderly companions. "And after pointing the finger at all the spreaders of rumors, the profiteers, the conjurors of price rises, the jugglers of price drops, the whole army of acrobats bivouacked at the Villa Gonzague, I'll show the Regent—by pointing, gentlemen, by pointing—the disappointed ambitions, the venomous jealousies. The finger points at men too arrogant or egotistical to learn to shut up, the anxious plotters, the white-haired lunatics trying to revive the Fronde uprising, the followers of Madame du Maine, the hangers-on at Cellamare's villa! The finger points at the ridiculous or despicable conspirators who want to drag France into some grandiose war to recover the positions they lost or the honors they miss, the flatterers of everything that was, the bad-mouthers of everything that is, the sycophants of what's to come, the worn-out puppets, the over-the-hill schemers who even describe themselves as the ruins of the great age, the foolish old Gerontes who are also gullible Jocrisses."

No one was left to listen to him. The last to go, old Barbanchois and La Hunaudaye, limped away together—the Baron of La Hunaudaye with gout in his right leg, the Baron of Barbanchois with gout in his left leg.

The little man in black laughed silently. "The finger points! The finger points!" he murmured. Then he drew from his pocket a parchment sealed with the royal crest, and sat down at the abandoned gaming table to read. The document began with the words, *Louis, by the grace of God King of France and Navarre, etc...* At the bottom it was signed *Philippe, Duke of Orléans, Regent*, and was witnessed by Secretary of State Le Blanc and Monsieur de Machault, the Chief of Police. "Perfect!" said the hunchback when he'd finished reading. "For the first time in twenty years we can lift our head and look people in the eye and throw our name back in our pursuers' teeth. I promise we'll make good use of it!"

V. The Pink Dominoes

Between the formal opening and the signatures, the parchment sealed with the crest of France held a valid safe-conduct, granted by the government to the Chevalier Henri de Lagardère, formerly of the late king's light cavalry. The decree followed the form recently adopted for diplomatic agents without publicly acknowledged credentials, and gave the Chevalier de Lagardère permission to come and go anywhere in the kingdom under official protection, and to leave French territory safely at any time, no matter what. "No matter what!" said the hunchback several times. "The Regent may have his quirks, but he's honest and he keeps his word."

He checked his pocket watch and got up. The Indian tent had two entrances. A few steps away from the second opening a path led through the flowerbeds to the rustic lodge of Master Le Bréant, doorkeeper and garden watchman. The decorators had made use of the lodge, like everything else: its façade had been prettied up and was lit by a reflector placed in a linden tree at the end of the path. On a normal night it was a dark, lonely, hidden spot that the Royal Guard kept a close eye on. Now when the hunchback came out of the tent he saw all of Gonzague's followers gathered in front of the flowerbeds, where they'd regrouped after their rout. They were talking about him. Oriol, Taranne, Nocé, Navailles, and the others made an effort to laugh, but Chaverny was thoughtful. The hunchback apparently had no time to waste, because he came straight toward them, admiring the decorations through his pince-nez just the way he had when he arrived. "No one can do these things like the Regent!" he muttered. "Delightful! Delightful!"

The rakes moved aside to let him pass. He pretended to recognize them suddenly. "Ha, ha! All the others left too. The finger points! He, he, he! The finger points! You know? That's the freedom of a masked ball. Gentlemen, your humble servant."

Only Chaverny still stood in his way. The hunchback doffed his hat and tried to walk on, but Chaverny stopped him. The rest of Gonzague's followers laughed.

"Chaverny wants his fortune told," said Oriol.

"Chaverny's found his master," added Navailles. "Someone even more acid-tongued and talkative then he is!"

"A word, if you please, sir," said Chaverny to the hunchback.

"All the words you wish, marquis."

"That thing you said—'Some parties have no morning after'—does it apply to me personally?"

"To you personally."

"Please explain it to me, sir."

"I don't have time, marquis."

"I could force you to."

"I dare you to! Monsieur de Chaverny dueling with and killing Aesop, known as Jonah, the hunchback who lived in Monsieur de Gonzague's dog kennel—that would certainly crown your reputation!"

But still Chaverny put out his hand to block his way. The hunchback took the hand in both of his and shook it. "Marquis," he said quietly, "You're better than you act. During my time in beautiful Spain, where we've both traveled, I once saw something remarkable: a noble warhorse caught by Jewish peddlers and harnessed with their pack mules. It was in Oviedo. When I passed that way again, the warhorse had died on the job. Marquis, you're out of place here. You'll die young, from the strain of trying to turn yourself into a rascal."

He walked on, and soon vanished behind the shrubberies. Chaverny was left standing still, his chin on his chest.

"He's finally gone!" cried Oriol.

"That little man is the devil incarnate," said Navailles.

"Look how anxious Chaverny is!"

"What trick did that damned hunchback play on him?"

"Chaverny, what's up?"

"Chaverny, tell us what happened!"

They gathered around him. Chaverny looked at them distractedly, and spoke unawares. "Some parties have no morning after!"

The music from the palace had paused between two minuets. The crowd in the garden had grown even denser, and lots of flirtatious couples were pairing off. Monsieur de Gonzague, tired of waiting for the Regent to receive him, had gone back inside. His charm and his sparkling conversation made him a favorite of the ladies, who often said that even without wealth and rank Philippe de Gonzague would have made a distinguished courtier; so you can imagine that the combination of his princely title—whose legitimacy was questioned only by a few timid voices—and his millions—which were doubted by no one—did him no harm. Though he was close to the Regent, he didn't adopt the disheveled look fashionable at the time. His conversation was courteous and discreet, his manner dignified, and yet the villain took every advantage: the Duchess of Orléans held him in high esteem, and the young king's tutor, Father Fleury, who badmouthed everyone, considered him almost a saint.

Court gossips had retold, in full and with elaborations, all that had happened earlier that day at the Villa Gonzague. Most of the ladies thought Gonzague's treatment of his wife went beyond heroism. The man was a holy apostle, a martyr! Twenty years of patient suffering! Twenty years of inexhaustible kindness in the face of unending scorn! Less beautiful tales than that had been made immortal by the ancient chroniclers. The princesses already knew of Monsieur de Gonzague's magnificent flight of eloquence at the family council. The Regent's mother, a good-natured soul, candidly gave him her big Bavarian hand; the Duchess of Orléans complimented him; the pretty little Abbess of Chelles promised to remember him in her prayers; and the Duchess of Berry told him he was a holy fool. As for the poor Princess of Gonzague, everyone wanted to stone her to death for making such a fine man suffer. As we all know, it was in Italy that Molière found the perfect name for his hypocrite: Tartuffe.

In the midst of his glory, Gonzague suddenly noticed his long-faced man Peyrolles standing in a doorway. Peyrolles never looked giddy with joy, but now his face resembled a distress flag. He looked pale, stunned, and he used his handkerchief to mop sweat off his temples. Gonzague called him over. Peyrolles awkwardly crossed the room and whispered a few words in his master's ear. Gonzague rose quickly and—with that ready wit peculiar to great villains from south of the Alps—said aloud, "The Princess of Gonzague has arrived at the ball? I'll hurry to meet her." Peyrolles himself was taken aback. "Where will I find her?" Gonzague asked him. Peyrolles didn't know what to say, so he just bowed and led the way.

"Some men are just too good!" said the Regent's mother with an oath she'd brought with her from Bavaria. The princesses tenderly watched Gonzague's hurried exit. Poor man!

"What do you want?" asked Gonzague when they were alone.

"The hunchback is at the ball," said Peyrolles.

"I know that, by God, since I'm the one who gave him his invitation."

"You don't know enough about him."

"How am I supposed to learn more?"

"I don't trust him."

"So don't trust him. Is that all?"

"He was with the Regent tonight, for over half an hour."

"The Regent?" Gonzague was surprised, but he quickly recovered. "No doubt he had lots to tell him."

"Lots indeed, and I'll let you be the judge of it." And Peyrolles reported the whole scene that had taken place inside the Indian tent.

When Peyrolles was through, Gonzague laughed with pity. "All those hunchbacks have such wit!" he said nonchalantly. "But it's a wit as strange and deformed as their bodies. They're always staging pointless theatrical scenes. The man who burned down the temple at Ephesus so people would talk about him must've been a hunchback."

"That's all you make of this!"

"Unless..." Gonzague grew thoughtful. "Unless that hunchback is trying to extort a high price."

"He's exposing us, my lord!" said Peyrolles vehemently.

Gonzague smiled sidelong at him. "Poor boy," he murmured, "what are we going to do with you? Can't you see this hunchback is zealously acting in our interests?"

"No, my lord, I admit, I don't see that."

"I don't like zeal. He's due for a sharp dressing down. But the fact is, he's given us an excellent idea."

"If your lordship would care to explain..."

They were walking in the arbor where the Rue Montpensier now runs. Gonzague casually took Peyrolles's arm. "First, tell me what happened at the Rue du Chantres."

"Your orders were carried out to a T. I didn't return to the villa until I'd seen the chaise start off toward Saint Magloire with my own eyes."

"And Doña Cruz?—I mean Mademoiselle de Nevers."

"She must be here."

"Find her. The royal ladies expect her. I've prepared the ground, and she'll be a tremendous success. Now, about that hunchback. What did he tell the Regent?"

"That's what we don't know."

"Well, I know, or I can guess. He told the Regent, 'Nevers's murderer lives.'"

Peyrolles couldn't help saying, "Shh!" while he shook from head to foot.

"He did well," went on Gonzague, unmoved. "Nevers's murderer is alive. Why would I hide the fact, I the husband of Nevers's widow, I the natural judge, I the legitimate avenger? Nevers's murderer is alive! I wish the whole court were here to hear me say it."

Peyrolles was sweating heavily.

"And since he's alive—God's blood, we'll find him!" Gonzague stopped and looked his factotum in the eye. Peyrolles was trembling, and nervous tics convulsed his face. "Do you understand?" said the prince.

"I understand we're playing with fire, my lord."

Gonzague suddenly lowered his voice. "That's the hunchback's idea. And, my word, it's a good one! But—how did he get the idea, and by what right does he claim to know more about it than we do? We'll clear that up. People as clever as he is are destined for an early grave."

Peyrolles looked up eagerly: finally something that didn't sound like Greek to him! "Tonight?"

Gonzague and Peyrolles had reached the central arcade of the arbor, from which they could see the long avenue of illuminated trees leading to the statue of the Mississippi River deity in the middle of the fountain. A woman wearing a mask and in proper court dress under a large black domino cloak came toward them from the other side of the arbor on the arm of an old man with white hair. As they entered the arcade, Gonzague pushed Peyrolles back into the shadows. The masked woman and the old man crossed the arcade.

"Did you recognize her?" asked Gonzague.

"No," replied Peyrolles.

"Dear judge," the masked woman was saying just then, "please don't escort me any further."

"Will the princess have need of my services again tonight?" asked the old man.

"You'll find me here again in an hour."

"It's Chief Judge de Lamoignon!" murmured Peyrolles.

The judge bowed to his companion and went away down a side alley.

Gonzague said, "The princess gives every impression of not yet having found what she's looking for. Let's not lose sight of her."

The masked woman, who was indeed the Princess of Gonzague, pulled up the hood of her domino and headed toward the fountain. The crowd stirred feverishly again at word of the arrival of the Regent and of Mr. Law, the second man of the kingdom; the little king didn't count yet.

"Your lordship hasn't given me the honor of an answer yet," insisted Peyrolles. "About the hunchback, is that for tonight?"

"So that hunchback has you scared, eh?"

"If you'd heard him like I did..."

"Talking about tombs opening and ghosts and divine justice? I've heard it all before. I want to talk to that hunchback. So, no, not for tonight. Tonight we're going to follow the course he's laid out for us. Listen hard and try to understand: tonight, if he keeps the promise he made to us—and he will, I'm sure of it—we'll keep the promise he made to the Regent in our name. A man will be coming to the ball, my lifelong enemy, the man who makes you tremble like a woman."

"Lagardère!" murmured Peyrolles.

"Under these glowing lamps, before this crowd—which is already stirred up waiting for who knows what great drama before the night's over—we'll rip off that man's mask and we'll say, 'Behold the murderer of Nevers!'"

"Did you see that?" asked Navailles.

"On my honor, it looks like the princess," replied Gironne.

"Alone in this crowd," said Choisy, "without an escort or a servant!"

"She's looking for someone."

Chaverny snapped out of his melancholy reverie. "My God, look at that pretty girl!"

"Where? In the pink domino? Venus herself!"

"That's Mademoiselle de Clermont, looking for me," said Nocé.

"Conceited fop!" cried Chaverny. "Can't you see it's General de Tessé's wife, and she's looking for me while her husband's running around after the tsar?"

"Fifty louis says it's Mademoiselle de Clermont!"

"A hundred says it's the general's wife!"

"Let's go ask her which one she is."

The two fools ran to her together—but only then did they notice, following the unknown beauty at a little distance, two fellows with rapiers a yard and a half long, sauntering along with their fists on their hips and their masked noses in the air.

"Damn!" Chaverny and Nocé cried together. "It's neither Mademoiselle de Clermont nor the general's wife—it's an adventure!"

All of Gonzague's followers had gathered not far from the fountain pool. A visit to the caterer's staff carrying liquor and pastries had restored their good humor. Oriol, that newly made gentleman, itched to do something impressive to earn his spurs. "Gentlemen," he said, rising onto his tiptoes, "isn't that actually Mademoiselle Nivelle?" The others kept up a running gag of never responding when Oriol mentioned Nivelle. In the last six months he'd spent fifty thousand écus on her. Without the mean-spirited jokes their love lives provoke, wealthy financiers run the risk of being too happy in this world.

The unknown beauty seemed quite disoriented in the middle of the crowd. She looked everywhere, her confusion obvious even behind her mask. The two bold fellows walked side by side ten steps behind her.

"Let's behave ourselves, Brother Passepoil!"

"Cocardasse, my distinguished friend, let's behave ourselves!"

"God's hat! This is no time for playing around!"

That hunchbacked devil had addressed them in Lagardère's name. Somehow they knew a stern and watchful eye was on them. They were as solemn and rigid as soldiers on sentry duty. To be able to move around at the ball as ordered by the hunchback, they'd gone back for their new doublets, and released old Françoise and her grandson Berrichon at the same time.

For an hour now, poor Aurore, lost in the crowd, had been looking in vain for Henri. When she saw the Princess of Gonzague she almost approached her, because she felt scorched by the eyes of all the lunatics, and she was growing afraid. But what could she say to be taken into the protection of one of those great ladies, who were so much at home at a ball like this? Aurore didn't dare. Anyway, she was in a hurry to get to the rendezvous spot at Diana's Circle.

"Gentlemen," said Chaverny, coming back, "it's neither Mademoiselle de Clermont, nor the general's wife, nor Nivelle, nor anyone we know. It's a wonderful brand-new beauty. A little commoner wouldn't carry herself like a queen the way she does; a girl from the sticks could sell her soul to the devil and still not have that enchanting grace; a lady of the court wouldn't have been so delightfully embarrassed. I have an idea."

"Let's hear it, marquis!" they all cried, and the giddy circle closed around Chaverny.

"She's looking for someone, right?" he said.

"That's pretty clear," said Nocé.

"But she's not being too obvious about it," added Navailles.

And all the others agreed, "Yes, yes, she's looking for someone."

"Well, gentlemen," continued Chaverny, "whoever he is, he's a lucky rascal!"

"Agreed. But that's not an idea."

"It's unfair," he went on, "that such a treasure should be monopolized by some nobody who's not part of our gang!"

"Unfair! Wrong! Improper! Outrageous!"

"I therefore propose that the beautiful girl not find the man she's looking for."

"Bravo!" they all cried. "Chaverny's come to his senses again!"

"I propose specifically," he went on, "that instead of her nobody the beautiful girl finds one of us."

"Bravo again! Bravissimo! Long live Chaverny!" They almost lifted him to their shoulders in triumph.

"But which one of us will she find?" asked Navailles.

"Me! Me! Me!" they all cried at once—even Oriol, the newly minted gentleman, without any consideration for Nivelle's rights.

Chaverny gestured regally for silence. "Gentlemen, this discussion is premature. Once we've gotten the girl away from her guards, we can play dice, or faro, or rock-paper-scissors, or draw straws to decide who'll have the honor of keeping her company."

Such a wise suggestion could only be met with general approval.

"Attack!" cried Navailles.

"One moment, gentlemen!" said Chaverny. "I claim the honor of leading the expedition."

"Granted! Granted! Attack!"

He looked around. "The challenge is to make no noise. The garden's full of Royal Guards, and it'd be a shame to get thrown out before supper's served. We need a trick. Do any of you with good eyesight see a pink domino on the horizon?"

"Mademoiselle Nivelle has one," offered Oriol.

"There go two, three, four!" cried the group.

"I'm taking about a pink domino we know."

"Mademoiselle Desbois is over there!" cried Navailles.

"Cydalise is over there!" said Taranne.

"We only need one. I choose Cydalise, because she's about the same size as our beautiful girl. Bring me Cydalise!"

Cydalise was on the arm of an old domino, a duke and peer at least, and decrepit as can be. They brought Cydalise to Chaverny.

"Darling," he said, "Oriol—who's now a gentleman—will give you a hundred pistoles if you help us. We need to distract two vicious old dogs over there, and you'll be the bait."

"Will it be good for a laugh?" asked Cydalise.

"Sidesplitting," said Chaverny.

VI. The Daughter of the Mississippi

Oriol didn't object to the part about the hundred pistoles, but only because he'd been referred to as a gentleman. Cydalise, an excellent girl, liked nothing better than a little mischief: "As long as it's good for a laugh, I'm in." It didn't take long to explain the plan to her. A moment later she slipped from group to group through the crowd and reached her spot, between our two masters of arms and Aurore. At the same time, General Chaverny sent one platoon out to confront Cocardasse and Passepoil, while another platoon maneuvered to cut off Aurore.

Cocardasse was the first to be elbowed. He swore a mighty "God's hat!" and put his hand on his rapier.

But Passepoil whispered, "Let's behave ourselves!" Cocardasse bit his tongue.

Now a vigorous shove almost toppled Passepoil, and his eyes lit up.

"Let's behave ourselves!" said Cocardasse.

Just as humble Trappist monks greet and part from each other with the same stoic words, "Brother, we must die!" now these two said over and over, "Crooked ace!"—"Let's behave ourselves!"

A heavy heel came down on Cocardasse's ankle, while Passepoil was tripped a second time by a sheathed sword poked between his legs. "Let's behave ourselves!" But our two bravos' ears were burning.

"Thunder and lightning, baldy," murmured Cocardasse at the fourth offense, looking pitifully at Passepoil, "I think I'm going to lose my temper!"

Passepoil was wheezing like a seal, and he didn't answer. But when Taranne came back around for another attack he got a colossal slap.

Cocardasse gave a deep sigh of satisfaction: he wasn't the one who'd started it. With one swing of his fist he sent both Gironne and the entirely innocent Oriol rolling in the dirt. A brawl followed, lasting only a moment—but it was long enough for the second platoon, led by Chaverny himself, to surround Aurore and steer her away.

Cocardasse and Passepoil, having routed their attackers, looked ahead and saw the familiar pink domino: it was Cydalise, earning her hundred pistoles. Happy to have gotten away with throwing a few punches, the two swordsmen followed Cydalise and reminded each other triumphantly, "Let's behave ourselves!"

Meanwhile, Aurore, disoriented and no longer seeing her two guards, was forced to go where the men around her went. The group, pretending to be driven along by the crowd, moved gradually toward the grove of trees that lay between the fountain pool and Diana's Circle. In the center of that grove stood Le Bréant's lodge. Narrow pathways curved through the flowerbeds in the English style then coming into fashion, but the crowd mostly followed the wider alley-ways and stayed off those paths. The vaulted arbor immediately around Le Bréant's lodge was especially deserted, and that's where the group led poor Aurore.

Chaverny lifted his mask. Aurore cried out, recognizing her young man from Madrid. At her cry the lodge door opened. On the sill stood a tall masked man wrapped in an ample black domino and holding a naked sword.

"Don't be afraid, charming lady," said Chaverny. "These gentlemen and I, one and all, are your admiring servants." As he spoke he tried to slip his arm around Aurore's waist. She called for help, but only once, because from behind her Albret put a silk handkerchief over her mouth. Still, that single cry was enough. The man in the black domino switched his sword to his left hand. With his right, he grabbed Chaverny by the scruff of the neck and flung him ten paces away. Albret met the same fate. A dozen swords were drawn. Switching his own sword back to his right hand, the man in the black domino disarmed Gironne and Nocé with two whip flicks. When he saw that, Oriol didn't hesitate: the new-made gentleman earned his spurs by running away, shouting "Help!"

Montaubert and Choisy attacked. Montaubert fell to his knees with his ear split open; Choisy, not as lucky, got slashed right across his face. The Royal Guard was coming, drawn by the noise. The band of troublemakers, all of them more or less beaten up, scattered like a flock of starlings. The Royal Guards found no one under the arbor—because the man in the black domino and the girl had vanished as if by magic, leaving only the sound of Le Bréant's lodge door closing.

"God's death!" said Chaverny when he found Navailles in the crowd, "what a heave! I'd like to meet that fellow again, just to compliment him on his grip."

Gironne and Nocé showed up, their heads hanging. Choisy was off in a corner with a bloody handkerchief pressed to his cheek. Montaubert hid his mangled ear as best he could. Half a dozen others had injuries to conceal. Only brave little potbellied Oriol was unharmed. They all exchanged hangdog looks. The expedition had gone badly, and each of them wondered who that brutal fighter could be. They knew the Paris fencing clubs intimately. Those clubs weren't flourishing as they had at the end of the previous century: nobody had the time now. Among the rapier virtuosos they knew, not one could have thrown a dozen swordsmen into disarray, and—to be honest—done it without much trouble. The man in the black domino hadn't even bothered to clear the encumbrance of his own long cloak out of his way. He'd only barely lunged a couple of times, quite calmly. A master, without a doubt! He must be a stranger: no one at the fencing clubs, including the provosts and the teachers, had his amazing skills.

Earlier they'd been talking about that Duke of Nevers, killed in the flower of his youth. He was a man whose memory lived on in all the fencing clubs, who could draw faster than thought, who had a foot of steel, an eagle eye. But he was dead, and all of them could bear witness that the man in the black domino was no ghost. There'd been another man in Nevers's time, a fencer greater than Nevers himself, a man in the late king's light cavalry named Henri de Lagardère. But what did it matter what the terrifying swordsman's name was? The only sure thing was that our rakes had met bad luck tonight. The hunchback had beaten them with his tongue, the man in the black domino with his blade. They needed revenge twice over.

"The ballet! The ballet!"

"His Royal Highness! The princesses! Look! Look!"

"Mr. Law! Look! Mr. Law, with Lord Stair, Ambassador of Queen Anne of England!"

"Stop pushing, damn it! There's room for everybody!"

"Oaf! Wise-ass! Clodhopper!" And so forth—the truest and dearest pleasure of a crowd: ribs smashed, feet crushed, women smothered! From deep inside the crowd came shrill cries; short women especially love to drown themselves in a crowd. They can't see a thing, they suffer like martyrs, but they can't keep away from the torture.

"Mr. Law! Look, there's Mr. Law going up onto the Regent's dais!"

"The one in the pearl-gray domino is Madame de Parabère."

"The one in the puce domino is the Duchess of Phalaris."

"Look how red Mr. Law's face is! He must've had a good dinner!"

"Look how pale the Regent is! He must've gotten bad news from Spain!"

"Silence! Shut up! The ballet! The ballet!"

The orchestra seated around the fountain pool struck up its first piece with a legendary down bow that was still being talked about in the boondocks fifteen or twenty years ago. The tiered dais stood on the side nearest the palace and facing away from it, like a hillside abloom with women. On the opposite side, by means of a slow invisible mechanism, rose a painted backdrop, of course depicting a Louisiana landscape: virgin forests stretching their giant trunks to the sky, vines winding around the trees like boa constrictors, prairies reaching to the horizon, blue mountains, and that enormous river of gold, the Mississippi, father of waters. Its banks were filled with cheerful scenes, using lots of the soft green that eighteenth century painters loved so much. Delightful Edenic woods were interspersed with moss-draped caves where Calypso could have waited comfortably for aloof young Telemachus.

But instead of nymphs from classical mythology there was an attempt at more appropriately local color: Indian girls wandered under the beautiful shade trees wearing fringed shawls and crowns of shining feathers. Young mothers gracefully hung the cradles of their newborns from the branches of sassafras trees swaying in the breeze. Warriors fired arrows or threw tomahawks. Old men smoked calumets around the council fire. As the backdrop rose, so did a number of other pieces of scenery—either decor or practical, in backstage jargon—so that the statue of the Mississippi at the center of the pool found itself all but surrounded by a magnificent landscape. Applause from top to bottom of the tiered stands, applause from one end of the garden to the other.

The entrance of Mademoiselle Nivelle as the Daughter of the Mississippi, the starring role in the ballet, drove Oriol crazy. He happened to be standing between the barons of Barbanchois and La Hunaudaye, and he elbowed each of them. "Well, what do you think of that?"

The two barons, both of them up on their tiptoes like herons, looked down at him scornfully.

"Isn't that stylish?" Oriol went on. "Isn't it artistic? Isn't it graceful? Isn't it splendid? Isn't it gold-spangled? The skirt alone cost me a hundred and thirty pistoles, the wings were thirty-two louis, the sash is worth a hundred écus, and I had to sell stock for the tiara! Bravo, my beloved! Bravo!"

The two barons exchanged a look over his head. "Such a pretty thing!" said Barbanchois.

"Getting her wardrobe from such a nobody!" said La Hunaudaye.

And they exchanged another sad look over Oriol's powdered wig, and said in unison, "Where are we all headed, baron? Where are we all headed?"

But Oriol's first bravo had triggered a roar of applause. Nivelle looked ravishing, and she danced a delightful dance at the river's edge, among the water lilies and the wild oats. Mr. Law must be a great man indeed to have invented a country where people danced like that! The crowd turned to offer him their smiles. The crowd was in love with him; the crowd couldn't have been happier.

But two men present didn't share in the general joy—two souls in torment. For about ten minutes Cocardasse and Passepoil had scrupulously followed Cydalise in her pink domino. Then suddenly the pink domino had vanished as if the earth had opened up and swallowed her. That was behind the fountain pool, at the mouth of a sort of tent made of sheets of embossed paper representing palm branches. When Cocardasse and Passepoil tried to get in, two Royal Guards barred the way, crisscrossing their bayonets under the bravos' chins. The tent was the dressing room for the ladies of the corps de ballet.

"God's hat! Friends..." began Cocardasse.

"Back!" came the answer.

"Brothers..." tried Passepoil.

"Back!"

They looked at each other pitifully. The charge was clear enough: they'd let the bird entrusted to them fly away. All was lost!

Cocardasse held out his hand to Passepoil. "Well, friend," he said with deep sadness, "we did our best."

"We're just out of luck, that's all," said Passepoil.

"Crooked ace! We're done for! Eat well, drink well, as long as we're here, and then—*vaya con Dios*, as they say in Spain."

Passepoil sighed heavily. "I'll just beg him to finish me off with one good blow to the chest. It can't matter to him."

"Why the chest?" asked Cocardasse. Passepoil had tears in his eyes, which didn't improve his looks; Cocardasse had to admit, at this critical moment he'd never seen an uglier man than his baldy.

But here's what Passepoil replied, modestly lowering his lashless eyelids. "Distinguished friend, I want to die from a blow to the chest because, since I've been accustomed to pleasing the ladies, I'd hate to think one or two persons of the fair sex to which I've dedicated my life might see me disfigured in death."

"Sweetheart!" muttered Cocardasse. "Poor little babe!" But he couldn't bring himself to laugh.

They began to pace around the fountain pool like two sleepwalkers unable to see or hear.

The ballet entitled "The Daughter of the Mississippi" was certainly peculiar, like nothing else since the invention of ballet. The Daughter of the Mississippi, in the lovely person of Nivelle, after fluttering through the reeds and the water lilies and the wild oats, called graciously to her companions, no doubt the nieces of the Mississippi, who came running with wreaths of flowers. All the savage ladies—among them Cydalise, Desbois, Duplant, Fleury, and other prancing starlets of the era—danced a number together, to universal satisfaction. The dance expressed their happiness and freedom on those flowering banks.

Suddenly horrible Indians, half-naked and wearing horns, leaped out of the reeds. We don't know how close their kinship was to the Mississippi, but they looked awful. Leaping, gesticulating, performing terrifying dance steps, the savages surrounded the girls and made ready to finish them off with their hatchets, intending to eat them. To explain all that, executioners and victims together danced a minuet that got an encore.

But just when the girls were about to be eaten, the violins fell silent and a bugle fanfare sounded in the distance. A band of French sailors ran out onto the beach, boldly dancing a brand-new jig. The savages, still dancing, shook their fists threateningly, and the ladies danced harder than ever and raised their hands to heaven. There was a dancing battle, during which the captain of the French and the chief of the savages engaged in single combat in the form of a pas de deux. The victory of the French was represented by a bourrée, the rout of the savages by a courante, followed by garlands clearly symbolic of the coming of civilization to those untamed lands.

But the best part was the finale. All that came before it was nothing compared to the finale. The finale alone proved the author of the libretto was a man of genius. Here was the finale: the Daughter of the Mississippi, dancing with unflappable dedication, tossed aside her garland and took up a cardboard chalice. She danced her way up the steep path leading to the statue of her father, the deity. There she stood en pointe on one foot and filled her chalice with the waters of the river. Pirouette. Then the Daughter of the Mississippi poured the magical water she had drawn over the Frenchmen dancing below. A miracle! It wasn't water falling from the chalice, it was a rain of gold coins. Shame on those who didn't get the subtle, well-conceived allusion! Now came a feverish dance on the banks of the river while picking up the gold coins, followed by a ballroom dance involving the nieces of the Mississippi, the sailors, and even the savages, who'd come back better behaved and threw their headdresses of horns into the river. It was a wild success. When the corps de ballet had exited through the reeds, three or four thousand voices cried out passionately, "Long live Mr. Law!"

But it wasn't over: now there came a cantata. And who sang the cantata? Can you guess? It was the statue of the river deity. The statue was actually Signor Angelini, star countertenor at the Opéra. Of course, some people think cantatas are tedious doggerel, and the ill-groomed bards who write them should confine their rhymed platitudes to pastry icing. But we don't agree. A flawless cantata is as good as a tragedy. That's our opinion, and we're sticking to it. The cantata was even more inventive than the ballet, if that were possible. It referred to Mr. Law with true French ingenuity:

Sent by the gods to Gallic shores
Th'immortal Caledonian son
Brings opulence with harmony.

There was also a verse about the young king, and a couplet about the Regent. Everybody had to be made happy. When the river deity had finished his cantata he was relieved of his duties, and the ball resumed.

Monsieur de Gonzague had felt obliged to be in his place on the dais during the ballet. His conscience made him fear a change in the Regent's manner toward him; but His Royal Highness greeted him warmly—no doubt he hadn't yet been informed. Before he went up onto the dais, Gonzague had ordered Peyrolles to keep an eye on his wife the princess, and to send him warning if any stranger approached her. No word came during the performance, so everything must be proceeding smoothly.

After the show Gonzague went to meet Peyrolles at the Indian tent by Diana's Circle. The princess was inside, alone, seated apart, waiting. Gonzague was about to withdraw, so as not to scare off by his presence the prey he planned to take in a trap—when our giddy group of rakes burst into the tent, laughing wildly. They'd already forgotten their misadventures, and were making fun of the ballet and the cantata. Chaverny imitated the grunting of the savages. With outrageous melismatic turns Nocé sang, "Sent by the gods to Gallic shores," etcetera.

"Was she ever a hit!" cried Oriol. "Encore! Encore! A lot of the credit goes to her costume!"

"And therefore to you!" said the others. "Let's weave a crown for Oriol! Th'immortal son of the Place Maubert!"

257

They fell silent at the sight of Gonzague. All, except Chaverny, came forward to greet him with the fawning attitudes of courtiers.

"Here you are at last, cousin," said Navailles. "We were getting worried."

"No ball's complete without our dear prince!" cried Oriol.

"Well, cousin," said Chaverny seriously, "do you know what's going on?"

"A lot's going on," answered Gonzague.

"What I mean is, has anyone told you what happened right here a little while ago?"

"I gave his lordship a report," said Peyrolles.

"Did he tell you about the man with the pirate's cutlass?" asked Nocé.

"We can joke later," said Chaverny. "The Regent's goodwill is my last asset, and I only have it second-hand. I need my illustrious cousin to stay in favor at court. If he can help the Regent with his investigation..."

"We're all at the prince's disposal," said Gonzague's other followers.

"Besides," Chaverny went on, "this Nevers business, surfacing again after so many years, has caught my interest like a fantastic novel. Do you have any suspects, cousin?"

"None." Then, as if an idea had just struck him, Gonzague added, "Actually... there is a man..."

"What man?"

"You're too young to have known him."

"What's his name?"

"That man," said Gonzague as if thinking aloud, "could certainly say whose hand struck poor Philippe de Nevers."

"What's his name?" repeated several voices.

"The Chevalier Henri de Lagardère."

"Is he here?" cried Chaverny impulsively. "Then he must be our man in the black domino!"

"What's that?" asked Gonzague eagerly. "You saw him?"

"Just some foolishness. We don't know this Lagardère from Adam, cousin, but if by chance he were here at the ball..."

"If he were here at the ball," Gonzague finished for him, "I'd make it my business to point out to His Royal Highness Nevers's murderer!"

Behind him a man's voice said solemnly, "Here I am!"

Gonzague started so violently that Nocé had to hold him steady.

VII. The Arbor

Gonzague froze for a moment without turning. His followers were stunned speechless at the sight of their patron so perturbed. Chaverny frowned and put his hand on his sword guard. "Is this the man named Lagardère?"

Gonzague finally turned and looked. The man who'd said, "Here I am!" stood erect, unmoving, his arms crossed. He wasn't masked. Gonzague said quietly, "Yes, that's him."

The princess—who since the beginning of this scene had stayed seated, lost in thought—seemed to rouse herself at the mention of Lagardère's name. From now on she listened, but she still didn't dare come forward. This was the man who held her fate in his hands.

Lagardère wore court dress of white satin with silver embroidery. He was still handsome Lagardère, Lagardère handsomer than ever. Without losing suppleness, his figure had grown in substance and dignity. His face shone with manly intelligence and noble will. The fire in his eyes was tempered by a certain sad and gentle resignation. Suffering is good for great souls; he was a great soul, and he had suffered. But he had a body of bronze. Just as wind, rain, snow, and storms all slide off the hard brow of a statue—time, weariness, sorrow, joy, and passion had slid off his brow without a trace. He was handsome, he was young, and the golden tan the Spanish sun had given his cheeks went well with his blond hair. It was a hero's juxtaposition: the soft hair framing the proudly sunburned features of a warrior. Other men present were dressed as splendidly as he, but not one of them carried himself so well. Lagardère looked like a king.

Without bothering to respond to Chaverny's blustering gesture, Lagardère glanced toward the princess, as if to say, "Wait for me." Then he grabbed Gonzague by the arm and pulled him aside. Gonzague didn't resist.

Peyrolles said quietly, "Gentlemen, be at the ready." They drew their rapiers.

The princess rose and stood between her husband and Lagardère on one side and Gonzague's followers on the other.

Since Lagardère hadn't spoken, Gonzague said, "What do you want from me, sir?"

He was held by a hand of steel. Not only could the prince not free himself, but—strangely—Lagardère, without changing his impassive expression, now began to squeeze Gonzague's hand, crushing it in a tightening vise.

"You're hurting me!" Gonzague murmured, sweat already running down his brow. Lagardère said nothing and squeezed harder. Gonzague gave a muffled cry of pain. Against his will, the curled fingers of his right hand straightened out. Then Lagardère, still silent and impassive, pulled off Gonzague's glove.

"Are we going to allow this, gentlemen?" cried Chaverny, and he stepped forward with his sword raised.

"Tell your men to stand at ease!" ordered Lagardère.

Gonzague turned to his followers. "Gentlemen, please, don't get involved in this."

His hand was bare. Lagardère laid his finger on a long scar that began at the base of Gonzague's wrist. "I'm the one who did this!" he murmured with deep feeling.

"Yes, it was you," replied Gonzague through clenched teeth. "I haven't forgotten. Why remind me?"

"This is the first time we've met face to face, Monsieur de Gonzague," said Lagardère slowly. "It won't be the last. I had my suspicions, but I needed proof. You murdered Nevers!"

Gonzague laughed shakily. "I'm the Prince of Gonzague," he said quietly, but with his head held high. "I have millions, enough to buy all the justice that remains on earth, and the Regent sees only through my eyes. You have just one asset against me: your sword. Go ahead and draw, I dare you!" He glanced toward his followers.

"Monsieur de Gonzague, your hour hasn't yet come. I'll choose the place and the time. I told you once, 'If you won't come to Lagardère, Lagardère will come to you.' You didn't come, so here I am. God is just, and Philippe de Nevers will be avenged." He let go of Gonzague's wrist, and the prince retreated several paces. Lagardère was done with him. He turned to the princess and bowed to her respectfully. "Madame, I'm at your service."

The princess went to her husband and whispered in his ear, "If you try anything against this man, sir, you'll find me in your way!" Then she returned to Lagardère and gave him her hand.

Gonzague was strong enough to hide the fury that made his blood boil. Rejoining his followers, he said, "Gentlemen, that man wants to take away your fortune and your future in one stroke. But he's mad, and fate has delivered him into our hands. Follow me!" He left the tent and walked straight to the steps of the Regent's rooms, and had the door opened.

In the palace and under the lavish tents set up in the courtyards, supper had just been announced. The garden was deserted: no one remained among the flowerbeds, and only a few stragglers in the avenues of trees. Among them we would have recognized the Baron of Barbanchois and the Baron of La Hunaudaye, trying to hurry as they limped along, saying over and over, "Where are we all headed, baron, where are we all headed?"

"To supper!" answered Cydalise as she went by on the arm of a musketeer.

Lagardère and the Princess of Gonzague were soon alone in the beautiful arbor that ran behind the Rue de Richelieu.

"Sir," said the princess, her voice trembling with emotion, "I just heard your name spoken. After twenty years, your voice has awakened a poignant memory in me. It was you, it was you, I'm sure of it, who took my daughter in your arms at the Castle of Caylus-Tarrides."

"It was I."

"Why did you trick me then, sir? Answer truthfully, I beg you."

"Because God in His goodness inspired me, Madame. But it's a long story, whose details you can hear later. I defended your husband, I heard his dying words, I saved your child, Madame. Do you need to hear more to trust me?"

The princess looked at him. "God has marked your face with trustworthiness," she murmured. "But I know nothing, and I've been tricked so often."

Her words almost offended him, and he answered coldly, "I have the proofs of your daughter's birth."

"That expression you used: 'Here I am!'"

"I learned it, Madame—not from your husband, but from his murderers."

"You said it then, in the moat at Caylus?"

"And by doing so, Madame, I gave your daughter a second chance at life."

"Then who said it near me, earlier today, in the great hall of the Villa Gonzague?"

"Another me."

The princess seemed to be searching for words. The first meeting between Aurore's savior and Aurore's mother ought to have been one long and fervent outpouring. Instead they seemed to be engaged in one of those diplomatic face-offs that usually end in fatal rupture. Why? Because between them lay a treasure they both coveted. Because the savior had rights, and the mother did too. Because the mother—a poor woman broken by sorrow, but also a proud woman toughened by solitude—was mistrustful. And because the savior, confronted by this woman who hid her own feelings, was equally prey to fear and mistrust.

"Madame," continued Lagardère coldly, "do you have any doubt about your daughter's identity?"

"No. Something tells me my daughter, my poor daughter, really is in your hands. What reward do you want for that immense good deed? Don't be afraid to ask too much: I'd give you half my life." It was the mother who spoke, but also the recluse, who gave offense without knowing it. She no longer understood the world.

Lagardère held back a bitter answer, and bowed without speaking.

"Where's my daughter?"

"First you have to agree to listen to me."

"I think I understand you, sir. But I already told you..."

"No, Madame," he interrupted harshly, "you don't understand me. And I'm beginning to fear you don't have what it takes to understand me."

"What do you mean?"

"Your daughter isn't here, Madame."

"She's at your house!" cried the princess with a haughty gesture. Then she reconsidered. "It's clear enough. You've watched over my daughter since her birth, and she's never left you?"

"Never, Madame."

"So naturally she's at your house. Of course you have servants?"

"When your daughter turned twelve, Madame, I took on an old and faithful servant of your first husband's, Dame Françoise."

"Françoise Berrichon!" she cried eagerly. She took Lagardère's hand. "Sir, that's the act of a gentleman, and I thank you!" Her words struck Lagardère to the heart like an insult, but the princess was too deeply preoccupied to notice. "Take me to my daughter. I'm ready to follow you."

"But I'm not ready."

She pulled her arm out from under his. "Ah!" she said, all of her suspicions returning at once. "You're not ready!" She looked him in the face fearfully.

"Madame, there are great dangers around us."

"Around my daughter? I'm here, I'll protect her."

"You?" Lagardère couldn't help raising his voice. "You, Madame?" His eyes burned, and he willed himself to look down. "Haven't you asked yourself a mother's natural question: why did this man wait so long to bring me back my daughter?"

"Yes, sir, I did wonder."

"But you haven't asked me, Madame."

"My happiness is in your hands, sir."

"And you're afraid of me?" She didn't answer. Lagardère smiled sadly. "If you'd asked me that question," he said, his firm tone somewhat tempered by compassion, "I would've answered frankly, within the bounds of respect and courtesy."

"I am asking you. Tell me, and if you like, set aside courtesy and respect."

"Madame, if I've waited so many years to bring you back your child, it's because in the depths of my exile I heard some news—strange news that at first I couldn't believe, and which was in fact unbelievable: Nevers's widow had changed her name, Nevers's widow was now the Princess of Gonzague!" She hung her head and blushed. "Nevers's widow!" he repeated. "Madame, when I inquired, when I knew without a doubt it was true, I asked myself, can Nevers's daughter find a home at the Villa Gonzague?"

"Sir!" she tried to interrupt.

"There are many things you don't know. You don't know why the news of your marriage shocked my conscience like a sacrilegious act. You don't know why the thought of the daughter of the man who was my friend for an hour, who called me brother in his dying breath—the thought of her at the Villa Gonzague felt like an insult to the dead, a foul impious blasphemy."

"And won't you tell me, sir?" The princess's eyes began to shine.

"No, Madame. This first and last meeting will be short, and will cover only essentials. I can see now, with sadness but with resignation, we're never going to understand each other... When I heard that news, I asked myself another question. Knowing better than you do the power of your daughter's enemies, I asked myself, how can she protect her child, when she hasn't been able to protect herself?"

The princess hid her face in her hands. "Sir, sir," she cried, her voice interrupted by sobs, "You're breaking my heart!"

"God knows that wasn't my intention, Madame!"

"You don't know what kind of man my father was, you don't know the torment of my isolation, the pressures he used, the threats..."

Lagardère bowed deeply. "Madame," he said with sincere respect, "I know the sacred love you had for the Duke of Nevers. The twist of fate that put your daughter's baby basket into my hands made me an involuntary party to the secrets of a great heart. I know you loved him deeply, intensely. You must be a noble woman, because you were a brave and faithful wife. And yet, you gave in to force."

"To make my first marriage and the birth of my daughter official."

"French law can't do that retroactively. I have the real proof of your marriage and of Aurore's birth."

"Give them to me!"

"I will, Madame. As I was saying, in spite of your resolve, in spite of your still-fresh memory of lost happiness, you gave in to force. Well! Couldn't—and can't—the force used against the mother be used in turn against the daughter? Didn't I—and don't I—still have the right to consider my protection preferable to anyone else's? I who have never given in to force, I who have treated a sword as a toy since I was young, I who say to violence: welcome, you're my element!"

For a few seconds the princess said nothing, and stared at him with genuine fear. "Am I right?" she said finally in a low voice. "Are you going to refuse me my daughter?"

"No, Madame, I'm not going to refuse you your daughter. I've come four hundred leagues and risked my life to bring her to you. But my course is laid out in advance. For eighteen years I've been protecting your daughter. She owes me her life ten times, because I've saved it ten times."

"Sir, sir," cried the poor mother, "should I love you or hate you? My heart goes out to you, and you rebuff it. You've saved my daughter's life, you've protected her..."

"And I'll go on protecting her, Madame," he interrupted coldly.

"Even against her mother!" said the princess, drawing herself up.

"Maybe. It depends on her mother."

A flash of resentment lit her eyes. "You're toying with my distress!" she murmured. "I don't understand. Explain."

"I came here to explain, Madame, and I'm eager to finish explaining, so please listen carefully. I'm not sure what you think of me; I believe you think ill of me. But sometimes people use anger as an excuse to shirk a debt of gratitude. With me, Madame, there's no shirking. My course is laid out in advance, and I'm following it—too bad for whatever gets in the way. You have to reckon with me in more than one way. I have my rights as her guardian."

"Her guardian!"

"What else would you call a man who carries out someone's dying wish by ruining his own life and sacrificing himself entirely for another person? The word guardian isn't adequate, is it? That must be why you objected to the term—either that or your own troubles have blinded you, and you don't see that the oath I fulfilled to the letter and the eighteen years of constant protection have given me an authority equal to yours."

"Oh! Equal!"

"Greater than yours," he went on, raising his voice. "The formal authority delegated by her dying father is enough to make up for your authority as her mother, and on top of that I have the authority earned at the cost of half my life. All that gives me only one right, Madame: to watch over the orphan with even more care, even more affection, even more solicitude. I intend to exercise that right even with regard to her own mother."

"Then you don't trust me?" she murmured.

"This morning, Madame, you said—I was there, hidden in the crowd—you said, 'If my daughter has forgotten her proud blood, even for a moment, I'll veil my face and say, nothing of Nevers now remains alive.'"

"Are you saying...?" she broke in, frowning.

"You have nothing to fear, Madame. Under my protection Nevers's daughter has remained as pure as the angels of heaven."

"Well, sir, in that case..."

"Well, Madame, though you have nothing to fear, I on the other hand..."

The princess bit her lip. Clearly she wouldn't be able to hold back her anger much longer.

"I arrived happy, confident, full of hope," he went on. "That speech froze my heart, Madame. Without that speech, your daughter would already be in your arms." He grew more animated. "Really? That was your first thought! Even before you saw your daughter, your only child, pride already spoke louder in you than love! The noble lady showed off her coat of arms, when I was looking for the mother's heart! I tell you, I'm afraid. Though I'm not a woman, Madame, I have a different concept of what a mother's love is; and if I was told, 'There's your daughter, the only child of the man you adored—she wants to press her face to your bosom, you'll mingle your tears of joy—' if they told me that, Madame, I think I'd have exactly one impulse, only one, an impulse that would make me giddy and mad with joy—to embrace and kiss my child!"

The princess wept, but pride made her hide her tears. "You don't know me, and yet you judge me!"

"In a word, yes, Madame, I judge you. If it was for myself, I'd give it time. But it's for her, and I can't afford to wait. In that house, where you're not in control, what will be that child's fate? What guarantees can you give me, against your second husband and against yourself? Speak, answer my questions. What kind of new life have you prepared for her? What new happiness will take the place of the happiness she'll lose? She'll have high rank, won't she? She'll be rich. She'll have greater honors, though less joy. More arrogance, but less tranquil goodness. Madame, that's not what we came for. We'd give up all the world's greatness, all of its riches, all of its honors, for one word spoken from the heart, and we're still waiting for that word. Where's your love? I don't see it. Your pride quivers, but your heart is silent. I'm afraid, I tell you, afraid not of Monsieur de Gonzague but of you, of you, her mother! That's where the danger lies—I can tell, I can feel it. And if I can't protect Nevers's daughter against that danger, the way I protected her against all the rest, I'm forsworn to the dead!"

He stopped to wait for an answer. She remained silent.

He made an effort to calm down. "Madame, forgive me. My duty requires me, my duty obligates me above all, to make conditions. I want Aurore to be happy. I want her to be free, and rather than see her enslaved..."

"Say it, sir!" Her tone suggested that she felt provoked.

He came to a halt. "No, Madame, I won't say it, out of respect for you. You've understood me well enough."

The princess smiled bitterly. Then, drawing herself up and looking into his face, she said to the stunned Lagardère, "Mademoiselle de Nevers is the richest heiress in France. When you think you've got that prey in your clutches, it's worth fighting for. I've understood you, sir, much better than you know."

VIII. Another Conversation

They'd reached the end of the arbor by Mansard's wing of the palace. It had grown late. The happy sound of clinking glasses increased steadily, but the lights were dimming, and even the rising raucous voice of drunkenness signaled the approaching end of the ball. The garden was more and more deserted, and it seemed nothing would disturb the conversation between Lagardère and the Princess of Gonzague—nor was there any sign they would come to agreement. The princess's defiant pride had struck a harsh blow, and at that moment she congratulated herself. Lagardère lowered his head.

"If I seemed cold, sir," she went on with even greater haughtiness, "if you didn't hear me utter the joyful cry from the heart you talk about so much, it's because I understood it all. I knew the battle wasn't over, and it was too soon for a victory song. As soon as I saw you, my blood ran cold. You're handsome, you're young, you're free of family ties. Your capital consists of your adventures. It must've occurred to you this was the way to make your fortune in one stroke."

"Madame," he cried, his hand on his heart, "God above is my witness and will avenge me for your insults!"

She responded angrily, "Do you dare claim you never had that ridiculous hope?"

There was a long silence. The princess looked defiantly at Lagardère. He blushed and grew pale in turn. Then in a deep, serious voice he went on. "I'm just a poor gentleman. Am I a gentleman? I have no name—my name comes from the ruined villa I took refuge in at night when I was an abandoned child. Yesterday I was a banished man. And yet you're right, Madame, I did have that hope—not a ridiculous hope, a holy and radiant hope. What I'm confessing to you today, Madame, was still a mystery to me yesterday: I didn't know my own mind..."

She smiled sarcastically.

"I swear to you, Madame, on my honor and on my love!" he cried, stressing the last word, and she looked at him with hatred.

"Even yesterday," he went on, "as God is my witness, I had only one thought—to return to Nevers's widow the sacred burden entrusted to me. I'm telling the truth, Madame, and it doesn't matter whether you believe me, because I have control of the situation and the power to decide your daughter's fate. During all my weary days of struggle, did I have time to examine my own heart? I was happy with what I had to do, and my devotion was its own reward. Aurore was my daughter. When I left Madrid to come to you, I wasn't sorry: I imagined that at the sight of me Aurore's mother, overcome with joy, would open her arms and embrace me while I was still dusty from traveling. But along the way, as the hour of separation neared, I felt something inside me like a wound opening, growing, infecting. My lips still tried to say the words 'my daughter!' But my lips lied: Aurore is no longer my daughter. I looked at her with tears in my eyes. She smiled at me, Madame—alas, poor little saint, unwittingly and without meaning to—she gave me a smile different from the one a father gets."

The princess waved her fan and murmured through clenched teeth, "Now you're going to tell me she's in love with you."

"If that's not my hope," he answered warmly, "may I drop dead right here!"

She sank onto one of the benches that lined the arbor. Her breast heaved. From that moment her ears were closed to argument, and she felt nothing but rage and resentment. Lagardère was her daughter's seducer! Her anger was even greater because she didn't dare express it: when you hand your purse to a beggar holding a blunderbuss, it's important not to offend him. This Lagardère, this rogue, acted like he didn't want to haggle for gold. "Does Aurore know her family name?" she asked.

"She thinks she's a foundling I took in," he said without hesitation. The princess lifted her head. He went on, "I see that gives you hope, and you can breathe easier. When she learns the difference in our rank..."

"But will she ever learn it?" she asked mistrustfully.

"She will, Madame. Do you think I want her to be free from you, only to be chained to me? Swear to me, with your hand on your heart, 'By Nevers's memory, my daughter will live with me in perfect freedom and safety.' Swear that, and I'll let you have her."

The princess hadn't expected that, and yet she wasn't won over. She suspected some new trick, and wanted to meet cunning with cunning. Her daughter was in this man's power; the important thing was to see her daughter.

Watching her hesitate, Lagardère said, "I'm waiting!"

Abruptly, to his surprise, the princess held out her hand. "Take it, and forgive a poor woman who's always been surrounded by enemies and sell-outs. If I've been mistaken about you, Monsieur de Lagardère, I'll make it up to you on bended knee."

"Madame..."

"I owe you a lot, I admit. This isn't the way we should've met again, Monsieur de Lagardère. Maybe you were wrong to speak to me the way you did. Maybe on my part I showed too much pride. I should've told you right away that what I said at the family council was directed at Monsieur de Gonzague and was prompted simply by the looks of the girl they were passing off as Mademoiselle de Nevers. I lost my temper too quickly. But suffering embitters you, as you well know—and I've suffered so much!"

Standing before her, he bowed respectfully.

"Plus which," she went on with a sad smile, "because every woman is above all an actress, I'm jealous of you—couldn't you tell? That provokes anger. I'm jealous of you for all you took from me: her affection, her infant cries, her first tears, her first smile. Yes, I'm jealous! I've lost eighteen years of her precious life! And you're bargaining with me over what's left. Well, will you forgive me?"

"I'm happy, so happy to hear you talk like this, Madame."

"You thought I had a heart of marble? Let me just see her! I'm in your debt, Monsieur de Lagardère, I'm your friend, and I promise not to forget it."

"I'm nothing, Madame, it's not about me."

"Give me back my daughter!" she cried, rising. "I promise everything you've asked for, on my honor and in Nevers's name!"

A darker sadness clouded Lagardère's face. "You've promised, Madame. Your daughter is yours. I ask only for time to let her know and get her ready. She's a tender soul, and too strong a shock might shatter her."

"Will you need long to prepare her?"

"I'm asking for an hour."

"So she's nearby?"

"She's in a safe place, Madame."

"And can I at least know..."

"Where I live? Why? In an hour Aurore de Nevers won't live there anymore."

"Then do as you wish. Goodbye, Monsieur de Lagardère. Do we part as friends?"

"I've never stopped being yours, Madame."

"I do feel that I could like you. Goodbye, and be hopeful."

Lagardère seized her hand and kissed it passionately. "I'm yours, Madame, body and soul!"

"Where will I find you?"

"At Diana's Circle, in an hour."

She moved away. As soon as she left the arbor she stopped smiling and began to hurry across the garden. "I'll have my daughter back!" she cried madly. "I'll have her! And never, never will she see that man again!" She headed toward the Regent's rooms.

Lagardère was also mad—mad with joy, with gratitude, with affection. "Be hopeful—I heard her clearly. She said, be hopeful. Oh, how wrong I was about that woman, that saint. She said, be hopeful. Did I ask her for that much? I bargained over her happiness, I mistrusted her, I thought she didn't love her daughter enough. Oh, how I'll cherish her! And what joy it'll be to put her daughter into her arms!"

He walked back through the arbor toward the fountain pool, now unlit and deserted. In spite of his fever of joy, he took care to make sure he wasn't followed. Two or three times he turned into side alleys , then retraced his steps at a run. Then he went straight to Le Bréant's lodge in the woods. Before he entered, he stopped and looked carefully all around. No one had followed him. All the nearby flowerbeds were empty. He heard only, from the direction of the nearby Indian tent, the sound of footsteps rapidly fading into the distance. It was an opportune time. He put the key in the lock, opened the lodge door, and went in.

At first he didn't see Aurore. He called and got no answer. But soon, by the light of a string of lamps outside that illuminated the interior of the lodge, he saw her waiting at a window, listening. He called to her.

Aurore left the window and ran to him. "Who was that woman?" she cried.

"What woman?" he said in surprise.

"The one who was just with you."

"How do you know that, Aurore?"

"That woman is your enemy, Henri, isn't she? Your mortal enemy!"

He began to smile. "What makes you think she's my enemy, Aurore?"

"You're smiling, Henri? I must have been wrong. Good! Forget about that, and tell me fast why I've been kept prisoner here in the middle of a ball! Are you ashamed of me? Am I not pretty enough?" Coquettishly she spread open her domino and let the hood fall to her shoulders, revealing her charming face.

"Not pretty enough! You, Aurore?" It was said admiringly, but with a somewhat absentminded admiration.

"The way you said that!" she murmured sadly. "Henri, you're hiding something. You seem upset, preoccupied. Yesterday you said it would be my last day of living in ignorance—and yet I know nothing more now than yesterday." He looked at her distractedly. She smiled. "But I'm not complaining. You're here now. I can't remember ever having waited so long for you. I'm happy—you're finally going to show me the ball."

"The ball's over."

"It's true: I can't hear the happy music that reached all the way here and cheered up a poor recluse. For a while now I've seen no one go by on the paths—except that woman."

"Aurore," he said solemnly, "please tell me why you thought that woman was my enemy."

"Now you're scaring me! Can it be true?"

"Answer me, Aurore. Was she alone when she passed by?"

"No. She was with a splendidly dressed gentleman. He wore a blue sash."

"Did she say his name?"

"She said your name. That's why I thought to ask you if she'd just been with you."

"Answer me, Aurore. Did you overhear what she said as she was passing under the windows?"

"Only a few words. She was angry, and acted like a crazy person. She addressed him as 'my lord.'"

"My lord!" he echoed.

"'If Your Royal Highness doesn't help me...'"

"That was the Regent!" he said with a start.

Aurore clapped her little hands with childish glee. "The Regent! I saw the Regent!"

"'If Your Royal Highness doesn't help me...'" he resumed. "And then?"

"After that I couldn't hear."

"Was it later she said my name?"

"It was earlier. I was at the window. I thought I heard it—but I think I hear your name everywhere, Henri. She was still far away. As she came closer she said, 'Force! Only force can crush that unshakeable will!'"

"Ah!" He let his arms drop to his sides. "She said that?"

"Yes, she said that."

"That's what you heard?"

"Yes. But you've gone so pale, Henri, and your eyes are burning!"

Indeed he was pale, and his eyes burned. A dagger to the heart wouldn't have hurt him more. His brow darkened. "Violence!" He restrained his voice. "Violence after trickery! Egotism! Perversity of the heart! To repay evil with good is the act of a saint or an angel. To repay evil with evil, or good with good, that's ordinary human justice. But to repay good with evil—in Christ's name, that's vile and treacherous, an impulse that can only come from Hell. She was deceiving me! I understand it all now. They're going to try to outnumber me. They'll separate us..."

"Separate us!" she echoed, leaping on the word like a young lioness. "Who? That pathetic woman?"

"Aurore," he said, putting his hand on her shoulder, "you must say nothing bad about that woman."

The expression on his face just then was so strange she drew back in fear. "In heaven's name! What's wrong?"

Lagardère held his head in his hands. Aurore came closer and tried to throw her arms around his neck. He pushed her away with a kind of dread. "Leave me alone! Leave me alone! It's awful! There's a curse around us, and a curse on us!"

Tears sprang into her eyes. "You don't love me anymore, Henri!" she stammered.

He looked at her again, half crazed. He clasped his arms, and sad laughter shook his chest. Ah!" he said, rocking like a drunk, overcome in both mind and body at once. "On my honor, I don't know, I don't know anymore. What's in my heart? Night? Emptiness? Love or duty—tell me, conscience, which is to be?" He dropped onto a chair, murmuring in the plaintive tone of a man deprived of reason, "Conscience, conscience, which is it to be? Duty or love? My death or my life? Does that woman have rights? And I—don't I have rights too?"

The words fell inarticulately from his lips, and Aurore caught none of it. But she saw his distress, and it broke her heart. "Henri, Henri," she said, kneeling before him.

"Those sacred rights aren't for sale," he continued, now collapsing after his fever. "They aren't for sale, even at the cost of a life. I gave my life, it's true. What am I owed for that? Nothing!"

"In God's name, Henri, dear Henri, calm down and explain!"

"Nothing! And did I do it so I would be owed something? What's my devotion worth? It's madness! Madness!" She held his hands in hers. "Madness!" he repeated indignantly. "I built on the sand; a gust of wind knocked down the fragile tower of my hopes; my dreams are ended!" He felt neither the gentle pressure of Aurore's fingers nor her hot tears running down his hands. "Why did I come here?" He mopped his brow. "Did anyone here need me? What am I? Isn't that woman right? I raised my voice, I spoke like a madman. How do I know you'd be happy with me?—Are you crying?"

"It makes me cry to see you like this, Henri," stammered the poor girl.

"If, later, I saw you crying, it would kill me."

"Why would you see me crying?"

"How do I know? Aurore, Aurore, who can understand a woman's heart? Do I even know if you love me?"

"If I love you!" she cried, drawing herself up fiercely. He watched her intently. "You ask me if I love you?" she repeated. "You, Henri?"

Lagardère lifted one hand to Aurore's lips, and she kissed it. He withdrew it as if from a flame. "Forgive me. I'm upset. And yet I have to know. You yourself don't know, Aurore, but I have to know! Listen carefully, think carefully: the stakes of the game are the happiness or the misery of the rest of our lives. I beg you, answer from your conscience, from your heart."

"I'll answer as I would to my father."

He turned white and closed his eyes. "Don't call me that!" he stammered so quietly she could barely hear him. "Never call me that!" After a pause he raised his tear-stained eyes. "My God! It's the only thing I taught her to call me! Who does she see in me, if not her father?"

"Oh, Henri!" Aurore blushed prettily.

"When I was a child," he reflected aloud, "men of thirty seemed old." His gentle voice shook. "How old do you think I am, Aurore?"

"What does your age matter, Henri?"

"I want to know what you think. How old?" He waited like a criminal anticipating arrest.

Love, that powerful, terrifying passion, can be strangely childish. Her heart pounding, Aurore lowered her eyes. For the first time Lagardère saw that her maidenly modesty had been aroused, and the gates of heaven seemed to open for him.

"I don't know how old you are, Henri. But what I called you before—Father—have I ever been able to say it without smiling?"

"Why would you smile? I could be your father."

"But I could never be your daughter, Henri."

The ambrosia on which the immortal gods got drunk was vinegar and bile next to that enchanting voice. And still Lagardère pressed on, wanting to savor his happiness to the last drop. "I was older than you are now when you were born, Aurore. I was already a man."

"It's true, since you could hold my baby basket in one hand and your sword in the other."

"Aurore, my beloved child, don't see me through your gratitude, see me as I am."

She laid her beautiful trembling hands on his shoulders and contemplated him at length. "I know nothing in the world," she said finally, a smile on her lips and her eyes half closed, "nothing better, nothing nobler, nothing handsomer, than you!"

IX. In Which the Ball Ends

At this moment especially, with happiness crowning Lagardère's brow in radiance, it was true: he looked as young as Aurore herself, and as handsome as she was beautiful. If you'd seen her—the maiden in love, veiling the fire in her eyes behind the fringe of her long lashes, her breast heaving, a smile full of feeling on her lips—if you'd only seen her! Chaste and noble love, the saintly affection that binds two beings tightly into one and joins two hearts—love, the hymn God in his goodness allows us to hear on earth—love, that manna brought by the dew of heaven—love, which can beautify ugliness itself—love, which frames beauty with a divine halo—love crowned and transfigured Aurore's gentle face.

Lagardère pressed his fiancée to his own beating heart. There was a long silence, in which their lips never touched, but their eyes spoke. "Thank you! Thank you!" he murmured. "Tell me, Aurore, have I always made you happy?"

"Yes, very happy."

"And yet today you were crying, Aurore."

"You knew that, Henri?"

"I know everything that concerns you. Why were you crying?"

She tried to evade the question. "Why do girls cry?"

"You're not like other girls. When you cry—please, why were you crying?"

"Because you were gone, Henri. I see you so rarely. And also, because of a thought..." She hesitated and looked away.

"What thought?"

"I'm just silly, Henri," she stammered in confusion. "The thought that there are beautiful women in Paris, and that all those women must want to please you, and that maybe..."

"Maybe?" he echoed, still thirsty for his blissful cup of nectar.

"That maybe you loved someone else." She hid her blushing face in his chest.

"Could God grant me such a blessing?" he murmured ecstatically. "Should I believe..."

"You should believe I love you!" She muffled on her lover's chest the frightening sound of her own voice.

"Aurore, you love me! Can you feel my heart beating? Oh, can it be true? But are you sure, Aurore? Do you know your own heart?"

"It speaks, and I listen."

"Yesterday you were a child."

"Today I'm a woman. Henri, Henri, I love you!"

Lagardère pressed her hands to his heart.

"And you?" she asked.

With trembling voice and tears in his eyes, he could only stammer, "Oh, I'm so happy! I'm so happy!"

Then a cloud crossed his brow, and, seeing the cloud, she stamped her foot rebelliously. "Now what?"

"What if someday you have regrets?" he said quietly, lowering his head.

"What regrets could I have, if you stay with me?"

"Listen. Tonight I tried to raise one corner of the curtain that hid the splendor of the world from you. You've seen the court, luxury, lights, you've heard the sounds of merrymaking. What do you think of the court?"

"The court is beautiful. But I haven't seen everything, have I?"

"Do you feel made for this life? Your eyes are shining. Would you enjoy this world?"

"With you, yes."

"And without me?"

"Nothing without you!"

He pressed her joined hands to his lips. Still he went on, "Did you see all the smiling women going by?"

"They looked happy, and very pretty."

"Those women are happy indeed. They have castles and mansions..."

"When you're in our house, Henri, I like it better than a mansion."

"They have friends."

"Don't I?"

"They have families."

"You're my family." Aurore gave all those answers without hesitation, and with a candid smile on her lips. She spoke from the heart.

But Lagardère wanted to test her to the limit. After a silence he summoned all his courage. "They have mothers."

Aurore grew pale. Her smile vanished. A tear formed in her half-closed eyes. He let go of her hands, and she clasped them to her heart. "A mother!" she said, her eyes turning to heaven. "I'm often with my mother. Next to you, Henri, it's my mother I think about most." Her beautiful eyes seemed to express a prayer. "If I had my mother here, with you, Henri, if I heard her call you her son!—oh, what greater joy than that could Paradise offer?" After a short pause she went on, "But if I had to choose between my mother and you..." Her breast heaved with emotion.

He waited, anxious, breathless.

"Maybe what I'm going to say is wrong," she went on with effort. "I say it because it's what I think. If I had to choose between my mother and you..." She didn't finish, but collapsed in his arms, crying in a voice choked with tears, "I love you! Oh, I love you! I love you!"

Lagardère drew himself up. With one hand he held her gently against his chest, while with the other he seemed to call on heaven as his witness. "God

274

who sees us," he cried exultantly, "God who hears us and judges us, you've given her to me. I receive her from you, and I swear she'll be happy!"

Aurore opened her eyes and showed her white teeth in a wan smile.

"Thank you! Thank you!" said Lagardère, bringing her forehead to his lips. "Just look how happy you've made me: I'm laughing, I'm crying, I'm giddy, I'm crazy! Ah, you're mine, Aurore, all mine!—But what was I saying before? Pay no attention to what I said, Aurore. I lied! I'm young. I'm bursting with youth, strength, life. We'll be happy, happy a long time! My darling, there's no doubt other men of my age are older than I am. Do you know why? I'll tell you. Other men do what I was doing before your baby basket crossed my path: they have love affairs, they drink, they gamble, who knows what. Men as rich as I was—rich in enthusiasm, rich in foolhardy courage—foolishly throw away the treasures of their youth. You came along, Aurore, and instantly I turned into a miser. A lucky intuition made me stop spending my heart's wealth. I hoarded my heart, to save it all for you. I locked my wild youth away in a strongbox. I gave up loving or wanting anything. All my love has lain dormant, like Sleeping Beauty—and now it awakens, fresh and hale: my heart's only twenty! You're listening, you're smiling, you think I'm crazy. I'm crazy with joy, it's true, but I know what I'm saying.

"What did I do all those years? I spent every one of them watching you grow and blossom. I spent them watching as your heart awakened. I spent them finding all my joy in your smile. In God's name, you were right! I'm of an age to be happy, of an age to love you! You're mine! We'll be all in all to each other! You were right again: besides the two of us, there's nothing in the world. We'll go hide away somewhere unknown, far away, very far from here! I'll tell you what our life will be: love overflowing the cup, love, always love... But say something, Aurore, say something!"

She'd listened with rapture. "Love!" she echoed, as if in a happy daydream, "always love!"

"Crooked ace, baldy!" said Cocardasse, holding the Baron of Barbanchois by his feet, "this old codger's heavier than he looks!"

Passepoil had hold of the same Barbanchois by the head. The baron was an austere, disgruntled man, deeply repelled by the decadence of the Regency; but right now he was as drunk as half a dozen tsars touring France. The Baron of La Hunaudaye had persuaded Cocardasse and Passepoil to take Barbanchois home, for a small fee. They were crossing the dark, empty gardens.

"Hey!" said Cocardasse when they'd come a hundred paces from the tent where supper had been served. "Let's take a break!"

"I concur," said Passepoil. "The old-timer's big and the money's small."

They set Barbanchois down on the lawn. Partly awakened by the cool of the evening, he took up his familiar refrain. "Where are we all headed? Where are we all headed?"

"Damn!" said Cocardasse. "This old drunk sure asks a lot of questions, sweetheart!"

"We're headed to our own funeral," sighed Passepoil with resignation.

They sat down together on a bench. Passepoil drew a pipe from his pocket and calmly began to fill it. "If that was our last supper, at least it was a good one."

"It was a good one." Cocardasse struck a light. "God's hat! I ate a bird and a half, all by myself."

"Ah, that bird across from me, with powdered blonde hair and feet small enough to hold in the hollow of my hand!"

"First-rate! God's blood! And the artichoke hearts all around it, thunder and lightning!"

"And a waist you could put two hands around! Did you notice?"

"I liked mine better," said Cocardasse solemnly.

"What!" protested Passepoil. "That cross-eyed redhead?" He meant Cocardasse's neighbor at table.

Cocardasse seized him by the scruff of his neck and stood him up. "Baldy, I won't allow you to insult my supper. Say you're sorry, God's life, or I'll split you in two without mercy."

To console themselves for their troubles, they'd both drunk twice as much as the austere baron. Passepoil, tired of his friend's tyranny, wouldn't apologize. They drew, and swung their swords wildly at each other without hitting anything. Then they grabbed each other by the hair, and wound up falling onto Barbanchois, who woke again and sang out, "Where are we all headed, Good Lord? Where are we all headed?"

"Hey!" said Cocardasse, "I forgot all about this old trash."

"Let's take it with us."

But before they picked up their burden again they embraced warmly, weeping a flood of tears. If you think they'd left supper without filling up their flasks, you don't know them. They both knocked back a good mouthful, sheathed their swords, and picked up the baron. Barbanchois was in the middle of dreaming he was at a ball at the Castle of Vaux le Vicomte given by Superintendent Fouquet for the young King Louis XIV, and he was sliding under the table after supper. "Other times, other customs," says the lying proverb.

"And you didn't see her again?" asked Cocardasse.

"Who? The girl across from me?"

"No, the little minx in the pink domino."

"Not a trace. I checked all the tents."

"Crooked ace! I went all the way into the palace, and let me tell you, baldy, they were staring at me. I saw pink dominos all over the place, but not ours. I tried to talk to one of them, but she tweaked my nose and called me a boogeyman's corpse. 'Damn!' I said. 'You jumped-up fishwife! I guess my noble friend the Regent is letting just about anybody in!'"

"And did you see him?"

Cocardasse lowered his voice. "No, but I heard people talking about him. The Regent didn't come to supper. He spent more than an hour in private with Gonzague. All the flunkies we saw this morning at his villa are whimpering and threatening. God's blood, if they can fight half as well as they can sing, our poor little Parisian's in trouble!"

Passepoil sighed. "I'm afraid they're going to take care of him for us."

Stopping short in the lead—which drew a complaint from Barbanchois—Cocardasse said, "Brother, you can be sure our rascal will come out all right. He's gotten through worse!"

"The pitcher can only go to the well so many times before..." murmured Passepoil.

He didn't finish the proverb. They heard footsteps from the direction of the fountain pool. Entirely from habit, our two bravos threw themselves into a thicket: their first impulse was always to hide. The footsteps drew nearer. It was a group of armed men, led by the Marquis of Bonnivet, Madame de Berry's equerry and a notorious cutthroat. As the men advanced along the alley they put out the lamps. Soon Cocardasse and Passepoil could overhear them.

"He's in the garden," said an officer of the Royal Guard. "I questioned all the sentries and the guards at the gates. His costume was easy to recognize. No one saw him leave."

"Twenty devils!" said a soldier. "That fellow sure asked for it! I watched him shake Monsieur de Gonzague the way you shake a tree to get apples."

"That boy must be a countryman of mine," murmured Passepoil, softened by a familiar Norman expression.

"Be ready, men," said Bonnivet. "You know he's dangerous company!"

They moved off into the distance. Another group was patrolling by the palace, and a third by the arbor behind the houses along the Rue Neuve des Petits Champs. Everywhere they went they put out the lamps on their way. Some sinister deed appeared to be intended in that frivolous place of pleasure.

"Baldy," said Cocardasse, "it's him they're after."

"That seemed clear to me," said Passepoil.

"I already heard them saying in the palace that our rascal had roughed up Gonzague. He's the one they're looking for."

"And to help find him, they're putting out the lights?"

"Not to find him, to get the better of him."

"It's forty or fifty against one. I swear, if they don't get him this time..."

"Brother, they won't get him. That little rascal has the devil in him. What I'm thinking is, we go find him too, and we offer him our services."

Passepoil, a cautious man, couldn't help wincing. "This isn't the time."

"Crooked ace! Are you arguing with me?" cried Cocardasse angrily. "It's now or never. And if he doesn't need our help, he'll answer us with the Nevers attack. We're at fault."

"It's true. We're at fault. But it's a hell of a bad business!"

The upshot was that the Baron of Barbanchois never reached his bed: that gentleman was nicely deposited on the ground, and went on sleeping. Where and how he awoke will be revealed later in the story. Cocardasse and Passepoil set off searching.

It was a dark night. The only lamps still lit in the garden were those around the Indian tents. Lights came on in the upstairs windows of the Regent's rooms. A window opened. The Regent himself came out onto the balcony and said to his servants invisible below, "Gentlemen, I'll have your heads if you don't take him alive!"

"God help us," muttered Bonnivet, whose platoon was then by Diana's Circle. "If the bandit overheard that, he'll cut us to pieces!"

Admittedly, the patrols were going about their work without much enthusiasm. Monsieur de Lagardère had such a fearful reputation as a devil incarnate that every soldier there would happily have made his will. That swashbuckler Bonnivet would rather have fought two dozen young provincial noblemen—thrushes, as they were called in those days in the gambling dens and on the dueling grounds and wherever they were gobbled up—than faced this job.

Lagardère and Aurore had just come to the decision to flee. Lagardère had no idea what was going on in the garden. He hoped the two of them would be able to leave through the door guarded by Le Bréant. Lagardère had put his black domino back on, and Aurore had once again hidden her face under her mask. They left the lodge.

Two men were kneeling outside the door. "We did what we could, chevalier," said Cocardasse and Passepoil together. They'd emptied their flasks to give themselves courage. "Forgive us!"

"Anyway," added Cocardasse, "that damned girl in the pink domino was like a will o' the wisp!"

"Sweet Jesus!" cried Passepoil. "Here she is!"

Cocardasse rubbed his eyes.

"On your feet!" ordered Lagardère. Then suddenly he noticed the muskets of the Royal Guard at the other end of the alley. "What's this mean?"

"It means you're trapped, poor boy!" answered Passepoil. He'd found such indiscreet language at the bottom of his flask.

Lagardère didn't ask for an explanation; he'd guessed it all. The ball was over, that's what shocked him. The hours had passed for him like minutes—he'd lost track of the time—he'd let it get late. His plan for escape depended entirely on the bustle of the ball. "Are you with me, completely and sincerely?"

"In life, in death!" said the two bravos, their hands on their hearts. They weren't lying. The sight of that rascal of a little Parisian, right after they'd drained their flasks, finished the job of making them drunk.

Aurore trembled for Henri, without thinking of herself.

"Have the sentries been pulled from the doors?" he asked.

"They've been reinforced," said Cocardasse. "We'll have to play close to the chest, God's blood!"

Lagardère considered. "Would you happen to know Master Le Bréant, the doorkeeper at the Laughter Court?"

"Like the back of our hand," said Cocardasse and Passepoil together.

Lagardère gave a disappointed shrug. "Then he won't open his door for you."

Our two bravos nodded at the impeccable logic of that: only someone who didn't know them would ever open the door to them.

Meanwhile a muffled noise arose in the bushes nearby, like the sound of men approaching cautiously from all sides. Lagardère and his companions could see nothing, because the lamps were out in all the nearby alleys, and the flower-beds were completely dark.

"Listen," said Lagardère, "we have to stake everything on one throw. Don't worry about me: I can take care of myself, and I brought a disguise that'll fool my enemies. Take the girl. Go into the Regent's vestibule and turn left. Master Le Bréant's door is at the end of the first corridor. Pass by in your masks and say, 'We're with the man in the garden, in your lodge.' He'll open the door. Go wait for me behind the oratory chapel at the Louvre."

"Got it!" said Cocardasse.

"One more thing. Are you men enough to die rather than hand over this girl?"

"Crooked ace! We'll smash everything in our way!" promised Cocardasse.

"Look out, insects!" added Passepoil with unaccustomed pride.

And together they both said, "This time you'll be pleased with us."

Lagardère kissed Aurore's hand. "Courage! This is our final ordeal."

She left, escorted by our two bravos. They had to cross Diana's Circle.

"Well, well," said a soldier. "Here's a girl who's taken her time finding her way out!"

"Boys," said Cocardasse, "this lady is with the corps de ballet." With a firm arm he pushed aside the men in front of him, and added shamelessly, "His Royal Highness awaits us!" The soldiers laughed and made way.

But in the shade of a line of potted orange trees bordering the corner of the Regent's wing, two men were hiding: the Prince of Gonzague and his factotum Peyrolles. They were waiting for Lagardère, whom they expected to show up any moment. Gonzague spoke a few words into Peyrolles's ear. The latter joined half a dozen rascals with long swords waiting in ambush behind the trees. All of them jumped out to follow our two bravos, who were just climbing the steps, still escorting the girl in the pink domino.

As Lagardère had expected, Le Bréant opened the door to the Laughter Court—but he opened it twice: once for Aurore and her escort, and a second time for Peyrolles and his men.

Lagardère had snuck to the end of the path to see if his fiancée would get into the building safely. When he tried to return to the lodge, he found his way blocked: a line of Royal Guards closed off the avenue.

"Hold it, chevalier!" cried their leader. "Don't try to resist, I beg you. You're surrounded." It was true. From all the nearby shrubberies came the ring of musket butts on the ground.

"What do you want with me?" Lagardère hadn't even drawn his sword. The brave Bonnivet, who'd tiptoed up behind him, threw his arms around him. Lagardère didn't try to break free, and asked again, "What do you want with me?"

"By God, friend," said Bonnivet, "you're about to find out!" Then he said to the troops, "Forward, men! To the palace! I hope you'll be my witnesses that I made this crucial arrest single-handed."

There were at least sixty of them. They surrounded Lagardère, and carried rather than led him to the Regent's rooms. Then the door to the vestibule was closed, and in the garden not a living soul remained—except the Baron of Barbanchois, snoring like an honest man on the damp grass.

X. Ambush

The room known as the big office, or more properly the outer office, was a fairly large hall where Philippe d'Orléans was in the habit of receiving his ministers and the Regency Council. It held a round table covered with a silk spread, an armchair for the Regent, another armchair for the Duke of Bourbon, chairs for the other permanent members of the council, and folding chairs for the secretaries of state. Over the main door hung the coat of arms of France crossed with the charge of Orléans. Every evening after dinner the affairs of the kingdom were settled here, a little carelessly: the Regent dined late and the Opéra began promptly, so there really wasn't much time.

The room was already full when Lagardère was brought in. It looked a little like a tribunal: Messrs de Lamoignon, de Tresmes, and de Machault stood around the Regent, who was seated. The dukes of Saint-Simon, Luxembourg, and Harcourt stood by the fireplace. There were guards at all the doors.

The triumphant Bonnivet glanced in a mirror and wiped the sweat off his brow. "We had some trouble," he said quietly, "but we got him in the end! Ah, he's a devil!"

"Did he put up much of a struggle?" asked Machault, the Chief of Police.

"If I hadn't been there," said Bonnivet, "God knows what might have happened."

The window alcoves were full of people you'd recognize: old General de Villeroy, Cardinal de Bissy, Minister d'Argenson, Secretary of State Le Blanc, and so on. A few of Gonzague's followers had shown up: Navailles, Choisy, Nocé, Gironne, and fat little Oriol, who was completely hidden behind Taranne. Chaverny was talking with Monsieur de Brissac, who was asleep on his feet after three nights of drinking. A dozen or more men armed to the teeth stood behind Lagardère. Only one woman was present: the Princess of Gonzague, seated at the Regent's right.

"Sir," said the Regent curtly as soon as he caught sight of Lagardère, "our safe-conduct didn't include permission to come disturb our festivities and insult in our own house one of the highest lords in the kingdom. You also stand accused of having drawn your sword on the grounds of the Palais-Royal. You've very quickly made us repent our clemency."

From the moment of his arrest, Lagardère's face had been like marble. He replied coldly and respectfully, "My lord, I'm not afraid to repeat what was said between Monsieur de Gonzague and me. As for the second charge, it's true, I drew my sword. But it was to defend a lady. Several among those here could attest to that."

Half a dozen of them could have done so, but only Chaverny spoke up. "It's true, sir." Lagardère glanced at him in surprise, while his companions glared at him reproachfully.

But the Regent, tired and ready for bed, didn't want to dwell on these trifles. "Sir, we could have forgiven you all of that. But be warned, there's one thing for which we won't forgive you. You promised you'd give Madame de Gonzague back her daughter. Is that true?"

"Yes, my lord, I promised."

"You also sent me a messenger who made me the same promise in your name. Do you admit that?"

"Yes, my lord."

"I suppose you realize you're facing a tribunal. Ordinary courts can't adjudicate the crime you're accused of. But, sir, I swear you'll be punished if you deserve it. Where is Mademoiselle de Nevers?"

"I have no idea."

"He's lying!" cried the princess impulsively.

"No, Madame. I promised more than I could deliver, that's all."

A disapproving murmur ran through the room.

Looking around him, Lagardère raised his voice. "I'm not acquainted with Mademoiselle de Nevers."

"Impudence!" cried the Duke of Tresmes, Governor of Paris.

"Impudence!" echoed all of Gonzague's followers.

Monsieur de Machault, raised in the sensible traditions of the police, immediately suggested they proceed to torture. Why overthink things?

The Regent glared at Lagardère. "Think carefully about what you say."

"My lord, careful thinking can neither add to nor subtract from the truth. I told the truth."

"Will you tolerate this, my lord?" said the princess, unable to hold back. "On my honor, on my salvation, he's lying! He knows where my daughter is, since he told me so himself a little while ago, not far from here, in the garden!"

"Answer!" ordered the Regent.

"Then, as now," answered Lagardère, "I told the truth. I still hoped to keep my promise then."

"And now?" stammered the princess, beside herself.

"Now I no longer hope to."

She fell back in her seat, exhausted.

The serious members of the company—the ministers, the members of the courts, the dukes—examined with curiosity this strange individual about whom they'd heard so much in their youth: handsome Lagardère, the cutthroat Lagardère! This calm, intelligent man didn't come across like a common sword wrangler. A few of them, the more observant, tried to find what lay behind his apparent ease. They saw a sad and deeply considered resolve.

Gonzague's followers felt too insignificant here to make much noise. They'd gotten in thanks to their patron, who was a party to the dispute—but their patron hadn't shown up.

The Regent continued, "And it was merely out of vague hopes that you wrote to the Regent of France? When you wrote, 'Your friend's daughter will be returned'"

"I hoped it would be so."

"You hoped!"

"Man is liable to error."

The Regent glanced toward Tresmes and Machault, who seemed to be his advisors.

"But, my lord," cried the princess, gesticulating, "can't you see he's stealing my child! He has her, I swear! He's keeping her hidden! On the night of the murder, he was the one I gave my daughter to—I remember it! I know it! I swear it!"

"Do you hear that, sir?" said the Regent.

Lagardère's pulse pounded imperceptibly in his temples. Sweat dampened his hair. But he answered without losing his cool, "The princess is mistaken."

"Oh!" she cried madly, "And to be unable to refute this man!"

The Regent began, "It would only take one witness..."

But he broke off, because Lagardère had drawn himself fully erect, and thereby attracted the attention of Gonzague, who'd just come in through the main door. Gonzague's entrance made a brief stir. Staying by the door, he bowed to his wife the princess and to the Regent from across the room. His eyes met Lagardère's.

As if delivering a challenge, Lagardère said, "Then let the witness show himself, and let the witness dare identify me!"

Everyone could see that Gonzague blinked as if he couldn't look the accused man in the eye. But he managed to smile, and everyone thought he might be looking away out of pity. Still, the room remained silent. There was a slight movement at the door. Gonzague stepped to the threshold, and Peyrolles's jaundiced face appeared out of the shadows.

"We have her!" said Peyrolles quietly.

"And the documents?"

"And the documents."

Gonzague's cheeks reddened with joy. "God's death! Wasn't I right to tell you that hunchback was worth his weight in gold?"

"I swear, I'll admit I was wrong about him. He did us quite a favor!"

Meanwhile Lagardère was saying, "No one answers, my lord, as you can see. Since you're the judge, be fair. What do you find before you right now? A wretched gentleman as disappointed in his hopes as you are. I thought I could count on a feeling that's normally purer and stronger than any other. I made my promise with the recklessness of a man who expects a reward." He paused, and went on with some effort, "Because I thought I had the right to a reward." In spite of himself his eyes fell, and his voice stuck in his throat.

"What kind of man is that?" old Villeroy asked d'Argenson.

"Either a great soul, or the lowest of all villains."

With enormous effort Lagardère got hold of himself. "Fate played a trick on me, my lord, that's my crime. What I thought I possessed got away from me. I'll sentence myself, and go back into exile."

"That's convenient!" said Navailles.

Machault was whispering to the Regent.

"I throw myself at your knees, my lord..." began the princess.

"Stop, Madame!" the Regent interrupted with an imperious gesture that silenced the room. He turned again to Lagardère. "You're a gentleman, sir. At least you claim to be. What you did was unworthy of a gentleman. Let your punishment be your own shame. Your sword, sir!"

Lagardère mopped the sweat that bathed his brow. When he undid his sword belt, a tear ran down his cheek.

"God's blood!" muttered Chaverny, moved without knowing why. "I'd rather see him killed!" At the moment Lagardère surrendered his sword to Bonnivet, Chaverny averted his eyes.

The Regent continued, "We no longer live in olden times, when knights convicted of a felony had their spurs broken. But nobility still exists, thank God, and loss of rank is the cruellest punishment a soldier can face. Sir, you have lost the right to wear a sword. Make way, gentlemen, and let him through. This man is no longer worthy to breathe the same air as you."

For a moment it looked like Lagardère was about to topple the columns of that room, like Samson, and bury the Philistines under the rubble. At first his powerful face expressed such terrible wrath that the men nearby moved aside from fear rather than in obedience to the Regent's order. But then anguish followed anger, and anguish in turn gave way to that cold resolve he'd shown since he was brought in. He bowed. "I accept Your Royal Highness's verdict and will not appeal." A distant solitary retreat, and Aurore's love—that was the picture that passed before his eyes. Was that not worth martyrdom? He started across the silent room toward the door.

The Regent said very quietly to the princess, "Don't worry, he'll be tailed."

At the center of the room Lagardère found himself facing Gonzague, who'd just left Peyrolles.

"Your Highness," said Gonzague, "I bar this man's way."

In extreme agitation, Chaverny looked as if he wanted to throw himself at Gonzague. "Ah, if Lagardère still had his sword!"

Taranne nudged Oriol. "Chaverny's gone nuts."

"Why do you bar this man's way?" asked the Regent.

"Because your understanding was mistaken, my lord," replied Gonzague. "Degradation from nobility is not the proper punishment for murderers!"

There was a great stir in the room, and the Regent stood up.

"This man is a murderer!" went on Gonzague, laying his naked sword blade on Lagardère's shoulder—and you can be sure he had a firm grip on the pommel. But Lagardère made no attempt to disarm him.

In the midst of the general uproar—because Gonzague's followers cried out and made as if to charge—Lagardère burst out laughing. He simply pushed aside the blade, grabbed Gonzague's wrist, and shook it hard enough that the sword dropped. Then he led, or rather dragged, Gonzague to the table. Displaying Gonzague's hand, forced open by pain, Lagardère pointed to a deep scar. "My mark! I recognize my mark!"

The Regent's look was black. All of them held their breath.

"Gonzague's done for!" murmured Chaverny.

But Gonzague's audacity now rose to magnificence. "Your Highness, I've been waiting for this for eighteen years! Philippe, our brave friend, will finally be avenged. I got this wound defending Nevers's life."

Lagardère let go, and his arms dropped to his sides. For a moment he stood there, floored, while all around a great cry rose up: "Nevers's murderer! Nevers's murderer!"

And Navailles and Nocé and Choisy and all the rest said to each other, "That rascal of a hunchback was right!"

The princess covered her face with her hands in horror. She felt faint and couldn't move.

At a sign from the Regent, the soldiers, led by Bonnivet, surrounded Lagardère, and finally he seemed to wake up. "Villain!" he growled like a roaring lion, "Villain! Villain!" Then, just as Bonnivet was about to grab him by the collar, he pushed him away. "Back!" he cried in a voice like thunder. "Death to the man who touches me!" He turned to the Regent. "My lord, I have Your Royal Highness's safe-conduct." As he spoke he drew the document from the pocket of his doublet and unfolded it. "*Free, no matter what!*" he read in a loud voice. "You wrote it, you signed it!"

"This is an unexpected..." began Gonzague.

"But in a case of trickery..." added Messrs de Tresmes and de Machault.

The Regent silenced them all with a gesture. "Would you give cause to those who say Philippe d'Orléans doesn't keep his word? It's written, it's signed; this man is free. He has forty-eight hours to get across the border."

Lagardère didn't move.

"You heard me, sir," said the Regent harshly. "Leave!"

Slowly Lagardère tore up the document and threw the pieces at the Regent's feet. "My lord, you don't know me. I give you back your word. Of the freedom you offer me, and which is my right, I keep only twenty-four hours. That's all I'll need to unmask a villain and let a just cause triumph. Enough of these humiliations! I hold up my head, and on the honor of my name—you hear, gentlemen, on the honor of Henri de Lagardère, whose honor is as good as yours—I promise and swear that by this time tomorrow Madame de Gonzague will have her daughter and Nevers will have his revenge—or I'll be Your Royal Highness's prisoner! You can summon the judges." He bowed to the Regent, and with one arm he moved aside the men who surrounded him. "Make way! I claim my right."

Gonzague had preceded him and was gone.

"Make way, gentlemen," said the Regent. "And you, sir, tomorrow at this hour you'll appear before your judges, and, by God, justice will be done!"

Gonzague's followers, with no role left to play here, shuffled toward the door.

For a moment the Regent remained pensive. Then, resting his forehead on his hand, he said, "Gentlemen, this is an odd business!"

"A bold rascal!" murmured Machault, the Chief of Police.

"Either that or a knight in shining armor from the days of yore," the Regent reflected aloud. "We'll find out tomorrow."

Alone and unarmed, Lagardère went down the main staircase of the Regent's apartment. In the vestibule he found Peyrolles, Taranne, Montaubert, Gironne—all those who'd committed themselves unconditionally in support of Gonzague. Three mercenaries blocked the corridor leading to Le Bréant's quarters. In the center of the vestibule stood Gonzague, sword in hand. The main door leading to the garden had been left open. It all reeked of an ambush.

But Lagardère paid no attention: the downside of his bravery was that he felt invulnerable. He walked straight up to Gonzague, who raised his sword. "Not so fast, Monsieur de Lagardère. We need to talk. All the exits are blocked, and no one can hear us, except my faithful friends here. God's blood! We can talk openly." Gonzague gave a wicked, sarcastic laugh.

Lagardère waited with his arms folded.

"The Regent has opened his doors to you," went on Gonzague, "but I'm closing them. I was as much Nevers's friend as the Regent was, and I have as much right to avenge his death. Don't call me a villain, it's pointless. Everybody knows losers at the card table throw insults around. Monsieur de Lagardère, shall I tell you something that'll ease your conscience? You thought you were lying—baldly lying— when you said you didn't have Aurore."

Lagardère's face changed.

"Well," went on Gonzague, cruelly savoring his triumph, "you were only guilty of a slight inaccuracy, a nuance, a trifle. It would've been more correct to say, 'I no longer have Aurore.'"

"If I believed that..." said Lagardère, clenching his fists. "But you're lying. I know you!"

"If you'd put it that way," continued Gonzague calmly, "it would've been the exact truth."

Lagardère flexed his knees as if preparing to spring on him, but Gonzague aimed his sword between Lagardère's eyes and murmured, "Get ready, men!"

Then he went on in the same mocking tone, "My God, we've won the round handsomely. Aurore is ours."

"Aurore!" choked Lagardère.

"Aurore, and a few other things..."

At those words, Lagardère trembled and threw himself at Gonzague, who fell heavily backward. Lagardère leaped over him and vanished into the garden.

Gonzague got back up with a smile. "No way out?" he asked Peyrolles, who was waiting outside the garden door.

"No way out."

"How many?"

"Five."

"Good, that's enough. He has no sword."

They both stepped outside to listen. In the vestibule the prince's followers, pale and sweating, listened too. They'd come such a long way since yesterday! Up to now only gold had stained their hands. Now Gonzague wanted them to get used to the smell of blood. It was a slippery slope, and they were sliding down it.

Gonzague and Peyrolles stopped at the foot of the steps. "They're taking their time!" murmured Gonzague.

"It just feels long," said Peyrolles. "They're over there, behind the tent."

The garden was as dark as the inside of an oven. The only sound was the tent canvas flapping sadly in the autumn breeze.

"Where did you catch the girl?" asked Gonzague, as if he wanted to talk just to make the time pass.

"Rue du Chantre, right at her door."

"Was she well guarded?"

"Two tough blades, but they took off when we told them Lagardère was finished."

"You didn't see their faces?"

"No, they kept their masks on the whole time."

"And where were the papers?"

Before Peyrolles could answer, a cry of agony came from behind the Indian tent, in the direction of Le Bréant's lodge. Gonzague's hair stood on end.

"That might be one of ours," murmured Peyrolles, and he shivered.

"No. I recognized his voice."

At that moment five black shadows emerged from Diana's Circle.

"Who's in charge?" asked Gonzague.

"Gendry," answered Peyrolles.

Gauthier Gendry was a big, well-built fellow who'd been a corporal in the Royal Guard. "It's done," he said. "We need a stretcher and two men to get him out of here."

They could hear him in the vestibule. Our lansquenet players, our small-time rakes, had not a drop of blood left in their veins. Oriol's teeth chattered hard enough to crack.

"Oriol! Montaubert!" called Gonzague. They both came. "You'll carry the stretcher." Seeing them hesitate, he added, "We all killed him, since we all profited from his killing."

They needed to hurry before the Regent dismissed his guests. Even though the usual way out was through the main door at the other end of the building, leading to the Fountain Court, someone familiar with the palace might take it into his head to exit by way of the Laughter Court.

Together Oriol, his heart failing him, and Montaubert, full of resentment, picked up the stretcher. Gendry led them into the shrubbery.

"Well, how about that!" said Gendry when they reached the far side of the Indian tent. "And yet the rascal was certainly dead!"

Oriol and Montaubert were on the verge of fleeing. Montaubert was the kind of gentleman capable of many small sins, but who'd never dreamt of a real crime. Oriol, a peaceable coward and a decent fellow, was terrified of blood. Yet here they both still were, and the others were waiting: Taranne, Albret, Choisy, Gironne...

Gonzague saw this as a way to guarantee their silence. They'd surrendered themselves to him, and existed only through him. To retreat would be to lose everything—and would also provoke the vengeance of a man who stopped at nothing. If they'd been told at the start, "This is where you'll wind up," possibly not one of them would have taken the first step. But the first step had been taken, and the second. And at that moment many a commoner and many a gentleman proved that the line between moral squalor and real crime is awfully fine. They couldn't retreat! And their banal excuse was that Gonzague had said, "If you're not with me, you're against me." The worst part was, they'd left that state of common honesty in which we act from fear of our conscience, not from fear of a man. They would certainly have recoiled from committing murder with their own hands; but they found themselves without the moral force to object out loud to murder committed by another.

Gendry said, "He must've crawled away to die nearby." He felt the ground around him and began searching on all fours. He went all the way around the lodge, whose door was locked. Twenty-five paces away he stopped and said, "Here he is!"

Oriol and Montaubert brought the stretcher over.

"When you think about it," said Montaubert. "The thing's already done. We're not doing any harm."

Oriol's tongue seemed paralyzed. They helped Gendry load onto the stretcher a body that was lying on the ground right in the middle of a flowerbed.

"He's still warm," said Gendry. "Go!"

They went. But on the way something frightened them: as they passed Le Bréant's rustic lodge they heard the crunching of dry leaves, and they would have sworn that short, hurried footsteps had followed them since then. In fact as they climbed the Regent's steps the hunchback was right behind them. He was very pale and seemed to have trouble standing up, but he was still laughing his harsh shrill laugh.

When Oriol and Montaubert reached the building with their load, Gonzague dismissed most of his followers. Pointing to the body, over which Gendry had thrown a cloak, the hunchback said to Gonzague—who didn't notice the change in his voice—"Well, well! So he showed up?"

Gonzague slapped him on the shoulder, and the hunchback staggered and almost fell.

"He's drunk!" said Gironne.

They all entered the building. Le Bréant didn't ask the name of the gentleman who had to be carried out because he'd drunk too much; the staff at the Palais-Royal were discreet and tolerant.

It was four in the morning. The lamps, no longer burning, just smoked. The group of rakes scattered in all directions. Gonzague went back to his villa with Peyrolles.

Oriol, Montaubert, and Gendry had the job of carrying the corpse to the Seine. They took the Rue Pierre Lescot. When they'd gotten that far, the two rakes lost heart. For a bribe of one pistole apiece, Gendry allowed them to leave the body on a pile of trash. He took back his cloak, and they dropped the stretcher a little further on, and then they all went home to bed.

That's why, the next morning, the Baron of Barbanchois, oblivious to everything that had happened the night before, woke up in the gutter on the Rue Pierre Lescot, in a state that needs no description. It was his "corpse" that Oriol and Montaubert had carried on their stretcher. The baron didn't brag about his adventure, but his hatred for the Regency only intensified. In the days of the late king he'd slid under the table twenty times and nothing like this had ever happened to him. On his way home to the baroness—who'd no doubt been worried about him—he said to himself, "What manners! To play a trick like that on a man of my rank! I ask you, where are we all headed?"

The hunchback was the last to leave, going out by Le Bréant's little door. It took him a long time to cross the Laughter Court, though it wasn't far. Between the Fountain Court and the Rue Saint Honoré he had to stop and sit down several times on doorsteps. When he stood up again his chest heaved and he gave a kind of whimper. They'd been mistaken in the vestibule: the hunchback wasn't drunk. If Gonzague hadn't had a lot on his mind, he would have noticed that the hunchback's cackle didn't sound quite right tonight.

From the Palais-Royal to Monsieur de Lagardère's house in the Rue du Chantre was only a short distance, but it took the hunchback ten minutes to do it. He could barely make it. He had to climb the spiral stairs leading to Master Louis's rooms on all fours. From outside he'd seen that the street door was broken wide open. The door to Master Louis's rooms too was wide open and broken. The hunchback entered the first room. The door to the second room—the room no one ever entered—had been broken down. The hunchback leaned against the doorframe, gasping. He tried to call Françoise and Jean-Marie, but his voice wouldn't sound. He fell to his knees and crawled to the trunk that used to hold the packet of documents, sealed with three royal seals, that we've described several times. The trunk had been broken open with an ax. The packet was gone. The hunchback slid to the floor like a sick man on the point of death.

The bell tower of the Louvre oratory rang five o'clock. The first light of dawn appeared. Slowly, very slowly, the hunchback pulled himself upright. He managed to unbutton his black wool shirt, and from under it he pulled out a white satin doublet horribly soaked in blood, as if that splendid doublet, wadded up, had been used to stanch a serious wound. Whimpering and crying out weakly, he dragged himself to a cupboard, where he found linen and water enough to clean the wound that had stained the doublet. The doublet was Lagardère's, but the wound bled from the hunchback's shoulder. He bandaged it as well as he could and drank a mouthful of water. Then he crouched down, feeling some relief.

"All right!" he murmured. "I'm alone! They've taken everything—my weapons and my heart!" His head dropped heavily into his hands. When he straightened up he said, "Stand by me, O God! I have twenty-four hours to restart from scratch the work of eighteen years!"

PART FIVE: THE MARRIAGE CONTRACT

I. The House of Gold Again

At the Villa Gonzague they'd worked through the night. The partitions were up. In the morning each vendor arrived to furnish his own four feet by four. The new cubicles in the great hall filled the air with the acrid smell of sawed pine. Construction in the garden was finished too. Nothing remained of the former magnificence. A few humiliated trees lingered here and there, and a few statues stood at the crossroads of the half dozen streets of sheds that had been laid out across the flowerbeds. On a marble pedestal at the center of a small open area facing the steps of the villa, not far from Médor's former kennel, stood a damaged statue of Modesty. Fate makes jokes like that. Who knows whether, in a future century, some guileless monument will mark the spot where our Stock Exchange now stands? By dawn the whole place was full, and the crowd included plenty of courtiers. Even a newborn art is already an art: they bid up, bid down, bought, sold, lied, stole—did business.

The heavy shutters on Madame de Gonzague's windows overlooking the garden were closed. The prince's, on the other hand, were covered only by their curtains of silk with gold brocade. Daylight hadn't reached either prince or princess—nor Monsieur de Peyrolles, whose rooms were under the roof: he was still in bed, though not asleep. He'd just finished counting his take from the night before, and adding it to the contents of a substantial strongbox he kept by his bed. Faithful Peyrolles was rich. He was a miser—or more accurately he was greedy; because, while he loved money passionately, it was only for the sake of the good things money can buy. It goes without saying that he had no prejudices: he accepted money from anyone, and he counted on being a great lord by the time he reached old age. He was Gonzague's Dubois: the Regent's Dubois wanted to be a cardinal; we don't know exactly what that discreet Peyrolles's ambition was, but the English already had a name for it—Milord Million. Peyrolles just wanted to be Cardinal Million.

Gauthier Gendry was giving Peyrolles a report, telling him how those two poor recruits, Oriol and Montaubert, had carried Lagardère's corpse all the way to the Marion Arch and thrown it in the river. Peyrolles always kept half of what his master gave him to pay the rascals he hired. He paid Gendry and dismissed him; but before he left Gendry said, "Good company's getting scarce. Under your windows there's an old soldier from my regiment who might be able to give us a hand now and then."

"Named?"

"The Whale. He's as strong and as dumb as an ox."

"Sign him up. Just as a precaution, because I sure hope we're through with all this violence."

"And I hope the opposite," said Gendry. "I'll go sign him up." He went down to the garden, where the Whale was busy as usual, trying in vain to fight the rising popularity of his happy rival, Aesop, known as Jonah.

Peyrolles got up and went to his master—where he found to his surprise he wasn't the first to arrive. The Prince of Gonzague was meeting with our two friends Cocardasse Junior and Brother Passepoil. In spite of the early hour, both were well turned out and freshly brushed, and they'd already made a stop at the kitchen.

"Well, rogues," said Peyrolles as soon as he saw them, "what did you do last night at the ball?"

Passepoil shrugged, and Cocardasse turned his back. "As much of an honor and a joy as it is to serve a distinguished patron like yourself, my lord," said Cocardasse, "it's exactly as much of a pain to have to deal with that gentleman. Isn't that right, baldy?"

"My friend has read my mind," said Passepoil.

Gonzague looked exhausted. "You heard me: you have to get me word this morning, reliable word, tangible proof. I want to know if he's alive or dead."

Cocardasse and Passepoil bowed the deep graceful bow that made them the most distinguished cutthroats in Europe. They passed stiffly by Peyrolles and exited.

"May I beg to know, my lord," said Peyrolles, already ashen, "to whom you refer when you say 'alive or dead'?"

"I'm talking about the Chevalier de Lagardère." Gonzague dropped his weary head back onto his pillow.

Peyrolles was stunned. "But how is there any doubt? I already paid Gendry."

"Gendry's a wicked rascal, and you're slowing down, Peyrolles. We've been had. While you were asleep I've already been at work this morning. I saw Oriol, and I saw Montaubert. Why didn't our men go with them all the way to the Seine?"

"The job was done. My lord, it was your own idea to make two of your friends..."

"Friends!" spat Gonzague with such scorn that Peyrolles was silenced. "I did the right thing," went on the prince, "and you're right, they're my friends. God's death! They have to believe they're my friends. Who can you take advantage of, if not your friends? I want to checkmate them, you understand? I want them tied up with triple knots, I want them in chains. If that murderer Count Horn had just had a hundred blabbermouths behind him, the Regent would've covered his ears: the Regent wants nothing more than to be left in peace. It's not that I'm afraid of ending up like Count Horn—" He broke off at the sight of Peyrolles staring intently at him. Gonzague gave a slightly forced laugh. "Good God! Look who's already got goose bumps!"

"Has it come to the point where you're worrying about what the Regent might do?"

Gonzague rose on one elbow. "Listen, I swear to God if I go down, you'll hang!"

Peyrolles stepped back three paces, his eyes bulging.

Gonzague burst out laughing. "You're the king of tremblers! In all my life I've never been as secure at court as I am now. But you never know what can happen. If I'm attacked, I want my defenses ready. I want to be surrounded, not by friends—friends are nothing anymore—but by slaves. Not slaves bought, but slaves in chains: creatures who live by my breath, so to speak, and who know my death would kill them."

"As far as I'm concerned," stammered Peyrolles, "your lordship had no need to..."

"It's true. I've owned you a long time. But the others? You know there are some big names in that bunch? You know supporters like that are a shield? Navailles has a ducal lineage, Montaubert is related to the Mole de Champlâtreux family, nobility of the robe whose voices ring like the bells of Notre-Dame! Choisy is Mortemart's cousin, Nocé is related to the Lauzuns, Gironne to Cellamare, Chaverny to the princes of Soubise."

"Oh, as for him..."

"He'll be tied up like the rest. It's just a matter of finding a leash that appeals to him. If we can't find one," Gonzague went on darkly, "too bad for him! But let's finish the list: Taranne is Mr. Law's personal protégé, that buffoon Oriol is the nephew of Secretary of State Le Blanc, Albret is Monsieur de Fleury's cousin. That idiot the Baron of Batz is part of the Princess Palatine's circle. I didn't pick my people blindly, believe me. Vauxménil gets me the Duchess of Berry; I have the Abbess of Chelles by way of little Saveuse. God's blood, I know they'd all sell me out for thirty pieces of silver, every one of them. But since last night I've had them in my hands, and by tomorrow morning I want them under my feet." Gonzague threw back his covers and jumped out of bed. "My slippers!"

Peyrolles knelt immediately and put on his master's slippers with perfect goodwill. When that was done he helped the prince into his dressing gown. He was a beast of many uses.

"I'm telling you all this, Peyrolles, because you're one my friends too."

"Oh, my lord! Are you going to compare me to them?"

"Not at all! Not one of them deserves that." Gonzague smiled bitterly. "But I think of you as such a perfect friend that I can talk to you the way I'd talk to my confessor. It can be a relief to confide in someone. Anyway, we were saying we need them bound hand and foot. The rope I've put around their necks only went on loosely; we'll tighten it. You'll see right away how urgent it is: we were betrayed last night."

"Betrayed! By whom?"

"By Gendry, by Oriol, and by Montaubert."

"Is that possible?"

"Anything's possible as long as the noose isn't choking them."

"And how does your lordship know...?"

"I know nothing, except our rascals didn't do their job."

"Gendry just told me he took the body to the Marion Arch."

"Gendry lied. I know nothing—I'll even admit I'm having trouble letting go of the hope that I was rid of that devil Lagardère."

"So why do you doubt it?"

From under his pillow Gonzague pulled out a rolled-up piece of paper. He unrolled it slowly. "I know almost no one who'd want to play a joke on me," he murmured. "Making the Prince of Gonzague the butt of a practical joke like this would be a dangerous thing to try."

Peyrolles waited for a fuller explanation.

"Plus, on the other hand," went on Gonzague, "at least that Gendry is competent. We heard the scream of agony..."

"What does that paper say, my lord?" asked Peyrolles, his fears rising.

Gonzague handed him the unrolled paper, and Peyrolles read eagerly. The message consisted of a list:

Captain Lorrain—Naples
Staupitz—Nuremberg
Pinto—Turin
El Matador—Glasgow
Jugan—Morlaix
Faenza—Paris
Saldaña—ditto
Peyrolles—...
Philippe of Mantua, Prince of Gonzague—...

The last two names were written in either red ink or blood. No location was given for them, because the avenger didn't yet know where they'd meet their punishment. The first seven names, written in black ink, were each marked with a red x. Gonzague and Peyrolles knew what that mark must mean.

Still holding the paper, Peyrolles shook like a leaf. "When did you get this?" he stammered.

"Early this morning, but not before the gates were opened, because I could already hear the racket those idiots are making inside and out."

There was in fact a stupefying din. They hadn't yet learned from experience how to run a stock exchange and how to give a fine air of propriety to a gambling den. Everybody was shouting at the same time, and the chorus of voices boomed like the roar of a mob.

But Peyrolles had other things to worry about. "How did it come?"

Gonzague pointed to the window above his bed, one of whose panes was broken. Peyrolles understood, and looked around on the carpet, where he soon saw a rock lying among the shards of glass.

"That's what woke me," said Gonzague. "I read it, and that's when it occurred to me that Lagardère might've gotten away."

Peyrolles bowed his head.

Gonzague went on, "Unless this bold move was carried out by some ally of his, unaware of what had happened to his master."

"Let's hope," murmured Peyrolles.

"Anyway, I immediately summoned Oriol and Montaubert. I played innocent, I kidded them, I pressed them, and they admitted they dropped the body on a pile of trash in the Rue Pierre Lescot."

Peyrolles slammed his fist on his knee. "That's all it took! A wounded man can recover."

"We'll soon get to the bottom of this. That's what Cocardasse and Passepoil went out to do."

"You really trust those two rascals, my lord?"

"I trust no one, Peyrolles, not even you. If I could do it all myself, I wouldn't use anyone else. They got drunk last night. They were wrong, and they know it—even more reason for them to behave themselves now. I had them come, and I ordered them to find the two bravos who were there last night, guarding the little adventuress who calls herself Aurore de Nevers." Gonzague couldn't help smiling as he said her name, but Peyrolles remained as solemn as an undertaker. "And to move heaven and earth," continued Gonzague, "to find out if our bête noire got away again."

He rang, and to the servant who came he said, "Have my chaise made ready!" Then he said, "You, Peyrolles, go to the princess so you can convey to her, as usual, my profoundest respects. Make sure to keep your eyes open. Report back on what things are like in the princess's antechamber, and on her chambermaid's tone of voice."

"Where will I find your lordship?"

"First I'm going to the pleasure house. I'm eager to see the little adventuress from the Rue du Chantre. Apparently she and that crazy Doña Cruz are old friends. Then I'm going to Mr. Law's house, because he's been neglecting me. Then I'll show my face at the Palais-Royal. It's not a good idea for me to stay away—who knows what kind of slander's being spread about me."

"All that'll take a while."

"All that'll be quick. I need to see our friends, our good friends. It won't be an idle day, and I'm planning a little supper for tonight—but we'll talk about that later." He went toward the window and picked up the rock from the carpet.

"My lord," said Peyrolles, "before I leave you, allow me to warn you against those two rascals..."

"Cocardasse and Passepoil? Poor Peyrolles, I know they've treated you badly."

"It's not about that. Something tells me they're treacherous. And look, if you need proof: they were part of that business in the moat at Caylus, and yet I don't see their names on that death list."

Gonzague, who'd been eyeing the rock pensively, quickly unrolled the paper again. "It's true," he murmured, "their names aren't here. But if it's Lagardère who made the list, and if those two rascals were Lagardère's men, he would've put their names at the top just to hide the con."

"Much too subtle, my lord. In a fight to the death you can't neglect anything. Since yesterday you've been gambling blind. That odd creature, that hunchback, who wormed his way into your business before you knew it..."

"That reminds me, I have to get him to come clean with me." Gonzague looked out the window. At the same moment, the hunchback, standing outside his kennel, threw a sharp glance up at Gonzague's windows. When he saw the prince, the hunchback lowered his eyes and bowed respectfully.

Gonzague considered the rock again. "We'll clear this up," he murmured. "We'll clear it all up. I feel like today will make up for last night. My chaise is here, Peyrolles. Go, and I'll see you later!"

Peyrolles obeyed. Meanwhile Gonzague got into his chaise and had himself taken to Doña Cruz's pleasure house.

As he followed the corridor toward Madame de Gonzague's apartment, Peyrolles said to himself, "I no longer feel the foolish affection I once had for France, my beautiful homeland. With money you can make a homeland anywhere. My piggy bank's almost full, and in twenty-four hours I can steal whatever more I want from the prince's money chests. The prince seems to be stumbling. If things don't pick up between now and tomorrow, I'll pack my bags and go find a climate that's healthier for my delicate constitution. Hell, the bomb won't have time to go off between now and tomorrow."

Cocardasse and Passepoil had promised to outdo themselves to resolve Gonzague's doubts, and they were as good as their word. We'll catch up with them not far away, in a dive on the Rue Aubry le Boucher, eating and drinking like horses. Their faces shone with joy.

"He isn't dead, God's life!" said Cocardasse, holding out his goblet.

Passepoil filled it and echoed, "He isn't dead." And they drank to the health of the Chevalier de Lagardère.

"Ah, thunder and lightning!" went on Cocardasse. "He deserves to beat us with the flat of his sword for all the stupid stuff we've done since yesterday evening!"

"We were drunk, brother. Drunkards are gullible. Besides, we left him in quite a pickle!"

"Is there any pickle bad enough for that darling little rascal?" cried Cocardasse enthusiastically. "Crooked ace! If I saw him now greased up like a chicken going into the oven, I'd still say, 'God's blood! He'll get out of it!'"

"The fact is," murmured Passepoil, taking little sips of his plonk, "he's a good student. It reflects well on us for having contributed to his education!"

"Brother, you've put into words the very feelings in my heart! Hell, let him beat us with the flat of the sword as much as he wants—I'm his, body and soul!"

Passepoil set his empty glass on the table. "Distinguished friend, if I were allowed to make an observation, I might tell you your intentions are good, but your fatal weakness for wine..."

"God's death!" interrupted Cocardasse. "Listen, baldy, you were three times as drunk as I was."

"Fine, fine, if that's how you're going to take it—hey, barmaid! Another jug!"

The barmaid was built like a barrel, and Passepoil wrapped his long, thin, crooked fingers around her waist.

Cocardasse watched him compassionately. "As far as that goes, poor fellow, you see a mote in your neighbor's eye—why not take the beam out of your own, scum!"

Before the interview with Gonzague that morning, they'd been so convinced of Lagardère's violent end that at dawn they'd gone straight to the house on the Rue du Chantre, where they'd found the doors broken open and the lower floor empty. The neighbors knew nothing about what had become of the pretty girl or of Françoise and Jean-Marie Berrichon. Upstairs, next to the trunk, whose lock had been broken, they'd found a puddle of blood. It was clear: the villains who'd attacked the girl in the pink domino they were supposed to guard last night had told the truth—Lagardère was dead!

But Gonzague himself had now given them new hope, by sending them out to find the body of his mortal enemy. Obviously Gonzague must have his reasons—and that was enough to lead our two friends to drink merrily to the health of Lagardère still alive. As for the second part of their mission—to find the two bravos who'd guarded Aurore—the job was done.

Cocardasse poured himself another round. "We'll have to make up a story, baldy."

"Two stories. One for you, one for me."

"Well, I'm half Gascon and half Provençal, and stories come easily to me."

"And I'm from Normandy, by God! We'll see who comes up with the better story!"

"You're challenging me, aren't you, sweetheart?"

"In a friendly way, brother. It'll be a battle of wits. But don't forget our story has to include finding the corpse of the little Parisian."

Cocardasse shrugged. "God's hat!" he muttered as he sucked down the last drop of the second jug. "Poor baldy's trying to one-up his master!"

It was too soon to go back to the Villa Gonzague—they had to allow time for the search. Cocardasse and Passepoil set themselves, each of them, to concocting his own story. We'll see which of the two was the better storyteller. Meanwhile they fell asleep with their heads on the table, and it would be hard to say which of the two deserved the trophy for most vigorous and resonant snoring.

II. A Regency Stock Swindle

The hunchback had been one of the first to arrive at the Villa Gonzague, and as soon as the gates opened he went in, followed by a little assistant who carried a chair, a money box, a mattress, and a pillow. The hunchback seemed to be furnishing his kennel as if he meant to live there, as his winning bid gave him the right to do. He had in fact taken over all of Médor's rights, including the dog's right to sleep in his kennel.

The occupants of the sheds in Gonzague's garden wanted to pack forty-eight hours into every day. There wasn't time to satisfy their appetite for trade. On the way to work or going home, they speculated. They met for dinner, to speculate while they ate. Only the hours of sleep were lost. Isn't it a shame that man, a slave to physical need, can't speculate in his sleep?

Volume was up. The ball at the Palais-Royal had made a big impression. Of course not one of the speculators had set foot inside the ball; but a few, perched on the balconies of nearby houses, had eavesdropped on the ballet—everyone was talking about the ballet. The Daughter of the Mississippi drawing water from her eminent father's urn, water that turned to gold coins: what an excellent, delightful allegory, something distinctly French that suggested to what height would rise in future centuries the dramatic genius of a nation that, born clever, had already created musical comedy! At supper, between the pears and the cheese, a new stock issue had been granted. These were the granddaughters. They were already going for ten percent over face value before they were print-ed. The mothers were white, the daughters were yellow, the granddaughters would be blue—the color of the sky, of distant vistas, of hopes, of dreams. No matter what people say, there's a profound poetry in a stock coupon register!

Most of the shops at the crossroads in the shanty town were liquor stands, whose owners sold ratafia spirits with one hand and speculated with the other. A lot of drinking was going on: it added energy to the trading. From time to time happy speculators took a round over to the Royal Guards posted as sentries on the main avenues. That was an assignment in high demand, as good as duty in the Porcherons red-light district.

Porters and servants constantly carried in loads of merchandise that they piled in the sheds or outside in the middle of the streets. Porters got paid astonishing fees. The only thing nowadays that can compare to the fees on the Rue Quincampoix is the going rate in San Francisco, the city of gold fever, where they say sufferers from gold fever will pay as much as two dollars to have their shoes shined. The Rue Quincampoix had surprisingly much in common with California.

Our century has invented nothing new in the way of folly. People weren't after gold or silver, or even goods; the mania was for scraps of paper. White ones, yellow ones, mothers, daughters, and finally those precious angels about to be born, the blue granddaughters—those sweet shares whose cradle was already surrounded by so much attention—that's what was being called for loudly on all sides, that's what everyone wanted, that's what provoked the general delirium.

Think about it: a louis is worth x number of francs today; tomorrow it'll still be worth x francs—whereas a granddaughter with a face value of a thousand livres, worth only a hundred pistoles this morning, by tomorrow night might be worth two thousand écus! Down with money—heavy, old-fashioned, static! Long live paper, light as air, precious paper, magical paper, which even while stuck at the bottom of a wallet can undergo a mysterious alchemist's transmutation! Raise a statue to the great Mr. Law, a statue as high as the Colossus of Rhodes!

Aesop, known as Jonah, took advantage of the craze. His back—that convenient writing desk, Nature's gift—wasn't idle for a moment. Six-livre coins and pistoles dropped steadily into his leather purse. But his profits left him impassive: he was already a hardened financier. He didn't look happy this morning; he looked sick. To anyone kind enough to inquire he answered, "I tired myself out last night."

"Whereabouts, Jonah?"

"At the Regent's. He invited me to his ball."

They laughed, they signed, they paid him; it was a blessing.

Around ten in the morning an immense cheer, like a terrible thunderclap, rattled the windows of the Villa Gonzague. The cannon that announces the birth of a sovereign's son and heir doesn't even come close to making that much noise. Trampling each other and swooning, the crowd clapped and shouted and threw their hats in the air in gusts and spasms of joy. The blue shares, the granddaughters, were born! Those fresh, adorable virgins were popping off the presses of the royal printers. It was enough to make the Rue Quincampoix collapse! The granddaughters, the blue shares, the newborns, carried the august signature of the assistant treasurer, Labastide!

"Right here! At ten over par!"

"Fifteen!"

"Twenty, over here, in cash!"

"Twenty-five, payable in wool from Berri!"

"In spices from the Indies—in raw silk—in Bordeaux wine!"

"By God, no pushing, granny! Shame on you, at your age!"

"Listen to the creep, insulting women! Have you no shame?"

"Make way, make way! A shipment of bottles from Rouen!"

"Make way! Heavyweight linen from Quintin, for thirty over par!"

The cries of women who'd been knocked down, of small men who'd been smothered, the squealing of tenors, the rumbling of basses, the trading of well-aimed blows—those blue shares were greeted with a welcome they fully deserved!

Oriol and Montaubert came down the steps from the villa doors. They'd just seen Gonzague, who'd given them a harsh dressing-down. They were silent and shamefaced.

"He's no longer a patron," said Montaubert as they reached the garden.

"He's a master," grumbled Oriol. "One who's leading us where we don't want to go. I'd sure like to..."

"Me too!"

A servant in the prince's livery intercepted them and gave them each a small sealed envelope. They broke the seals: each envelope contained a bundle of blue stock shares. Oriol and Montaubert stared at each other.

"God's blood!" said Oriol, already perking up. He stroked his lace ruff. "I call that sensitive and thoughtful."

"He has ways of doing things," said Montaubert affectionately, "that are like nobody else's."

They counted their granddaughters: a reasonable number.

"Let's mingle," said Montaubert.

"Let's mingle," agreed Oriol.

Their scruples were already far behind them; ahead lay happiness. They heard a sort of echo: "Mingle, mingle!" The whole giddy gang was coming down the steps: Navailles, Taranne, Choisy, Nocé, Albret, Gironne, and the others. Each of them, on arriving, had been given the same consolation prize and conscience-quieter. They all gathered together.

"Gentlemen," said Albret, "look at all these peasant merchants with écus spilling out of their boots. If we work together we can corner the market today and score a windfall. I have an idea..."

"Let's work together, let's work together!" they all cried.

"Am I included?" asked a harsh little voice that seemed to come from the Baron of Batz's pocket. They turned. It was the hunchback, currently lending his back to a dishware dealer who was happily trading away his entire business inventory for a dozen scraps of paper.

"What the hell!" said Navailles, backing away. "I don't like that creep."

"Get lost!" said Gironne rudely.

"Gentlemen, your servant," said the hunchback politely. "I've paid my rent, and the garden is as much mine as yours."

"To think," said Oriol, "this imp, who was such a nuisance to us last night, is nothing but a nasty walking desk!"

"Thinking—listening—talking!" The hunchback put emphasis on each word. He bowed, smiled, and wandered away.

Navailles' eyes followed him, and he murmured, "Yesterday I wasn't afraid of that little man."

"That's because yesterday we were still free to make our own choices," said Montaubert quietly.

"Your idea, Albret, tell us your idea!" cried several voices. They all crowded around Albret, who spoke with animation for several minutes.

"Excellent," said Gironne. "I get it."

"It's zuperb," said the Baron of Batz. "I ket it. But chust exblain again..."

"No need," said Nocé. "To work! In an hour the trick has to be done."

They scattered. About half of them left through the courtyard leading to the Rue Saint Magloire, to take the long way around to the Rue Quincampoix. The others, singly or in twos and threes, wandered here and there, chatting casually about current events.

After a quarter of an hour Taranne and Choisy came back in through the gate that opened onto the Rue Quincampoix. They elbowed their way vigorously through the crowd, calling out to Oriol, who was standing with Gironne. "It's a panic!" they shouted. "Hysteria! They're going for thirty or thirty-five at the Venetian Club, forty or even fifty at Foulon's! In an hour they'll be at a hundred! Buy! Buy!"

In his corner the hunchback chuckled. "We'll throw you a bone to gnaw, small fry," whispered Nocé in his ear. "Just be good."

"Thanks, worthy sir," he replied humbly. "That's all I need."

Meanwhile in the blink of an eye the news had spread that by the end of the day the blues would reach a hundred over par. A crowd of buyers came forward. Albret—who had all of the group's shares in his hands—sold them in bulk at fifty apiece. And he took orders to buy more at the same rate at the stroke of two o'clock.

Just then, through the same gate leading onto the Rue Quincampoix, appeared Oriol and Montaubert with long faces. "Gentlemen," said Oriol to those who asked him what the matter was, "I don't think I should spread the terrible news—it might make the market drop."

"And no matter what we do," added Montaubert with a deep sigh, "it'll happen fast enough anyway."

"Swindlers! Swindlers!" shouted a fat trader whose pockets were stuffed with granddaughters.

"Shut up, Oriol!" said Montaubert. "See what you've done?"

But an eager, curious crowd was already pressing around them. "Please, gentlemen, tell us what you know!" people cried. "That's the honest thing to do!"

Oriol and Montaubert were as silent as fish.

"I'll dell eferyzing!" said the Baron of Batz, who'd just arrived. "Grash! Grash! Grash!"

"Crash? Why?"

"I'm telling you, they're swindlers!"

"Silence, fat man! Why is it a crash, Monsieur de Batz?"

"I ton't know," said the baron sadly. "Vivty berzent trop!"

"Fifty percent drop?"

"In den minudes!"

"In ten minutes? But that's a collapse!"

"Ja, a gollabse! A tisastre! A banig!"

"Gentlemen, gentlemen," said Montaubert calmly, "let's not exaggerate."

"Twenty blues at fifteen over par!" shouted someone nearby.

"Fifteen blues, fifteen, at ten over par and on credit."

"Twenty-five at par."

"Gentlemen, gentlemen, this is madness!" said Montaubert. "The abduction of the young king hasn't yet been officially confirmed."

"And there's no proof Mr. Law has absconded," added Oriol.

"Or that the Regent is being held prisoner in the Palais-Royal," concluded Montaubert sadly.

There was a stunned silence, followed by the sound of a thousand screaming voices. "The young king kidnapped!—Mr. Law fled!—The Regent a prisoner!—Selling thirty shares at fifty under par— Eighty blues at sixty under!—A hundred!—A hundred and fifty!"

"Gentlemen, gentlemen," said Oriol, "don't be hasty."

"I'll sell all I've got at three hundred under!" cried Navailles, who in fact had none left. "Will you take them?"

Oriol refused with a firm wave. Immediately the blues fell to four hundred under par.

Montaubert went on, "They didn't keep a close enough eye on the du Maines, who had allies. Chancellor d'Aguesseau was in on it, and Cardinal de Bissy, and Monsieur de Villeroy, and General de Villars. They were funded by the Prince of Cellamare. De Malestroit, Marquis of Poncallec, the richest man in Brittany, caught the king on his way to Versailles and took him to Nantes. The king of Spain is now crossing the Pyrenees with three hundred thousand men— that, unfortunately, has been confirmed."

"Sixty blues at five hundred under par!" came a cry from the ever-growing crowd.

"Gentlemen, gentlemen, don't be hasty! It takes time to get an army from the Pyrenees all the way to Paris! Besides, it's just rumors! Nothing but rumors!"

"Rumors, rumors," echoed the Baron of Batz. "I'fe zdill kot eine zhare. I'll zell it fur vife huntret vranks! Here!"

No one wanted the baron's share, and the bidding continued in loud voices.

"At the very worst," said Oriol, "if Mr. Law hasn't fled..."

"But who exactly is holding the Regent prisoner?" someone asked.

"You're asking me more than I know, good people," said Montaubert. "I'm neither buying nor selling, thank God! It seems the Duke of Bourbon was unhappy. They're also saying it was the clergy, because of the constitutional business. Some people claim the tsar is mixed up in all this, and he wants to proclaim himself king of France."

There was a cry of horror. The Baron of Batz offered his share at a hundred écus. As the general panic crested, Albret, Taranne, Gironne, and Nocé, who were holding the group's collective cash, made a small purchase and were immediately noticed. People pointed them out to each other: that quartet of idiots was buying! In the blink of an eye the crowd surrounded them, besieged them, smothered them.

"Don't tell them your news," someone whispered to Oriol and Montaubert.

Oriol could hardly keep from laughing. "Poor fools!" he murmured, pointing with pity at his own accomplices. Then he addressed the whole crowd. "I'm a gentleman, my friends. I've shared my news *gratis pro Deo*. Do what you want with it—I wash my hands of it."

Taking kindness even further, Montaubert called to the naive quartet, "Buy, my friends, buy! If the rumors are false you'll make a killing."

People were signing papers two at a time on the hunchback's hump. He was taking payment with both hands, and now wanted nothing but gold. "Cash out now for a profit!" was the general cry. What had been considered par for the blue shares or granddaughters was five thousand livres, the rate at which they were issued, though their face value was only a thousand livres. In twenty minutes they'd fallen to a few hundred francs. Taranne and his men cleaned up. Their wallets swelled like the hunchback's leather purse—and Jonah himself laughed quietly as he lent his back to all these feverish transactions.

The trick was done. Oriol and Montaubert vanished. Soon people arriving breathless from all sides said, "Mr. Law is at his villa.—The young king is at the Tuileries.—The Regent is having lunch."

"Swindle! Swindle! Swindle!"

"Zvindle! Zvindle! Zvindle!" echoed the Baron of Batz, outraged. "Those vools said it was all a zvindle!"

There were people who hung themselves.

On the stroke of two o'clock, Albret showed up to deliver the shares he'd presold earlier at the rate of five thousand five hundred francs apiece. In spite of the people who'd hung themselves, in spite of the people who'd gone bankrupt while beating themselves up and tearing out their hair, Albret turned another fabulous profit. While he was signing a bank transfer on the hunchback's hump, Albret slipped a purse into his hands. Jonah cried out, "Come here, Whale!" The old veteran came, because he'd seen the purse. The hunchback threw it in his face.

Those of my readers who find the trick played by Oriol, Montaubert, and company too elementary should look at Berger's footnotes to Father Choisy's *Secret Memoirs*, where they'll see that even more primitive swindles met with great success. The retelling of those hoaxes entertained the man on the street. Pulling off a barefaced fraud was, besides a way to make a fortune, a way to make a name as a wit. Stock swindles were excellent jokes that made everybody laugh—except the ones who'd hung themselves.

While our tricksters had gone off somewhere to divide the loot, the Prince of Gonzague and his faithful Peyrolles came down the steps from the villa. The sovereign was paying a visit to his vassals. Frantic speculation had resumed, at new rates, based on new rumors, more or less fake. The House of Gold, rocked for a moment by a spasm, had pulled itself together and was doing fine.

Monsieur de Gonzague carried a large envelope, from which hung three seals on silk ribbons. When the hunchback spotted it, his eyes widened and the blood rose to his pale face. He didn't move, and went on working, but his eyes remained fixed on Peyrolles and Gonzague.

"What's the princess doing?" asked Gonzague.

"The princess didn't sleep last night," replied Peyrolles. "Her chambermaid heard her saying over and over, 'I'll search all of Paris! I'll find her!'"

"God!" murmured Gonzague. "If she ever found that girl from the Rue du Chantre, all would be lost."

"Is there a resemblance?"

"You'll see: like two peas in a pod. You remember Nevers?"

"Yes. A handsome young man."

"She's definitely his daughter, and as pretty as an angel. The same eyes, the same smile."

"She's already smiling?"

"She's with Doña Cruz; they know each other. Doña Cruz is comforting her. The sight of that child moved me. If I had a daughter like her, Peyrolles, I think maybe... But that's nonsense! What do I have to feel sorry for? Have I done wrong for its own sake? I have a goal and I'm moving toward it. If something gets in the way..."

"Too bad for it!" murmured Peyrolles with a smile.

Gonzague rubbed the back of his hand across his brow.

Peyrolles touched the sealed envelope. "Does your lordship think we found the right thing?"

"Without a doubt. The seal of Nevers, and the seal of the Caylus-Tarrides parish chapel!"

"You think these are the pages torn from that famous register?"

"I'm sure of it."

"Your lordship could settle the question by opening the envelope."

"Are you crazy? Break the seals? Beautiful intact seals? By God, each of these seals is worth a dozen witnesses. We'll break the seals when it's time, Peyrolles, when we present Nevers's real heiress to the family council."

"The real one?" blurted Peyrolles.

"The one we're going to make into the real one. And all the evidence that comes out of this envelope will be consistent."

Peyrolles bowed his head. The hunchback watched them.

"But what'll we do with the other girl, my lord?" continued Peyrolles. "By which I mean, the one with Nevers's eyes and smile?"

"Damned hunchback!" cried whatever speculator was currently signing papers on Aesop's hump. "Can't you hold still?" The hunchback had indeed shuffled to move closer to Gonzague.

The prince was considering. "I've given it some thought," he said as if to himself. "In my place, Peyrolles, what would you do with that girl?"

Peyrolles smiled his shifty, equivocal smile. Gonzague must have understood, because he said, "No, no, not that! I have another idea. Who would you say is the furthest gone, the most debased of all our entourage?"

Peyrolles didn't hesitate. "Chaverny."

"Hold still, hunchback!" said another speculator.

"Chaverny!" Gonzague's face lit up. "I like the boy, but he bothers me. That would rid me of him."

III. The Hunchback's Whim

Our lucky speculators, Taranne, Albret, and company, having finished dividing the spoils, began to reappear in the crowd. People's new respect seemed to make them a cubit or two taller.

"Where is that dear boy Chaverny?" asked Gonzague.

Just as Peyrolles was about to answer, a terrible uproar broke out in the crowd. Everyone ran toward the steps, where two Royal Guards were dragging a poor fellow by the hair.

"Counterfeiter!" people shouted. "It's forgery!"—"It's an outrage!"—"Falsifying the mark of credit!"—"Desecrating the symbol of public trust!"—"Perverting the exchange! Ruining business!"

"Drown the counterfeiter! Drown the scum!" Fat little Oriol, Montaubert, Taranne, and the rest screamed like eagles. To be without sin before casting the first stone may have been good enough for Our Lord's time! The poor man, terrified and half dead, was dragged before Gonzague. His crime: he'd passed off a white share as a blue share, to take advantage of the slight premium attached to the more fashionable new shares.

"Have mercy! Have mercy!" he cried. "I didn't realize the enormity of the crime."

"My lord," said Peyrolles, "the place is crawling with counterfeiters."

"My lord," added Montaubert, "you need to make an example of him."

And the mob shouted, "Outrage! Infamy! Counterfeiter! Villain! No mercy!"

"Throw him out," said Gonzague, turning away.

The mob immediately grabbed the poor wretch, crying, "To the river! To the river!"

It was five o'clock. The first bell marking closing time rang in the Rue Quincampoix. The daily occurrence of regrettable incidents had prompted the authorities to ban stock trading after dusk, and it was always at this last moment that the gambling fever reached its peak of delirium. It looked like a free-for-all. People grabbed each other by the collar. Voices rose and mingled until you could hear nothing but one great howl.

God knows, the hunchback had plenty to do, but his eyes never left Gonzague. He'd overheard Chaverny's name.

"They're going to close! They're closing!" cried the mob. "Hurry! Hurry!" If Aesop had had several dozen humps, what a fortune he could have made!

"What did you want to tell me about the Marquis of Chaverny, my lord?" asked Peyrolles.

In return for their bow, Gonzague gave his followers a haughty condescending nod. Since last night he'd grown and they'd shrunk. "Chaverny?" he said absently. "Ah, yes, Chaverny. Remind me later that I need to talk to that hunchback."

"And the girl? Isn't it risky to leave her at the little house?"

"Very risky. She won't stay there long. While I'm thinking of it, Peyrolles: we'll have supper with Doña Cruz—a gathering of old friends. Get everything ready." He whispered a few words into Peyrolles's ear.

The factotum bowed and said, "It'll suffice, my lord."

"Hunchback!" cried another unhappy signer. "You're hopping around like a little madman! You've forgotten how to do your job. Gentlemen, we'll have to hire the Whale again."

As Peyrolles was moving away Gonzague called him back. "And find me Chaverny. I need Chaverny, dead or alive!"

The hunchback shook his hump while someone was signing on it. "I'm tired," he said. "There's the bell. I need to rest."

The bell was indeed ringing, and the doorkeepers went by jangling their big keys. A few minutes later the only sound was that of locks turning. Every tenant had a lock, and all the goods that hadn't sold or been traded stayed inside the sheds. The guards urged on the stragglers. Our band of confederated speculators, Navailles, Taranne, Oriol, and company, had gathered around Gonzague with their hats off. The prince's eyes were on the hunchback, who sat on a curbstone outside his kennel, giving no sign that he planned to leave, and calmly counting the contents of his big leather sack with at least the appearance of great pleasure in the task.

"We came by this morning to find out how you were, cousin," said Navailles.

"And we were delighted to hear you weren't feeling too worn down after last night," added Nocé.

"There's one thing that wears you down faster than revelry, gentlemen, and that's worry."

"The fact is," said Oriol, who was determined to get a word in, "the fact is that worrying—that's how I am too—when you worry—" Usually Gonzague would be kind enough to come to the rescue of any of his courtiers who was floundering, but this time he let Oriol twist in the wind.

On his curbstone the hunchback laughed. When he'd finished counting his money he twisted the neck of his sack and tied it up carefully with string. Then he got ready to withdraw into his kennel.

"Come on, Jonah," said one of the watchmen. "Are you planning to sleep here?"

"Yes, I am, friend. I've brought everything I need."

The watchman laughed, and all the gentlemen joined him—except for Gonzague, who remained serious.

"Come on, come on!" said the watchman. "No jokes, little man. Scram, on the double!"

The hunchback closed the door in his face. The watchman began kicking the kennel. The hunchback's pale face appeared at the round window under the roof. "I claim justice, my lord!" he cried.

"Justice!" cried all the gentlemen cheerfully.

"Too bad Chaverny's not here," added Navailles. "We could've given him the solemn job of passing sentence."

Gonzague gestured for silence. "Everybody out at the sound of the bell. That's the rule."

"My lord," replied Aesop, known as Jonah, with the crisp, precise delivery of a lawyer summing up his case, "I beg you to consider that I'm not like everybody: not everybody has rented your dog kennel."

Some cried, "Well put!" Others said, "What does that prove?"

"Yes or no," went on the hunchback, "was Médor in the habit of sleeping in his kennel?"

"Well put! Well put!"

"If—as I can demonstrate—Médor was in the habit of sleeping in his kennel, and if I've paid thirty thousand livres to assume Médor's rights and privileges, then I claim the right to do as he did, and I won't leave here unless I'm carried out by force."

This time Gonzague smiled, and nodded his agreement. The watchman withdrew.

"Come here," said the prince.

The hunchback immediately came out of his kennel and approached, bowing like a sociable fellow.

"Why do you want to live in there?" asked Gonzague.

"Because it's safe, and I have money."

"You think you made a good bargain for that kennel?"

"A priceless bargain, my lord. I knew that in advance."

Gonzague put his hand on the hunchback's shoulder, and the hunchback cried out in pain. That had happened once the night before, in the vestibule of the Regent's rooms.

"What's wrong with you?" asked Gonzague in surprise.

"A souvenir of the ball, my lord. A strain."

"He danced too much," said the gentlemen.

Gonzague gave them all a scornful look. "You want to make fun of him, gentlemen, and maybe I do too. But what if we're wrong, and what if instead he's making fun of us?"

"Oh, my lord..." said the hunchback humbly.

"I call it as I see it, gentlemen," went on Gonzague. "Behold your master." They began to protest. "Behold your master!" he said again. "He was more useful to me all by himself than the rest of you put together. He promised us Monsieur de Lagardère at the Regent's ball, and we had Monsieur de Lagardère."

"If your lordship had given us the job..." began Oriol.

Gonzague ignored him. "Gentlemen, you can't make Monsieur de Lagardère come and go at your beck and call. I hope we won't have occasion soon to relearn that."

They all looked at each other, puzzled.

"Let's speak plainly," said Gonzague. "I plan to make this fellow here one of my people; I trust him." The hunchback swelled with pride. The prince went on, "I trust him, and I'll say it in front of him, as I'll say it in front of you, gentlemen. If Lagardère isn't dead, we're all in mortal danger."

There was a silence. The hunchback seemed more surprised than anyone. "Did you let him get away?" he murmured.

"I don't know. My men are late. I'm worried. I'd give a lot to know what I'm up against."

The followers around him tried to keep countenance. The braver ones managed it: Navailles, Choisy, Nocé, Gironne, and Montaubert had all shown their mettle. But the three financiers, especially Oriol, turned pale, and the Baron of Batz turned green.

"Thank God there are enough of us and we're strong enough..." began Navailles.

"You have no idea what you're talking about," interrupted Gonzague. "I hope none of you trembles more than I do if we finally have to strike hard."

"By God, your lordship!" they cried, "we're all with you!"

"I know that, gentlemen," he answered curtly. "I'm counting on it."

If any of them was reluctant, he didn't show it.

"Meanwhile," went on Gonzague, "let's settle old business. Friend, you did us a big favor."

"It was nothing, my lord!"

"Please don't be modest. You did good work. Claim your pay."

The hunchback was still holding his leather sack; he began twisting it. "Really," he stammered, "there's no need..."

"God's head!" cried Gonzague. "Are you about to ask for some enormous reward?"

The hunchback looked him in the eye and said nothing.

"I've already told you," said the prince with growing impatience, "I accept nothing for nothing. I think favors done for free turn out to be expensive, because they conceal betrayal. I want you to ask for payment."

"Come on, Jonah," cried the gang. "Make a wish! He's the king of genies!"

"Since your lordship insists..." said the hunchback with growing embarrassment. "But how can I dare ask your lordship for that?" He lowered his eyes, twisted his sack, and stammered, "Your lordship will make fun of me, I know he will!"

"A hundred louis says our friend Jonah's in love!" cried Navailles.

There was a long laugh. Only Gonzague and the hunchback took no part in the joke. The prince was sure he'd need the little man again. Gonzague was greedy, but no miser: money cost him nothing, and when he needed to he could spread it around with both hands. Right now he was maneuvering to reach two goals: to make this mysterious man his instrument, and to know him better. His followers, far from bothering him, were helping him to establish more clearly his benevolence toward the hunchback.

"Why shouldn't he be in love?" he said seriously. "If he's in love, and if it's in my power, I swear I'll make him happy. There are services that can be paid for with something besides money."

"My lord," said the hunchback with emotion, "I thank you. Love, ambition, curiosity—what can I call the passion that torments me? These men are right to laugh: I'm tormented!"

Gonzague held out his hand. The hunchback kissed it, but his lips trembled. He went on in a tone of voice so odd that the rakes' laughter faded away. "Curiosity, ambition, love—who cares what you call the illness? Death is death, whether by fever or poison or the sword."

Suddenly he shook his thick hair, and his eyes shone. "Man is small, but he moves the world! Have you ever seen the ocean, the great ocean in a fury? Have you seen tall waves wildly tossing their foam at the veiled face of the sky? Have you heard that deep hoarse voice, deeper and hoarser than thunder itself? It's enormous—enormous! Nothing can resist it, not even a granite shore, which wears away little by little, eroded by the tide. I'm telling you, and you know it: it's enormous! Well—there's a plank floating, suspended over the deep, a frail plank that shakes and creaks. And what's on that plank? An even frailer creature, that from a distance looks smaller than a dark bird off the coast, and at least a bird has wings. That being is Man. He doesn't tremble. Who knows what magic power underlies his weakness: it comes from heaven, or from hell. Man says—that naked midget, without claws, without fur, without wings—Man says, 'I command,' and the ocean is tamed!"

They all listened. Those around him thought the hunchback's face had changed. "Man is small," he went on, "so small! Have you ever seen a bonfire's blazing locks of hair? The copper sky over the thick, heavy dome of rising smoke? It's a dark night, but distant buildings stand out from the shadows in that other, awful dawn, and nearby walls turn pale as they look on. Have you seen the façade? It's monumental, and enough to make you shiver: the façade as see-through as a grille, its empty window frames and doorframes all gaping holes opening onto the inferno, like the double or triple rows of teeth of the monster called fire! It's grand, it's as angry as a storm, it's as menacing as the sea. There's no fighting it. It reduces marble to dust, it twists or melts iron, it makes cinders of the giant trunks of ancient oaks. Well! On that smoking, crackling, incandescent wall, amid the rippling flames whipped by the abetting wind, there stands a shadow, a dark object, an insect, an atom: Man. He's not afraid of fire, any more than of water. He's king, and he says, 'I command!' The impotent fire consumes itself and dies."

311

The hunchback mopped his brow. He glanced slyly around him, and suddenly gave his familiar little dry crackling laugh. "He, he, he!" he chuckled, as his listeners started. "He, he, he! I'm small, but I'm a man. Why shouldn't I be in love, gentlemen? Why shouldn't I be curious? Why not ambitious? I'm no longer young—I've never been young. You think I'm ugly, don't you? I used to be even uglier. That's the privilege of ugliness: it fades with age, just like beauty. Your loss is my gain, and in the grave we'll all be alike."

Looking around at Gonzague's followers, he cackled. "What's worse than ugliness? Poverty. I was poor, and an orphan—I suppose my father and mother were afraid of me the day I was born, and put my baby basket out on the street. I opened my eyes to see gray sky overhead, a sky that dropped cold rain on my poor shivering little body. What woman gave me her milk? I could've loved her. Stop laughing! If anyone in heaven is praying for me, it's her! My first memory is of pain after a beating; I knew I was alive because the whip tore my flesh. My bed was the sidewalk. My food was whatever the stray dogs left in the gutter. A good school, gentlemen, a good school! If you only knew how inured I am to evil! Goodness surprises me, and intoxicates me like the drop of wine that goes straight to the head of a man who's always drunk water."

"You must be full of hatred, friend," murmured Gonzague.

"He, he! Yes, my lord, full. I've met happy people who are nostalgic for their childhood. Even as a child my heart was filled with anger. You know what I envied? The happiness of others. Others were good-looking, others had parents. Did those others at least feel pity for one who was alone and broken? No. All the better! What shaped my character, what hardened it and tempered it, was mockery and scorn. Sometimes that kills; it didn't kill me. Abuse taught me my own strength. Once I was strong, was I bad? Gentlemen, those who were my enemies are no longer here to testify."

There was something so odd and unexpected in his words that everyone was silent. Our rakes, taken aback, had lost their mocking smiles. Gonzague, surprised, listened attentively. The effect was like the chill produced by the threat of an invisible enemy.

"As soon as I was strong," went on the hunchback, "I wanted to be rich. For ten years, maybe more, I worked amid laughter and jeering. The first shekel is hard to earn, the second less so, the third comes by itself; twelve shekels make a sou, twenty sous make a livres. I sweated blood to earn my first gold louis; I still have it. I look at it when I'm tired and discouraged. Seeing it reawakens my pride, and it's pride that motivates men. Sou by sou, livre by livre, I hoarded money. I didn't eat my fill; but I drank my fill, because water from the public fountain is free. I wore rags, I slept rough, my treasure grew—I hoarded and hoarded!"

"So you're a miser?" interjected Gonzague, as if it satisfied his curiosity or gave him pleasure to find a weakness in this odd creature.

The hunchback shrugged. "I wish, my lord! If only God had made me a miser! If only I could love those poor écus the way a lover loves his mistress! That's real passion! I could devote my life to satisfying it. What's happiness, if it's not having one goal in life, one reason for working and living? But you can't choose to be a miser. For a long time I hoped to become a miser, but I couldn't, and I'm not one."

He sighed, and folded his arms. "I had one day of joy—one single day. I'd just counted up my treasure, and I spent a whole day wondering what to do with it. I had twice, three times as much as I'd thought. I said giddily over and over, 'I'm rich! I'm rich! I can buy happiness!' I looked around—and saw no one. I looked in the mirror: wrinkles and white hair. Already! Already! Wasn't it just yesterday I was a child being beaten? 'The mirror's lying!' I said, and I broke the mirror. A voice called out, 'Well done! That's the way to treat anyone tactless enough to tell the truth!' And the same voice said, 'Gold is handsome! Gold is young! Sow gold, hunchback! Sow gold, old man! And you'll harvest youth and beauty!' Whose voice was that, my lord? I knew I'd gone crazy. I went out and wandered the streets in search of one benevolent look, one smiling face. 'Hunchback! Hunchback!' said the men to whom I held out my hand. 'Hunchback! Hunchback!' said the women to whom I held out my poor virgin heart. 'Hunchback! Hunchback! Hunchback!' And they laughed. People who say money rules the world are lying!"

"You should've shown off your money!" cried Navailles, while Gonzague listened pensively.

"I did show it off. Hands reached out, not to shake mine, but to go through my pockets. I wanted to invite home friends, a mistress; I drew no one but thieves. You're smiling again; but I wept—I wept blood. But I only wept for one night. Friendship, love—just luxuries! Let me have pleasure, let me at least have everything in this world that's for sale!"

"Friend," broke in Gonzague coldly and haughtily, "can I finally hear what it is you want from me?"

"I'm getting there, my lord." The hunchback's tone of voice changed again. "Once more I emerged from my sanctuary, still shy, but passionate. Now I wanted pleasure. I became philosophical. I wandered along, hunting for the trail, sniffing the air at street corners, trying to figure out where the mysterious voluptuous wind was coming from."

"And?" said Gonzague.

The hunchback bowed. "Prince, the wind was coming from your place."

313

IV. The Gascon and the Norman

It was said in a light and playful way. That rascal of a hunchback seemed to have a gift for orchestrating the collective mood. The rakes around Gonzague, and even Gonzague himself—so serious just a moment ago—burst out laughing. "Ha, ha!" said the prince. "The wind was coming from here!"

"Yes, my lord. I came running. Even from the gates I knew I was at the right place. Who knows what scent had reached my brain—probably the scent of aristocratic, opulent pleasure. I stopped to savor it. It's like a drug, my lord; I like it."

"Lord Aesop isn't repelled!" cried Navailles.

"What a connoisseur!" said Oriol.

The hunchback looked him in the eye. "You who carry loads around in the night," he said quietly, "you understand that to satisfy his desires a man is capable of anything."

Oriol grew pale.

"What's he mean by that?" cried Montaubert.

"Explain yourself, friend," ordered Gonzague.

"That won't take long, my lord," replied the hunchback pleasantly. "You know I had the honor of leaving the Palais-Royal last night at the same time as you. I saw two gentlemen harnessed to a stretcher. That's not normal, so I figured they must be getting well paid to do it."

"Does he know...?" began Oriol without thinking.

"What was on the stretcher?" broke in the hunchback. "Of course. An elderly drunken baron, to whom I later lent my arm to help him back to his house."

A look of total astonishment spread across the faces of all the rakes. Gonzague himself lowered his eyes and reddened. "And do you also know what became of Monsieur de Lagardère?" he asked quietly.

"He, he! Gauthier Gendry has a sound blade and a sound hand," replied the hunchback. "I was nearby when he made his attack. The blow struck home, I give you my word. The men you've sent out for information can tell you the rest."

"They're awfully late getting back!"

"It takes time. Master Cocardasse and Brother Passepoil..."

"You know them?" Gonzague was taken aback.

"My lord, I know everybody slightly."

"God's blood! Friend, are you aware I don't like men who know so many and so much?"

"It can be dangerous, I admit," said the hunchback calmly. "But it can also be useful. Let's be fair. If I hadn't known Monsieur de Lagardère..."

"Hell if I'd make use of that man," murmured Navailles behind Gonzague.

He thought he hadn't been overheard, but the hunchback replied, "You'd be wrong." But all of them silently agreed with Navailles.

Gonzague hesitated. As if he meant to toy with the prince's ambivalence, the hunchback went on, "Before I was interrupted, I was about to forestall your suspicions. When I stopped at the entrance to your villa, my lord, I too hesitated, I had second thoughts, I was uncertain. Here was heaven, the heaven I wanted, not the Church's heaven but Mohammed's. Every delight at once: beautiful women, good wine, nymphs crowned in flowers, ambrosia with a head of foam. Was I ready to do anything—anything—to gain admission to this voluptuous Eden, to shelter my insignificance under the skirts of your princely cloak? That's what I asked myself before I came in; and then I came in."

"Because you felt ready to do anything?" asked Gonzague.

"Anything!" said the hunchback firmly.

"Good God! What a raging appetite for rank and pleasure!"

"I've been dreaming of it for forty years. My desires have been incubating under gray hair."

"Listen," said Gonzague, "nobility can be bought—just ask Oriol!"

"I don't want the kind of nobility that's for sale."

"Ask Oriol how much a title weighs."

The hunchback showed off his hump with a comical gesture. "Does a title weigh as much as this?" Then he went on more seriously, "A title, a hump—two burdens that crush only the weak-minded! I'm too insignificant a person to be compared to an important financier like Monsieur Oriol. If his title crushes him, too bad for him: my hump doesn't bother me. General de Luxembourg is a hunchback! Did the enemy see his back at the Battle of Neerwinden? Pulcinella, the hero of Neapolitan comedy, the invincible man no one can stop, has a hump on his stomach as well as one on his back. The Spartan poet Tyrtaeus was lame and hunchbacked; Vulcan, forger of lightning, was hunchbacked and lame. Aesop—whose glorious name you've given me—had a hump, the hump of wisdom. The Titan Atlas had a hump that was the globe itself. Without calling mine the equal of any those illustrious humps, I'd say it's worth, at the going rate, an income of fifty thousand écus. Where would I be without it? It's precious to me: it's made of gold!"

"It's made of wit, at least, friend," said Gonzague. "I promise you'll be a gentleman."

"Many thanks, my lord. When?"

"Damn! He's in a hurry!" they all said.

"It takes time," said Gonzague.

"They're right," replied the hunchback. "I'm in a hurry. I beg your pardon, my lord—you just told me you don't like favors done for free, and that gives me license to demand my payment right away."

"Right away! But that's impossible."

"Allow me—this isn't about a title of nobility." Drawing closer, the hunchback said slyly, "I don't need to be a gentleman to sit next to Monsieur Oriol, say, at your little supper tonight."

They all laughed, except Oriol and Gonzague. The prince frowned. "You know about that too!"

"Just a word or two overheard by chance," murmured the hunchback modestly.

The others were already crying out, "We're having supper? We're having supper?"

"Oh, prince," went on the hunchback earnestly, "I'm suffering the curse of Tantalus! I can see a small house: its hidden entrances, its shaded garden, its boudoirs with soft light coming in through discreet curtains. There are paintings on the ceilings, nymphs and cupids, butterflies and roses. I can see the gilded parlor! I can see it! A parlor for Epicurean parties full of laughter. I can see the chandeliers—they're dazzling." He shielded his eyes with one hand. "I can see the flowers, I can breathe in their scent—and what's that, next to the excellent wine overflowing the cups while a bevy of beautiful women..."

"He's already drunk," said Navailles, "and he hasn't even been invited yet."

"It's true." The hunchback's eyes shone. "I'm drunk."

"If your lordship wishes," whispered Oriol in Gonzague's ear, "I can let Mademoiselle Nivelle know."

"She already knows." Then, as if to inflate even further the hunchback's grandiose whim, Gonzague said, "Gentlemen, this will be no ordinary supper."

"What'll there be?"

"Guess."

"Actors in a play?"—"The tsar?"—"Mr. Law?"—"The monkeys from the Saint Germain fair?"

"Better than that, gentlemen! Give up?"

"We give up."

"There'll be a wedding."

The hunchback started, but they attributed that to his great envy. "A wedding?" he echoed, clasping his hands and looking away. "A wedding following a little supper?"

"A real wedding," said Gonzague, "a real wedding with solemn ceremony."

"And who's getting married?" they all asked.

The hunchback held his breath. Just as Gonzague was about to answer, Peyrolles appeared on the steps, crying, "Hurrah! The men are finally back!" Behind him came Cocardasse and Passepoil, wearing the calm proud expression so well suited to useful men.

"Friend," said Gonzague to the hunchback, "we're not done, you and I. Stick around."

316

"I await your lordship's orders." The hunchback headed back to his kennel. He was thinking, wracking his brains. When he'd entered his kennel and shut the door, he dropped onto his mattress. "A wedding," he murmured, "a scandal! But it can't be a pointless parody—this man does nothing without a reason. What's behind this sacrilege? His plan eludes me, and time's running out!" He buried his head in his clenched hands. Then he went on with strange intensity, "Ah, whether he says yes or no, I swear to God I'll be at that supper!"

"Well, well, what's the news?" cried Gonzague's followers, full of curiosity. This Lagardère business was starting to interest them personally.

"These two bravos will speak only to his lordship," said Peyrolles.

Cocardasse and Passepoil, well rested after a long day asleep at a tavern table, were as fresh as roses. They advanced proudly through the ranks of the lesser rakes and, coming right up to Gonzague, bowed to him with the extravagant dignity of genuine masters of arms.

"Come on, now," said Gonzague, "spit it out."

Cocardasse and Passepoil looked at each other.

"After you, my distinguished friend," said Passepoil.

"Not at all, sweetheart," answered Cocardasse. "After you."

"God's blood!" cried Gonzague. "Are you going to keep us hanging?"

They began to talk at the same time, loud and clear. "My lord, to show ourselves worthy of the honor and trust..."

"Stop!" cried Gonzague, stunned. "One at a time."

There followed another polite round of "after you" before Passepoil finally said, "Being younger and of lesser rank, I'll obey my distinguished friend and speak. I'll start by stating that I carried out my mission successfully. If I've been more successful than my distinguished friend, it's not on account of greater merit on my part."

Cocardasse smiled proudly and stroked his enormous mustache. We haven't forgotten that these two rascals were competing to tell the better lie. Before we watch them spar with eloquence like Virgil's Arcadians, we should say that they weren't completely at ease. When they'd left the tavern they'd gone back a second time to the house on the Rue du Chantre. No news of Lagardère. What had become of him? Cocardasse and Passepoil had not the slightest idea.

"Be brief," ordered Gonzague.

"Concise and precise," added Navailles.

"Here it is in a nutshell," said Passepoil. "The truth never takes long to tell, and in my opinion people who overcomplicate things are just doing it to mystify their listeners. And if that's what I think, it's because I have my reasons. Life experience—but let's not get distracted. So, I went out this morning on your lordship's orders. I and my distinguished friend here said to each other, 'Let's double our chances and each go his own way.' We therefore split up at the Holy Innocents' market. What my distinguished friend did, I don't know. I went to the Palais-Royal, where the workers were already taking down the decorations. Everybody was talking about a pool of blood they'd found between the Indian tent and Le Bréant the gardener and doorkeeper's little lodge. So that was good news: certainly a sword thrust had been delivered. I inspected the pool of blood myself. It looked reasonable. Then I followed a trail of footsteps—ah, you've got to have eyes for that kind of thing!—from the Indian tent to the Rue Saint Honoré, going through the vestibule of the Regent's rooms. The servants said, 'Hey, did you lose something?' and I said, 'Yes, my mistress's portrait,' and they laughed like the idiots they are. If I'd had a portrait made of each of my mistresses, I swear to God I'd have to pay a mint in rent for a big enough storeroom!"

"Cut to the chase," said Gonzague.

"I'm doing my best, my lord. Here's a good thing: so many horses and carriages go by on the Rue Saint Honoré that the trail had been erased. So I went straight to the river..."

"Which way?"

"By way of the Rue de l'Oratoire."

Gonzague and his followers exchanged a glance. If Passepoil had named the Rue Pierre Lescot, the scene of Oriol and Montaubert's stupid escapade, he would immediately have lost all credibility. But Lagardère might well have gone by way of the Rue de l'Oratoire.

Passepoil went on ingenuously, "Noble prince, I'm telling you just the way I would tell my confessor. The trail picked up again on the Rue de l'Oratoire, and I followed it to the riverbank. There, nothing more. But I saw some sailors talking, and I approached them. One of them, with a Picardy accent, said, 'There were three of them. The gentleman was wounded, and after they took his purse they threw him off the top of the Louvre embankment.' I said, 'Friends, did you get a good look at the gentleman?' They didn't want to answer, because they thought I might be a police informer. But I said, 'I'm part of the household of that gentleman, Monsieur de Saint Saurin, a native of Brie and a good Christian.' Then they said, 'God have mercy on his soul! We saw it all.'—'How was he dressed, friends?'—'He was wearing a black mask, and a white satin doublet.'"

The listeners murmured and nodded. Gonzague seemed to approve. Only Cocardasse kept his skeptical smile. He thought to himself, "My little baldy's an excellent son of Normandy, God's blood. But crooked ace, crooked ace, our turn will come!"

"Here's a good thing!" continued Passepoil, encouraged by the success of his story so far. "If I don't express myself like a literary man, it's because my job is to hold a sword, not a pen, and also because I'm a little intimidated by your lordship's presence—I'm just being honest. But in the end the truth is the truth: do your duty and never mind what people say! So I go down alongside the Louvre, passing between the river and the Tuileries, all the way to the gate at La Conférence. I follow the Cours la Reine, the Debilly footbridge, the Passy tow-

318

path; I pass the Point du Jour market and the Sèvres bridge. I had a theory, as you'll see. I reach the Saint Cloud bridge."

"The nets!" murmured Oriol.

"The nets," echoed Passepoil with a wink. "The gentleman has put his finger on it."

"Not bad, not bad," said Cocardasse to himself. "We might end up being able to make something of that rascal Passepoil!"

"And what did you find in the nets?" asked Gonzague, frowning doubtfully.

Passepoil unbuttoned his doublet. Cocardasse's eyes widened: he hadn't expected this. What Passepoil pulled out from under his doublet he hadn't found in the nets at Saint Cloud. He'd never in his life seen the nets at Saint Cloud. It's even possible that, like today, the nets at Saint Cloud were just an urban legend. What Passepoil pulled out from under his vest he'd found in Lagardère's own room in his house, on their first visit there that morning. He'd picked it up without any definite purpose, just out of his habit of leaving nothing lying around. Cocardasse hadn't even noticed. It was nothing less than the white satin doublet Lagardère had worn to the Regent's ball. Passepoil had dunked it in a bucket of water at the tavern. He held it out to Gonzague, who recoiled in horror. All of them felt the same, because Lagardère's spoils were perfectly recognizable.

"My lord," said Passepoil modestly, "the body was too heavy, so this is all I could bring."

"God's hat!" thought Cocardasse. "I'd better pull myself together! The little rascal has a touch of genius!"

"So you saw the body, Passepoil?" asked Peyrolles.

"I beg your pardon," said Passepoil, drawing himself up. "Have you and I been shepherds together? I don't 'Peyrolles' you. Don't 'Passepoil' me—except if his lordship pleases."

"Answer the question," said Gonzague.

"The river at that spot is deep and turbulent. God knows I'd never affirm as a fact something I hadn't seen with my own eyes!"

"Well, I was waiting for that!" cried Cocardasse. "If my cousin had lied, God's blood, I'd never have talked to him again!" He turned to Passepoil and gave him a courtly bow. "But you didn't lie, little baldy! For God's sake, how could the body be in the nets at Saint Cloud, since I just saw it at least two leagues away from there, on dry land!"

Passepoil lowered his head. All eyes turned to Cocardasse. "Friend," he said, still addressing his companion, "with his lordship's permission I'd like to salute your honesty. Men like you are rare, and I'm proud to call you my brother in arms."

"Drop it," said Gonzague. "I want to ask this man a question." He pointed to Passepoil, standing in front of him with an expression of innocence and candor. "What about those two bravos? The ones guarding the young woman in the pink domino. You have no news of them?"

"I confess, my lord, I devoted all my time to the other business."

"Crooked ace!" shrugged Cocardasse. "Don't ask the poor boy for more than he can deliver. My friend Passepoil did all he could. And listen, Passepoil, I heartily approve. I'm happy with you, little baldy—but let's not claim you're on my level. Ha! That'd be an exaggeration!"

"You had more luck?" asked Gonzague skeptically.

"*Un per poco*, my lord, as they say in Florence. When Cocardasse is on the trail—God's blood!—he comes up with more than just some rags fished up from the bottom of the river!"

"Let's hear what you did."

"First, prince, I talked to those two rascals, just like I have the honor to be talking to you right now. *Secondo*, secondly, I saw the body..."

"You're sure?" Gonzague couldn't help interjecting.

"Really? Speak! Speak!" added the others.

Cocardasse put his fist on his hip. "All right. Let's proceed in an orderly fashion. I take pride in my work, and people who think just anybody could do what I did are nuts. You can be pretty good, like cousin Passepoil here, and still not reach my level. You need innate talent, plus acquired skill, plus specialized knowledge. Instincts, God's death! A good eye, nose, ear, foot, arm, heart. Crooked ace—I've got all that! When I left my dear friend at the Holy Innocents' market, I said to myself, 'Well, Cocardasse, sweetheart, let's think a bit. Where do you find swordsmen?' So I went from door to door and poked my nose in everywhere. You know the Moor's Head tavern, over on the Rue Saint Thomas? It's always full of hardware! Around two o'clock, two rascals came out of the Moor's Head. 'Greetings, neighbors!' says I. 'Greetings, Cocardasse!' (I know all those fellows like family.) 'Follow me, boys!' I led them onto the embankment on the other side of Saint Germain l'Auxerrois, in the old abbey moat. We had a little chat, *un per poco*, about tierce and quarte. Good God! They won't be guarding anybody else, by day or by night!"

"You killed them?" Gonzague was struggling to make sense of the story.

Cocardasse stretched out twice, miming two deep lunges. Then he resumed his proud stately posture. "Ha!" he said boldly. "There were only two of those sweethearts! God's hat! I've gobbled up plenty more!"

V. The Invitation

Passepoil eyed his distinguished friend with a mixture of admiration and affection. Cocardasse had barely begun his lying, but already Passepoil was honest enough with himself to admit defeat: this gentle, good-natured, modest soul, free from bitterness, was almost as commendable for his humble virtues as Cocardasse was for his showier qualities.

Gonzague's followers exchanged astonished looks. There was a silence, undercut by long whispers.

Cocardasse gave the points of his enormous mustache an impressive curl. "Your lordship gave me two tasks. And from one I proceed to the other. When I split up with Passepoil I said to myself, 'Cocardasse, sweetheart, tell the truth: where do you find bodies? By water!' Well then! Before hunting down my two rascals, I took a little stroll along the Seine. But you've got to be an early riser, and the sun was already hitting the Châtelet Fortress. Nothing on the banks of the Seine, and nothing floating in the river besides corks! *Caramba*—we'd missed the boat. It wasn't altogether my fault, but who cares, God's hat! I said to myself, 'Cocardasse, my boy, you'll die of shame if you go back to your honorable master like a dunce, without having carried out his little errands. *Va bene!* Keep looking and something'll turn up!' I'd passed the Pont Neuf, strolling along with my hands behind my back, and I said, 'Thunder and lightning—that statue of Henri IV is perfect right where it is!' I headed up into the neighborhood of Saint Jacques. Hey, Passepoil!"

"Cocardasse?"

"By the way, you remember that little carrot-topped Provençal rascal Massabiou, from La Canebière, who picked pockets outside Notre-Dame?"

"Sure—the one who got hanged?"

"No, God's life! A sweet good-hearted boy! Anyway, Massabiou makes a living selling fresh meat to surgeons."

"Get on with it," said Gonzague.

"Well, my lord, all trades are honorable—but if I'm wasting his lordship's time, God's blood, I can be as silent as a fish!"

"Get to the point," ordered Gonzague.

"The point is, I ran into little Massabiou coming down through the neighborhood on his way to the Rue des Mathurins. 'Greetings, little Massabiou,' says I.—'Greetings, Cocardasse,' says he.—'How's things, lazybones?'—'All's well, rascal, and you?'—'All's well. And where might you be coming from, sweetheart?'—'From the hospital over there, delivering merchandise.'"

Cocardasse paused. Gonzague had turned to face him. Everyone listened eagerly. Passepoil felt a little like falling to his knees to worship his distinguished friend.

"You notice," went on Cocardasse, knowing he had them now, "the rascal was coming from the hospital, and he still had his big sack over his shoulder. 'See you around, friend!' says I. And while Massabiou headed downhill I continued uphill to the Val de Grâce hospital."

"And?" broke in Gonzague. "What did you find?"

"I found Professor Jean Petit, surgeon to the king, dissecting, for the instruction of his students, the cadaver sold to him by that little scoundrel Massabiou."

"And you saw it?"

"With my own eyes, God's blood!"

"Lagardère?"

"No doubt about it. Crooked ace! The spitting image of his blond hair and his figure and his face. The scalpel was in him." Then he added gruesomely, "Even the sword wound!" and pointed cynically to his own shoulder, because he could see doubt clouding their faces. "The wound! For masters of arms like us, wounds are as recognizable as faces!"

"It's true," said Gonzague.

It was what they'd been waiting to hear. A long joyful murmur ran through the group, "He's really dead! Really dead!"

Gonzague himself gave a deep sigh of relief and echoed, "Really dead!" He tossed his purse to Cocardasse, who was surrounded, questioned, congratulated.

"That'll put some sparkle in the champagne!" cried Oriol. "Here, good man, take this." All of them wanted to give something to Cocardasse, the hero— who, in spite of his pride, accepted with open hands.

A servant came down the steps. Daylight was already fading, and the servant held a torch in one hand, while in the other he carried a silver tray on which lay a letter. "For your lordship," he said. The followers made way for him. Gonzague took the letter and opened it. They could see his face change, then immediately recover. He looked sharply at Cocardasse. Passepoil got goose bumps.

"Come here!" said Gonzague to Cocardasse, who promptly stepped forward. "Do you know how to read?" asked the prince with a bitter smile. And while Cocardasse was spelling out the words Gonzague went on, "Gentlemen, here's late-breaking news."

"News of the dead man?" cried Navailles. "Too much of a good thing can't hurt."

"What does the deceased say?" asked Oriol, who was turning into a wit.

"Listen, and you'll find out. Read it out loud, master of arms!"

They all gathered around. Cocardasse didn't have much education, but he knew how to read, if he took his time. Still, in these circumstances he needed help from Passepoil, who wasn't much more of a scholar himself. "Draw alongside, brother," said Cocardasse. "I'm seeing double."

Passepoil approached and cast his eyes over the letter. He reddened—but in truth it looked like he was blushing with pleasure, and likewise it looked like Cocardasse was struggling not to laugh. But that was just for a moment. They bumped elbows. They understood each other.

"Well, isn't this just something!" cried honest Passepoil.

"Crooked ace! You have to see it to believe it!" said Cocardasse, looking concerned.

"What is it? What is it?" came the cry on all sides.

"You read it, Passepoil. I've lost my voice. Well! I call that a miracle!"

"You read it, Cocardasse. It's given me goose bumps!"

Gonzague tapped his foot.

Cocardasse drew himself up and said to the servant, "Give me some light, rogue!" When the torch had been brought close enough, he read in a loud, clear voice, *"Prince, to settle at one time all of our various accounts, I'm inviting myself to your supper tonight. I'll be there at nine o'clock."*

"Signed?" cried a dozen voices together.

Cocardasse finished with, *"Chevalier Henri de Lagardère!"*

They all repeated the name, which from now on was like that of a boogeyman. A great silence fell. The envelope that had held the letter also contained an object, which Gonzague took before anyone could identify it. It was the glove that Lagardère had pulled off his hand at the Regent's. He clutched it. He took the letter back from Cocardasse. Peyrolles wanted to speak, but Gonzague pushed him away. "Well," he asked the two bravos, "what do you say to that?"

"I say," replied Passepoil gently, "that Man is frail and subject to error. I told the strict truth. And anyway, this doublet is irrefutable evidence."

"But this letter is refutable?"

"Crooked ace!" cried Cocardasse. "I'm telling you, that rascal Massabiou can confirm that I met him on the Rue Saint Jacques. Send for him! And is Professor Jean Petit surgeon to the king, or is he not? I saw the body, I recognized the wound..."

"But this letter?" Gonzague frowned.

"These jokers have been deceiving you for quite a while now," murmured Peyrolles in his ear.

Gonzague's followers stirred and whispered.

"This is too much," said fat little Oriol. "The man's a magician."

"He's the devil!" cried Navailles.

Suppressing the fever that was making his heart pound, Cocardasse murmured, "God's hat! He is a man, isn't he?"

"He's Lagardère!" murmured Passepoil.

"Gentlemen," went on Gonzague in a different tone of voice, "there's something incomprehensible behind this. No doubt we've been deceived by these men..."

"Oh, my lord!" protested Cocardasse and Passepoil at the same time.

"Silence! I've been sent a challenge, and I accept it!"

"Bravo!" said Navailles weakly.

"Bravo, bravo!" the others repeated grudgingly.

"If his lordship will allow me to advise him," said Peyrolles, "instead of the supper you planned..."

"We'll have that supper, by God!" interrupted Gonzague, lifting his head.

"Then," insisted Peyrolles, "at least lock the doors."

"Doors open! Doors wide open!"

"That's the spirit!" said Navailles again.

There were some good blades among them: Navailles himself, Nocé, Choisy, Gironne, Montaubert, and a few others. The financiers were the exception.

"You all wear swords, gentlemen," went on Gonzague.

"So do we!" murmured Cocardasse to Passepoil with a wink.

"Would you know how to use them if you had to?" asked Gonzague.

"If he comes alone..." began Navailles without bothering to conceal his hesitation.

"My lord, my lord," said Peyrolles, "this is a job for Gauthier Gendry and his men!"

Frowning, his lips trembling, Gonzague surveyed his followers. "On my life," he said to himself, "they'll do it! I need them to be my slaves, or the whole powder keg will go up."

"Copy me," said Cocardasse quietly to Passepoil. "Now's the time."

They both advanced, solemnly draped in their swashbucklers' cloaks, and stopped in front of Gonzague. "My lord," said Cocardasse, "thirty years of honorable conduct—to call it no more than that—testify in favor of two good men whom appearances now seem to accuse. A single day cannot tarnish the luster of an entire life! Look at us! The Supreme Being has left on every face the mark of honesty or treachery. By Satan's body, look at us, and then look at our accuser, Monsieur de Peyrolles."

Cocardasse was superb, and his Provençal-Gascon accent lent a certain flavor to his well-chosen words. As for Passepoil, he shone with his usual modesty and candor. That wretch Peyrolles seemed to have been designed to serve as a contrast. In the last twenty-four hours his chronic pallor had shifted toward gray-green. He was like a textbook illustration of those bold cowards who tremble when they strike, and have loose bowels when they commit murder. Gonzague was pensive.

Cocardasse went on, "My lord, you who are great, you who are mighty, Your Excellency, you can judge from on high. You didn't just meet your humble servants today—remember the moat at Caylus, where we were together."

"Silence!" cried Peyrolles, terrified.

Gonzague looked calmly at his followers. "These gentlemen have already figured it out. Whatever they don't yet know, we'll tell them. These gentlemen count on us, as we count on them. We make mutual allowances. Each of us knows the others."

Gonzague emphasized those last words. Was there a single one of those rakes without some stain on his conscience? A few of them had already needed Gonzague's intercession in their tangles with the law—and besides, their actions the night before had made them all accomplices. Oriol felt faint; Navailles, Choisy, and the other aristocrats lowered their eyes. If even one of them had objected, that would have been enough, and the others would have followed him; but not one objected. Gonzague was privately grateful for the lucky absence of the little Marquis of Chaverny: for all his faults, Chaverny wasn't a man who could be silenced. Gonzague intended to be rid of him tonight—permanently.

"I just want to point out to your lordship," resumed Cocardasse, "that old servants like us shouldn't be condemned lightly. Passepoil and I have lots of enemies, as do all good men. Here's my opinion, which I'll submit to your lordship in my usual straightforward way: I say it can only be one thing or the other—either the Chevalier de Lagardère has been resurrected, which to me seems unlikely, or this letter is a forgery, a hoax by some scoundrel to make trouble for two good men. That's what I say, thunder and lightning!"

"My distinguished friend has so eloquently spoken my own thoughts," said Passepoil, "that I'm loath to add a single word."

"You won't be punished," said Gonzague, his mind elsewhere. "Get lost."

They didn't move.

"Your lordship has misunderstood us," said Cocardasse with dignity. "Alas! It's too bad!"

Hand on heart, Passepoil added, "We don't deserve to be treated this way."

"You'll be paid," said Gonzague impatiently. "What more do you want?"

"What we want, my lord?" Cocardasse spoke with that quaver in the voice that comes only from the heart. "What we want? Full and complete proof of our innocence, crooked ace! I can see you don't know who you're dealing with!"

"No—oh no," said Passepoil, with entirely genuine tears in his eyes, "you just don't know!"

"What we want is to be cleared resoundingly. To achieve that, here's what I propose: the letter says Monsieur de Lagardère will come confront you tonight at your supper. We claim Monsieur de Lagardère is dead. Let events decide! We give ourselves up as your prisoners. If we've lied and Monsieur de Lagardère shows up, we consent to die—isn't that right, Passepoil, sweetheart?"

"With pleasure!" replied Passepoil, bursting into tears.

"If, on the contrary, Monsieur de Lagardère doesn't show up, then our honor is restored! Your lordship wouldn't refuse to let two good men continue to devote their existence to him!"

"Agreed!" said Gonzague. "You can accompany us to the pleasure house. Events will decide."

The two bravos seized his hands and kissed them effusively. "It's in God's hands!" they said together as they straightened up like a pair of righteous men.

But at that moment Gonzague's attention was elsewhere, scornfully taking in the pitiful faces of his followers. He turned to Peyrolles. "I ordered that Chaverny be sent for!"

Peyrolles left immediately.

"Well, gentlemen," continued Gonzague, "what's wrong with you? God forgive me, you've gone as white and tongued-tied as ghosts!"

"It's a fact," murmured Cocardasse. "They're not dancing for joy!"

"Are you scared?" went on Gonzague.

The gentlemen bridled, and Navailles said, "Careful there, my lord!"

"If you're not scared, then do you just not feel like following me?" No one answered, and Gonzague cried, "Be careful there yourselves, my gentleman friends! Remember what I told you yesterday: passive obedience! I'm the head, you're the arms. We have a pact."

"No one's planning to break the pact," said Taranne, "but..."

"But nothing! I don't want to hear it. Think carefully about what I've told you, and what I'm about to tell you. Yesterday you could've walked away from me; today you can't—you know my secret. Today, whoever isn't with me is against me. If someone fails to answer the summons tonight..."

"Nobody will fail," said Navailles.

"Good thing! We're very close to the goal. You think I've been rattled; you're wrong—I'm half again as strong as I was yesterday. Your share has doubled: without your knowing it, you're already richer than dukes and peers. I want my supper to be a success; it has to be."

"It will be, my lord," said Montaubert, who was among the souls already damned. The promise contained in Gonzague's last words rallied the waverers.

"I want it to be fun!" added the prince.

"It will be, by God, it will be!"

"Speaking for myself," said Oriol, who was chilled to the marrow of his bones, "I'm already feeling jolly. We'll have some laughs."

"We'll have some laughs! We'll have some laughs!" echoed the others, putting on a brave face. Just then they saw Peyrolles returning with Chaverny.

"Not a word about what's happened, gentlemen," said Gonzague.

"Chaverny! Chaverny!" they all shouted, affecting the warmest good cheer. "Hurry up, we're waiting for you!"

Hearing Chaverny's name, the hunchback—who'd been still for so long in his kennel—seemed to awaken. His face appeared in the round window over his door. Cocardasse and Passepoil noticed him at the same time.

"Look out!" said Cocardasse.

"On our toes," said Passepoil.

"Here I am," said Chaverny.

"Where've you been?" asked Navailles.

"Not far, just beyond the church. So you need two concubines at a time, cousin?"

Gonzague grew pale.

The face at the little kennel window brightened, then vanished. The hunchback crouched behind his door, both hands on his heart to calm its beating. Those last words had struck him like a beam of light.

"You fool! Incorrigible fool!" cried Gonzague almost gaily. His pallor had given way to a smile.

"I didn't pry much," said Chaverny. "I just climbed the wall to take a stroll around Armida's enchanted garden. But it turns out there are two Armidas, and neither one of them has a Rinaldo."

Gonzague's continued calm in the face of Chaverny's insolent flight of wit surprised them all. "Did you like them?" they asked, laughing.

"I adore them both. But what's up, cousin? Why did you send for me?"

"Because you're needed tonight, to be in a wedding party."

"Bah! Really? Somebody's getting married? Who?"

"A girl with a dowry of fifty thousand écus."

"Cash?"

"Cash."

"Wow, what a pile! Who with?" Chaverny looked around the circle.

"Guess." Gonzague was still laughing.

"I see a lot of necks ready for the yoke. Too many. I can't guess.—Oh! Yes, I can! Is it me?"

"Bingo!" said Gonzague. They all burst out laughing.

The hunchback quietly opened his door and stood on the threshold. He no longer had the thoughtful, eager, intent expression he wore earlier—now his face was that of Aesop, known as Jonah, and he cackled.

"And that dowry?" asked Chaverny.

"Here it is." From inside his doublet Gonzague pulled a bundle of stock shares. "All ready."

Chaverny hesitated for a moment. The others, laughing, congratulated him. The hunchback came forward slowly. He dipped his pen in ink, handed Gonzague the pen and the small board he used as a desk, and bent over to present his hump. Gonzague paused before endorsing the shares. "Do you accept?"

"Hell, yes!" replied Chaverny. "You've got to settle down sometime."

While Gonzague was signing he said to the hunchback, "Well, friend, are you still set on your little whim?"

"More than ever, my lord."

Cocardasse and Passepoil watched with mouths wide open.

"Why more than ever?" asked Gonzague.

"Because I know the groom's name, my lord."

"And why does his name matter?"

"Hard to say; some things you can't explain. For example, how can I explain to you why I'm convinced that, without me there, Monsieur de Lagardère won't carry out his boastful promise?"

"So you were listening."

"My kennel's right there. My lord, I served you once."

"Serve me twice, and you'll never want for anything."

"That's up to you, my lord."

"Here you go, Chaverny," said Gonzague, handing him the bundle of signed shares. Then he turned to the hunchback. "You'll be at the wedding; I'm inviting you."

They all clapped. Cocardasse exchanged a glance with Passepoil and murmured, "The fox in the henhouse! God's hat! They're right, we'll have some laughs!"

Gonzague's followers surrounded the hunchback and congratulated both him and the bridegroom. Aesop bowed in thanks to the prince. "My lord, I'll do my best to show myself worthy of this great favor. As for these gentlemen, we've already bandied words. They've got some wit, but not as much as I do. He, he! Without failing in the respect I owe your lordship, I'll provide some laughs. You'll see the hunchback at table—he's a regular life of the party! You'll see! You'll see!"

VI. The Parlor and the Boudoir

On the Rue Folie Méricourt in Paris, at the time of Louis Philippe, an example still survived of the precious, fussy architecture of the early years of the Regency. It contained a hint of fantasy, a hint of Greek, a hint of Chinese. Architects did their best to derive each design from one or another of the four Hellenic styles, but the results looked more like gazebos than like the Parthenon. They were bijou houses, candy boxes. At the Fidèle Berger candy factory they still make lots of those cardboard boxes, mostly hexagonal but with Turkish or Siamese bulges, whose pleasing shape brings joy to buyers with good taste.

The Prince of Gonzague's little pleasure house looked like a gazebo disguised as a temple. The face-powdered Venus of the eighteenth century would have set her altar there. It had a small white colonnade flanked by two small white wings, above whose Corinthian columns a second story hid behind a terrace. The third story rose directly over the square center of the building, in the form of a six-sided belvedere with a roof like a Chinese hat. Aficionados of the day considered it bold. Modern owners of a certain kind of cute villa in the Paris area think they invented that confectioner's style; they're mistaken—the Chinese hat and the belvedere have been around since Louis XV's childhood. But gold thrown at them in abundance gave the eccentricities of that time a look our more economical villas can't match, however cute they may be. Austere good taste might condemn the exteriors of those gorgeous birdcages; but they were adorable, elegant, and fashionable. As for the interiors, we all know the lavish sums great lords love to pour into their little houses.

Gonzague, richer by himself than half a dozen very great lords put together, couldn't have avoided falling victim to fashionable extravagance. His folly was considered a marvel. From a great hexagonal parlor, whose six sides formed the base of that belvedere, four doors opened onto four bedrooms or boudoirs, which would have given the house a trapezoidal shape without the built-in greenhouses. The last two sides held French doors leading to open terraces filled with flowers. The design was so exquisitely refined that only three or four places in Regency Paris could match it.

We're afraid we might be describing it badly. To put it more clearly: let the reader imagine a ground level that's a flowerbed, and then cut out of that flowerbed—without worrying about the odd angles—a central six-sided room flanked by four square boudoirs arranged kitty-corner like the blades of a windmill, with the two main sides opening onto the flowerbed. Leaving aside closets and so on, the odd angles themselves formed an interior flowerbed leading to the terraces and allowing fresh air, when desired, to enter with the daylight. The Duke of Antin himself had designed this precious little Saint Andrew's Cross, for his ancillary folly in the village of Miroménil.

The ceiling and the friezes in the parlor of Gonzague's folly were by Louis van Loo and his son Jean-Baptiste, then at the pinnacle of French painting. Two youngsters had painted the paneling, one of them only fifteen: Jean-Baptiste's younger brother Charles-André van Loo, and Jacques Boucher. The latter, a student of old Master Lemoine, was made famous by it, because he put so much charm and voluptuous abandon into his two pieces, Vulcan's Nets and The Birth of Venus. The four boudoirs were decorated with copies of works by Albani and Primaticcio, done by Louis van Loo, the father. The two terraces, in white marble, held antique statuary, no other kind being wanted; and the staircase, also marble, was considered Oppenordt's masterpiece. All of it was princely in the full sense of the word.

It was about eight in the evening. The promised supper was in progress, and the parlor was full of light and flowers. The table glowed beneath the chandelier, and the chaos of serving platters showed that the battle had long since begun. The company consisted of our band of rakes, among whom the little Marquis of Chaverny stood out for premature drunkenness: it was only the second course, and he'd already pretty much lost his mind. Choisy, Navailles, Montaubert, Taranne, and Albret held their wine better, sitting up straight and being careful not to say anything stupid. The Baron of Batz, silent and rigid, seemed to have drunk nothing but water.

Of course there were ladies present, and of course those ladies were mostly from the Opéra: first Mademoiselle Fleury, a favorite of Gonzague's; then Mademoiselle Nivelle, the Daughter of the Mississippi; then that round, plump Mademoiselle Cydalise, a sweet girl, with a mind like a sponge for soaking up ballads and jokes and turning them into nonsense on request; and Mesdemoiselles Desbois, Dorbigny, and half a dozen other young ladies who were strangers to inhibition and narrow-mindedness. They were all beautiful, young, sparkling, bold, silly, and ready for a laugh even when they'd rather cry. That's the nature of work: if you hire a lawyer you expect him to defend you. A glum dancing girl is a pernicious failure, to be shunned. Some say the hardest part of those saddening and sometimes sad lives spent wriggling in pink chiffon like fish in a pan is never having the right to cry.

Gonzague was absent: he'd just been summoned to the Palais-Royal. Apart from the seat that awaited his return, three other chairs were empty. One belonged to Doña Cruz; she'd fled as soon as Gonzague left, after bewitching everyone around the table—though she'd kept the party from reaching quite the shrill pitch that was supposedly normal by the first course at a Regency revel. No one knew whether Gonzague had forced her to come, or whether the giddy girl had forced him to make room for her. What was clear was that she'd been dazzling, and everyone adored her—except Oriol, who remained Nivelle's loyal slave.

The second empty chair had yet to be sat in. The third was that of the hunchback, Aesop, known as Jonah, whom Chaverny had just defeated at single combat, the weapons being glasses of champagne. At the moment of our arrival, Chaverny, taking advantage of his victory, was piling coats, cloaks, and ladies' shawls on top of the poor hunchback where he lay in a large wing chair. The hunchback, dead drunk, wasn't complaining: he was buried so deep in that pile of clothing that he ran the risk of smothering. In any case, it was just as well: the hunchback had failed to keep his promise—he'd been taciturn, moody, nervous, preoccupied. What good was a mere living desk? Down with the hunchback! See if he'd get invited to a supper like that again!

They'd all wondered repeatedly, before getting drunk, why Doña Cruz had come. Gonzague wasn't in the habit of leaving things to chance. Up to now he'd hidden away this Doña Cruz as carefully as if he were her Spanish guardian. That he now brought her to supper with a dozen good-for-nothings was, to say the least, odd. Chaverny had asked if she was his bride-to-be; Gonzague had shaken his head. Chaverny had asked where his fiancée was; Gonzague had answered, "Be patient!" What did Gonzague hope to gain by treating the girl this way—a girl he planned to present at court under the name of Mademoiselle de Nevers? That was his secret. Gonzague said what he felt like saying, nothing more.

They'd all drunk heavily. The ladies had grown very jolly, except for Nivelle, who was a melancholy drunk. Cydalise and Desbois were singing a dirty song; Fleury was going hoarse shouting for violins. Oriol, as round as a ball, was boasting about his amorous conquests, without anyone believing him. The rest drank, laughed, wept, sang: the wine was excellent, the food delicious, and none of them remembered the threats hanging over this Belshazzar's feast. Only Monsieur de Peyrolles retained his usual Lenten manner: a celebratory mood, whether respectable or not, had no effect on him.

"Will anyone be kind enough to shut up Monsieur Oriol?" asked Nivelle, sad and irritable. Among any ten ladies of pleasure, at least five pass the time this way.

"Shut up, Oriol!" they all cried.

"I'm not talking as loud as Chaverny," objected Oriol. "Nivelle's just jealous. I won't tell her any more of my indiscretions."

"Naive boob!" murmured Nivelle, gargling champagne.

"How many did he give you?" Cydalise asked Fleury.

"Three, darling."

"Blues?"

"Two blues and a white."

"Will you see him again?"

"Never! He doesn't have any more!"

"Ladies," said Desbois, "I've got to warn you about that little Mailly, who wants to be loved purely for himself!"

"Horrifying!" cried all the women present. The blasphemous pretension was enough to make them ask, like the Baron of Barbanchois, "Where are we all headed? Where are we all headed?"

Chaverny had returned to his seat. "If that rascal Aesop wakes up, I'll drown him." He looked heavily around the room. "I don't see the Zeus of our Olympus! I need him here so I can explain my situation to you."

"No explanations, for God's sake!" said Cydalise.

"I need to." Chaverny swayed in his seat. "It's a delicate business. Fifty thousand écus is not exactly the mines of Peru! If I wasn't in love..."

"In love with whom?" interrupted Navailles. "You haven't even met your fiancée."

"That's where you're wrong! Let me explain my situation..."

"No, no!"—"Yes, yes!" mumbled the company.

"A ravishing little blonde," Oriol was telling Choisy, who was asleep. "She was following me around like a poodle—impossible to ditch her! You can imagine, I was afraid Nivelle would see us together. Tigers ain't in it for jealousy like Nivelle's. Anyway..."

"Then if you won't let me explain," cried Chaverny, "just tell me where Doña Cruz went! I want Doña Cruz!"

"Doña Cruz! Doña Cruz!" they all called. "Chaverny's right, we demand Doña Cruz!"

"You could at least call her Mademoiselle de Nevers," said Peyrolles curtly.

Laughter drowned him out, and they all said, "Mademoiselle de Nevers, that's right! Mademoiselle de Nevers!" In an uproar, they rose.

"My situation..." began Chaverny.

They all fled from him and ran to the door by which Doña Cruz had left.

"Oriol!" said Nivelle. "Here, now." He didn't have to be told twice. He was only sorry none of the others had witnessed the liberties she took. "Sit here by me," she ordered, yawning wide enough to dislocate her jaw, "and tell me the story of Donkey Skin. I'm sleepy."

"Once upon a time..." began the obedient Oriol.

"Did you gamble today?" Cydalise asked Desbois.

"Did I ever! If it hadn't been for my footman Lafleur, I'd have had to sell my diamonds."

"Lafleur? How so?"

"As of yesterday Lafleur's a millionaire, and as of today I'm under his protection."

"I've seen him," cried Fleury. "A good-looking fellow!"

"He bought the Marquis of Bellegarde's horses and carriage, after the marquis fled the country."

"And he bought the Viscount of Villedieu's house, after the viscount hanged himself."

"Are people talking about him?"

"I'd say so! He did a cute thing—made a scene worthy of the Duke of Branca. Today as he was leaving the House of Gold, his carriage was waiting for him in the street. Out of habit, he got up behind!"

"Doña Cruz! Doña Cruz!" called the gentlemen.

Chaverny rapped on the door of the boudoir into which they thought the charming Spanish girl had withdrawn. "If you won't come out," he threatened, "we'll put you under siege!"

"Yes, yes! A siege!"

"Gentlemen, gentlemen!" remonstrated Peyrolles.

Chaverny grabbed him by the collar. "If you don't shut up, you old owl, we'll use you as a battering ram to force the door!"

Doña Cruz had locked the door of the boudoir when she withdrew, but she was no longer there. A hidden staircase led from that room down to the ground floor, and Doña Cruz had gone downstairs to her bedroom. There, on a sofa, trembling and with her eyes red from crying, lay poor Aurore. Aurore had now been in this house for fifteen hours; without Doña Cruz she would have been dead of misery and fear. Doña Cruz had come to see her twice already since the start of supper.

"Any news?" asked Aurore weakly.

"Monsieur de Gonzague's been summoned to the palace. There's nothing to be afraid of, poor dear sister. It's not so awful upstairs, and if I didn't know you were here—worried, sad, upset—I'd be having a great time."

"What are they doing up there? I can hear them all the way down here."

"Stupid stuff. They're laughing their heads off, the champagne is flowing. The gentlemen are jolly, witty, charming—one of them especially, the one they call Chaverny."

Aurore drew her hand across her brow, as if trying to recall a memory. "Chaverny!" she echoed.

"Young, splendid, afraid of neither God nor the devil. But I'm not allowed to spend too much time with him: he's engaged."

"Ah!" said Aurore absently.

"Guess with whom, dear sister!"

"I have no idea. What does it matter?"

"It certainly matters to you—you're the one that young Marquis of Chaverny is engaged to!"

Aurore slowly raised her pale face and smiled sadly.

"I'm not joking," insisted Doña Cruz.

"Any news of him?" murmured Aurore. "Sister, little Flor, you haven't brought me any news of him?"

"I known nothing, absolutely nothing."

Aurore's beautiful head dropped to her chest, and she wept. "Yesterday, when those men attacked us, they were saying, 'He's dead! Lagardère is dead!'"

"As far as that goes, I'm sure he's not dead."

"What makes you so sure?" asked Aurore eagerly.

"Two things. First, they're still afraid of him up there. Second, that woman—the one they wanted to give me as my mother..."

"His enemy? The one I saw last night at the Palais-Royal?"

"Yes, his enemy. I recognized her easily from your description. The second reason, as I was saying, is that she's still hunting for him just as relentlessly. Today when I went to complain to Monsieur de Gonzague about the outrageous way I was treated at your house on the Rue du Chantre, I saw that woman there, and I heard her. She was saying to some white-haired lord who was coming out of her apartment, 'It's my business and my duty and my right. I'm keeping my eyes open, and he won't get away from me. And when the twenty-four hours are up, he'll be arrested—if I have to do it myself!'"

"Oh, that's got to be the same woman! I recognize her by her hatred. A couple of times already I've had the idea..."

"What idea?"

"Nothing, I don't know, I'm crazy."

"I have one thing more to tell you," said Doña Cruz hesitantly. "It's almost a message I'm delivering to you. Monsieur de Gonzague's been good to me, but I no longer trust him. Whereas you I love more and more, my poor little Aurore." She sat next to her friend on the sofa. "Monsieur de Gonzague certainly told me this so I'd pass it on to you."

"What did he say?"

"A little while ago, when you cut me off to ask about your handsome Chevalier de Lagardère, I was in the middle of telling you they want to marry you off to the young Marquis of Chaverny."

"By what right can they marry me off?"

"I don't know, but they don't seem too worried about whether or not they have the right to. Gonzague drew me into conversation. In the middle, he dropped these exact words: 'If she cooperates, she'll save from mortal danger everything that's most precious to her in the world!'"

"Lagardère!"

"I do believe he was referring to Lagardère."

Aurore hid her face in her hands. "There's like a fog over my thoughts," she murmured. "Will God have no mercy on me?"

Doña Cruz pulled her close. "Didn't God put me here next to you?" she said gently. "I'm only a woman, but I'm strong and I'm not afraid of dying. If they attacked you, Aurore, you'd have someone to fight for you."

Aurore returned her embrace. Now they began to hear the tumult of voices calling for Doña Cruz. "I have to go!" said the gypsy girl. Then, feeling Aurore suddenly trembling in her arms, she added, "Poor dear child, gone so pale!"

"I'm afraid here when I'm alone," stammered Aurore. "The servants, the ladies' maids, all frighten me."

"There's nothing to be afraid of. The servants and the ladies' maids know I love you, and they think I have a powerful influence over Gonzague." She stopped and reflected. "At times I think so too. Sometimes I have the feeling Gonzague needs me."

Upstairs the noise redoubled. Doña Cruz rose and picked up the glass of champagne she'd set on the table.

"Advise me! Guide me!" said Aurore.

"There's still hope if he really needs me!" cried Doña Cruz. "We have to play for time."

"But what about this marriage? I'd rather die a thousand times!"

"There's always plenty of time for dying, dear sister."

She made a move to go, but Aurore held her back by her dress. "Are you abandoning me so soon?"

"Can't you hear them calling for me?" But then Doña Cruz stopped. "Did I tell you about the hunchback?"

"No. What hunchback?"

"The one who got me out of here yesterday by ways even I didn't know, the one who led me right to your door—he's here!"

"At the supper?"

"At the supper. I remembered what you told me about the strange creature who's the only person allowed into your handsome Lagardère's rooms."

"It must be the same man!"

"I'd swear to it! I went near him to tell him that in case of trouble he could count on me."

"And?"

"He's the oddest hunchback who ever took advantage of the right to do whatever he wants. He pretended not to recognize me. I couldn't get a word out of him. He was completely preoccupied with those ladies, who made fun of him and forced him to drink too much, till he slid under the table."

"So they have women up there?"

"Sure!"

"What kind of women?"

"Great ladies," replied the gypsy girl innocently, "the Parisian ladies I dreamt about in Madrid! Here the ladies of the court sing and laugh and drink and swear like musketeers. It's delightful!"

"Are you sure they're ladies of the court?"

Doña Cruz was almost offended.

"I'd like to have a look at them," said Aurore. "Without being seen," she added with a blush.

"And wouldn't you also like to have a look at that cute little Marquis of Chaverny?" asked Doña Cruz teasingly.

"Sure," said Aurore simply. "I'd be happy to see him."

Laughing, without giving her time to think it over, Doña Cruz grabbed her arm and pulled her toward the hidden staircase. Upstairs, only the thickness of a door separated the two girls from the party. Amid the clinking of glasses and the shouts of laughter they could hear twenty voices shouting, "Put the boudoir under siege! Attack! Attack!"

Monsieur de Peyrolles, unaccredited proxy for the master of the house, found his authority ignored. Chaverny and a few others had already dismissed him. He was now powerless to control the uproar. On the other side of the door Aurore, more dead than alive, bitterly repented having left her hiding place. But the bold and mischievous Doña Cruz laughed: it would take a lot more than that to scare her! She blew out the candles in the boudoir—not for her own sake but so no one looking in from the parlor could see Aurore. Doña Cruz pointed to the keyhole. "Have a look!" But Aurore's curiosity had long since faded.

"How long are you going to drop us all for that girl?" asked Cydalise.

"I hope she's worth it!" added Desbois.

"The marchionesses are jealous," said Doña Cruz.

Aurore had her eye to the keyhole. "Marchionesses, them?" she said skeptically.

Doña Cruz shrugged knowingly. "You don't know this court!"

"Doña Cruz! Doña Cruz! We want Doña Cruz!" came the shout from the parlor.

The gypsy girl smiled with naive pride. "They want me!"

The door shook. Aurore quickly drew back, and Doña Cruz now put her eye to the keyhole. "Ha, ha, ha! That poor Peyrolles is quite a sight!"

"The door's resisting," said Navailles.

"I heard voices," added Nocé.

"Get a crowbar! A wrench!"

"Why not cannons?" said Nivelle, waking partway. Oriol almost passed out laughing.

"I have a better idea!" cried Chaverny. "A serenade!"

"With glasses and cutlery and bottles and plates!" offered Oriol, gazing at his Nivelle. She'd fallen back asleep.

"Isn't that little marquis a charmer?" murmured Doña Cruz.

Aurore came to the door again. "Which one is he?"

Instead of answering, Doña Cruz said, "But I can't see the hunchback anymore."

"Are you in there?" shouted Chaverny.

With her eye now at the keyhole, Aurore tried to recognize her admirer from the Calle Real in Madrid, but so great was the chaos in the parlor that she couldn't do it. "Which one is he?"

"The drunkest one of all."

"Here we go! Here we go!" roared the crowd. Almost all had risen, even the ladies, and they all held their instruments of choice. Cydalise had a hotplate, on which Desbois was beating. Even before the singing began, the racket was almost unbearable. Peyrolles tried to object mildly, and Navailles and Gironne grabbed him and hung him from a coat hook for now.

"Who's going to sing?"

"Chaverny! Chaverny! Chaverny's going to sing!" And the little marquis, pushed along from one person to another, was thrown against the door.

At that moment Aurore recognized him, and recoiled.

"Bah!" said Doña Cruz. "Just because he's a little tipsy! That's fashionable at court. He's charming."

With a drunken gesture Chaverny called for silence, and they all obeyed. "Ladies and gentlemen, before we go on, I insist on explaining my situation."

There was a storm of boos. "No speeches! Sing or shut up!"

"My situation is simple, even if at first glance it seems..."

"Down with Chaverny! Penalty! Hang Chaverny next to Peyrolles!"

"And why do I want to explain my situation?" continued Chaverny with the unflappable persistence of a drunk. "Because morality..."

"Down with morality!"

"...Because circumstances..."

"Down with circumstances!" Cydalise, Desbois, and Fleury encircled him like three she-wolves. Nivelle was asleep.

"If you won't sing," cried Navailles, "recite some tragic verse."

There were loud protests.

"If you sing," said Nocé, "we'll let you explain your situation."

"You swear?" asked Chaverny solemnly.

They all struck a pose from the Oath of the Horatii. "We swear, we swear!"

"In that case," said Chaverny, "let me explain my situation first."

Doña Cruz was holding her sides, but in the parlor they were getting angry, and talking about hanging Chaverny out the window by his feet. People certainly had a good time in the eighteenth century.

"It won't take long," he went on. "Basically, my situation is clear. I haven't met my bride, so I can't hate her. I'm fond of women in general, so it's a love match."

Twenty voices burst over him like thunder. "Sing! Sing! Sing!"

He took a plate and a knife out of Taranne's hands. "Here's some light verse, composed by a young man."

"Sing! Sing! Sing!"

"Just a few simple couplets, but pay attention to the chorus!" And then, gravely beating time on his plate, Chaverny sang:

"If a woman has married two husbands,
You blame her—but I think it's funny.
Yet a man with two wives is an outrage to me,
Because women today cost real money!"

"Not too bad, not too bad!" said the critics.

"Ask Oriol what the going rate is!"

"Here comes the chorus!
Yet a man with two wives is an outrage to me,
Because women today cost real money!"
"Who's going to bring me a drink?" said Nivelle, waking with a start.
"Did you like the song?" Oriol asked her.
"It's stupid as all get out!"
"Bravo! Bravo!"
"Don't be afraid," said Doña Cruz to Aurore, who was hanging onto her.
"The second verse! Courage, Chaverny!"
He continued:
"*At the Bank that belongs to the Regent,*
You'll find everything—not counting gold!"
That irreverence gave Peyrolles such a desperate start that he unhooked himself and fell flat on his face. "Gentlemen, gentlemen!" he said as he rose, "in the name of the Prince of Gonzague..."
But no one was listening.
"It's a lie!" cried some.
"It's the truth!" said others.
"Mr. Law has all the riches of Peru in his vaults!"
"No talking politics!"
"Yes!"
"No!"
"Long live Chaverny!"
"Down with Chaverny!"
"Gag him!"
"Taxidermy him!" And the ladies began zealously breaking the plates and glasses.
"Chaverny, come give me a kiss!" cried Nivelle.
"Well, excuse me!" protested Oriol.
"He's raising our value," mumbled Nivelle, closing her eyes again. "He's a nice little marquis. He says in Paris women cost real money—but that's still underbidding. Men are like tenant farmers: if I see a man holding back a single pistole at the bottom of his sack, I'm furious!"
In the boudoir Aurore hid her face in her hands and said in a changed voice, "I'm cold, I'm cold to the bottom of my heart. To think they want to hand me over to a man like that!"
"Bah!" said Doña Cruz. "I'd know how to make him as gentle as a lamb. You don't think he's nice?"
"Take me away from here! I want to spend the rest of the night in prayer."
Aurore swayed, and Doña Cruz had to hold her up. The gypsy girl had the best heart in the world, but she just didn't share her friend's revulsion—this was the Paris she'd dreamt of. "Come on!"

Meanwhile Chaverny, taking advantage of a short silence, asked tearfully to be allowed to explain his situation.

As they went down the stairs Doña Cruz said, "Dear sister, let's play for time. Pretend to cooperate, and trust me. Rather than leave you in the lurch, I'll marry that Chaverny myself!"

"You'd do that for me?" cried Aurore with a naive burst of gratitude.

"God, yes! Now go ahead and pray, since that soothes you. As soon as I can get away I'll come find you."

With nimble feet and a light heart, Doña Cruz ran back up the stairs, her champagne glass at the ready. "Of course," she murmured, "it's just to help her—but life with that Chaverny would be full of laughs. What could be better?"

When she reached the closed door to the parlor she stopped to listen. Chaverny was saying in an aggrieved tone, "Did you or did you not promise I could explain my situation?"

"Never! Chaverny's gone too far! Throw him out!"

"Really, gentlemen," said Navailles, "we have to attack! That girl is insulting us!"

Doña Cruz seized the moment and opened the door. She stood on the threshold, cheerful and smiling, with her glass held high. She was greeted with long loud applause. "Come now, gentlemen," she said, holding out her empty glass, "a little more oomph! You call that making a racket?"

"We're trying," said Oriol.

"You're feeble noisemakers," she went on, draining her glass again. "I couldn't even hear you through this door!"

"Is that true?" cried several of the humiliated rakes. They thought they'd been keeping all of Paris awake.

Chaverny eyed Doña Cruz admiringly. "Charming!" he murmured. "Adorable!"

Oriol wanted to say the same thing, but Nivelle woke and pinched him hard enough to make a bruise. "Will you shut up!" He tried to get away, but the Daughter of the Mississippi held him by the sleeve. "Pay the penalty! A blue one!"

Oriol pulled out his wallet and handed her a brand-new blue share, while Nivelle sang, "*Because women today cost real money!*"

Meanwhile Doña Cruz was glancing around, looking for the hunchback. She felt instinctively that, in spite of his rebuffing her, he was secretly an ally. But she couldn't ask anyone here about him. Instead, to learn whether the hunchback had accompanied Gonzague, she asked, "Where's his lordship?"

"His carriage is back," said Peyrolles, returning. "He's just giving orders."

"For violins, I hope!" said Cydalise.

"Are we really going to dance?" cried Doña Cruz, already blushing with pleasure.

Desbois and Fleury threw her a scornful glance.

"I remember the days," said Nivelle pompously, "when we always found something under our plates when we came here." She lifted her plate. "Nothing! Not so much as a grain of millet! Ah, ladies, the Regency's in decline!"

"The Regency's over the hill!" agreed Cydalise.

"The Regency's fading! If we'd each gotten two or three blues for dessert, would Gonzague even have noticed the cost?"

"What are these blues?" asked Doña Cruz.

How can we describe the collective astonishment? Imagine a modern-day supper at the House of Gold, with a party of sugar-daddies and gold-diggers, and imagine one of the ladies not knowing what a mortgage was. It's impossible. Well, Doña Cruz's candid innocence was just as unbelievable. Chaverny fumbled quickly in the pocket where he'd put the dowry. He pulled out a dozen shares and put them into Doña Cruz's hands.

"Thank you," she said. "Monsieur de Gonzague will reimburse you for them." Then she spread them out in front of Nivelle and the others, and said with delightful grace, "Ladies, here's your dessert."

The ladies took the shares, and agreed with each other that the girl was despicable.

"Now then," went on Doña Cruz, "it wouldn't do for his lordship to find us asleep! A toast to the Marquis of Chaverny! Your glass, marquis!"

Chaverny held up his glass and sighed deeply.

"Look out—he's going to explain his situation!"

"Not to you," he answered. "The only listener I want is the charming Doña Cruz. The rest of you aren't smart enough to get it."

"But basically, your situation is clear," interjected Nivelle. "Your situation is, you're drunk." They all burst out laughing. It looked like Oriol might choke.

"Damn it!" cried Chaverny, smashing his glass on the table. "Do any of you here dare make fun of me? Doña Cruz, I'm not kidding: in this place you're like a star from the sky fallen among street lamps."

Loud protest by the ladies.

"Now you've gone too far!" said Oriol.

"Shut up," said Chaverny. "Comparing you to a street lamp is an insult to street lamps. Anyway, I'm not talking to the rest of you. I command Monsieur de Peyrolles to put an end to all your indecent chatter—and might I add that the only time I've liked him in my whole life was when he was hung up on that coatrack, where he belonged." He softened, and went on with tears in his eyes, "Yes, that's where he belonged. But coming back to my situation." He took Doña Cruz's hands in his.

"I know it perfectly well, marquis," she said. "Tonight you're marrying a wonderful girl."

"Wonderful?" asked the chorus.

"Wonderful," she repeated. "Young, witty, good, and perfectly ignorant of the blue papers."

"I sense an epigram coming!" said Nivelle.

"You get into a post-chaise," went on Doña Cruz, still addressing Chaverny. "You carry away your bride..."

"Ah! If only it were you, sweet girl!"

Doña Cruz filled his glass to the brim.

"Gentlemen," said Chaverny before drinking, "Doña Cruz has just explained my situation, better than I could've myself. It's a romantic situation."

"Drink up," she laughed.

"Wait. For a long time now I've been pondering an idea."

"Let's hear it! Let's hear Chaverny's idea!"

He stood up and posed like an orator. "Gentlemen, several seats are empty here. That one is my cousin Gonzague's, this one is the hunchback's. Both of them have been here. But what about that one?" He pointed to the seat directly across from Gonzague's, in which indeed no one had sat since the beginning of supper. "Here's my idea: I want someone to sit there, and I want it to be my bride!"

"Quite right! Quite right!" came the cry from all sides. "Chaverny's idea's a good one. The bride! The bride!"

Doña Cruz tried to take Chaverny's arm, but nothing could distract him. "What the hell!" he mumbled, holding onto the table with his hair falling into his face. "Am I drunk?"

"Drink up and be quiet!" she whispered in his ear.

"I'll drink, star of heaven. Yes, as God is my witness, I'll drink. But I won't be quiet. My idea's a good one, and it follows from my situation. I call for the bride, because—listen, all of you!"

"Listen! Listen! He's as handsome as the god of eloquence!" said Nivelle, waking up all the way.

Chaverny pounded his fist on the table and shouted, "I say it's absurd—absurd!"

"Bravo, Chaverny! Splendid, Chaverny!"

"Absurd, I say, to leave a seat empty..."

"Excellent! Excellent! Bravo, Chaverny!" The whole company applauded.

He struggled mightily to keep to his train of thought. "...To leave a seat empty," he concluded, clutching the tablecloth, "if you're not expecting someone."

Just as a salvo of hurrahs was about to greet that labored conclusion, Gonzague appeared at the door. "In fact, cousin," said the prince, "I do expect someone."

VIII. A Peach and a Bouquet

The Prince of Gonzague looked somber and even worried. They all put their glasses down on the table and stopped smiling.

Chaverny slumped in his chair. "Cousin, I've been waiting for you, to talk to you a little about my situation."

Gonzague came to the table and took away the glass Chaverny was raising to his lips. "Stop drinking!"

"What the hell?" protested Chaverny.

Gonzague threw the glass out the window. "Stop drinking."

Chaverny stared at him, his eyes wide with surprise. The rest of the company sat back down. On many a face the high color of incipient drunkenness gave way to pallor. The one thought they'd held at bay since the start of the party now loomed over them again, and it was Gonzague's worried look that had brought it back.

Peyrolles tried to sidle up to his master, but Doña Cruz got there first. "A word, please, my lord."

Gonzague kissed her hand and stepped aside with her.

"What's all this about?" murmured Nivelle.

"I'm beginning to think we're not going to have violins," said Cydalise.

"It can't be bankruptcy," said Desbois. "Gonzague's too rich."

"Stranger things have happened!" said Nivelle.

The gentlemen kept out of the conversation. Most of them looked thoughtfully down at the tablecloth. But Chaverny, oblivious to the sober anxiety that had suddenly filled the room, sang a bawdy street ballad.

Oriol mumbled in Peyrolles's ear, "Is it bad news?" Peyrolles turned his back on him.

"Oriol!" called Nivelle. He came immediately to heel, and the Daughter of the Mississippi said, "When the prince is through with that girl, tell him we're requesting violins."

"But..."

"Silence! You'll do it, because I say so!"

Gonzague wasn't through, and the longer the silence lasted the more obvious grew the mood of discomfort and sadness. Genuine cheer had never been the prevailing tone at this party: if you thought these people were truly having a good time, then we've failed in drawing the picture. They'd done their best; wine had made their voices louder and their faces redder; but behind their bursts of artificial laughter their anxiety had never faded, even for a moment. And all it took to make the hollow merriment fall flat was Gonzague's frown. What Oriol had said out loud, they were all thinking: there was bad news.

Gonzague kissed Doña Cruz's hand again. "Do you trust me?" he said in a fatherly tone.

"Of course, my lord," she replied with a pleading look. "But she's my only friend, my sister!"

"I can refuse you nothing, dear child. In an hour, no matter what, she'll be free."

"Really, my lord?" she cried joyfully. "Let me go give her the good news."

"Not now. Stay here. Did you tell her what I wanted?"

"This wedding? Of course. But she's bitterly against it."

"My lord," stammered Oriol, set in motion by an imperious wave from Nivelle, "I'm sorry to intrude, but the ladies are calling for violins."

"Forget it!" said Gonzague, pushing Oriol away with his hand.

"Something's up!" murmured Nivelle.

Gonzague squeezed both of Doña Cruz's hands in his. "Just one thing more: I wish I could have saved the one she loves."

"But, my lord, if you can explain to me how this marriage will help Monsieur de Lagardère, I'll pass on what you say to poor Aurore."

"That's all settled. I can't add anything more to what I've said. You think I'm in control of events? In any case, I promise you there'll be no coercion."

He tried to move away, but she held him. "I beg you, let me go back to her. Your secrecy frightens me."

"Right now I need you here."

She was surprised. "Me?"

"Things are going to be said here that the ladies shouldn't hear."

"And am I going to hear them?"

"No. They're not about your friend. This is your home; do your job as hostess and take the ladies into the other lounge."

"I'm ready to obey, my lord."

Gonzague thanked her and returned to the table. All of them tried to read his face. He motioned to Nivelle, and she came to him. "You see that child," he said, indicating Doña Cruz, who remained pensively at the far end of the parlor. "Distract her, and make sure she pays no attention to what goes on in here."

"Are you throwing us out, my lord?"

"We'll bring you back in later. In the little lounge there's a wedding gift basket."

"I understand, my lord. Can we have Oriol?"

"No, not even Oriol. Go!"

"Darlings," called out Nivelle, "Doña Cruz would like us to go see her wedding presents."

The ladies all rose and followed Doña Cruz into the small lounge on the opposite side of the parlor from the boudoir in which we previously saw the two friends. In that lounge, indeed, they found a wedding gift basket. The ladies gathered around.

Gonzague glanced at Peyrolles, who went to close the door behind the ladies.

No sooner was the door closed than Doña Cruz returned to it, but Nivelle ran over and led her back by the hand. "It's up to you to show us everything, angel. We're holding you to it."

In the parlor, only the men remained. There was silence while Gonzague took his seat—a silence deep enough to wake Chaverny. Since no one spoke, he mumbled to himself, "I remember seeing two beautiful creatures in the garden. Am I really going to marry one of them, or am I dreaming? I swear I can't tell." Then suddenly he called out, "Cousin! It feels like a funeral in here! I'm going to go see the ladies."

"Stay here!" ordered Gonzague. Then he surveyed the company. "Have we all kept our heads?"

"Totally kept our heads," they all replied.

"By God, cousin!" cried Chaverny. "You're the one who wanted us to drink!" He was right: Gonzague's idea of keeping their heads was entirely relative—he wanted hot heads and steady hands. Except for Chaverny, they all qualified.

Gonzague had already given Chaverny an appraising look, shaking his head with displeasure. Now he glanced at the clock. "We have just half an hour to talk. No time for foolishness. I'll speak on your behalf, marquis."

When Gonzague had ordered him to stay, Chaverny had sat back down, not in his chair, but on the table. "Don't worry about me, cousin," he said with a drunk's solemnity. "You'd just better hope no one here is drunker than I am. I'm a little preoccupied with my situation, that's all."

"Gentlemen," cut in Gonzague, "we'll get by without him if we have to. Here's the deal. Right now a girl is getting in our way. In our way, you hear me? In the way of all of us, because from now on our interests are bound together tighter than you know. You might say my destiny is yours. I've taken steps to make sure the tie that binds us is nothing less than a chain."

"We couldn't stick any closer to your lordship than we already do," said Montaubert.

"Right, right," they all said, but without enthusiasm.

Gonzague went on, "That girl..."

"Since things seem to be getting serious," interrupted Navailles, "we deserve a little clarity. Is the girl your men kidnapped yesterday the same one who was mentioned at the Regent's?"

"The one Monsieur de Lagardère promised to bring to the Palais-Royal?" added Choisy.

"In other words, Mademoiselle de Nevers?" said Nocé.

Chaverny's expression changed, and he muttered to himself in an odd tone of voice, "Mademoiselle de Nevers!"

Gonzague frowned. "What does her name matter to you? She's in our way, and she has to be moved out of our way."

Silence. Chaverny lifted his glass, but set it down again without drinking.

"I'm appalled by bloodshed, gentlemen," went on Gonzague, "as much as and even more than you. Violence has never worked out for me. Therefore, no more violence: I prefer kindness. Chaverny, it's costing me fifty thousand écus plus your travel expenses to soothe my conscience."

"That's a high price," grumbled Peyrolles.

"I don't get it," said Chaverny.

"You will. I'm giving that beautiful girl one chance."

"Is she Mademoiselle de Nevers?" asked Chaverny, mechanically picking up his glass again.

"If she likes you..." began Gonzague instead of answering.

"As for that, she'll like me." And Chaverny drank.

"Good! In that case she'll marry you of her own free will."

"I wouldn't have it otherwise."

"Me neither." Gonzague smiled equivocally. "Once you're married you'll take your wife to some provincial backwater, and you'll make the honeymoon last forever—unless you'd rather come back sooner, by yourself."

"And if she says no?"

"If she says no, then my conscience will be clear. She'll be free." In spite of himself, as Gonzague spoke the last word his eyes fell.

"You said before that you'd give her only one chance," murmured Chaverny. "If she accepts my hand, she lives. If she refuses my hand, she's free. I don't get it."

"Because you're drunk," said Gonzague curtly.

The others kept silent. Under the sparkling chandeliers that lit up the playful paintings covering the ceiling and the walls, amid the empty bottles and the wilted flowers, hovered an ominous feeling. From time to time they could hear the women laughing next door, and that laughter pained them.

Gonzague alone had a smooth brow and a cheerful smile. "I assume you other gentlemen understand me?"

No one answered, not even that hardened villain Peyrolles.

"I guess you need it explained," went on Gonzague, still smiling. "I'll be brief, since we don't have much time. Let's start with the axiom in the case: the very existence of that child means our utter ruin. Don't look skeptical—it's the truth. If I lost Nevers's inheritance tomorrow, the next day we'd all be fugitives."

"Us!" they all cried.

"You, gentlemen." Gonzague drew himself up. "All of you, without exception. This isn't about your old peccadillos. The Prince of Gonzague keeps up with the times; he's got account books like any merchant; and you're all in the

Prince of Gonzague's account books. Peyrolles is excellent at that kind of thing! My bankruptcy would be followed by your total ruin."

All eyes turned to Peyrolles, who didn't flinch.

"Plus which," went on Gonzague, "after what happened yesterday... But why make threats? You're bound tightly to me, and you'll follow me into adversity like faithful companions. So now we need to find out how much in a hurry you are to prove your devotion."

Again no one spoke.

His smile grew more mocking. "Clearly you understand me. Was I wrong to count on your intelligence? The girl will be free. I said it, and I hold to it: free to leave this place, free to go wherever she wants. Yes, gentlemen. Does that surprise you?"

They stared at him in stunned puzzlement. Chaverny, looking grave, drank slowly. There was a long silence.

For the first time Gonzague filled his own glass and those of his neighbors. "I've often told you, friends," he went on lightly, "that good customs, fine manners, great poetry, exquisite perfumes, all came to us from Italy. Italy isn't well enough known here. Listen and learn." He drank a mouthful of champagne. "Here's an anecdote from my youth—sweet years that'll never return. Count Anibal of Canossa, one of the Amalfi princes, was a cousin of mine, a good fellow, believe me, and my partner on many an escapade. He was rich, very rich. Judge for yourselves: my cousin Anibal had four castles on the Tiber, twenty farms in Lombardy, two villas in Florence, two in Milan, two in Rome, and all of the famous gold tableware of our respected uncles the Allaria cardinals. I was my cousin Anibal's sole heir, but he was only twenty-seven and looked like he would live to a hundred. I've never seen anyone in better health. You look cold, friends. Drink up, please—have a drink to put some heart in you."

They obeyed; they needed it.

"One night I invited my cousin Anibal to my vineyard at Spoleto, a delightful spot—and the vines! Ah, such vines! We spent the evening on the terrace, savoring the scented breeze and talking, I believe, about the immortality of the soul. Anibal was a stoic, except when it came to wine and women. He left by beautiful moonlight, hale and hearty. I can still see him getting into his carriage. He was obviously free, wasn't he? Free to come and go, at will: to a ball, to a supper—to whatever there is to do in Italy—to a lovers' tryst, but also free to stay..." Gonzague emptied his glass. And then, with all eyes on him, he concluded, "My cousin Count Anibal took advantage of that last freedom, and stayed."

The company stirred. Chaverny clutched his glass convulsively. "He stayed!" he echoed.

Gonzague picked a peach out of the fruit basket and tossed it to him. The peach landed on Chaverny's lap. "Learn from Italy, cousin!" said Gonzague. Then he corrected himself. "Chaverny's too drunk to understand me, and no doubt that's for the best. Gentlemen, learn from Italy." He rolled peaches across the table until every man had one. Then in a clipped curt tone he said, "I forgot to mention one trivial detail: before he left me, my cousin Count Anibal of Canossa shared a peach with me."

Every one of them quickly put down the peach he was holding. Gonzague refilled his glass. Chaverny did the same.

"Learn from Italy," said Gonzague a third time. "That's the only place they really know how to live. It's been a hundred years since they used the stupid stiletto. What good is violence? In Italy, if, say, you want to move aside a girl who's in your way, as in our case, you find a gallant man who agrees to marry her and take her off to who knows where. Very good; that's our case too. If she accepts, end of story. If she refuses, that's her right, here as in Italy. So then you bow to the ground and beg her pardon for presuming, and you respectfully escort her out. On the way out, purely out of gallantry, you give her a bouquet." As he spoke, Gonzague picked up a bouquet of real flowers from the centerpiece of the table. "Who can refuse a bouquet?" he went on, arranging the flowers. "She leaves, just as free as my cousin Anibal, free to go where she pleases, to her lover, to a friend, back home... But also free to stay."

He held out the bouquet. All of his guests drew back with a shudder.

"She stays?" said Chaverny through clenched teeth.

"She stays," said Gonzague coldly, looking him in the eye.

Chaverny stood up. "Are those flowers poisoned?" he cried.

Gonzague burst out laughing. "Sit down—you're drunk."

Chaverny passed a hand across his sweating brow. "Yes," he murmured, "I must be drunk. Otherwise..." He reeled. His head spun.

IX. The Ninth Stroke

Gonzague cast a masterful eye around the company. "Chaverny's not himself; I forgive him. But if any of the rest of you..."

"She'll say yes," stammered Navailles for his own peace of mind. "She'll accept Chaverny's hand."

It was a timid enough protest, amounting to very little—but the others managed not even that much. The threat of ruin had carried the day. Shame is like the Sphinx's victims: it drops dead fast. And it drops fastest and farthest in an age of wheeling and dealing. Gonzague knew that from now on he could do anything: these men were all his accomplices—he had an army. He put the bouquet back in the centerpiece. "Enough about that; we're all agreed. There's something more serious. It's not yet nine o'clock."

"Has your lordship heard any news?" asked Peyrolles.

"Nothing. But I've taken steps. All the approaches to this house are protected. Gendry and five of his men are guarding the alley door; the Whale and two others are at the garden gate; Lavergne and five more men are standing watch in the garden. And in the vestibule all the servants are armed."

"What about those two jokers?" asked Navailles.

"Cocardasse and Passepoil? They aren't stationed anywhere. They're waiting here, like us." He pointed to the entrance from the terrace, where the torches had been extinguished and the door left wide open since his arrival.

"Who are they waiting for, and who are we waiting for?" asked Chaverny suddenly, a spark of intelligence flaring in his dulled eyes.

"You weren't there yesterday when I got that letter, cousin?"

"No. Who are you expecting?"

"Someone to sit there." Gonzague pointed to the chair that had remained empty since the start of supper.

"The alley, the gardens, the vestibule, the terrace, crammed with swordsmen!" said Chaverny with a scornful wave. "All that for one man?"

"One man named Lagardère," said Gonzague with unintended emphasis.

"Lagardère!" echoed Chaverny. And mostly to himself he added, "I hate him! But he had me in his power, and he took pity on me."

Gonzague was leaning toward him to hear better, and shook his head. Then he straightened up. "Gentlemen, do the measures I've taken seem like enough?"

Chaverny shrugged and laughed.

"Twenty to one," murmured Navailles. "That seems fair."

"By God!" cried Oriol, reassured by the size of the garrison. "We weren't afraid!"

"So," said Gonzague, "you all think that to watch for him, ambush him, and take him dead or alive, twenty men are enough?"

"Too many, my lord, too many!" came the cry from all sides.

"In that case, you all agree in advance that none of you will blame me later for not being cautious enough?"

"I'll take that pledge," cried Chaverny. "What's lacking certainly isn't caution!"

"I needed your agreement," said Gonzague. "And now do you want to hear what I think?"

"Tell us, my lord, tell us!" They'd gone back to drinking.

Gonzague stood up. "I think," he said slowly and gravely, "nothing can stop him—nothing. I know the man. Lagardère said, 'I'll be with you at nine o'clock.' So at nine o'clock we'll see Lagardère face to face. I know it; I'd swear to it. There's not an army that could stop Lagardère from keeping an appointment. Will he come down the chimney? Will he burst in through a window? Will he pop up out of the floor? I don't know. But at the appointed hour, neither earlier nor later, we'll see him seated at this table."

"By God!" cried Chaverny. "Let me at him, but man to man."

"Shut up," said Gonzague harshly. "When I want to watch dwarves wrestle giants I go to the fair." Turning to the others he resumed, "I'm so deeply sure of what I'm saying, gentlemen, that a little while ago I tested the mettle of my rapier." He drew his sword and flexed the supple, shining steel blade. He glanced at the clock. "It's almost time. Follow my example. I warn you, you can count on nothing but your own swords."

All eyes had followed his, and they stared at the face of the magnificent pendulum clock that rumbled in its rosewood case. The hands stood almost at nine o'clock. The men ran to get their swords, which they'd left scattered about on the furniture.

"Let me at him!" said Chaverny again. "In single combat!"

"Where are you going?" said Gonzague to Peyrolles, who was headed toward the terrace.

"To close that door," said his prudent factotum.

"Leave the door. I said it would stay wide open, and wide open it'll stay." Gonzague turned to the rest of his companions in arms. "That'll be our signal, gentlemen. If the double doors close, you can rejoice: it means 'the enemy is beaten.' But as long as they stay open, look out."

Peyrolles got in the back row, with Oriol, Taranne, and the other financiers. Next to Gonzague stood Choisy, Navailles, Nocé, Gironne—the aristocrats. Chaverny, on the opposite side of the table, stood nearest to the door. All of them had their swords in their hands and their eyes on the dark terrace. This solemn anxious wait certainly hinted at the magnitude of the man who was coming.

The gears of the clock made their usual grinding sound just before striking the hour.

"Ready, gentlemen?" said Gonzague, his eye on the door.

"Ready!" they answered as one. They'd just done a head count: courage is often a question of numbers.

Standing his sword up with its point stuck in the parquet floor, Gonzague lifted his glass from the table and said with a swagger—at the very moment the clock rang out the first stroke of nine—"A toast to Monsieur de Lagardère! Glass in one hand and sword in the other!" He raised his glass.

"Glass in one hand and sword in the other!" echoed the chorus. Then they stood silent, glasses filled to the brim, blades in hand. They waited, eyes peeled, ears pricked. In the silence they heard some kind of metallic clash from outside. The clock struck slowly: it seemed to take a hundred years to ring out its nine strokes. On the eighth, that metallic sound from outside stopped. On the ninth, both panels of the double doors slammed shut.

They gave a long hurrah and lowered their swords.

"To Lagardère dead!" cried Gonzague.

"To Lagardère dead!" echoed the company, and they drained their glasses. Only Chaverny didn't move and didn't speak.

But just as Gonzague was bringing his glass to his lips, he started. In the middle of the room the capes and cloaks piled onto the hunchback began to shift and rise. Gonzague had forgotten all about the hunchback—and anyway he wasn't aware of what had happened to him. The prince had said, "I don't know if he'll come down the chimney or burst in through a window or pop up out of the floor, but at the appointed hour he'll be here." At the sight of the shifting pile Gonzague stopped drinking and stood en garde.

From under the coats came a burst of shrill dry laughter. "I'm on your side, gentlemen!" said a harsh voice. "Present and accounted for!" It wasn't Lagardère.

Laughing, Gonzague murmured, "It's our friend the hunchback."

The hunchback skipped around, grabbed a glass, and mingled with the drinkers who were toasting. "To Lagardère!" he cried. "The coward must've known I was here! He didn't dare show up!"

"To the hunchback! To the hunchback!" laughed the chorus. "Long live the hunchback!"

"He, he! Gentlemen," he said ingenuously, "someone who didn't know your valor as well as I do, and who saw you so cheerful, might think you'd just had a good scare. But what do those fellows want?" He pointed to the closed double doors, in front of which stood Cocardasse and Passepoil as still as statues. They looked triumphant.

"We come to hand over our heads," said Cocardasse sarcastically.

"Chop 'em off," added Passepoil, "and send two more souls to heaven."

"Honor restored!" cried Gonzague joyfully. "Give those fellows a glass—they'll toast with us!"

Chaverny gave them the look of loathing you wear when facing the hangman. He moved away from the table as they approached it. "I swear," he said to

Choisy, who was next to him, "I think if that Lagardère had shown up I'd have switched to his side."

"Shush!" said Choisy.

The hunchback, who'd overheard, pointed out Chaverny to Gonzague. "Is your lordship quite sure of that man?"

"No."

Cocardasse and Passepoil were clinking glasses with the gentlemen. Chaverny, now sobered up, listened while Passepoil explained about the blood-stained white doublet and Cocardasse retold the story of the anatomy class at the Val de Grâce hospital.

"This is despicable!" said Chaverny, pushing right up to Gonzague. "They're obviously talking about a murder!"

"What?" The hunchback feigned surprise. "Where's this fellow been?"

Cocardasse raised a mocking, insulting glass to Chaverny, who turned away in horror.

"God's blood!" went on the hunchback. "The gentleman seems to have very peculiar qualms!"

The rest of the company kept quiet.

Gonzague put his hand on Chaverny's shoulder. "Be careful, cousin," he murmured. "You've drunk too much."

"On the contrary, my lord," said the hunchback in his ear, "I think your cousin hasn't drunk enough. Believe me, I know what I'm talking about." Gonzague eyed him suspiciously. The hunchback laughed and nodded like a man who's sure he's right.

"All right," said Gonzague, "you might be right. I'll hand him over to you."

"Thank you, my lord," said the hunchback. Then he approached Chaverny, glass in hand. "Will you also refuse to toast with me? It's a rematch!"

Chaverny began to laugh, and held out his glass.

"To your wedding, handsome bridegroom!" cried the hunchback.

They sat down facing each other, the circle of partisans and judges already gathering around them: their bacchanalian duel was starting again.

After the evening's long debauch every man here in this parlor felt a weight lifted from his heart, an enormous weight: Lagardère was dead, since he'd broken his braggart word—and Lagardère alive but skipping out on the rendezvous was impossible! Gonzague himself no longer doubted it. And if he ordered Peyrolles to make the rounds outside and check on the sentinels, that was only out of an abundance of Italian caution. It never hurts to be careful. The armed men stationed outside had been hired for the whole night, and it would cost nothing extra to leave them at their posts.

The more afraid the guests had been, the happier they were now. This was the real start of the party. Their appetites awoke, along with their thirst. The merriment absent earlier now flowed in from all sides. By God, our aristocrats

352

couldn't remember ever having trembled, and our financiers were now as brave as Caesar. But for every foolishness, just as for every sin, a scapegoat must be found. Poor fat little Oriol was the chosen victim: he had to atone for the collective cowardice. He was heckled and squelched, and all of their trembling and pallor and faintheartedness was heaped on his head. Oriol alone had trembled—the gentlemen were all agreed on that. He resisted like a demon, and challenged them all to duels.

"The ladies! The ladies!" they cried. "Why not bring back the ladies?"

At a sign from Gonzague, Nocé opened the door to the lounge. The ladies returned like a flock of birds escaping from an aviary, all talking at once, complaining of the long wait, laughing, crying, simpering.

Indicating Doña Cruz, Nivelle said to Gonzague, "What a little snoop! I had to pull her away from the keyhole a dozen times."

"My God!" said Gonzague innocently, "what could she have seen? We sent you darlings away for your own good. You don't like to hear us talk about business."

"Have we been brought back for a reason?" cried Desbois.

"Is it finally time for the wedding?" asked Fleury.

And Cydalise, putting one hand on Cocardasse's bearded chin and the other on Passepoil's blushing cheek, asked, "Are you the violinists?"

"God's hat!" said Cocardasse, standing as rigid as a sentry. "We're gentlemen, cutie pie!"

And Passepoil shuddered from head to foot at the touch of that soft, sweet-smelling hand. He tried to speak, but couldn't.

Gonzague kissed the tips of Doña Cruz's fingers. "Ladies, we have no secrets from you. If we had to deprive ourselves of your presence for a moment, it was just to settle the preliminaries of tonight's wedding."

"So it's true!" cried all the silly girls. "Can we watch the play?"

Gonzague gestured in protest. "This is a serious union," he said solemnly—as if the setting and the company in themselves didn't contradict him. Turning to Doña Cruz he added, "It's time to go warn your friend."

She gave him a look of concern. "You promised me, my lord," she murmured.

"I'll keep all my promises." As Gonzague led Doña Cruz to the door he added, "She can say no; I won't take that back. But for her sake and that of someone else I won't name, you'd better hope she says yes."

Doña Cruz didn't know what had happened to Lagardère, and Gonzague counted on that. She had no conception of this godless impostor's depths of hypocrisy. Still, she stopped in the doorway. "My lord," she said pleadingly, "I have no doubt you're acting from motives that are noble and worthy of you. But very odd things have been going on since yesterday. We're just two poor girls, without enough experience to solve riddles. Out of friendship for me, my lord, and out of compassion for that poor child I love and who's in distress, tell me—

just a word of explanation—a single word to enlighten me and help me overcome her resistance. I'd be better equipped if I could tell her in what way this marriage can protect the life of the one she loves."

Gonzague stopped her reproachfully. "Don't you trust me, Doña Cruz, and doesn't she trust you? I say it's so, and you believe me. If you say it's so, she'll believe you." Then he added imperiously, "And make it quick. I'm waiting for you." He bowed, and Doña Cruz withdrew.

Just then an uproar broke out in the parlor—shouts of delight and bursts of laughter.

"Bravo, Chaverny!" cried some.

"Hang in there, hunchback!" cried others.

"Chaverny's glass was fuller!"

"No cheating! It's a battle to the death!"

And the ladies cried out, "They're going to kill themselves! They're crazy!"

"That little hunchback is a devil."

"If he's got as many blue shares as they say," murmured Nivelle, "I'll admit I've always had a thing for hunchbacks."

"But look how much they're soaking up!"

"They're a couple of funnels! A couple of sponges!"

"A couple of hollow legs! Bravo, Chaverny!"

"Hang in there, hunchback! A couple of bottomless pits!"

The hunchback and Chaverny sat face to face, surrounded by an ever-tightening circle. It was their second trial of strength. The influence of English ways, which began to be felt at that time, had made this kind of drinking tournament fashionable. A dozen empty bottles scattered around them attested to the blows delivered—or rather swallowed—on each side. Chaverny was as white as a sheet; his bloodshot eyes looked ready to pop out of their sockets. But he was used to this kind of jousting. In spite of his modest height and trim belly, he was an impressive drinker, with exploits beyond counting. The hunchback, on the other hand, glowed with high color, and an extraordinary light sparkled in his eyes. He got excited, he talked—not a good thing, as we all know: chatter can inebriate you almost as much as wine. In a serious contest a champion drinker should keep silent—after all, consider fish! The odds seemed to favor the marquis.

"A hundred pistoles on Chaverny!" cried Navailles. "Aesop's going to crawl back under the coats!"

"I'm all right!" protested the hunchback, swaying on his chair.

Seeing that, Nivelle said, "My whole wallet on Chaverny!"

"What's in the wallet?" asked the hunchback between swigs.

"Five blue shares—my entire fortune, alas!"

"Ten against them!" cried the hunchback. "Pass the wine."

"Which one do you like best?" murmured Passepoil in his friend's ear, looking in turn at Cydalise, Nivelle, Fleury, Desbois, and the other ladies.

"The sweetheart's going to drown, God's life!" answered Cocardasse without taking his eyes off the hunchback. "I've only known one man who could drink like that."

Aesop stood up; they thought he was going to fall. But he sat merrily on the table and looked all around in his cynical, mocking way. "Don't you have bigger glasses?" he cried, flinging his into the distance. "Drinking out of these nutshells, we might be here all night!"

X. The Hunchback Victorious

Let's return to the bedroom on the ground floor where we saw Aurore and Doña Cruz earlier, when the supper had just begun. Aurore, alone now, knelt on the carpet, but she wasn't praying. The noise from upstairs had just intensified with the duel between Chaverny and the hunchback, but Aurore paid no attention. She was daydreaming, and her beautiful eyes, tired from weeping, stared at nothing. So deep was her reverie that she didn't hear the slight noise Doña Cruz made as she came into the room and tiptoed closer and kissed the back of Aurore's hair. Aurore turned her head slowly, and her poor pale cheeks and her eyes dimmed by tears wrung Doña Cruz's heart.

"I've come to fetch you."

"I'm ready," answered Aurore.

Doña Cruz wasn't expecting that. "Have you been thinking it over?"

"I prayed. When you pray, things that are confused become clear."

Doña Cruz eagerly drew close. "What became clear?" she said, from affectionate interest rather than out of curiosity.

"I'm ready," said Aurore again, "ready to die."

"It's not a question of dying, poor dear sister."

"It's been a long time since I first had the idea," said Aurore in bleak discouragement. "I'm the curse on him, I'm the danger that always threatens him, I'm his angel of doom. Without me he'd be free, he'd be at peace, he'd be happy!"

Doña Cruz listened uncomprehendingly.

"Why didn't I do yesterday what I'm thinking of doing today?" Aurore wiped away a tear. "Why didn't I run away from his house? Why am I not dead?"

"What are you talking about?"

"Flor, dear sister, you don't know how different today is from yesterday. I've seen heaven opening up for me. A whole life of wonderful joys and holy delights appeared for me. He loved me, Flor."

"And you only found that out yesterday?"

"If I'd known it earlier, God only knows whether we would have undertaken the pointless dangers of this journey. I wasn't sure, I was afraid. Oh, how foolish we are, sister! We should tremble, and not rejoice, when we're offered joys so great they'd bring the blessings of heaven down to earth. That's impossible, you see: happiness can't be found here below."

"But what've you decided to do?" broke in Doña Cruz, whose gifts didn't run to mysticism.

"To obey, so as to save him."

Delighted, Doña Cruz stood up. "Come! The prince is waiting for us." Then a cloud veiled her smile. "You know, I spend my time performing heroics with you. Of course I don't feel love the way you do, but I do feel love in my own way—and I keep running into it."

Aurore looked surprised and puzzled.

"Don't worry," Doña Cruz smiled, "I won't die of it, I promise. I expect I'll be in love this way more than once before I die. I know if it weren't for you I still wouldn't have given up on that king of knights errant, handsome Lagardère! But I also know that, besides handsome Lagardère, the only man who's made my heart beat is that fool Chaverny."

"What!"

"I know, I know, he's frivolous. But what can you do? Apart from Lagardère I hate saints. That monstrous little marquis has gotten into my head."

Smiling, Aurore took her hand. "Dear sister, your heart's worth more than your words. And anyway, why should you have the proud sensitivity of the high-born?"

Doña Cruz pursed her lips and murmured, "So I guess you don't believe in my noble birth?"

"I'm the one who's Mademoiselle de Nevers," Aurore answered calmly.

The gypsy girl's eyes widened. "Lagardère told you?" she murmured, not even thinking to dispute it: she wasn't ambitious.

"No—and that's the only thing in my life I can blame him for. If he'd told me..."

"Then who did?"

"No one. I just know it, that's all. Since yesterday, various events starting when I was a child have taken on new meaning for me. I've remembered things, I've drawn comparisons. The conclusion arrived by itself. The baby asleep in the moat at Caylus while her father was being murdered, that was me. I can still see the look on Henri's face when we visited that sinister spot! Didn't Henri make me kiss Nevers's marble face at the Saint Magloire cemetery? And that Gonzague, whose name has followed me since childhood, that Gonzague who's going to deal me the final blow today, isn't he married to Nevers's widow?"

"But he's the one who wanted to reunite me with my mother!"

"My poor Flor, we won't be able to figure it all out, I know. We're children, and God has kept our hearts pure, so how can we plumb the depths of depravity? And what good would it do? I don't know what Gonzague meant to use you for, but you were a tool in his hands. I've seen it since yesterday, and listening to me now, you see it yourself."

"It's true," murmured Doña Cruz, her eyes half closed and her brow furrowed.

"Just yesterday, Henri told me he loved me."

"Just yesterday?" said Doña Cruz in surprise.

"Why was that? Was there some obstacle between us? And what could that obstacle be, except the touchy, scrupulous honor of the most principled man in the world? It was my high birth, and the great wealth I was heiress to, that separated him from me." Doña Cruz smiled. Aurore looked her in the eye with austere pride. "Will I be sorry I told you all this?" she murmured.

"Don't scold me." Doña Cruz threw her arms around Aurore's neck. "I was smiling because I would never have considered that to be an obstacle—since I'm not a princess."

"I wish to God I weren't either!" Aurore had tears in her eyes. "Greatness has its rewards and its burdens. I'm going to die at twenty, having know nothing of greatness but sorrow." With a gentle gesture she closed her friend's mouth before she could protest again, and went on, "I'm calm. I trust in the goodness of God, who won't test us beyond our capacity. Though I speak of dying, don't worry that I'm going to hasten my final hour. Suicide is a crime without atonement, that closes the doors of heaven. If I didn't go to heaven, where would I wait for him? No—others will carry out my release. That's not a guess, I know it."

Doña Cruz had gone pale. Her voice changed. "What do you know?"

"I was here all alone," said Aurore slowly, "going over everything I've just told you, and more besides. There's plenty of proof. It's because I'm Mademoiselle de Nevers that I was kidnapped yesterday, it's because I'm Mademoiselle de Nevers that the Princess of Gonzague is hounding Henri with her hatred. And you know, Flor, that's the thought that robbed me of all my courage. The idea of standing between my mother and him, two enemies, pierced my heart like a dagger. Will the hour come when I have to choose? Who knows? Since the time I learned my father's name, I've had my father's spirit. I see my duty for the first time, and that voice—the voice of duty—is already as strong in me as the voice of happiness itself. Yesterday I knew of nothing on earth that could separate me from Henri. Today..."

"Today?" prompted Doña Cruz. Aurore turned aside and wiped away a tear. Doña Cruz watched her and was moved; without a struggle, without regret, she gave up the shining illusions Gonzague had inspired in her. She was like a child waking with a smile from the golden chimeras of a beautiful dream. "Dear sister, you're Aurore de Nevers. I believe it. There aren't many duchesses who could have a daughter like you. But you said something earlier that worried and frightened me."

"What did I say?"

"You said, 'Others will carry out my release.'"

"I forgot. So here I was, all alone, my head bursting and feverish—and I guess it was the fever that gave me courage—and I left this room and went upstairs the way you showed me, using the hidden stairs and the corridor, and I reached the boudoir where the two of us were before, and I went up to the door behind which those men were calling you. The noise had stopped. I put my eye to the keyhole. There wasn't a single woman at the table."

"They sent us away."

"Do you know why, Flor?"

"Gonzague told us..."

"Ah!" Aurore shuddered. "So that man giving orders to the others was Gonzague?"

"That was the Prince of Gonzague."

"I don't know what he told you, but he must've lied."

"Why would you think that, sister?"

"Because if he'd told you truth, you wouldn't have come to get me, dear Flor."

"Then what's the truth? You're driving me crazy!"

There was a silence. Aurore seemed to be lost in thought, her head pressed to her friend's bosom. Then she went on, "Did you notice the flowers on the table?"

"Yes, pretty flowers."

"And didn't Gonzague tell you, 'If she says no, she'll go free'?"

"His very words."

Aurore put her hand on the gypsy girl's hand. "Well, it was that Gonzague who was talking when I looked through the keyhole. The guests listening to him were still, silent, pale. I put my ear to the keyhole instead of my eye. I heard..."

There was a sound at the door.

"You heard?" prompted Doña Cruz. Aurore didn't answer.

Monsieur de Peyrolles, pale and unctuous, stood in the doorway. "Well, ladies? We're waiting for you."

Aurore rose immediately. "Lead the way."

As they climbed the stairs, Doña Cruz drew close to her and whispered, "Keep going! What about those flowers?"

Aurore squeezed her hand and smiled calmly. "Pretty flowers, like you said. Monsieur de Gonzague has the gallantry of a great lord. When I say no, not only will I go free, but I'll get a bouquet of those pretty flowers."

Doña Cruz stared at her. She could tell that behind those words lay something tragic and menacing, but she couldn't figure out what.

"Bravo, hunchback! We'll call you the king of carp!"

"Hang in there, Chaverny! You can do it!"

"Chaverny just spilled half a glass down his shirtfront—that's cheating!"

There was a cry of joy: someone had brought the big glasses the hunchback had called for—a pair of Bohemian tankards, used for iced drinks in the summer, each of them holding at least a quart. The hunchback emptied a bottle of champagne into his. Chaverny tried to do the same, but his hands shook.

"Are you going to make me lose my five granddaughters, marquis?" cried Nivelle.

"That Nivelle would've been great at the 'Better he died!' speech from Corneille's *Horace*," said Navailles.

"Hell!" said the Daughter of the Mississippi. "I worked hard enough to earn that money!"

Bets were being taken all around the circle, and the bettors mostly agreed with Nivelle. Fleury, not the gambling type, ventured the opinion that it was time to call a halt, but she was shouted down.

"We're just getting started," laughed the hunchback. "Help the marquis fill his glass."

Nocé, Choisy, Gironne, and Oriol were gathered around Chaverny, and they filled his tankard to the brim.

"Alas," sighed Cocardasse, "what a waste of God's good wine."

As for Passepoil, his blank stare moved admiringly from Nivelle to Fleury to Desbois and back, and he murmured passionate words to himself. How could such a tender, sensitive being not inspire interest in the ladies?

"Your health, gentlemen!" The hunchback raised his enormous tankard.

"Your health!" stammered Chaverny. Gironne and Nocé had to support his shaking arm.

The hunchback lifted his tankard to everyone around the circle. "This toast must be drunk to the bottom in one draft without stopping for breath." He brought the tankard to his lips and drank without haste, but in a single draft. They all clapped like mad.

Chaverny, already being held up by his seconds, also drained his tankard—but everyone could tell it was his final effort.

"One more!" proposed the hunchback, cheerful and at ease as he held out his tankard.

"Ten more!" said Chaverny, swaying.

"Hang in there, marquis!" cried the gamblers. "Don't look at the chandelier!"

Chaverny laughed idiotically. "Everybody stay calm," he stammered. "Stop the seesaw and keep the table from spinning."

Nivelle, that brave soul, now got more actively involved. "Sweetie pie," she said to the hunchback, "I was joking. They'd have to kill me before I'd bet against you." She stuffed her wallet into her pocket and raked Chaverny with a scornful glare as she moved away.

"Let's go! Let's go!" said the hunchback. "A drink! I'm thirsty!"

"A drink!" echoed Chaverny. "I could drink the ocean! Just stop the seesaw!"

The tankards were refilled. The hunchback raised his with a firm grip. "To the ladies!"

"To the ladies!" murmured Passepoil in Nivelle's ear.

Chaverny made a supreme effort to lift his arm, but the full tankard slipped from his shaking hand, to Cocardasse's great indignation. "Crooked ace!" he muttered. "People who waste wine should be locked up!"

"A redo!" said Chaverny's supporters.

The hunchback staunchly held out his tankard to be refilled. But Chaverny's eyelids had begun to beat like the wings of martyred butterflies when children pin them to the wall. It was the end.

"You're weakening, Chaverny!" cried Oriol.

"Chaverny, you're rocking!"

"Chaverny, there you go!"

"Hurrah for the little man! Long live Aesop!"

"Let's carry the hunchback around for a victory lap!"

The general uproar was followed by a great silence. Chaverny, no longer being held up, rocked back and forth on his chair, while his limp hands tried in vain to find anything to take hold of. "Nobody said the house was going to collapse," he murmured. "It seemed so well built. That's not fair!"

"Chaverny's lost it!"—"Chaverny's crumbling!"—"Chaverny's uprooting!"—"Down goes Chaverny!"—"Chaverny's vanished!"

He slid under the table. A second hurrah rang out. The victorious hunchback raised the tankard that had just been filled for the loser, and drank it standing on the table. He was as solid as a rock. The applause almost brought down the building.

"What's all this?" asked Gonzague, drawing close.

The hunchback hopped lightly down from the table. "You gave him to me, my lord."

"Where's Chaverny?"

With one foot the hunchback nudged Chaverny's legs where they stuck out from under the table. "Here he is."

Gonzague frowned and murmured, "Dead drunk! This is too much—we needed him."

"For the wedding, my lord?" And the hunchback actually clutched his lace ruff just like a nobleman and tucked his hat under his arm as he bowed.

"Yes, for the wedding."

"God's blood!" said the hunchback indifferently. "You lose one, you gain one. Such as I am, my lord, I wouldn't be sorry to settle down, and I'll volunteer for the job."

A great burst of laughter greeted this unexpected offer. Gonzague examined the hunchback, who stood firmly before him, still holding his empty tankard. Pointing to Chaverny, the prince asked quietly, "Do you know what taking his place will involve?"

"Yes, I know what's involved."

"And you feel up to it?"

The hunchback smiled—a smile both arrogant and cruel. "You don't know me, my lord. I've done harder things than that."

XI. Italian Flowers

The company had returned to the table and begun drinking again. "Great idea!" they all said. "We'll marry off the hunchback in Chaverny's place."

"That's way more entertaining—the hunchback'll make an excellent groom!"

"And imagine the look on Chaverny's face when he wakes up a widower!"

Oriol was making friends with Passepoil, by order of Nivelle, who'd taken that shy debutant under her wing. No more foolish standoffishness: Cocardasse was toasting with everyone like an equal; it felt natural to him, and he didn't make too much of it. Here as everywhere, he behaved with a dignity beyond praise. But—"Crooked ace!"—fat little Oriol had tried to advance to first names with him, and was severely rebuffed.

The Prince of Gonzague and the hunchback stood a little to one side. Gonzague was still observing the little man carefully, and seemed to be reading his secret thoughts through the mocking mask of his face.

"My lord," said the hunchback, "what guarantee do you need?"

"First I want to know how much you've guessed."

"I don't have to guess, I was there. I heard the parable of the peach, the story about the flowers, the encomium to Italy." He pointed to the armchair where the coats were still piled.

Gonzague followed his finger. "Yes, I see," he murmured, "you were right there. So why the playacting?"

"I wanted to be sure, and I wanted to think. Chaverny was never the right man."

"It's true. I have a fondness for him."

"Fondness is always a mistake, because it creates risk. Chaverny's sleeping now, but he'll wake up."

"I'm aware of that," murmured Gonzague. "But never mind Chaverny. What do you say to the parable of the peach?"

"Nice, but too vivid for your cowards."

"And the story about the flowers?"

"Elegant, but still too vivid. They got scared."

"I'm not talking about those gentlemen. I know them better than you do."

"I'm aware of that," said the hunchback in turn.

Gonzague smiled at him. "Answer for yourself."

"I appreciate anything that comes from Italy. I've never heard a more delightful anecdote than the one about Count Canossa at the Spoleto vineyard; but I wouldn't have shared it with these men."

"So you think you're tougher than they are?"

The hunchback just smiled and didn't bother to answer.

"Well?" called Navailles. "Is the marriage all arranged?"

Gonzague silenced him with a gesture.

"That little creature must be worth his weight in blue shares," said Nivelle. "I'd marry him in a second!"

"You'd be Madame Aesop," said Oriol, cut to the quick.

"Madame Jonah!" added Nocé.

"Bah! The king of the gods is Plutus the god of wealth." Nivelle pointed to Cocardasse. "You see this fellow? With a little Mississippi powder I could turn him into a prince."

Passepoil was jealous. Cocardasse puffed himself up. "Well, the sweetheart shows good taste! She's got a thing for me, God's hat!"

Meanwhile Gonzague asked the hunchback, "What do you have that Chaverny doesn't?"

"Experience. I've been married before."

"Ah!" Gonzague looked at him more sharply.

The hunchback rubbed his chin and didn't lower his eyes. "I've been married, and I'm a widower."

"Ah!" said Gonzague again. "And what advantage does that give you over Chaverny?"

The hunchback flushed slightly. "My wife was beautiful," he said quietly. "Very beautiful."

"Young?"

"Very young. Her father was poor."

"I get it. Did you love her?"

"Madly! But we weren't together long." The hunchback's face darkened again.

"How long?"

"A day and a half."

"That's odd. Explain."

The little man gave a forced laugh. "Why explain, if you get it?" he murmured.

"I don't get it."

The hunchback lowered his eyes and seemed to hesitate. "Maybe I'm wrong after all. Maybe you only need a Chaverny!"

"Explain, I said!"

"Did you explain the story of Count Canossa?"

Gonzague put a hand on his shoulder.

"It was the day after our wedding," said the hunchback. "I'd given her a day to think it over and get used to my appearance. She couldn't do it."

He grabbed a glass off a side table and looked at the prince. Their eyes met. The hunchback's eyes expressed such merciless cruelty that Gonzague murmured, "So young, so beautiful—you felt no pity?"

With a sudden spasm, the hunchback smashed the glass on the side table. "I want to be loved!" he said with real ferocity. "To bad for women who can't do it!"

For a moment the prince remained silent. The hunchback had regained his cold, mocking demeanor. Then Gonzague nudged the sleeping Chaverny with his foot. "Hey there, gentlemen!" he cried. "Who's going to carry this man out of here?"

The hunchback's chest rose. He struggled to hide his triumph.

Navailles, Nocé, Choisy, and all of Chaverny's friends made a last effort to save him. They shook him, they called to him. Oriol threw a pitcher of water in his face. The ladies were kind enough to pinch him till he bruised. And with great goodwill they all cried, "Wake up, Chaverny, wake up! Somebody's stealing your bride!"

"And you'll have to give back the dowry!" added Nivelle, her mind always on practical matters.

"Chaverny, Chaverny, wake up!" All in vain.

At a sign from Gonzague, Cocardasse and Passepoil lifted the defeated marquis onto their shoulders to take him away. As they passed the hunchback he said very quietly, "Don't harm a hair of his head, on your lives, and deliver the letter to its address." Cocardasse and Passepoil carried their burden out.

"We did what we could," said Navailles.

"We were loyal friends to the end," added Oriol.

"But there's no doubt the hunchback's wedding is much funnier," said Nocé.

"Marry off the hunchback! Marry off the hunchback!" cried the ladies.

In one bound Aesop leaped onto the table.

"Silence!" they all cried. "Jonah's going to make a speech!"

"Ladies and gentlemen," said the hunchback, gesturing like a lawyer at the High Court, "I'm touched and flattered to the bottom of my heart by the interest you've condescended to take in me. Certainly the knowledge that I'm unworthy of it should prompt me to keep silent..."

"Excellent!" said Navailles. "He talks like a book!"

"Jonah," said Nivelle, "your modesty just makes your fine qualities stand out even more."

"Bravo, Aesop! Bravo! Bravo!"

"Thank you, ladies. Thank you, gentlemen. Your willingness to indulge me gives me the courage to try to be worthy of it, and worthy also of the generosity of the illustrious prince to whom I'll owe the favor of my bride."

"Excellent! Bravo, Aesop! A little louder!"

"Use your left hand a little more when you gesture!" said Navailles.

"Recite some suitable poetry!" cried Desbois.

"Dance a minuet! A jig on the tablecloth!"

"If you have any gratitude at all, Jonah," said Nocé with great feeling, "perform the scene of Achilles and Agamemnon."

"Ladies and gentlemen," replied Aesop seriously, "those are all stale old things. I mean to demonstrate my gratitude with something better. I mean to give you some contemporary theater, a premiere performance!"

"From the works of Jonah! *Bravissimo*! He's written a play!"

"I'm going to write one, ladies and gentlemen; but for now it'll be improvised. I mean to show you how the art of seduction is stronger even than nature itself..."

The cheer that followed almost shattered the parlor windows.

"He's going to teach us a lesson in flirtation!" they cried.

"*The Art of Pleasure*, by Aesop, known as Jonah!"

"He's got Aphrodite's girdle in his pocket!"

"Cupid's tricks, jokes, graces, and arrows!"

"Bravo, hunchback! Hunchback, you're splendid!"

He bowed all around and concluded with a smile, "Bring out my bride, and I'll do my best to entertain the company."

"I'll get you a job at the Opéra, if you want!" cried Nivelle enthusiastically. "We're short on clowns!"

"The hunchback's bride!" shouted the gentlemen. "Bring on the hunchback's bride!"

At that moment the door to the boudoir opened. Gonzague called for silence. Doña Cruz entered, holding up a tottering, deathly pale Aurore. Monsieur de Peyrolles followed them. The sight of Aurore prompted a long admiring murmur. That first glance made the gentlemen forget all about the wild romp they'd planned. No one even responded when the hunchback, peering at her through his pince-nez, said cynically, "By God, my bride's a beauty!"

From the bottom of all those hearts—more numb than evil—rose a feeling of compassion. For a moment even the ladies felt pity, so great was the deep sadness and the gentle resignation on that charming virginal face. Looking around at his army, Gonzague frowned. Then Taranne, Montaubert, Albret, and all those lost souls were ashamed of their feelings and said, "That hunchback's a lucky devil!"

That was certainly what Passepoil thought as he came back in with Cocardasse. But that first lustful impulse gave way to surprise when both of them recognized the two girls from the Rue du Chantre: the girl Cocardasse had seen on Lagardère's arm in Barcelona, the girl Passepoil had seen on Lagardère's arm in Brussels. Neither of our two bravos was in on the secret of the performance, and what was about to take place remained a mystery to them—but they knew something strange was going to happen. They nudged each other and exchanged a glance that meant, "Look out!" They didn't need to check to be sure their rapiers weren't stuck in their sheaths. When the hunchback gave him a quick look, Cocardasse answered with a slight nod. "All right," he muttered to Passepoil, "the little fellow wants to know if his letter got delivered. We didn't have far to go."

Doña Cruz looked around the room for Chaverny. "Maybe the prince changed his mind," she murmured to her friend. "I don't see Chaverny."

Aurore just shook her head sadly without raising her lowered eyes; clearly she expected no mercy. When Gonzague turned their way, Doña Cruz took Aurore by the hand and led her forward. The prince was pale, though he affected a smile. The hunchback stood next to him, doing his best to strike a gallant pose and twisting his lace ruff with a triumphant air. Doña Cruz's eyes met his; she tried to look a question at him, but he remained impassive.

"Dear child," said Gonzague in a voice everyone thought sounded different, "has Mademoiselle de Nevers told you what we expect of you?"

Without lifting her eyes, but with her head held high, Aurore answered in a firm voice, "I'm the one who's Mademoiselle de Nevers."

The hunchback started so violently that even in the general surprise his reaction was noticed. "God's blood!" he cried, quickly mastering his emotions. "My bride's of a good family!"

"His bride?" echoed Doña Cruz.

Whispers ran through the room. The ladies didn't feel the jealous dislike for the newcomer that they had for the gypsy girl. On Aurore's ingenuous, innocently proud head, the Nevers name seemed fitting.

Gonzague turned angrily to Doña Cruz. "Was it you who put that lie in this poor child's mind?"

"Ah!" said the disappointed hunchback. "So it's a lie? Too bad! I would've liked to be allied to the house of Nevers."

There were a few laughs, but overall the mood was chilly. Peyrolles was as dour as a beadle in mourning.

"Not I," answered Doña Cruz, who wasn't intimidated by the prince's anger. "But what if it's true?" Gonzague shrugged scornfully. "Where's the Marquis of Chaverny?" went on Doña Cruz. "And what's the meaning of this man's words?" She pointed to the hunchback, who was keeping his composure as he stood among Gonzague's followers.

"Mademoiselle de Nevers," said Gonzague, "your role in all this is over. If you're in a mood to abandon your rights, I'm still here—thank God—to protect them. I'm your guardian; everyone here was at the family tribunal that met yesterday; they constitute almost a majority. If I'd listened to the prevailing opinion, I might've been less forgiving toward a brazen, shameless imposture. But I was guided by the goodness of my heart and the peaceful ways of my life. I didn't want to turn a comedy into a melodrama."

He stopped. Doña Cruz understood nothing: for her his words were empty sounds. Maybe Aurore understood better, because a sad, bitter smile came to her lips. Gonzague looked around at the company. All eyes were lowered, except those of the ladies, who listened with curiosity, and those of the hunchback, who seemed impatient for the end of the sermon.

"I'm speaking directly to you, Mademoiselle de Nevers," went on Gonzague, still addressing Doña Cruz, "because you're the only one here who needs to be persuaded. My honorable friends and advisors share my opinion; my words express their thoughts." No one objected. "What I said before about wanting to avoid harsh punishment will explain the presence of these ladies. If it were a matter of making the punishment fit the crime, they wouldn't be here."

"What crime?" asked Nivelle. "We're all in suspense, my lord!"

"What crime?" echoed Gonzague, pretending to master his indignation. "Surely it's a serious matter, considered a crime under the law, to worm your way into a prominent family to take fraudulent advantage of the opening created by a missing or deceased heir!"

"But poor Aurore hasn't done anything!" cried Doña Cruz.

"Silence! This pretty little adventuress needs to be reined in and mastered. As God is my witness, I wish her no harm. I'm spending a small fortune to wind up her game nicely: I'm marrying her off."

"About time!" said the hunchback. "Here comes the wrap-up."

"And I say to her," went on Gonzague, taking the hunchback's hand, "here's an honest man who loves you and who aspires to the honor of being your husband."

"You tricked me, my lord!" cried Doña Cruz, flushed with anger. "He's not the one! Who could possibly give herself to a creature like him?"

"If he had a lot of blue shares..." said Nivelle only half to herself.

"That's not polite! Not polite at all!" murmured the hunchback. "But I hope the young lady will soon change her mind."

"You!" cried Doña Cruz. "I'm onto you! You're the one who's pulling all the strings in this business. And now I know you're the one who gave away where Aurore was hiding."

"He, he, he!" The hunchback gave a self-satisfied chuckle. "He, he, he! By God, I'm certainly capable of having done it. My lord, this girl talks too much. She's keeping my bride from answering."

"Now if it was the Marquis of Chaverny..." began Doña Cruz.

"Let it go, dear sister," said Aurore in the clear, cold tone she'd used at the start. "If it was Monsieur de Chaverny, I'd refuse him just as I refuse this man."

The hunchback didn't seem at all put out. "Sweet angel, that's not your final word."

Doña Cruz stepped between him and Aurore. She was spoiling for a fight with someone. Gonzague had resumed his lofty, careless air.

"No answer?" said the hunchback, stepping forward, hat under his arm, hand on his ruff. "It's because you don't know me, darling. I'm ready to spend my entire life at your feet."

"All right, now you're overdoing it," said Nivelle.

The other ladies listened and waited. Women have a sixth sense, like second sight. They were dimly aware that behind this farce, unfolding painfully in spite of the star clown's efforts, lay some terrible tragedy. The gentlemen, who knew where this was headed, grimaced with artificial cheer. But you can't summon joy at will; and joy stubbornly stayed away. When the hunchback spoke, his harsh, grating voice got on all their nerves. When the hunchback said nothing, the silence felt sinister.

"Well, gentlemen," said Gonzague suddenly, "why aren't you drinking?"

They filled their glasses quietly; no one was thirsty.

"Listen to me, dear child," said the hunchback. "I'll be your little hubby, your lover, your slave..."

"What a nightmare!" said Doña Cruz. "Speaking for myself, I'd rather die!"

Gonzague stamped his foot and glared at his protégée.

"My lord," said Aurore with the calm of despair, "don't drag this out. I know the Chevalier Henri de Lagardère is dead."

A second time, the hunchback started as if he'd received a sudden shock. He said no more, and a deep silence fell on the room.

"And who has informed you so thoroughly, mademoiselle?" asked Gonzague with great courtesy.

"Don't question me, my lord. Let's get to the end of this, which has all been laid out in advance. I accept it. I welcome it."

Gonzague seemed to hesitate. He wasn't expecting to be asked for the Italian bouquet, and yet he'd seen Aurore's hand reach toward the flowers. He stared at her—so beautiful and so young. "Would you rather have a different husband?" he murmured in her ear.

"My lord, you sent me the message that if I refused I'd go free. I'm asking you to keep your word."

"And you know about..." he began, still whispering.

"I know," said Aurore, finally lifting her saintly eyes to his. "And I'm waiting for you to offer me those flowers."

XII. Hypnosis

Of all those present, only Doña Cruz and the ladies didn't understand the horror of the situation. All of the rakes, both financiers and noblemen, had ice in their veins. Cocardasse and Passepoil kept their eyes fixed on the hunchback, like two stock-still hunting dogs. Amid those surprised, worried, curious ladies, amid those men filled with disgust but lacking the strength to break their chains, Aurore remained calm. She glowed with the gentle, radiant beauty and the deep resigned sadness of a saint undergoing her ultimate trial on this sinful earth and already gazing at heaven.

Gonzague's hand reached toward the flowers, but then fell back. He wasn't ready for this. He'd expected some kind of struggle, at the end of which the supposed gift of the flowers to the girl would seal the complicity of his followers. But, confronted by this beautiful sweet creature, Gonzague's wickedness was disarmed. What was left of his heart rose up; Count Canossa had only been a man.

The hunchback fixed his glittering eyes on the prince. The clock struck three in the morning. Out of the silence came a voice behind Gonzague: one rascal present had a heart too dried out to beat. Monsieur de Peyrolles said to his master, "The family tribunal will reconvene tomorrow."

Gonzague turned his head and murmured, "Do what you want."

Peyrolles picked up the bouquet of flowers whose purpose Gonzague himself had described.

Filled with a nameless dread, Doña Cruz whispered in Aurore's ear, "What were you telling me about those flowers?"

"Mademoiselle," said Peyrolles at the same time, "you're free to go. All of the ladies have bouquets. Permit me to offer one to you." He did it awkwardly, and his face dripped with treachery. Nevertheless, Aurore reached out to take the flowers.

"God's hat!" said Cocardasse, wiping his brow. "There's some mischief going on!"

Doña Cruz, her eager eyes on Peyrolles, instinctively reached out—but another hand had anticipated hers. Thrust roughly away, Peyrolles staggered back to the wall. The bouquet dropped from his hands, and the hunchback calmly trampled it underfoot. A weight was lifted off all their chests.

"How dare you!" cried Peyrolles, drawing his sword.

Gonzague eyed the hunchback suspiciously.

"No flowers!" said the little man. "From now on I alone have the right to give my fiancée presents. Hell, you all look like people who've just seen lightning strike! It's just a bouquet of wilted flowers! I let things go this far just to make a point." To Peyrolles he said, "Sheath your sword, friend, and make it snappy!" He turned to Gonzague. "My lord, tell that knight of the doleful countenance to stop spoiling our fun. Good heavens! I admire you: throwing in the towel like that, breaking off negotiations. Allow me not to give up so fast."

"He's right! He's right!" cried the company. They all grasped at a way out of the nightmare. There'd been no joy at Gonzague's supper that night. It goes without saying that Gonzague himself expected the hunchback's initiative to fail—but it gave him a precious few minutes to think.

"I'm right, by God! I know it!" cried the hunchback. "What did I promise you all? A lesson in the fencing match of love! And you acted without me! And you didn't even let me say a word! I'm attracted to this girl, I want her, I'll have her."

"Excellent!" said Navailles. "That's telling 'em!"

"Let's see," said Oriol, carefully turning a witty phrase. "Let's see if you're as good in a love bout as in a drinking bout."

"We'll be the referees," added Nocé. "Let the battle begin!"

The hunchback looked at Aurore, then around the circle—while she, exhausted by the supreme effort she'd just made, sagged in Doña Cruz's arms. Cocardasse pushed a chair forward, and Aurore collapsed into it.

"It doesn't look good for poor Aesop," murmured Nocé.

Since Gonzague wasn't laughing, they remained serious. The ladies were interested only in Aurore—except for Nivelle, who thought to herself, "I have a feeling that little man is as rich as Croesus."

"My lord," said the hunchback, "allow me to beg a favor of you. You're much too great a nobleman to have meant to play a practical joke on me. If you tell a man to run, you can't start by tying his feet together. The first condition for success here is to be alone with her. Have you ever known a woman to soften when she's surrounded by gawkers? Be reasonable—it's impossible."

"He's right," cried the chorus.

"All these people are frightening her," he went on. "I feel at a disadvantage myself, because in love talk, tenderness, passion, enthusiasm all border on the ridiculous. How can I speak in a way that'll melt a woman—in front of a jeering audience?"

As he delivered this self-satisfied, conceited speech, with one fist on his hip and one hand on his ruff, the hunchback was truly comical. If it weren't for the sinister breeze blowing that night through Gonzague's pleasure house, they would certainly have laughed. They tried to laugh a little.

"Grant his request, my lord," said Navailles.

"What's he asking for?" said Gonzague, still lost in thought.

"That my fiancée and I be left alone," replied the hunchback. "I'm only asking for five minutes to overcome this charming girl's disgust."

"Five minutes!" they cried. "Listen to him! You can't refuse him that much, my lord!"

Gonzague said nothing. The hunchback stepped forward and quickly whispered in his ear, "My lord, you're being watched. You'd put to death anyone who betrayed you the way you're betraying yourself!"

"Thank you, friend," said the prince, his face changing. "That's good advice. Clearly I'm going to owe you a lot, and I think you'll be a great lord before you die." Then to the others he said, "Gentlemen, I was only thinking of you. Tonight we won a round, a terrible one. It looks like tomorrow our troubles will be over, but we don't want to miss stays coming into port. Forgive my absent-mindedness, and follow me." He'd contrived to smile, and all of their faces lit up.

"Let's not go too far away," said the ladies. "We need to be able to spy on them."

"Out on the terrace," said Nocé. "We can leave the doors ajar."

"Get to work, Jonah! The coast is clear!"

"Outdo yourself, hunchback! We'll give you ten minutes instead five, but watch in hand!"

"Gentlemen," said Oriol, "the betting is on!" They'd gamble on anything and about anything; the odds were quoted at a hundred to one against Aesop.

As he passed by Cocardasse and Passepoil, Gonzague said, "If the pay was right, would you two go back to Spain?"

"We'd do anything your lordship asked," replied our two bravos.

"Then don't go away," And the prince went to join the crowd of his followers. Cocardasse and Passepoil had no intention of going anywhere.

When everyone had left the parlor, the hunchback faced the doors to the terrace, behind which he could see the gawkers lined up three rows deep. "Very good!" he called playfully. "Perfect! That way you won't bother me at all. Don't bet too hard against me, and keep an eye on your watches." He crossed the parlor to the doors. "I was forgetting one thing. Where's his lordship?"

"Here," said Gonzague. "What is it?"

"Do you have a justice of the peace or a notary ready?" asked the hunchback with splendid seriousness. They couldn't help themselves, and a burst of laughter filled the terrace. "We'll see who gets the last laugh," he murmured.

Impatiently Gonzague replied, "Hurry it up, friend, and don't worry: there's a royal notary in my office."

The hunchback bowed and returned to the two girls. Doña Cruz watched him approach with a kind of horror. Aurore still had her eyes lowered. The hunchback knelt in front of her chair.

Rather than watch the show—such a hit with his followers—Gonzague paced alongside Peyrolles. They stopped at the far end of the terrace.

"People come back from Spain," Peyrolles was saying.

"People die in Spain, just like in Paris," murmured Gonzague. After a short silence he went on, "We've missed our chance here. The women would figure it out. Doña Cruz would talk."

"Chaverny..."

"He'll keep quiet."

They exchanged a glance in the darkness, and Peyrolles asked for no further explanation.

"When she leaves here," went on Gonzague, "she has to go free, perfectly free—as far as the next corner."

Suddenly Peyrolles leaned forward, listening.

"That's just the lookout going by," said Gonzague.

There was a sound of weapons clashing in the garden, but it was quickly drowned out by a great stir on the terrace.

"It's astonishing!" the company cried, "it's a miracle! Are we seeing things? What the devil is he telling her?"

"By God," said Nivelle, "it isn't hard to guess. He's telling her how many shares he has."

"But just look!" said Navailles. "Who took that hundred to one bet?"

"Nobody," said Oriol. "I'll give you fifty to one now. How about twenty-five?"

"No thanks! Look! Look!"

The hunchback was still on his knees by Aurore's chair. Doña Cruz tried to step between them, but the hunchback waved her off, saying, "Keep out of it."

He'd spoken quietly, but in so strikingly different a voice that Doña Cruz, her eyes wide, couldn't help drawing back. The harsh, shrill sounds they were used to hearing out of that mouth had given way to the deep, gentle, melodious voice of a man. That voice spoke Aurore's name. Doña Cruz felt her friend start weakly in her arms and murmur, "I'm dreaming."

Still kneeling, the hunchback said again, "Aurore!"

She hid her face in her hands. Thick tears ran between her trembling fingers. Doña Cruz stood with her head thrown back, her mouth agape, her eyes staring. It seemed to the onlookers at the half-open terrace doors like they were witnessing some kind of hypnosis.

"By heaven!" cried Navailles. "It's almost miraculous!"

"Shh! Look! The other girl seems to be drawn as if by some irresistible force!"

"The hunchback must have something—a talisman or an amulet!"

Only Nivelle could put a name to what the hunchback had; that lovely girl had firm opinions, and believed in the supernatural power of blue shares.

What they were saying outside was true: as if against her will, Aurore leaned toward the voice that called to her. "I'm dreaming! I'm dreaming!" she stammered between her sobs. "It's awful! I can't tell anymore!"

"Aurore!" said the hunchback a third time. And just as she was about to speak, he silenced her with an imperious gesture. "Don't turn your head," he said gently. "We're on the very edge of the abyss: one move, one gesture, and all is lost."

Doña Cruz felt weak-kneed, and had to sit down next to Aurore.

"I'd give twenty louis to know what he's telling them!" cried Navailles.

"By God!" said Oriol. "I'm beginning to think—and yet he hasn't given her anything to drink."

"A hundred pistoles on the hunchback, at even odds!" offered Nocé.

The hunchback went on, "You're not dreaming, Aurore. Your heart has not deceived you. It's me."

"You!" she murmured. "I don't dare open my eyes. Flor, dear sister, look for me!"

Doña Cruz kissed her forehead and whispered, "It's him!"

From between the slightly parted fingers hiding her face, Aurore ventured a glance. Her heart leapt, but she managed to stifle her first cry. She stayed still.

The hunchback looked quickly toward the terrace door. "Those men don't believe in heaven, but they believe in hell. It's easy to fool them by pretending to be evil. Instead of obeying your heart, Aurore, my beloved, obey whatever bizarre power it is that they imagine to be the work of the devil. Act as if you're hypnotized by the conjuring motions of my hand." He made a few passes in front of her face, and she obediently leaned toward him.

"She's almost there!" cried Navailles, stunned.

"She's almost there!" echoed the chorus.

Fat little Oriol ran to the far end of the terrace. "My lord, you're missing the best part!" he cried, out of breath. "Hell if it isn't worth a look!"

Gonzague let himself be dragged toward the door. "Shh! Shh! Don't disturb them!" said the watchers as the prince joined them. They made room for him. He stood silent with astonishment.

The hunchback continued to wave his hands. Aurore, swept along under his spell, leaned closer and closer to him. He was right: those who don't believe in God often have faith in the kind of hogwash that in those days came especially from Italy—philters, charms, occult powers, magic.

Even Gonzague, with his intelligence, murmured, "That man knows some evil spell!"

Passepoil, nearby, crossed himself ostentatiously. Cocardasse muttered, "The rascal must have some grease from a hanged man! Crooked ace! It's obvious!"

"Slowly, very slowly, move your hand," the hunchback whispered to Aurore, "as if an invincible power were forcing you to give it to me against your will."

Aurore's hand came away from her face and dropped slowly and mechanically. If the watchers on the terrace could have seen her charming smile! But they saw only her heaving breast and the back of her lovely head in its mass of hair. They watched the hunchback with increasing terror.

"God's hat!" said Cocardasse. "The little hussy is giving him her hand!"

And all of them said in astonishment, "He can do whatever he wants with her! He's a demon!"

"Crooked ace!" added Cocardasse with a glance at Passepoil. "It's the kind of thing you have to see to believe!"

"I'm seeing it," said Peyrolles behind Gonzague, "and I don't believe it."

"What? By God!" they protested on all sides. "You can't deny the evidence!"

Peyrolles shook his head angrily.

"Let's leave nothing to chance," went on the hunchback quietly. He must have had his reasons for counting on Doña Cruz's complicity. "Gonzague and his sidekick are watching now. We have to fool them too. When your hand touches mine, Aurore, you should start and look around in surprise. Well done!"

"I played that scene in *Beauty and the Beast*, at the Opéra," said Nivelle, shrugging. "I acted surprised better than that girl, didn't I, Oriol?"

"You were delightful, as always. But what a shock that poor girl must have felt when their hands met!"

"That proves there's antipathy and diabolical subjugation involved!" Taranne opined solemnly.

The Baron of Batz, an educated man, said, "Ja! Andibady! Ja, ja! Tiapoligal zuptiucation! A zagrament! Ja, ja!"

"Now," said the hunchback, "turn stiffly toward me—slowly, slowly." He stood up and fixed his eyes on her. "Rise like an automaton. Good! Look at me, take one step, and fall into my arms."

Aurore obeyed. Doña Cruz sat as still as a statue.

The onlookers pushed the doors wide open and burst into applause. Aurore's beautiful head rested on the chest of Aesop, known as Jonah. The crowd of spectators flooded noisily back into the parlor.

"Only five minutes!" cried Navailles, watch in hand.

"Did he turn the pretty señorita into a pillar of salt?" asked Nocé.

The hunchback gave his dry little laugh and said to Gonzague, "Nothing to it, my lord."

"My lord," said Peyrolles from the other side, "something doesn't make sense here. This fellow must be an accomplished con man—be on your guard."

"Are you afraid he's going to vanish your head?" asked Gonzague. Then he turned to the hunchback. "Bravo, friend! Can you share the recipe?"

"It's for sale, my lord."

"And will the spell hold until the wedding?"

"Till the wedding, yes, but not beyond."

"How much do you want for your talisman, hunchback?" cried Oriol.

"Almost nothing. But to make it work you need a precious commodity."

"What commodity?"

"Smarts," answered Aesop. "Better go shopping, sir."

Amid applause, Oriol withdrew into the crowd.

Choisy, Nocé, and Navailles surrounded Doña Cruz and peppered her with questions. "What did he say?"—"Was he speaking Latin?"—"Did he have a phial in his hand?"

"He spoke Hebrew," said the gypsy girl, who was gradually recovering.

"And that pretty girl understood him?"

"Perfectly. He stuck his left hand in his pocket and pulled out something that looked like—how can I put it?"

"A ring studded with jewels?"

"More like a bundle of shares!" said Nivelle.

"It looked like a pocket handkerchief," said Doña Cruz, turning away.

"By God, you're a valuable man, friend." Gonzague put his hand on the hunchback's shoulder. "I admire you."

"Not bad for a beginner, eh, my lord?" he answered with a modest smile. "But please ask the gentlemen to back up—further!—further, if you please! Don't crowd me! I've been hassled enough. Where's the notary?"

"Send for the royal notary!" ordered Gonzague.

XIII. Signing the Contract

The Princess of Gonzague had spent the whole of the previous day in her rooms, but a succession of visitors had interrupted the solitude to which she'd sentenced herself for so many years. Starting in the morning, she'd written a number of letters. Her visitors hastily brought her their replies in person. In that way she received Cardinal de Bissy; the Duke of Tresmes, Governor of Paris; Monsieur de Machault, the Chief of Police; Chief Judge de Lamoignon; and Minister d'Argenson. She asked each of them for help and support against Monsieur de Lagardère, the pretended gentleman who'd kidnapped her daughter. To all of them she reported her meeting with that Lagardère, who—furious at not getting the exorbitant reward he dreamt of—had taken refuge in bold lies. They were all outraged at Lagardère, and in fact they had good reason to be. The wisest of the princess's counselors felt that the very promise made by Lagardère, the promise to produce Mademoiselle de Nevers, had been his first deceit. But the promise had been worth testing.

In spite of the respect they all feigned for the name of the Prince of Gonzague, clearly the events of the previous day's assembly had left them all with a bad impression of him. There was some dark mystery about the whole business that none of them could fathom, but that inspired alarm in each of them. Zeal always contains an element of curiosity. Cardinal de Bissy had been the first of them to sniff out some great scandal, but the smell had gradually reached all the rest. And as soon as they started on the trail of the mystery, the hunt began in earnest. All of them swore not to be satisfied with anything short of a definite answer. They advised the princess to go straight to the Palais-Royal to make everything known to the Regent. And they advised her above all not to make accusations against her husband.

Toward midday she got into her chaise and was taken to the Palais-Royal, where she was admitted right away: the Regent awaited her. He granted her an unusually long audience. She made no accusations against her husband. But the Regent questioned her, which he hadn't been able to do in the confusion of the ball. And the Regent—his memories of Philippe de Nevers, his best friend, his brother, having been brusquely reawakened in the last two days—naturally wound back through the years and brought up that sinister business at Caylus, which to him had never been made clear. It was the first time he'd spoken face to face like this with his friend's widow. The princess made no accusations against her husband; but by the end of the audience the Regent was left sad and thoughtful. And yet the Regent went on to receive Gonzague twice—that day and that night—and didn't bring it up with him. Those who knew Philippe d'Orléans understood: suspicion had dawned in the Regent's mind.

On her return from her visit to the Palais-Royal, the princess found her apartment full of friends. All those who'd advised her not to accuse her husband wanted to hear what the Regent had decided to do about the prince.

Though instinctively he felt a storm coming, Gonzague didn't see all the clouds gathering on his horizon. He was so powerful, so rich! And the doings of that night, say, would be so easy to deny the next day: the bouquet of poisoned flowers would sound like a joke, a leftover from the days of Madame de Brinvilliers the poisoner; the tragicomic wedding would be a joke too, and anyone claiming the hunchback's instructions were to murder his bride would just make people split their sides laughing. Fairy tales! Nothing got gutted these days except wallets.

But the storm wasn't coming from there—it was coming from the Villa Gonzague. The long sad drama of the eighteen years of forced marriage might be reaching a resolution. Something was stirring behind the black-curtained altar where every morning Nevers's widow attended the Mass for the dead. A ghost was rising in the midst of her unprecedented mourning. The current crime would never be believed, because it had too many witnesses, all of them accessories. But an ancient crime, no matter how deeply buried, almost always manages to break through the worm-eaten coffin lid.

The princess's answer to her counselors was that the Regent had inquired about the circumstances of her marriage and what had come before it. She added that the Regent had promised to make Lagardère talk, if necessary under torture. The counselors fell back on Lagardère, with the secret hope that he'd provide answers; they all knew or suspected that Lagardère had been involved in the night scene that had opened this interminable tragedy twenty years before. Monsieur de Machault promised his police officers, Monsieur de Tresmes his troops, the judges their court investigators. We're not sure what a cardinal could put up to match that, but His Eminence offered what he had. Lagardère would just have to look out.

Toward five o'clock in the evening, Madeleine Giraud came to her mistress, who was sitting alone, and gave her a message from the Chief of Police, informing the princess that Monsieur de Lagardère had been killed the previous night as he left the Palais-Royal. The letter ended with words that by now were turning into a litany: "Don't make accusations against your husband." The princess spent the rest of the evening in feverish solitude.

Between nine and ten, Madeleine Giraud came back with a new note, this one in an unknown hand. It had been brought by two unprepossessing strangers who looked a lot like cutthroats, one of them tall and insolent, the other short and ingratiating. The note reminded the princess that the twenty-four hours granted by the Regent to Monsieur de Lagardère would end at four the next morning. It went on to tell the princess that at that hour Monsieur de Lagardère would be at Monsieur de Gonzague's pleasure house. Lagardère at Gonzague's! Why? How? And what about the letter from the Chief of Police announcing his death? The princess ordered her carriage, and had herself driven to the Villa Lamoignon on the Rue Pavée Saint Antoine. An hour later twenty Royal Guards, led by a captain and four officers from the Châtelet, were gathered in the courtyard of the Villa Lamoignon.

We haven't forgotten that the occasion for the supper hosted by Gonzague at his little pleasure house behind Saint Magloire was a wedding—the wedding of the Marquis of Chaverny with an unknown young lady for whom the prince was putting up a dowry of fifty thousand écus. The groom had agreed, and we know Gonzague thought he had reason to be confident the bride wouldn't refuse. Naturally the prince had taken steps beforehand so nothing would delay the planned union. The royal notary, a genuine royal notary, had been summoned. Even better, the priest, a genuine priest, was waiting in the sacristy of Saint Magloire. The point was not to fake a wedding: Gonzague needed a lawful marriage, one that would give the husband power over his wife, so that at the husband's order the wife could be sent into perpetual exile.

The prince had told the truth: he didn't like bloodshed. But, when other means failed, he'd never retreated from bloodshed. At one point it seemed like the night's adventure was going wrong. Too bad for Chaverny! But since the hunchback had stepped forward things were looking up. The hunchback was obviously a man ready for anything. Gonzague had sized him up at a glance: he was one of those people who are happy to make all mankind pay for the misery they themselves have suffered, and who hold against other men the heavy cross God set on their shoulders. Most hunchbacks are mean, thought Gonzague. Hunchbacks want revenge. Lots of hunchbacks are cruel and clever, because for them this world is enemy territory. Hunchbacks have no pity—because who had any on them? Ignorant mockery hits them so hard at so young an age that a protective callous forms around their hearts. Chaverny was no good for the job that had to be done. Chaverny was just a fool; wine made him strong, generous, brave. Chaverny was capable of loving his wife, and of kneeling repentantly before her after beating her. Not the hunchback. The hunchback would bite only once, but that one bite would be fatal. The hunchback was a real find.

When Gonzague called for the notary, his followers all wanted to show their zeal, and Oriol, Albret, Montaubert, and even Cydalise rushed out ahead of Cocardasse and Passepoil, who found themselves alone for a moment under the marble colonnade.

"Baldy," said Cocardasse, "before the night's over it's going to hail..."

"Blows!" finished Passepoil. "The weathervane points toward sword strokes."

"Crooked ace! My hand's itching! How about you?"

"Hell—it's been a while since we danced, distinguished friend."

Instead of going into the ground floor rooms, they opened the outside door and went out into the garden. There was no sign of the men Gonzague had placed in ambush in front of the house. Our two bravos went as far as the arbor where Monsieur de Peyrolles had found the bodies of Saldaña and Faenza the day before. They noticed with surprise that the little gate leading to the alleyway was wide open. There was no one in the alley. They looked at each other.

"Well, hell, it can't be that rascal of a Parisian who did this," murmured Cocardasse, "since he's been upstairs in that room since early in the evening."

"Do we really know what he's capable of?"

They heard some kind of vague noise from the direction of the church.

"Stay here," said Cocardasse. "I'll go have a look."

While Passepoil stood guard at the little gate, Cocardasse slipped along the garden walls. The garden ended at the Saint Magloire cemetery, which he could see was full of Royal Guards.

"Well, baldy," he said when he came back, "if we're having a dance, there'll be plenty of violins!"

Meanwhile Oriol and his companions burst into Gonzague's apartment, where the royal notary, Master Griveau, Senior, slept peacefully on a sofa, near a side table holding the remains of an excellent supper. I don't know why our century has turned against notaries. They're generally clean, healthy, well fed, polite, witty at home, and blessed with a good eye for a whist hand. They exhibit good table manners and old-fashioned courteous chivalry. They're gallant toward rich old ladies, and few Frenchmen look better in white tie and tails, which go so well with gold-framed glasses. It won't be long till the pendulum swings the other way, and we'll all agree that a young blond notary, of solemn and gentle appearance, and whose incipient potbelly hasn't yet grown to its full size, is one of the prettiest flowers of our civilization.

Griveau—notary and scribe and file clerk to royalty and at the administrative offices in the Châtelet—had the additional honor of being a devoted servant to the Prince of Gonzague. He was a fine man of forty: plump, healthy, rosy-cheeked, smiling, a pleasure to look at. Oriol took him by one arm, Cydalise by the other, and together they dragged him back to the upstairs parlor at the pleasure house.

The sight of a notary always brought out Nivelle's tender side: it's notaries who make bequests between living people legal and official. Griveau, a sociable man, bowed with great decorum to the prince and the ladies and the gentlemen. He had with him the draft of a marriage contract, prepared in advance, but it began with Chaverny's name. That had to be fixed. At Peyrolles's invitation, Griveau sat at a small table, drew pen and ink and scraping knife from his pocket, and got to work.

Gonzague and most of the company had stayed around the hunchback. "Will it take long?" the little man asked the notary.

"Master Griveau," laughed the prince, "you understand the natural impatience of a young bridegroom."

"Give me five minutes, my lord," said the notary.

The hunchback crumpled his ruff with one hand. With the other he stroked Aurore's beautiful hair. "Exactly as long as it takes to seduce a woman!" he said triumphantly.

"Since we've got a little time," cried Gonzague, "let's drink! A toast to the happy hymeneals!"

They uncorked more champagne. This time it seemed like real joy might break out. Their fears had fled, and they all felt good.

Doña Cruz herself filled Gonzague's glass. "To their happiness!" she said, clinking cheerfully.

"To their happiness!" echoed the laughing circle, and they drank.

"By the way," said the hunchback, "is there a poet around to compose my wedding verses?"

"A poet! A poet!" they all cried. "Send for a poet!"

Griveau put his pen behind his ear. "I can't do everything at the same time," he said softly and discreetly. "When I've finished the contract I'll improvise a few rhyming couplets."

The hunchback bowed deeply in thanks.

"Poetry from the Châtelet records office," said Navailles. "Romantic ballads from a notary. Don't deny it—we're living in the golden age!"

"Who wants to deny it?" said Nocé. "Fountains will flow with almond milk and sparkling wine."

"Out of thistles will grow roses," added Choisy.

"Naturally, since out of file clerks now flow verses!" The hunchback puffed himself up with smug arrogance. "And the occasion for all this wit is my wedding!" Then he stopped. "But are we going to be like this? For shame! The bride's not dressed. And me, God's blood, I'm a disgrace! My hair isn't done, my cuffs are wrinkled. The bride's toilette, by God! Didn't I hear something about a wedding gift basket, ladies?"

Nivelle and Cydalise had already gone to the lounge next door, and they returned with the basket. Doña Cruz took charge of Aurore's toilette. "Make it snappy! The night's almost over! We need time to go dancing!"

"What happens if they wake her up, Aesop?" asked Navailles.

The hunchback had a mirror in one hand, a comb in the other. Before answering he said to Desbois, "Darling, just do something with the back of my hair!" Then he turned to Navailles. "She belongs to me, dear children, the way you all belong to Monsieur de Gonzague—or rather to your ambitions. She belongs to me the way Oriol belongs to his vanity, the way pretty Nivelle belongs to her greed, the way you all belong to your cute little capital crime! Darling Fleury, please retie my hair bow."

"Done!" said Griveau just then. "Ready to sign."

"Have you written in the names of the bride and groom?" asked Gonzague.

"I don't know them."

"Your name, friend?" the prince asked the hunchback.

"You go ahead and sign, my lord," he answered lightheartedly. "And you sign too, gentlemen—I hope you'll all do me that honor. I'll write in my name myself. It's an odd name, and it'll make you laugh."

"Now that you mention it," said Navailles, "what the hell is his name?"

"Go ahead and sign, please. My lord, I'd like to have your shirt cuffs as a wedding present."

Gonzague immediately took off his lace cuffs and tossed them to him, then went to the table to sign. The gentlemen were all racking their brains to come up with the hunchback's name.

"Don't bother trying," he said as he fastened on Gonzague's cuffs. "You'll never get it. Monsieur de Navailles, what a splendid embroidered handkerchief!"

Navailles gave him his handkerchief. Then each of them wanted to add something to his toilette: a pin, a buckle, a bit of ribbon. He let them do it, and admired himself in his mirror. Meanwhile one by one the gentlemen signed the contract; Gonzague's name was at the top.

"Go see if my bride's ready!" said the hunchback to Choisy, who was fastening a ruff of Mechlin lace around his neck.

Just then they all cried, "The bride! Here comes the bride!"

Aurore appeared in the doorway dressed in bridal white and with symbolic orange blossoms in her hair. Though she was perfectly lovely, her pale, strangely frozen features still made her look like a beautiful statue. She remained under the spell. A long murmur of admiration greeted her.

The hunchback clapped his hands with delight. "By God! I've got a gorgeous bride! It's our turn, sweetheart, our turn to sign!"

He lifted her hand out of those of Doña Cruz, who was supporting her. Everyone expected Aurore to show some sign of revulsion, but she followed him with perfect docility. As he went toward the table where Griveau had made everyone else sign, the hunchback, seeing Cocardasse and Passepoil returning, caught Cocardasse's eye, winked, and quickly brushed his hand down his side. Cocardasse must have understood, because he blocked the hunchback's way and cried, "God's hat! Something's missing from your toilette, sweetheart!"

"What? What could it be?" they all cried.

"What could it be?" said the hunchback himself innocently.

"Crooked ace!" said Cocardasse. "Since when does a gentleman get married without his sword?"

"It's true! It's true!" cried the honorable company as one. "Correct the oversight! A sword for the hunchback! He's not comical enough as he is!"

Navailles looked around at their rapiers for a good fit, while the hunchback fussed and murmured, "I'm not used to it, it'll get in the way."

Among all those swords for show, one sword was made for fighting: the long, tough blade belonging to Peyrolles, who was never in fun. Navailles took Peyrolles's sword, like it or not.

"There's no need, there's no need!" said the hunchback.

Playfully they fastened the belt onto him. Cocardasse and Passepoil noticed that at the moment he touched the sword guard his hand trembled involuntarily with joy—but they were the only ones who noticed. When the sword was strapped on, the hunchback stopped protesting: it was a done deed. But the weapon now hanging at his side suddenly gave him a surfeit of pride. He marched back and forth, preening like such a buffoon that they all burst out laughing. They surrounded him to embrace him, they squeezed him, they spun him around like a doll—he was a wild success. He good-naturedly let them do it. But when he reached the table he said, "Careful, careful! You're rumpling my clothes. Don't press my bride so close, please, and give me some room, gentlemen, friends, so we can make the contract official."

Griveau was still seated at the table. He held his pen ready at the top of the contract. "Your last names, please, first names, title, date of birth..."

The hunchback gave his chair a little kick, and the notary cum scribe cum file clerk looked up.

"Have you signed yet?" asked the hunchback.

"Of course," said Griveau.

"Then go in peace, my good man," said Aesop as he pushed him aside. Then he sat down solemnly in the notary's place, and the company all laughed. From now on, everything the hunchback did was automatically hilarious.

But Navailles wondered, "Why the devil does he want to write in his own name?"

Peyrolles was whispering to Gonzague, who shrugged. Peyrolles was worried by what he saw going on, and Gonzague mocked him and called him a nervous Nelly.

"You'll see!" said the hunchback in answer to Navailles. And then with his dry little cackle he added, "You'll be amazed. You'll see, you'll see. Meanwhile have a drink."

They took his advice and recharged their glasses. He began filling in the blanks with a large steady hand. "Damn this sword!" he said, trying to shift it to a less awkward position. Another burst of laughter. He was getting more and more tangled up in his battle gear. The big sword seemed to affect him like an instrument of torture.

"He's going to sign!" cried some.

"He's not going to sign!" cried others.

Losing his patience, the hunchback drew the sword from its sheath and set the naked blade next to him on the table. More laughter.

Cocardasse squeezed Passepoil's arm. "God's blood!" he muttered, "the bow is raised!"

"Get ready for the violins!"

The clock was about to strike four.

"Sign, mademoiselle," said the hunchback, holding out the pen to Aurore. She hesitated; he looked at her. "Sign your real name, since you know it," he murmured.

Aurore bent over the paper and signed. Doña Cruz, leaning over her shoulder, gave a start of surprise.

"Is it done? Is it done?" asked the onlookers.

Quieting them with a gesture, the hunchback took the pen in turn and signed. "It's done," he said. "Come see: it'll amaze you!"

They all rushed forward. The hunchback had dropped the pen and carelessly picked up the sword.

"Look out!" murmured Cocardasse.

"It's time!" answered Passepoil stoutly.

Gonzague and Peyrolles reached the table first. When they read the heading of the contract they recoiled three steps.

"What is it?" cried the company behind them. "What's his name? What's his name?"

The hunchback had promised to amaze them all. He kept his word. At that moment his twisted legs straightened out, his torso grew, and the sword stood squarely in his hand.

"Crooked ace!" muttered Cocardasse. "The rascal did all kinds of contortionist tricks at the Fountain Court when he was little!"

As he rose the hunchback threw back his hair, and atop that straight, robust, elegant body a handsome, noble face shone forth. "Come read the name!" he said, casting a sparkling eye around the stunned crowd. As all eyes followed the movement of his sword, with its tip he pricked the signature.

The room was filled with an uproar consisting of one name: "Lagardère! Lagardère!"

"Lagardère," he said. "Lagardère, who never misses an appointment he's made!"

In that first stunned moment, when they were thrown into confusion, he might have been able to break through the ranks of his enemies. But he didn't move. With one hand he pressed Aurore trembling against his chest. With the other he held his sword high. Cocardasse and Passepoil stood behind him, swords drawn. Gonzague drew in turn, and all his followers did the same. They were at least ten to one. Doña Cruz tried to thrown herself between the two sides, but Peyrolles grabbed her around the waist and pulled her away.

"This man must not leave here, gentlemen!" said Gonzague, his lips pale and his teeth clenched. "Attack!"

Navailles, Nocé, Choisy, Gironne, and the other noblemen charged impetuously.

Lagardère hadn't even put the table between him and his enemies. Without letting go of Aurore's hand, he covered her and put himself en garde. Cocardasse and Passepoil flanked him to right and left.

"Let's do it, sweetheart!" said Cocardasse. "We've been fasting for more than six months! Let's do it! Thunder and lightning!"

"Here I am!" cried Lagardère with his first lunge.

A few seconds later Gonzague's men drew back, leaving Gironne and Albret lying on the floor in a pool of blood. Lagardère and his two bravos, unharmed, still as statues, waited for the second wave.

"Monsieur de Gonzague," said Lagardère, "you tried to stage a parody of a wedding. But the marriage is official—it even has your signature."

"Attack! Attack!" cried the prince, frothing at the mouth in his fury. This time he led his men forward.

The clock struck five. There was a great noise outside, and loud knocking on the exterior doors, and a voice cried, "In the name of the king!"

What a strange scene the night's festivities had left behind in that parlor: the table was covered with food and half-empty bottles; overturned glasses lay scattered here and there, mixing spilled wine with the splashed blood of battle; at the far end, next to the lounge where the wedding gift basket had been kept—and which now sheltered the notary Griveau, more dead than alive—the group consisting of Lagardère, Aurore, and the two masters of arms stood silent and still; in the middle of the room Gonzague and his men, brought up short by that cry—"In the name of the king!"—stared at the doors in horror; in every corner hid the ladies, mad with fear; between the groups lay two bodies in a dark red puddle.

Whoever was knocking at Gonzague's door at this hour of the night no doubt anticipated a slow response. It was the Royal Guards and the officers from the Châtelet we met before, first in the courtyard of the Villa Lamoignon and then in the Saint Magloire cemetery. They'd come prepared. When they'd knocked three times, they pried the doors off their hinges and threw them aside. The tramp of marching soldiers reached the parlor.

Gonzague felt cold to his very marrow. Was this the law coming for him? "Gentlemen," he said as he sheathed his sword, "there's no resisting the king's men." But then he added very quietly, "For now."

Captain Baudon de Boisguiller of the Royal Guard appeared in the doorway. "Gentlemen, in the name of the king!" He bowed coldly to Gonzague, then stood aside to let his soldiers come into the parlor, followed by the officers from the Châtelet.

"What's the meaning of this, sir?" asked Gonzague.

Boisguiller looked at the two bodies on the floor, then at Lagardère and his two bravos, all three of them still sword in hand. "Good God!" he murmured. "They did say he was a mighty soldier!" Turning to Gonzague he said, "Prince, I'm here tonight on your wife the princess's orders."

"So it's the princess my wife who..." began Gonzague furiously.

He didn't finish. Nevers's widow appeared on the threshold, dressed in her usual mourning. At the sight of the ladies from the Opéra, and the predictable paintings on the walls, and all the mingled debris of food and debauchery and battle, the princess dropped her veil over her face. "I didn't come for you, sir," she said to her husband. Then she approached Lagardère. "Monsieur de Lagardère, your twenty-four hours are up. Your judges have gathered. Surrender your sword."

"And this woman is my mother!" stammered Aurore, hiding her face in her hands.

"Gentlemen," said the princess, turning to the soldiers. "Do your duty."

Lagardère dropped his sword at Boisguiller's feet. Gonzague and his people hadn't made a move or uttered a sound. Though Boisguiller pointed to the door, Lagardère, still leading Aurore by the hand, approached the princess. "Madame, I was sacrificing my life to protect your daughter."

"My daughter!" echoed the princess, her voice shaking.

"He's lying!" said Gonzague.

Lagardère ignored the insult. "I asked for twenty-four hours to bring Mademoiselle de Nevers back to you," he said slowly, his proud handsome face lifted to dominate courtiers and soldiers alike. "The twenty-fourth hour has struck. Here is Mademoiselle de Nevers."

The cold hands of mother and child met. The princess opened her arms. Aurore fell into them, weeping. A tear came to Lagardère's eye. "Protect her, Madame," he said, mastering his sorrow with an effort. "Love her. She has no one now but you!"

Aurore tore herself from her mother's arms to run to him. He gently pushed her away. "Farewell, Aurore. Our wedding will have no morning after. Keep that contract, which makes you my wife in the eyes of men, just as you've been since yesterday in the eyes of God. The princess will forgive you this unsuitable match, made with a dead man."

One last time Lagardère kissed Aurore's hand. Then, after bowing to the princess, he headed to the door, saying, "Lead me to my judges!"

PART SIX: THE TESTIMONY OF THE DEAD

I. The Regent's Bedroom

It was eight o'clock in the morning. The Marquis of Cossé, the Duke of Brissac, the poet La Fare, and three ladies—among whom old Master Le Bréant, doorkeeper at the Laughter Court, thought he'd recognized the Duchess of Berry—had just left the Palais-Royal by the little door we've mentioned several times. The Regent was alone in his bedroom with Father Dubois and, in the presence of the future cardinal, he was getting ready for bed. They'd had supper at the Palais-Royal, just like at the Prince of Gonzague's; that was the fashion. But the supper at the Palais-Royal had ended on a happier note.

Serious, worthy writers in our own times have tried, under various pretexts, to rehabilitate the reputation of Father Dubois: first, they say, because the pope made him a cardinal—but the pope didn't always get to choose the cardinals he made; second, they say, because the eloquent, virtuous Massillon was a friend of his—but that would hold more weight if it could be proved that virtuous men never have a weakness for rascals, whereas as long as there's been history, history has delighted in proving the opposite. Anyway, if in fact Father Dubois was a little saint, then God owes him a special place in heaven—because never has a man been martyred by such copious slander.

Drinking made the Regent sleepy. He was asleep on his feet this morning; while his valet took care of him, Father Dubois, half drunk—or apparently so, because we won't swear to anything—sang the praises of English ways. The Regent was fond of the English, but he was barely listening, and instead urging his valet to hurry up.

"Go to bed, Dubois," he said to the future cardinal. "You're wearing out my ears."

"I'll go to bed later. But do you know the difference between your Mississippi and the Ganges? Between your fleets and their flotillas? Between your log cabins in Louisiana and their mansions in Bengal? Do you realize your Indies are a lie, and they've got the real land of the Arabian Nights, the source of inexhaustible treasures, the country of perfumes, its sea floor paved with pearls, its mountains studded with diamonds?"

"Dubois, esteemed tutor, you're drunk. Go to bed."

The priest laughed. "No doubt Your Royal Highness is stone cold sober? I won't say another word: study the English, and tighten your bonds with them."

"God's life!" cried the Regent. "You've more than earned the commission Lord Stair pays you so dependably. Go to bed, Father."

Muttering, Dubois picked up his hat and headed to the door. But it opened before he got there, and a servant announced Monsieur de Machault.

"I'll see the Chief of Police at noon," said the Regent grumpily. "These people are toying with my health; they'll be the death of me."

The servant insisted, "Monsieur de Machault has important news..."

"I've already heard it. He's here to tell me Cellamare is hatching plots, King Philip of Spain is a wicked man, Alberoni would like to be pope, Madame du Maine would like to be regent. At noon, or better yet at one! I don't feel well."

The servant left. Dubois came back to the middle of the room. "If you had the support of England, you could dismiss all those petty second-rate conspiracies."

"I swear to God, rascal! Will you get out of here?"

Dubois didn't seem to mind. Again he headed to the door, and again it opened before he got there.

"Secretary of State Le Blanc," announced the servant.

"To hell with him!" The Regent stepped barefoot onto a stool to climb into bed.

The servant closed the door halfway, but then put his mouth to the opening and added, "The Secretary of State has important news."

"They all have important news." The Regent laid his spinning head on a pillow trimmed with Mechlin lace. "They like to pretend to be afraid of Alberoni or the du Maines. They think it makes them important, but it just makes them a nuisance, that's all. I'll see Monsieur Le Blanc, along with Monsieur de Machault, at one. No, better make it two. I feel like I could sleep soundly till then."

The servant left. The Regent closed his eyes. "Is that priest still here?" he asked his valet.

"I'm going, I'm going," said Dubois.

"No, come here, Father. You can put me to sleep. Isn't it odd that I can't get a minute's peace to rest? Not a minute! They show up as soon as I go to bed. You can see I'm dying in harness, can't you, Father? But that doesn't bother them."

"Would His Royal Highness like me to read to him?"

"No, on second thought, scram. Make my apologies to those gentlemen. I spent all night working. I've got a migraine, as usual, from writing by lamplight." He sighed heavily. "It's all killing me, literally, and the king is going to make me go to his levee, and Monsieur de Fleury will purse his lips like a dowager countess. But even with the best will in the world, you can't do everything. God's blood! Governing France is no job for an idler!"

His head burrowed deeper into his pillow. His breathing grew steady and heavy. He was asleep. The priest exchanged a glance with the valet, and they both began laughing. When the Regent was in a good mood, he called Father Dubois a rascal. The budding cardinal had much of the nature of a lackey.

When Dubois left, he found Machault and Le Blanc still in the anteroom. "His Royal Highness will see you at three," said the priest. "But if you want my advice, wait till four. We had supper very late, and His Royal Highness is a little tired."

Dubois's entrance had interrupted a conversation between the Chief of Police and the Secretary of State. "That rascal!" said Machault when Dubois was gone. "He doesn't even know how to cover for his master's weaknesses."

"That's exactly how His Royal Highness likes his rascals," said Le Blanc. "But do you know the facts about that business at the Prince of Gonzague's pleasure house?"

"I know what my officers reported to me. Two men dead: Gironne's youngest son, and the financier Albret. Three men arrested: a veteran of the light cavalry named Lagardère, and two cutthroats whose names don't matter. The princess barging into her husband's hideaway by force and in the name of the king. Two girls—anyway the whole thing is a mystery, an enigma worthy of the Sphinx."

"One of those girls must be Nevers's heiress."

"Who knows. One was produced by Gonzague, the other by that Lagardère."

"Does the Regent know what happened?" asked Le Blanc.

"You heard the priest. The Regent was having supper till eight this morning."

"When the news does reach him, Gonzague had better look out."

Machault shrugged and said again, "Who knows? Either Gonzague keeps the Regent's favor, or he loses it."

"But His Royal Highness showed no mercy in that business of Count Horn."

"That was a matter of the Bank's reputation," said Machault. "The Rue Quincampoix was calling for someone to be made an example of."

"But here as well, powerful interests are in play: Nevers's widow..."

"No doubt, but Gonzague's been the Regent's friend for twenty-five years."

"The Burning Court had to be summoned last night," said Le Blanc.

"For that Lagardère, and at the request of the Princess of Gonzague."

"You think His Royal Highness is determined to cover up for the prince?"

Machault cut him off. "Personally, I'm determined to think nothing at all until I know whether or not Gonzague has lost favor. That's the key."

As he was finishing, the door to the antechamber opened. The Prince of Gonzague entered alone and without attendants. The three gentlemen kissed each others' hands profusely.

"Isn't it morning yet at His Royal Highness's?" asked Gonzague.

"We've been refused entry," said Machault and Le Blanc together.

"In that case, I'm sure it's closed to everyone," said Gonzague ingratiatingly.

"Bréon!" called the Chief of Police to a servant. "Go announce the Prince of Gonzague to His Royal Highness."

Gonzague gave Machault a suspicious look—a look both officials noticed. "Did he leave particular instructions on my behalf?" There was an anxious note to the question.

The Chief of Police and the Secretary of State bowed and smiled. Machault answered, "It's just that His Royal Highness, whose door is closed to his ministers, would of course get pleasure and relaxation from the company of his best friend."

The servant Bréon returned and said in a loud voice, "His Royal Highness is willing to receive the Prince of Gonzague."

All three lords reacted with surprise—equal in degree, but for quite different reasons. Gonzague, troubled, bowed to the two officials and followed Bréon.

"His Royal Highness'll never change!" grumbled the disappointed Le Blanc. "Pleasure before business."

Machault smiled mockingly. "A single piece of evidence can point to quite different conclusions."

"At least you can't deny that Gonzague's favor..."

"Teeters on the brink of collapse!"

Le Blanc looked at him in surprise.

Machault went on, "Unless his favor has reached its apogee."

"Explain yourself, sir. You're too subtle for me."

"Yesterday," said Machault simply, "the Regent and Gonzague were good friends, and Gonzague sat here in the antechamber with us for over an hour."

"And from that you deduce..."

"God forbid I deduce anything! But while the Duke of Orléans has been Regent, the Burning Court has done nothing but bookkeeping. It put down its sword and picked up slate and chalk. But now it's been served up some red meat—this Lagardère. That's a first step. I'll see you later, sir. I'll be back at three."

In the corridor leading from the antechamber to the Regent's bedroom, Gonzague had only a moment to think. He used the time well. The encounter with Machault and Le Blanc had entirely changed his strategy; they'd said nothing, and yet when he left them Gonzague knew a shadow hung over his fortunes.

He might have feared a worse reception: the Regent held out his hand, and Gonzague—instead of bringing it to his lips as some courtiers did—clasped it in both of his and sat beside the bed without asking permission. The Regent still had his head on his pillow and his eyes half closed, but Gonzague could tell he was being observed carefully.

"Well, Philippe," said the Regent in a tone of affectionate teasing, "now everything's come out."

Gonzague's heart pounded, but he gave no sign of it.

"You were unhappy, and we knew nothing about it!" went on the Regent. "That shows at least a lack of trust."

"It was a lack of courage, my lord," said Gonzague quietly.

"I understand. Nobody likes to expose his family wounds to the open air. The princess suffers from ulcers, so to speak."

"Your lordship must be familiar with the power of slander."

The Regent propped himself on one elbow and looked his oldest friend in the eye. A cloud crossed his prematurely lined brow. "I've had my honor slandered, my probity slandered, my love for my family slandered—everything that's precious to a man, slandered. But I can't figure out why you, Philippe, choose to remind me of something my friends try to help me forget."

Gonzague lowered his head. "My lord, I beg you to forgive me. Misery is selfish: I thought only of myself, not of Your Royal Highness." Shaking his head, he went on so quietly the Regent could barely hear him. "You and I, my lord, are used to making light of matters of the heart. I've been guilty of it, and I've got no right to complain. But there are some feelings..."

"All right, all right, Philippe! You're in love with your wife. She's a beautiful and noble woman. We've made fun of that a few times, it's true, when we're drunk, but we've also made fun of God..."

"We were wrong, my lord," interrupted Gonzague in turn, in a different voice. "God will have his vengeance."

"What a way to react! Is there something you want to tell me?"

"Lots, my lord. Two men were killed at my pleasure house last night."

"The Chevalier de Lagardère, I bet!" cried the Regent, sitting up suddenly, no longer sleepy. He frowned at Gonzague. "If you did that, Philippe, I swear, you did wrong! You're just confirming people's suspicions..."

The prince drew himself up to his full height. His handsome face shone with pride. "Suspicions!" he echoed, as if he couldn't contain his impulsive scorn. Then he added earnestly, "So your lordship has had suspicions against me?"

"Well, yes," said the Regent after a short silence. "I've had suspicions. They weaken when you're here, because you've got the look of an honest man. Let your words quell them completely: I'm listening."

"Will your lordship do me the favor of telling me what your suspicions have been?"

"There are old ones, and new ones."

"The old ones first, if your lordship will deign to share them."

"Nevers's widow was rich, you were poor. Nevers was our brother..."

"And so I shouldn't have married Nevers's widow?"

The Regent rested his head on his knees and didn't answer.

Gonzague lowered his eyes. "My lord, as I've already said, we've been too used to poking fun, and matters of the heart ring false between us."

"What are you trying to say? Explain yourself."

"I'm trying to say, if there's one action in my life that does me honor, it's that. Our beloved Nevers died in my arms, as you know; I told you that. You also know I was at Caylus Castle to overcome the blind stubbornness of the old marquis, who was bitterly against our Philippe for having taken his daughter from him. The Burning Court, which I'll come back to later, already heard my testimony this morning."

"Ah! Tell me, what verdict did the Burning Court render? So Lagardère wasn't killed at your place?"

"If your lordship would let me go on..."

"Go on, go on. I want the truth, I warn you, nothing but the truth!"

Gonzague bowed coldly. "I'm addressing Your Royal Highness, no longer as a friend, but as my judge. Lagardère wasn't killed at my pleasure house last night. Instead it was Lagardère who killed the financier Albret and Gironne's youngest son."

"Ah!" said the Regent a second time. "And how did Lagardère come to be at your house?"

"I think the princess could tell you that."

"Be careful! She's a saint."

"One who hates her husband, my lord!" said Gonzague with feeling. "I have no faith in the saints Your Royal Highness canonizes."

He'd scored a point: the Regent smiled instead of getting angry. "Come now, Philippe, maybe I've been a little hard on you—but you've got to realize, there's scandal. You're a nobleman of high rank. Scandals on high make noise, enough noise to shake the throne. And I'm sitting near enough to the throne to feel it. Let's get back on track. You claim your marriage to Aurore de Caylus was a good deed; prove it."

With well-feigned warmth Gonzague replied, "Is it a good deed to carry out the last wish of a dying man?"

The Regent stared at him openmouthed. There was a long silence. Then he murmured, "I believe you—you wouldn't dare lie to me about that."

"The way you're treating me, my lord, this interview will have to be the last between us. People of my family aren't in the habit of being spoken to like this, even by princes of the blood. When I've washed away the stain of the accusations against me, I'll say farewell forever to the friend of my youth, who rebuffed me in my misery. You believe me; good, that's enough for me."

"Philippe," murmured the Regent, his voice betraying deep emotion, "just answer the accusations, and I swear, you'll see I still love you!"

"So, I'm accused?" The Regent made no answer. Gonzague went on with the dignified calm he was so good at faking. "If your lordship will interrogate me, I'll answer."

The Regent thought for a moment before speaking. "You witnessed the bloody drama in the moat at Caylus?"

"Yes, my lord. I risked my life to fight for my friend and yours. It was my duty."

"It was your duty. And you heard his dying breath?"

"With his last words, yes, my lord."

"I want to know what he said to you."

"I had no intention of withholding it from Your Royal Highness. Our poor friend said to me, and I repeat it word for word, 'Be a husband to my wife, so you can be a father to my daughter.'" Gonzague's voice was steady as he delivered this unholy lie.

The Regent was lost in thought. His intelligent, pensive face looked tired, but all signs of drunkenness had vanished. "You did well to carry out a dying man's wish. It was your duty. But why did you let almost twenty years go by and never mention it?"

Gonzague didn't hesitate. "I love my wife, as I've already told your lordship."

"And why would that love seal your lips?"

Gonzague lowered his eyes and managed to blush. "Speaking out would've amounted to accusing my wife's father," he murmured.

"Ah! So the murderer was the Marquis of Caylus?"

Gonzague bowed his head and sighed heavily.

The Regent fixed a sharp, eager eye on him. "If the Marquis of Caylus was the murderer, what do you have against Lagardère?"

"What we have, in Italy, against a bravo whose stiletto was hired to commit a murder."

"Monsieur de Caylus had hired Lagardère's blade?"

"Yes, my lord. But that menial assignment lasted only a day. On his own initiative, Lagardère traded it for the active role he's played persistently for eighteen years. For his own motives, Lagardère stole Aurore de Caylus's daughter and the papers proving her birth."

"Then what were you claiming yesterday at the family council?"

Gonzague deliberately gave his smile a bitter edge. "My lord, I thank God for allowing this interrogation. I considered these questions beneath me, and that was a mistake. You can only beat an enemy who shows himself; you can only dismiss an accusation that's been uttered. The enemy shows himself, the accusation is uttered—all the better! You've already made me throw the light of truth on the dark places my conjugal devotion preferred to leave in shadow; now you're going to make me expose to you the virtuous side of my life—the noble, Christian, humbly devout side. I've rendered good for evil, my lord, patiently,

393

unwaveringly, for almost twenty years. I've labored night and day in silence, at work that often put my life in danger; I've invested my immense fortune; I've muffled the call of my own ambitions; I've sacrificed all that remained of my strength and my youth; I've poured out my own blood..."

The Regent gestured impatiently.

Gonzague went on, "You think I'm boasting, don't you? Listen to my story, my lord, you who were my friend, my brother, as you were friend and brother to Nevers. Listen to me carefully, impartially. I've chosen you as arbiter, not between the princess and me—God forbid! Against her I seek no judgment—nor between me and that rogue Lagardère! I rate myself too highly to put myself in the scales with him. But between you and me, my lord, between the two survivors of the three Philippes: between you, Duke of Orléans, Regent of France—with quasi-royal power enough to avenge the father and protect the child—and me, Philippe de Gonzague, a mere gentleman, with no means to carry out that sacred twofold mission besides my heart and my sword! I make you my arbiter, and when I'm done I'll ask you, Philippe d'Orléans, whether it's you or Philippe de Gonzague whom Philippe de Nevers applauds and smiles down on from up there at the feet of God!"

II. The Speech for the Defense

The attack was bold, the thrust well aimed: it struck home. The Regent lowered his eyes under Gonzague's stern look. The latter, long used to verbal jousting, had prepared this moment in advance; the tale he was about to tell wasn't improvised.

"Would you dare claim that I fell short in what I owed to friendship?" murmured the Regent.

"No, my lord. But, forced as I am to defend myself, I'm merely going to contrast my behavior with yours. We're alone, and Your Royal Highness will have no cause to blush."

The Regent had regained his composure. "We've known each other a long time, prince. You're taking things pretty far. Be careful!"

Gonzague looked into his eyes. "Are you going to hold against me the love I showed our friend after his death?"

"If you've been wronged, you'll have justice. Speak."

Gonzague had hoped he'd be angrier: the Regent's calm cost him an oratorical flourish he'd been counting on. But even so he continued, "To my friend, to that Philippe d'Orléans who loved me yesterday and whom I cherished, I would've told my story a different way. But as Your Royal Highness and I now stand, a clear, succinct summary will do. The first thing I have to tell you is, this Lagardère is not just a cutthroat of the most dangerous sort, a kind of hero to his peers, but also a cunning, clever man, able to carry out an ambitious plan over many years, and stopping at nothing to reach his goal.

"I don't think he meant at first to marry Nevers's heiress. For that he would've had to wait fifteen or sixteen years after taking her across the border— too long. So, clearly his first plan was to hold her for an enormous ransom; he knew Nevers and Caylus were rich. Having pursued him relentlessly since the night of the crime, I know every single thing he's done: for him, possession of the child simply raised hopes of a great fortune. My own efforts made him change tack; he must've realized pretty quickly, from the way I was hunting him, that any kind of sordid deal was out of the question. I crossed the border soon after he did, and caught up with him near the small town of Benasque, in Navarre. Though there were lots of us, he managed to get away. He changed his name, and fled deeper into Spain.

"I won't tell you in detail about all our various encounters. His strength, his courage, his skill, are astonishing. Besides the wound he gave me in the moat at Caylus, while I was defending our poor friend,"—and here Gonzague drew off his glove to reveal the scar made by Lagardère's sword—"besides this wound, I carry the mark of his hand in several places. There isn't a fencing master who could stand up to him. I'd hired an entire army, because I wanted to take him alive, so he could attest to the identity of my precious young ward. My army included the most famous swordsmen in Europe! Captain Lorrain, Jugan, Staupitz, Pinto, Pépé El Matador, Saldaña, Faenza—they're all dead."

The Regent stirred.

"They're all dead," repeated Gonzague, "dead by his hand!"

"Are you aware," murmured the Regent, "that he too claims to have been charged with the mission of protecting Nevers's child and avenging our poor friend?"

"I am aware, because, as I've said, he's a bold and clever impostor. I hope Your Royal Highness, weighing competing claims, will have the presence of mind to take the source of each into account."

"And so I will," said the Regent slowly. "Go on."

"Years went by. Note that this Lagardère never tried to get either a letter or a message to Nevers's widow. Faenza, a capable man, whom I'd sent to Madrid to keep an eye on the kidnapper, came back with an odd report that I'll draw Your Royal Highness's attention to: he said Lagardère, who was going by Don Luis in Madrid, had traded his prisoner for a girl some gypsies from Léon sold him. Lagardère was afraid of me, he could tell I was on his trail, and he wanted to trick me. From that point on he raised the gypsy girl, while Nevers's real daughter lived with the gypsies in their camp.

"I didn't believe Faenza. That prompted my first visit to Madrid. I found the gypsies in the canyons around Cerro del Baladron, and I was convinced Faenza hadn't lied to me. I saw the girl, whose memories were still fresh. We made plans to seize her and take her back to France—she was delighted at the thought of seeing her mother again. On the night set for the abduction, to allay suspicion my men and I ate dinner with the chief in his tent. We'd been betrayed: those unbelievers have strange powers. In the middle of dinner our eyesight went blurry and we all fell asleep. When we woke it was morning, and we found ourselves stretched out on the grass in the Baladron canyon. The tents were gone, the campfires had burned down to coals, and the Léon gypsies had vanished."

Gonzague had arranged his story so it always ran right alongside the truth, so dates and locations and characters matched. His lie was pinned to the truth—in such a way that if Lagardère or Aurore were questioned their answers would be bound to line up with his version somewhere. According to him, both Lagardère and Aurore were impostors, and therefore both had reason to twist the facts.

The Regent still listened, impassive and attentive.

"That was a great opportunity missed, my lord," went on Gonzague with the sound of pure sincerity that made him so eloquent. "If we'd succeeded, what past tears and present miseries would've been spared! I say nothing of the future, which is in God's hands. I went back to Madrid: no trace of the gypsies. Lagardère had gone away, leaving the gypsy girl he'd substituted for Mademoiselle de Nevers to be raised at the Convent of the Incarnation.

"My lord, you're trying to suppress any reaction to what I'm telling you. You don't trust yourself to speak out the way you're usually happy to do. I'm trying to keep it short and simple. But I can't help interrupting my story to tell you your mistrust and your bias won't make any difference: the truth will prevail. From the moment you agreed to hear me out, the question was settled— I've got enough and more than enough to persuade you.

"Before I go on with the story, I have to make an important observation. At first, Lagardère switched the children to baffle my pursuit; that's clear. He still meant to take back Nevers's heiress at a certain point, to make use of her to further his designs. But then his plans changed. His about-face can be explained in a word: he fell in love with the gypsy girl. From then on, the real Nevers girl was doomed. It was no longer a matter of ransom. The horizon expanded. The bold rogue now dreamt of placing his mistress on the ducal seat and marrying Nevers's heiress."

The Regent stirred uneasily under his covers. The plausibility of any claim varies according to the morals and character of the listener. Philippe d'Orléans might not have bought Gonzague's storybook devotion or his labors of Hercules to fulfill his promise to a dying man, but this new scheme of Lagardère's struck him between the eyes and dazzled him. The Regent's circle of acquaintance and his own temperament made him resistant to tragic themes—but romantic comedy came naturally to him. He was struck: struck enough not to notice how skillfully Gonzague had woven together the premises of his hypothetical argument, struck enough not to see that switching the children was itself one of the storybook plot points he'd dismissed. For him, suddenly the whole story was tinged with a shade of truth. The adventurer Lagardère's ambition was such a logical outcome of the situation that it coated everything else with plausibility.

Gonzague was well aware of the effect he'd produced, but he was clever enough not to take advantage of it right away. In the last half hour he'd become convinced that the Regent knew, minute by minute, all that had happened in the past two days, and as a result Gonzague was pivoting his attack. The Regent was rumored to have at his disposal another police force, one not under Monsieur de Machault's command. Gonzague had often thought there might be a couple of informers even among his own herd of toadies. (The word "mouche" for informer was fashionable under the Regency; its modern form, "mouchard," is no longer acceptable in polite usage.)

Simply out of prudence, Gonzague was betting on the worst case: he was playing under the assumption that the Regent had already seen every card in his hand. "Believe me, my lord, I don't attach more importance to that point than it deserves: given Lagardère's intelligence and boldness, it had to turn out that way, and it did. I had proof of that even before Lagardère reached Paris; since then, the abundance of new evidence has made the older proofs redundant. The Princess of Gonzague—whom no one would accuse of giving me much support—can tell Your Royal Highness all about it.

"But let's get back to the facts. Lagardère was away for two years, by the end of which the gypsy girl, educated by the Sisters of the Incarnation, was transformed. It's when he came back and saw her that Lagardère must have conceived the plan we're talking about. Things changed: the alleged Aurore de Nevers now had a house, a maid, a page, all to keep up appearances. Oddly, the real Nevers girl and her replacement knew each other and were friends. It's hard to believe Lagardère's mistress was in good faith, but it's not impossible: he's clever enough to have kept that pretty child completely in the dark. What's certainly true is that he objected to receiving the real Nevers girl at his house in Madrid, and forbade his mistress to see her—because of her loose morals."

Here Gonzague laughed bitterly. "At the family council the princess said, 'If my daughter had forgotten her proud blood, even for a moment, I'd veil my face and say, nothing of Nevers now remains alive!' Those were her very words. Alas, my lord, the poor child thought I was making fun of her poverty when I spoke to her for the first time about her lineage. But a mother can't deny the valid rights of her child based on superficial scruples; you'd be naive to think otherwise, in my opinion—and if you don't agree with me, the law will set you straight. Did Aurore de Nevers ask to be born under a fraudulent paternity? Her mother committed the original fault. The mother can complain about the past; that's all. The child has her rights, and the dead Nevers has one last living heir— Two! I meant to say two!" Gonzague hastened to recover his slip. "Your face changed, my lord! Allow me to say that the warmth of your heart shows on your face. And let me ask you, what slandering voice could make you forget thirty years of devoted friendship in a single day?"

The Regent meant to sound stern, but his voice gave away his doubts and his emotion. "Prince, I can only repeat my own words: just answer the accusations, and you'll see I'm your friend."

"But what am I accused of?" cried Gonzague, feigning an angry outburst. "A crime committed twenty years ago? A crime committed yesterday? Has Philippe d'Orléans ever believed, for an hour, a minute, a second—I have to know, I have to!—have you ever believed, my lord, that this sword..."

"If I'd ever believed it..." murmured the Regent, frowning and reddening.

Gonzague seized his hand and pressed it to his own heart. "Thank you!" he said with tears in his eyes. "You hear that, Philippe! I'm reduced to thanking you for not adding your voice to the others accusing me of infamy!" He drew himself up, as if he were ashamed of his own emotions. "Forgive me, my lord, I won't forget myself again. I know what I'm accused of, or at least I can guess. My struggle against that Lagardère has led me into actions the law disapproves; if the law attacks me, I'll defend myself. Besides, there's the fact of Mademoiselle de Nevers being found in a house of pleasure.

"I don't expect that what I have left to say will demand much more of Your Royal Highness's attention. Your lordship no doubt remembers being surprised by my request to be made ambassador to Madrid. Till then I'd carefully steered clear of politics. After what we've been discussing, you can't be surprised anymore: I wanted to return to Spain with an official title that would put the Madrid police at my disposal. Within a few days I located the dear child who's now the last hope of a great family. Lagardère had completely abandoned her—what use did he have for her? Aurore de Nevers was earning a living as a dancer on the streets. My intention was to seize, in one stroke, both of the girls as well as the adventurer. The adventurer and his mistress got away; I brought back Mademoiselle de Nevers."

"The one you claim to be Mademoiselle de Nevers," corrected the Regent.

"Yes, my lord, the one I claim to be Mademoiselle de Nevers."

"That's not good enough."

"Allow me to think it is, since your lordship himself has ruled in my favor. I didn't act lightly. At the risk of repeating myself, I'd say, I've been working at this for almost twenty years! What was required? The presence of both girls and of the impostor. We've got them: all three of them are in Paris..."

"Not by your doing," interrupted the Regent.

"By my doing, my lord, entirely by my doing. When did Your Royal Highness receive your first letter from that Lagardère?"

"Did I say...?" began the Regent haughtily.

"If Your Royal Highness won't answer, I'll answer for you. The first letter from Lagardère, the one asking for a safe-conduct, written from Brussels, reached Paris at the end of August: about a month after Mademoiselle de Nevers was in my hands. Don't treat me worse than an ordinary defendant, my lord— grant me at least the use of evidence. For almost twenty years, Lagardère lay low. You think he didn't need a reason for suddenly wanting to come back to France exactly then? And you think the reason wasn't my capture of the real Nevers girl? If I have to dot every i, could Lagardère have thought anything besides, 'If I let Gonzague move the late duke's heiress into the Villa Lorraine, what hope would I have left? And what use would I have for this pretty girl, who was worth millions yesterday but tomorrow will be a gypsy girl poorer than I am?'"

"One could make the opposite case," objected the Regent.

"That Lagardère, seeing I was about to pass off a fake heiress, wanted to bring forward the real one?"

The Regent nodded.

"Well, my lord, either way, it would still prove Lagardère's return was my doing. That's all I ask. In fact, here's what I was thinking: Lagardère will follow me no matter what. He'll fall into the hands of the law, and the mystery will be solved. I'm not the one, my lord, who gave Lagardère the means to enter France and gave him protection from the law."

"Did you know Lagardère was in Paris when you asked for my permission to summon a family tribunal?"

"Yes, my lord," replied Gonzague without hesitating.

"Why didn't you warn me?"

"By moral principle and under God, I claim to have done no wrong. Before the law, which is to say before you, my lord, if you wish to embody the law, my hopes fade. Under the pitiless letter of the law, an unfair judge could condemn me. I should've asked for your advice—and for your help too. That may seem obvious, but do I need to explain to you why I hesitated? I hoped to end the unfortunate antagonism there's always been between the princess and me: by my good deeds I hoped to overcome her violent aversion to me—which is unmotivated, I swear on my honor! I hoped to bring about peace before anyone alive even suspected there'd been war. That's a valid reason; surely, my lord, I who know better than anyone the sensitive, tender heart hidden under your affectation of skepticism, surely I can offer a reason like that to you.

"But there was another reason, a childish one maybe—if taking pride in a duty accomplished can be considered childish. I'd begun this great and sacred task alone; for half my life I'd pursued it alone; at the hour of victory I was reluctant to let anyone, even you, my lord, share that victory with me.

"At the family council I understood from the princess's attitude that she'd been warned against me. Lagardère didn't wait for my attack—he fired first. My lord, there's no shame in admitting it: trickery isn't my strong suit. Lagardère outplayed me and won. I think you already know he concealed himself among us under a bold disguise." Gonzague went on scornfully, "Maybe his trick succeeded from its sheer crudeness. It has to be said, the fellow's old trade had given him uncommon skills."

"I don't known what work he did."

"He was a street acrobat before he was a murderer. Right here outside your windows, in the Fountain Court, do you remember a miserable child who made his living doing contortions, and disarticulating his joints, and even imitating a hunchback?"

"Lagardère!" murmured the Regent as a memory returned. "It was while the late king's brother was still alive. We used to watch him out this window: little Lagardère!"

"I wish to God you'd remembered that two days ago! But going on: as soon as I suspected he was in Paris, I picked up my plan where I'd left off. I tried to seize the two impostors and the documents Lagardère had stolen from Caylus Castle. In spite of all his skill, Lagardère or the hunchback couldn't stop me from carrying out most of my plan: he saved himself, but I got my hands on the girl and the papers."

"Where's the girl?"

"With the poor deceived mother: with Madame de Gonzague."

"And the papers? I'm warning you, this is where you're in real danger, prince."

"Danger? Why, my lord?" Gonzague smiled arrogantly. "I couldn't imagine being—for a quarter of a century!—the companion, the friend, the brother of a man of whom I had such a poor opinion! You think I've already falsified the papers? The envelope itself, sealed with three seals, all three of them unbroken, will answer for my integrity, which you doubt. The papers are in my hands. In exchange for a detailed receipt, I'm ready to deliver them into yours."

"I'll expect them from you this evening."

"I'll be ready this evening—as I am now. But let me finish. After that seizure, Lagardère was beaten. It was that damned disguise that changed everything. I myself brought the enemy into my house. I'm fond of freaks, as you know, and I think it was Your Royal Highness's tastes that rubbed off on me back when we were friends. That hunchback showed up to rent my dog kennel for an outrageous amount. He struck me as an exotic creature. In short, I was hoodwinked—why deny it? That Lagardère is the king of contortionists. Once he was in the sheepfold, the wolf showed his teeth. I was blind to it, and it was one of my trusted servants, Monsieur de Peyrolles, who took it upon himself secretly to warn the Princess of Gonzague."

"Could you prove that?"

"Easily, my lord, with Peyrolles's testimony. But the Royal Guard and the princess arrived too late for my poor friends Albret and Gironne. The wolf had struck."

"So this Lagardère was alone against all of you?"

"There were four of them, my lord, counting my cousin the Marquis of Chaverny."

"Chaverny!" The Regent was astonished.

Gonzague went on lying. "He'd known Lagardère's mistress in Madrid while I was ambassador. I have to tell your lordship, this morning I asked for and got a warrant from Minister d'Argenson for Chaverny's arrest."

"And the other two?"

"The other two have also been arrested. They're just a couple of masters of arms, known to have taken part in the past in Lagardère's debauchery and misdeeds."

"Then the only thing left to explain is your behavior last night in front of your friends."

Gonzague looked up at him with well-feigned surprise. He paused a moment before answering, with a mocking smile, "So the rumors I heard have really been circulating?"

"I have no idea what you heard."

"Bedtime stories, my lord, accusations so wild—but is this really appropriate, considering Your Royal Highness's great wisdom and my own dignity?"

"I wear my wisdom lightly, prince. Put it aside for a moment, along with your dignity. Speak on."

"That's a command, and I'll obey. While I was with Your Royal Highness last night, apparently the carousing at my pleasure house reached extravagant heights. They forced open the door to my private apartment, where I was sheltering the two girls with the intention of entrusting them both to the princess this morning. I don't need to tell your lordship who the instigators of the violence were; my drunken friends took part in it. There was a drinking contest between Chaverny and the so-called hunchback. The trophy was to be the hand of the gypsy girl he's trying to pass off as Mademoiselle de Nevers. When I got back I found Chaverny lying on the floor and the victorious hunchback with his mistress. A marriage contract had been drawn up and was covered with signatures—among which my own had been forged!"

The Regent gave Gonzague a look that seemed intended to penetrate to the bottom of his heart. Gonzague had just fought a desperate battle. When he came into the Regent's bedroom he might have expected his patron and friend to be a little icy with him—but he hadn't counted on this long and awful explanation. Of the lies he'd skillfully woven together, of his towering pile of deceit, three quarters had been improvised. Not only was Gonzague presenting himself as a victim of his own heroic actions, but he was contradicting in advance the word of the only three people who could testify against him: Chaverny, Cocardasse, and Passepoil.

Philippe d'Orléans had loved this man as dearly as he was capable of loving anyone; they'd been intimate friends since childhood. That wasn't necessarily to Gonzague's advantage: all those long years of intimacy might have made the Regent wary of his friend's great skill. And that was in fact the case. Maybe Gonzague's clear and seemingly precise answers would have been enough to persuade him—if they'd come out of another mouth.

Though history rightly condemns him for a great many vices, the Regent did have an innate sense of justice. We can surmise that the sad and solemn memory that overhung this particular case brought his true nobility of character to the fore. Punishment was finally coming to the murderer of Philippe de Nevers—whom Philippe d'Orléans had cherished like a brother. And Nevers's disinherited daughter was finally going to be granted her name, her fortune, and her family. The Regent was tempted to believe Gonzague's words. If he resisted, it was out of virtue—he wanted his conscience clear in this matter. All of his thinking could be summed up in his words at the start of the interview: "Just answer the accusations, and you'll see I love you." If Gonzague answered the accusations, let his enemies beware!

"Philippe," said the Regent hesitantly after a long silence, "as God is my witness I'd be happy to keep a friend. Slander may have wronged you, because lots of people envy you."

"What they envy I owe to your lordship's goodness," murmured Gonzague.

"You're protected against slander by your high rank and by the great intelligence I admire in you. Please answer one last question. What was the meaning of that story about your inheriting from Count Anibal of Canossa?"

Gonzague put his hand on the Regent's arm. "My lord," he said simply and seriously, "my cousin Anibal died while Your Royal Highness was traveling in Italy with me. Please, don't stoop lower than the limit beyond which insults turn into absurdity and deserve nothing but scorn, even if they come out of the mouth of a mighty prince. This morning Peyrolles told me, 'They've sworn to destroy you. They'll talk His Royal Highness into holding you responsible for all the ancient sins of Italy. You'll be another Borgia. Poisoned peaches, flowers whose blossoms have been steeped in fatal *aqua tofana...*'"

Gonzague broke off, then went on, "My lord, if you need a speech for the defense before you can absolve me, go ahead and condemn me, because disgust seals my lips. I'll sum up, and leave you to confront three facts: Lagardère is in the hands of the law; the two girls are with the princess; I've got the pages torn from the chapel registry at Caylus. You're the head of state. With those ingredients in hand, solving the case becomes so easy that I can't help giving way a little to pride when I consider that I'm the one who shone light into the darkness!"

"The truth will indeed come out. I myself will preside at the family tribunal tonight."

Gonzague eagerly clasped both of the Regent's hands in his. "I'd come here precisely to ask you to do that. In the name of the man to whom I've devoted my whole life, I thank you, my lord. Now I have to beg forgiveness for speaking out maybe a little too much to the head of a great state. But no matter what happens, my punishment is this: tonight Philippe d'Orléans and Philippe de Gonzague will see each other for the last time."

Old friendships are robust, and the Regent pulled him close. "It's no loss of face for a prince to make public atonement. If need be, Philippe, I hope you'll be satisfied with the Regent's apology."

Gonzague slowly shook his head. His voice shook. "Some injuries no balm can heal." He stood up suddenly and looked at the clock. The interview had lasted three long hours. "My lord," he said firmly and coldly, "you won't get any sleep this morning. Your Royal Highness's antechamber is full. Out there, they're wondering whether I'll leave here in even greater favor than before, or whether your soldiers will escort me to the Bastille. I'm wondering the same thing. I ask Your Royal Highness for one of two favors, and let the choice be yours: either send me to prison to protect me, or give me some special public sign of your friendship to restore to me, even if just for today, all the credit I've lost. I need it."

The Regent rang the bell and said to the servant who entered, "Send everybody in." Then, at the moment all the summoned courtiers appeared at the door, he pulled Gonzague close and kissed his brow, saying, "Until tonight, Philippe, my friend!"

The courtiers moved aside to make way, and bowed to the ground as the Prince of Gonzague withdrew.

III. Three Floors of Cells

The Burning Courts date back to the mid-1500s, when François II established one in each Appellate Court to try cases of heresy. The sentences of those extraordinary courts were without appeal and could be carried out within twenty-four hours. The best known Burning Court was the committee of inquiry appointed by Louis XIV during the Poisoning Scandal. The name carried over into the Regency, but the duties changed. Several committees of the Appellate Court of Paris, meeting simultaneously, were named Burning Courts, but the mania of the day wasn't heresy or poison but finance, so under the Regency the Burning Courts tried financial crimes. They served as courts of auditors, whose job was to check the accounts and verify the receipts of treasury agents. After the fall of John Law they were even renamed the Audit Courts.

There was, however, another Burning Court, which met at the Châtelet while Le Blanc was renovating the Appellate Courthouse and the Conciergerie prison. That court first sat in 1716, for Longuefort's trial, and rendered a number of famous verdicts—against the paymaster Le Saulnois de Sancerre for counterfeiting the royal seal, to cite just one. In 1717 the court comprised five associate judges and one chief judge. The deputies were the lords Berthelot de Labaumelle, Hardouin, Hacquelin-Desmaisons, Montespel de Graylnac, and Husson-Bordesson, the auditor. The chief judge was the Marquis of Ségré. The court could be summoned by order of the king at a day's notice, or even from one hour to the next, and its members were required not to leave Paris.

The Burning Court had been summoned the night before, at the request of His Royal Highness the Duke of Orléans. The summons announced that the session would begin at four o'clock in the morning, and that the judges would learn the name of the accused from the bill of indictment. At half past four the Chevalier Henri de Lagardère appeared before the Burning Court at the Châtelet and was charged with corruption of a minor and murder. Testimony was heard from the Prince and the Princess of Gonzague, but they contradicted each other so thoroughly that, after sitting for an hour, the court—though it was used to reaching a verdict on the flimsiest of evidence—adjourned to gather more information. Three more witnesses were to be heard: Messrs de Peyrolles, Cocardasse, and Passepoil.

Monsieur de Gonzague met one on one with each of the associate judges and the chief judge. The king's counsel had called for the appearance of the girl who'd been kidnapped, but the court declined: Gonzague had persuaded them that Nevers's daughter was in some form or other under the influence of the accused—an aggravating factor in a trial for kidnapping the heiress of a duke and peer! They'd expected to take Lagardère to the Bastille, where middle-of-the-night executions were carried out. But the postponement meant they had to find him a cell nearer the courtroom, so he could be within reach of the judges.

They put him on the fourth floor of the Tour Neuve, the "new tower," so named because Monsieur de Jaucourt had finished rebuilding it toward the end of Louis XIV's reign. Standing at the northwest corner of the Châtelet fortress, its embrasures overlooking the quay, it was only half the size of the old Magne Tower, which had collapsed in 1670, bringing down a section of the ramparts. It was where they usually put condemned prisoners before sending them to the Bastille. The Tour Neuve, a delicate red-brick structure, contrasted oddly with the dark dungeons around it. A drawbridge on the third floor connected it to the old ramparts, which formed a terrace in front of the great hall of the administrative courts. The dungeons—or really the cells—were neat and tidy, and were tiled, like most bourgeois apartments of that time. Clearly they were meant only for temporary detention, and except for the big locks on the doors, no doubt a holdover from the old tower, nothing suggested a government prison.

When he locked up Lagardère after the trial was suspended, the jailer told him he was being held in solitary. Lagardère offered him twenty or thirty pistoles he had on him, to provide him pen, ink, and paper. The jailer took the thirty pistoles and gave him nothing in exchange, promising only to deposit the money with the court.

Lagardère, now locked in, sat still for a moment, racked by thought. Here he was—captive, paralyzed, powerless—while his enemy had power, wealth, freedom, and the open favor of the head of state. The trial that night, which lasted about two hours, had begun right after the little supper at Gonzague's pleasure house. It was already light when Lagardère reached his cell. He'd served on guard duty at the Châtelet more than once long ago, before he joined the royal light cavalry, and he knew the layout. There should be two cells below his.

He took in his miserable domain at a glance: a butcher block, a pitcher, a loaf of bread, a bale of straw. They'd left him his spurs. He took one off and pricked his arm with the prong of the buckle. That gave him ink. A corner of his handkerchief provided the paper, and a blade of straw served as his pen. With tools like that you write slowly and clumsily, but you can write. Lagardère wrote a few words. Then, again using the prong from the buckle of his spur, he began to work loose one of the tiles of his cell floor.

He was right: there were two cells below his. In the first one the little Marquis of Chaverny, still drunk, slept the sleep of the righteous. In the one below that, Cocardasse Junior and Brother Passepoil, stretched out on the straw, waxed witty and philosophical on the fickleness of fate and the changeability of fortune. Now they had nothing but a chunk of dry bread—they who'd supped with a prince last night! Cocardasse still licked his lips as he recalled the fine wine he'd drunk. As for Passepoil, he had only to close his eyes to see passing before him, as if in a dream, the cute snub nose of Nivelle, the Daughter of the Mississippi; the smoldering eyes of Doña Cruz; Fleury's gleaming hair; or Cydalise's teasing smile. If Passepoil had only known the nature of Mohammed's Paradise, he would have abandoned the faith of his fathers and turned Muslim, led on by lust. And yet he had his good points.

Chaverny too was dreaming, but in a different vein. Sprawled on his straw, his clothes bedraggled, his hair disheveled, he tossed and turned like a demon. "Another round, hunchback," he was saying, "and no cheating! You're just pretending to drink, rascal! I see wine trickling down your collar! God's blood—wasn't Oriol satisfied with one insipid chubby-cheeked face? Now he seems to have two, three, five, seven, like the Lernaean Hydra! Come on, hunchback, let's bring out two more barrels, nice and full! You drink one, you sea sponge, and I'll drink the other! But, my God, get that woman off my chest: she's heavy! Is she my wife? I must be married!" Suddenly he looked unhappy. "It's Doña Cruz, I recognize her. Hide me! I don't want Doña Cruz to see me like this. Take back your fifty thousand écus—I want to marry Doña Cruz." And on he thrashed. Sometimes the nightmare caught him by the throat with a drunkard's foolish blissful laugh.

He couldn't hear the slight sounds coming from above his head—it would have taken a cannon to wake him. But the sounds continued: the ceiling was thin. After a few minutes plaster dust began to rain down. Chaverny felt it in his sleep, and slapped his face a few times, as if to drive away an annoying insect. "Pesky flies!" A chunk of plaster hit him on the cheek. "Hell and damn! Stupid hunchback! You dare throw breadcrumbs at me? I'm happy to drink with you, but don't presume!" A small black hole appeared in the ceiling directly above him, and a chunk of plaster hit him on the forehead. "Are we children, throwing rocks at each other?" he cried angrily. "Hey, Navailles! Grab the hunchback's legs. We're going to dunk him in the pond."

The hole in the ceiling grew larger, and a voice seemed to issue from heaven. "Whoever you are, please answer a companion in misery! Are you in solitary too? Is no one from outside coming to see you?"

Chaverny was still asleep, but more lightly: another half dozen chunks of plaster on his face and he'd wake up. Hearing the voice in his dream and responding to who knows what, he said, "God's death! She's not a girl whose affections you can toy with! She wasn't in on that little performance at the Villa Gonzague, and at the pleasure house my villain of a cousin made her think she was with noble ladies." He went on solemnly and seriously, "I'll swear to her virtue. She'll be the world's most charming marquise!"

"Hey!" came Lagardère's voice overhead. "Didn't you hear me?"

Tired of talking in his sleep, Chaverny snored a little.

"I know there's someone down there!" said the voice overhead. "I see something moving."

Some kind of package came through the hole and struck Chaverny's left cheek. He leaped to his feet, holding his jaw in both hands. "You wretch! You dare slap me?" Then whatever phantom he was seeing vanished. He looked around his cell, stunned. "Hmm," he murmured, rubbing his eyes, "I don't seem to be able to wake up! Obviously I'm still dreaming!"

The voice overhead said, "Did you get the package?"

"All right," said Chaverny, "the hunchback's hiding somewhere. He's playing some kind of practical joke on me. But this room has a hell of a grim feel to it!" He looked straight up and cried as loud as he could, "I see your hole, damned hunchback! I'll get you back for this! Go tell them to open up!"

"I can't hear you," came the voice. "You're too far from the hole. But I see you and I recognize you. Monsieur de Chaverny, though you've spent your life in bad company, I know you're still a gentleman. That's why I saved you from being murdered last night."

Chaverny's eyes widened. "It's not exactly the hunchback's voice," he thought. "But what's all this about murder? And who dares treat me like he's my protector?"

"I'm the Chevalier de Lagardère," said the voice, as if in answer to his thoughts.

"Ah!" said Chaverny in surprise. "Talk about someone who's hard to kill!"

"Do you know where you are?"

Chaverny shook his head vigorously.

"You're in the Châtelet prison, on the third floor of the Tour Neuve."

Chaverny ran to the embrasure that let dim daylight into his cell. His arms dropped to his sides.

The voice went on, "You must've been picked up at home this morning, because of an arrest warrant..."

"Obtained by my dear devoted cousin!" grumbled Chaverny. "I seem to remember expressing some distaste last night for certain outrages..."

"Do you remember your champagne duel with the hunchback?"

Chaverny nodded.

"That was me playing the part of the hunchback."

"You? The Chevalier de Lagardère!"

"When you were drunk, Gonzague gave orders to make you disappear. You were in his way. He's afraid of the little bit of decency left in you. But the two bravos who got the job were my men. I countermanded the order."

"Thanks! It's all a little hard to believe—even more reason to believe it."

"The thing I dropped down is a message. I wrote a few lines on my hand-kerchief in blood. Do you have some way to get that note to the Princess of Gonzague?"

Chaverny's gesture said "None." He picked up the package to see how a scrap of soft cloth could have given him such a violent, well-placed blow. Lagardère had knotted a brick into the handkerchief. "So you were trying to fracture my skull!" he muttered. "But I must've been fast asleep if they brought me here without my knowing it." He untied the handkerchief, folded it, and put it in his pocket.

"I may be mistaken," said the voice, "but I believe you're willing to help me." Chaverny nodded. "Chances are, I'm going to be executed tonight. So let's hurry. If you have no one to give the message to, do what I did: dig through the floor, and let's trust to fate on the next level down."

"What did you use to dig your hole?"

Lagardère didn't hear him, but he must have guessed, because his spur, now white with plaster dust, dropped at Chaverny's feet. He got straight to work, and went at it with enthusiasm. As his drunken fatigue wore off, he got more and more fired up at the thought of all the harm Gonzague had meant to do him. "If we don't settle accounts today, it won't be my fault!" And he worked furiously, digging a hole ten times as big as he needed for passing on the note.

"You're making too much noise, marquis!" said Lagardère at his hole. "Be careful, they're going to hear you!"

Chaverny was pulling out bricks, plaster, and laths, and bloodying his hands.

"God's blood!" said Cocardasse on the level below, "what kind of a dance are they holding up there?"

"It might be some poor wretch who's being strangled and trying to resist," replied Passepoil, whose thoughts were melancholic this morning.

"Well, if he's being strangled he has the right to resist. But I think it sounds more like some neighborhood madman who's being kept in prison before they send him to the Bicêtre asylum."

There was a loud noise, followed by a muffled crack, and part of the ceiling came down. The plaster falling between our two friends raised a thick cloud of dust.

"Let's commend our souls to God," said Passepoil. "We're without our swords, and I fear they're coming to do us harm."

"Fool! They'd come through the door! Hey, somebody's there!"

"Ahoy!" cried Chaverny, who could fit his entire head through the hole in the ceiling.

Cocardasse and Passepoil looked up at the same time.

"There are two of you in there?"

"As you can see, marquis," said Cocardasse. "But, thunder and lightning, what's all this mess for?"

"Move your pile of straw under the hole so I can jump."

"Nix! Two's enough in here."

"And the jailer doesn't seem like a fellow with a sense of humor," added Passepoil.

But Chaverny went on rapidly widening his hole.

"Crooked ace!" said Cocardasse, watching him. "Who builds prisons like that!"

"It's nothing but mud and spit!" said Passepoil scornfully.

"The straw! The straw!" cried Chaverny impatiently.

Our two bravos didn't move. Finally Chaverny thought to mention Lagardère's name, and immediately they piled their straw in the middle of the cell.

"Is that rascal with you?" asked Cocardasse.

"You have news of him?" asked Passepoil.

Without answering, Chaverny poked his legs through the hole. He was slim, but his hips got stuck against the rough edges of the opening and wouldn't pass. He made frantic efforts to force his way through, and the sight of his wildly wriggling legs made Cocardasse laugh. Passepoil, ever prudent, put his ear against the door to the corridor. Meanwhile Chaverny squeezed his body through little by little.

"Come here, squirt!" said Cocardasse. "He's going to fall, and it's far enough to break his ribs."

By eye Passepoil reckoned the distance from ceiling to floor. "It's far enough for him to break us, if we're stupid enough to act as his mattress!"

"Bah! He's so scrawny!"

"Maybe so, but a fall of a dozen or more feet..."

"Crooked ace, baldy! He's coming on behalf of the little Parisian! Get into position!"

Passepoil obeyed. He and Cocardasse joined their strong arms above the pile of straw. A moment later there came another muffled crack from the ceiling. The two bravos closed their eyes—and as Chaverny dropped, his sudden weight on their outstretched arms pulled them all into an involuntary tight embrace. All three rolled on the floor, blinded by the flood of plaster that came down after the marquis.

He was the first to rise, laughing and shaking himself off. "You're a good pair of fellows. The first time I saw you I took you for pure gallows meat, begging your pardon. Since there are three of us, let's force the door, overpower the jailers, and fly the coop."

"Passepoil!" said Cocardasse.

"Cocardasse!" replied Passepoil.

"Do you think I look like gallows meat?"

"And how about me?" murmured Passepoil, resentfully eying the newcomer. "That's the first time that insult has been..."

"Crooked ace! The little sweetheart will answer for it when we get outside. Meanwhile, I like him and I like his idea. Let's force the door, God's life!"

But just as they were about to throw themselves against the door, Passepoil stopped them. "Listen," he said, tilting his head to hear better.

They heard a noise in the corridor. In a moment all the fallen plaster had been pushed into a corner and hidden behind the straw, now restored to its usual place. A key squeaked loudly in the lock.

"Where can I hide?" Chaverny was laughing in spite of his predicament.

From outside came the loud echoing sound of bolts being drawn. Cocardasse quickly pulled off his doublet, and Passepoil did the same. Chaverny hid as best he could, half under straw and half under their doublets. The two masters of arms, now in shirtsleeves, faced off against each other and pretended to be boxing.

"Come on, baldy!" cried Cocardasse. "One! Two! Go!"

"Touché!" laughed Passepoil. "If only we had our rapiers to pass the time."

The heavy door turned on its hinges. Two men, a turnkey and a warden, stood aside to make way for a third person in splendid court dress. "Don't go away," said the latter as he pushed the door closed. It was Monsieur de Peyrolles in all his finery. Having recognized him at first glance, our two bravos paid him no attention and went right on boxing.

When he left the little pleasure house that morning, that excellent Peyrolles had counted his money again. All of his hard-won gold, all of his stock shares carefully filed away in his money box, had revived his plan to leave Paris and retire to the peaceful countryside to savor a landowner's happiness. He saw darkness gathering on the horizon, and his instincts said, "Go!" But there couldn't be much risk in staying another twenty-four hours. That fallacy will forever be the downfall of greedy men: twenty-four hours is so short! They don't reflect that those hours contain one thousand four hundred and forty minutes, each of which lasts sixty times longer than it takes for a rascal to give up the ghost.

"Morning, friends." Peyrolles glanced at the door to make sure it had stayed ajar.

"Greetings, pal!" answered Cocardasse as he threw a terrible punch at Passepoil. "How's things? We were just saying, me and this trash, that if we had our rapiers back we could at least pass the time."

"Take that!" Passepoil planted his fist in the middle of his friend's stomach.

"How do you like it in here?" asked Peyrolles mockingly.

"Not bad, not bad," said Cocardasse. "Anything new in town?"

"Not that I know of, friends. So you really want to get your rapiers back, eh?"

"Just out of habit," said Cocardasse simply. "When I don't have Petronille I feel like I'm missing a limb."

"And what if, when you got your swords back, you could get out of here too?"

"God's hat! That'd be sweet! Right, Passepoil?"

"And what would we have to do for that?" asked Passepoil.

"Not much, friends, not much at all. Just thank a man you've always considered an enemy, but who's got a fondness for you."

"And who might this fine man be, God's blood?"

"Myself. Think about it, old comrades—we've known each for over twenty years!"

"Twenty-three years on Michaelmas," said Passepoil. "On the night of the archangel's feast day, behind the Louvre, I gave you two dozen with the flat of my sword on behalf of Monsieur de Maulévrier."

"Passepoil!" cried Cocardasse sternly. "Such disagreeable memories, and beside the point now. I myself have often suspected that Monsieur de Peyrolles was secretly fond of us. Say you're sorry, God's life, and make it snappy, rascal!"

Passepoil obediently left his spot in the middle of the room and approached Peyrolles, hat in hand. Just then the watchful Peyrolles noticed the spot where plaster dust had left a white mark on the floor. Naturally he looked up at the ceiling, and at the sight of the hole he grew pale. But he said nothing, because Passepoil, still smiling humbly, was already between him and the door. But Peyrolles did instinctively back toward the pile of straw, so as to protect his rear. Yes, he was facing two strong resolute men, but the jailers were in the corridor and he had his sword. As Peyrolles stopped, with his back to the pile of straw, Chaverny lifted Passepoil's doublet, which had been covering him, and poked out his smiling face.

IV. Old Acquaintances

At this point we should tell the reader what Monsieur de Peyrolles had come to Cocardasse and Passepoil's prison cell for, since he hadn't had time to explain it himself. Our two bravos were summoned—though not by the Prince of Gonzague—to appear as witnesses before the Burning Court at the Châtelet. Peyrolles's assignment was to make them an offer so dazzling that their consciences couldn't hold out: a thousand pistoles each, right now, in advance, in cash—not even to accuse Lagardère, but just to say they'd been nowhere near Caylus the night of the murder. Gonzague had reasoned that the deal was the more attractive because Cocardasse and Passepoil wouldn't be eager to admit they'd been there anyway.

Here's why Peyrolles never had a chance to show off his negotiating skills: the Marquis of Chaverny had lifted his mischievous head from under Passepoil's doublet while Peyrolles, busy keeping an eye on our two bravos, had his back to the pile of straw. Chaverny winked and signaled to his allies, who carefully drew nearer.

"Crooked ace," said Cocardasse, pointing to the hole in the ceiling. "Putting two gentlemen in a cell that's so badly roofed seems a little negligent."

"Time marches on, and standards keep slipping," said Passepoil mildly.

"Comrades," cried Peyrolles anxiously as he watched them getting nearer, one from the right and one from the left, "no tricks! If you force me to draw my sword..."

"For shame!" sighed Passepoil. "Drawing your sword against us!"

"Unarmed men!" agreed Cocardasse. "God's beard, that's not right!"

They came closer still. But before calling for help—which would have broken off the negotiations—Peyrolles thought he should match actions to words, and he laid his hand on his sword guard. "Come now, boys, what's going on? You were trying to escape through that hole, by giving each other a leg up, and you couldn't do it.—Stop right there! One more step and I draw!"

But there was another hand on his sword guard—a milk-white hand, encircled by wrinkled lace, that belonged to Chaverny, who'd managed to get up out of his hiding place and was now standing behind Peyrolles. The sword slipped suddenly into his hands, and Chaverny, seizing Peyrolles by the collar, set the point of the blade at his throat. "One word and you're dead, clown!" he said quietly.

Spittle formed on Peyrolles's lips, but he was silent. Using their neckcloths, Cocardasse and Passepoil tied him up in less time than it takes to write it.

"And now?" said Cocardasse to Chaverny.

"Now, you stand to the right of the door, this good fellow to the left, and when the two jailers come in, both hands around their throats."

"So they're going to come in?" asked Cocardasse.

"Just get in position! Monsieur de Peyrolles will serve as the bait."

The two bravos quickly placed themselves at the wall, one on each side of the door. With the point of his sword at Peyrolles's throat, Chaverny ordered him to call for help. Peyrolles shouted, the two jailers rushed into the cell, and Passepoil took the turnkey while Cocardasse took the warden. After muffled gasps, both fell silent, half strangled. Chaverny shut the cell door, found ropes in the turnkey's pockets, and made handcuffs for both men.

"Crooked ace!" said Cocardasse. "You're the most delightful gentleman I've ever met!"

Passepoil added his own milder praise, but Chaverny was in a hurry. "To work! We're not yet on the streets of Paris! You, the Gascon, strip the turnkey as naked as a worm and put on his clothes. You, the Norman, do the same for the warden."

Cocardasse and Passepoil looked at each other. "Well, this is awkward," said the former. "I don't know if it's appropriate for gentlemen..."

"I'm about to dress up in the clothes of the most shameful crook I know!" cried Chaverny, pulling off Peyrolles's splendid doublet.

"Distinguished friend," ventured Passepoil, "the day before yesterday we put on..."

Cocardasse cut him off with a dreadful gesture. "Enough, man! I command you to forget that painful occasion. Anyway, that was in the service of our little rascal."

"It's in his service today too."

Cocardasse sighed heavily and stripped the turnkey, who was gagged. Passepoil did the same to the warden, and soon our two bravos were dressed. Never since the time of Julius Caesar, said to be the original builder of this ancient fortress, had the Châtelet held within its walls two finer-looking jailers.

Meanwhile Chaverny had put on Peyrolles's doublet. "Boys," he said, now playing the part of Gonzague's factotum, "I've finished my business with these two wretches. Please escort me out to the street."

"Do I look a little like a warden?" asked Passepoil.

"Uncannily," said Chaverny.

"Well, then," said Cocardasse without trying to hide his humiliation, "do I look more or less like a turnkey?"

"Like two peas in a pod," said Chaverny. "Let's go—I have a message to deliver."

The three of them left the cell, which they locked and double locked, not forgetting the bolts. Peyrolles and the two jailers stayed there, securely bound and gagged. Our story does not report what their thoughts were under those difficult, painful circumstances.

Our three prisoners, meanwhile, reached the end of the first corridor unhindered: it was empty.

"Don't hold your head so high, Cocardasse," said Chaverny. "I worry about your villainous mustaches."

"God's blood! You could mince me up as fine as ground meat, and you still couldn't get rid of my good looks!"

"We'll have 'em till we die," added Passepoil.

Chaverny pulled Cocardasse's wool cap further down over his ears, and taught him how to hold his keys. They were coming to the door to the inner courtyard.

The courtyard and the covered galleries were full of people: the chief judge, the Marquis of Ségré, was treating his associate judges to dinner while waiting for the court session to resume, and the Châtelet was in a great stir. Covered dishes, portable stoves, baskets of champagne went by, all coming from the Suckling Calf tavern, established two years earlier by the chef Le Preux right on the square by the Châtelet.

Chaverny went first, his hat low over his eyes. "My good man," he said to the doorkeeper at the inner courtyard, "you've got a couple of dangerous rascals down the corridor in number nine. Keep an eye on them!"

The doorkeeper mumbled and doffed his hat. Cocardasse and Passepoil crossed the inner courtyard without hindrance. In the guardroom Chaverny played the part of a tourist visiting the prison: he examined everything through his pince-nez and solemnly asked a number of stupid questions. He was shown the cot where Count Horn had rested for ten minutes, along with his friend Father de La Mettrie, following his final hearing. Chaverny seemed very interested.

Now they only had to make it across the main courtyard. But right at the start Cocardasse almost knocked over a pot boy from the Suckling Calf who was carrying a platter of blancmange. Our bravo threw out a loud "God's hat!" that made everybody turn around. Passepoil shook down to the marrow of his bones.

"Friend," said Chaverny sadly, "the boy meant no harm, and you could've done without blaspheming the name of our Lord and Savior."

Cocardasse looked abashed, and the sentries took Chaverny for a very decent young gentleman.

"I don't recognize that Gascon turnkey," muttered the gatekeeper. "Those damn southerners seem to weasel their way in everywhere!"

The gate stood open just then to make way for a fine roast pheasant, the centerpiece for the Marquis of Ségré's dinner. No longer able to control their impatience, Cocardasse and Passepoil strode through the opening.

"Stop them! Stop them!" cried Chaverny.

The gatekeeper leaped to his feet—and was felled by the heavy ring of keys Cocardasse planted in the middle of his face. At the same moment our two bravos took off, and vanished at the Lanterne crossroads.

The carriage that had brought Monsieur de Peyrolles still waited by the gate; Chaverny recognized Gonzague's livery. He leaped onto the running board, still crying at the top of his lungs, "Stop them, by God! Can't you see they're getting away? Anyone fleeing like that is up to no good! Stop them! Stop them!" Taking advantage of the uproar, he leaned out the window on the other side and called, "To the Villa Gonzague, rascal, on the double!" The horses took off. When the carriage reached the Rue Saint Denis, Chaverny mopped the sweat off his brow and began to laugh, holding his sides. Good old Peyrolles was giving him not only his freedom but a carriage to take him in comfort to his destination.

He was headed to that same somber, sparsely furnished room in which we first saw the Princess of Gonzague the morning before the family council. The trappings of mourning were the same: the altar draped in black—where the funeral Mass in memory of the late Duke of Nevers was held daily—still supported its large white cross lit by six candles. But something had changed: some note of joy, still timid and barely perceptible, had slipped in among the dour decor; some mysterious smile lit up the mourning. The altar was flanked by flowers, and yet this wasn't early May, when the dead husband's birthday was observed. The open curtains let in a ray of soft autumn light.

There was company in the princess's private chapel, lots of company, though it was still morning. A beautiful girl slept stretched out on the daybed. Her perfectly formed face lay partly in shadow, but sunlight played on the rich mass of her shining golden brown hair. Next to her, with her hands folded and with tears in her eyes, stood the princess's chambermaid, faithful Madeleine Giraud. She'd confessed to Madame de Gonzague that the miraculous warning the princess had found in the margin of the *Miserere* in her book of hours—the note that read *Come protect your daughter* and that evoked after twenty years the private signal of happy rendezvous and young love, Nevers's motto, "Here I am!"—had been put there by Madeleine herself, acting for the hunchback.

Instead of scolding her, the princess had embraced her. Madeleine was as happy as if her own child had been found. The princess sat at the far end of the room, with two women and a teenage boy. Around them lay the scattered pages of a manuscript, and the box that had held them. Those lines—written in the burning hope that someday they'd come into the hands of an unknown but beloved mother—had reached their destination. It was clear from her eyes, reddened by happy, loving tears, that the princess had already read those pages.

As for how the box and its sweet contents had entered the Villa Gonzague, no need to ask: one of the women was old Dame Françoise Berrichon, and the boy twisting his cap slyly and awkwardly in his hands was young Jean-Marie, Aurore's page, the reckless, talkative boy who'd dragged his grandmother away from her duty and led her into temptation among the gossiping housewives of the Rue du Chantre. The other woman stood slightly apart; beneath her veil you would have recognized the bold kind features of Doña Cruz. Her mischievous face now expressed deep sincere feeling.

"That one's not my son," said Dame Françoise in her mannish voice, pointing to Jean-Marie. "He's the son of my own poor boy. And I can tell your ladyship, my Berrichon was a whole different matter! He was five foot ten, and brave—he died a soldier."

"And you were in service with Nevers, good woman?" interjected the princess.

"All the Berrichons, from father to son, since the world began! My husband was equerry to Duke Amaury, Duke Philippe's father. And my husband's father, Guillaume Jean-Nicolas Berrichon..."

The princess interrupted again. "But it was your son who brought me that letter at Caylus Castle?"

"Yes, my lady, it was him. And God knows, he remembered that night all his life. He'd met—he told me so himself many a time—in the Ens Forest he'd met Dame Marthe, your old duenna, who was keeping the baby. Dame Marthe recognized him from having seen him at the young duke's castle when she took your messages there. Dame Marthe said to him, 'Somebody at Caylus Castle has found everything out; if you see Mademoiselle Aurore, tell her to be careful.' Berrichon was caught by the bandits and saved by the grace of God. It was the first time he ever saw the Chevalier de Lagardère everybody was talking about. He told us Lagardère was as handsome as the Archangel Michael in the church at Tarbes!"

"Yes," murmured the princess absently, "he's handsome."

"And brave!" Françoise grew animated. "A lion!"

"A real lion!" agreed Jean-Marie.

Françoise glared at him, and he shut up. "Anyhow," she went on, "that's what my poor boy Berrichon told us. And since Nevers and that Lagardère had a rendezvous to duel, and since that Lagardère defended Nevers for a whole half hour against more than twenty devils, begging your ladyship's pardon, all armed to the teeth..."

The princess motioned to her to stop. She was worn down by all these sad memories. Her tear-filled eyes turned to the candle-lit altar. "Philippe!" she murmured, "my beloved husband! It was only yesterday! The years have passed like hours! It was only yesterday. My wounded heart bleeds and will not heal."

Doña Cruz observed her immense grief with an admiring spark in her eye. In her own veins ran the kind of hot blood that makes hearts beat faster and lifts spirits to heroic emotions.

Françoise shook her head maternally. "What's past is past. We're all mortal. You can't beat yourself up for what's done and gone."

Jean-Marie turned his cap in his hands. "Listen to my grandma preach!"

"Anyhow," went on Françoise, "when the Chevalier de Lagardère came back to the area, it must be five or six years ago now, to ask me if I wanted to serve the duke's daughter, I said yes right away. Why? Because my son Berrichon had told me how things had gone. The dying duke called the chevalier by name and said, 'My brother! My brother!'"

The princess pressed her hands to her heart.

"And also," went on Françoise, "'Be a father to my daughter, and avenge me.' Berrichon never lied, my lady. Besides, why would he have lied? So Jean-Marie and I went along. The Chevalier de Lagardère knew Mademoiselle Aurore was now too grown up to live alone with him."

"And he wanted the lady to have a pageboy," added Jean-Marie.

Françoise shrugged and smiled. "The boy's a blabbermouth, begging your pardon, my lady. So we left for Madrid, which is the capital of the Spanish country. Damn—I got tears in my eyes when I saw that poor child, I tell you true! The spitting image of the young lord. But hush! We had to keep quiet. The chevalier wouldn't listen to reason."

"And the whole time you were with them..." The princess hesitated. "That man, Monsieur de Lagardère..."

"Lord God, my lady!" Françoise turned purple. "No, no, on my hope of heaven! I might think the same thing you're thinking, since you're a mother—but you see, over the course of six years I learned to love the chevalier as much as and more than what family's left to me. If anyone but you dared to suspect him—but I beg your pardon..." She curtseyed. "Here I am forgetting who I'm talking to. But he's a saint, my lady, and your daughter was as safe with him as she'd have been with her mother. Nothing but sweet, pure respect and goodness and affection!"

"You're right to defend someone who deserves no blame," said the princess coldly. "But give me details. My daughter lived apart?"

"Alone, always alone, too much alone, because it made her sad. And yet, if he'd listened to me..."

"What are you trying to say?"

Françoise glanced over at Doña Cruz, who hadn't moved. "Listen. A girl who sings and dances out on the Plaza de Santa Ana isn't a fit companion for a duke's heiress..."

The princess turned to Doña Cruz. A single tear shone in the girl's long lashes.

"You have no other criticism of your master?"

"Criticism?" cried Françoise. "That's not a criticism. Anyway, the girl didn't come often, and I always kept an eye out..."

"That's all, my good woman," interrupted the princess. "I thank you. You may withdraw. From now on you and your grandson will be part of my household."

"On your knees!" cried Françoise, roughly pushing Jean-Marie down.

The princess stopped this excessive display of gratitude. At a sign, Madeleine Giraud led the old woman and her grandson away. Doña Cruz also turned to go.

"Where are you going, Flor?"

Doña Cruz thought she'd misheard.

"Isn't that your name? Come, Flor, I want to embrace you."

The girl hesitated, and the princess rose and took her in her arms. Doña Cruz felt her face bathed in tears.

"She loves you," murmured the happy mother. "It says so there, in those pages that will never leave my bedside—those pages in which she poured out her heart. You're her gypsy girl, her first friend. You're luckier than I was: you knew her as a child. She must've been lovely. Tell me about it, Flor." Without giving the girl a chance to answer, she went on with a mother's deep impulsive passion, "Everything she loves, I want to love. I love you, Flor, my second daughter. Embrace me. And you, could you love me? If you knew how happy I am, and how much I want the whole world to be happy! That man—you hear me, Flor?—even that man, who stole my child's heart away from me: well, if that's what she wants, I feel I could even love him!"

V. A Mother's Heart

Doña Cruz smiled through her tears. The princess pressed her passionately to her heart. "You might think, darling Flor," she murmured, "that I shouldn't presume to hug you like this yet. Don't get angry: it's her I'm kissing on your brow and on your cheeks." She moved away to get a better look at Doña Cruz. "You danced on the streets as a little girl?" she said absently. "You had no family. Would I have loved her any less, if I'd found her like this? My God, my God! Reason is folly! The other day I said, 'If Nevers's daughter had forgotten her proud blood, even for a moment...' No! I won't finish. My blood runs cold at the thought that God might've taken me at my word. Come give thanks to God, Flor, my gypsy girl, come!"

She drew the girl toward the altar and knelt down. "Nevers! Nevers!" she cried, "I have our daughter! Ask God to see the joy and gratitude in my heart!"

Her closest friend wouldn't have recognized her now. Returning blood flushed her cheeks. She was young, she was beautiful, her eyes shone, her lithe body twisted and shook, her voice was soft and charming. For a moment she was lost in her own ecstasy. "Are you a Christian, Flor? Yes, I remember, she said so, you're a Christian. God is good, isn't He? Give me both your hands and feel my heart."

"Ah!" Doña Cruz dissolved in tears. "If I had a mother like you, Madame!"

The princess drew her to her heart again. "Did she talk to you about me? What did you talk about? When you first met her, she was still small." She broke off, because her emotions made her talk nonstop. "You know, I think she's afraid of me. I'll die if that keeps up. You'll speak to her about me, Flor, darling Flor, I beg you!"

Doña Cruz smiled through her tears and pointed to the scattered pages of Aurore's manuscript. "Madame, haven't you seen from that how much she loves you?"

"Yes, yes—can I even express what I felt while I read it? My daughter isn't sad and somber like me. She's got her father's joyful spirit. But I—I who've wept so much—I used to be joyful. The house I was born in was a prison, and yet I laughed, I danced, right up to the day when I met the man who would take all my joy and laughter with him to the grave." She passed a hand across her burning brow. Suddenly she asked, "Have you ever watched a poor woman go crazy?"

Doña Cruz looked at her with concern.

"Don't be afraid, don't be afraid—happiness is such a new thing for me! I wanted to say, Flor: did you notice? My daughter's like me—her joy vanished the day she fell in love. There are plenty of tear stains on those final pages."

She took the gypsy girl's arm to return to her seat. She often turned toward the daybed where Aurore still slept, but some inchoate emotion seemed to keep her away. "She loves me, there's no doubt. But the smile she remembers, the smile above her cradle, is that man's smile. Who gave her her first lessons? That man. Who taught her the name of God? That man again! Oh, I beg you, Flor, my darling, never tell her how much anger and jealousy and resentment I still feel against that man!"

"That's not your heart speaking, Madame," murmured Doña Cruz.

The princess squeezed her arm with sudden intensity. "It is my heart! It is my heart! On holidays they went out to the fields around Pamplona together. He played with her like a child. Is that a man's job? Isn't that a mother's place? When he came home from work he brought her a toy or a sweet. What could I have done to match that, if I'd been poor and in exile with my daughter? He knew very well he was taking—was robbing me of—all her affection!"

"Oh, Madame!" Doña Cruz tried to interrupt.

"Are you defending him?" The princess eyed her suspiciously. "Are you on his side?" She went on with bitter disappointment, "I can see you love him better than you love me—you too!"

Doña Cruz lifted the hand she was holding to her own heart.

Tears flowed from the princess's eyes. "Oh, that man, that man!" she stammered through her sobs. "I was a widow, I had nothing left but my daughter's love!"

To this, the ultimate injury to maternal love, Doña Cruz had no response. She understood it—she, a girl devoted to pleasure, a giddy girl who yesterday was ready to take a gamble on life's adventure: in her heart lay the seeds of every kind of jealous passionate love.

The princess had returned to her seat. She picked up the pages of Aurore's manuscript and turned them over absently, saying slowly, "How many times did he save her life?" She was about to go through the manuscript, but she stopped after the first pages. "What's the point?" she said, defeated. "I only gave her life once!" Her eyes sparkled fiercely. "That's true, that's true!—She's his much more than she's mine!"

"But you're her mother, Madame," said Doña Cruz gently.

The princess raised her anxious, suffering eyes. "What do you mean by that? You're just trying to comfort me. To love your mother is a duty. If my daughter loved me merely out of duty, I think it would kill me!"

"Madame, Madame, reread the pages where she talks about you. Such affection! Such loving respect!"

"I remember, Flor, darling. But something keeps me from rereading those lines I kissed so passionately. My daughter is stern; she makes threats. When she begins to suspect that the obstacle between her and her beloved is her mother, her words cut like a sword. We read it together—you remember what she says. She talks about arrogant mothers..." The princess trembled all over.

"But you're not that kind of mother, Madame."

"I was!" she murmured, hiding her face in her hands.

Across the room Aurore de Nevers moved on her daybed and mumbled indistinct words. The princess started. She rose and crossed the room on tiptoe, motioning to Doña Cruz to follow her, as if she felt a need for support and protection. The worry that constantly pierced her joy, the fear, the remorse, the obsession—whatever name we'd give to the strange anguish that troubled the poor mother's heart and spoiled her joy—was both childish and distressing. She knelt at Aurore's side, while Doña Cruz stood at the foot of the bed. For a long time the princess gazed at her daughter's face, and stifled her own sobs.

Aurore was pale. Her restless sleep had undone her hair, which fell around her onto the carpet. The princess gathered up the strands of hair in both hands and kissed them with her eyes closed.

"Henri!" murmured Aurore in her sleep. "Henri, my beloved!"

The princess turned so pale that Doña Cruz moved quickly to support her—but the princess pushed her away with a pained smile. "I'll get used to it. If only she spoke my name in her dreams as well!"

She waited. Her name didn't come. Aurore's lips were parted, and she breathed heavily.

"I'll be patient," said the poor mother. "Maybe another time she'll dream of me."

Doña Cruz knelt before her. The princess smiled at her with a resignation that lit her face with sublime beauty. "You know, the first time I saw you, Flor, I was surprised that my heart didn't leap toward you. Yet you're beautiful, in the Spanish way I expected to see in my daughter. But look at her forehead—look!" Gently she moved aside the heavy hair that half-covered Aurore's face. "You don't have that," she said, touching Aurore's temples. "That's from Nevers. When I saw her, and that man said, 'This is your daughter!' my heart didn't hesitate. It was as if Nevers's voice suddenly came down from heaven and said, like him, 'It's your daughter!'"

Her eager eyes took in Aurore's features. "When Nevers slept his eyelids fell like that, and I often saw that line around his lips. Something about her smile is even more like him. Nevers was very young, and people said he had a somewhat feminine beauty. But what struck me most of all was her eyes. Oh, it's as if the fire of Nevers's glance has been relit! Proofs? Their pitiful proofs! God put our name on this child's face. It's not Lagardère I trust, it's my heart."

The princess had spoken very quietly, but at Lagardère's name Aurore started slightly.

"She's going to wake up," said Doña Cruz.

In a kind of terror, the princess rose. When she saw her daughter was about to open her eyes, she quickly drew back. "Don't tell her right away I'm here! We have to be careful."

Aurore stretched out her arms. Her lithe body stiffened unconsciously, as is common on awakening. Suddenly her eyes opened wide, and she glanced around the room in astonishment. "Ah! Flor, you're here. I remember. So I wasn't dreaming." She rubbed her face with both hands. "This isn't the room we were in last night. Was that a dream? Did I see my mother?"

"You saw your mother."

The princess, who'd retreated as far as the mourning-draped altar, had tears of joy in her eyes. Her daughter's first thought had been of her—her daughter hadn't yet spoken of Lagardère. She thanked God with all her heart.

"But why do I ache like this?" asked Aurore. "Every movement hurts, and every breath tears at my chest. At the Convent of the Incarnation in Madrid, after my terrible illness, when the fever and delirium were over, I remember feeling like this. My head was empty but I felt a weight on my heart. Every time I tried to think, my dazzled eyes saw stars and my poor head felt ready to burst."

"You had a fever," said Doña Cruz. "You were very sick." She glanced at the princess as if to say, come, it's your turn to speak. But the princess stayed where she was, her hands clasped, shyly adoring her child from a distance.

"I don't know how to put it," murmured Aurore. "It's like a weight crushing my thoughts. I'm always on the point of cutting through the veil of shadows encircling my poor wits, but I can't do it, I can't!" Her head fell weakly back on the cushion. "Is my mother angry with me?" As she spoke her eyes lit suddenly. Just for a moment she understood the situation, but then the fog over her thoughts thickened, and her beautiful eyes dimmed.

The princess had started at her daughter's last words, but she silenced Doña Cruz with an imperious gesture. Then she drew near with the quick, light step she must have had when she was a young mother and the cry of her child called her to the crib. She drew near. Cradling the back of her daughter's head, she kissed her brow.

Aurore began to smile. The strange mental crisis she was going through was most evident at that moment. She was happy—but with an everyday, habitual, calm, mild happiness. She gave her mother a kiss, like a child accustomed to giving and getting the same kiss every morning. "Mother," she murmured, "I dreamt of you, and all night long in my dream you were weeping." Then she broke off. "But why's Flor here? Flor has no mother. But so much can happen in one night!" It was the battle once again, and her wits struggled to tear away the veil. She gave up, beaten by the overwhelming painful weariness. "Let me see you, Mother. Come close, take me on your lap."

Laughing and crying, the princess sat on the daybed and took Aurore in her arms. How to describe her feelings? Does any language have words to condemn or disparage that holy crime, the selfishness of the maternal heart? The princess possessed her whole treasure: her daughter on her lap, weak in body and mind, a child, a poor child. The princess could see Flor weeping helplessly, but she herself was happy, and slightly mad, and she rocked Aurore in her arms, and in a murmur she sang some song of perfect tenderness. And Aurore laid her head on her breast. It was charming and pitiful. Doña Cruz averted her eyes.

"Mother," said Aurore, "ideas are spinning around me and I can't take hold of them. It seems like it's you who doesn't want me to see clearly. And yet I feel there's something in me that isn't me. I should behave differently with you, Mother."

"You're pressed to my heart, child, dear child," said the princess in a voice like a prayer. "Don't look for anything beyond that. Rest on my breast. Be happy with the happiness you give me."

"Madame, Madame," whispered Doña Cruz in her ear, "when she wakes it'll be awful!"

The princess waved her away impatiently. She wanted to fall asleep in this strange voluptuous state, though it was also a torture. No need for anyone to remind her all this was nothing but a dream!

"Mother," went on Aurore, "I think if you spoke to me the blindfold would drop from my eyes. If only you knew how I'm suffering!"

"You're suffering!" echoed the princess, pressing her tighter to her breast.

"Yes, I'm suffering deeply. I'm terribly afraid, Mother, and I don't know, I don't know." Her voice was choked with tears, and she pressed her beautiful hands to her face.

The princess felt a jolt in the chest that was pressed to hers.

"Oh, oh!" cried Aurore, "let me go! I should be on my knees before you, Mother. I remember—an odd thing!—a moment ago I imagined I'd never left your breast." She looked up at her mother with wild eyes. The princess tried to smile, but face was filled with horror. "What's wrong? What's wrong, Mother? You're happy to have found me, aren't you?"

"Am I happy, darling child?"

"Yes, that's it—I had no mother, and you found me."

"And God who reunited us, my child, will never part us again!"

"God!" Aurore's wide eyes stared at nothing. "I couldn't pray now—I can't remember my prayers."

"Would you like to say your prayers with me?" asked the princess, latching eagerly onto this distraction.

"Yes, Mother. Wait, there's something else."

"Our Father, who art in heaven," began the princess, clasping Aurore's hands between her own.

"Our Father, who art in heaven," repeated Aurore like a small child.

"Hallowed be Thy name."

This time, instead of repeating after her, Aurore stiffened. "There's something else," she murmured. Her clenched fingers pressed her sweat-soaked temples. "Something else. Flor! You know what it is—tell me!"

"Dear sister," stammered Doña Cruz.

"You know! You know!" Aurore blinked away tears. "So no one wants to help me!" Suddenly she sat up and looked her mother in the eye. "That prayer, Mother," she said, articulating every word, "are you the one who taught me that prayer?"

The princess lowered her head and moaned.

Aurore fixed her burning eyes on her. "No, it wasn't you." She made a supreme effort to think. A terrible cry escaped her. "Henri! Henri! Where's Henri?"

She stood up, and gave the princess a fierce, magnificent look. Doña Cruz tried to take her hands, but she pushed her away with a man's strength. The princess wept, her head on her lap.

"Answer me!" cried Aurore. "What have they done with Henri?"

"I've been thinking only of you, my child," stammered the princess.

Her head high and fire in her eyes, Aurore whirled toward Doña Cruz. "Have they killed him?"

No answer. Aurore turned back to her mother, who slid to her knees and murmured, "You're breaking my heart, child. Have pity on me."

"Have they killed him?"

"Him! Always him!" cried the princess, wringing her hands. "There's no room in this child's heart to love her mother!"

Aurore stared at the floor, and she reflected out loud, "They won't tell me if he's been killed!"

The princess stretched out her arms to her, then fell back in a swoon.

Aurore—her face crimson, her eyes tragic—held her mother's hands. "On my salvation, I believe you, Madame. You did him no harm. All the better for you, if you love me the way I love you. Because if you'd done him harm..."

"Aurore! Aurore!" interrupted Doña Cruz, putting her hand over her friend's mouth.

"I'm speaking," said Aurore with haughty dignity. "I'm not making threats. My mother and I have known each other only a few hours; we should meet each other heart to heart. My mother's a princess, I'm a poor girl—that gives me the right to talk back to her. If my mother were poor, weak, abandoned, I wouldn't have stood up, and I would've spoken to her only on my knees."

She kissed the princess's hands. Her mother gazed at her admiringly. How beautiful she was! And how the deep anguish that troubled her heart without lessening her pride put a halo around her virgin's face! Virgin, we said correctly—but a virgin bride, with all the strength and majesty of a wife.

"You're all the world to me, my child. Without you I'm weak, I'm abandoned. Judge me, but with the mercy you owe to those who suffer. You blame me for not removing the blindfold that clouded your reason. But you loved me when you were delirious—and it's true, it's true, I feared your waking!"

Aurore glanced toward the door.

424

"Do you wish to leave me?" cried the frightened mother.

"I have to. Something tells me Henri needs me and is calling me right now."

"Henri! Always Henri!" murmured the princess in despair. "Everything for him, nothing for your mother!"

Aurore fastened her fiery eyes on her. "If he were here, Madame," she said gently, "and you were far away, your life in danger, I'd speak to him only of you."

"Is that true?" cried the princess, delighted. "Do you love me as much as him?"

Aurore held her in her arms and murmured, "How could you not have known that before, Mother?"

The princess covered her with kisses. "Listen, I know what it is to love. My dear, noble husband, who hears me now and whose memory fills this room, must be smiling at the feet of God as he sees to the bottom of my heart. Yes, I love you more than I loved Nevers, because a wife's love is mingled with a mother's love. It's you—but also him in you—that I love, Aurore, my fondest hope, my happiness. Listen! I'll love that man, so that you can love me. I know, because you wrote it, that you'd stop loving me if I rejected him. Well then, I'll open my arms to him."

Suddenly she turned pale, because she'd seen Doña Cruz going into the small room whose door opened behind the daybed.

"You'll open your arms to him, Mother?" insisted Aurore.

The princess was silent, and her heart pounded. Aurore tore herself from her arms, and the princess dropped into a chair.

"You're no good at lying!" cried Aurore. "He's dead! You think he's dead!"

Before the princess could answer, Doña Cruz returned, wearing her cape and veil. She blocked Aurore's move to the door. "Do you trust me, dear sister? Your strength is no match for your courage. Everything you'll want to do, I can do." Then turning to the princess she said, "Please call for your carriage, my lady."

"Where are you going, dear sister?" asked Aurore faintly.

Doña Cruz answered firmly, "Madame de Gonzague is about to tell me where I need to go to save him."

VI. Condemned to Death

Doña Cruz waited by the door. The mother and daughter faced each other. The princess had just ordered her carriage. "Aurore," she said, "I didn't need to wait for your friend's advice to act. She spoke for you, and I don't hold it against her. But what did the girl think—that I prolonged your confusion to keep you from taking action?"

Doña Cruz couldn't help reproaching herself.

"Yesterday," went on the princess, "I was that man's enemy. Do you know why? He'd taken my daughter, and appearances strongly suggested that Nevers had died by his hand."

Aurore straightened up, but her eyes fell, and she turned so pale that her mother stepped forward to support her. "Go on, Madame, I'm listening," said Aurore. "I can see by your face you already know it was slander."

"I read your journal, my child. It's an eloquent defense. The man who sheltered so pure a heart under his roof for twenty years couldn't be a murderer. The man who brought me back a daughter whose like I couldn't have hoped for, even in the most extravagant dreams of maternal love, must have a conscience without stain."

"Thank you on his behalf, Mother. Have you no other proofs?"

"Yes: I have the testimony of a worthy woman and her grandson. Henri de Lagardère..."

"...My husband, Mother."

"Your husband, my child," said the princess, lowering her voice, "didn't attack Philippe de Nevers, he defended him."

Her coldness melting suddenly away, Aurore threw her arms around her mother's neck and covered her face with kisses.

"That's for him!" said the princess, smiling sadly.

"That's for you!" cried Aurore, bringing her mother's hands to her lips. "For you, whom I've finally found, dear Mother! For you, whom I love, for you, whom he will love. So what did you do?"

"The Regent has my letter, explaining Lagardère's innocence."

"Thank you, oh, thank you! But then why isn't he here now?"

The princess motioned for Doña Cruz to approach. "I forgive you, child," she said, kissing the girl's brow. "The carriage is ready. It's you who'll go fetch the answer to my daughter's question. Go now and come back quickly—we'll be waiting for you."

Doña Cruz hurried away.

"Well, my dear," said the princess, leading Aurore to a sofa, "have I sufficiently mortified the fine lady's arrogance you faulted me for even before you

426

knew me? Am I obedient enough to the peremptory orders of Mademoiselle de Nevers?"

"How good you are, Mother..." began Aurore as they sat.

The princess interrupted her. "I love you, that's all. Before I was afraid of you, but now I fear nothing: I have a talisman."

Aurore smiled. "What talisman?"

The princess observed her for a moment in silence. Then she said, "To love him so you love me."

Aurore threw herself into her mother's arms.

Meanwhile, Doña Cruz had crossed Madame de Gonzague's parlor and reached the antechamber when she heard an uproar. People were arguing loudly outside on the stairs. A voice she thought she recognized was scolding Madame de Gonzague's footmen and chambermaids, who seemed to be huddled like an army against the closed door, preventing entry to the apartment.

"You're drunk!" cried the footmen, while the chambermaids added shrilly, "Your shoes are full of plaster dust and your hair is full of straw! A fine way to appear before a princess!"

"God's blood, villains!" cried the besieger's voice. "Who cares about plaster or straw or being presentable! You can't be too particular to get out of where I've come from!"

"Did you come from a tavern?" asked the footmen.

"Or from the clink?" suggested the chambermaids.

Doña Cruz had stopped to listen through the door.

"Insolent rabble!" cried the voice. "Go tell your mistress that her cousin, the Marquis of Chaverny, wishes to see her immediately!"

"Chaverny!" echoed Doña Cruz in surprise.

On the other side of the door the servants conferred. They'd finally recognized Chaverny in spite of his strange clothes and the plaster soiling the velvet of his shoes. They all knew he was Gonzague's cousin. But it seemed as if the marquis found their deliberations too protracted: Doña Cruz heard the sounds of a struggle, and the thumping noise a human body makes as it falls down the stairs. Then the door flew open and Chaverny appeared, dressed in Monsieur de Peyrolles's finery.

"Victory!" he cried, pushing back the flood of the besieged of both sexes as they threw themselves on him again. "Hell if these rascals haven't come near to making me lose my temper!"

He slammed the door in their faces and bolted it. As he turned he saw Doña Cruz. Before she could back away or resist, he seized both her hands and kissed them, laughing. He acted impulsively, without premeditation, and nothing surprised him. "Sweet angel," he said—while she pulled away in a mixture of delight and embarrassment—"I dreamt of you all night. It happens that this morning I'm too busy to make you a formal proposal. So I'll skip the preliminaries and fall straight to my knees before you, and offer you my heart and my hand." He did indeed kneel in the middle of the antechamber.

Dona Cruz hadn't been expecting this, but she was no more embarrassed than he was. "I'm in a hurry too," she said, struggling to remain serious, "so please let me by."

Chaverny stood back up and embraced her boldly, like those comic servants Frontin and Lisette embracing on stage. "You'll be the most gorgeous marquise in the world! So it's settled. Don't think I'm acting recklessly—I thought it over the whole way here."

"Don't I have to give my consent?" she objected.

"I considered that. If you don't consent, I'll abduct you. Anyway, enough said about settled business. I come with important news, and I need to see Madame de Gonzague."

"She's with her daughter, and receiving no one."

"Her daughter! Mademoiselle de Nevers! My bride-to-be last night, that charming girl, by God! But you're the one I love, and I'd marry you today. Listen to me, darling, I'm serious: if Mademoiselle de Nevers is with her mother, that's all the more reason I should go in."

"Impossible!"

"Nothing is impossible for a French chevalier!" said Chaverny solemnly.

He took the gypsy girl in his arms, and—as they put it in those days—stealing half a dozen kisses, he moved her aside. "I don't know the way, but the god of adventure will guide me. Have you read any novels by La Calprenède? Doesn't a man carrying a message written in blood on a scrap of cloth go anywhere he wants?"

"A message written in blood!" she echoed, no longer laughing.

Chaverny had already reached the parlor. Doña Cruz ran after him, but she was too late to stop him from opening the door to the private chapel and reaching the princess unannounced. There, Chaverny's manners changed: even giddy noblemen know their world. He remained on the threshold and bowed respectfully. "Madame, noble cousin, I've never had the honor of laying my compliments at your feet, and you don't know me. I am the Marquis of Chaverny, Nevers's cousin by way of Mademoiselle de Chaneilles, my mother."

At the name of Chaverny, Aurore pressed against her mother in fear. Doña Cruz came in behind the marquis.

The princess rose angrily. "And what are you doing here, sir?"

He turned to Aurore almost in supplication. "I've come to atone for the faults of a scatterbrain I know—a madman whose name is pretty close to mine. Instead of making Mademoiselle de Nevers an apology she couldn't accept, I'm buying forgiveness by bringing her a message." He went down one knee before Aurore.

The princess frowned. "A message from whom?" Aurore, trembling and blushing, had already guessed.

"A message from the Chevalier Henri de Lagardère." Chaverny drew from his breast the handkerchief on which Lagardère had scrawled a few words in blood.

Aurore tried to rise, but she dropped back weakly on the sofa.

"Is he...?" began the princess when she saw the bloodstained scrap of cloth.

Chaverny kept his eyes on Aurore, whom Doña Cruz was now supporting. "The note looks gruesome, but don't be afraid. When you have neither ink nor paper..."

"He's alive!" murmured Aurore with a deep sigh. Then she lifted her tear-filled eyes to heaven and thanked God. She took the handkerchief, stained with Henri's blood, from Chaverny's hands and pressed it passionately to her lips. The princess turned away—the final revolt of her pride. Aurore tried to read, but tears blinded her, and anyway the fabric had soaked up the blood and the letters were almost illegible. The princess, Doña Cruz, and Chaverny all tried to help her, but the sprawling symbols, intermingled and diffused, told them nothing.

"I'll read it!" Aurore wiped her eyes on the handkerchief itself. She went to the window and knelt with the cloth spread out. And indeed she read:

To the Princess of Gonzague. I beg to see Aurore once more before I die!

Aurore stopped cold. When her mother helped her up, she said to Chaverny, "Where is he?"

"In the Châtelet prison."

"He's been sentenced?"

"I don't know. All I know is, he's in solitary."

Aurore tore herself from her mother's embrace. "I'm going to the Châtelet prison."

"You have your mother with you, my child," murmured the princess reproachfully. "From now on your mother is a guide and support to you. You didn't speak from your heart—your heart would have said, Mother, take me to the Châtelet prison."

"What!" stammered Aurore. "You'd agree to that?"

"My daughter's husband is my son. If he succumbs I'll mourn him. If he can be saved I'll save him!"

The princess led the way to the door. Aurore held her, kissed her hands, and bathed them with her tears. "May God reward you, Mother!"

The high court at the Châtelet had dined copiously and at length. The Marquis of Ségré had a well-earned reputation as a fine host. He was a gourmet of exquisite taste, a fashionable judge, and a perfect gentleman. His associate judges, from Lord Berthelot de Labaumelle down to young Husson-Bordesson—the court auditor, with only an advisory role—were epicures: well fed, with hearty appetites, and more at home around a table than on a dais. Let's grant them this much: the second session of the Burning Court ran a lot shorter than dinner. Of the three witnesses scheduled to be heard, two had defaulted—those escaped prisoners, Cocardasse and Passepoil by name. Only Monsieur de Peyrolles had given his deposition. The evidence he gave was so detailed and so damning that the proceedings had been surprisingly simplified.

Everything was a little ad hoc just then at the Châtelet. The judges missed the comforts of the Appellate Courts. For a cloakroom the Marquis of Ségré had to make do with a dark closet attached to the courtroom and separated only by a partition from the alcove all the associate judges used to freshen up. It was awkward, and the judges were used to better facilities than that in even the shabbiest provincial courts.

The courtroom opened, by way of French doors, onto the bridge that connected the brick Tour Neuve to the main fortress at the level of the cells where Chaverny had been held. Convicts had to pass by this courtroom on their way back to prison.

"What time do you have, Monsieur de Labaumelle?" asked Ségré through the partition.

"Two o'clock, judge."

"The baroness must be waiting for me! Damn these double sessions! Ask Monsieur Husson to see if my chaise is at the door."

Husson-Bordesson took the stairs four at a time. That's what you have to do when you want to move up in a serious career.

"You know," said Hacquelin-Desmaisons meanwhile, "that witness, Monsieur de Peyrolles, expressed himself very well. Without him we'd have had to deliberate till three."

"He's Monsieur de Gonzague's man," said Labaumelle. "The prince chooses his people well."

"What's this I hear about Gonzague being in disgrace?" asked Ségré.

"No, no," said Hacquelin, "this morning Gonzague had the Regent's little levee all to himself. That's favor built on solid rock."

"Rascal! Crook! Beggar! Good-for-nothing!" cried Ségré: that was his usual way of greeting his valet, who got back at him by pilfering from him. "Remember, I'm going to the baroness's and my hair has to be perfect!"

Just as the valet was about to go to work on him, a bailiff entered the judges' shared alcove. "Someone to see the chief judge."

Ségré heard through the partition and shouted, "I'm not here, by God! To hell with whoever it is!"

"It's two ladies," said the bailiff.

"Two petitioners? Throw 'em out!... How are they dressed?"

"Both of them in black, and veiled."

"The look for lost causes! How did they get here?"

"In a carriage with the Prince of Gonzague's crest."

"Well, hell!" said Ségré. "But that Gonzague wasn't exactly at ease when he was testifying... Still, since the Regent... Have them wait. Husson-Bordesson!"

"He went to see if your lordship's chaise was at the door."

"Never around when you need him!" grumbled the grateful Ségré. "That numbskull won't go far!" He raised his voice. "Are you dressed, Monsieur de Labaumelle? Do me the favor of going and entertaining those two ladies. I'll be with 'em in a moment."

Labaumelle, who was in shirtsleeves, threw on a big tailcoat of black velvet, slapped on his wig, and headed off for duty.

To his valet Ségré said, "You realize if the baroness doesn't like my hair, you're fired! My gloves! A carriage with the Prince of Gonzague's crest! Who could those stuck-up dames be? My hat, my walking stick! Why is there a crease in my collar, rascal? You ought to be broken on the wheel! Get me a bouquet for the baroness. Get there ahead of me, jackass!"

The judge crossed through the alcove shared by his five associates, nodding in response to their respectful bows. Then he stepped into the courtroom like a true palace dandy. It was a waste: the two ladies waiting for him with Labaumelle—the latter sitting as silent as a clam and as rigid as a sentry—took no notice of his elegant appearance. Ségré didn't recognize them; all he knew was they weren't actresses from the Opéra, like the girls Gonzague usually favored.

"Whom do I have the honor of addressing, sweet ladies?" he asked, pirouetting and doing his best to come off like a gallant swordsman. Labaumelle, released, returned to the changing room.

"Your Honor," replied the taller of the two veiled women, "I am the widow of Philippe de Lorraine, Duke of Nevers."

"Huh?" said Ségré. "But I thought Nevers's widow had married the Prince of Gonzague."

"I am the Princess of Gonzague," she replied with a kind of revulsion.

The judge made three or four courtly bows, and rushed off to the antechamber. "Chairs, villains! I can see I'll have to fire all of you one of these days!"

The bailiffs, the footmen, the clerks, the legal assistants, the runners, and all the palace rats from nearby cells were thrown into an uproar by his tone, and in the resulting commotion a dozen armchairs showed up.

"There's no need, Your Honor," said the princess, who remained standing. "My daughter and I have come..."

"Damn!" interrupted Ségré, bowing. "A lily bud! I wasn't aware that the Prince of Gonzague..."

"This is Mademoiselle de Nevers!" said the princess solemnly.

Ségré looked away uneasily, and bowed.

The princess went on, "We've come with information for the court..."

"Allow me to say that I can guess what it is, sweet lady," interrupted the judge yet again. "The work we do here sharpens and refines the wit, if I may use the expression, to a remarkable degree. It surprises people. From a word we can guess the sentence; from a sentence, the whole book. I predict you've come with further proof of the guilt of that villainous..."

"Sir!" said the princess and Aurore together.

"Superfluous! Superfluous!" Monsieur de Ségré pinched his lace ruff with delicate refinement. "It's done. The wretch will murder no more!"

"So you've heard nothing from His Royal Highness?" asked the princess dully. Aurore, almost fainting, leaned on her mother.

"Nothing at all, my lady, but there was no need. It's done, and well done. We rendered the verdict half an hour ago."

"And you heard nothing from the Regent?" repeated the princess, floored. Aurore trembled and shook beside her.

"What more do you want? That he be drawn and quartered on the Place de Grève? His Royal Highness disapproves of that kind of public execution, except to make an example in cases of bank fraud."

"So he's condemned to death?" stammered Aurore.

"What else, dear child? You want us to put him on bread and water?"

She collapsed onto a chair.

"What's wrong with the precious darling?" asked the judge. "Madame, girls don't like to hear about this kind of thing. But I hope you'll excuse me, the baroness awaits, and I have to run. I'm delighted to have been able to give you the details in person. I beg you, kindly tell the Prince of Gonzague it's all irrevocably settled. The sentence is without appeal, and tonight... Sweet lady, I kiss your hands with all my heart. Please assure Monsieur de Gonzague he can always count on his most devoted servant."

He bowed and pirouetted, and on his way to the door he shook his legs, as was then the fashion. On his way downstairs he said to himself, "I'm one step closer to chief justice! That Princess of Gonzague is on my side—with all her heart!"

The princess still stood staring at the door by which Ségré had left. As for Aurore, she looked like she'd been struck by lightning. She sat stiffly in the armchair, her eyes seeing nothing. No one was left in the courtroom. The mother and daughter thought neither of talking together nor of inquiring further: they were like statues.

Suddenly Aurore raised her arm and pointed to the door by which the judge had left, the door leading to the court and to the magistrates' exit. "He's here!" she cried in a voice that seemed no longer to belong to a living being. "He's coming. I recognize his footsteps."

The princess listened but heard nothing. She looked at her daughter, who cried again, "He's coming, I can tell. Ah, if only I could die before he dies!"

Moments later, the door opened and guards entered, leading the Chevalier Henri de Lagardère, his head bare and his hands bound before him. A few steps behind him followed a Dominican friar carrying a cross.

Tears ran down the princess's cheeks, but Aurore stood dry-eyed and still. At the sight of the two women, Lagardère stopped near the door. He smiled sadly and nodded in greeting. "Just a word, sir," he said to the officer with him.

"We have strict orders."

"I am the Princess of Gonzague, sir!" The poor mother advanced toward the officer. "His Royal Highness's cousin! Don't refuse us!"

The officer looked at her in surprise. Then he turned to his prisoner. "Only to satisfy a dying man's last request. Make it fast!" He bowed to the princess and retired to the next room, followed by his troops and the friar.

Lagardère came slowly toward Aurore.

VII. The Final Meeting

The door remained open, and they could hear a sentinel pacing in the corridor, but they were alone in the courtroom: their final meeting would have no witnesses. Aurore rose and stood up straight to receive Lagardère. She kissed his bound hands, then presented her brow—as white as marble—and he pressed his lips to it without a word. Tears finally ran down her cheeks when she saw her mother moving aside to weep.

"Henri! Henri! So this is how we were destined to see each other again!"

Lagardère gazed at her as if he were trying concentrate all his love, all the tenderness that had been the focus of his life for years, into these last moments. "I've never seen you so beautiful, Aurore," he murmured, "and your voice has never reached so sweetly all the way to the bottom of my heart. Thank you for coming. My hours in captivity passed quickly: you filled them, and the dear remembrance of you watched over me. Thank you for coming, thank you, my beloved angel!" He turned toward the princess. "Thank you, Madame. To you above all, my thanks. You could've refused me this last joy."

"Refused you!" cried Aurore impulsively.

The prisoner glanced from the daughter's proud face to the mother's bowed head, and he understood. "This isn't right. It shouldn't be this way, Aurore. For the first time, my lips and my heart have cause to reproach you. I can see you gave the orders, and your obedient mother came. Don't answer, Aurore. Time's running out, and I can't give you much more instruction. Love your mother; obey your mother. Today despair gives you an excuse, but tomorrow..."

"Tomorrow, Henri," Aurore said firmly, "if you're dead, I'll be dead!"

He drew back a step and looked at her sternly. "I had one consolation, almost a joy: to tell myself as I departed this world, 'I leave my life's work behind me, and in heaven Nevers will extend his hand to me, because he'll have seen I left his daughter and his wife happy.'"

"Happy! Happy without you!" Aurore laughed madly.

"But I was mistaken. I won't have that consolation, and you're robbing me of that joy! I labored for twenty years, only to see my work destroyed at the final hour. This interview has lasted long enough. Farewell, Mademoiselle de Nevers!"

The princess had quietly drawn near. Like Aurore, she kissed the prisoner's bound hands. "And it's you!" she murmured. "You who plead my cause!" Aurore crumpled into her arms. "Don't punish her!" the princess went on. "It's me, my jealousy, my arrogance..."

"Mother, Mother!" cried Aurore. "You're breaking my heart!"

434

They collapsed together onto a large armchair. Lagardère remained standing before them. "You're mother's wrong, Aurore. You're wrong, Madame. Your arrogance and your jealousy were prompted by love. You're Nevers's widow—and who forgot that for a moment? I did! Only one person is at fault, and that's me." His noble face grew sad and solemn. "Listen to me, Aurore. My crime only betrayed itself for a moment, and its excuse was the mad, radiant, thousand-fold precious dream in which I saw the gates of Paradise open. But that crime was great enough to wipe out twenty years of devotion. For a moment—a single moment!—I wanted to tear a daughter away from her mother!"

The princess lowered her eyes, and Aurore hid her face in her mother's breast.

"God has punished me," he cried. "God is just. I will die."

"But is there no recourse?" cried the princess, feeling her daughter weakening in her arms.

"I'll die just when my life, a struggle for so long, was about to open like a flower. I've done wrong, and the punishment is harsh. God is even angrier with those who tarnish a good deed with a crime—that's what I realized in prison. What right did I have to defy you, Madame? I should have brought her straight to you, happy and smiling, by the front door of your villa. I should have left you to embrace each other. Then she would have told you she loved me and I loved her. And I would have fallen at your feet and begged you to bless us both." He knelt slowly, and Aurore did the same. "And you would have done it, wouldn't you, Madame?"

The princess hesitated—unable either to bless them or to reply.

"You would have done it, Mother," said Aurore very quietly, "just as you're going to do it now at this fatal hour."

They both bowed their heads.

The princess, her cheeks bathed with tears, lifted her eyes to heaven. "Lord God, perform a miracle!" Then she kissed their heads, which touched each other. "Children! Children!"

Aurore rose and threw herself into her mother's arms.

"Now we've been engaged twice, Aurore," said Lagardère. "Thank you, Madame. Thank you, Mother! I never thought I could cry tears of joy in this place!" He stood up, and his expression changed. "And now it's time for us to part, Aurore."

She turned deathly pale—she'd almost forgotten.

"Not forever," he smiled. "We'll see each other at least once more. But you must step aside, Aurore; I need to talk to your mother."

Aurore pressed his hands to her heart, and moved away to a window alcove.

"Madame," he said when they were alone, "any moment now that door's going to open, and I still have several things to tell you. I think you're being honest with me. You've forgiven me. But would you agree to honor the wish of a dying man?"

"Whether you live or die, sir—and you'd live if it took all the blood in my body to do it—I swear on my honor I'd refuse you nothing." She stopped to consider. "Nothing. I'm trying to think if there's anything in the world I could refuse you, and there's nothing!"

"Then listen to me, and let God reward you with your dear daughter's love! I'm condemned to death, I know, though they have yet to read out my sentence. No one's ever reversed the final sentence of the Burning Court.—No, I'm wrong, there's one case: under the late king, the Count of Bossut, who'd been condemned to death for poisoning the Elector of Hesse, had his life spared because an Italian, Grimaldi, who was already sentenced for other crimes, wrote to Madame de Maintenon and confessed. But in my case the real criminal isn't going to confess—and anyway that wasn't what I wanted to talk to you about."

"Still, if there remained any hope..."

"There's no hope. It's three in the afternoon. The sun sets at seven. Toward dusk an escort will come to take me to the Bastille. At eight I'll be taken to the execution yard."

"I understand! Along the way, if we had friends..."

He shook his head with a sad smile. "No, Madame, you don't understand. Let me be clear, because I don't expect you to guess. Between the Châtelet, from where I'll start, and the courtyard at the Bastille, where my final journey will end, there'll be one stop: the Saint Magloire cemetery."

"The Saint Magloire cemetery!" The princess trembled.

Lagardère gave a slightly bitter smile. "Doesn't the murderer have to make public atonement at the tomb of his victim?"

"You, Henri! You, Nevers's protector! You, our help and salvation!"

"Not so loud, Madame. At Nevers's tomb there'll be a chopping block and an ax. I'll have my right hand cut off there."

The princess hid her face in her hands. At the other end of the room, Aurore knelt weeping in prayer.

"That's unjust, isn't it, Madame? And though I don't bear a famous name, you can understand the torment, in my last hour, of leaving behind such a shameful memory!"

"But why such a pointless act of cruelty?"

"Judge Ségré said, 'You can't go around killing a duke and peer like he's just anybody! We have to make an example of you!'"

"But, my God, it wasn't you! The Regent won't allow..."

"The Regent could do anything he pleased before the court passed sentence. Now, unless the real perpetrator confesses... But please, Madame, let's not worry about that. Here's my last request: you can turn my death into a martyr's hymn of thanksgiving; you can rehabilitate me in the eyes of all. Would you do it?"

"Would I? You're asking me to! What must I do?"

He lowered his voice further. In spite of her solemn agreement, his voice shook. "The front steps of the church are near the tomb. If Mademoiselle de Nevers were there by the church door, in a wedding dress; if there were a priest in his vestments; if you too were there, Madame; and if my escort had been bribed to grant me a few minutes to kneel at the altar rail... "

The princess drew back, her legs tottering.

"I'm frightening you, Madame..."

"Go on! Go on!" Her voice shook.

"If, with the consent of the Princess of Gonzague, the priest blessed the union of the Chevalier Henri de Lagardère and Mademoiselle de Nevers..."

"On my salvation," interrupted the princess, drawing herself up, "it will happen!"

Lagardère's eyes shone. He tried to kiss her hands, but she declined; and instead Aurore, turning at the sound, saw her mother holding the prisoner in her arms.

Others saw it too, because at that moment the courtroom door opened and the officer and his men entered.

The princess, paying no attention, went on in a kind of passionate exhilaration, "And who'll dare say that Nevers's widow, who has dressed in mourning for twenty years, allowed her daughter to marry her husband's murderer! That's good thinking, Henri, my son! Don't say anymore I haven't understood you!"

This time it was Lagardère whose eyes filled with tears. "Ah, you understand!" he murmured. "And you've made me bitter at losing my life! I thought I was losing only one treasure..."

"Who'll dare say it?" she went on. "The priest will be there, I swear it. It'll be my own confessor. The escort will give us time, if I have to sell all my jewels, if I have to hand over to the pawnbrokers the wedding ring I got at Caylus! And once the union has been blessed, the priest and the mother and the bride will follow the condemned man through the streets of Paris. And I'll say..."

"Silence, Madame, for God's sake!" he said. "We're no longer alone."

The officer came forward, staff in hand. "Sir, I've overstepped my authority. I'll ask you to follow me."

Aurore ran to Lagardère to give him a farewell kiss. The princess leaned in and whispered in his ear, "Count on me! But besides that, can nothing else be done?"

Lagardère was already turning to join the officer, but he paused in thought. "Listen. It's not even really a chance. But the family tribunal meets at eight. I'll be very near there. If somehow I could be brought into His Royal Highness's presence, in the midst of the tribunal..."

The princess squeezed his hand and said nothing. Aurore fixed her sad eyes on Lagardère as the soldiers surrounded him again and the dismal Dominican friar took up his place next to him. The procession vanished out the door leading to the Tour Neuve.

The princess took Aurore by the hand and pulled her away. "Come, child, all is not yet lost—God wouldn't want this shameful crime to take place!"

More dead than alive, Aurore heard nothing. As they climbed into their carriage, the princess said to the coachman, "To the Palais-Royal! On the double!"

At the moment their carriage set off, another carriage, waiting beneath the ramparts, also began to move. Through the window an excited voice called to the coachman, "If you don't reach the Fountain Court before the princess's carriage, you're fired!" Inside that second carriage, in a change of clothes, sprawled Monsieur de Peyrolles, in an unmistakably ugly mood. He too had come from the Châtelet courts, where he'd spit fire and brimstone after having spent two thirds of the day locked up.

His carriage overtook the princess's at the Trahoir crossroads and reached the Fountain Court first. Peyrolles leaped out and rushed through Le Bréant's lodge without a word. When Madame de Gonzague presented herself and requested an audience with the Regent, she was curtly refused out of hand. She thought of attending His Royal Highness's public departure or return—but it was getting late, and first she had to keep her promise to Lagardère.

The Prince of Gonzague was in his private study, where we first saw him when Doña Cruz visited him. On a table covered in papers lay his unsheathed sword. He was in the process of putting on—without the help of his valet—one of those light vests of chain mail that can be worn under clothing. To do so he'd taken off, and was about to put back on, a suit of court dress in black velvet without decoration. His cordon of rank hung from the arm of a chair.

Now that trouble and worry bore down heavily on him, the ravages of time—which normally he disguised with so much skill—told clearly on his face. His barber had neglected to arrange his black hair over his temples, revealing the sad retreat of his hairline and the wrinkles bunched at the corners of his eyes. He was tall, but now he slumped like an old man, and his hands shook as he fastened his armor.

"He's been sentenced! The Regent allowed it to go forward. Is he that morally indifferent, or did I really manage to persuade him? I've lost weight around the chest; my coat of mail is too loose. But I've put on weight around my waist; the mail's too tight over my stomach. Is this really old age? He's a strange creature—a joking prince, querulous, idle, cowardly. If he's not careful, though I'm the eldest, I might be the last survivor of the three Philippes! He made a mistake with me, God's death! He made a mistake! When you've got your foot on an enemy's neck, you'd better not take it off—especially when your enemy's name is Philippe of Mantua! Enemy! All beautiful friendships end that way. If

Damon and Pythias hadn't died young, they'd have found plenty of reasons to cut each other's throats when they grew up."

The coat of mail was fastened. Gonzague put on his doublet, his cordon of rank, and his sword belt. Then he ran a comb through his hair before putting on his wig.

"And that simpleton Peyrolles!" He shrugged. "There's a fellow who just wants to escape to Milan or Madrid! The fool's got millions! Sometimes it's a pleasure to drain your own leaches dry—he's like something I saved up for a rainy day."

Someone knocked lightly three times on the door leading to the library.

"Come in," said Gonzague. "I've been expecting you for an hour."

In the doorway appeared Monsieur de Peyrolles, who'd taken the time to go change his clothes. "Don't bother scolding me, my lord: it was beyond my control—I just got out of the Châtelet prison. Luckily those two rascals, in making a run for it, did exactly what I went there to bring about anyway: they didn't show up at the trial, so I was the only witness. The job's done. In an hour that demon from Hell will have his head chopped off, and tonight we can sleep soundly."

Gonzague had trouble following all that, so Peyrolles summarized his misadventures at the Tour Neuve, and the escape of the two masters of arms and Chaverny. The latter name made the prince frown, but there was no time to linger over details. Then Peyrolles reported seeing the Princess of Gonzague and Aurore coming out of the courtroom. "I got to the Palais-Royal only seconds ahead of them, but that was enough. Your lordship owes me for two stock shares worth five and a quarter livres, at today's exchange rate; I slipped them into Monsieur Nanty's hands to deny entry to the ladies."

"Well done. And the other business?"

"Taken care of. Post horses for eight o'clock, arranged all the way to Bayonne, by courier."

"Well done." Gonzague drew a parchment from his pocket.

"What's that?"

"My appointment as a secret envoy on royal assignment, signed by Minister d'Argenson."

"Done on his own initiative?" murmured Peyrolles in surprise.

"They think I'm more in favor than ever; I made sure of that. And in fact, by God, are they wrong? I must be pretty secure, Peyrolles, for the Regent to have let me go free. Pretty secure! If Lagardère's head falls, I'll reach such heights all of you will have vertigo. The Regent won't be able to do enough to make amends to me for his suspicions today. I'll hold him to it, and if he tries to bluster his way out of it—once Lagardère, that Sword of Damocles, is no longer hanging over my head—God's death! I've saved up enough blue, white, and yellow shares to suck the Bank down the drain!"

Peyrolles nodded his approval, as was his place and his duty. "Is it true His Royal Highness will preside over the family tribunal?"

"I persuaded him to do it," replied Gonzague boldly, because he deceived even his loyal servants.

"And what about Doña Cruz? Can you count on her?"

"More than ever. She swore to appear at the session." Peyrolles looked him in the eye, and Gonzague smiled mockingly. "If Doña Cruz suddenly disappears," he murmured, "what can I do? I have enemies who'd like that. But it's enough that the girl did exist—the members of the tribunal saw her." Peyrolles began a question, but Gonzague cut him off. "We'll see how things go this evening, Peyrolles. The princess could've gotten in to see the Regent without worrying me in the least. I have my commission as envoy and, even better, I still have my freedom, after being accused of murder—accused by implication. I've had a whole day to maneuver. Without realizing it, the Regent has made me a giant! God's blood! The minutes pass slowly; I'm impatient."

"Then your lordship is sure of victory?" asked Peyrolles deferentially. Gonzague's only answer was an arrogant smile. "So why the summons to your vassals and all their vassals?" insisted Peyrolles. "Out in the hall I saw all our people fully equipped—equipped to take the field, by God!"

"They're here by order."

"You expect a battle?"

"Back home in Italy," said Gonzague offhandedly, "even the greatest generals make sure to protect their rear. Every medal has a flip side. Those gentlemen are my rear guard. Have they been waiting long?"

"I don't know. They saw me go by and didn't say a word."

"How do they seem?"

"Like beaten dogs or schoolboys in detention."

"Nobody's missing?"

"Nobody but Chaverny."

"Peyrolles, while you were in prison, something happened here. I could put you—even you, my friend—through hell if I felt like it."

"If your lordship will just tell me..." began Peyrolles, already quaking.

"It'd be a bore to explain it twice. I'll explain it in front of everybody."

"Shall I go alert the gentlemen?" asked Peyrolles eagerly.

Gonzague eyed him sidelong. "God's death!" he muttered. "I don't want to put temptation in your way—you'd skip town!" He rang, and a servant appeared. "Send in the gentlemen who are waiting!" Turning back to the downcast Peyrolles, he added, "I think it was you, the other day, in the heat of your zeal, who said, 'My lord, if we need to we'll follow you into Hell!' Well, we're on our way now, so let's enjoy the ride!"

VIII. Former Gentlemen

There wasn't a lot of variety among Gonzague's followers. Chaverny stood out among them: he'd had a little bit of genuine devotion to the prince. With Chaverny now out of the picture, there remained Navailles, who'd been somewhat seduced by Gonzague's more dazzling qualities; and Choisy and Nocé, who were gentlemen of real character and breeding. As for the others, they'd attached themselves to the prince entirely from self-interest and ambition. Oriol the fat little financier, Taranne, the Baron of Batz, and all the rest would have betrayed Gonzague for substantially less than thirty pieces of silver. Still, even they weren't really criminals; to tell the truth, there wasn't a criminal among them—they were just rakes gone astray. Gonzague had taken them as they came. They'd followed his lead, willingly at first, and then by force. They didn't enjoy doing evil, but it was mostly the danger that bothered them. Gonzague understood them perfectly. He wouldn't have swapped them for hardened criminals: they were exactly what he needed.

As they all came in together, what struck them first was the look on the faces of the master and his factotum: Peyrolles's sad and Gonzague's arrogant. During the hour they'd been waiting in the hall, they'd entertained God knows how many theories. They'd studied Gonzague's position with a magnifying glass. Some of them had shown up with vague ideas of rebellion, because the previous night had made a grim impression on them—but all the talk at court was of the Prince of Gonzague rising ever higher in favor. This was no time to turn their backs to the sun. It was true that other rumors had made the rounds. The Rue Quincampoix and the House of Gold had given a lot of thought to Monsieur de Gonzague today. They said His Royal Highness had heard from informers, and during the whole night of revelry that had ended in bloodshed the walls of Gonzague's pleasure house had been as if made of glass. But one piece of news predominated: the Burning Court had passed judgment, and the Chevalier Henri de Lagardère was sentenced to death. Every one of those gentlemen knew at least a little about the past. That Gonzague must be powerful!

Choisy had arrived with strange news: that very morning Chaverny had been picked up at his villa and put into a carriage with an officer and some soldiers—the familiar start to a journey leading to the Bastille, by means of a passport in the form of an arrest warrant. They hadn't discussed Chaverny much, because each of them was looking out for himself, and anyway each of them distrusted all the rest. But the general mood was unmistakable: discouragement, weariness, and disgust. They wanted to halt on the slippery slope. And among all of Gonzague's followers there might not have been one who hadn't come that evening with secret thoughts of breaking the pact. Peyrolles had been right: they were literally dressed for war—boots, spurs, battle swords, traveling cloaks.

Gonzague had stipulated the gear when he summoned them, which only intensi-fied their anxious, agitated desire to draw back.

"Cousin," said Navailles as he led them all in, "here we are at your orders once again."

Gonzague gave him a patron's smile and nod. The others rendered the prince their usual respectful bows. Without inviting them to sit down, he looked around the circle. "Good," he murmured. "I see nobody's missing."

Nocé spoke up. "Albret, Gironne, and Chaverny are missing." There was a silence while they all waited for their master's response.

Gonzague frowned slightly. "Gironne and Albret did their duty," he said curtly.

"Damn, cousin!" said Navailles. "That was a brief funeral oration. We're subjects only of the king."

"As for Monsieur de Chaverny," continued Gonzague, "he got a touch of the scruples, and I had to cashier him."

"Will your lordship be so good as to explain what you mean by 'cashier'?" said Navailles. "We heard mention of the Bastille."

"The Bastille is a big place," murmured Gonzague with a cruel smile, "with plenty of room for others."

At that moment Oriol would have given up his title of nobility—so recent and so precious to him—and half the shares he owned, and the love of Made-moiselle Nivelle into the bargain, to wake from this nightmare. Over in the cor-ner by the chimney stood Peyrolles, unmoving, sorrowful, silent. Navailles glanced inquiringly around at his companions.

"Gentlemen," said Gonzague in a new tone of voice, "I suggest you not think about Monsieur de Chaverny or anyone else. You have work to do. Be-lieve me, you should be worrying about yourselves." As he looked around the circle, they all lowered their eyes.

"Cousin," said Navailles quietly, "every word you speak sounds like a threat."

"Cousin," answered Gonzague, "my words are clear. It's not I who threat-ens you, it's fate."

"What's going on?' asked several voices.

"Not much. It's the last round of the game, and I need all my cards."

The circle tightened unconsciously around him, and Gonzague waved them back with an almost regal gesture. Standing with his back to the fireplace, he assumed an orator's pose. "The family tribunal meets tonight, and His Royal Highness the Regent will preside."

"We know that, my lord," said Taranne, "and we're all the more surprised at how you told us to dress. This is no way to appear at such a gathering."

"True enough, because I won't be needing you at the tribunal."

There was a general cry of surprise, and they all looked at each other.

"Is this about swordplay again?" said Navailles.

442

"Maybe."

"My lord," said Navailles firmly, "Speaking only for myself..."

"Don't speak, even for yourself, cousin! You've stepped out onto a slippery bridge. I warn you: I don't even need to push you to make you fall—all I have to do is stop holding your hand. If you still want to say something, Navailles, at least wait until I've explained our position to everybody."

"I'll wait until your lordship has explained," murmured Navailles. "But I want to warn you in turn: we've had time to think things over since last night."

Gonzague eyed him for a moment with pity, then collected himself. "I don't need you at the tribunal, gentlemen; I need you elsewhere. Court dress and rapiers for show would be useless for what you have to do. A man's been sentenced to death, but you know the Spanish proverb: 'Between the cup and the lip, between the ax and the neck...' Right now the executioner awaits a man..."

"Monsieur de Lagardère," said Nocé.

"Or me," said Gonzague coldly.

"You? You, my lord?" they all cried. Peyrolles stood up, appalled.

"Stop shaking," said Gonzague with an arrogant smile. "It's not up to the executioner. But with a demon like that—I'm talking about Lagardère—who managed to find himself powerful allies even from inside his prison cell, only one thing can make me safe: dirt, six feet deep, covering his corpse. As long as he's alive, his arms in chains but his wits at liberty, as long as his mouth can open and his tongue can speak, we need one hand on the sword, one foot in the stirrup, and we need to keep our heads!"

"Our heads!" cried Nocé, straightening up.

"By God," cried Navailles, "This is too much, my lord. If you're just speaking for yourself..."

"I swear," muttered Oriol, "things are getting ugly, and I can't take it anymore." He took a step toward the door, which was open—but outside Gonzague's apartment, in the vestibule leading to the great hall of the Villa Gonzague, stood armed Royal Guards. Oriol backed up, and Taranne closed the door.

"Don't worry about them, gentlemen," said Gonzague. "Those men are just here as an honor guard to receive the Regent. You won't leave here by way of the vestibule. Now, I said 'our heads' and that seemed to upset you."

"My lord," said Navailles, "you're going too far. Threats aren't going to work with men like us. We've been your faithful friends as long as we were on a course gentlemen could follow. Now it looks like a matter for Gauthier Gendry and his cutthroats. Farewell, my lord!"

"Farewell, my lord!" echoed the whole circle.

Gonzague laughed bitterly. "And you too, Peyrolles!" he said, seeing his factotum slipping in among the crowd trying to flee. "Ah, I had your number, gentlemen! Well, my faithful friends, as Monsieur de Navailles put it, just one more thing. Where are you going? Don't you know that door leads straight to the Bastille?"

Navailles already had his hand on the doorknob. He withdrew it, and rested it on his sword.

His arms folded, standing calmly amid all the frightened faces, Gonzague laughed. He stared them all down with scorn. "Can't you see this is exactly what I expected from such honest men? Haven't you heard I had the Regent all to myself from eight this morning till noon? Don't you know the winds of favor are blowing toward me at gale force?—blowing so hard they might break me, but not before they break you, my faithful friends, I swear! If this is my last day in power, I have no regrets: I've made good use of my last day. Your names—all of your names—are on a list. That list is on Monsieur de Machault's desk. At a word from me, every name on that list is a lord of high rank; at a different word from me, it's a list of banished men."

"We'll take our chances," said Navailles. But his voice was weak, and the others kept silent.

"'We'll follow you, we'll follow you, your lordship!'" said Gonzague, mimicking their words from a few days earlier. "'We'll follow you meekly, blindly, gamely! We'll form a holy battalion around you!' Who was singing that song, the one whose tune every traitor knows? You or me? And now, at the first gust of wind from the storm, I look around in vain for a soldier—one single soldier from the holy battalion! Where are you, my faithful followers? Running away? Not yet, God's death! I'm coming behind you, and I'll pass my sword through the guts of any runaways."

Navailles opened his mouth to speak, but Gonzague cut him off. "Silence, cousin! I don't have the patience to listen to any more of your bluster. You all handed yourselves over to me, freely and fully. I took you, and I'm keeping you. Oh, this is too much, you say? Oh, I've gone too far, you say? Ha, ha! It seems I have to chart my course very circumspectly for you gentlemen to be willing to follow it. Ha, ha! You throw Gauthier Gendry at me—you, Navailles, who live off me; you, Taranne, bloated with my handouts; you, Oriol, a buffoon passing for a man, thanks to me; and all the rest of you: my dependents, my creatures, my slaves, since you sold yourselves, since I bought you!"

He towered over even the tallest of them by a foot, and his eyes flashed. "This isn't your problem? You want me just to speak for myself? I swear to God, my scrupulous friends, this is your problem, the biggest and most serious problem you have, your only problem right now. I let you have some cake, you ate it eagerly, and too bad for you if the cake was poisoned! Your piece will taste just as bad as mine! If that isn't morality, I don't know what is—right, Batz, you strict philosopher? Why did you all cling to me? I assume it was to climb as high as I did. Well then, climb, God's death! Climb! Are you dizzy? Climb, climb some more, climb right onto the scaffold!"

444

There was a general shiver. All eyes were fastened on Gonzague's frightening face. Oriol, whose knees were knocking together, couldn't help repeating the prince's last word. "The scaffold!"

Gonzague glared at him with unspeakable scorn. "The noose for you, peasant." Then he bowed sarcastically to Navailles, Choisy, and the rest. "But you, gentlemen, who are of the nobility..." He paused and stared at them, his scorn overflowing. "You, Nocé, a gentleman, a fine soldier's son, and a stockjobbing courtier! You, Choisy, a gentleman! You, Montaubert, a gentleman! You too, Navailles, a gentleman! You a gentleman likewise, Baron of Batz!"

"Gottamn it!" muttered the baron.

"Shut up, creep! Gentlemen, I challenge you to look at yourselves, not only without laughing like the augurs of ancient Rome, but without blushing to the whites of your eyes! Gentlemen, you?! No: clever financiers, quicker with a pen than a sword." His face changed. He stepped closer, and every one of them drew back. "Tonight..." He lowered his voice. "It's not yet dark enough to hide your ashen faces. Look around at each other, trembling, anxious, caught as if in a trap between my victory and my defeat—my victory that would become yours, my defeat that would crush you."

He'd reached the door leading to the vestibule where the Regent's soldiers waited. He took hold of the doorknob. "I'm through. Repentance is expiation, and you seem full of good intentions. You can achieve martyrdom by going through this door. Shall I open it?"

The only answer was silence. Then Montaubert was the first to speak. "What's the job, my lord?"

Gonzague looked them all up and down. "You too, cousin Navailles?"

"Whatever your lordship wishes," he replied, his face pale and his eyes lowered.

Gonzague held out his hand to him, and then addressed them all in the tone of a father sorry to have to scold his children. "Fools that you are—you've reached port and you were going to founder at the final pull of the oars! Listen to me and repent. No matter how the battle turns out, I've made you safe in advance: tomorrow you'll either be the greatest men in Paris, or you'll be on your way to Spain carrying plenty of gold and high hopes. King Philip of Spain awaits us, and who knows whether his minister Alberoni won't lower the Pyrenees in a sense different from the way Louis XIV wanted to!"

He glanced at his pocket watch. "At this very hour, Lagardère is leaving the Châtelet prison, on his way to the Bastille for the final act of the play. But he won't go straight there: the sentence requires him to make public atonement at Nevers's tomb. The forces arrayed against us consist of two women and a priest; against them your swords can do nothing. A third woman, Doña Cruz, is floating between the two sides—at least I think so. She wants to be a noble lady, but she doesn't want her friend to get hurt. She's a weak reed, and she'll get broken. The two women are the Princess of Gonzague and her alleged daughter Aurore. I needed to get my hands on that Aurore, so I've allowed the plot that will deliver her to us to go forward. Here's the plot: the mother, the daughter, and the priest are waiting for Lagardère at the Saint Magloire church. The girl has put back on her wedding dress. I assume, just as you would, the idea is to stage some scene to provoke the Regent's clemency: a wedding *in extremis*, and then the virgin widow throwing herself at His Royal Highness's feet. We can't let that happen; that's the first half of the job."

"Easy enough," said Montaubert. "We just have to keep them from playing the scene."

"You'll be there, and you'll block the way into the church; that's the second half of the job. If our luck turns, and we have to flee, I have gold—enough for all of you—and on that I give you my word of honor. I also have the king's commission, which will open all doors to us." He unfolded the document and showed them Minister d'Argenson's signature. "But I need more than that. We have to take our living ransom, our hostage, with us."

"Aurore de Nevers?" said several voices.

"Between you and her there'll be nothing but a church door."

"But on the other side of that door," said Montaubert, "if our luck has turned, won't there be Lagardère?"

"And me facing Lagardère!" said Gonzague solemnly. He slapped his sword. "The time has come to call on this! My blade's as good as his, gentlemen—it was quenched in Nevers's blood!"

Peyrolles's head spun. That confession made aloud proved to him his master was burning his boats.

There was a loud noise from the vestibule, and the Royal Guards cried, "The Regent! The Regent!"

Gonzague opened the door to the library and shook hands with those around him. "Gentlemen, stay calm. In half an hour it'll be over. If all goes well, you just have to keep the procession from climbing the steps of the church. Call for help from the crowd, and scream 'Sacrilege!' It's one of those words that never fails. If things go badly, remember this: from the cemetery where you'll be waiting for me you can see the windows of the great hall here. Keep an eye on those windows. If you see a candlestick move up and down three times, force the church doors and attack! I'll join you the minute after I give you the signal. Is that clear?"

"Perfectly clear," they answered.

"Since he knows the way, follow Peyrolles, gentlemen, and get to the cemetery through the villa gardens."

They all went out. Gonzague was left alone, mopping his brow. "Whether he's a man or a devil, that Lagardère is doomed." He crossed the room, heading toward the vestibule, but paused in front of a mirror. "That little adventurer hasn't got a chance. A foundling against a prince! Let's go play those odds!"

Behind the closed door of the Saint Magloire church, the Princess of Gonzague supported her daughter, who was dressed in white and wearing a bridal veil and a wreath of orange blossoms. The priest had on his vestments. Doña Cruz knelt in prayer. In the shadows stood three armed men. The steeple clock rang eight, and in the distance they could hear the tolling of the death knell at the Sainte Chapelle, announcing the departure of the condemned man. The princess thought her heart would break.

Aurore, though whiter than a marble statue, had a smile on her lips. "The time has come, Mother."

The princess kissed her brow. "I know we need to part now," she murmured, "but I felt you were safe as long as your hand was in mine."

"Madame," said Doña Cruz, "we'll watch over her. The Marquis of Chaverny has vowed to defend her with his life."

"Crooked ace!" muttered one of the three men. "The little sweetheart didn't even mention us, brother!"

Instead of going straight to the door, the princess crossed to where Chaverny, Cocardasse, and Passepoil stood. Before she could speak a word, Cocardasse said, "God's blood! This little gentleman here can be a devil when he wants, and he'll be fighting under the eyes of his beloved. And we two, this rascal Passepoil and myself, we'd fight to the death for Lagardère. It's understood, God's hat! Now go do your part!"

IX. The Dead Man Speaks

The great hall of the Villa Gonzague glowed with light. From the courtyard came the sound of horses belonging to the Savoy hussars. The vestibule was full of Royal Guards. The Marquis of Bonnivet was in charge of guarding the doors. Clearly the Regent meant to give this family occasion as much prestige and importance as possible. The seats arranged on the dais held the same cast as two days earlier: the same dignitaries, the same magistrates, the same high lords. But behind Monsieur de Lamoignon's chair sat the Regent on a sort of throne. Around him sat Minister Le Blanc, Minister d'Argenson, and the Count of Toulouse, Governor of Brittany.

The parties in the case had changed places: when the princess entered, she was seated next to Cardinal de Bissy, who was now on the judges' right hand; whereas Monsieur de Gonzague sat at a table lit by two candlesticks—at the very spot where his wife's chair had been two days earlier. That way Gonzague sat with his back against the curtains concealing the little door the hunchback had used to get into the first session, and facing one of the windows that looked toward the Saint Magloire cemetery. The hidden door was unknown to the organizers of the gathering, and therefore unguarded. It goes without saying that all the commercial alterations that had disfigured this great and noble hall had vanished completely, and the curtains and the wall hangings concealed every trace of them.

When the Prince of Gonzague had come in, before his wife, he'd bowed respectfully to the judge and to the company. People noticed that His Royal Highness had nodded back at him in a very friendly way.

Then the Count of Toulouse, one of Louis XIV's sons, went to meet the princess at the door—as instructed by the Regent, who took a few welcoming steps toward her himself, and kissed her hand.

"Your Royal Highness didn't deign to receive me today," said the princess. She stopped as she saw the look of surprise on his face.

Gonzague followed their encounter out of the corner of his eye while he pretended to devote his attention to sorting the papers he'd set down on his table. Among those papers lay a large parchment envelope closed with three hanging seals.

"Your Royal Highness likewise didn't deign to reply to my message," went on the princess.

"What message?" whispered the Regent.

The princess unconsciously glanced toward her husband. "My letter must've been intercepted..."

"Madame," interrupted the Regent. "Nothing is settled, everything remains in question. Act without fear, according to your conscience. From now on, no one can stand between you and me." Then, taking leave of her, he raised his voice. "This is a great day for you, Madame, and it's not just for the sake of our cousin Gonzague that we wished to witness this family gathering. The hour has come for Nevers's revenge: his murderer will die."

"Ah, my lord!" said the princess. "If only you'd gotten my message..."

As he led her to her seat, the Regent murmured quickly, "Everything you ask for I will grant." Then he went on in a louder voice, "Gentlemen, take your seats, if you please."

When he'd reached his own seat, Chief Judge de Lamoignon stood and whispered a few words in his ear.

"Forms and procedures," replied the Regent. "Yes, I'm a great admirer of proper forms, and everything will take place according to procedure. I hope at last we'll be able to acknowledge Nevers's genuine heiress."

So saying, he sat down and put on his hat, leaving the management of the debate to the Chief Judge. Lamoignon called first on Monsieur de Gonzague.

Something odd was going on outside. The wind was from the south. From time to time the toll of the mournful death knell at the Sainte Chapelle seemed to be coming from the next room, and they could hear some kind of indistinct noise in the distance: the tolling bell had summoned a crowd, and the crowd had taken up its position in the streets. When Gonzague rose to speak, the bell tolled so loudly that for a few moments he was forced to remain silent. Outside the shouts of the crowd greeted the death knell.

"Your Excellency, gentlemen," began Gonzague, "I've lived my whole life in the open. Underhanded maneuvers have always gotten the better of me: I can never foil them, because I lack an instinct for trickery and deception. You know that until recently I sought the truth with a certain zeal. That fine zeal has cooled. I'm weary of the accusations piling up against me in the shadows. I'm weary of always finding my way blocked by blind suspicion and cowardly contemptible slander. I've already presented the girl I maintained—and still maintain more than ever—to be Nevers's genuine heiress. I look in vain for her now: her rightful seat is empty. Your Royal Highness knows that as of this morning I've resigned her guardianship—so whether or not she joins us now is of no matter to me. I have only one object: to show all of you on which side of this dispute stand good faith, honor, and nobility of spirit." He picked up the parchment envelope from the table. "I bring the proof called for by the princess herself— the page ripped from the Caylus chapel registry. There it is, under triple seal. As I am submitting my evidence, I call on the princess to submit hers."

He bowed once again to the company and sat down. There were some whispers from the back rows. Gonzague lacked the enthusiastic supporters he'd had here last time. But why would he need them? He was asking for nothing, except a chance to prove his integrity. And that proof lay on the table—material, incontrovertible proof.

The Regent leaned down between Chief Judge de Lamoignon and General de Villeroy. "We await the princess's reply."

"If the princess had confided her intentions to me..." began Cardinal de Bissy.

The princess rose. "My lord, I have my daughter, and the proof of her birth. Look at me, all of you who saw me in tears, and you'll understand from my joy that I've found my child."

"The proof you speak of, Madame..." began Chief Judge de Lamoignon.

"That proof will be submitted to the council," she interrupted, "as soon as His Royal Highness has granted the petition humbly presented to him by Nevers's widow."

"Nevers's widow has not yet presented me any petition," said the Regent.

The princess turned her steady gaze on Gonzague. "Friendship is a fine and beautiful thing. For the last two days everyone with my interests at heart has been telling me, 'Don't accuse your husband, don't accuse your husband.' I assume they mean that one powerful friend amounts to an impenetrable shield around the prince. So I'll make no accusations, but I'll say that I addressed a humble petition to His Royal Highness, and that it was deflected by an unknown hand."

Gonzague allowed himself a calm, resigned smile.

"What did you request of us, Madame?" asked the Regent.

"My lord, I invoked another friendship. I didn't accuse, I pleaded. I wrote Your Royal Highness that the public atonement prescribed at the tomb wasn't enough."

Gonzague's face changed.

"I wrote Your Royal Highness," she went on, "that there was another public atonement—greater, worthier, fuller—and I begged him to order that right here where we are, in the Villa Nevers, before the head of state and before this illustrious assembly, the condemned man, on his knees, should hear his sentence read aloud."

Gonzague had to half-close his eyes to hide their fire. The princess was lying, and Gonzague knew it, because he had her letter in his pocket—the letter she'd sent to the Regent and that Gonzague himself had intercepted. In her letter the princess gave the Regent her formal guarantee of Lagardère's innocence. That was all. Why the lie? What broadside was she hiding behind this bold feint? For the first time in his life Gonzague felt ice in his veins from some terrible unknown danger. He felt like the ground under him was mined and about to blow up. But he didn't know how to find the bomb in time to stop it going off. He sensed the abyss under him—but where? Night had fallen. Any move might betray him. He knew all eyes must be on him. With a mighty effort he stayed calm. He waited.

"That would not be the normal procedure," said Chief Judge de Lamoignon to the princess.

450

Gonzague could have kissed him.

"Can the princess offer us any reasons for..." began General de Villeroy.

"I'm addressing His Royal Highness," she interrupted. "The law has taken twenty years to find Nevers's murderer; surely the law owes something to the victim who's waited so long for vengeance. Mademoiselle de Nevers, my daughter, cannot enter this house until satisfaction has been given in full. And I'll deny myself all rejoicing until I've seen the stern faces of our ancestors look down from their family portraits at the humiliated, beaten, punished culprit!"

There was silence. Chief Judge de Lamoignon shook his head no. But the Regent hadn't yet spoken, and seemed to be thinking.

"What does she expect to gain by bringing Lagardère here?" wondered Gonzague to himself. A cold sweat drenched his hair. He even missed his followers.

"What does the Prince of Gonzague think about it?" asked the Regent suddenly.

Before answering, Gonzague summoned a careless smile. "If I had an opinion—and why would I have an opinion about such an odd whim?—it would look like I just wanted to contradict the princess's wishes. Except that it would delay carrying out the sentence, I see neither benefit nor harm in granting her request."

"There'll be no delay," said the princess, listening to the noise of the crowd outside.

"Do you know where to find the condemned man?" the Regent asked her.

"My lord!" protested Chief Judge de Lamoignon.

"By slightly bending the letter of procedure, sir," said the Regent crisply and energetically, "sometimes you can better match its spirit."

In answer to the question, the princess merely pointed to the windows. The muffled noise outside grew louder.

"The condemned man can't be far!" murmured Minister d'Argenson.

The Regent summoned Bonnivet and briefly spoke to him aside. Bonnivet bowed and withdrew. The princess had sat back down. Gonzague eyed the company with a look he thought was calm; but his lips trembled and his eyes burned.

From the vestibule came the sound of armed men. Impulsively they all stood—so great was the curiosity inspired by that bold adventurer whose story had been told and retold since the day before. Some of them had seen him at the Regent's ball, when His Royal Highness had taken away and broken his sword, but to most of them he was unknown. When the doors opened and they saw him—as beautiful as Christ, surrounded by soldiers, his hands bound at his chest—there was a long murmur. The Regent kept his eyes on Gonzague, who showed no reaction. Lagardère was led to the foot of the dais. Behind him came the bailiff with the sentence, which, according to procedure, was to have been read partly at Nevers's tomb, for the cutting off of the hand, and partly at the Bastille, for the beheading.

"Read it," ordered the Regent.

The bailiff unrolled the parchment. The gist of the sentence was this:

Here ye, here ye, the accused, the witnesses, the royal prosecutor. In light of proofs and proceedings, this court sentences Henri de Lagardère, esquire, calling himself a chevalier, convicted of murder against the person of the high and mighty Prince Philippe de Lorraine Elbeuf, Duke of Nevers, to punishment herewith: 1) that public atonement be followed by mutilation by broadsword at the feet of the statue of the aforementioned prince and lord Philippe, Duke of Nevers, at the cemetery in the parish of Saint Magloire; 2) that the head of the aforementioned esquire, Henri de Lagardère, be struck off by act of the executioner, in the courtyard of the Bastille, etcetera.

When the bailiff was done reading, he stepped back behind the soldiers.

"Have you been given satisfaction, Madame?" asked the Regent.

The princess stood so abruptly that Gonzague unwittingly did the same. He looked like a man preparing himself for a sudden blow.

"Speak, Lagardère!" cried the princess, filled with unmistakable exhilaration. "Speak, my son-in-law!"

It was as if an electric current had run through the room. All of them expected to witness something extraordinary, something unprecedented. The Regent was on his feet, his cheeks flushed, his eyes fixed on Gonzague. "Are you shaking, Philippe?"

"No, God's death!" he replied, planting his feet boldly. "Neither today nor ever!"

The Regent turned to Lagardère. "Speak, sir!"

"Your Highness," said the condemned man, his voice calm and ringing, "the sentence against me cannot be appealed. Not even you have the power to pardon me, and I want no pardon. But you have the duty to render justice, and I want justice!"

It was incredible to see all the white hair shake on all those eagerly listening old heads. Chief Judge de Lamoignon was moved in spite of himself, because the contrast between the two faces—that of Lagardère and that of Gonzague—provided some kind of astonishing lesson. Reluctantly the judge spoke. "To alter a sentence rendered by a Burning Court requires a confession by the culprit."

"We'll have the culprit's confession," said Lagardère.

"Then hurry up, friend," said the Regent. "I'm impatient."

"So am I, my lord. But allow me first to say, everything I promise, I deliver. I'd sworn on my honor that I would return to Madame de Gonzague the child she entrusted to me; at the risk of my life, I did it!"

"And blessings on you a thousandfold!" murmured the princess.

"I'd sworn," he continued, "to hand myself over to your justice after twenty-four hours of freedom; at the appointed hour I surrendered my sword."

"It's true," said the Regent. "Since then I've had my eye on you—and on other people."

Gonzague ground his teeth: even the Regent must be in on it!

"Thirdly," said Lagardère, "I'd sworn I would prove my own innocence before you all by unmasking the real culprit. Here I am, and I will now fulfill my last vow."

Gonzague was still holding the parchment envelope with the three red wax seals he'd stolen from the house in the Rue du Chantre. It was now his sword and his buckler. "My lord," he said brusquely, "I think this comedy has gone on too long."

"I don't believe you've been accused of anything yet," said the Regent.

"An accusation, from the mouth of that madman?" said Gonzague, trying for scorn.

"That madman's about to die," said the Regent sternly. "The words of a dying man are sacred."

"If you still don't know what that man's words are worth, my lord, I'll hold my peace. But believe me, men like us—we mighty nobles and lords and princes and kings—we're seated on thrones whose bases are crumbling. This little entertainment Your Royal Highness is indulging yourself in today will set a dangerous and inauspicious example. To allow a wretch like him..."

Lagardère turned slowly toward him.

"To allow a wretch like him," went on Gonzague, "to confront me, a prince of the realm, without witnesses or proofs..."

Lagardère took a step toward him. "I have my witnesses, and I have my proofs."

"Where are your witnesses?" cried Gonzague, his eyes racing around the room.

"Don't bother looking for them. I have two witnesses. The first is here: it's you!"

Gonzague tried for a pitying laugh, but only produced a frightening spasm.

"The second," went on Lagardère, his cold fixed stare enveloping the prince like a cage, "the second is dead and buried."

"The dead and buried can't speak," said Gonzague.

"They can when God grants it!"

A hush fell around them—the hush of tightened throats and chilled blood. No ordinary man could have silenced all those mocking skeptics: nine out of ten of them would have greeted with scornful, incredulous laughter even the start of an argument that seemed to rely on phenomena beyond the natural order. It was an age of doubt: doubt reigned supreme, whether dressed up in the frivolous tone of salon conversation or draped in academic robes as learned philosophical doctrine. Ghosts seeking vengeance, empty graves, bloodstained shrouds—those terrors of the previous century just made people nowadays guffaw.

But it was Lagardère who spoke, and it's the actor who carries the scene. His solemn voice reached into their hearts and touched fibers long dead or numbed. The grand, noble beauty of his pale face froze the mockery on all their lips. No one dared look into those eyes that held Gonzague writhing and spellbound. Only Lagardère, from the depths of his passion, could defy their fashionable skepticism; only he could invoke ghosts at the height of the eighteenth century, before the Regent's court, before the Regent himself. None of them could remain indifferent to the solemn shock of this face-to-face contest. All mouths hung open, all ears strained to hear. When Lagardère paused for breath, the whole crowd exhaled in a long murmur.

"Those are my witnesses," he resumed. "The dead and buried will speak, I swear it—on my own head. As for my proofs, there they are, Monsieur de Gonzague, in your hands. My innocence lies inside that triple-sealed envelope. You proffered that document yourself—the means of your own downfall. You can't withdraw it, it belongs to the law, and the law now presses in on you from all sides! To secure that weapon—which now will strike you—you broke into my home like a thief in the night: you broke down my door and picked the lock of my strongbox—you, the Prince of Gonzague."

"My lord," said Gonzague, his eyes bloodshot, "silence this wretch!"

"Defend yourself, prince!" cried Lagardère in a mighty voice, "instead of asking for my mouth to be shut! We'll both be allowed to speak—you as well as I, I as well as you—because death stands between us, and because His Royal Highness said, 'The words of a dying man are sacred.'" He held his head high.

Gonzague instinctively picked up the parchment envelope, which he had set on the table.

"There it is!" said Lagardère. "It's time. Break the seals—break them, I tell you! Why are you shaking? There's nothing inside but a sheet of parchment: the birth certificate of Mademoiselle de Nevers."

"Break the seals!" ordered the Regent.

Gonzague's hands seemed paralyzed. Perhaps by design, perhaps by chance, Bonnivet and two of his Royal Guards had drawn closer, so that they stood between Gonzague's table and the tribunal; all three of them faced the Regent as if awaiting his orders. Gonzague hadn't yet obeyed, and the seals remained intact.

Lagardère took another step toward the table, his eyes sparking like a steel blade. "You're guessing there's something else inside, aren't you, prince?" he said in a low voice, and the whole company seemed to lean closer to listen. "I'll tell you what there is. On the reverse of the parchment are three lines, written in blood. That's how the dead speak!"

Gonzague shook from head to foot, and spittle appeared at the corners of his mouth. The Regent leaned over Villeroy's head and rested his fist on the judges' table.

Lagardère's voice rang out over the mute emotion of the whole assembly. "God took twenty years to tear away the veil. God didn't want the avenger's voice to cry out in solitude—so God has brought together all the mighty of the kingdom, under the head of state himself. The time has come! The night of the murder, Nevers was with me. It was before the battle, just a minute before. He could already see the shining blades of the murderers creeping up in the shadows from the other side of the bridge. He said his prayers. Then, on that parchment there, with fingers dipped in blood drawn from his own veins, he wrote three lines describing in advance the coming crime and the name of the murderer."

Gonzague's teeth chattered. He backed away to the end of the table, and his clenched hands seemed ready to crumple the envelope that would now betray him. When he reached the second candlestick he lifted it and lowered it three times without taking his eyes off Lagardère's. It was the signal to his followers.

"Look!" whispered Cardinal de Bissy to Monsieur de Mortemart, "he's lost his mind!"

No one else spoke. They all held their breath.

"The name is there!" Lagardère raised his bound hands and pointed to the parchment. "The real name, written out in full. Break the seal, open the envelope, and let the dead man speak!"

Gonzague, his eyes rolling, his brow bathed in sweat, glanced wildly toward the tribunal. Bonnivet and his men blocked the way. Gonzague stood with his back to the candlestick, and behind him his shaking hands blindly sought the flames. The envelope caught fire.

Lagardère could see it, but instead of raising the alarm he said, "Read it! Read it out loud! Let's find out whether the murderer's name is mine or yours!"

"He's burning the documents!" cried General de Villeroy, who could hear the parchment crackling.

In the uproar that followed, Bonnivet and his men turned to face Gonzague. The Regent rushed forward. "He burned the documents! The documents that held the murderer's name!"

Lagardère gestured to the fragments of parchment burning on the floor. "The dead man has spoken!"

"What was written there?" cried the Regent, whose emotions were at their peak. "Say it right now and we'll believe you, because this man has just condemned himself."

"Nothing!" said Lagardère. They were all stunned. "Nothing!" he said again in a ringing voice. "Nothing, you hear, Monsieur de Gonzague? I tricked you, and your tortured conscience stumbled into my trap. You burned the document that I threatened would testify against you. Your name wasn't on it, but you've just written it there yourself. That was the voice of the dead man—the dead man spoke!"

"The dead man spoke!" murmured the whole assembly.

"By trying to destroy the proof, the murderer betrayed himself," said General de Villeroy.

"The culprit has confessed!" said Chief Judge de Lamoignon reluctantly. "The verdict of the Burning Court can be voided."

Up to this point, the Regent, choked by indignation, had kept silent. Suddenly he cried, "Murderer! Murderer! Arrest that man!"

Quicker than thought, Gonzague drew his sword. In one bound he crossed in front of the Regent and landed a thrust squarely in Lagardère's chest. Lagardère cried out and staggered back, and the princess caught him in her arms.

"You won't have the satisfaction of your victory!" growled Gonzague, bristling like a maddened bull. He spun around, knocked down Bonnivet in passing, then turned again and confronted the soldiers rushing at him. He backed up slowly while fighting off ten blades at once. The soldiers gained ground. Just when they thought they had him cornered against the drapes, Gonzague flung aside a curtain and vanished as if through a trapdoor. They could hear a key turning in the lock outside.

Lagardère was the first to throw himself against the door, which he knew from having used it on the day of the first family tribunal. His hands were free: Gonzague's treacherous lunge had cut the rope that bound them, and otherwise had wounded him only slightly. The door was locked tight.

Just as the Regent was ordering a pursuit of the fugitive, a shattered voice rose from the far end of the great hall. "Help! Help!" Doña Cruz, disheveled and in disarray, fell at the feet of the princess.

"My daughter!" cried the princess. "Something's happened to my daughter!"

"Men... in the cemetery..." gasped Doña Cruz, out of breath. "They're forcing the church doors. They're going to kidnap her!"

All was confusion in the great hall, but one voice rose over the tumult like a clarion call. It was Lagardère saying, "A sword, in God's name, a sword!"

The Regent drew his own and put it into Lagardère's hands.

"Thank you, my lord. And now open the window, and call out to your men not to stop me, because the murderer has a head start on me, and too bad for anyone who gets in my way!"

Lagardère kissed the blade, brandished it over his head, and vanished like a flash.

X. Public Atonement

The middle-of-the-night executions carried out behind the walls of the Bastille weren't necessarily secret, just not open to the public. Aside from those that history knows and notes, carried out without due process by the king's authority, all other executions followed legal sentencing and a more or less regular procedure. The inner courtyard of the Bastille was a place of execution just as official and acknowledged as the Place de Grève. The executioner known only as Monsieur de Paris had the sole privilege of chopping off heads there. There were lots of reasons to hate the Bastille, lots of legitimate reasons, but the common people of Paris begrudged it most for concealing its scaffold. If you've entered La Roquette Prison these days on a night of capital punishment, you know whether or not the people of Paris have been cured of their barbaric taste for the macabre.

That night the Bastille was due, yet again, to hide away the final agonies of Nevers's murderer, sentenced by the Burning Court of the Châtelet. But it wouldn't be a total loss: the public atonement at the victim's tomb and the hand chopped off by the executioner's broadsword were worth something. They at least were open to all. The tolling of the death knell at the Sainte Chapelle had stirred up the poorer neighborhoods of the city. News didn't have the same ways to spread that it does now, but for that very reason people were eager to see and to know. In the blink of an eye the streets around the Châtelet and the palace were crowded. When the procession emerged from the Cosson gate, facing the Rue Saint Denis, ten thousand gawkers already lined the way. No one in the crowd knew the Chevalier Henri de Lagardère. Usually there'd be someone in the mob who could put a name to the face of the victim, but tonight no one knew anything. Still, ignorance doesn't put a stop to talk; on the contrary, it opens up the field to theorizing. In place of one name nobody knew, they found a hundred. Conjectures collided. Within a few minutes, every possible crime— political or other—had been heaped on the head of the handsome soldier with his hands bound who walked, beside his Dominican confessor, between four guards from the Châtelet, swords drawn. The monk, with gaunt face and fiery eye, pointed to heaven with his iron crucifix, which he held up like a broadsword. Before and behind them rode the courthouse archers.

Some voices in the crowd could be heard.

"He comes from Spain, where Alberoni paid him a thousand doubloons to come stir up trouble in France."

"Say, he looks like he's listening carefully to the monk."

"Hey, Madame Dutuit, think about the wig you could make with all that gorgeous blond hair!"

"Apparently," said someone in another group, "the Duchess of Maine summoned him to Sceaux to carry out her plans. He was supposed to kidnap the young king the night the Regent gave his ball at the Palais-Royal."

"And do what with the young king?"

"Take him away to Brittany, put His Royal Highness in the Bastille, proclaim Nantes as the capital of the kingdom..."

And a little further on, "He was waiting for Mr. Law in the Fountain Court, planning to knife him as he was getting into his carriage..."

"How awful if he'd succeeded! Overnight, everybody in Paris would've been a pauper!"

When the procession passed the corner of the Rue de la Ferronnerie, a chorus of women let out a piercing shriek: La Ferronnerie was a continuation of the Rue Saint Honoré, and Mesdames Balahault, Durand, Guichard, and all the rest of the gossips from the Rue du Chantres just had to stroll down their street to get there. At the same moment they all recognized the mysterious sword engraver, master to old Dame Françoise and little Jean-Marie Berrichon.

"Well," cried Mother Balahault, "didn't I tell you he'd come to a bad end?"

"We should've turned him in right away," said Mother Guichard, "since no one could figure out what was going on at his house."

"He looks like butter wouldn't melt in his mouth!" said Mother Durand.

They talked about the little hunchback and the pretty girl who sang at the window. And out of the goodness of their hearts they all said, "You can't say he didn't get what's coming to him!"

The crowd couldn't get much ahead of the procession, because no one knew where it was going. Neither the archers nor the guards said a word: officials of that kind have always enjoyed frustrating the mob by their self-important discretion. As long as they hadn't passed the market at Les Halles, clever people thought the victim was headed to the pillory by the charnel house at Les Innocents. But then they passed Les Halles. The head of the procession led the way along the Rue Saint Denis as far as the corner of the little Rue Saint Magloire. The vanguard of the crowd then saw two torches burning at the entrance to the cemetery, which set off new conjectures—but those conjectures soon gave way to an event already known to our readers: the arrival of an order from the Regent to bring the condemned man to the great hall of the Villa Nevers. The whole procession entered the courtyard of the villa. The crowd filled the Rue Saint Magloire and settled down to wait.

Saint Magloire had first been the chapel of the Benedictine abbey of that name, until the monks were moved to new quarters at Saint Jacques du Haut Pas; then it became a house of repentance; and it had now been a parish church for a century and a half. It had been rebuilt in 1630, and Monsieur, brother and heir to King Louis XIII, had laid the cornerstone. The sanctuary was small, and sat in the middle of the largest cemetery in Paris. The hospital to its east also had a public chapel, and as a result the small winding alley that climbed from the Rue Saint Magloire to the Rue aux Ours was called the Rue des Deux Églises.

The wall surrounding the cemetery had three entrances: the main gate opened onto the Rue Saint Magloire, a second onto the Rue des Deux Églises, and a third onto an unnamed cul-de-sac leading back around behind the church to the Rue des Deux Églises and bordering the garden of Gonzague's pleasure house. There was also a small breach in the wall to give passage to the procession of Saint Gervais's relics.

Though shabby and little used, the church itself survived into the early years of our own century, its doors opening onto the street at the spot where the house at 166 Rue Saint Denis now stands. Two doors opened onto the cemetery, which by then hadn't been used for burials for a number of years: most of the dead were buried outside Paris. Only four or five noble families still maintained their sepulchers at Saint Magloire—notably the Nevers family, which held the funerary chapel in fief. As we've said, that chapel stood a little distance from the church proper, surrounded by tall trees; the shortest way to get there was from the Rue Saint Magloire.

About twenty minutes had passed since the procession reached the courtyard of the Villa Gonzague. It was now dark, and from the cemetery could be seen both the brightly lit windows of the great hall of Nevers and the windows of the church, through which a dim light shone vaguely. The murmuring of the crowd squeezed together on the street came in gusts.

To the right of the funerary chapel lay a vacant area planted with ornamental trees that had now filled out and grown tall, so that it looked like a thicket—or more exactly, like one of those abandoned gardens that within a few years begin to resemble virgin forest. The Prince of Gonzague's followers were waiting there, and their horses stood ready on the cul-de-sac leading to the Rue des Deux Églises.

Navailles held his head in his hands; Nocé and Choisy leaned against a cypress tree; Oriol sat on the grass, sighing deeply; Montaubert, Taranne, and Peyrolles stood talking quietly. Those last three were lost souls—not more devoted than the rest, but more compromised. No one will be surprised to learn that since they'd gotten here Gonzague's friends had openly discussed whether desertion was still possible. Every one of them, from first to last, had in his heart already broken the chain that tied them all to their master. But all of them still counted on his support, and all of them feared his vengeance. They knew Gonzague would show them no mercy. They remained so deeply convinced of his unshakeable favor with the Regent that they took Gonzague's behavior to be some kind of playacting: they thought he'd faked the supposed danger as a way to tighten the bit in their mouths, or even to test them. There's no doubt that if they thought Gonzague was finished, they wouldn't have hung around for long.

The Baron of Batz had crept along the cemetery walls almost to the villa, and reported back that the procession had stopped and the crowd was blocking the street. What could it mean? Was the story of public atonement at Nevers's tomb just an invention by Gonzague? It was getting late: a few minutes ago the clock at Saint Magloire had rung a quarter to nine—and at nine Lagardère's head was due to drop in the Bastille courtyard. Peyrolles, Montaubert, and Taranne kept their eyes on the windows of the great hall, and especially on the one where a single bright light shone next to the tall silhouette of Gonzague.

Not far away, behind the north door of the Saint Magloire church, waited another group. Madame de Gonzague's confessor stood at the altar. Aurore, kneeling, looked like one of those sweet statues of prostrate angels on a tomb. Cocardasse and Passepoil stood motionless, sword in hand, flanking the doors. The Marquis of Chaverny and Doña Cruz talked quietly.

A couple of times Cocardasse and Passepoil thought they'd heard suspicious noises from the cemetery. They both had good eyesight, yet when they pressed their faces to the small barred window in the door they saw nothing: the funerary chapel hid the ambush party from them. The eternal flame burning at the tomb of the last Duke of Nevers lit the inside of the vault and threw everything around it into greater darkness.

But suddenly our two bravos started; Chaverny and Doña Cruz fell silent; and Aurore said distinctly, "Mary, Mother of God, have mercy on him!" Some sound—puzzling, though very close—had reached their waiting ears.

In the thicket, the entire ambush party was on the move. His eyes fixed on the windows of the great hall, Peyrolles said, "Heads up, gentlemen!"

And then they all watched as the candlestick rose and fell three times. It was the signal to attack the church doors. There was no room for doubt or ambiguity—and yet Gonzague's followers still hesitated. Before, they hadn't believed in the crisis the signal would supposedly announce. Now they saw the signal they still didn't believe it had been necessary: Gonzague was just toying with them, Gonzague just wanted to rivet the chain around their necks. As that feeling grew stronger, it was their fear of Gonzague—at the very hour of his downfall—that made them decide to obey.

"After all," said Navailles, talking himself into it, "it's just a kidnapping."

"And our horses are close by," added Nocé.

"It's just a brawl, and we're not risking much," offered Choisy.

"Let's go!" cried Taranne. "His lordship needs to find the job done."

Montaubert and Taranne each picked up a heavy iron crowbar. The whole group ran forward, Navailles in the lead and Oriol in the rear. At the first blow the peaceful church doors gave way. But behind stood a second line of defense: three naked blades.

At that moment a loud crash came from the direction of the villa, as if something had collapsed on the crowd waiting in the street.

The swords struck only once. Navailles wounded Chaverny, who'd taken a reckless step forward; he fell, with one knee on the ground and a hand to his chest. Now that he recognized him, Navailles stepped back and dropped his sword.

"All right then," said Cocardasse, who'd been hoping for better sport than this. "God's blood! Show us your hangers!"

No one had time to respond to his bluster. Rushing footsteps thudded on the cemetery lawn. A whirlwind passed by—a whirlwind! The church steps were swept clean. Peyrolles let out a cry of agony; Montaubert gasped; Taranne stretched out his arms, dropped his sword, and fell backward. And yet it was only one man, his head and arms bare, holding nothing but a sword. His voice rang out in the silence. "Let all those who are not accomplices of the murderer Philippe de Gonzague withdraw!"

Shadows slipped away into the night. No one spoke. The only sound was of hoof beats galloping away down the gravel of the alley leading to the Rue des Deux Églises.

Lagardère—for it was he—stepped through the doorway and saw Chaverny fallen. "Is he dead?"

"No, if you please," replied the little marquis. "God's death, chevalier! I've never seen lightning strike!—I get goose bumps thinking about that street in Madrid—You're more demon than man!"

Lagardère embraced him, and shook hands with both bravos. The next moment Aurore was in his arms.

"To the altar!" cried Lagardère. "We're not done here! Lights! The hour awaited for twenty years is about to sound—Hear me, Nevers, and look upon your avenger!"

When he left the villa, Gonzague had found his way blocked by an impenetrable barrier: the crowd. Only Lagardère had been able to force his way through, charging straight ahead like a wild boar through that human thicket. Lagardère got through, but Gonzague went around, which was why Lagardère, who started second, got there first. Gonzague entered the cemetery by the breach in the wall. The night was so dark he had trouble finding his way to the funerary chapel. When he reached the spot where his followers were to wait in ambush, his eyes were drawn to the bright windows of the great hall. The hall was still lit, but it was vacant; the dais was deserted, and the empty gilded chairs shone.

"They're after me," he said to himself, "but they won't get me in time!"

When he turned back to the thicket of trees around him, with eyes still dazzled by the bright light from the windows, he thought he saw his companions standing on all sides; every tree trunk looked like a man. "Hey there, Peyrolles!" he said quietly. "Is it over already?" Silence. He rapped the pommel of his sword against the dark shape he'd taken for his factotum. His sword struck the rotten trunk of a dead cypress. "Anyone here? Did they all leave without me?"

He thought he heard a voice answer, "No," but he wasn't sure, because his own feet were making the dry leaves rustle. A muffled noise rose and grew from the direction of the villa. Gonzague choked back an oath. "I'm going to find out what's going on!" he cried, skirting around the chapel to rush toward the church.

But before him stood a tall shadow, and this one was no dead tree. The shadow held a naked blade.

"Where are they? Where are the others?" asked Gonzague. "Where's Peyrolles?"

With the tip of his sword the man pointed to the foot of the chapel wall. "Here's Peyrolles."

Gonzague bent down, and cried out: his hand had touched warm blood.

"Montaubert's over there," said the man, pointing to the cypress grove.

"Dead?"

"Dead." Then with his toe the man nudged a body that lay between him and Gonzague. "That's Taranne. Dead."

The noise grew louder. From all sides came the sound of footsteps approaching, and now lit torches could be seen beyond the thicket of trees. Gonzague ground his teeth. "So Lagardère beat me here?" He took a step back, no doubt to flee, but now bright red light from behind him suddenly lit Lagardère's face. The prince turned and saw Cocardasse and Passepoil coming around the corner of the chapel, holding torches. The three corpses stood out against the darkness. From the direction of the church came more torches. Gonzague recognized the Regent, followed by the chief magistrates and all the lords who'd taken part in the family tribunal only a few minutes before.

The Regent said, "Let no one over the walls of this cemetery! Post guards everywhere!"

"God's death!" Gonzague gave a broken laugh. "We're being granted closed ground for single combat, like in the days of chivalry! For once in his life, Philippe d'Orléans has remembered he's the descendant of knights! So be it! Let's wait for the tourney referees!"

Even as Lagardère was answering, "All right, let's wait," without warning Gonzague lunged treacherously at his stomach. But in some hands a sword is like a living being that defends itself instinctively. Lagardère's sword rose, parried the thrust, and riposted. Gonzague's chest gave off a metallic sound. His coat of mail had done its job. Lagardère's sword shattered. Then, without retreating even a foot, Lagardère dodged his adversary's dishonorable follow-up thrust, whose momentum carried Gonzague right past him. At the same time, Lagardère took Cocardasse's rapier, which the latter held out to him by its point. That move had caused the combatants to trade places, and Lagardère now stood flanked by the two masters of arms. Gonzague, whose lunge had carried him almost to the doors of the funerary chapel, now turned again, which put the Regent and his people behind him.

The combatants went back en garde. Gonzague was a formidable swordsman, and he only had to protect his head, but Lagardère seemed to be toying with him. At the second pass, Gonzague's rapier flew from his hand. When he bent to pick it up, Lagardère stepped on it.

"Ah, chevalier!" said the Regent as he reached them.

"My lord," said Lagardère, "our forefathers called this the judgment of God. We're not believers anymore, but disbelief doesn't kill God any more than blindness snuffs out the sun."

The Regent spoke in a low voice with his ministers and counselors.

"It wouldn't be advisable to let this prince's head drop on the chopping block," volunteered Chief Judge de Lamoignon.

"Nevers's tomb is right here," said Lagardère, "and the expiation he was promised will come to pass. Nevers is owed public atonement—and it's not my hand being cut off by the executioner's broadsword that'll do it." He picked up Gonzague's sword.

"What are you doing?" asked the Regent.

"My lord, this is the sword that struck Nevers. I recognize it. This sword will punish Nevers's murderer!" Lagardère threw Cocardasse's sword at Gonzague's feet; trembling, the prince seized it.

"God's hat!" muttered Cocardasse. "The third stroke kills the rooster!"

The whole family tribunal formed a circle around the combatants. When they went back en garde, the Regent, maybe unconscious of what he was doing, took the torch out of Passepoil's hands and held it high—Philippe d'Orléans, Regent of France!

"Remember his body armor!" murmured Passepoil behind Lagardère.

There was no need. Lagardère had been transfigured. His tall form stretched forth, the wind lifted his long hair, his eyes shot daggers. He forced Gonzague back to the chapel doors. Then his sword flashed as it followed the quick circle leading to a first-position riposte.

"The Nevers attack!" said the two masters of arms together.

Gonzague fell, and rolled to the foot of the statue of Philippe de Nevers. A bleeding hole pierced his forehead. The Princess of Gonzague and Doña Cruz supported Aurore. Nearby a doctor bandaged the Marquis of Chaverny's wound. They were at the doorway of the Saint Magloire church. The Regent and his suite climbed the steps. Lagardère stood between the two groups.

"My lord," said the princess, "here is Nevers's heiress, my daughter, who tomorrow will be Madame de Lagardère, if Your Royal Highness permits it."

The Regent took Aurore's hand, kissed it, and set it in her beloved's hand. "Thank you," he said to Lagardère, while he almost reluctantly faced the tomb of the friend of his youth. Then, steadying his voice, which had shaken with emotion, Philippe d'Orléans straightened up and said, "Count of Lagardère, only the king, when he reaches his majority, can make you Duke of Nevers."

THE END

APPENDIX ONE
THE PAUL FÉVAL, *FILS* SEQUELS

Paul Féval's eldest son was also a novelist, also named Paul Féval. In French, following the similar Alexandre Dumas father-son model, they're known logically enough as Féval *père* ("father") and Féval *fils* ("son"). Féval *fils*'s specialty was what we would now call mashups: d'Artagnan versus Cyrano de Bergerac, a near-Tarzan versus a near-Sherlock Holmes, that kind of thing. Starting in 1893—five years after his father's death (mercifully?)—Féval *fils* began building out the *Hunchback* franchise; over the next forty years he wrote seven sequels and one prequel to his father's most famous novel. Note that Féval *père* was himself no stranger to novel series and wrote lots of sequels to his other big hit, *Les Habits Noirs* ("The Black Coats"), but he chose never to return to *The Hunchback* in the decades following its initial success.

Though at first he spiraled his way gently into the series by constructing the Lagardère family's later years (a "next generation" approach), eventually Féval *fils* took on the challenge of a story that would immediately follow the events in *The Hunchback*: a particular challenge because—as you know since you just read it—Féval *père* ended his novel with the clear triumph of the hero and the no-doubt-about-it death of the villain.

In Hollywood they solve that problem by showing in the sequel how the villain escaped through a trapdoor seconds before we saw the building blow up in the first movie. With no such elbow room, Féval *fils* did what he had to, and just rewrote the whole last chapter on the occasion of the republication of Féval *père*'s *Le Bossu* in 1905. In brief, in the rewrite, while Gonzague remains exposed as Nevers's murderer, Lagardère is unable to stop him from carrying out Plan B. Taking Aurore and Doña Cruz hostage, Gonzague flees for Spain along with Peyrolles and all the usual suspects. All? No. Chaverny is firmly on Lagardère's side—and Navailles, repentant after wounding Chaverny at the church door, has now joined the good guys too. The stage is set for the Lagardère-Gonzague struggle to go on and on until cancellation looms. (A more detailed plot synopsis of each book follows below.)

In fact, the Féval *fils* sequels—none of them translated into English—are a lot like a TV series spun off from a hit movie: but think *Legally Blonde*, not *M*A*S*H*. The characters and the situations persist, but they've been thinned down to their simplest tics. And certainly the somewhat repetitive action hardly ever slows down for one of Féval *père*'s ruminations on life and culture in Regency France (you may find that a plus)—or for a long heartfelt conversation, or really for anything at all. The sequels read like scripts for a cape and sword *telenovela*.

One interesting change is that, whether out of personal taste or because he was writing fifty years later, under different rules, Féval *fils* is a lot more unbuttoned than his father. One example will give you the idea: during an almost-gang-rape of a barmaid by Gonzague's followers, somebody shouts, "We'll have her! Stretch her out on the table stark naked! We'll throw the dice between her breasts!" (The winner at dice will be first in line; she escapes by getting them all too drunk to move.) It's like reading the "adult" fan-fiction version of a childhood favorite.

The plot synopses below follow the internal chronological order of the story, rather than the order of publication. So first comes the prequel.

La Jeunesse du Bossu [The Hunchback's Boyhood] (1934).

Féval *fils* actually wrote this one last. Unlike in *Lagardère's Wild Ride* (the immediate sequel to the original novel), in this case he was able to dovetail his story neatly with the scattered hints his father had sketched out vaguely in *The Hunchback*, without forcing awkward changes or contradictions.

In Italy in 1682 (seventeen years before the start of the original book), the Duke of Mantua, Prince of Gonzague—a distant cousin of the Gonzague we know—with the help of his factotum, young Peyrolles, steals the dukedom of Guastalla by poisoning the old duke and then ambushing and murdering the rightful heir, René de Lagardère, and his wife (Guastalla's daughter). But Peyrolles fails at his part—finishing off René's own infant son and heir—and baby Henri escapes in care of a family servant, Suzon Bernard. She raises Henri in secrecy and poverty and never tells him who he is. At nine, Henri joins a traveling circus (making Suzon come with him), and learns contortionism and trick voices. In Paris she takes him to live in the ruins of the Villa Lagardère; so the name he adopts is, unwittingly, his own. He dives for coins and performs as a contortionist; old Madame Bernard sells pastries. (This is the point where little Henri indirectly entered the original story.)

Jump to 1692, and new characters. Myrtille, queen of the Paris criminal underworld, deals in gun running and human trafficking for the pirates based in Tortuga. She drugs Olivier de Sauves, a gentleman down on his luck, and ships him off as a slave to the pirates. Her thugs, Joel de Jugan and Scarface, go to drown Olivier's little girl, Armelle; but Henri saves her and brings her to the humble street theater where he now works, featuring performing dogs, a clown, Henri doing contortions and a hunchback act—and soon his adopted little "sister" Armelle as singer and dancer. Meanwhile Olivier, though a captive, saves the pirate ship in a storm and is appointed captain by a pirate chief nicknamed Tourmentin. The pirate kingdom on Tortuga turns out to be more like a republic of freedom and equality. Olivier excels as a polite and almost nonviolent pirate, the "gentleman of the sea." Still, how will he find his daughter?

Underworld queen Myrtille discovers Henri and Armelle, and has her thugs burn down the theater tent. Henri saves a noble lady, the Countess of Montboron, from the fire; she's grateful. Old Madame Bernard, feverish on her deathbed, babbles about the evil Duke of Mantua and tells Henri he really is a Lagardère; then she dies. Henri goes to the fencing academy to study with Cocardasse and Passepoil.

On to 1696: the Duke of Mantua comes to Paris to hang out with the Three Philippes, of whom his cousin Gonzague is one. At the fencing academy, Mantua hears about the great Lagardère: uh-oh. They duel outside Paris; Henri stabs him dead. (Peyrolles goes to work for the other Gonzague.) Henri is attacked by Myrtille's men, but the pirate Tourmentin is back home and takes his side: Tourmentin knows where Olivier is, Henri knows where Armelle is. Myrtille has ties to the king's mistress, Madame de Maintenon. Maintenon denounces Henri to the king as Mantua's murderer; but that same day in the forest Henri and Tourmentin have fortuitously saved Louis XIV from assassins— so Henri is forgiven and reappointed to the cavalry.

Olivier returns to France to negotiate an alliance with Louis: royal navy and pirates together against Spain. Myrtille claims Henri seduced and abducted Armelle from her care; Olivier vows revenge. By now Armelle and Tourmentin (who's really Viscount of Varcourt) have fallen in love. Olivier spots Henri and tries to kill him—but all is explained in time. For Myrtille it's too late to escape to Tortuga, so she shoots her husband and hangs herself. By now Olivier and the Countess of Montboron have also fallen in love. So there will two weddings when Olivier and Varcourt return from the joint naval expedition. But poor Henri returns alone to his regiment: his childhood is over now—what adventures lie ahead?

In linear story order, this is where Féval *père*'s original *The Hunchback* would go—but with the ending changed to make possible everything that now follows.

Les Chevauchées de Lagardère [Lagardère's Wild Ride] (1909).

Besides changing the ending, Féval *fils* shifts the whole time frame of the original story by a year—it's now 1718 instead of 1717—so he can work in the real-life Cellamare Conspiracy. (Féval *père* alludes to it repeatedly in *The Hunchback*, but says it's beyond the scope and time of his story; not anymore!) Basically, King Philip V of Spain—with lots of help from the Regent's French enemies—plotted to replace the Duke of Orléans as Regent to young King Louis XV, and thereby make himself de facto ruler of both France and Spain.

As explained above, in the new improved ending of *The Hunchback* Gonzague takes Aurore and Doña Cruz hostage and heads for Spain, with Lagardère (and Cocardasse and Passepoil) in hot pursuit: the "wild ride" of the title. At Bayonne Gonzague sets a trap, but it's foiled—using a secret tunnel at the bottom of a well—by a brave Basque innkeeper, Jacinta, whose brother Antoine Laho now joins the good guys. They survive an ambush at a pass in the Pyrenees, with the help of a gypsy girl, Mariquita (a childhood friend of Flor's). In Spain, Gonzague hides Aurore and Doña Cruz in an old castle, with Peyrolles to guard them.

Meanwhile the Regent sends Chaverny to Spain to warn the French ambassador to leave: the Cellamare plot has been exposed, and war looms. Chaverny saves the ambassador, then seeks news of Lagardère and friends. Mariquita turns out to be the daughter of the old man at that castle; she and Doña Cruz are reunited. Mariquita can't find Lagardère, but she meets Chaverny and tells him about the castle. Meanwhile Lagardère and his men happen upon a witches' Sabbath in the mountains—and massacre thirty unarmed warlocks (they let the hundred naked witches escape). Lagardère learns that war's been declared (it's the War of the Quadruple Alliance, for anyone keeping track); he dutifully crosses the border to join the French army. He single-handedly secures the surrender of Hondarribia. From Chaverny he learns about the girls in the castle, and abandons the war to ride there. But just before he reaches the castle, an earthquake topples it: is Aurore dead?

Mariquita (1922).

Now Féval *fils* replays the cliffhanger collapse of the castle from the inside: Mariquita has helped Aurore and Doña Cruz escape; her old father duels Peyrolles, knowing he himself will be killed—and when he is, Mariquita blows up the castle to finish off Peyrolles. But she herself is buried alive; by the time she gets out, and finds Lagardère outside, she's gone mad and can tell him nothing. Peyrolles also survives the explosion, and gets away.

Meanwhile Chaverny, Cocardasse, Passepoil, and Laho split up to find Lagardère. Laho finds Aurore and Doña Cruz gypsy-dancing on the streets to earn their way to France. But Peyrolles also finds them; in his attempt to get them back, both he and Laho are wounded. Laho hides the girls at a nunnery. For a while everybody wanders around Spain, fleeing or pursuing or convalescing. Lagardère leads Mariquita back across the same mountain pass where she first met him; she regains her reason and her memory—but Gonzague's rakes show up, and Lagardère is wounded while protecting her. The original gypsy band from Cerro del Baladron shows up, and the old crone Mabel nurses Lagardère at an abandoned hideaway—which turns out to belong to Laho's sister Jacinta.

The war's over. Gonzague and all his followers run into all the good guys (still looking for Lagardère) plus the girls, now retrieved from the nunnery: the big face-off happens just outside Jacinta's hideaway, and Gonzague and his people flee when convalescent Lagardère appears. Lagardère and Aurore are finally reunited, as are Chaverny and Doña Cruz. After they all leave for France,

Mariquita—in love with Lagardère but sworn to restore him to Aurore—drops dead from a broken heart.

So the titular character is dead, and the couples are back together: the end? No, just halfway. On the way back to Paris (now joined by the Princess of Gonzague too) they survive several attacks by Peyrolles's hired men—led by Gauthier Gendry, and including the sons of Jugan and Pinto, whom Lagardère killed in the original book—aiming to re-kidnap Aurore (though by this point Gonzague's motive for abducting her is unclear). The Regent ennobles Lagardère: now he's the Count of Lagardère. At a grand ball, Jugan Jr and Pinto Jr fail to kill Lagardère and Aurore by dropping a really big chandelier on them—but they almost hit the Regent, and now he's mad: he sends Lagardère to Spain to escort a royal wedding party (a double princess swap to seal the peace), along with a diplomatic demand that the king expel Gonzague.

Lagardère doesn't show up in Madrid, but an eccentric little mute Turkish hunchback follows the French princess's party to the king's palace and pitches a tent. He cuts wonderful freehand caricature silhouettes, and becomes an instant favorite at court. Suspecting it's Lagardère again, Gonzague's rakes attack the little Turk on a dark street. Now the king's favorite Turk can't be found. An unknown elderly provincial Spanish nobleman shows up at the royal wedding and claims he saw Gonzague's rakes kill the Turk. The king needs a pretext to expel Gonzague anyway; he accuses Gonzague of ordering the Turk's murder. The elderly nobleman reveals that he's Lagardère—and also the Turk, therefore not murdered—but Gonzague and gang are still going to be expelled tomorrow, unless Lagardère (as he promises) kills Gonzague and Peyrolles in a duel first. The bad guys are put under house arrest overnight—but Gonzague leads them out by a secret tunnel, and they escape to London.

Cocardasse et Passepoil (1923).

While Lagardère is in Madrid playing Turk, back in Paris Cocardasse and Passepoil are supposed to be helping Chaverny and Laho protect Aurore and Doña Cruz. (None of them knows where Lagardère went, and in fact he barely figures in most of this book.) The two swordsmen get drawn into a series of face-offs and altercations with Gendry's gang; Gendry's aim is to eliminate Aurore's watchdogs so he can get at her, for Gonzague's still opaque reasons. After one fight, Gendry's men throw the masters of arms into a canal to drown (they don't); a brothel servant girl named Mathurine saves Passepoil, and it's true love. Jean-Marie Berrichon convinces the gossips on the Rue du Chantre that the hunchback was a wizard from Mississippi and Aurore nothing but a wind-up automaton, then he and Françoise move in with the whole gang at the Villa Nevers; he gets fencing lessons from Cocardasse and Passepoil.

Gonzague and followers leave London and return to France in disguise: Gonzague and Peyrolles as rich Dutch merchants, and the six rakes as miscellaneous pilgrims, street acrobats, and gypsies; they even steal a dancing bear for the gypsy act. In Paris, disguised, Gonzague is puzzled to learn that Lagardère isn't back: why would he still be in Spain? He sends Gendry and sundry bandits into an epic battle against Cocardasse and friends outside the city gates. The good guys are outnumbered (though Berrichon kills young Jugan)—but a little hunchbacked beggar joins in, and by the end pretty much all of Gendry's people are killed, including Gendry himself; only the Whale and young Pinto limp away. Yes, it's Lagardère—sadly, he wasn't the dancing bear. He tells his men to keep his presence a secret and follow the orders of any hunchback they meet (it'll be him). As part of his getup, Lagardère carries around a small mysterious animal in a rucksack, to which he feeds raw meat. Meanwhile Gonzague doesn't believe Lagardère would play that tired old hunchback routine yet again; he doubts he's back.

A new character, libertine Baroness Liane de Longpré, has become Aurore's unlikely new friend, but she's really an enemy: secretly she used to be Gonzague's mistress. She spots Gonzague in town and tells him she can help him with general spying and treachery against Aurore. How does she know him in Dutch merchant disguise? She recognizes his ring, the one with the poison dispenser.

At this promising point, about three quarters of the way through the book, an odd thing happens—as if Féval *fils* lost a hundred pages of his manuscript in a taxi, and rather than try to rewrite them he just summarizes a few major points in a paragraph without bothering to pay off the rest. So: thinking Lagardère is there, Gonzague burns down the St. Germain fair, killing hundreds—but not Lagardère, who's reunited (offstage) with Aurore; among the dead is Liane de Longpré, stabbed: so no payoff to the elaborate frenemy plot, no payoff to the poison ring, nor to the gag of all the real hunchbacks in Paris being mistaken for Lagardère, nor to the animal in the rucksack. Lagardère pursues Gonzague—now wanted for arson too—but he slips away again. All that in about a paragraph...

On the occasion of his majority and the end of the Regency (putting us now in real-life 1723), young King Louis XV and the Regent attend the double wedding—Lagardère and Aurore, Chaverny and Doña Cruz—at the Saint Magloire Church. Gonzague and all of his followers are waiting in the cemetery. After the weddings, there's a final battle by the Nevers crypt: all of the rakes are killed—but not before fat little Oriol kills young Berrichon (shocker!)—and Peyrolles too is killed. In a near cut and paste of the original ending of *The Hunchback* (the ending Féval *fils* denied us in his 1905 rewrite), the Regent and the king watch Lagardère duel and kill Gonzague: vengeance for Nevers!

Le Fils de Lagardère [The Son of Lagardère] (1893).

This novel, like the next one (*The Nevers Twins*)—these being the first two sequels Féval *fils* wrote to *The Hunchback*—is itself divided into two named volumes, each of which is at least as long as any of the other books in the series.

Volume One, *Le Sergent Belle-Épée* (*Sergeant Beautiful-Blade*), jumps forward about twenty years, to 1745 and the end of the War of the Austrian Succession. In Flanders, old Cocardasse, now in the army, meets a young sergeant who knows the Nevers attack. He doesn't, however, know his own family name or origins: he's just Philippe, nicknamed Sergeant Beautiful-Blade. Cocardasse introduces him to Chaverny and Flor (now Marquise of Chaverny), and to their daughter, Olympe; she and Philippe are smitten. Meanwhile young Philippe keeps being attacked by German thugs led by a man named Mathias Knauss.

Philippe tells Cocardasse he was raised by fishermen who rescued him at the age of four from a shipwreck that killed the Englishman who was with him and who just called him "Philippe." When he was fifteen his adoptive fisherman parents died, and he went to Paris to seek his fortune. He befriended Boniface, son of Passepoil and Mathurine. Passepoil now keeps a fencing academy, and he taught Philippe, who soon surpassed him and earned the nickname "Beautiful-Blade." At eighteen, Philippe and Boniface joined the French Guards. Just before they left for war, Philippe met an old bearded man on the street who was struck by his looks and drew out his story. Shortly after that began all the attempted murders by Knauss. Philippe was heroic in the capture of Prague (real-life 1742) and promoted to sergeant.

By now Cocardasse has realized Philippe must be Lagardère's son, and the old bearded man must be Peyrolles—who somehow survived (and based on the chronology in *The Hunchback's Boyhood* must now be in his mid-eighties). Before Cocardasse can explain who he is, Philippe gets a message from a man named Baron Posen that his adoptive sister Marine (the fisherman's daughter) has tried to kill herself; Posen saved her. Philippe races from Flanders to Paris, where he learns that Marine was drugged and raped and abandoned by an Italian named Count Zéno; Philippe rushes off to challenge him to a duel.

The second half of this volume is all flashback to explain how we got to this point. Henri de Lagardère is savagely murdered in 1727 in a mysterious ambush. Shattered by insane grief, his widow Aurore comes to depend heavily on Bathilde, a favorite new chambermaid hired as nanny to Philippe; Aurore even includes Bathilde in her will. Soon little Philippe sickens and dies. Bathilde persuades Aurore to have the body embalmed; conveniently she even knows an embalmer. For fifteen years Aurore withdraws to mourn in near-madness in the country. But in 1742 she returns to Paris with suspicions of foul play. She hires a private detective, Baron Posen, who seems to know what she wants without asking. Posen and Cocardasse break into the crypt and steal the child's coffin. In the presence of Aurore and her dear friends the Chavernys and their daughter Olympe, Posen opens the coffin—and smashes the embalmed corpse against the wall: it's a metal and plaster dummy! Philippe lives!

Posen explains: Back in 1726 he was a quack pharmacist. Bathilde persuaded him to help her drug little Philippe, and craft the dummy, and make the switch in the coffin—all ostensibly to save the child by letting his enemies think he was dead. Though he never knew who the boy was (and therefore couldn't confess), Posen reformed and became a detective. But recently he recognized Bathilde at a gambling den run by Count Zéno, the Venetian ambassador. Now Posen advises Aurore not to let Bathilde know they're onto her. Meanwhile he and Cocardasse will go search the world for Philippe.

Now comes another flashback, showing how Peyrolles survived the end of *The Hunchback*—meaning the original Féval *père* ending, since Féval *fils* wouldn't have the nerve to rewrite that until 1905. (In fact much of the backstory here depends on the original ending, since some of the later-written sequels that follow the revised ending precede in story order the earlier-written sequels that don't; if that sounds confusing, that's because it is.) Regrouping in hiding in Belgium, and vowing vengeance on Lagardère and all his family, Peyrolles smothers little Bathilde's father with a pillow, adopts the orphaned girl, and hires Knauss, a cutthroat ex-student of Staupitz.

Back in Paris incognito after four years, Peyrolles gets Bathilde hired in Aurore's household, and lures Lagardère into an ambush. Against Knauss's fifteen armed men, complete with lasso and scythe, Lagardère goes down fighting, but he goes down. Years pass... then Peyrolles runs into young Philippe on the street—the spitting image of Lagardère. He confronts Bathilde: she admits the long-ago "embalmed" dummy swap. She gave the child to a humble English family, but later heard they all drowned in a Channel shipwreck—so little Philippe died anyway. Nope, says Peyrolles, and he sics Knauss on Sergeant Beautiful-Blade's trail.

Volume Two, *Le Duc de Nevers* (*The Duke of Nevers*), resumes the present-day story where it left off halfway through Volume One: Philippe goes to confront Zéno, but can't get at him in the Venetian embassy. Cocardasse and Passepoil reunite to help Philippe. Oddly, Cocardasse and Passepoil haven't seen each other in twenty years, though they've both been in Paris; also oddly, Passepoil never noticed Philippe's resemblance to Lagardère when he was teaching him fencing.

Bathilde has secretly been Zéno's mistress; he covets the inheritance she'll get from Aurore (as does Peyrolles). All three meet to plot Philippe's death—to clear the way for that inheritance—but Posen spies on them and learns all. Posen and Cocardasse and Passepoil still won't tell Philippe who he is, or even warn him, because they want to catch the villains red-handed first. So they let Bathilde lure Philippe to her quarters at the Villa Nevers, and into Peyrolles's trap—but now she falls in love with the man she saved as a child, and when Peyrolles and Zéno and Knauss burst in to kill him, she pushes Philippe into a secret chamber with a hidden exit. The bad guys are waylaid by Philippe's friends; young Boniface kills Knauss, but both Peyrolles and Zéno escape. Meanwhile Philippe can't find the secret exit, and wanders around the Villa

Nevers until he recognizes his old nursery, and even sees his sleeping mother, before fleeing.

Posen finally brings Aurore up to date (she didn't even know they'd found Philippe); mother and son are reunited. They all go to Versailles to confront Peyrolles and Zéno, who are there attending Madame de Pompadour while also plotting to burn down the Villa Nevers and kill everybody. Zéno gets away, but Philippe catches Peyrolles. Though Aurore urges him to avenge his father on the spot, Philippe takes pity on the pathetic old man and leaves him to the law; but Peyrolles takes advantage of the king's arrival to slip away again. The king makes Philippe Duke of Nevers, as the Regent had promised his father.

Posen and Boniface infiltrate Zéno's gambling den and learn the arson plot; Boniface even joins the recruits for the job. Meanwhile Peyrolles, angry with Bathilde for saving Philippe from his trap, boasts that he smothered her father with a pillow; so she does the same to him. Then Bathilde returns to confess all to Aurore and Philippe, starting with Peyrolles's death, and vows atonement. The Villa Nevers catches fire... but it's quickly put out, because Posen and Boniface diverted Zéno's gang of killers into that same secret exit, where they're trapped. Zéno is still at large in the villa, and Philippe goes to find him, but he gets away.

A month later, Philippe de Lagardère and Olympe de Chaverny are married in the presence of everybody, including King Louis XV and Philippe's grandmother the Princess of Caylus/Nevers/Gonzague. Poor adopted sister Marine is there too—and she knows she's pregnant after Zéno's rape. (Zéno had diplomatic immunity and fled to Venice.) Bathilde has become a nun. Cocardasse moves in with Passepoil and Mathurine; she beats them both regularly.

Les Jumeaux de Nevers [The Nevers Twins] (1895).

Volume One, *Le Parc-aux-Cerfs* (*The Deer Park*), jumps ahead another eighteen years, to 1763. Marine is now abbess of the convent where Bathilde is a nun. Marine's daughter (by Zéno), Louise, has now entered the nunnery after being raised by Philippe and Olympe alongside their twins, Blanche and Henri de Nevers. Henri's best friend, young Viscount of Dizons, has fallen in love with Louise (who thinks the abbess is her "aunt").

The Deer Park (the real-life Parc-aux-Cerfs) is King Louis XV's Versailles love nest, where he debauches a revolving harem of teen beauties—girls provided by his rival and competing procuresses and ex-mistresses, Madame de Pompadour and the Marquise of Coislin, each seeking the king's favor by offering him the choicest girls. So far, so historical... Now Pompadour and Coislin separately have Blanche and Louise, respectively, abducted from the convent to be pimped to the king. Henri and Dizons find out, and rush to Versailles.

Blanche is a prisoner at the Deer Park. The king makes his move on her—he's incognito as a Polish prince, and he won't let her tell him who she is—but he can tell she's nobility, and he respects her honor (for now). He persuades her that he can intercede with the king for her father, who's supposedly in trouble... but only if she's nice to him, the prince. She's a gullible innocent and believes him. Meanwhile Louise is a prisoner at Coislin's estate—but Coislin is now Zéno's mistress, and (though Zéno himself engineered the convent kidnap) when he sees Louise he can tell she's Marine's daughter, and therefore his. The shock of having almost pimped his own daughter reforms him instantly. Zéno tries to stop Coislin, but she badly needs her new offering to trump Pompadour's, so she stabs him dead with a hat pin and hides the body.

Henri and Dizons climb a garden wall and talk to Blanche (without naming the king), but she's been gas-lighted so completely she doesn't believe them. At a masked costume ball, Blanche and Louise are reunited, and Blanche finally grasps the whole twisted setup. Pompadour whisks both girls away to the Deer Park: whichever new beauty the king prefers, she'll get the credit. Henri and Dizons arrive at the ball too late—where'd everybody go?—but a mystery man in an astrologer costume not only explains all but seems to know everything about them too. They rush off to the Deer Park, accost the king and some duke outside, and sword-fight them. But you can't attack the king! They're arrested and sent to the Châtelet prison.

That night Zéno, not dead, comes to and confronts Coislin; she thinks he's a ghost and falls off a balcony to her death. To hide her body, Zéno gets help from that same astrologer, who knows all about Zéno's wicked past too. The astrologer—actually the detective Baron Posen—explains to Philippe and Olympe that the girls are in the king's harem and the boys are in prison, but everybody will be fine, even Dizons, who dueled the king—because he's actually another of Louis's bastards by another seduced and abandoned conquest, and Posen has proof. Still, Philippe rushes to Versailles to save the girls—but he doesn't have to: when the king learns accidentally that Blanche is a Nevers (unthinkable!), he has both girls sent home, and banishes La Pompadour; Coislin is already dead and beyond punishment. Blanche goes back to her mother, Louise goes back to the abbess (her "aunt"); but Henri and Dizons are still prisoners in the Châtelet.

In Volume Two, *La Reine Cotillon* (*The Petticoat Queen*), Henri and Dizons—who think they face torture and execution for attempted regicide, though in fact they've already been pardoned through Philippe's intercession—break out of the Châtelet and flee the country... to Québec, which has just been lost to the English in the Seven Years' War. Five years pass (so it's now 1768). Madame de Pompadour dies; she never recovered from the king's displeasure at her pimping him Blanche de Nevers. Louis XV's new mistress—the next "Petticoat Queen"—is the real-life Madame du Barry.

The king, out hunting, is almost killed by a wild boar but is saved by two Canadian backwoodsmen dressed in buckskin and fur: Henri and Dizons, home incognito after five years. They soon learn they were pardoned, but they keep up the buckskin and fake names anyway, for no good reason; also for no good reason, they have yet to go home to see their families—who haven't known for five years if they're alive or dead, much less where: Féval *fils* fails to explain why they couldn't write a letter even once from Québec... but onward!

The grateful king invites the heroic Canadian boys to Versailles, where Henri and Madame du Barry fall madly in love at first sight. (Being the aged king's mistress doesn't mean she loves him.) Baron Posen, who has seen through the backwoods Québécois act and is tailing the boys, overhears a plot by du Barry's libertine pal the Duke of Fronsac to win a bet by luring two virtuous, innocent beauties to one of du Barry's notorious debauches. Posen deduces that Fronsac means Blanche and Louise (because who else?). But rather than prevent the scheme, Posen encourages it: he hopes that seeing the sinful side of du Barry's life will snap Henri out of his lovestruck folly. So Posen arranges for the girls to go to the "supper" thinking they'll be reunited with Henri and Dizons; and posing as the mysterious "astrologer" he orders the boys to accept du Barry's invitation to the same party.

At the supper du Barry and Henri flirt and declare their undying love: she's ashamed of her loose past and notorious present; he knows all about it (who doesn't?) and doesn't care. Meanwhile in the next room Blanche and Louise are confronted by the usual rakes and loose girls from the Opéra—whom Fronsac has asked to behave until he can win his bet, but who can't help themselves. Blanche and Louise panic at the looming threat of depravity and call for help, and Henri and Dizons rush in, followed shortly by Cocardasse and Passepoil (now aged seventy-five at least), whom Posen has sent as backup. Henri and Fronsac duel; Fronsac is wounded, which is enough to uphold Blanche's honor. As Posen planned, Henri is so shocked by the debauchery surrounding du Barry that he renounces her forever—though he's still in love and so is she. Later Dizons and Louise are married by her father, who used to be Count Zéno but is now a monk. Later still, in the Terror of 1792, Madame du Barry goes to the guillotine with Henri de Nevers's name on her lips.

Mademoiselle de Lagardère (1929).

Speaking of which... the next book—though not next in writing order, since there's a thirty-five-year gap—begins in 1794 at the height of the Terror. Appropriately, this is the grimmest and most political of the whole series, and Féval *fils*'s politics are staunchly Bonapartist: the Jacobins are bloodthirsty monsters, the fatuous exiled royalists have learned nothing, and only Napoleon can restore order and save France. Much more than in any of the other stories, Féval fils roots the action in the fine-grained details of historical events, and real people far outnumber fictional characters in the cast. His titular character, Zelig-like, is present in the background at, and intervenes in, just about all the key moments of the period.

Henri de Nevers was killed by a Jacobin mob in 1791. His teenaged daughter, Marie de Lagardère, escaped to America before returning in disguise as Rita Zinetta, the leader of a small traveling circus actually composed of other exiles—notably an excitable seven-foot six-inch giantess and a scholarly, dandyish midget. In true Lagardère fashion, "Rita" is a bareback rider, acrobat, fencer, dancer, lion tamer, and sharpshooter; in fact this book features a lot more pistols than swords—and no capes.

Robespierre is at the height of his tyrannical power. Marie de Lagardère is a 1789 moderate democrat, and she loathes the regicide Convention butchers—but to save France she holds her nose and joins their anti-Robespierre Thermidor plot. She meets young General Bonaparte, the hero of Toulon, when he attends the circus; she falls for him hard. At a gathering of the Thermidor plotters he shows up and flirts with her; but later in public he seems indifferent. Meanwhile the circus troupe's juggler and tightrope walker, Count Florac, loves her unrequited—though she does notice his slight resemblance to Napoleon...

The Thermidor plotters assign Marie to seduce Robespierre: not to murder him Corday-style, but to confuse and distract him so he can't thwart their plans. She beats Robespierre at chess, and he's attracted; but she says the way to her heart is for him to be forceful and dominating at the Convention. Besotted, he goes to address the Convention to impress her—mistake! The Thermidor plotters engineer his downfall. It takes the circus troupe's elephants to drive off the Paris mob come to save him, but eventually Robespierre goes to the guillotine.

Napoleon is assigned to restore order in Paris; Marie persuades him not to fire on the Jacobin mob, and also persuades the mob to disperse. Later she runs into the Viscount of Bresle, a secret emissary from the exiled Louis XVIII—and when he tries to rape her she gets a taste of the ugliness and entitlement of the royalist faction: surely only Napoleon can save what's good in the Revolution! Five years go by (so it's 1799); Napoleon, victorious everywhere, is now First Consul. Marie uncovers the royalist Chouans plot to kill Napoleon with a bomb in a barrel on a cart—Bresle is involved—and she sword-fights them in the Paris catacombs, but they get away. Napoleon's police chief wants the bomb plot to go forward—as an excuse to eliminate the Consul's enemies, both Jacobin and royalist—but he's noticed Florac's uncanny resemblance too, and he gets Florac to impersonate Napoleon a second time (Florac was already the amorous "Napoleon" at the Thermidor meeting). Marie tries in vain to stop the bomb going off—but Napoleon is elsewhere and safe, and actually Florac in disguise survives too, thanks to her.

Bresle lures both Marie and Napoleon separately into a trap; but the circus giantess, now Napoleon's official food taster, sends Florac once again in his place. Marie duels and defeats Bresle. She finally discovers it's Florac playing Napoleon, and that she's loved him all along. The real Napoleon shows up; since Marie and her troupe have saved him over and over, he awards her the Legion d'honneur and pinches her earlobe. Marie de Lagardère—the last of the

Nevers line—marries Florac; can wedding bells be far behind for the giantess and the midget?

La Petite-Fille du Bossu [The Hunchback's Granddaughter] (1931).

Technically, it should be "great-granddaughter," since the original Henri de Lagardère begat Philippe begat Henri begat Marie, who repeats as the heroine of this installment. But anyway! Féval *fils* leapfrogs most of the Napoleonic era between books, and this story begins with the defeated French outside Moscow in flames in 1812. Knowing he'll be overthrown if word of his failure reaches Paris while he's still in Russia, Napoleon leaves his army and rushes west to beat the news, incognito. But not incognito enough, because a spy and traitor—the villain Bresle, who somehow survived that sword-fight with Marie—has alerted the Russians, and Napoleon's carriage is pursued across the steppe by Cossacks. At an inn on the way Napoleon meets the familiar circus troupe (on tour in the wake of the Grande Armée) and recruits them all as his escort. A wild chase across Europe follows, complete with ambushes in Poland and treachery in Prussia and six weeks of starvation in a Strasbourg dungeon for Marie and Florac and the giantess, until the clever midget can get them out. Meanwhile in those six weeks Napoleon has been defeated and exiled to Elba.

Marie and her circus friends retire from public life to the Lagardère estate, where Marie and Florac (now Duke of Lagardère-Nevers) left their eight-year-old son, Henri-Napoleon de Lagardère, godson to You Know Who. When Napoleon himself returns from Elba, Marie faces a dilemma: while she's personally devoted to the Emperor (no longer in love, of course, since that confusion got cleared up in the last book), she realizes Napoleon in power means endless war, and is that good for France? But when he appeals directly for her help in Belgium, loyalty trumps philosophy: she and the whole gang join Napoleon for the Hundred Days. At Waterloo he sends Marie as a courier to launch the counterattack that would save the day—but the traitor Bresle, working for the Prussians though mostly motivated by his wish to rape and murder Marie, prevents her getting through, and the day is lost.

The second half of the novel is all about trying to rescue Napoleon from his exile on Saint Helena. (Marie de Lagardère is still a constitutional monarchist by principle, but she's heard the Emperor is being badly treated, and she thinks he deserves to live out his days as a private citizen in the United States.) The brainy midget comes up with a plan, inspired by his American friend Robert Fulton, that involves a newfangled oceangoing steamship and even a pedal-powered submarine: it's like we wandered into a Jules Verne novel. But Bresle has spies, and knows their plans. He sets fire to their unfinished steamship while it's still in dry-dock. Because of Bresle's constant counterplots, it takes them several years and countless restarts in one country after another, but finally they build both the steamship and the submarine—which the midget steers while the giantess pedals: still no wedding bells for them. Marie comes ashore on Saint

Helena and is affectionately reunited with Napoleon; but he knows he has only days left to live (stomach cancer), and he declines to escape.

Marie and Florac long ago sold their country estate and spent their entire fortune on the Saint Helena rescue caper, so they're reduced to living in genteel poverty in the old Villa Lagardère in Paris—boyhood home to the original Henri. The circus troupe turns Cocardasse and Passepoil's old fencing academy into a gym, where they teach young Henri-Napoleon physical culture. Marie and Florac welcome the July Revolution of 1830: new king Louis Philippe is a close friend. Bresle attacks the couple on the street, and Marie (now in her mid-fifties, but she's still got it) finally kills him with the Nevers attack.

Paul Féval *fils* died before writing the further adventures of young Henri-Napoleon Lagardère; but research done by that scholarly circus midget (really) in the Lagardère family archives supplied him with the material to write *The Hunchback's Boyhood*—thus closing the long loop, stretching in story time from the 1680s to the 1830s, of the whole series of prequel and sequels to his father's best-known novel, *The Hunchback*.

Stuart Gelzer
Santa Fe, 2020

APPENDIX TWO
THE HUNCHBACK ADAPTATIONS

Stage

After the great success of his novel, Paul Féval wrote a theatrical version in collaboration with Auguste Anicet-Bourgeois (1806-1871), a popular French dramatist with whom he had collaborated on *Les Mystères de Londres, ou Les Gentilhommes de la Nuit* (1849).[6] The theatrical version of *Le Bossu* was a drama in five acts and twelve tableaux, published by Michel Lévy *frères* and performed for the first time on September 8, 1862, in Paris, at the Théâtre de la Porte-Saint-Martin, with Gravier in the role of Lagardère.

The very same play was restaged on 16 December 1949 at the Théâtre Marigny (Paris) by Jean-Louis Barrault with Pierre Brasseur in the role of Lagardère, and then again on 12 October 1973 at the Théâtre Montansier (Versailles) and the Théâtre des Célestins (Lyon) by Jacques-Henri Duval with Jean Marais (who had played the part in the 1959 motion picture) as Lagardère.

Other stage adaptations include:

* 1888: an opéra-comique written by Henri Bocage & Armand Liorat with music by Charles Grisart;

* 1908: *Le Fils de Lagardère* [The Son of Lagardère], a drama in four acts and eleven tableaux adapting the sequel by Paul Féval, *fils*;

* 2008: a new version of *Le Bossu*, adapted by Éric-Emmanuel Schmitt and performed at the Abbey of Villers-la-Ville;

* 2014: yet one more version adapted by Pierre Naftule & Pascal Bernheim; and finally,

* 2015: another version adapted by Valérie de La Rochefoucauld.

Cinema

Le Bossu was first adapted for the screen as an uncredited silent short film made in 1909, then expanded in 1912 in a version (a.k.a, *Les Aventures de Lagardère*) directed by André Heuzé starring Henry Krauss as Lagardère. This version was remade in 1923, also with Henry Krauss.

---

[6] Available from Black Coat Press. Anicet-Bourgeois also wrote a *Rocambole* play in 1864, also available from Black Coat Press.

Paul Féval, *fils*'s *Le Fils de Lagardère* [The Son of Lagardère] was adapted in 1913 by Henri Andréani with Maxime Léry as the eponymous Philippe de Lagardère.

A new version of *Le Bossu* (known as *The Duke's Motto* in English) was made in 1925 by Jean Kemm starring Gaston Jacquet, and another in 1934 by René Sti, starring Robert Vidalin.

The first "modern" adaptation was Jean Delannoy's in 1944, starring Pierre Blanchar as Lagardère.

Paul Féval, *fils*'s *Le Fils de Lagardère* was also adapted in Italy in 1952 as *Il figlio di Lagardere* [The Son of Lagardère] by Fernando Cerchio with Rossano Brazzi as the eponymous Philippe, while in Spain, *El Juramento de Lagardere* [Lagardère's Oath] was made in 1955 by León Klimovsky starring Ernesto Bianco.

The version that most fans of the book would call definitive was made in 1959 by André Hunebelle (who later directed three Fantômas cult movies), starring Jean Marais (of *Beauty and the Beast* fame) as Lagardère and French comic Bourvil as Passepoil.

The latest version of *Le Bossu* was made in 1997 by Philippe de Broca with Daniel Auteuil in the role of Lagardère.

Television

Arguably the best filmed adaptation of *The Hunchback* was a 1967 television series produced by the First Channel of the then-ORTF French Television network. Entitled *Lagardère*, it was comprised of six episodes of 50 minutes, directed by Jean-Pierre Decourt and starring Jean Piat as the eponymous hero.

1. Le petit Parisien
2. Aurore
3. Le bal du Régent
4. Les noces du Bossu
5. Le défilé de Poncorvo
6. La vengeance de Lagardère

The first four episodes adapt *The Hunchback*, while episodes 5 and 6 borrow (somewhat clumsily) from Paul Féval *fils*'s *Les Chevauchées de Lagardère* and *Maraquita*.

A new version was produced in April 2005, also entitled *Lagardère*, comprised of two episodes of 100 minutes each, directed by Henry Helman and starring Bruno Wolkowitch as Lagardère.

JEAN PIAT

dans

LAGARDERE

D'APRÈS L'ŒUVRE DE PAUL FEVAL PÈRE ET FILS
ADAPTATION ET DIALOGUES DE MARCEL JULLIAN
RÉALISATION DE JEAN-PIERRE DECOURT

AVEC

JACQUES DUFILHO · JEAN-PIERRE DARRAS · SACHA PITOEFF
RAYMOND GEROME · MARCO PERRIN · JACQUES BALUTIN
ET MICHÈLE GRELLIER · NADINE ALARI

DIRECTEUR DE LA PHOTOGRAPHIE GEORGES BARSKY
ARCHITECTE DÉCORATEUR JEAN D'EAUBONNE
MUSIQUE DE JACQUES LOUSSIER

EN COULEURS
GRAND-ECRAN

www.ingramcontent.com/pod-product-compliance
Lightning Source LLC
Chambersburg PA
CBHW030644120726
47905CB00001B/52